About the Author

Jackson J. Radley was born in London in 1951. He was educated in South London at Kingston Polytechnic and now lives in East Sussex.

HYPERION

To my parents

Jackson J. Radley.

HYPERION

AUSTIN MACAULEY
PUBLISHERS LTD.

A CIP catalogue record for this title is available from the British Library.

ISBN 978 184963 687 2
2nd Edition

www.austinmacauley.com

First Published (2014)
Austin Macauley Publishers Ltd.
25 Canada Square
Canary Wharf
London
E14 5LB

Printed and bound in Great Britain

Acknowledgments

My thanks to Susan Woolcott.

HYPERION

The Father of the Dawn, the Sun and the Moon.

Fanatics have their dreams wherewith they weave
A Paradise for a sect...

John Keats

BOOK ONE

PART ONE

THE CONSTITUTION OF ATHENS

"Christ's bollocks"!

Leila Kumar broke away from what she was doing and walked across the observation room towards the source of the profanity. Lenny West commanded a liberal variety of expletives and the conservative quality of his latest one was in deference to her known dislike of such language.

"What is it?" she enquired of her junior officer.

"Look at these readings, Captain."

She stood behind the seated West and peered over his shoulder at the illuminated figures emerging from the machine. The wall of graphs and charts in front of them indicated a sudden increase in temperature and pressure of the magma chamber. She turned and looked at the large image that occupied the entire end of the observation room. The massive volcano two hundred kilometres below the ship showed no outward sign of unusual activity; just a series of small eruptions at regular intervals. At that moment another ejection peppered the slopes with glowing bombs of magma, just as it had done for the last six days. A pyroclastic flow cascaded down the steep slope in an avalanche of sulphurous dust that choked the thin atmosphere of Vega Delta. It all looked normal. She turned back to the figures; temperature and pressure were still increasing at an alarming rate; some warning lights started flashing red.

"What do you want to do, Captain?"

She passed her hands through her spikey, black hair as she thought. The landing party still had two days work to do down there; it would be expensive to bring them back prematurely. "What's causing that? There shouldn't be any pressure increase like that. The volcanic plug was breached with the first eruption."

West shook his head. "I don't know. It shouldn't be happening. It's a sodding mystery, that's for sure. Maybe there's another volcano; I mean one inside the other."

Captain Kumar rolled her eyes; the question had been rhetorical and she had not expected to receive an uneducated opinion from her junior officer. She had little time for West although she was always careful to maintain her professional inscrutability in his presence. "Mr West, you are not a volcanologist, therefore your opinion is of little value in this situation."

West detected another put-down and wondered, not for the first time, why the captain didn't like him. He pressed his lips together glumly while she contacted the landing party where First Officer Johansen, the ship's volcanologist, was conducting a survey and collecting samples for mineralogical analysis.

The face of Alex Johansen appeared. "Yes, Captain."

"Alex, have you seen the current readings of the magma chamber?"

"No, we're sort of busy down here."

"Take a look at them, will you?"

Johansen glanced down; she saw his eyes widen in surprise. That doesn't look right." He commanded some more data to appear, frowning deeply as he read the figures. "The composition of the magma chamber appears to have suddenly changed."

"What does that mean?"

"I can't be certain but the most likely cause is an upwelling of fresh magma from the mantle; it's what we call a plume."

"What does that mean?" repeated Leila Kumar with studied patience.

Johansen scratched his head. "I'm not sure; I've never seen anything like it; at least not this rapid and on this scale."

"Well, you're the volcanologist, what do you think it means?"

Johansen considered. "It could be dangerous; it's difficult to predict. The pressure from below could force the magma chamber to the surface."

"A large eruption?"

"You could say that; perhaps more of a cataclysm really."

"What sort of time-frame would you estimate?"

Johansen shrugged. "Could be a day; maybe as little as a few hours. It's hard to say."

As he spoke a violent shudder passed through the vehicle and his image shook for a few seconds.

"What was that?" said Kumar.

"A quake; we've had a few in the last couple of hours. It's normal."

The captain bit her lip; a decision had to be made and she was in no doubt that the safety of the landing party trumped any commercial considerations. "I want you out of there now."

"We're over two hundred kilometres away from the thing," protested Johansen. "We haven't finished."

"I don't care. Leave immediately."

Her first officer seemed strangely reluctant. "Are you sure? It's probably just a local spike in pressure."

"What if it's not? I'm not gambling the lives of six of my crew members; I'm commanding you to leave."

Johansen seemed to be deliberating upon further argument, but he knew the force of his captain's will. She was a decisive commander who they all respected but she would have no truck with dissent. "Very well, I'll pick up the survival gear from the safety chamber and then head back."

"You will not; you will take off immediately," she returned in a voice that betrayed rising impatience.

"It's valuable; we can't leave it; it might be destroyed."

"First Officer Johansen, I'm telling you to leave now. THIS MOMENT."

Johansen passed her a look that she fancied resembled resentful defiance. He nodded and cut the communication.

Alex Johansen was not happy. The captain was panicking and making a wrong decision. The life support in the survival chamber excavated at the beginning of their mission to the surface of Vega Delta was not something that could be just left behind as if it had no value. He had to retrieve it and she would thank him for it later when she had calmed down and applied rational thought to the matter. The loss of equipment meant docked pay and he was not a fan of docked pay; in fact, the very thought of it made him feel quite queasy. But, unpalatable as it may be, the loss of money was not the primary source of concern on Johansen's mind for hidden in the chamber was something of which he was deeply ashamed but now realised that he could not bury and leave behind as he had intended.

Ever since he could remember Alex Johansen's father had imbued him with a love for ancient Greece. He was an archaeologist famed for the discovery of a ceremonial sword attributed to Alexander the Great; a jewel-encrusted weapon unearthed in the lands to the north of the Tigris River. He named his son after the conqueror of Persia and, when he was old enough, took him on many digs to the Middle East, the Levant and Greece. Alex was a keen student and had read the entire works of Sophocles and Plato before he was eight years old. But of all the ancient writers it was the work of Aristotle that he revered the most. Aristotle was the teacher of Alexander the Great, who was himself taught by Plato and Plato by Socrates. What a line! A ribbon of genius running through the thread of history. And it was Aristotle that had brought him to his present predicament.

"Well, you heard her."

Johansen recovered himself with a start. Sara Clark was sitting next to him, her gentle face filled with anxiety.

"Aren't you going to take off?"

"She's wrong," he replied. "The volcano's still quite stable. There's time to pick up the gear from the chamber. Wake the others up while I go and get it."

Second Officer Clark stared at him in disbelief. She had a soft spot for Johansen; he wasn't a bad looking chap. Late thirties in appearance, pure Scandinavian stock, blond hair, blue eyes; unusual in an age of racial impurity.

"She gave you a direct order," she protested. "I heard her."

Johansen rose. "I know. Do as I say, go and wake the others up and then prepare for take-off."

"She's not going to be happy; not at all."

"She'll get over it," he said as he passed her and went directly down to the air-lock anti-chamber. There he stripped down to his underpants and climbed into the E.V.A. suit reserved for him. He checked all the functions on the heads-up display before stepping into the compartment itself. It closed behind him and he heard the hiss of the escaping air as it began to match the exterior pressure. A green light appeared and he touched it with his gauntlet. He began to descend the short distance to the surface of the planet. Between the two rear legs of the lander he could see the broad, flat horizon of Vega Delta, the fourth planet from the star. There was no colour to speak of, just endless shades of dusty grey which blurred into the heavy blackness of the starry sky. The distant, fragile light of Vega itself was not visible. In a world of perpetual dusk it was night. He moved forward, planting his feet carefully in the fine dust of the surface. The survival chamber was just a few metres beyond the ship; an excavation three metres below the surface formed by the melting and then compacting of the basalt crust. A standard procedure carried out by every landing party entering hostile environments. As he approached a trapdoor sprung open and light shone like the beam of a torch into the blackness above the chamber. He glanced behind him at the insect-like silhouette of the lander. They would all be watching, intruding on this private business. Damn them.

"Why haven't they taken off?"

Not in the thirty-two years of the expedition had Lenny West ever seen his captain so agitated. "Get me that lander."

"They're not replying to my signal, Ma'am."

"I'm the captain of this ship," stated Leila Kumar imperiously. "Override the normal channel, use emergency protocol."

"Okay."

The sheepish face of Second Officer Clark appeared. "Captain?"

"What the devil is going on? Why haven't you left the surface?"

"The number one is outside," replied Clark hesitantly.

The captain's face visibly drained; she glanced down at the readings of the magma chamber and struggled for equilibrium. There had been a sudden and startling increase in both pressure and temperature. "Tell him to get back inside immediately."

"He said we had plenty of time."

"Did he? Well, he's wrong. The readings are off the chart, you're about to run out of time."

"He's in the chamber."

"BUGGER HIM!" she exploded making West jump out of his skin. He had never heard the captain swear before. Not one word in thirty-two years.

"BUGGER, BUGGER BUGGER!" she continued. "BUGGER HIM TO......," she searched for a suitable destination, "BUGGERY."

"Captain!" shouted West pointing at the display.

"Get out of there now!" screamed the captain.

"But the number one."

"Leave him, you've run out of time."

Clark's face twisted in agony. She engaged the landers motors just as the mountain blew itself to pieces with the power of a million atomic bombs.

The captain and West turned to the monitor display and watched the entire mountain and its surroundings collapse in on itself before blasting into the thin atmosphere of Vega Delta. The whole planet shook triggering quakes across its entire surface.

"Are you clear?" enquired the captain.

The crackle of electrical interference filled the observation room as they waited anxiously. A minute passed and then a faint voice struggled through. "Clear."

The blast front shook the lander and they heard the ominous sound of debris peppering its outer shell as it reached the upper atmosphere. Suddenly all hell broke loose inside the craft; a klaxon began to wail; lights flashed and emergency breathing apparatus burst from above. The crew grabbed them and strapped them on to their faces. Instinctively they began to pray as the lander continued to rise in the buffeting storm. And then nothing beyond the whisper of escaping air; the buffeting ceased and they were surrounded with the velvet blackness of space.

Sara Clark sat in the pilot seat stunned at the closeness of their escape. Never in the entire mission had they ever been exposed to danger; the captain was very cautious and they all had reason to be thankful for it. She calmed herself, tried to breath normally and glanced around at the four faces of the landing party; they were grim and drained. No one spoke. In thirty-two years they had never lost a crewmember, now they had lost the first officer. It was a bitter blow but at least they had escaped.

In the tomb of the survival chamber Alex Johansen felt the rocks shudder and then violently convulse, throwing him to the ground. It seemed to him that minutes passed as he was tossed like a boat in stormy waves as the blast front passed through the surrounding rocks. The temperature inside the chamber soared. Desperately he lunged for the survival unit and activated it. Cold air flooded the chamber as the sickening rocking motion began to subside. When he was able, he stood and inspected the walls. They were intact and might remain so providing there were no more major events. He turned on his communicator. Just static, exactly what he would have expected. He hoped to God that the others had got away in time; they would certainly all be dead by now if they hadn't. Damn his luck! If the mountain had just held for a few more minutes they would have all got away safely. Now he was stranded and they would have no way of knowing if he had survived, at least not until the atmospheric disturbances had subsided and that could take many days.

He wondered what the captain would do and various scenarios entered his head. If the lander had been destroyed would she risk the remaining one? Probably not, he thought. But what if they'd got away? He tried to put himself in her position but hope clouded rationality. He had to have some prospect of rescue otherwise why wait? Why not just turn off the machine, remove his helmet and give himself over to the heat and poison. He wondered, ghoulishly, which would kill him first. It would be a close run thing.

After about an hour the temperature in the chamber had stabilized and poisonous, irradiated atmosphere had been replaced by breathable air. To make himself comfortable Johansen removed his E.V.A. suit and began to turn his thoughts to mundane matters of survival. The unit would function for about three hundred days. It would provide him with nutrition in the form of tablets taken once every twelve hours and water mainly extracted from his recycled urine. A long time, three hundred days, stuck in a hole on your own. He smiled grimly; of course, he would probably go mad with solitude long before the unit gave out and, if eventually rescued, would emerge like some long-bearded, lank-haired prisoner from an oubliette, blinking at the unaccustomed light. Except there was no light above, just an enormous, impenetrable dust-cloud of violent, swirling gas and poison. He knew that. There would be no communication, no landing, for some time.

The chamber walls were still too hot to touch so he spread his E.V.A. suit on the floor of the chamber and up the wall so that his skin would not come into contact with it. For some time he brooded further on the nature of his predicament until it occurred to him that, until that moment, he had not given a thought to the cause of it. He looked up and could just make out the faint outline of the cover to the small niche he had fashioned to accommodate the treasure; virtually invisible unless someone knew it was there. The casket would still be inside; it could survive practically anything, protecting its precious contents from harm. He had intended to leave it here, as if somehow the act of concealment would assuage the guilt of its unethical and illegal acquisition, but when it had come down to it, he had realised that he could not be parted from it. He had to retrieve it, even in the face of mortal danger. Now, here he was and Fate had decided; they would be buried together, Alex Johansen and his guilty treasure in everlasting communion.

Captain Leila Kumar had exceedingly beady, dark eyes and a large hooked nose that, from certain angles, gave her the aspect of a witch. Had she also been furnished with a pointed, protruding chin and a hairy wart the image would have been complete and she could have frightened naughty children for a living. She had neither wart nor oversized chin, but for Second Officer Sara Clark the beady eyes were more than enough to produce a childish anxiety, especially when they were turned on her, as they now were.

"So, Officer Clark, you are proposing to take a lander into the Maelstrom beneath us, effect an extremely hazardous landing, undertake an even more hazardous expedition in order to extract a crewman who is unlikely to have survived. Have I got that correct?"

Clark slumped. They were alone together in the observation room; the muffled sound of conversation filtered from the crew lounge down the corridor and filled the pregnant silence between the two women. "That's about it, Captain.," replied Clark quietly, hopelessly.

"May I ask does anyone else share your suicidal enthusiasm?"

Clark slumped further. "No, Captain."

"Then listen to me. In the entire history of humanity no manned spacecraft has ever been as far into deep space as we now are. Should anything go wrong we are way beyond any reasonable expectation of rescue and I will not, I repeat not, ever sanction any action that jeopardises the safety of this ship, its crew or this mission. Am I clear?"

Clark nodded resignedly.

"With the absence of Johansen, you are now acting first officer and I expect total professionalism."

"Of course, Captain."

"And rationality," added Kumar with some emphasis. Besides, the fate of Johansen is not my principal source of concern right now."

"What do you mean?"

Liela Kumar sat back in her chair and drew her fingers into a steeple at her chin; an act that usually preceded a difficult announcement. "We seem to have lost contact with base."

Clark looked puzzled. "You mean we have no reception?"

"No, there is nothing wrong with our equipment, I had the 'Obi' check it thoroughly."

"What did it say?"

"That there was nothing wrong at our end. The quarterly communication had not been sent."

"Have they ever missed before?"

"They're not allowed to."

"How overdue is it?"

"Two days."

"Perhaps they've had equipment failure at their end."

Kumar shook her head. "They have massive back-up on Argentu Station." She dropped her voice to a whisper. "Do not speak of this to the crew, but the last com., ninety-two days ago, was very strange. Much of it was garbled; full of non-sequiturs, as if the sender was drunk. It mentioned that they had received no communication from Earth for almost three months. That much was clear at least."

"Three months!"

"Yes. That is why I was so keen to receive this next one. I was hoping for an explanation."

"That com. would have been over five years old."

"We're five point six two light years from Argentu Station actually."

Clark puffed her cheeks and blew. "Makes you wonder, doesn't it?"

The captain nodded slowly. "That's why I've decided to abort the mission. We're going home."

Clark blinked in surprise. "Have you consulted the 'Obi'?"

"It's my decision; the ship's on board intelligence system has nothing to do with it."

"Are you sure?"

"The 'Obi' is designed to protect us and act in our interests. It is not its place to second guess a captain's decision."

Clark passed her a sceptical look; she wasn't so sure. "The Company won't like it," she ventured.

"The Company isn't here, we are."

"When are we leaving?"

"In four hours. I thought we'd have a brief commemoration for Johansen and then head for Argentu Station."

At the mention of his name, Clark glanced at the image behind her captain. The dust cloud had wrapped itself around the planet like a shroud, but the thermal image showed what was going on beneath it. Fiery quakes had rent the crust into a mosaic, magma poured from the enormous caldera that had once been a volcano some twenty-five kilometres high. Huge tongues of molten rock slurped towards the site of the chamber and would soon bury it under their heavy flow. If he was down there and still alive there would soon he no hope for him at all.

"Well, what is there to say? We all knew Alex Johansen, a steady and likeable person and a proficient first officer. He certainly had his faults, but who among us can make any claim to perfection." Captain Kumar smiled reflectively at the assembled crew in the muster room. Most of the faces were appropriately glum, a few looked as if they would rather be somewhere else. "We live in close proximity when we are not in stasis and, although I know this is not a fashionable view in these times of individuality, but I think of our company as family and Alex Johansen was part of our family. I propose we take a few moments of silence to remember him as he passes into the hands of God." To offer an example the captain shut her eyes and bowed her head in prayer; most of the crew followed her lead; some more awkwardly than others. A minute later she spoke again. "As you know I have decided to return to Argentu Station. This will shorten our mission by approximately seven years with inevitable consequences to your salaries. I haven't made this decision lightly. You were all aware of the deteriorating situation on Earth before we left, I have not hidden from you the disturbing despatches from Argentu Station, but now it would appear that we have lost contact with Argentu itself."

A buzz of disquiet ran through the crew. Edwards, a junior researcher, stood up and spoke first. "What do you mean? How can we loose contact?"

"The last despatch is two days overdue," replied the captain.

Edwards sat down heavily; he had an uncle on Argentu.

"Are there any other questions or observations?" asked the captain.

The room fell silent.

"Very well, we will depart immediately."

One hour later Leila Kumar and Acting First Officer Clark were, once again, closeted in the observation room. This time the door was shut so that they could not be overheard.

"It must be Johansen, it won't let us leave without him."

The captain brooded while Clark let the statement hang in the silence. She had never seen Kumar at such a loss; she had always known what to do in any situation. Eventually the captain shook her head. "I can't accept that. The 'Obi' can't possibly know if Johansen is still alive and it wouldn't sanction risking crew to retrieve him even if it did know. It must be something else."

"And you've had absolutely nothing from it?"

"Nothing. It has simply stopped responding."

Clark's face assumed a look of puzzlement. "It must be malfunctioning."

"Look around you; everything is normal; it is functioning perfectly."

"But it doesn't make any sense. It has to act in the best interests of all the crew; it cannot function in any other way. Can it?" She added with a questioning look.

"That's what we have always understood; now I'm no so sure."

"Can't we disable it? Bypass it somehow? There must be a way."

"None that I know of. The 'Obi' controls every aspect of the ship; the environment; the propulsion units; the communication system; everything right down to the last microcircuit."

"Even us," added Clark.

"We all signed up to it."

"That's true." She glanced over the head of her captain at the projected image of the planet below. The dust cloud still obscured the surface but the image showed that, below it, the wall of magma had advanced to within ten kilometres of the chamber. It had slowed down significantly as the rock cooled and solidified in the freezing atmosphere forming vast cliffs over which the fresh outpourings tumbled glutinously. "It'll soon cover the chamber," she said.

Captain Kumar turned towards the image. "Yes," she replied wistfully.

"You know the atmospheric conditions down there have eased. Wind velocity is less than one-twenty."

"I see that. Are you suggesting a landing?"

"It's feasible; you know it, I know it and the 'Obi' knows it."

Kumar noticed the particular emphasis on the last five words. "You persist in thinking that we are being detained here because of Johansen? Because he might still be alive down there."

"That is what I hope; the alternative is too awful to contemplate."

Kumar sat back in her chair and formed steeple with her fingers beneath her chin as she contemplated. Both knew what the other was thinking; that the contamination afflicting Earth had reached Argentu Station and they were being protected from themselves by the on board intelligence. "It's extremely risky," she said at length.

"Agreed, but we don't have much time; the magma wall is advancing." She observed her captain deliberating and detected a chink in the wall of her opposition to a rescue. Clark knew that Johansen was still alive, at least she felt it strongly and the thought of leaving him down there to die alone disturbed her greatly. "There's no reason why we shouldn't try," she added.

"There are many reasons," returned the captain brusquely. "I suppose you've canvassed for volunteers already."

Clark nodded.

"Very well, I'll sanction it. We don't seem to be going anywhere and you may be right. If he has not survived you will still need to bring him back. Do you understand?"

"Yes."

"You'll need a crew of two; that's all I'm prepared to risk."

During his enforced entombment time oppressed on Alex Johansen for there was little to do other than monitor the conditions of his cell and sit and ruminate on the forlorn situation in which he found himself. Ironically he had not even been able to enjoy the sight of the treasure that had cost him his life; the rock covering the cavity in which it lay had fused shut with the heat and movement of the cataclysm and he had no instrument to hand that was capable of breaking it open. A punishment for his wickedness; tortured by the unobtainable proximity of that which he most treasured.

It had dawned on him some time ago that Captain Kumar would be unlikely to risk a lander in the conditions that prevailed outside and so he would be forced to bide his time. And then it occurred to him that the magma field surrounding the cataclysm might spread as far as the chamber, in which case it would be all over for he would surely burn to death as it stripped the hatch from the entrance and encroached into the survival chamber itself. The machine would be useless against that kind of force. Alex Johansen did not want to die like that and so he rested his thoughts on the hope that the captain would wait for a respite in the atmospheric conditions and the restriction of the magma field.

He turned out the light and slept; a troubled sleep that lasted no more than four hours. When he awoke he checked the readings on the equipment. The surrounding rock temperature had begun to decrease and now he could touch the walls with his bare hand. He looked up at the entrance hatch but could see nothing through the small transparency at its centre. He sat back on his E.V.A. suit and looked up at the fused cover of the niche. It had not budged and showed no sign of weakness. The treasure was well and truly trapped. Perhaps, he speculated, it was as well; it would be safe there, no one could ever destroy it, it would exist for all time. He took comfort in the thought and in the notion that he, of all men, would be the last to have seen it.

Another shudder passed through the chamber as the crust split again a thousand kilometres away. It reminded him of the deadly conditions outside and on the scales of hope and doubt, another weight fell on the side of doubt. He placed himself in the captain's chair and speculated; would he risk a rescue? He hoped he would but knew he wouldn't.

On the fourth day of his confinement Alex Johansen awoke. He was back on Earth in his parent's house; he was unwrapping a gift; faces looked down at him expectantly; it was his ninth birthday and the family had gathered in the sitting room of the house near Stockholm. Outside the large window the snow was falling; he had never seen such a thing; it had not snowed in Stockholm for a generation. He wanted to go out and play in it but he could not escape the smiling faces. Sara Clark said, "come in Alex," and offered her hand to take him away. Where were they going? Out into the snow?

He opened his eyes with a start. What was Sara Clark doing at his ninth birthday? He had no special connection with her, or indeed, with any other person. The Company had seen to that during sterilization when they had also been rendered impotent and stripped of libido. The Company did not tolerate emotional complications between male and female crewmembers. So why had Sara Clark invaded his waking dream?

The communicator on the survival unit cracked into life and through the heavy static he heard her voice. But this time he was awake.

"Come in Alex."

"Yes," he practically shouted for joy, forgetting the correct response.

"Are you injured?"

"No, repeat no."

"Good. We're going to blow the hatch; it's fused shut. Are you wearing your suit?"

"No, repeat no."

"Put it on: we don't have much time."

"Understood."

Johansen hurriedly climbed into his suit, checked that all the seals and life supports were functioning correctly and, taking cover, indicated that he was ready. The shaped charge blew the entire hatch mechanism away from the rock; it flew high and landed some distance away. A cloud of hot dust swirled into the chamber obliterating his vision; he switched on his view filter, picked up the survival unit and headed for the space below the entrance where the faces of Sara Clark and Chin Sen, the microbiologist, peered down at him.

"Leave the unit, we haven't time," shouted Clark; she had just received a warning that another magma flow was on its way. They had three minutes to get out of there.

Johansen pushed it up the ladder towards them. "Take it, take it," he insisted.

They didn't have time to argue. She and Chin Sen reached down and pulled it up to the surface. Johansen climbed out into the swirling eddies of dust. The heat hit him like a club; the huge wall of solidifying magma was less than fifty metres away. He activated the ladder and it folded into itself making a small, light portable package. Clark and Chin Sen had already started back to the lander with the survival unit; their bodies now no more than shadows in the swirling dust. A faint light blinked on the survival unit they carried between them; he took a heading from it ran as fast as the suit would allow.

As the lander took off they saw how close they had come to destruction. The magma plain was a sea of molten rock flowing like water towards the cliff edge. As they rose through the dust they saw the first wave tumble over the precipice and splash into the dust where they had so recently stood. A moment later the chamber was swallowed up.

Alex Johansen had not expected his conversation with his captain to characterised by any joy at his survival and in this his expectations were soundly justified. Her tone was stony, admonishing.

"You disobeyed a direct order and placed the lander, its crew and yourself in serious and unnecessary danger. Your actions caused endangerment not only once but twice and I have to tell you I have found them inexplicable."

"I understand, but...."

"I haven't finished. It is in my power to demote you and to recommend that fifty per cent of your remuneration be withdrawn and I am minded to do both unless you can furnish me with a credible cause for mitigation. What do you say?"

Alex Johansen stared at the deck of the observation room where they were alone, as if expecting some revelation to emerge from beneath his feet. But no such revelation came to him and he was reduced to his rather incredible explanation. "I just thought we had more time; I didn't want to leave the equipment; I was responsible for it."

"You were responsible for making sure that your crew and the lander were safe. You failed."

"I know, I'm sorry."

"Sorry! Sorry! You can't be sorry out here; out here we deal with certainties. We are not cavaliers; things only work when orders are followed."

"I understand, I truly do."

"Well I don't. Since the beginning of this mission you have been an exemplary officer; I had no reason to doubt you; you have carried out all your duties with calm professionalism at all times. But down there, on that planet, something changed and I would like to know what that was."

"It was a misjudgement."

"Rubbish!"

The room fell into an expectant silence as Johansen debated the merit of telling her the truth. Had the circumstances been different he would never have done so, but now what was there to lose?

"Have you heard of the philosopher, Aristotle?"

"You and your Greeks," she replied contemptuously. The entire crew were well acquainted with his obsession. "Of course I've heard of Aristotle."

"In the fourth century B. C. Aristotle composed a treatise on the constitution of Athens; a masterpiece of historical importance. A copy of it crossed the Mediterranean to the library in Alexandria in Egypt where further copies were made. At one time the Library was very extensive, containing practically all the knowledge of the western world; its importance to humanity could not be denied, but much of it was destroyed by fire during the invasion of the city by Julius Caesar in 47 B.C. Further destruction took place in 391 A.D. during the reign of Theodoseus the Great when the Library was sacked by a mob of fanatical Christians."

"This is all ancient history," interrupted Kumar impatiently.

Johansen held up his hand to stay her impatience. "No, I'm telling you this so that you might correctly understand the magnitude of my crime."

Her eyes bulged in incomprehension at the mention of the word 'crime', as if an alien monster had suddenly appeared in his place. Johansen ignored her and continued.

"The contents of the Library were thought lost and indeed they were until an almost complete papyrus containing the Constitution of Athens was unearthed in Egypt at the end of the nineteenth century. It was brought to the British Museum in London where it stayed for over two centuries until it was lent out to an exhibition of antiquities in Kinshasa, Central Africa where it was destroyed in a disastrous fire. But it was not entirely destroyed; one small fragment survived and was sold at auction. It passed through many hands over the next decades until it came into the possession of a very good friend of mine. When he showed it to me I knew I had to possess it. I would have paid anything he asked but he would not sell it to me. So I stole it."

Captain Kumar's jaw dropped. "You stole it!"

"Yes. To my everlasting shame, I stole it and because of what I did my friend killed himself."

"You stole it!" repeated Kumar as if unsure that she had heard him correctly.

Johansen nodded gravely. "I could not live with the shame and so I sought to bury it in the survival chamber. I intended to leave it there but when it came to the point I realised I could not be without it. It was that which I was trying to retrieve, not the equipment."

"You endangered yourself, your crewmates and the lander for a piece of paper?"

"Papyrus," corrected Johansen.

"Whatever. Where is it?"

"Still down there."

Kumar let out an ironic snort. "I am several leagues beyond mystified."

"I thought you wouldn't understand."

"You are quite correct. Under normal circumstances I would bust you down to nothing and place you in immediate stasis; your contract would be terminated and no remuneration given, but these aren't normal circumstances are they?"

"No, they are not."

"I had hoped that rescuing you would be the answer, but it seems that that is not the case. The 'Obi' still does not respond to any command I give it; we are stranded."

"I wondered why you risked the rescue."

"Be under no illusion, I would not have sanctioned it had it not been a possible solution to our situation."

"I would not have blamed you in any way had you left me down there."

"I would hope not. However, we are where we are and there appears to be no solution."

"Perhaps there shouldn't be a solution."

"What do you mean?"

Johansen scratched his head. "The 'Obi' must act for the preservation of the crew."

"Yes, that is its overriding directive."

"Communication has ceased from Earth and now Argentu Station. Perhaps it is preserving us by keeping us here."

He saw by the expression on her face that this had already occurred to her.

"I hope to the very core of my heart that that is not the reason," she replied almost inaudibly.

He looked up reflectively at the image of the spreading magma field far below. It had long since swallowed up the survival chamber but the outpourings had decreased and the advance of the magma field had almost halted.

"Do not imagine that your shame is buried with that object," said Kumar, following his gaze.

"I don't."

She became suddenly reflective; her mood softened. "I do not propose to inform the crew of your crime; I see nothing to be gained by it."

"Thank you."

"It is something that must weigh heavily on you and you alone."

"It does."

"Then that is some small justice, I suppose."

Johansen smiled weakly and took comfort in the thought that the fragment would be preserved forever or rather preserved until Vega exploded and consumed its own system of planets billions of years from now. He, Alex Johansen was the last to see it and that was how it would be until the end of time.

But Alex Johansen was wrong for he was not the last human being to see the surviving fragment of Aristotle's Constitution of Athens. He could not have foreseen that the arc of human history would eventually bring men back to that very place on Vega Delta where he had placed the precious object. For over one-hundred-and-twenty-thousand years the fragment rested in its tomb waiting to play its part; waiting until a man would reach into its protecting casket and bring it into the light of a different sun. Waiting for a man from a world so distant in time and space that he belonged to a civilisation having no knowledge of the true source of humanity; a man who belonged to a civilisation intolerant of dissent, steeped in a doctrine of human origin based on myth and superstition allowing no place for evidence and scientific reason. The fragment of The Constitution of Athens fell into the hands of the one individual with the ability to recognise it for what it was and to use it to change the course of human history. His name was Solon Bru.

PART TWO

AGON

I

Twenty five million years ago, the molten currents and eddies that churned beneath the equatorial crust of Agon caused a small fissure to appear on the surface of the planet. At first, this geological event was of small significance, but, as time passed, the pressures below began to exploit the weakness and the fragile skin of Agon opened and a vast gash appeared in the parched, primeval landscape. Volcanoes burst forth at its margin, forming towering peaks of ash and magma which were then rent asunder as the fissured land collapsed into the mantel to be consumed in the boiling heart of the planet. And then, as though its anger had been sated, the world began to cool, the volcanoes ceased their poisonous belching and the land became still. The turmoil that had gripped Agon for over two million years was ended, but it had left an indelible scar on the landscape in the form of a great rift valley that extended for over two thousand kilometres.

As time passed, a more forgiving season embraced Agon. The climate cooled and rain poured into the valley, flooding it with life-giving water and creating a vast sea that lapped against the towering walls of solidified magma. Primitive plants colonized the shoreline and clung to the cliff ledges and the valley gradually turned green and temperate.

It was in this green and temperate valley, over three thousand years ago, that men first walked on Agon. It was here that they first built their primitive villages and cultivated the fertile ledges that had formed at the base of the cliffs. These were simple men with few demands beyond survival. In their ignorance, they worshipped the sun, the water and the land, for it was these elements that gave them life and prosperity. The population grew and eventually a city was founded and in that city men began to turn away from the old gods and look for new ideas.

And so, in time, a prophet, who was born of the sea itself, came among them. His name was Minnar and he taught them that he was the essence of the Spirit of Creation and that they should worship him. He taught them that they were created from the waters of the sea; he taught them of life after death and the judgement of their sins that was to come to all men. He taught of the sin of polyphony and complex rhythm, decreeing that only devotional plainchant was to be heard from the mouths of men and that dancing was the surest path to damnation. He spoke of abstinence in all matters of the flesh, saying that only those who followed him in purity, eschewing the contamination of female company could achieve the highest plain of ecstasy in the Afterworld. These laws with many others, he wrote down in a document that became the known as 'The Book of Minnar'. This book was taken up by a small but devout faction of adherents who evangelised it among the superstitious population with promises of life beyond corporeal death.

But the city elders grew frightened of his power and fearful of his message and so they took him to a high cliff, bound him and weighed him down with rocks and threw him into the sea from whence he came. At that very moment, according to scripture, there was a terrible shaking of the ground and the mountains began to fall into the sea. The city was destroyed and the life-sustaining waters of the sea drained away until all that remained was a lake, trapped in the deepest recesses of the valley.

The Elders, in fear and contrition, commanded the building of a great temple on a pinnacle of rock called Imbar that had once been an island in the sea. They ordered the smashing of all the primitive instruments for the making of music and banned their manufacture on pain of death. They banned dancing!

But all their prayers to the spirit of Minnar were unanswered, for the waters gradually turned foul and famine visited the cursed people. The region was abandoned except for the temple, which grew into a shrine, enticing pilgrims and, eventually, the construction of a new city to serve them.

Over two thousand years after the death of Minnar, Solon Bru gazed across the glassy surface of the lake. The long day of Agon was closing and the vivid sun touched the parched valley walls with a sanguineous hue that appeared to make them bleed into the dark, putrid waters. The lake was now known as the Sea of Creation and from the apron of his high, cliff dwelling Bru had an unparalleled view across its sterile waters to the distant shore and the City of Imbar with its crumbling towers shining like bloody fangs in the declining sun.

It was the very place that Minnar had lived and died and had taught of the creation of Mankind. It was here that men had first emerged from the waters and walked upon the land. The irony of his situation was not lost on Bru. He was an exile from his home world and known to be a heretic. The Elders of Agon had chosen this revered location for him so he that could look upon it every day and eventually come to realize his error. They believed he would recant his heresy and embrace the One True Faith.

He took a large swig of the bitter distillation that passed for wine on Agon and tossed the rest over the wall of the apron. The droplets glinted like red jewels in the sun and tumbled two hundred metres to the dusty floor of the valley below. Then, as an afterthought, he tossed the goblet over after them, turned and wearily walked past his vehicle and into the cool interior of his home.

Inside he entered his sleeping quarters and pulled off the grimy tunic he had been wearing for three days. He noticed, with distaste, the odour of his own body and caught sight of his image in the reflector. At seventy-six years of age he was in the prime of his life; at an age when the rash vigour of youth had matured into a deeper physical strength. But the image that stared back at him belied these attributes and for the first time, he saw what he would become in old age. The skin around his sharp, grey eyes had begun to wrinkle and sag and the furrows of his brow had deepened into sun-starved crevasses that extended almost to his temples where grey variegated his dark brown hair. He scowled at the image and ambled towards his ablution area.

The particle bombardment cleaned his skin and made it tingle pleasantly. Revived a little, he dressed himself in a fresh tunic and swallowed a stimulant. He could not think of sleep; not yet anyway.

He returned to his living quarters to discover his wife Rhell. She was seated, as usual, on the floor, cross-legged and straight-backed, patiently waiting for him.

He had been expecting her arrival, but not this soon. This was most inconvenient. He spoke first, as was the custom on Agon.

"I greet you, but I was not expecting your presence here."

"My father brought me, Sir."

"Why?" He noticed her eyes did not meet his; she fixed her gaze on his naked feet.

"My father thought you would need nourishment, you have been away. He thought you would require me."

This did not surprise Bru, the old man would have instructed her to find out where he had been. He would have to report his son-in-law's movements to the appropriate authority. "I do not require you," he said shortly.

"But your meal Husband, I must prepare it."

"The simulant will do it."

"No Sir, it is my duty."

"I release you from it. You will return to your father's home by my vehicle."

She looked up at him imploringly. "No Sir, please, I may not go home."

Bru frowned in surprise; she had never defied him before. She looked terrified as her dark eyes began to moisten while she pulled at her long, black hair, as was her habit when she was nervous. She was not handsome, even by the modest standards of Agon, and at thirty-six had been well past the acceptable age of marriage when their union had been arranged. But she was tolerable company and in the nine years of their marriage had proved biddable and willing to accept the inevitable limitations of their relationship. He had even developed a manner of affection for her which had caused him to take the trouble to give her a rudimentary education, a practice against both law and custom on Agon where women were not permitted to read or write. The fiercely misogynistic culture of his adopted world had always discomforted and mystified him and he had never fully come to terms with it. The social and economic exclusion of over half the population seemed to him a tragic waste of human potential that must inevitably compromise the economic viability of Agon. But he was a guest here and there was nothing he could do about it beyond flouting the law privately and teaching his wife. She had accepted the lessons with reluctant grace and prospered modestly. It had been their secret and it had been her pleasure to accede to his wishes. She had never questioned or defied him before, but something was making her practically shake with fear.

"Very well," he said at length, "you may stay for a while."

"Thank you, Sir," she whispered as she rose and left without meeting his eye.

Deep in thought he watched her leave. What did they suspect? Had he made any mistakes? Anything at all that would arouse suspicion? He paced the room and reflected, trying to recall any action that might have betrayed him. He could think of none.

Presently she returned with his meal and placed it on a low table near the threshold to the terrace where she knew he liked to sit. The vermillion rays of the setting sun shimmered on the walls of the sparse, elegant dwelling like the flames of a campfire. Only her soft footsteps broke the intense silence. He sat cross-legged on a floor cushion and began to eat while she observed him from a distance. At length he started the conversation.

"How is your family?"

"My father and brothers are well, Sir."

The omission of any mention of the female members of the family was quite normal and Bru knew better than to ask. "I am glad to hear it," he replied.

There was a silence before she continued in a somewhat tentative manner. "My father was concerned by your absence; he wondered what had become of you."

"I thank your father for his concern but my absence was quite normal."

There was a pause before she probed further. "My father said you had failed to deliver four lectures at the Institute. This is not usual for you."

He glanced up from his meal. She was staring out at the evolving sky and would not look at him. "I arranged an adequate substitute to deliver the lectures."

"This was not normal."

She was getting reckless, on the very edge of permitted intercourse. He resumed eating. *What of it?* he thought. *They will eventually find out where he had been; why not let her bear the news?*

"I was with my researcher Engin Par, in the north, at a retreat he keeps. We were engaged in some difficult astro-geological theory that required a complete lack of distraction. I am sure your father will understand and I hope this will relieve his concern."

He did not look at her but could feel her relief from across the room. The tension in the atmosphere eased and he heard her whisper, "Thank you, Sir."

She had done her duty to her father by honouring his command to find out where her husband had been. He had done her the kindness of telling her and as she sat in the pregnant silence and gazed out beyond the terrace, she reflected on the first time she had set eyes on this strange being, her husband.

At thirty-six she had resigned herself to spinsterhood. Although high born, she knew she was not desirable and could not expect to receive offers of marriage from the most eligible quarters. Her father had already refused three offers from individuals deemed to be unsuitable, describing them as 'low rank fortune hunters'. She despaired at his reticence, but his judgement was vindicated when he solicited an offer from Solon Bru.

It was the duty of all the men of rank on Agon to marry and, although an alien and naturally unsympathetic to the institution of marriage, Bru had finally been prevailed upon to accept a union. Bru was Suran, an exile from a world quite unlike her own. She discovered that Surans were a slight, pale-skinned, androgynous people who had a pathological aversion to hair and were thus universally bald. They were disgusted by any form of physical contact and relied on technology to perpetuate their race. Her brothers had laughed at her, telling her that she was betrothed to a 'dickless, hairless freak', but when, at the marriage ceremony, she saw him for the first time, she was surprised to discover that her future husband was neither slight nor hairless. Solon Bru was just under two metres tall, well-built and had a fine head of cropped, dark brown hair. Indeed, he might have been taken for a native except for his beard, which was neatly trimmed instead of the full growth traditional on Agon and his intense, grey eyes that had glanced disinterestedly in her direction as she had entered the marriage chamber.

Solon Bru looked so masculine, so normal, that despite her father's warnings, she entertained thoughts of conjugal bliss. But in this, she was deceived, for despite his appearance, Bru was essentially a Suran. In the nine years of their marriage he had never touched her, nor shown the slightest inclination to do so and she had never seen him in any other state than fully clothed. She had the good sense and grace to accept this, for there were other compensations. Though distant he was kind, considerate and patient. He was liberal and did not require of her the strict confinement of a normal spouse. He was superior in virtue to her brothers and yes, even to her father and treated her as a person not as a chattel. In short, he was the best man she knew. Had Bru been less emotionally obtuse, he might have discerned that she had come to love him very much.

Her husband finished his meal and, for while sat in contemplative silence. A slight breeze wafted across the terrace and curled down the valley towards the city, carrying away the last of the day's breathless heat. Bru was never garrulous, but this evening he seemed more taciturn than usual, as if he was contemplating some intractable problem. At last he spoke again.

"And your father, I trust he is well?"

For a moment she did not know how to respond; he had asked her about her family earlier.

"He is well, Sir," she replied, not wishing to draw his attention to a mistake.

He realized his error and turned towards her. "I believe I have already enquired after your father's health. Forgive me."

"There is nothing to forgive," she uttered demurely.

He was about to speak again but was forestalled by an incoming communication. It was from his assistant, Engin Par. *What does he want now?* thought Bru, as he rose to receive the communication in his study. He had only just left him in his squalid, little retreat in the north.

Rhell watched him leave and close the door to his study behind him. There was an uneasy quality about him that she could not quite measure. She wondered at her father's particular insistence that she obtain news of Bru's whereabouts, but it was not a woman's place to question the ways of men. She stood and went to the low table to clear away the remains of her husband's meal.

Inside his study Bru accepted the communication and a three-dimensional life-sized image of Engin Par appeared before him. Par's normally alarmed expression had developed new heights of distress. His bony frame, shrivelled with years of worry, buckled before his employer. He gestured imploringly. "Doc... Doc, have you seen it?"

"Seen what exactly?" replied Bru with forced patience. He found his assistant's constant state of angst wearing. These past three days alone with him had been something of a trial.

"The newscast, of course... The newscast. Have you seen it? They know... they know. Oh Lord! What are we going to do? What are we going to do?" Tears welled in his eyes, he grabbed nervously at his thinning, gingery hair.

"To which newscast do you refer?"

Par shot him a look of surprise through his tears. "You mean you haven't seen it yet? It's the main item on Inter-World; it's everywhere."

"Remain connected," said Bru, deleting the squirming image of his assistant and commanding Inter-World to appear. He slumped in his chair and waited patiently for the nugget of news to escape the deluge of publicity.

"We now return to sector ninety-three for the latest report on the destruction of Station Two Eleven."

He sat up sharply whilst the commentary continued over the image of a field of debris glinting in the stark light of a nearby star.

"The Station was destroyed by a catastrophic explosion timed at zero, zero, eleven two five..."

Bru calculated the time; it was two days ago.

"There are thought to be no survivors from the three hundred and twenty six registered on board. We have, as yet, no explanation of what happened here. An inspection team from Barta Magnus is expected shortly. Station Two Eleven was owned by The Odin Recovery Company of Barta Magnus. It was primarily engaged in the resale, and salvage of interplanetary craft. A spokesperson for The Company said..."

Bru cut the transmission and stared, grim faced, into the void where it had been. Could there possibly be a connection between this disaster and his activities? It was impossible to be sure but the coincidence was alarming. The station had been destroyed just four days after Par had left it. He composed himself and returned to his assistant.

"Have you seen what they did? Have you? Oh shit! They know Doc... they know. It must have been Evangelists; who else could it have been? They must have followed me. Oh Lord! I can't bear it." Par dissolved into fresh paroxysms, biting his hand while tears and snot ran down his face and into his wispy excuse for a beard.

"Pull yourself together," said Bru sharply." There is nothing to suggest that this is the work of Evangelists or that it has any connection to us. You followed my instructions regarding your departure and return to Agon?"

Par nodded dejectedly. "Yes, I did, absolutely."

"Good, in that case we have nothing to fear. You could not have been detected; I assure you nobody knows anything about what we have found, especially not the Evangelists."

Par let out a final sob. "You know what they would do to us if they found out?"

Bru knew well enough what happened to apostates. Their executions were degrading, public and long drawn out. They were designed to maintain loyalty to the Faith through fear. As a Suran and a diplomat he would not suffer such a public fate, but he had no doubt that he would suffer privately. The Elders of Agon would be forced to render him to the Evangelists and he would simply disappear.

"They will not find out," he said with quiet authority. "Are you still working on the casket?"

Par nodded.

"Meet me at the Institute and bring it with you. We will decide what is to be done when you arrive."

"Shall I come straight away?"

"Yes, straight away."

"Alright."

Par's image faded and left Bru alone in his study. For the first time in his life he wasn't sure what to do. Had he made a mistake? Had Par been detected and followed? Could someone have found out what they had obtained on Station Two Eleven? It just seemed impossible to him that after forty-seven years he could still be worthy of such scrutiny. If they were still watching him it might follow that they would also be watching his assistant. He considered contacting Par to warn him of his thoughts, but concluded that it would only make him even more neurotic and irrational. Best to leave it until he saw him in person, then they would decide what to do.

He walked distractedly back into his living area. Rhell was seated, crosslegged on a floor cushion, waiting for him. "Is everything well Sir?" she asked.

He almost started at the sound of her voice; he had forgotten she was there. "Everything is well," he replied hastily. "I'm afraid we must forgo our conversation this evening, I am required at the Institute."

She made a poor attempt at concealing her disappointment. "May I stay here, Sir?"

He looked down at her and their eyes met briefly; he knew how much she treasured her time away from her father's house. "If you wish, although I do not know when I will return."

"I will wait," she replied as he walked past her and out on to the terrace. She watched his vehicle rise gracefully into the air and head away from her towards the city. She kept her eyes on it until it became just another light in the emerging star field of the sky.

II

Engin Par was, by no means, assured by Bru's apparent lack of concern. His natural disposition had brought him to a state of near hysteria and his vivid imagination entertained all sorts of macabre punishments and tortures that his frail body would have to endure before the blessed release of death. He reflected bitterly on his own stupidity and naivety for enthusiastically embracing Bru's passion for ancient mysteries. Why had he not seen that it would lead him to question and eventually abandon his faith and to expose himself as an apostate? What, a matter of hours ago had been an adventure, an excitement in his dull life, had now become a nightmare and the fruit of his sacrilege was now about to fall on his own head. He had convinced himself (and it was an easy job) that he was about die in the most appalling way.

He picked up the small casket from the makeshift analysis table they had set up in his retreat and contemplated destroying it. But what good would that do? It was already too late for that and if he were wrong Bru would be furious. He turned it over in his hands, caressing its smooth, featureless surface with his fingers and acquainting himself anew with the perfection of its engineering. Even now, when he knew exactly where it was, he could not see the join where the body and the lid came together. Only the analytical power of the finest instruments Bru had brought with him from Suran had revealed how to open it; a combination of pressures applied in a certain sequence to each of its corners. And yet there were no obvious working parts; the mechanism was in the structure itself, a hydrocarbon construct completely unknown to science. They could not even accurately date the object, its matrix was so alien; but, by its provenance, they knew was that it was very, very old.

And when, at last, they had solved the puzzle that kept it secure, it had smoothly opened to reveal something quite extraordinary, a thin fragment of material with strange markings on its surface. Bru had carefully lifted the object from the casket with a pair of tweezers and placed it between two sterile transparencies that he had sealed. He had then placed it on the analysis table for a better look.

"What is it?" Par had asked.

"The destroyer of lies; it's the destroyer of lies," came the reply and his friend and mentor had looked at him and smiled.

Par had been surprised by Bru's request that he should take the casket straight to his retreat where he would join him. Knowing Bru's natural Suran fastidiousness, it worried him, somewhat, that his basic accommodation would not meet with his boss's approval. He was right, even though he had tidied it up as best he could Bru still declared it to be squalid and depressing. "Never mind," he said, "it is remote and we will not be disturbed here."

They had worked on the casket for three days before discovering its secret. When, at last, they had opened it, Bru declared that he had better return to allay any suspicions. He took the fragment and left the casket for Par to continue work.

It was soon after the departure of his mentor that Par saw what had happened to Station Two Eleven and everything changed.

He stuffed the casket into his grubby tunic and took one last look about the rudimentary cabin. He knew that he would never see it again for he had decided not to meet Bru at the Institute but to throw himself on the mercy of the priests of Imbar. They might just be able to protect him from the Brothers of Mercy, the Evangelists. He would never be allowed to leave the Temple and would have to spend the rest of his life making devotions, but at least he would be alive and the priests weren't such a bad lot. It gave him pause that he would have to denounce his friend, the man who had trusted him and given him so much, but it was also Bru who had led him down this dangerous path and by that logic he justified the betrayal.

With a beating heart, he opened the cabin door a fraction and peeked out. A zephyr winding its way up the valley sang through the needles of the trees. It was a beautiful sound that Par loved, but now it only served to mask the movements of his enemies. He waited awhile and detected nothing moving in the darkness and then he stepped out and hurried down the winding path that led to his waiting vehicle.

Par owned a vehicle that had once been in public service. It was large, dishevelled and unkempt and had seen better days, but it was robust and reliable and rarely required maintenance. He climbed in, relieved at having made it safely and sat in the front seat. He placed the casket next to him and commanded the craft to take him to the Temple of Imbar. It shuddered and rose into the cold night air and he watched his retreat disappear as the star-tousled forest swallowed it up.

As he sped south towards the city, he stared fixedly ahead, his mind in increasing turmoil. What if he was wrong and Bru was right and the Evangelists knew nothing of their activities? To denounce a friend was not very admirable and he always fancied himself better than that. Was he being rational or was it just paranoia? His mind churned, at one moment attracted to one course of action, at the next attracted to another. He was so engrossed that, at first, he did not notice the strange, sickly, sweet odour that had begun to creep into his nostrils. Then he became aware of it, the unmistakable waft of incense that took him back to his youth and the long hours of worship in the temple. He wondered what piece of discarded detritus would generate such a smell; then he realized that he was not alone.

"Do not turn around, my son." The voice was soft and mellifluous, as if chanting an incantation.

He felt the blood drain from his body as fear paralysed him and stifled a cry in his throat.

The voice came close to his ear and he could feel warm breath on his skin. "I have come for you, Engin Par. I have come to grant you salvation."

Par tried to speak but no words escaped his dry mouth. He felt the warmth of his own urine as it trickled down his leg.

"Do not be afraid, Engin Par, for I am here to release you of your burden."

"Yes take it," he managed a broken whisper and fumbled for the casket.

A large, powerful hand stayed his skinny arm. "These trinkets are for fools. Close your eyes and pray. Do you recant your blasphemy, my son?"

"Yes... yes."

"Do you confess to the sin of apostasy?"

"Yes... I confess.

"Are you now truly the servant of He Who Knows and Sees All?"

"Please, I am a poor..."

"He knows what you are, my son. The Lord Minnar sees it all. He knows of your transgressions and sees into the darkest recesses of your soul. He has asked for your release and now I will obey His command and release you, Engin Par."

A wave of elation shot through Par's body; he was to be spared. "Release," he spluttered.

"Yes my son. I will release you to stand before him and be judged."

Par felt the powerful hands clamp around his scrawny neck and heard the soft flow of an incantation as the grip began to tighten. The brief elation of reprieve was banished, not by panic but by a calm resignation. His body felt so heavy, as though it would melt into the fabric of the craft. He did not struggle; he just gazed at the endless vault of the night sky before him. It was beautiful, so beautiful. For the first time in his adult life he was not afraid of anything.

III

The Institute of Science occupied the one hundred and first level of the Great Tower in the City of Imbar. There were six other towers of lesser stature in close proximity, each being surrounded by a tangled network of crude, squalid, mudstone buildings and heaving markets in which all manner of commodities could be obtained for the right price. The towers were an expression of a bygone, more prosperous age, an age of hope in which Imbar attempted to capitalize on its position and kudos as the cradle of mankind. But the economics of the depleted equatorial region had defeated the dreams of the city elders and the small wealth of Agon had drifted to more temperate climes.

The seven towers themselves had seen better days. One had been entirely abandoned and left to crumble, whilst two others had been declared unsafe with several unsuccessful attempts having been made to clear them of squatters and criminals. Large, ugly cracks in their fabric were evidence of frequent quakes that split the thin crust of the planet below Imbar. Only the temple remained impervious to geological assault. Its gaudy, overblown edifice stayed intact on a volcanic plug that had once been an island in the sea.

It had been something of a coup for the governing body of the Institute to entice Bru to their backwater of learning. His acceptance of their offer of a position as the head of astro-geology had greatly surprised them for they were not aware that he had been given very little choice in the matter. Bru was unique, for no other Surans had left that academic paradise for as long as anyone could remember. To make him comfortable they funded, at considerable expense, the construction of a dwelling located at a suitably remote distance from the city. They knew he would require solitude, at least until he acclimatized himself to the populous conditions on Agon.

He repaid their faith and expense with diligence, publishing numerous, influential treatises with the Institute's name on them and attracting to the faculty a cohort of distinguished professors. Apart from the Temple, the Institute was the only organ of distinction in Imbar and the governors of it were very pleased with their Suran exile.

Bru landed his vehicle at the high port, in a place reserved for him and walked the short distance to his research rooms at the Institute. A couple of students noticed him and nodded deferentially. It was late and the place was almost deserted. Once inside, he secured the door and went to his safe. He opened it and took out the fragment and gazed at it, as though it had some mesmeric spell over him. It was no more than six centimetres by four with two straight and two ragged edges where the material had been torn. The markings on its surface, which were truncated at the torn edges, were obviously a form of writing, but it was alien script and of insufficient quantity to attempt an interpretation. It intrigued him but he would never know what the words said.

He carefully placed the object on his workbench. All his instruments were dedicated to the analysis of rocks, minerals and crystals and they were not suitable for the delicate work required here. He was impatient to obtain a more complete analysis but that meant taking it to the one place he must not go.

He had to return to Suran.

The apprehension of such a thought troubled him for some time until it occurred to him that Par was overdue. He contacted him but could get no reply so he waited for a while and tried again. It suddenly struck him that Par might possibly betray him; the fellow was so agitated that he might be frightened into such a rash action. He cursed his lack of forethought and decided that he could not wait any longer. He had to find out where his assistant was and that meant invading the military systems of Agon. This was an extremely serious step for it would mean that, after it, he would have to flee and never come back. With grim resolution he went to his safe and took from it a small device he had illegally exported from Suran. It had rested securely at the bottom of his safe for forty-seven years and he had hoped that he would never have to use it, but now there it was, sitting innocently on his workbench.

He recited the code he had memorized and the small, grey cube instantly generated a menu of options in a light field above itself. Bru selected the system he wanted to invade and a moment later he had full control of it. It showed him that he had six point two three hours before the invasion would be traced back to his rooms. He gave it the code for Par's vehicle and the trace came through straight away. The vehicle had come to rest in a remote valley in the north about five hundred kilometres south of Par's cabin. He frowned; why would his assistant land in such a place? He accessed another system and brought up a real time image of the valley. He stared at in shock and disbelief. Smoke was rising from a large, black scar where a swathe of vegetation had been destroyed. He could see the carcass of the old craft burning at its centre.

"Check for human remains," he said in the desperate hope that Par might have escaped. His hopes were dashed; it indicated one human, deceased.

He felt himself weaken and had to sit down. His obsession and recklessness had led to the death of his assistant. He put his head in his hands and clenched his teeth while a sickening feeling of despair churned inside him. "Damn them," he hissed vehemently, but, in truth, he was cursing himself. He had miscalculated badly and now he knew he was in serious danger. There was no question about it; Par's fate had removed all doubt.

He tried to clear his mind and focus. He was a diplomat and that afforded him some privilege and immunity, but he had invaded the military systems of his hosts and that was something they were not likely to overlook or forgive. This was a worry but his most immediate concern was for the Brothers of Mercy, the Evangelists who might now know the nature of the threat he posed to the Faith and would stop at nothing to neutralize him. He decided that his best chance of escape was to get to the city of Aven, three hundred kilometres to the southeast. He knew somebody who would help him but it would not be an easy trip for he would not be able to use his own transportation. He would have to hire a vehicle on the black market and that meant entering the steaming favelas that surrounded the towers; not an inviting prospect.

He sent a brief, coded message to his contact in Aven then found his medical kit. Taking out a small phial of liquid, he dropped his pants and picked up the ancient fragment of material from his workbench. Pulling his scrotum to one side, he introduced it to the inside top of his left leg then carefully applied the contents of the phial to the area. A new skin formed over the object and took on the hue of his own. He observed the result with satisfaction; the tops of his legs were not hairy and the result was almost invisible.

He dressed himself and took one last look around the familiar room. He was about to depart when he was arrested by a communication. His heart rate shot up and he quickly declined acceptance but it over-rode him and came through anyway. A figure shimmered into the room. It was an Evangelist.

"Doctor Bru, forgive the intrusion."

The figure was dressed in the harsh, grey robes of the sect, similar to those worn by the Prophet. The close-cropped head turned slowly to face him and the grim face fixed him with malevolent eyes even though it could not see him. He stared in horror at it. It seemed to generate a malodorous physical presence in the room that turned his mouth dry.

"What do you want?" he spluttered.

"To offer our condolences; it is always difficult to lose a friend, even for someone of your race." A thin smile played on the lips of the image.

"Condolences? You murdered him."

"No Doctor Bru, *you* murdered him. Did you think we would not be watching you? Are you so arrogant and self-important that you think yourself immune? We always knew that you would eventually betray yourself. You are a blasphemer."

"I have never denied the Faith."

The Evangelist raised his voice. "You are a Suran and all Surans are condemned as impious. You should not have come here; you taint this sacred place with your foul stench."

Bru had heard enough; he was about to cut the communication when he realized that it was coming from his own home. Before he could speak again another sinister figure appeared dragging his wife by her long, black hair. Her eyes were wide with fear and she was breathing heavily.

Anger and loathing boiled up in him. "You will release my wife and vacate my home."

They ignored him and forced Rhell into a kneeling position in front of them. "This low creature is a blasphemer; her association with you condemns her. She is the lowest dust of the world. She has been taught to read," he added with particular menace.

Rhell was shaking; she shut her eyes, knowing what was about to happen.

Bru screamed desperately, "I demand you release…"

A large sword appeared from beneath the gown of the second Evangelist and flashed through the air in a high arc. Her head was parted from her body, which slumped to the floor as blood gushed from the severed arteries. The executioner held Rhell's dripping head aloft by her hair and made an incantation, but Bru did not hear it; he reeled and was violently sick.

On Agon, public decapitations were not uncommon, but Bru had never witnessed one. His head swam with the image that, for the rest of his life, he would never be able to expunge. He cut the communication without looking at it again and stood numbed, supporting himself on his workbench, his mind paralysed with the horror of what he had just seen. It was as though the world had folded in on him and buried him where no light or joy would ever touch him again. He was in a coffin, surrounded by death.

Slowly his eyes turned to the small, grey cube sitting impassively on his workbench. He stared at it, breathing heavily while his mind reorganized itself into an overpowering desire for revenge. The emotion developed and coursed through him and he activated the cube, releasing its full potential.

The chaos started almost immediately. The primitive systems of the tower went first and soon the tentacles of disruption began to spread throughout the city. Lights were extinguished and replaced by a dim, ruddy glow; alarms started to wail and confusion and panic began to spread. In the tower the docile, wealthy residents soon clogged the escape routes with their clambering bodies. Most thought it was a quake and they knew enough to get out of the old building; they had seen the fate of the other towers.

In the dim light, Bru found his rock hammer; a small, powerful atomic pulveriser he used to split and polish geological samples. He picked it up and adjusting it to a low setting, fired it at the door mechanism of his room. It melted and sealed him in his own laboratory; if they were waiting for him outside they would be disappointed. He picked up the grey cube and dropped it into a pocket in his tunic. Now he had to escape.

The Great Tower consisted of an agglomeration of residential, commercial and academic facilities, evolved over the years in a haphazard way. Bru had never concerned himself with what accommodation neighboured his. He knew that above his rooms the Institute occupied another level, but had no idea what was below him. Whatever type of accommodation it was he knew that it must be vacated by its occupants by now. He increased the power level of the rock hammer and fired it at a clear section of his laboratory floor. The operation was silent and, at first, there was no apparent effect, but the atomic bonds that held the material together began to fail and a section of floor about a metre in diameter began to sag. He turned off the rock hammer and stamped on the depression; it collapsed noisily into the void between the levels.

He eased himself into the hole and kicked away the rubble. He was now standing on the ceiling plate of what lay below. He spread his legs and fired the hammer at the area between them. The brittle material caved in with a crash and a cloud of dust. He covered his nose and mouth with his arm, knelt down and peered in.

The dim, ruddy light revealed an apartment dwelling of some quality, much as would be expected on the upper levels of the tower. He had broken into the main living area and, also as expected, there appeared to be no one at home. He eased himself into the hole he had made and dropped to the floor. He started for the exit that would lead him to the common areas, but as he crossed the floor, he became aware that he was not alone. Someone was watching him from the bedroom door. He swung round and saw that it was a female child, about twelve years old. She was wearing a pale, pink slip that barely covered her modesty; her blonde hair tumbled over her shoulders and framed a perfect face of fair skin. She observed him with a pair of startlingly blue eyes.

"What are you doing here?" she demanded in nasal voice that betrayed her origin. She was not a child of Agon.

Bru froze and stared. Why had she been left here?

"What are you doing here?" she repeated, "you did not explain."

"I'm just leaving and you should come with me; it's not safe here."

"I may not leave," she replied, "my daddy says so."

"Your daddy is wrong, you must leave. Come with me."

"My daddy is never wrong and you are an intruder," she replied flatly.

Bru looked at her carefully, she was too perfect. "I'm leaving," he said decisively but the girl moved with surprising speed and placed herself between him and the exit.

"You must not leave, you are an intruder. You must wait for my daddy to come back."

"Get out of my way," said Bru, advancing on her.

"Intruder!" she shrieked in her high, nasal voice and rushed at him.

He just had time to raise his rock hammer and fire it at her head. Her head exploded, showering him with warm gore, but the headless body closed on him and snapped its arms around his midriff like a vice. He was lifted off his feet as the thing started to march across the room, squeezing tighter and tighter as it went. The rock hammer fell from his grasp as he struggled to free himself from the deadly embrace. His back slammed against the wall as the grotesque cadaver marched blindly on. It was going to crush him to death. Desperately he plunged his arm into the neck cavity and down into the warm, gelatinous gore of the body. He felt for the beating heart, trapped within the composite of the ribcage, closed his hand around it and yanked with all his strength. It came free and he pulled it out through the neck. Immediately the grip eased and the marching stopped and thing began to wilt. They crashed to the floor and the arms went limp, while the body twitched violently before becoming still. He rolled free and lay there next to it panting.

He got to his feet and stared down at it. The slip had ridden up to reveal inappropriately mature genitals. He kicked the body to make sure it was entirely inert then he picked up his rock hammer and found the dressing room. He stripped off his tunic and used it to remove the gore from his face and arms then he carefully explored himself for broken ribs. He was sore and there would be severe bruising but nothing else too serious.

He washed himself with cold water then inspected the extensive wardrobe, which was entirely male. The degenerate occupant was about his size but the clothes were finer than he would have liked. He picked out a traditional, loose fitting gown in plain white and put it on. It fitted him well enough but without his pants he felt naked and vulnerable. He observed the result in the reflector; at least he could now pass for a native.

He retrieved the grey cube from his tunic and placed his old clothes in the atomizer, forgetting that it would not function now. It didn't matter; they were not likely to be found before he left the planet. He picked up the rock hammer and made his way to the exit of the apartment and sealed the door behind with a quick, low-level blast.

Outside, the common area was deserted. In the distance he could hear shouting and screaming and the melee of panic. There was a pungent whiff of smoke in the air from fires that had started on one of the lower levels. He made his way to the emergency escape shaft and looked down. A stairway wound its way into the murky depths. He began to descend, moving quickly, ignoring the pain in his ribs. Down and down he went, level after level, until each became a blur. At level fifty-two he encountered his first evacuees, two old men wheezing their way down the steps. He pushed past them and soon came across other escapees, as the trickle of humanity became a throng and eventually a river of bodies, clambering to get out. The pall of acrid smoke became stronger as fires that had started on the populous, labyrinthine lower levels took hold. People were hammering on doors that had jammed shut, sealing them in to their fate as the human river pushed on, ignoring their desperate cries.

Bru was carried down in the crush of the inadequate escape shaft. The sickening touch and smell of flesh pressed into him almost overwhelming him with nausea. He had not expected such disorganization and mayhem to result from the disruption, but it served him well to be one of a large anonymous crowd. How many would die in the neglected abdomen of the tower he knew not. He could not think of such things. He just had to get out, get away from all these people.

At level nine the crush eased as the choking stair shaft spilled out on to the wide apron that surrounded the tower. About four thousand people had already escaped and thronged the area, milling about in bewilderment. Many looked up at the smoke now generously billowing from various points in the façade; some were lying down injured and moaning; some were tending them; some were already dead.

Bru emerged gasping for air and began to push his way through the disorientated, noisy crowd. He made his way to the parapet of the apron where a long ramp led down to ground level and into the favela. The ramp was constantly garrisoned to prevent the disenfranchised people of the slums from gaining access to the elite of the tower; but now the garrison had turned their weapons inwards on the residents, commanding them to stay put for their own safety. But the people were not listening to the soldiers and surged forward in panic. There was a discharge of weapons and screams as some of the crowd fell. An angry mood quickly developed but the garrison stood firm against the swell of abuse while more and more people spilled out of the burning tower and packed the high apron.

Bru could see he was trapped and reasoned that the garrison had been instructed to contain the crowd because they were looking for him. An injured woman clawed at him for help; she was bleeding from an ugly head wound. He pushed her away in disgust. He had to think; he had to get away.

Suddenly the sound of a deep rumble silenced the crowd. It sounded like a quake but it was not. The building shuddered and a great plume of fire burst from the façade of the tower and lit up the night sky like a sun. A terrible roar followed as the explosion shattered a huge, black chasm into the fabric of the building. Debris cascaded down the face of the tower, crashing on to the apron and lacerating the crowd. Two men no more than a metre from Bru were hit and killed instantly; their blood splashed his gown and face. As a section of the structure above them failed, more debris fell and now the garrison could not stop the mob. They surged forward, ignoring the weapons and overwhelming the guards who were thrown over the wall to their deaths. They burst down the ramp and into the favela and with them, carried along in a river of fleeing humanity, went Solon Bru.

IV

The dichotomy of existence that persisted on Agon was the direct result of its poverty, and nowhere more so than the Divine City of Imbar in which the elite tower dwellers spent their lives in relative affluent comfort whist the vast majority of the population existed in penury.

As the original seat of human settlement, Agon had once enjoyed the fruits of a civilization grown from rudimentary villages around the Sea of Creation to the occupation of the entire planet where the temperate conditions enhanced harmonious industry. Over two billion people once dwelt on Agon, but war and greed plundered its resources and destroyed its once benign environment and reduced it to a vassal world on which less than forty million now existed.

It is not unusual to find that, for the maintenance of the power, a governing elite requires the military suppression of the disenfranchised majority; and so it was on Agon. It is also not unusual to find a boiling anger and resentment among the suppressed and so, when the unfortunate residents of the tower surged down the ramp and into the favela some were set upon, robbed and murdered by the waiting mob gathered there to witness the destruction of the hated tower. But many got through the gauntlet and disappeared into the labyrinth of slums that they had so recently despised.

Bru was lucky; his robe had been slashed by a knife but he was unharmed. Into the dark alleys he ran with a group that had detached themselves and escaped the baying mob. On they ran, scattering through the narrowing mud brick labyrinth until just three of them remained, he and two young men.

"What happened? Where are we?" gasped the younger, a beardless youth of about sixteen; his wild, nervous eyes anxiously searching the darkness.

"I don't know," replied the other, an older man, about twenty. "My wife is back there. I lost her in the crowd, and I don't know where she is."

"It's not safe here," said Bru, "I'm going on."

"Yes, we should move on," said the younger man, "where to?"

"Anywhere but here," replied Bru and turned to go just as another explosion racked the tower and a great flash of fire arced across the sky and lit the alley for a moment.

The older man's eyes widened as he saw the face of the man he was with. "You're The Suran!" he exclaimed.

"You're mistaken," replied Bru quickly.

"No I'm not, I know you. I was a student at the Institute. You *are* The Suran."

Bru cursed and began to move away from them but up ahead he caught sight of two figures in the deep shadows advancing towards them. He turned to find that three more had entered the alley from the other end. They were trapped. He felt for the rock hammer; it was gone, fallen through the rip in his robe. More men entered the alley from both ends. The younger man began to wail as he saw the dull flash of knives coming for them. *This is it*, thought Bru, *this is where it ends, in this filthy, degraded place, on this benighted planet.* He accepted it and what surprised him was how calm he felt. He was so tired, so physically and mentally exhausted that death would come as a welcome relief. He hoped it would not be too traumatic, that it would all be over quickly. He stood still and awaited his assailants.

"Stop!" screamed the older of his two companions, "you don't know who we are."

The leading assailant raised his long knife. "Filthy towermen," he growled, "I'm going to slice you up."

"Wait… no wait, this is the Suran; the richest man on the planet."

The assailant hesitated.

"It's him I tell you, we're together, we can make you rich," pleaded the man.

Cautiously, knife poised, the leader advanced. He was a pockmarked fellow with an ugly scar down the side of his face. He was about the same build and height as Bru.

"We're together; you'll be richer than you ever dreamed…"

A blow to the head cut off the man mid-sentence, he went down clutching his face, blood poured from his nose. The leader squinted at Bru's face through the darkness.

"You don't look like one of our kind. Is it true? Are you the Suran?"

Bru held his eyes unblinkingly. "Yes," he said.

A grin flashed across the face of the leader. "You're *my* Suran now," he said and before Bru knew what was happening he felt a sickening blow to the side of the head that seemed to loosen his brain and make it rattle around in his cranium. Hands grabbed him and dragged him down the alley, deeper and deeper into the favela. Behind him the screams of his two companions faded into the mudbrick canyons. Their deaths would not be easy.

V

When Bru regained his senses he found himself lying on a hard stone floor looking up at a soot-stained, vaulted ceiling. His head swam as he tried to get up; his brain pounded as if it was trying to escape his skull. He had never been hit before and the experience had shocked him. He slumped back in pain. After a while he became aware of a sound nearby; it sounded like thunder. Holding his head, he raised himself and tried to focus. A man sitting on a low cushioned ledge swam into view. He was middle-aged, fair-skinned and completely hairless, just like a Suran, but he was not a Suran for he was almost naked, his modesty saved only by the presence of a white loincloth. The sound of thunder was coming from the image on which he was concentrating. It was the image of the burning tower.

He tore his eyes away. "Ah, my Suran, you are back with us. Quite a business, isn't it?"

Bru made no reply.

"Do you know how many you have killed today?" He leaned forward, enjoying the moment. "Nearly three thousand and counting. You are to be congratulated."

"I don't know what you mean."

"You are too modest, Doctor Bru. You should acknowledge and enjoy your little victories."

Bru stared at his host, unable to conceal his disgust. The man was overweight with pronounced breasts and a swollen belly. He was clearly not suffering the privations of the favela. "You describe this as a victory?"

"Quite so. How did you do it?"

"As I said, it has nothing to do with me."

The man's flesh shook as he laughed and produced the invader and tossed it into the air and caught it in his small, fat hand. "Then what is this?"

Bru was silent. The man put it carefully down beside him. "It does not matter for the moment. But forgive me, I have not introduced myself, I am known here as Three Corners."

"I have heard of you. You are a felon."

"And I have heard of you, Doctor Bru. We foreigners should stick together don't you think? You despise them too, don't you? These peasants."

"I despise no one."

"You despise me. You cannot hide it, or is it all this exposed flesh that discomforts you? I know you Surans are so peculiar about such things."

"It is your house, not mine."

"Well observed, Doctor. You know I once lived there, in the great tower. We had a grand apartment on the one hundred and twenty first level, my wife and I. We lived like lords... like priests. A long time ago," he added wistfully, "before I was cast out. Unjustly cast out, to rot in this filthy hole. We have that in common, we are both exiles."

"We have nothing in common. What is your intention?'

Three Corners considered for a moment. "That depends on your value."

"I am a diplomat of Suran, they will respond to a ransom."

"I am not a fool, Doctor Bru. The exile of a Suran is extremely unusual, perhaps even unique. I do not pretend to know what transgression led to it, but I'll wager that the High Council of Suran would not be too distressed if you just disappeared." He waved a dismissive hand. "They are not likely to pay good money to get the likes of you out of a hole."

Bru remained silent: Three Corners' analysis was uncomfortably accurate; the High Council was not likely to come to his assistance. His captor stared at him expectantly, as if anticipating a revelation.

Bru allowed the silence to travel a little further before muttering, "I have some personal wealth."

Three Corners beamed; his plump, baby features waggled with pleasure. "There we are," he declared. "We have known each other for only a few moments and, already, we have come to a right understanding. An understanding of gentlemen," he added decisively.

"I have demands."

Three Corners feigned shock. "Are you sure you're in a position to issue demands?"

"You want money and I have some. I want to leave Agon."

"That is beyond my ability."

"In that case, you will get me to Aven."

"I might be able to arrange that." He produced a small tablet from nowhere and tossed it to Bru. "Display your portfolio and do not play me false, Suran."

Bru identified himself and authorized it to display the considerable value of his account on Agon, thankful that he had secreted the larger part of his fortune elsewhere. He threw it back to Three Corners who perused it while his jowls wobbled into a smile. "Well, well, who'd have thought it? Don't teachers do well for themselves." He fixed Bru with a malicious gaze that betrayed his true character. "The price is everything. All you have."

"Don't be ridiculous, that would leave me without means."

"I assure you, I am in earnest. I require it all."

"Will you leave me with nothing?"

Three Corners threw the tablet back. "I will leave you with your life. Confirm it."

"I will, when I am in Aven."

"Confirm it now, I will keep my word."

"And I will keep my money, until I'm in Aven."

A flash of anger was instantly suppressed by a forced smile. "Doctor Bru, you will not go to Aven, you will not even leave this room alive unless you confirm the payment now."

Bru regarded the hard-eyed face protruding from the repulsive flab. There seemed to him little choice. "What is to stop you from killing me the moment I confirm this financial arrangement?"

"Nothing, except honour. Without honour we are nothing, Doctor Bru."

It occurred to Bru that the commodity of honour would be rather scarce in these surroundings, but he was cornered and there was no alternative. He confirmed the payment.

Three Corners beamed. "There, that wasn't so bad, was it? Now I am rich and you are not. However you are rich in the way of the vital organs that remain inside you. Now you should get some rest, you have a long journey ahead."

"How so? Aven is only three hundred kilometres from here."

Three Corners laughed. "I don't have a flying machine Doctor Bru, I am but a poor man. At least, I was!"

He waved his hand as Bru stood with some difficulty. Two thugs entered.

"Return that to me," said Bru, pointing at the invader by the side of Three Corners. "It is no use to you, only I can command it."

"Ah this," he said picking it up. "I think I'll keep it for now. You've done enough damage for the time being. And, by the way, my apologies for your undignified treatment earlier, my men can be ruffians sometimes."

Bru took a last look at the small, grey cube. "The two men that were with me?"

"Do you really need to know, Doctor Bru?"

Bru nodded and was escorted from the smiling presence of Three Corners. They took him to a cell-like room that contained nothing but a bed roll on the floor and locked him in. He lay down, his mind racing. They had searched him while he was unconscious; the thought made him squirm, but they had not discovered the fragment hidden below the false skin on his thigh. But it had been too easy, even with the cleaning out of his Agon accounts it had just seemed to be too easy. And with that disquieting thought reverberating in his brain, he fell into a deep sleep.

Back in his chamber Three Corners smile disappeared as he watched the gowned figure approach.

"I'll take that," he said, stretching out a large, powerful hand.

Three corners reluctantly handed over the invader. "I did well."

The Evangelist pierced him with a look of distaste. "It was acceptable. He probably suspects, but he has no choice. His journey begins."

"Where do you think he will go?"

"He will betray his fellow conspirators, wherever they are. We will finally know the rotten source of this blasphemy."

Three Corners hesitated, but his curiosity got the better of him. "What exactly did he do?"

"That is not your concern."

"Of course, I just wondered, that's all. I just wish to serve you,"

"You will serve me with your silence."

"Of course... of course. I meant nothing, Brother Dax."

The Evangelist threw him a hell-freezing glance and turned to leave. Three Corners debated whether to risk asking the question most vital to him. Overcoming his fear he blurted, "And the money? Can I keep it?"

The Evangelist rounded on the obnoxious flesh heap and spat the answer through clenched teeth. "If nothing goes wrong, I will allow you to keep your worthless head."

VI

Solon Bru was vaguely aware of an unpleasant sensation as he groggily emerged from his deep sleep. He was being touched! Actually touched, shaken to his senses with some violence. He pushed the offending hand away as he regained consciousness and the horror of his situation returned in all its misery. He was still in the putrid cell in the bowels of the favela, still on the run, still homeless and stripped of everything he had known for the past forty-seven years.

"Get away from me," he growled. "Do not touch me."

The shaking stopped and he focused on its source, a lad of about twelve, grinning from ear to ear. "Get up," he said.

Bru raised himself painfully. His torso still hurt from the crushing and bruising from the arms of the simulant and his head still pounded from the blow that had knocked him senseless in the darkness of the favela. His mouth was so dry he could hardly swallow.

"I am to take you to Aven of Agon. We leave now."

Bru regarded the lad sceptically. "You?"

"Yes, me. What's wrong with that?"

"I was expecting a maturer escort."

The boy's grin disappeared and he suddenly looked older. "I'm fourteen, and I'll get you there. I am Gong Lat." He announced his name as though it should mean something to the world.

Bru struggled to his feet. "I am…"

"I know who you are, follow me."

They filed out of the cell and into a series of passages and alleys that twisted and turned in a seemingly endless tangle. Bru caught glimpses of hearth fires through ill-fitting doors; the tangy smell of cooking; muffled voices in the half light of the early morning. Few people were about, those that they met cast down their eyes respectfully as Gong Lat strode imperiously past them.

After some time they came to the edge of the city where the relative formality of the favela dissolved into a landscape of huge scrap heaps and steaming piles of detritus. Even in the cool of the morning the stench was horrific and Bru was obliged to cover his nose and mouth with his sleeve. Some early risers were already scouring amongst the filth; some huddled around camp fires, their emaciated faces caught in the flickering light; others still sprawled on the dusty ground or under rude shelters, catching the last moments of rest before the merciless grind of the coming day.

Gong Lat pulled out a sidearm and they continued to pick their way carefully through the hellish landscape. Bru knew of such places but was still shocked at what he saw. They stepped over a sleeping child sprawled carelessly in the path that wound between the heaps of rubbish. The child did not stir and Bru realized that it was dead. Then he noticed other corpses, lying abandoned, overtaken by exhaustion or murder; some naked; some being stripped by the ghouls who stalked the night time hours. The denuded bodies were thrown on to the heaps to become part of the decaying mass; legs, heads, arms and hands protruded from the rubbish, as though grasping their last moments of life. The smell of death was so overpowering it made his head swim. He had flown over this hell many times but had never looked down, never given a thought to the fate of the crawling mass of humanity below.

Three men appeared from behind a heap; Gong Lat raised his sidearm and they melted away. "Stay close," he said over his shoulder.

Bru did not need the instruction; he was right on the lad's heels. Never before had he been so glad to be close to another human being. As they pressed on the piles of filth diminished and eventually gave way to the cruel, rock-strewn desert that formed the floor of the Great Rift Valley. The stench faded in his nostrils and Bru was able to breathe easily at last. He turned and looked at the city. The light of the rising sun was catching the tip of the great tower still smoking from several ugly, blackened rents in its façade. He wondered if they would ever repair the building and what would become of the Institute. Probably it would be abandoned, and the tower left to rot as others had been by the indolent citizens of Imbar the Divine. Eventually the whole city would crumble to be consumed in a pit of chaos leaving only the shining temple on the headland of the Sea of Creation, standing proud surrounded by a latrine of human depravity.

Bru turned his back on it for the last time and followed the boy into a gulley where they stopped for a few moments' rest. They settled against a boulder and Gong Lat took a bottle from his backpack and handed it to him. Bru took it and drank. It tasted strange but it quenched his thirst and cooled his parched mouth. "What is this?" he said.

The boy eyed him curiously. "Water. We add things, so it doesn't kill us."

Bru returned his gaze and noticed the wide face and pale eyes of his companion. His hair was light brown indicating that he was not of pure Agon stock. He had a pleasantly mischievous face, which wore a permanently amused expression that belied his true character. He grinned easily, revealing (unusually), a perfect set of teeth, but it was a grin of menace rather than mirth and gave the impression that he could just as soon bite your jugular as greet you.

He stood up abruptly. "We move on."

"Where are we going?"

The boy pointed east, down the valley. "About five kilometres."

He set off and Bru followed him along the gulley. They were off the main track and below the level of the valley floor shimmering in the amber light of the rising sun above them. The world began to heat up and he was soon sweating in his robe as they picked their way along the boulder-strewn wadi. It was many years since he had walked such a distance and his body and feet were soon in rebellion so that he was obliged to stop frequently and swig the strange water while his companion looked on disdainfully.

At last the wadi opened into a clearing and they came to a small settlement consisting of several mud brick hovels. Bru remained outside while Gong Lat entered one of the huts. Some words were exchanged and he emerged with an elderly, toothless fellow dressed in filthy rags. He passed Bru a suspicious look and led them around the back of the hut to a ramshackle shed that he prized open to reveal a dusty vehicle. Bru observed in dismay as they pulled it into the light. It was an all-terrain cart of rudimentary design with two seats below a frame that might have once supported a canopy but was now open to the elements. The thing looked ancient, incapable of reaching the next village, let alone the three hundred kilometres to Aven.

"What is this?" he asked angrily, now convinced he had been tricked.

Gong Lat ignored him and loaded his backpack on to the rack behind the seats. "Get on," he said.

"I will not," replied Bru, "this wreck will strand us; we will die in the badlands, assuming you can get it going."

Gong Lat climbed into his seat behind the steering gear and strapped himself in. "It's this or walk. You choose."

Bru knew he had no choice and reluctantly climbed into the seat next to Gong Lat.

"You might want to strap yourself in," said the lad, handing him a pair of dark goggles, "and put these on, it's going to be a dusty ride."

He tossed the old peasant a coin and, covering him with a choking cloud of dust, careered off into the desert at an unexpectedly terrifying speed. Bru held on grimly as the cart swerved and plunged through the arid landscape while its driver grinned with impish delight.

"We will go south west," he announced over the raucous throb of the motor, "I know a way up the cliff. It's tricky but this will do it.'

Bru did not like the sound of the proposal but kept silent while the thing pummelled and shook him so violently that he thought his spine would shatter at any moment. When at last they stopped below the scarp for a break, he was so exhausted that he rolled out of his seat and lay gasping on the ground.

Gong Lat stood over him and laughed derisively. "You have to roll with it, Suran. Relax and just roll with it. Still think we won't get there?"

Bru struggled stiffly to his feet. "You might get my bones there, but they may not still be attached to me."

"I'm going for a piss; I suggest you do the same. We won't be stopping again before nightfall."

"Wonderful," said Bru and limped off behind a boulder.

The ascent of the cliff was alarming. They had turned into what looked like a blind canyon but the boy had insisted there was a way up near the end and that he had done it before. They made their way up a steep scree that led to a ledge that wound its way precipitously around the cliff face. Gong Lat was not grinning now as he guided the vehicle minutely along the friable edges of the ledge. Bru undid his harness, ready to jump clear in case the worst should happen, which looked to him very likely, for there were times when he could look over the edge at a sheer drop of hundreds of metres.

At last the gradient began to ease and they found themselves on the high plateau that surrounded the rift valley where the air was cooler and scrub-like vegetation clung to the barren soil. No people lived on the great central plateau. There were no farmers or nomads, no villages, not even a solitary hut punctured the endless, flat horizon. Nothing but hour after hour of soulless monotony.

They travelled in silence across the empty landscape until the sun neared the horizon and the cloudless sky turned to vermillion. Several times Bru had drifted into a troubled sleep but had been jolted awake as the cart swerved and shuddered over the rocky ground. At last the torture ceased and Gong Lat brought them to a halt in a shallow depression surrounded by low boulders.

"We will stop here for the night," he announced, dismounting and producing from his pants a long, vicious looking knife. He disappeared behind a boulder as Bru painfully eased himself from the cart and tried to work some life back into his aching body. Presently the boy came back clutching a bundle of scrub and placing it on the ground, lit it with a low charge from his firearm.

"I like a fire when I'm out here at night, it gets cold," he said and handed Bru the knife. "You get some more for burning while I unpack."

Bru took the blade and headed off to gather more kindling, when he returned Gong Lat had laid out some food on a dirty cloth next to the fire and was swigging wine from a flask.

"Took your time, Suran, thought you weren't coming back."

Bru threw down the kindling and sat down near the fire. "I am not skilled with a knife."

"Drink?" said the lad, offering the flask. Bru declined and Gong Lat grinned and pulled out another flask. "Go ahead, I haven't touched it."

Bru took it and drank; the raw bitterness of the liquor brought tears to his eyes and made him cough.

Gong Lat laughed. "Not the fine wine you've been used to Suran, is it? We call it Devil's Piss."

"It's well named."

"Have some food."

Bru observed the dubious picnic and realized how hungry he was. He had not eaten since the meal Rhell had prepared him the night before. Only the night before, he reflected ruefully. It felt like a lifetime ago. He picked up a piece of the food-cake and put it into his mouth. It was surprisingly good; sweet, with a perfumed, flowery taste.

"My Ma made it," Gong Lat informed him.

"It's acceptable."

Bru finished the cake and took another swig of the liquor. It burned its way down his throat but this time it felt good, the first mouthful having dulled his taste buds. The boy watched him intently as the last vestiges of the sun gave way to the effulgent night and the temperature began to drop.

Gong Lat broke the long silence. "It was you wasn't it? Lit up the tower."

"What?"

"That's why we're here isn't it? Getting you away from there."

"You've been misled."

"Don't think so. What a mess. Brilliant."

"How so? What is so marvellous about it? Thousands of people got killed."

"Good, I hate those fuckers, every one of them. They deserve to die. They take everything; suck us dry; leave us with nothing. I hate them."

"What do you know about it? You're still a child."

Gong Lat's face darkened in the flickering light. "I'm not a child, I'm a man fully grown. I've had sex many times."

"Any of those times with another human being?"

Suddenly Bru found himself staring at the end of a firearm with Gong Lat's angry eyes behind it. He recoiled in fear, convinced the boy was going to kill him, but Gong Lat's expression suddenly lightened, as if night had become day, and he laughed.

"A joke. You made a joke."

Bru nodded eagerly. "Yes, a joke."

"Alright, perhaps I won't kill you then."

"Were you going to?"

The boy shook his head. "No, my father ordered me to get you to Aven alive."

"Your father?"

"Three Corners."

"Three Corners is your father?"

"Yes, until I kill him. I will have to kill him; he will never give up the manor."

"Is that what you want? His little empire of skulduggery and murder."

"It's all I'm going to get. People like me don't get…"

His voice tailed off and he fell into a reflective mood as Bru studied him. Now he could see his father's features, younger and thinner and mixed with the darkening influence of his Agon mother. It was a surprisingly pleasing confluence.

Gong Lat threw another piece of brushwood on the fire and it crackled into life. It was the only sound in the world of cool, darkening peace. They were two beings alone in the vast empty plain of dust, scrub and starlight and it felt as though they were the last humans alive and nothing really mattered. "Twice," he said. "I've had sex twice. That's all."

Disarmed by the liquor and the sudden honesty of the boy, Bru found himself speaking before he could think. "Twice more than me." Instantly he regretted it, as Gong Lat was suddenly attentive.

"You've never done it?"

Bru shook his head. "I am a Suran, don't you know what that means?"

"I know that Surans aren't men or women, but something in between."

"Androgynous, that is correct."

"But you are not like that; my father said you were not. He said you are a man, right and proper."

Bru shuddered inwardly at the thought of having been so inspected. "That is true; I am unfortunate in that respect."

"But it's better to be a man. Men are more important, stronger."

"That is so on Agon, but not on Suran. On my world androgyny is prized, the purer the better. In character the population is essentially female."

"Fuck that, I'd kill myself."

"Some have, those that don't fit in."

"These 'androgoes', what do they look like? I mean underneath. The men have cocks don't they? And the women have holes, just like here. You couldn't get babies otherwise, you'd all die out."

Bru considered it. He had never before discussed this taboo subject with anyone; it would have been unthinkable, certainly on Suran, to broach the subject of reproduction other than in a purely academic way. But here it didn't seem out of place, indeed, he quite welcomed the discussion. "Suran cannot support a large population so a long time ago the rulers experimented with a form of eugenics to control it. They used chemical castration and engineered a population selected for physical neutrality because they found the subjects both docile and intelligent. Over time the need for sex disappeared altogether because it was not needed to sustain the population. What they ended up with is a world of less than five million on which there are no cities, towns or villages and every individual lives in isolation by design and inclination."

Gong Lat stared at him as if he had just been speaking in an entirely different language. "So the women don't have holes and tits and the men don't have cocks? What the fuck do they have then?"

"We do not refer to ourselves by gender. It is considered a deep insult. We do not expose ourselves to one another, but I suppose what you're asking is what is the physical norm of a Suran."

"I suppose."

"Essentially, a male body with female genitals."

"Blokes with cunts!" Gong Lat roared with laughter until tears rolled down his face. Bru laughed too, infected by the laughter of a peasant boy who saw only absurdity in his world and all it represented.

"I'd love to see that. What a freak show."

"You are not the first to think that, but it is natural to us."

Gong Lat wiped the tears of laughter from his eyes. "And they actually made the people like that?"

"A long time ago."

"But how come you aren't like that? I mean you've got a cock, you're a man aren't you?"

Bru nodded, "I am male, but it is quite rare on Suran to be so gender specific. There are others that could be described as female, but most are neither."

"Is that why they chucked you out? I mean you didn't fit in did you?"

"It was difficult for me, that's true, but it is not the reason I had to leave. I don't wish to discuss that subject."

"Fair enough."

They talked into the night, for the boy had many questions about this strange man and his even stranger world. He laughed at Bru's description of the Suran aversion to hair and their universal baldness; he listened attentively to Bru's description of his upbringing and education by a single person until he was twelve and independent; the traumatic separation and his solitary existence thereafter. He was agog that Bru's education lasted until he was twenty-seven and that it was undertaken under the sole tutelage of a powerful teacher called a *doyen*. His questions were at one time, frivolous, at others, incisive and Bru answered most of them with an unaccustomed candour, until, eventually, they could no longer keep themselves awake and they slept by the dying fire in that dusty hollow in the vast plain of Agon.

VII

The vision of his wife's decapitation shook him from his sleep and he woke up in a sweat even though he was cold. The fire was out and the sun was still a long way below the horizon when he opened his eyes onto the star-filled sky. The vision of the slack-jawed, blank-eyed expression of his wife's dead face, with her blood dripping from the severed neck as the Evangelist held it aloft, resounded and amplified in his mind until he could stand it no longer and, though still tired, he raised himself and ambled painfully away to urinate behind a boulder. The cold had crept into his bones during the night and he could not stop shivering. He had spent his entire life cushioned by technology and the privations of raw nature were alien to him. He had never slept in the open air, never been exposed to such prolonged cold, never had to sleep on anything other than the finest beds. This single night had taught him more about himself than he had ever wanted to learn. He was not in the prime of life; he was soft, and ignorant of many worldly things.

Gong Lat was still sleeping soundly, curled up next to the ashes of the fire with his thumb in his mouth. Bru stared at him and experienced a strange, fleeting sensation of affection. In all his previous relationships he had never experienced any emotional charge; they were acquaintances rather than friends. Even Engin Par, or his wife Rhell, whom he might have described as friends, were little more than respected associates to whom he attached no real emotional significance. Perhaps the emotional stringency of his Suran upbringing had been maintained by the quality of his existence on Agon. His aloofness, his isolation, had all been encouraged by deference and there had been no need for him to concern himself with the niceties of social intercourse. But the traumatic events of the last day were conspiring to strip away the carefully layered veneers of his character and a small kernel of humanity was beginning to emerge. The thought troubled him and he crept off to sit in the cart and await the end of the long night.

Gong Lat awoke just before dawn and rose with the lithe easiness of youth. They ate and drank in silence and set off just as the first sector of the sun turned the landscape into a mystical pink wilderness. Very little passed between them during the five bone-shaking hours of the journey. The boy, tight lipped, steered them through the relentless terrain, while Bru ruminated on the challenges ahead.

He was dozing when they finally stopped on the edge of a wide ravine. He opened his eyes and saw the city in the distance, spread like an ugly rash across the valley floor. Through it the grey river Aven meandered like an open sewer, its banks awash with teaming shanties and crumbling warehouses which had once been filled with the products of commerce but now stood neglected. Proudly above them stood the Temple of Aven, perched, like a monstrous cake, on a ziggurat in the centre of the city.

"Aven of Agon," announced Gong Lat unnecessarily. "I told you I would get you here."

"We are not yet there; do you expect me to walk from here?"

"No, we will be met and you will be taken into the city by another."

"That was not our arrangement."

"It will be safer for you to be seen with a native, rather than me. Do not worry, the contract will be honoured; our man here is reliable; one of the family. He comes now."

Bru turned to see a distant cloud of dust approaching them along the edge of the ravine. "Are you sure he's reliable?"

"Quite sure, he's my half brother. How are you going to get into the mission of Barta Magnus?"

"I'm not sure yet, I have a contact but it may be tricky."

The boy spoke almost inaudibly, "Take me with you."

"What?!"

"Take me with you. I want to leave here; I want to go to Barta Magnus."

Bru regarded the boy, who stared fixedly ahead. "I'm sorry, I can't do that."

"You mean you won't."

"I mean I can't."

Tears welled in his eyes. "I hate it here; I hate not having stuff, stuff that others get. I've seen how it is on Barta Magnus, how people live. They're not starving; they can have anything they want."

"That's not quite true. There's poverty on Barta Magnus too, they just don't let people see it."

"You're lying, I know you are."

"Surans don't lie," lied Bru. "You must believe me when I tell you that you can't come with me, you would surely be killed."

"I can look after myself."

"Against Evangelists?"

Gong Lat swallowed hard and dried his eyes. "Is that who's chasing you?"

"I believe so. They've already murdered my assistant and my wife, now they're after me. To be honest I don't know how I've got this far."

"That fat bastard that says he's my father should have told me it was Evangelists after you."

"Would you have refused to take me?"

"No, but I would have squeezed his balls for much more than he gave me. How much did you give him?"

"Everything I have."

"Miserable bastard, he told me he owed you, that this was a special favour."

"I never met your father before yesterday."

Gong Lat considered for a moment. "Everything you had, Suran? And you were rich, weren't you?"

"I was."

"And now he's got it all."

"Yes."

A furtive smile stole across the boy's face. "Perhaps I *will* go to Barta Magnus, after all."

"Perhaps," replied Bru and they waited in silence for Gong Lat's half brother to arrive in a swirl of dust.

Gong Che possessed nothing of his brother's good looks. He was a squat, swarthy specimen who had obviously run into trouble on many occasions for his face was a web of scars with one particularly vicious one running from his forehead, across his eye socket and down his cheek. He was several years older than Gong Lat but it was obvious from their greeting that he deferred to his younger brother, nodding frequently as they discoursed out of Bru's earshot. At length they were introduced.

"This is Gong Che, my brother," said the boy. "I have told him to get you to the mission of Barta Magnus."

"Greetings Gong Che," said Bru, bowing slightly.

Gong Che nodded peremptorily and stalked off to his cart which bore an unpromising resemblance to his brother's.

"Don't mind him, he'll do as he's told," said Gong Lat. "Don't tell him who's after you though, he won't like it. He's a cowardly little shit."

"I've no intention of mentioning it to anyone."

"Good. Well, this is where we part. Good luck to you, Suran."

He held out his arm for Bru to clasp but then remembered and withdrew it. Bru smiled and realized that something that only two day ago would have been distasteful to him now seemed quite natural. He offered his arm and the boy took it and they clasped in the traditional Agon way.

"Good luck to you, Gong Lat, and thank you for a most entertaining journey."

Gong Lat beamed and mounted his cart and was off in a cloud of dust. Bru watched him go with a tinge of regret, then turned towards the cart of his unfortunate brother.

They navigated the valley slope and plunged down into the cauldron of humanity that had spread itself across the flood plain. Aven was far more populous than Imbar the Devine and its filthy, degraded suburbs seemed to go on forever. They wove their way through the increasingly narrow, increasingly cacophonous, crowded streets, Gong Che, tight lipped and resentful, his scarred face a mask of hostility behind the goggles. Through gaps in the canyons of faceless tenements Bru caught glimpses of the looming walls of the great temple ziggurat as they neared the heart of the city. On and on they drove, through squalid alleys and squares until, at last, they came upon the walls of the mission compound, high and impregnable, like a fortress island of peace in a sordid sea.

Bru had been to the mission many times in his pseudo diplomatic capacity, but he had never approached it from the ground and certainly not from the city itself. Inside the walls one might have been on a different planet entirely, so stark was the contrast. Buildings of finely hewn and polished stone sat in a verdant park of pools and fountains where the well-dressed, well-fed mission staff strolled and discussed the urgent matters of the day. It was a place of culture and refinement where nothing of the brutal realities of its surroundings encroached.

Gong Che stopped the cart under the walls of the mission where a multitude of hopeful supplicants camped, sometimes for years, in the hope of migration to Barta Magnus. They crowded at the main gate and surged forward in a frantic press, waving applications whenever an official appeared. Sometimes two or three applications would be taken for consideration and, occasionally, one applicant would be successful, the fortunate soul being spirited away for a new life in the slums of Barta Magnus.

"How're you going to get into the mission?" said Gong Che, speaking to him for the first time.

Bru got out of the cart. "I'll find a way, I know somebody who works for the mission."

"Gong Lat said you were some big shot."

"Did he?"

"He did, so I said, 'what's a big shot doing driving through the desert with the likes of you'?"

"Did he tell you?"

"No. He said he would cut out my tongue if I told anyone about you."

Bru turned to go. "You should bear that in mind. Thanks for the transportation."

"Wait."

Bru turned back to face him and saw the ugly looking dagger he had drawn from his pants. Gong Che cracked a vicious smile at the alarm he had evidently caused. He proffered the knife.

"Take it, you will need it. Wear it where it can be seen, it may keep you alive long enough to get into the mission."

Bru took it. "Thanks."

"Don't thank me, it's Gong Lat's knife. If it was up to me, I'd slit you open with it."

With that parting shot, Gong Che abruptly turned the cart and disappeared into the labyrinth of the city streets. Bru watched him until he was out of sight then promptly plunged into the city himself, away from the mission of Barta Magnus and into the maze of back streets that surrounded it. Moving quickly, he negotiated the sunless alleys with the assurance of a native of the city, his memory serving him well to guide him to his destination.

Bru had never intended to go to the mission of Barta Magnus; it was far too obvious an escape route. He was suspicious of the ease at which he had escaped Imbar and fallen into the hands of Three Corners and he had little doubt that a way would be found for him to get into the mission, seemingly by chance. But Bru had always suspected that circumstances would arise in which he would be obliged to flee and, being cautious, he had planned for such an eventuality a long time before. He found the place just as dusk was beginning to spread its gloom over the city, a dingy door down a narrow alley that led nowhere else. He knocked and an elderly, grey-haired woman opened it.

"I thought I would be seeing you soon," she said as he slipped past her. "Are you sure you were not followed?"

"As sure as I can be. They will be expecting me at the mission of Barta Magnus."

"I see."

She picked up a small device and pointed it at him. "You're clean, there are no transmitters. What is that at the top of your right leg?"

"It's what this is all about."

She considered for a moment. "Will it destroy them?"

"It might, if I can get it to where it needs to go."

She smiled weakly. "Good, you Surans are the only real hope. Sit down I will get you some refreshments."

Bru gave himself up to a dusty seat in the corner of the single room while the woman gathered a selection of provisions. "Is everything ready, as stipulated?" he asked.

"Of course, exactly as you said."

"Good."

"There is a departure tonight to Barta."

"That will do. Do you have someone?"

She brought him the food and some crude wine. "Yes, he is a local."

Bru took a mouthful of the wine and shuddered; it was repulsive. The food was acceptable and he realized how hungry he was. She watched him intently as he ate.

"You are accused of the murder of your wife," she announced.

Bru looked up startled. "She was murdered by them, before my eyes."

"I suspected as much. That business in Imbar, the tower, that was you wasn't it?"

Bru nodded, "Sadly it was. Things did not go as I intended."

"These things happen in war. And we are at war, aren't we?"

"It might be described that way."

"They murdered my son and husband and now they've murdered your wife. That's my definition of war."

"Evangelists always liquidate the entire families of blasphemers, how did you escape?"

"I didn't, not completely. They pushed a sword into my body until it came out of my back while my son and husband were forced to watch. They thought I would die but I didn't. I wish I had died, I saw what they did to my beautiful son and husband; their screams that just went on and on; their blood showering over me until I thought I would drown in it. They did unspeakable things; things that no human being should be capable of doing to another. My son was sixteen years old, a child, what did he know of blasphemy? But that did not stop them. It took him a long time to die and even though I was in pain, I felt every moment of his agony. No Suran, I will never forget, not if I live for a thousand years, and I will never forgive."

"You carry a heavy burden but hatred and revenge are rarely good life companions."

"That's easy coming from a Suran, you despise emotion. Hatred is all I have left."

"I am sad for you, if I may be allowed that particular emotion."

"You know what I mean; you people are not so susceptible to their lies, you worship science and logic rather than idols and superstition. That is why you are the best hope."

"I pray you are right."

VIII

Some time later that night a man with the biometric profile of Solon Bru was observed boarding an interplanetary cruiser bound for Barta Magnus, a world eleven light years from Agon. The man enjoyed the delights and liberties of the cruiser for three days until his libidinous behaviour alerted the dullard that was tailing him to the fact that he could not be a Suran. His subsequent interrogation involved a great deal of discomfort but it revealed nothing of the old woman who had kindly given him the trip of a lifetime. No trace of her was ever found.

Solon Bru left Agon sometime soon after. There was no record of his departure though there was speculation that he assumed the guise of a weapons trader who suddenly disappeared under suspicious circumstances. There is also a possibility that he left as part of a party of pilgrims who had paid a visit to the desert shrine of Minnar. There are many other theories, some outlandish, some plausible, but none definitive. Solon Bru just disappeared and was never seen on Agon again.

PART THREE

SURAN

I

Of the one hundred and fifty-nine Doyens of Suran, Herton Lim was, by some measure, the most ancient. And although at one hundred and eighty-six years old, this crumpled and bent individual no longer took a hand in the governance of Suran, the aura of wisdom and infallibility was no less jealously guarded than it had been at the height of Lim's powers. It was, therefore, with no small amount of consternation, that this great teacher discovered, on this beautiful, sunlit morning, the extent of the wicked, duplicitous trick that had been perpetrated.

Only the previous day a life long devotion to parsimony was overcome when Lim had purchased, at great expense, a new research paper by Fry Toran of Barta Magnus entitled 'New Discoveries and Interpretations of First Civilization Artefacts'. Lim was unfamiliar with the author, but the list of academic qualifications was impressive and it was therefore, with great anticipation the tome was opened and read that morning. But it had not been long before a certain familiar ring was detected and Lim realized that the entire thing had been plagiarized from a work of a former student and had been lodged in the school library over twenty years before.

Lim was incandescent with rage, in truth, more at the waste of money rather than at the intellectual disappointment, and an inordinate amount of time was spent plotting revenge and retribution on the head of the charlatan Fry Toran of Barta Magnus.

"You will be exposed for the fraud you are," announced Lim to the smiling image of the blackguard. "Let us see if you'll still be smirking when I, Doyen Lim, have finished with you. You will be blacklisted, expunged from academia, eradicated without trace..." Thus Lim continued, preoccupied with vengeful thoughts and plans for a refund and a generous compensation for wasted time, so preoccupied in fact, that the time for the arrival of Jun Siu, the latest and final student of Lim's teaching career, found the doyen in want of preparation.

"You are late," announced Lim, as Jun Siu entered the sparse pristine study of his teacher.

Jun Siu bowed in the traditional way and regarded the teacher nervously. It was immediately obvious that Lim was out of humour.

"I said you are late."

"Honoured Doyen, I thought I was on time."

"Insufferable, you know I cannot abide lateness."

Jun Siu bowed again, a little lower this time. "Honoured Doyen, I apologize."

"Fewer apologies and more attention," snapped Lim. "What is that you are carrying?"

"It is the essay you requested yesterday on the molecular structure..."

"I know what task I set you yesterday, I am not a dotard. Give it to me."

Jun Siu stepped forward and tentatively offered the manuscript to his teacher, who snatched it away and perused it with a look of distaste. An awful silence fell as Jun watched the shrivelled figure read. Lim was often illtempered in the morning, but tended to lighten as their discussions progressed. But this morning Lim's mood did not lift and the doyen had barely read a quarter of the essay when it came hurtling back towards the unfortunate student's head, striking it before clattering to the floor.

"How old are you?" hissed Lim, ignoring the startled look of the student.

"I... I am nineteen, Honoured Doyen," stammered Jun, rubbing the spot where the manuscript had struck.

"And how long have I been your doyen?"

"Four point two nine years."

"And in this time you have learnt nothing... nothing. You insult me with this miserable work... this dross."

"Honoured Doyen..."

"Silence! Get out and take that excremental effort with you. You will return this afternoon with it and I shall expect no less than perfection."

"This afternoon?"

"Am I now required to repeat myself?"

"No, Honoured Doyen," replied Jun, recovering the writing tablet and retreating towards the study door. With a hurried bow the student was gone leaving Lim alone in the silence of the magnificent, Spartan study.

Perhaps a little harsh, thought Lim, as there was nothing particularly wrong with the essay. A lack of style and flair in the composition, but that was of no real significance at this stage in the course. There would have to be a rapprochement between them and that would be done this afternoon, perhaps with the offer of some drinking water in a goblet from the second best set or even an unmerited compliment, worked into the conversation. Lim shuffled around the large, illuminated analysis table that dominated the study and sat down in the heavily padded seat adjacent to it. The morning sun struck through the crystalline, domed roof of the room and played upon the twelve portraits of Lim's alumni, arranged in a row across one wall of the study. The faces smiled or frowned back, each according to their character, all except one, four from the end, where there was a conspicuous gap.

Lim required meticulous order and it had always been rather a bother that this gap had developed. It disturbed the equilibrium of the room, particularly when recalling the circumstances of the portrait's demise, how it had been torn from the wall and trampled underfoot in a transport of imperious rage and indignation. The doyen recalled the scene uncomfortably, so undignified and perhaps, even a little childish. Maybe it was time to think about replacing the image, possibly when the portrait of Jun Siu eventually joined the illustrious row. It would be good to have the full set and to look upon the human faces of a life's work.

With this resolve Doyen Herton Lim's attention returned to the denunciation of the fraudster Fry Toran of Barta Magnus, and began the letter that would surely bring the cad down. So freely did Lim's indignation take form that it was not long before the vituperative complaint was nearing completion and Lim was reading it through with some satisfaction.

"In conclusion, I demand the immediate restitution of the funds that have been ripped from the bosom of a respected academic who can ill afford them…" at which point Lim stopped to reflect that they might know who the wealthiest person on Suran was and decided to delete the last phrase. A new one was about to be inserted when an interruption came in the form of an announcement.

"Doyen Lim, you have a communication."

Lim had always disliked the obsequious, squeaky tone of the house system and its accent, not the crisp tones of Suran but the lazy drawl of Barta Magnus. Several complaints to the installers had brought no improvement.

"Communication? In the morning? Before lunch!"

"Affirmative."

"Why can't you just say 'yes'? Who is the caller?"

"The communicator will not be identified."

"The audacity! Refuse it."

"The communicator is insisting."

"What! Insisting? Insisting of a doyen and a High Council member?!"

"Affirmative."

"You inform the communicator, whoever that may be, that I, Doyen Lim, may not to be insisted upon."

"The communicator apologizes, but still insists."

"If this is my student, I will rip…"

"The communication is not from your student. Its source is a private craft approaching Suran."

Lim thought for a moment. "Ah! They are coming to replace you at last. My complaints have at last born fruit."

"That is unlikely, Doyen Lim."

"No doubt you are correct; your makers have shown little sympathy for my plight. They are hardly likely to send your replacement in a private craft. I am at a loss; I am expecting no visitors. Who can it be?"

"The communicator will not be identified."

"Blast you! We have established that."

"The caller will be identified when you accept the communication."

"That is obvious. But if they think I'm paying for it…"

"The charge has already been met."

"In full?"

"Affirmative."

This was good news at least. Lim brooded for a moment then bested by curiosity, accepted the call. The figure of a man shimmered into the study. Lim recoiled at the sight of the beard and dark hair that had indecently been left exposed. Revolting though it was, there was something vaguely familiar about it and Lim was induced to look more closely.

The image bowed and spoke. "Honoured Doyen, forgive the manner of my approach."

Lim's old, grey eyes nearly popped from their sockets, the voice was unmistakable. It was the disgraced alumnus Solon Bru.

Rendered speechless for a moment, Lim eventually stammered, "What is this? What is the meaning of it? The audacity…"

"Forgive me, but I come on a matter of gravest importance. I must have an audience."

"An audience! Have you left your wits on Agon? You have been abolished, expunged."

"I have left many things on Agon, Honoured Doyen, and I am aware that I am not a welcome sight, but I must insist on seeing you."

"You are very free with all this insisting. Do you not recall that I was forced to resign from the government because of you? I was disgraced; the School was disgraced, all because of you and your wilfulness. I will not see you, it is impossible."

Bru's voice remained calm, but there was an indefinable air of menace and resolve that Lim had not encountered before. "Honoured Doyen, I am coming to see you, if necessary as a supplicant, under your protection. In which case, the whole of Suran will know I am here."

"What! You wouldn't dare. I would be ruined, disgraced all over again."

"That would be your choice."

"You are a shameless ingrate; your residence on Agon has not improved you."

"Residence on Agon does not improve anyone."

Lim stared at the image and considered. "What is the nature of your business with me?"

"I cannot say."

"Impossible, insufferable."

"Honoured Doyen, I assure you it is of the utmost importance. I have suffered many privations and difficulties in order to seek this audience with you. People have died; I, myself was almost killed."

"I see you have not lost your penchant for melodrama."

"Honoured Doyen, please understand that I do not come here at a whim but by absolute necessity."

"Very well, I will grant you a brief audience tomorrow and then you must leave Suran immediately."

"No. I am coming to see you directly. I will arrive in two hours and twenty-three minutes. Please arrange the permit."

Lim was about to protest but Bru's air of desperation finally overcame the natural indignation of his former teacher. "Very well, I will arrange it."

Bru bowed and the image disappeared leaving Lim alone with an uncomfortable mixture of anger and curiosity.

II

Stannik Poon, the Junior Minister of Migration was not a doyen, but the product of an inferior school, at least by Lim's estimation, run by Doyen Ma, the minister of lower education and one of Lim's oldest rivals. Lim had dealt with the Junior Minister three years earlier when seeking access for the engineers that had installed the infernal house system and had detected a distinct air of condescension and lack of respect. This was particularly distasteful from an individual who had unjustifiably benefited from the nepotistic partiality of their doyen and been elevated beyond their station.

Suran, being both remote and insular, was rarely visited and immigration was not permitted, so the Minister was not overworked and Lim had no trouble making direct contact.

"Good morning, Honoured Doyen Lim, this is a pleasant surprise, indeed." Poon's obsequious image smiled indulgently. "We trust you are in good health."

Lim was immediately angered by the use of the personal pronoun 'we' when the Minister was clearly alone, but bottled it up and exchanged courtesies in the accepted manner. "Good day, Junior Minister, thank you for your concern, I am well."

"It gives me joy to hear it. And what may we do for you today?"

"I require an entry permit."

The Junior Minister's expression changed to a frown. "There is no liner due for fifty-six days and all permits have been issued."

"The permit is for a private craft."

The Junior Minister now looked concerned. "How many passengers?"

"One. Is there a problem?"

"This is most unusual; this is the second such request I have had today."

Lim was shocked but kept a steady countenance. Bru had applied to a rival doyen. This was beyond endurance. "From whom did you receive the other application?"

"We are not at liberty to give that information. What is the name of the arriving party?"

"A private citizen."

"We are required to know the identity…"

Lim interrupted with magisterial anger. "I am a doyen of Suran and a member of the High Council with the commensurate rights and privileges thereof. You will issue the permit without further questions."

The Junior Minister was visibly shaken. A look of confusion betrayed genuine shock. Lim was known to be prickly, but this was close to insulting. The Minister debated whether to pursue any further enquiries but decided to be content with reporting Lim's behaviour to the High Council. There was nothing to do but issue the permit.

"Very well, it is so issued."

"Good day, Junior Minister."

Lim cut the communication and boiled. Not only had Bru insulted and imposed himself in this unacceptable way, but had added the most grievous slight of applying to a rival. Lim had just over two hours to prepare the dressing down and it would be delivered in the most decisive manner.

III

During his escape from Agon, Solon Bru had suffered a great deal of mental anguish, but nothing seemed to compare to the apprehension he felt as his craft swept over the familiar landscape of dark, cycad forests and deep blue lakes that surrounded the glowing jewel of his alma mater. His heart was pounding as he came to land in the fine garden that enfolded the impressive structure and alighted into the crystalline air and early afternoon sun that used to give him such joy.

The door slipped aside and he walked into the elegant vestibule, arranged just as it had always been, over forty-seven years ago. Memories flooded back, mostly happy, of the latter stages of his course when he and Lim had become easy and familiar with each other and their discussions had assumed an intellectual freedom that transcended the difference in age and experience between them. If only it had not gone sour, if only he had been more cautious, how different would his life have been?

Bru walked into the study with trepidation and found Lim sitting on the chair of state, dressed in the full ceremonial gown. The shrivelled, bent figure did not stir but the eyes peering out of the lined face fixed him with a stare that seemed to emanate from the heart of the vast ice caps of Suran itself.

He bowed low. "Honoured Doyen, thank you for granting me this audience."

Lim made no reply letting the silence hang in the air like a primed guillotine.

"Honoured Doyen, please forgive…"

"Who was it?" Lim snapped.

"I… I crave your pardon."

"Who, I demand to know, who?"

"I don't know…"

"Your conspirator, do not deny it."

"I do not know what you are talking about."

"Ha! It is not enough for you to flagrantly jeopardize what is left of my reputation; you must also insult me by consorting with another doyen.

"Another doyen! What is this?"

"Do not deny it, you are a poor liar. Did you think I would be unable to obtain a permit? That I am so debased…"

"What is this about a permit?"

"Do not take me for a fool, Solon."

"Damn it! I really do not have any idea what you are talking about."

"Do not use profanities in my presence. You applied to another doyen for your entry permit."

"I did no such thing. Has another been issued?"

"You know it."

Bru felt himself grow cold. "Do you still keep a security system here?"

"What!"

"Can you secure the building?"

"I have the finest system available. Do not try to deflect me; I am wise to your tricks."

"Never mind that. Secure the building, right now."

Lim heard the fear and urgency in Bru's voice and ordered the domestic system to secure the building.

"Do you wish to purchase the luxury security system with the new organic filter option?" The squeaky drawl of the system grated Lim's nerves, especially as it was demanding more money for something that had already been paid for, but Bru forestalled the fresh onrush of indignation that was about to issue from his doyen by addressing it himself.

"Organic filter? What is that?'

"Honoured guest of Doyen Lim, the organic filter is an entirely new security concept. It prevents weapon ingress by atomizing anything that enters the dwelling that is not a living organism."

"Buy it, we may need everything."

"You are very free with my money Solon."

"We are in danger, Herton, I strongly urge you to purchase it whatever the cost."

Lim grudgingly ordered the upgrade while, without being invited, Bru sat down on the small, hard student seat across the analysis table, his tortured face lost in thought.

"What is this about, Solon?" In the face of perceived danger Lim's anger toward his former student had entirely dissolved. Now answers were needed.

Bru looked sorrowfully at the craggy face of his teacher. "I thought I had not been followed, it seems I was wrong."

"Followed by whom?"

"Evangelists."

Lim stiffened. "Evangelists?"

Bru nodded, "I fear I may have brought them to your door."

"Evangelists, on Suran? I hardly think so. Why do you think they are following you?"

"Because of what I have, what I have brought to you."

Bru stood and produced Gong Lat's knife from his tunic. "Please turn your head and shut your eyes, I have to disrobe."

Lim's eyes widened. "In my presence? Have you become a complete barbarian?"

"Please, it won't take a moment."

"This is highly irregular."

Making sure his doyen's eyes were tightly shut, Bru dropped his pants and carefully cut away the false skin that had entrapped the fragment to his inner thigh. He placed it on the analysis table and dressed himself.

"You may open your eyes now."

"Are you sure?"

"Quite sure."

Lim's eyes slowly opened as if not quite believing the assurance. Bru pushed the fragment across the table.

Lim peered at it. "What is it?"

"I don't know, I have not been able to analyse it properly, that's why I brought it here. What I can tell you though is that it is of human origin and it's over one hundred and twenty thousand years old."

Bru had never seen his doyen look so stunned. "Are you sure?"

"I am."

Lim inspected the fragment closely, turning it over and over in silence. "The markings must be a form of writing."

"Agreed, but there is insufficient to decipher any logical pattern."

"Yes, a pity. Let us see what it is."

Lim placed the fragment on to the analysis table and activated it. Immediately a projection of the chemical composition hovered above. Bru walked around the table and they scrutinized it together.

"It's certainly organic in origin," remarked Lim, "although these molecular compounds are completely unknown."

"Some type of plant?"

"Yes, but not a type known to natural science. Look at that! That's not vegetable matter."

Lim honed in on a small area of the fragment and magnified it ten thousand times, while the analyser probed deeper and deeper. "Sanity preserve us! That's a particle of human skin."

"Date it."

Lim did so and for the first time, the ancient, lined face broke into a smile. "You were right, Solon, it is one hundred and twenty two thousand, five hundred and seventy years old. It is over forty times older than any human evidence we have ever seen. Perhaps this is a trace of the person who made it. Just think of it, a human who lived all that time ago made this and we are looking at a piece of that very person. Incredible; just incredible. And look at the writing medium, what is that?"

"I don't know; it is something entirely different."

"This will require many days of analysis; we will have to go through it molecule by molecule."

"Yes, if we are allowed the time."

Lim looked up sharply. "We will not be disturbed here; this is Suran, not a wild outpost of degeneracy."

Bru nodded but made no reply; he had bitter experience of this type of complacency.

"And now," said Lim, suddenly turning off the analyser, "I will get us some refreshment and you will relate to me the circumstances by which you came to possess this extraordinary object."

Lim shuffled away, leaving Bru in the eerie tranquillity of the study. The weak afternoon sun danced upon the elegantly curved walls of the room and dappled the sparse furnishings with gold. For the first time Bru noticed the gallery of distinguished alumni and the gap where his portrait should have been. He smiled ruefully; he was not surprised.

Presently Lim returned carrying two goblets one of which was placed in front of Bru who noticed that the doyen's hand was shaking slightly and that the ends of the fingers were quite yellow. Bru had seen this before and knew what it was.

Doyen Lim had a terminal disorder and probably less than a year to live. This shocked Bru profoundly; he had always thought of his doyen as immortal. But now, in the presence of this frail, shrivelled person, he realized that the one great, dependable constant in his life would soon disappear forever.

He took a sip of the liquid in the goblet, while Lim sat down. As he suspected, it was plain water.

"Now we are comfortable, I would first like to know where this object was found."

"Sector KT153."

Lim looked puzzled and brought up a projection of the galactic chart. "That's in the Orestean Limb, over twenty thousand light years from here. It's not possible."

"You know that it is. We both know."

Lim looked up sharply. "What do you mean?"

"I mean the answer was in your library, where I found it."

Lim visibly shuddered. "The Fourth Proposition."

"The Fourth Proposition, this vindicates it; this proves it."

"You took a copy?"

"Yes."

Lim jumped out of the seat with surprising vigour and began to pace. "Reckless, I cannot believe that you, even you, would have been so foolish, so completely reckless. Has the copy now been destroyed?"

"No."

"Where is it?"

"On Agon, in a systems disrupter."

Lim became even more incredulous. "You exported a disrupter!?"

"Yes."

"It must be retrieved. Where is it?"

"I don't know; I left it in the City of Imbar."

"Is it primed?"

"Yes, if anyone tries to interfere with it, it will disseminate The Fourth Proposition to every system on Agon."

Lim stared at him, hardly able to believe it. "Do you have any idea what will happen if it does that?"

"Yes."

"I only hope I will not be alive to witness the consequences of what you have done."

Bru nodded and a reflective silence fell which was broken by the announcement of an approaching craft. They exchanged startled glances.

"If your fancy security systems don't work you may get your wish," whispered Bru.

IV

For the young scholar, Jun Siu, the day had started with promise. The essay had been completed satisfactorily, the sun was shining and the student looked forward to the daily instruction with glad anticipation. This had not always been the case, for Lim, uniquely among the doyens of Suran, required an audience every day and to be in the physical presence of another person so often was highly uncomfortable. Adding to this inconvenience, Lim was also very intimidating, with a permanently grim aspect and a liberal use of withering admonishments. But Jun Siu had won the scholarship over the candidacy of over two hundred others and was determined to make full use of the opportunity. Hard work had brought its rewards; even to the point of eliciting a couple of off-hand compliments from the great teacher and now the daily lesson, instead of a burden, had become a pleasure.

But today's meeting with Doyen Lim had been far from pleasurable. Never before had the doyen been so angered and violent and this was made more disturbing because Jun Siu did not fully understand the cause of the great teacher's distemper. As the small craft rose into the air above the school, Jun Siu rubbed the place on the forehead where the writing tablet had struck, there was going to be a lump. Tears welled and by the time the fifty kilometres to the modest, student dwelling had been completed, the unfortunate scholar was in quite a state of anxiety.

Jun's composure was not improved by the task that had been set. The unsatisfactory essay was read and then re-read; the facts were checked and the academic texts searched for anything germane that ought to have been added. Nothing could be found. This lack of progress, together with the unheard of imposition of having to visit the doyen twice in one day, had reduced Jun to a nervous wreck. And so, it was with great trepidation, that Scholar Siu climbed into the small craft and started the short journey back to the dwelling of Doyen Lim and it was the arrival of this craft that interrupted their momentous discussion.

"Identify the craft," said Lim

"The vehicle belongs to Jun Siu, your student," replied the obsequious house system.

The two of them breathed again. "You have a student?" said Bru.

"Why should I not?" replied Lim defensively.

"I thought you might have retired."

"I don't know why you should think that. I will direct Scholar Siu to leave."

"Don't do that, the student is already implicated, by association. This is most inconvenient; I had not thought to involve anyone else."

"'Inconvenient' is hardly the appropriate adjective. But you are correct; if you have been followed the student is compromised and should be admitted. My student is Jun Siu, come to the door with me and I will introduce you."

Jun's surprise at seeing an interstellar vehicle sitting in Lim's fine parkland was greatly increased when the door slid aside to reveal his teacher and another person of extraordinary appearance. Bru could not resist a smile at the open mouthed look of shock on the student's face. Jun Siu was small framed possessing the classic, delicate femininity of a Suran with fine features accentuated by large, blue eyes set in alabaster skin. It was as though all the most appealing aspects of the Suran race had been distilled into this one individual. Bru assessed that Jun Siu was exquisitely androgynous and experienced an unworthy pang of jealousy.

Jun only just remembered to bow in the traditional way.

Lim made the introductions. "This is my current student Jun Siu, and Jun Siu; this is my former graduate Solon Bru."

Jun looked up, puzzled; all the faces in the gallery were very familiar.

"The gap," Bru assisted.

Lim shuffled awkwardly. "Never mind that, enter; there is much to discuss."

At Lim's bidding Jun entered the building, at which point a most unfortunate thing happened. The student's clothing and the writing tablet were instantly vaporised.

It was hard to say who was more surprised. On seeing the unfortunate student naked, Lim let out a great scream of anguish and rushed away. Jun froze, barely able to comprehend what had happened. Bru was more surprised than shocked, for it was immediately obvious that Scholar Siu was in no way androgynous. The student was anatomically male to a degree that Bru would have thought impossible in a Suran.

Bru was so surprised that he was obliged to stare inappropriately before recalling himself and turning around. "I beg your pardon, Scholar Siu," he said and walked back into the study, leaving the stunned, naked student shivering in the vestibule.

Lim, in a torment of horror, acted with commendable alacrity and very soon a mechanoid with a fine gown and slippers was sent to the rescue. When Jun Siu finally entered the study, he looked bewildered and a little unsteady. Lim fussed excessively, apologizing and asking Scholar Siu if he was going to faint while Bru stood aside, unable to meet his eye.

"Don't just stand there, Solon, fetch some water, can't you see that the poor student is about to faint?"

Bru nodded and went off for the water. When he returned he found the boy sitting in the student seat, still conscious, with Lim still fussing about.

"Are you sure you don't require any medication? It is most unfortunate, most unfortunate. Ah! Water, that will help. Make sure you drink it all, most refreshing. When I catch up with the slippery evildoers that sold me this system, I will tear them to shreds; they will be cast into the foulest prison where they will remain for the rest of their worthless lives; they will be taken out and made to eat sand; they will be..."

"Honoured Doyen," interrupted Bru, "before any or all of these merited punishments are meted out, you should re-secure the dwelling."

"Are you mad? Look at the damage the cursed thing has done."

"Nevertheless, we should be prudent. Remember what we have here."

"Very well, but mark my words, there will be retribution and I will not stop until every last one of the blackguards that talked me into buying this system is exposed and punished."

In this manner Lim continued for some time, listing the increasingly severe degradations that the entrepreneurs of Barta Magnus could expect, while occasionally soliciting a bulletin of the student's condition.

Finally, Bru was obliged to interrupt. "Honoured Doyen, we should return to the matter in hand. We have a pressing matter to discuss here and now."

Lim was brought up short. "Yes, you are right, we should return to the matter we were discussing earlier, before this unfortunate business. Are you sure you are alright, Scholar Siu?"

"I think I'll be alright," replied the student weakly.

"Then Solon, you were about to tell me how this object came into your possession." Lim picked up the fragment and waved it towards the bewildered student. This object, Scholar Siu, is over one hundred and twenty two thousand years old and it was made by a human being. It was found in sector KT153; do you know where that is?"

"In the Orestean Limb."

"Correct."

"One hundred and twenty two thousand years? I don't understand."

"Doctor Bru will explain it to you now."

Bru regarded Scholar Siu, newly impressed; not even Lim had known the location of KT153. He turned to the doyen. "Do I have your permission to speak of The Fourth Proposition?"

Lim nodded a resigned affirmation with closed eyes.

"Very well. Scholar Siu, have you heard of The Fourth Proposition?"

"No, I have read the first three Propositions; I did not know there was a fourth."

"Then you will know that the first three Propositions concern the origin of the human species not as a divine construct but as a natural organic entity."

"Yes, they were refuted."

"Yes, mainly because there was no evidence of any evolutionary process and the primitive creatures so far discovered anywhere in the galaxy bear no resemblance to humans. The biological gap is too large. The conclusion, therefore, was that humans must be a divine creation. The first three Propositions served only to reinforce the tenets of the Faith, but the fourth was different. It was written about one hundred and fifty years ago, a brilliant and closely argued work that struck at the very heart of the Faith. It showed that, far from being a divine creation, humanity was implanted here by an earlier civilization; that no evidence exists because it emanated from a great distance and it sets out how this great distance could have been negotiated using human D.N.A. in stasis. It goes on to describe how the Angels of the First Book of Minnar, who gave Mankind language and mathematics, were actually robots whose function was to nurture the founding of new colonies.

"Needless to say, it was incendiary, a bomb at the very centre of the Faith that could not be refuted by the theologians. Their reaction was predictable. They proscribed it and murdered anyone who expounded it. Thousands were put to death until it was stamped out and all evidence of its existence removed. It was even expunged from the libraries of Suran under threat of war. The Fourth Proposition was lost to history for nearly a hundred years until I discovered a copy, hidden in the library of this school."

"You should not have been rummaging around like that," interrupted Lim.

"And you should have destroyed it, as you were supposed to," countered Bru, sharply.

"Your actions cost me my ministerial portfolio and sent you into exile."

"You abandoned me; you didn't stand up for your own principles."

Lim visibly bristled. "You fool; don't you realize I saved your life? The Council was ready to extradite you. You would have been taken to Kagan and executed. I argued that a dangerous precedent would be set, that Surans could not be executed. I managed to persuade them to make you a diplomat, to protect you. We nearly went to war, Solon."

Bru and Jun Siu stared at Lim in surprise; Bru, because he had never heard this before and Jun, because he could not believe that his doyen could be spoken to in such a way.

Lim went on. "The negotiations were difficult. They insisted you be placed in their charge so that you could do no more damage and we insisted that you would not be extradited to Kagan. In the end a compromise was struck and you were sent to Agon and specifically to the most holy site, so that every day you would be reminded of your heresy."

"I didn't know," muttered Bru.

"There's a lot you don't know, Solon. Of course, it was never suggested that you got the copy of The Fourth Proposition from me, they wouldn't have dared, but I was held responsible because I had not controlled you. I was forced to resign my government post and I have not spoken in the Council since."

"I'm sorry, I truly am."

"I doubt that, it is not in your character to be sorry for what you have done."

"That is unjust."

"Is it? Have you ever considered the cost of your actions?"

"You could have stopped me. But you didn't, did you?"

Lim stared at him angrily and was about to retort but with a change of mind, subsided into moody silence.

"I apologize, Doyen," said Bru quietly; he knew he had gone too far. "With your permission, I will continue."

Lim assented with a nod.

"When I arrived on Agon and took up my position at the Institute in the City of Imbar the Divine, in the Department of Astrogeology, I had not been there a year when the son of a wealthy industrialist was sent to me for instruction. His name... excuse me, I have become accustomed to using pronouns of gender... his name was Abel Arno; his father was the owner of Arno Mining Corporation of Barta Magnus. Abel was enthusiastic and gifted and a trust developed between us. Just before he graduated he came to see me in my home to tell me that his father had requested his return to Barta Magnus. I showed him the copy of the Fourth Proposition."

Bru noticed the sorrowful shake of his doyen's head but pressed on. "The effect the Proposition had on Abel was profound. It would be accurate to say that he became obsessed. I confess I did not discourage him while, at the same time, pressing upon him the need for secrecy. During one of our discussions, I suggested that, although the Proposition is not specific, the source of humanity might lie somewhere in the Orestean Arm."

"You extrapolated the line of settlement," said Lim.

"Essentially, yes."

Lim, noticing the puzzled look on the student's face, explained. "There are five original worlds of human settlement which were established over a period of about five hundred years. Agon is the oldest, with each subsequent occupation being slightly nearer the interior of the galaxy. It suggests a source towards the periphery."

"Allowing for galactic rotation, the KT regions looked a possibility," added Bru. "Abel left Agon and returned to Barta Magnus, but we kept in touch. Abel inherited the company after the death of his father twenty years later and he had not forgotten his obsession. He announced a vast expansion in mineral exploration using the new propulsion technology to reach regions that were not previously viable. He built and launched a large number of geological probes, many of which were secretly reprogrammed with a device that was designed to detect unnatural formations on and just below the surface of planets with reasonably stable crusts. The probes were redirected to the KT region and ostensibly lost. Five years later they arrived and started sending back data. Thousands of star systems were surveyed and nothing was found that could not be explained by natural processes.

"Abel was facing ruin and the probes began to shut down, but then one sent back the image of a tomb-like structure, buried under the edge of a magma flow. Abel gathered a small crew and left immediately, leaving behind his ruined company. I did not hear from him for ten years and then thirty days ago I got a coded message from a craft nearing the outer perimeter. It said, 'I bring you the destroyer of lies'.

"I waited to hear further, but I received no other messages. Then, twelve days ago, I learned that Abel's craft had been found abandoned beyond Station Two Eleven."

"The one that was destroyed recently?" asked Lim.

Bru nodded. "Yes. I sent my assistant there to obtain Abel's cargo. He bought a box that contained this fragment and several miscellaneous items of no importance. Of Abel, himself, there was no trace. None of the life pods were missing and according to the salvagers, the craft had been abandoned for over a year."

"They were lying to get round the statute, so they could sell it," said Lim.

"Probably."

"What happened to the box?" asked Jun Siu."

"I left it in the possession of my assistant who was murdered. It may have been destroyed, or it may be in the hands of our enemies."

"Your assistant, your former graduate; your associates are an unfortunate lot," said Lim.

Bru nodded ruefully and thought of his wife and the thousands in the great tower of Imbar. He hoped his doyen would never find out how many people had already lost their lives.

"The question is," continued Lim, "what is to be done?"

"Surely we must take it to the Council," said Jun.

Lim gave him a withering look. "And what would they do? Hand over the evidence to the priests of Kagan and offer our heads on a plate?"

"We could negotiate, you did before, I mean when Doctor Bru got into trouble."

Bru heard the measure of desperation in the student's voice; *He knows what's coming,* he thought.

Lim held up the fragment. "That was entirely different; we were dealing with a theory. This is not a theory; this is proof; hard evidence."

Jun pressed on, "Why can't it just be secured here? Nobody else needs to know."

"Scholar Siu, I'm afraid it is already too late for that," said Bru.

"Besides," added Lim, "we are researchers, it is our job to pursue the truth, our duty. The responsibility is mine, but I am too old to shoulder it, so it passes to you, Solon, and to you Scholar Siu."

Siu let out a plaintive wail. "No, please, I beg of you!"

"Silence! You will do as I direct."

Jun visibly shrank in his chair and Lim turned to Bru. "You know what you have to do. We now have the technology to get to the KT region; this was not the case when The Fourth Proposition was first published. The cost will be high but I will make the funds available. Go to Barta Magnus, there you will be able to purchase a suitable craft. Go and look; find the true source of Humanity. It will be an undertaking of great value to Mankind. I will keep the fragment here; do not worry, it will be quite safe."

"Yes, Doyen."

Lim got out of the chair and walked around the table. "Scholar Siu, stand up."

Jun stood and forlornly faced his doyen.

"Scholar Jun Siu, I renounce you. You are now and henceforth the subject of my heir, Doctor Solon Bru. Now leave us."

The boy's face twisted in agony and he walked out of the study.

Bru was stunned. "Your heir?"

"Yes, I named you upon your graduation; I saw no reason to change it. Now go, leave your student's vehicle here and get what's required for the journey. Clothing and a personal item may be of some comfort although I suspect you will have a sullen individual on your hands."

"Yes, Doyen, I don't know what to say."

"Nothing is appropriate. Goodbye, Solon."

Bru bowed. "Goodbye, Herton."

When he reached the door of the study, Lim added, "and Solon, don't corrupt him."

It wasn't until he recalled them later that Bru realized how strange his Doyen's last ever words to him were. A pronoun of gender had been used and it caused Bru to wonder if Lim had always known Jun's terrible secret.

V

Bru's vehicle rose above the glowing dome of Lim's dwelling and headed out, over the darkly verdant cycad forest towards Jun's residence. The boy sat next to him, staring fixedly ahead, tears running down his pale cheeks and dripping on to the incongruously elegant gown of his former doyen.

"I'm sorry," said Bru, "I did not intend this."

"Why did you come here? You could have gone anywhere." He angrily wiped his eyes with his sleeve. "How am I to graduate?"

"I can teach you everything you need to know, and more, I dare say."

"I don't want you to teach me, I already had a teacher, the best teacher. Why would I want you?"

"I am sorry that you have been obliged to accept an inferior scholarship, but I hope we can make the best of it."

"I don't want to make the best of it; I want my doyen to teach me."

"Your doyen has renounced you and now that cannot happen."

"Only because of you. Now I will never see my graduation."

"You would not have done anyway; our doyen has less than a year to live."

"That's a lie."

"Is it? You must have noticed the unsteady hands, the yellowing fingertips. I bet you looked up the symptoms."

Jun made no reply.

"Ironic really, since I am Lim's heir you might have been sent to Agon to finish your studies with me." Bru glanced at the delicate boy beside him and smiled. "You wouldn't have liked Agon, Scholar Siu."

"I wouldn't have gone, I'd have rather died."

The patchwork of lake and forest slipped past below them and they were soon descending into the small park that surrounded Jun's student dwelling.

Bru carefully checked the horizon for other vehicles and they landed.

"Change into more robust clothing and bring your coursework, nothing else."

They left the shuttle and Bru watched the boy trudge the short distance to his dwelling. He did not presume to follow him; sure that it would have caused further friction between them. Jun had almost reached the door when Bru became aware of heat rising through the soles of his boots. His hair stood on end and he bellowed, "Stop!"

But it was too late. The door slid open just as Jun turned around to see his unwanted, new teacher bearing down on him. He felt himself grabbed and propelled along like a doll. He screamed just as the massive pressure wave blew them both off their feet and the roar of the fireball passed over them. Great chunks of debris rained from the sky and thumped into the ground about them. A scalding lump of metal hit Bru on the arm and he yelped a curse. The air was filled with an impenetrable choking dust and acrid smoke.

Winded and shaking, Bru struggled to his feet. "Get up," he screamed, pulling the boy roughly to his feet. "Go."

They staggered out of the smoke and dust with streaming eyes. Some of the trees surrounding the dwelling had caught fire, their fronds burning like torches and igniting the mossy ground with cinders. Bru wiped his eyes and squinted through the smoke. A large crater had replaced Jun's dwelling and his vehicle had been blown over on to its back. He cursed vehemently; now it could only serve one purpose.

"Stay here," he commanded and, covering his nose and mouth, he ran towards the overturned shuttle. Jun watched him disappear into the vehicle and re-emerge a few moments later. He ran back to where the boy stood shaking within the blackened ceremonial gown of his former doyen.

"We have ten minutes to get clear," said Bru, panting heavily. "I suggest you start running."

"What?"

Bru grabbed him roughly by the collar and shoved him hard. "Run, damn you; unless you want to die right here."

Jun had had enough of being manhandled; he planted his feet and refused to move. "I'm not going anywhere," he declared resolutely.

Bru gnashed his teeth in frustration. "Fine. I've just primed a nuclear device. Enjoy the last ten minutes of your life, Scholar Siu."

He turned and ran towards the forest. Jun watched him go, boiling with resentment. He looked at the crater that had once been his home and the overturned shuttle that would soon vaporise the entire area; a moment later he was running just as fast as he could. They got almost two kilometres away when the awful white flash filled the sky and the ground convulsed. They dived into a ditch and laid face down, covering their heads with their arms as the air shook and the shock wave passed over, flattening the forest. The day turned to night as vicious whirlwinds whipped the lacerated forest into the air and screamed in their ears like a trapped and wounded monster. A firestorm swept over the land, igniting the torn fronds of trees, moss and even the soil of the forest floor as it swirled above them. They could not move and remained still for a long time, while the firestorm raged and eventually, abated, showering them with hot, choking dust and embers. The heat was unbearable; the oxygen was being consumed by the fire and Bru knew that they had to get out of there. He staggered to his feet and pulled Jun up by his gown. With their arms over their faces, the two ghost-like figures stumbled through the burning wasteland in a direction that Bru hoped would get them out of this hell.

Finally, after what seemed like ages, they began to come across trees still standing, the forest thickened and the dust thinned enough for them to see where they were going. They stumbled on until they found a small clearing and threw themselves to the ground, coughing and wheezing and trying to choke up the dust from their throats.

Bru hawked and spat out a bitter lump of debris and looked up at the billowing cloud, still rising into the sky, obscuring the sun. He saw the distant glint of a craft approaching. *Coming to see their handiwork,* he speculated, *I bet they weren't expecting that.* A small explosion could have been covered up, but not this. Questions would be asked in Council, the enemy would be forced to withdraw and Lim would be left alone, at least for a while. The doyen would assume they were dead though, and that was a sadness, but so would the enemy, and in that lay hope.

He approached the boy who was still kneeling on the ground coughing. "How far is the nearest water?"

"What insanity was that?" croaked Jun between coughing bouts.

"A little something I had prepared for emergencies. Crude but effective wouldn't you say?"

Jun turned his bespattered face towards his nemesis; he had a look of utter incomprehension in his dust-reddened eyes. "You brought a nuclear device to Suran?"

"Evidently."

"You are mad; beyond insane; there isn't a word to describe it. How could you have obtained such a thing?"

"With money and the right connections it is not that difficult. Now, where is the nearest water?"

Jun pointed. "About two kilometres."

"Come on, we have to wash off this dust before it corrodes our skin."

Covering their faces they pressed on until they cleared the blast area. Above them the cloud had reached the high atmosphere and was beginning to drift away to the south. As he ran, Bru allowed himself a rueful smile; he had miscalculated the force of the explosion; he should have allowed more time to escape.

They came upon the small lake, deep and blue with the dark fronds of the forest overhanging its fragrant, mossy shore.

"Wash the dust from your clothing and shoes and bathe thoroughly," said Bru, "and drink plenty of water."

Jun watched the loathed figure disappear into the forest to bathe at a respectable distance further along the shore and out of sight. He looked out across the shimmering water to the dark shore opposite and recalled the times he had swum across this beautiful lake, hidden in the forest, or walked around its softly lapping perimeter while contemplating the wise instruction of his doyen. Only this morning he had everything that a young Suran could wish for; a comfortable home; the patronage of one of the world's greatest teachers; solitude; a future. Now he had nothing.

He untied the gown and let it drop to the ground. Naked, he looked down at himself and at the hated appendage. Why couldn't he have been like other Surans? Why was he cursed with this physical aberration? With sudden clarity he knew what he would do. He stepped into the cool water and waded in until it was up to his chest, then, with a last look at the sky, he dove and struck down into the darkest depths, down and down he swam until the rippling, sunlit surface was distant roof above. Why should he ever come up again?

VI

Bru found a pleasant cove, two hundred metres from Jun and took his time, luxuriating in the coolness of the lake. His plans were in tatters and he had plenty of thinking to do. The loss of his craft now seemed to have effectively stranded him on Suran. If he tried to go to the authorities he would be immediately arrested and sent back to Agon and Lim might even be arraigned. He had to leave Suran undetected, but it would not be easy. He had to devise another plan and by the time he stepped from the water, he had the bones of it, although it was not, by any means, ideal.

He pulled on his cold, damp clothes and walked slowly back to the place he had left the boy. He called out at a distance to let him know of his approach, he didn't want any repeats of the unfortunate incident at Lim's door, but there was no reply. He moved closer and called again, but still heard no response. Surely Jun could not still be bathing. He waited and listened but could hear neither the sound of splashing nor any other sound except the gentle lapping of the water on the shore. It suddenly occurred to him that Jun might have run away so he returned to the place where he had left him to bathe. He found the boy sitting against a tree trunk looking out across the lake.

"Could you not have answered? I didn't know whether it was safe to return."

Jun threw him a moody glance. "Would you have cared?"

Bru ignored the insult. "Get up, we have to get moving."

"And go where?"

"To Dolon Export, about fifty kilometres east of here."

"Nobody is allowed to go to Dolon Export. Your plan, if you have one, is faulty."

"I know nobody is allowed there, that's precisely why we're going."

"It's illegal, I refuse."

"You will do as I direct, now stand up."

"What for? So you can touch me again?"

Bru pulled out his knife and stepped closer menacingly. "Touch you? I would sooner slit you from ear to ear."

"Go ahead, you savage. I want to die. Better that than going anywhere with you. Look at yourself; you're a barbarian, not a Suran."

Bru was taken aback. He turned away and quickly replaced the knife into his pants, ashamed at having lost control of himself. "You may be right, I have become a barbarian, and that's how I survived my exile. I do not intend to apologize for it. If you think I want your company any more than you want mine, you are mistaken, but, I am bound to take you with me because I cannot leave you behind. You already know too much."

"I didn't ask for any of this, I don't deserve it."

"What you asked for or deserve is of no importance. I remind you of our doyen's last injunction, you are bound to me and I am bound to go to KT153, or die trying."

The reminder of Lim's last words to him brought Jun reluctantly to his feet, Bru was right; his doyen's last injunction had to be obeyed. "You will kill us both."

"Then you will have got your wish to die, Scholar Siu."

They skirted the lake and struck due east towards Dolon Export. The sun slipped below the horizon and the daylight faded into a twilit night filled with stars. The twin moons of Suran rose and flooded the land with watery, silver light so that, even under the dense canopy of forest fronds, they were able to find their path over the soft, mossy undergrowth. No dwellings were allowed within fifty kilometres of Dolon Export, so they came across no other signs of life. After eight hours he could see that Jun was flagging and his own legs were feeling leaden, so they stopped. Bru sat down and rested his back against the trunk of a large fern and shut his eyes for a moment.

When he woke up the moons had set and the first hint of dawn was gathering in the east. He had slept for five hours.

He found Jun lying on the ground in a shallow depression, a few metres away. The boy was fast asleep. Bru called to him but he would not stir, so he picked up a clump of wet moss and threw it at him. It struck him on the head.

"What did you do that for?" he said angrily, struggling stiffly to his feet.

"You wouldn't wake up and I didn't want to touch you. Come on, we still have about five hours ahead of us."

"I'm hungry."

"So am I," said Bru, setting off.

"What are you going to do when we get to Dolon Export?"

"I don't know yet, it's some time since I was there."

"You've been there!"

"Once, when I was young."

"Even though you knew it wasn't permitted?"

Bru allowed himself a smile. "Yes."

"But why did you do it then?"

"I had to know what was there."

"I don't understand; you disobeyed a Council decree just because you wanted to?"

"That's about it."

This silenced Jun, never before had he encountered anything like this. It didn't seem possible that anybody would disobey the Council. This person he was following was a very strange creature indeed. How could his doyen ever have contemplated allowing this person to be the heir? It made him wonder if he had ever really understood Lim.

The day broke and they pressed on in silence. Bru tried to recall the geography of the area from the long trek he had made so many years ago. It was not possible to approach Dolon Export in a private craft of any sort, so it had been necessary to walk for over thirty kilometres each way. At last they came upon a lake that he remembered was about half an hour's walk from the port. Bru led the way along the southern shore where they had to traverse a stream that fed the lake. Here they stopped and drank and let their bare feet dangle in the soft water.

Bru noticed that Jun's feet were raw from Lim's ill-fitting slippers and it pleased him that the boy had not complained.

"Not far, we are almost there."

Jun nodded and kept his gaze on the rippling water. "What did you see at Dolon Export?"

"Ah! Do I detect the smell of rebellion?"

"No," replied the boy quickly, "I ask only because I am being forced to go there by you."

"Really? How disappointing. The truth is that I discovered very little at Dolon Export. It is a vast structure entirely populated by simulants; there are no humans there at all. It was not until I left Suran that I discovered the truth about what comes out of Dolon Export and why the Council Elders do not allow any of the population near it."

"What is it, what do they export?"

"Misery, Scholar Siu, pure misery, from the dark heart of Suran; misery that keeps you, Lim, and everyone on this planet in comfort and affluence.

"What do you mean?"

"Weapons, thousands upon thousands of weapons; sidearms, field weapons, anything that will kill or maim human beings.

"That's a lie. I don't believe you."

"It's the rotten, fetid kernel of our world. Everything we have; our lavish education; our fine dwellings; our beautiful parks; our solitude; all paid for with guns and death. And I must tell you, Scholar Siu, our esteemed council is not particular who is in receipt of these weapons. If they have credit, they get them."

"It's not true."

"It is, you will see for yourself."

"Our doyen would never agree to it. Our doyen would never be part of this."

Bru sighed. "Our doyen was a minister and is a member of the Council, I leave you to draw your own conclusions." He dried his feet on some moss and replaced his boots. "Never mind, Scholar Siu, Suran is a socialistic meritocracy and at least the proceeds go to culture and science, which is a lot more than can be said for most other worlds."

Jun did not choose to reply.

VII

Dolon Export lay in the hollow of an ancient meteor crater four kilometres across and nearly a hundred metres deep. In the centre stood one enormous, grey circular building shaped like a flattened dome, about two kilometres in diameter. Numerous portals surrounded one large one at the apex of the dome.

"Did you go inside before?" asked Jun as they stood looking down from the edge of the crater.

Bru shook his head. "No."

"How do you know we can get in? I don't see any doors."

"There are quite a few access points around the base of the perimeter."

"How do you know?"

"I have studied the plans; there was a copy in our doyen's library. That is why I wanted to see the place for myself."

"Why would our doyen keep a copy of the plans of this place?"

"I don't exactly know, but I suspect that Lim had a large hand in the design. Our doyen did a great deal of research into the control of gravitational fields and this is an anti-gravitational launcher. What you see here is just the tip of a huge structure that goes down over five kilometres into the crust below us. That is the power source and it generates enough to produce a beam of reverse gravity from the centre of that building. Anything in that beam literally falls into the sky."

"I have heard of this, but I thought it was just a theory."

"A theory made real, the only one of its kind as far as I know. It was too impractical and expensive, they never built another and the Council would never have allowed the technology to leave Suran."

"Have you ever seen a launch?"

"No, it would be the last thing you'd see, Scholar Siu. Look about you; there is no vegetation, nothing organic survives. That is why there are no humans here, at least one of the reasons."

"So what are we going to do?"

"We will withdraw to a safe distance, well beyond the tree line, and wait for a launch. After that we will have about two hours before it can recharge sufficiently for another launch. Plenty of time to get inside."

They retraced their steps, across the barren apron of land surrounding the crater, passing the strangely distorted trees of the forest edge. At about half a kilometre away the forest resumed a look of normality and they settled down to wait in a small clearing. Jun sat a small distance away and, through half-closed eyes, Bru could see the boy studying him, though whether from curiosity or revulsion, he could not tell. At least the open antipathy had subsided and Jun had reverted to the natural Suran character of unquestioning obedience and reverence for authority, and, at the moment, he was the authority. He shut his eyes and slept.

It wasn't the noise that awoke him, there wasn't any. It was the pressure, or rather a wave of disruption in the atmosphere that could not easily be described. He felt as though he was being both stretched and compacted at the same time; upside down and yet still the right way up. He looked up and the fronds above him seemed to distort and dance, lights popped and flashed in the thickening air. With horror, Bru realized they were too close.

Jun had already staggered to his feet and was swaying drunkenly. Bru screamed at him to get down but the words seemed to emerge from his mouth and hang in the thick air above him. He saw the boy fall, but he did not fall in a natural way, rather he floated to the ground in slow motion. Bru covered his head with his arms and buried his face in the mossy ground while pulse after pulse passed through his body and into the ground below.

It lasted just over four minutes, just long enough to send the craft beyond the planet's atmospheric envelope and into the vacuum of space. Then suddenly it stopped.

Bru tried to get up but his head was spinning and he could not coordinate his limbs. He retched several times but his stomach was empty and nothing came but bile. He spat and turned over. The afternoon sky spun and he tried to focus but it was a shimmering haze above him, as though a great, unseen hand was shaking the air. He shut his eyes and waited. When he reopened them the spinning, shaking sensation had subsided and he tried to raise himself. He retched again and slumped back down. Now he could see the blurred figure of the boy on all fours, retching and coughing. He could hear it too and thanked his luck that his eardrums had not burst.

After several minutes, Bru managed to raise himself and sat with his back against a fern while the world stopped spinning and shaking and his vision began to return. Jun was now lying on the ground, his eyes shut, quite still. Bru noticed that Lim's ill-fitting gown had come adrift, exposing the boy's right leg to his thigh, so he hauled himself away to face another direction. After fifteen minutes Bru was able to stand, but it was like learning to walk for the first time. He fell over a dozen times before he made it to the nearest trunk for support.

He waited several minutes, regaining his senses and balance before trying to move again. This time he didn't fall over and he was able to make it to where Jun was sitting. The boy looked frightful, his normal pallid colour now entirely drained, his face and gown soiled with vomit, his unfocused eyes staring blankly ahead.

Bru stood in front of him, swaying. "Can you stand?" The words came out like a drunkard's but the boy must have understood for he shook his head slowly. "Try," encouraged Bru, but Jun would not budge. Bru slumped to the ground; they were going to have to wait.

Twenty minutes later two figures staggered out of the forest and across the apron of desolation that led to the edge of the crater. The rocky sides were steep and their progress was slow as they picked their way down the slope. At one point Jun slipped and hit his head on a boulder. Bru reluctantly reached down to help him up, but the boy dealt him such a furious look that he quickly withdrew his hand. The fall broke the delicate skin of Jun's unprotected scalp and blood began to trickle down his temple as he struggled to his feet.

They reached the compacted, rocky floor of the crater and began to make their way towards the looming walls of the dome of Dolon Export. The two hours that Bru had estimated they would have before the possibility of another launch was almost up. He urged Jun on knowing they would not survive another launch, especially not in the crater itself, and they broke into a gentle run. He had now fully recovered his senses and it looked as though Jun had too.

The sun had just set when they finally reached the fluted wall of the great dome. Bru started to search the perimeter base for one of the access points that he recalled from the plans, but there were none. As they searched a sinking doubt began to overtake him and he racked his memory, trying to recall the plans and wondering if he had got it totally wrong. After about fifteen fruitless minutes he heard Jun say, "Look." The boy was pointing up at a point further along the wall. Bru looked and saw the outline of a large portal, the base of which was about four metres from the ground. Bru realized, with a sinking feeling of dismay, the access points were not for humans; they were for robots.

"We have to get back," said Jun, "this is hopeless. Didn't you realize?"

"No," replied Bru. He felt foolish; it should have been obvious that human access wouldn't ever be needed here. "We can't go back, Scholar Siu, there is no second plan, this is it; we have to get in."

"Well, we can't, unless you know of any other way."

"No, these are the only access points at this level."

"This is madness, I'm going; you do what you want."

"You're not going anywhere," said Bru, his voice suddenly hard.

"What are you going to do, float up there on a cushion of air? Even if you get up there, how are you going to get it open? It's hopeless. If there's another launch, we're dead, we have to get away."

"We're not going to open it, they are," said Bru and he picked up a large rock and hurled it at the door. "These are maintenance portals; something will open it and check for damage." He picked up another rock and launched it at the door; it fractured and rained to the ground in pieces. Bru threw again and again, with increasing desperation while Jun watched with ill-concealed disdain. At last Bru could throw no more and he ceased; the building had not even been slightly damaged; it was hopeless.

"Now, may we go?" said Jun with a level of sarcasm in his voice that Bru could stand no more. Frustration boiled in him and he turned on the boy with a murderous look on his face. Jun stepped back in alarm; he had never seen such raw anger, not even from Lim. It began to look as if he would actually be attacked, but, at that moment, he was saved by the sound of machinery coming from above. The door was opening.

It slowly eased out and upwards in a continuous, smooth movement as they watched. Then a machine emerged and began to ascend the dome wall.

Bru turned to Jun. "We don't have much time; you will do exactly as I say without argument or question. This will not be easy for either of us." He placed his back against the dome wall and linked his hands to form a cradle. "Start climbing."

With horror it dawned on Jun what Bru wanted him to do. He hesitated long enough to illicit a bellowed, 'Now!' from Bru. Jun started climbing, the closeness of this man's flesh almost made him gag but he was soon standing on Bru's shoulders. He felt big hands grab his feet and push him up the wall until his fingers just touched the bottom edge of the portal. He grabbed for it and held on, then, at the expense of a considerable effort, pulled himself up while Bru stood away and watched. Having checked the upper levels of the sector of the dome, the robot was beginning to descend. They had very little time.

Jun hauled himself inside and turned around to look down at Bru. He could not see a way that the man was going to get up. It was too far to jump and he certainly could not pull him up. "Now what?"

"Is there anything there to tie on to?"

Jun looked about him, he could see nothing. "No."

"Catch this." Bru threw him the knife and Jun managed to catch it without cutting himself on the fine blade, then he looked back down and what he saw filled him with a revulsion he had never come close to experiencing before. Bru was stripping! He tore off his tunic and then his pants and began to knot them together. He was stark naked, except for his boots. Jun was so shocked at what he saw that he gawped. The man was covered in hair, filthy, dark hair; his chest; his navel; his groin; even his legs. It was revolting beyond measure. Jun also couldn't help noticing that Bru was male, something he had always suspected, though Bru was more fortunate than he for his genitals were a lot more discreet. He shut his eyes quickly to spare himself more offence.

"Open your eyes, damn you," shouted Bru. "Now catch this."

He threw up the bundle of clothing and the boy caught it first time. "Now jamb the knife between the floor and the bulkhead and tie one sleeve to it securely."

Jun pushed the blade into the narrow gap between the floor of the portal and the inside of the wall. It went in up to its hilt and formed a reasonably firm anchor. Then he tied the sleeve to it, letting the rest fall over the side. Above him he could hear the approach of the maintenance robot returning after its fruitless mission.

"Hold the knife in place," shouted Bru, he could see the robot no more than twenty metres away, approaching fast. He jumped and grabbed the dangling leg of his pants and began to haul himself up with all his strength.

He arrived at the threshold of the portal just in time. The robot was almost back and he managed to scramble in, grabbing the knife and then rolling away as the robot entered and settled back into its place by the portal door. He got up and began to un-knot his clothes as the portal door began to close slowly.

Jun was pointedly looking away. "I have never seen anything so revolting," he said.

"You are young, give it time," replied Bru, pulling on his pants. "Anyway, what makes you think you're a joy to behold? Boy," he added provocatively.

Jun bristled. "How dare you... How dare you use a term of gender on me?"

"Why shouldn't I? It is quite obvious to me you are male. I saw that for myself."

"You look like a savage and you are one, to refer to that unspeakable incident in such a personal way. I cannot bear it."

"Do you think I enjoyed it? The sight of you revolted me. Neither of us are perfect Surans, are we, Scholar Siu?"

Bru saw the boy's pale skin flush with colour. The arrow had struck its target and now he would shut-up. He finished dressing and secured the knife in his pants just as the portal door closed on the last of Suran. "Come, we have a ride to find."

"And don't call me 'scholar' anymore; I'm no longer one, thanks to you."

"As you will," said Bru as he walked past him and off down the darkened passage.

VIII

At the end of the short passage they found themselves in a vast space. The visible dome was merely the roof and where they stood was the upper level of a complex, multi-layered structure into which each cargo vessel nestled. The light level was extremely dim and they could not see the floor of the port nearly two hundred metres below.

Bru squinted into the gloom towards the only light source, a pair of navigation lights on a vessel about four hundred metres away. They made their way carefully along the high level until they came to the vessel. Below him Bru could hear the soft whirr of machinery.

"They're loading this one." he said. "We need to get to a lower level."

They found their way down five levels until they came to an air lock door. Bru pressed the mechanism, it opened and a soft, blue light shone out into the gloom. They stepped inside and he closed the outer door and waited for the inner door to open.

The vast majority of cargo vessels that plied the vastness of space did so without human company, but international law still required each vessel to provide support for a minimum crew of twelve. This vessel was designed with the minimum specification arranged in a cramped and functional style. They made a cursory tour and found twelve small cabins and a common area with a galley and a place to eat. Jun found a cabin and disappeared into it without a word; he had not spoken since their last altercation. Bru was not unhappy about that, he found Jun's company trying and he wondered if their relationship could ever recover from their disastrous first encounter. He left the boy to his own devices and found a cabin for himself; slumped down on to the bed and was soon asleep.

Three hours later he was awoken by a vague sensation of movement, which lasted for about ten minutes, followed by a period of complete stillness. Then a slight shudder passed through the ship and he became aware of a brief sense of weightlessness before he fell upwards and hit the ceiling quite hard. By the time he struggled to his feet, he was beginning to become weightless. Bru had not experienced weightlessness before and he found himself flailing for control until he managed to grab the frame of the door. He floated into the common area and eventually found the control panel and activated the gravity. As it gained strength, he gradually came to rest on the floor.

Jun emerged from his cabin just as Bru opened the observation shields. His face was still bloody from the fall in the crater and there was an unpleasant smell of vomit about him. Neither spoke as, together, they watched the green, blue and white confection of Suran recede until it disappeared into the anonymous backdrop of stars. Bru noticed a tear had formed on the boy's cheek and conceded that it must be difficult for him to see the disappearance of his world. As for himself, he experienced quite different emotions, relief at having made it and apprehension for what might be ahead, for he was well aware that Suran exported arms to many places that were better left unvisited.

When he could no longer see his world, Jun returned to his cabin and shut the door. Bru decided to explore the galley and soon discovered that it was unstocked. This was disappointing but not entirely unexpected so he found his way to the survival deck where two six-man life pods were located. These had to be stocked, by law, with enough provisions for twenty-six days and Bru was relieved to find them both complete. He took one of the nutrient tablets to stave off his hunger pangs. It was entirely tasteless, but at least it would keep them alive.

During the next fifty hours of the journey Bru occupied himself with an investigation of the vessel. He attempted to discover their destination but was thwarted by a security code that he could not break. He knew also that he had to be very careful since any evidence of tampering would quickly bring an investigation. They just had to go where they were taken and from his observations, it appeared to be back toward Agon. In all this time he did not see Jun, nor was there any evidence that the boy had left his cabin. The rations that he had left out were untouched and, as far as he could see, the douche had not been used. Whereas this did not particularly concern Bru at a personal level, he was very well aware of the effects of starvation. If Jun wanted to starve himself to death, that was his prerogative, but a half starved and weakened companion was not an option at this time.

He knocked on Jun's cabin door, but there was no reply, so he opened it. The boy was on the bed, lying quite still with his eyes closed. The blood from his head wound still stained the pallid, drawn skin on the side of his face. Looking down at him, Bru was surprised to notice a distinct darkening of his pate indicating that his hair follicles had not been destroyed. He was awake but kept his eyes shut.

"Scholar Siu, if you wish to kill yourself I beg you do it in a swifter way than starvation. I do not wish to be saddled with an invalid. If you do not wish to kill yourself then take some nourishment, clean yourself up and assist me in getting us to KT153 as our doyen requested. That is all I have to say." He turned and left the room.

Two hours later Jun emerged. Bru threw him a cursory glance and pointed at the galley. Jun went over and took one of the nutrient pills then he made his way to the douche. When he emerged, both he and the gown were clean, but his demeanour was still sullen. He took a seat as far away from Bru as possible.

"Do you know where we are going yet?"

"No, perhaps you can help me work it out. Take a look."

Jun got up and stared out at the stars. "That's Vindus, that red giant; and that's the Fern Cluster; I'd say we are heading for one of the old worlds."

"I agree; could it be Agon?"

Jun shook his head. "No, we are not heading there, I can't tell where, though, not yet. Can't you get into the ship's system?"

"It's encoded. Anyway, we do not want to draw attention to ourselves."

Jun nodded and sat down. After some time he spoke again. "Is it permitted to ask you a personal question?"

"We have very little left to hide from each other. Go ahead."

Jun coloured a little at the reminder. "Why did you allow your hair to grow?"

"Agon is a hirsute society; all the men are bearded and proud of it. It took some time for my follicles to recover, but when they did, I allowed my hair to grow in order to fit in."

"I have not received any treatment."

"So I see. Why not?"

"I don't know exactly. I suppose I preferred the satisfaction of manual removal."

"That's very singular."

"Is it?"

"I assume so. Anyway, it is as well. Fastidious hairlessness is a unique, Suran trait and we don't want to draw attention to ourselves. You will allow it to grow."

Jun buried his head in his hands. "I will become a barbarian, like you."

"You'll get used to it. I did."

Bru did not have the heart to tell the boy what else was going to happen to his body now that he was free of the bromidic environment of Suran. Given the limited and slanted human biology instruction he would have received as a youth, Jun would be ill prepared for the blossoming of his sexuality. It was a subject better left buried and, anyway, they would probably both be dead before any physical developments were likely to occur.

IX

The long journey unfolded with little to occupy them. This forced them into each other's company more than would have been natural for either. Jun discovered in Bru a wide knowledge and phenomenal recall which he could not help but respect and Bru found Jun to be a willing pupil with an extraordinary ability to retain information, but, as yet, lacking in critical analytical skills. Their discussions ranged far and wide, into art and philosophy; mathematics and the sciences; and even into faith and the nature of religion itself. This brought them, quite naturally, into a discussion on The Fourth Proposition in which Bru described, in some detail, the nature of the Faith and why the Proposition had been so dangerous. This discussion ended in a revelation that Jun had not expected, when he asked why their doyen had retained a copy of The Fourth Proposition in the face of such risk.

"You are right to ask, Scholar Siu, for had it been discovered the High Priests would certainly have demanded the extradition of a doyen of Suran, which could not be allowed. There would probably have been war. But it is very difficult to give up one's own offspring, if you'll pardon the metaphor, for, you see, our doyen was the author of The Fourth Proposition."

Jun gave him a look of astonishment. "How do you know? Did our doyen tell you this?"

"Of course not; it could not be acknowledged; not even in confidence. But the style was unmistakably Lim's and why else would a copy have been kept? But there is something else. There is a long chapter relating to the Book of Minnar and other early scriptures that is not the work of our doyen. It was this chapter that caused most of the fuss for it constituted a direct challenge to the Faith. In the third book, for instance, we are introduced to the Guardians of Knowledge, 'which are neither male nor female', who lived amongst the first men. They are described as ageless and wise beyond the comprehension of Man. It also described how, after three generations, they vanished into a great light in the sky. Minnar, writing over five hundred years after the Creation of Man, describes many other miraculous events, all of which are accounted for, in The Fourth Proposition, as the work of sophisticated androids. The writer of this chapter was not a Suran."

"Not a Suran?"

"No, the knowledge of scripture is too deep for any Suran and there are references made to books that only the priests of Kagan, the seat of the Faith, had seen."

"So the second writer was from Kagan?"

Bru nodded. "It seems likely."

"But how would our doyen have known someone from Kagan? It is an extremely unlikely scenario."

"I agree, but I refer you to the gallery of Lim's alumni in the study. There is another face missing, quite apart from mine. Recall the beginning of Lim's doyenship, the first graduate."

"Mardon Fan, a great researcher. Fan died recently, did you know?"

"I did not know, but Fan, as you say, was a great researcher, and, yet, according to the dates of scholarship, Fan required almost twenty seven years of instruction in order to graduate. That is not credible."

Jun had to agree. "So our doyen was concealing an association?"

"And rightly so. An ill-judged association with a foreigner that resulted in the deaths of thousands; wouldn't you conceal it?"

"It was dishonest, but I can understand it. Did you try and find out who the other contributor was?"

"Yes, that was when I got into trouble. I made a cursory enquiry at the Kagan Mission on Suran and all hell broke loose because I mentioned The Fourth Proposition."

"That was foolish, to mention it."

"I had no idea it would produce such a reaction. How could I? Nobody knew anything about it, because it had been buried for a hundred years. Lim was furious, but I wonder, sometimes if I hadn't been manoeuvred. I am certain that Lim knew I was searching the library and that sooner or later, I would come across The Fourth Proposition."

"You think it was all done deliberately? Why?"

"Lim wanted someone to carry the torch, The Fourth couldn't be allowed to die and our doyen chose me. But I messed up, instead of pursuing the idea described in The Fourth, I pursued the authors and it caused another incident. I think that was why Lim was so angry; it wasn't part of the plan."

Jun did not like what he was hearing about his doyen, to whom he had always ascribed the highest integrity and ideals. First, the shocking involvement in the arms trade; now this. He was unable to deny the logic of Bru's argument and began to realize that he had been caught up in a tangle of deceit that had destroyed his life and expectations and the cause of it could be traced back to his own, duplicitous doyen.

"You think this has all been planned?"

Bru smiled. "I think 'plan' is too strong a word, maybe 'facilitation' would be more apposite."

"But where do I fit in?"

"You don't. You are collateral damage, Scholar Siu. I am sorry for you."

"I see."

"Do not be too downcast, we have begun a mission to discover the true source of Humanity, surely there is some merit in that."

Jun thought for a moment then conceded that there was.

X

On the sixty-third day of their confinement, Bru was in the galley, taking a nourishment pill with some water, when Jun entered in a state of agitation. The boy's appearance had altered considerably since they had boarded the freighter. His hair had grown and now covered his head in a light brown stubble and there was the faintest hint of down on his top lip. There was also muscle tone and a distinct masculinity about him where none had existed before. Bru suspected that he had been exercising after he had jokingly berated him for being weak and puny and no use in a fight. When Jun pointed out that Surans didn't fight, Bru had laughed and said, "I hope you're right." But the boy had taken the criticism to heart and had begun to address it.

The growth of his hair caused him great consternation and not a day went by without some reference to it. But that morning, in the galley, it was not becoming hirsute that was causing him great anguish; it was an entirely different manifestation of his absence from Suran.

"What's the matter with you?" asked Bru. "What errant follicle has appeared now?"

"Nothing," replied Jun and took his ration away into the common area and slumped into his usual seat.

Bru followed and sat opposite. "You know I cannot abide silent petulance, if I have offended you I would rather you speak."

"It is not you; it has nothing to do with you."

"That is a welcome change. What is it then?"

Jun sat forward and stared at the floor, clasping his hands. "I have become a barbarian."

"You have me at a disadvantage Jun, I have no idea what you mean."

The boy looked up at him, his eyes filled with tears. "What will become of me? I am disgusting."

Bru thought of a couple of good quips, but for once, held back. "You will have to be specific. What is the problem?"

Jun flushed, right to the top of his head. "My... my... you know was swollen when I awoke just now."

Bru looked at him stunned. "Good Lord! Already!"

"When I woke up… it was revolting, horrible…"

"Do not continue; I have the gist."

Jun rubbed the tears away with his sleeve. "I don't know what it means."

Bru silently cursed the stilted education of his home planet. "It is quite natural and nothing to be alarmed about."

"That's easy for you to say, you are not so cursed. You did not see it, it grew and became…"

"That will do; I do not require a description."

"Can you help me? I don't want it to happen again. It mustn't happen again."

"I'm afraid I can't help you. You will have to learn to accept it, for it will happen again."

"Can it not be prevented?"

"There are chemical suppressants, but not on this vessel. I'm afraid you will have to live with the affliction. I confess I am surprised, I had not thought the environmental effect of Suran would fade this quickly."

"Did it not happen to you?"

"Yes, but not until I had been a year on Agon."

"You see, I am a barbarian, even worse than you."

"I was twenty-nine when I left; my exposure to the environment of Suran was much greater than yours. You are but nineteen and bound to be more vigorous. Even so, this speed is surprising but then we have no precedent on which to rely."

"Is that supposed make me feel better?"

"That was not my aim; I was merely making an observation."

"I curse the day I was made like this. Why me?"

"That is a universal question that many of us ask of ourselves. The answer, of course, is, why *not* me? We are all unique, every single one of us, even on Suran where we have been genetically engineered. Even our predecessors recognized that, without variety, the human race would become sterile and die. You are a product of that essential variation, as am I, but I must tell you, what may be extraordinary on Suran is not extraordinary elsewhere and it is not generally considered desirable to be androgynous."

"I don't believe that."

"That is because you have never been exposed to other societies. Our education on Suran is highly technical, but it is also myopic. We are brought up to believe that our way is the only way and everything else is uncivilized. That works very well because it keeps us content in our superiority, but I must tell you, this philosophy is no use to you in the wider universe. You are going to change, accept it for it will not kill you."

Mercifully for Bru, that was the last time such an intimate subject was discussed and his limited expertise was not taxed further. From that time, Jun seemed more at ease with himself and even neglected the daily hair bulletins, much to Bru's relief. Two days later Jun smiled for the first time at one of Bru's weak jokes, and a day after that, he actually laughed at another. Their enforced confinement together had altered them both. Bru had discovered a tolerance for company that he would never have endured at any time in his life before and, although Jun would not have been his first choice of companion, he accepted him for what he was and made the best of it.

His need for solitude, though, was not as greatly diminished as Jun's, whose transformation was more dramatic. The sullen, insular boy that had started the journey seventy-odd days ago had disappeared and been replaced by a person of a more robust character. He became talkative and gregarious to a degree that discomforted the older man to such an extent that he was often obliged to hide from the boy or feign sleep in his own cabin. It was as though Suran had only placed a faint imprint on Jun and Bru wondered whether this was unusual or whether any other youth taken from its sterile environment would recover normal human behaviour so easily.

On the seventy-third day they were able to see that one star began to burn brighter in the cosmos. This was to be their destination. They tried to work out which it was, estimating the speed of the craft and their journey time and their position in the star region, and they narrowed it down to four possibilities. Jun thought it was probably Dax, Bru favoured Muran, but they were both wrong, for as the craft slowed on its approach to the system, it became obvious that the star was Cato and that meant they were going to the fifth planet, Tarnus.

This revelation immediately took Bru into one of the life pods, cursing that he had not prepared earlier. He had always known that Tarnus was a possibility, but had chosen to hope that it would not be their destination. Now that they knew it was, he had to act.

"What are you doing?" asked Jun, following him into pod two.

"We will need to re-program this pod. The safety landing sequence must be interrupted; we need to control the descent and landing."

"Isn't that dangerous?"

"Yes. We will use this pod to leave the ship before it orbits. We must not be discovered on board. We will land, obtain transport and get away from Tarnus as soon as possible."

"Is it a bad place?"

"It is no place for a Suran, or any other civilized human being."

PART FOUR

TARNUS

I

Unless it is governed by a powerful and purposeful intelligence, there is an unvarying direction to human society toward the degradation of once-pristine environments. This degradation may take the form of over-exploitation of resources; of overpopulation; of inappropriate and unsympathetic development; of pollution, and any number of actions that unconsciously combine to demote the human condition. But, by far the most devastating cause of degradation is conflict.

In the human diaspora many worlds had fallen prey to the ravages of war, but none were so devastated and so degraded as Tarnus, for the people of Tarnus would not live together. They fought and murdered each other and squandered the natural assets of their ancient world. They became addicted to violence and had made an industry of it to the extent that for over five hundred years Tarnus had known no peace. Its once-fertile surface had been laid to waste and vast areas were so poisonous that they had been rendered sterile. The towns and cities were ruins where the meagre population cowered in cellars and scraped by on what they could beg from the well-fed armies.

Into this nightmare world hurtled, like a meteor, the life pod containing Solon Bru and Jun Siu. Every warning light was flashing critical, every alarm klaxon was sounding, as they shot through the upper atmosphere like a fireball in the night and plunged towards the ground. The temperature of the exterior of the pod read over three thousand degrees and it was getting extremely hot inside.

"Slow us down," shouted Jun above the cacophony, "you have to slow us down."

"No. We must get to the surface as quickly as possible."

"You're going to kill us."

"Get into one of the stasis capsules; it will protect you if we crash."

"You mean *when* we crash," corrected Jun and, bracing against the lurching of the life pod, made his way to the capsule furthest from the cockpit.

At seven thousand metres Bru saw what he was looking for and targeted an area about two kilometres from what appeared to be a city. Then he threw the vehicle into auto-landing mode and climbed into one of the stasis capsules while the engines screamed.

The first small missile hit them at fifteen hundred metres and then a second at twelve hundred. The sturdy craft stayed intact as they were buffeted around in the night sky, before finally hitting the ground like a stone skimming across water and bouncing high into the air. On the second impact the craft began to break up and by the time it finally came to rest it had divided into four pieces with wreckage strewn along a path over two kilometres long.

Bru opened the stasis capsule that was still attached to the main part of the wreck. The nightime air was warm and foul, the remains of the pod steamed and crackled. They had landed in a swamp. He looked about him and through the dull, grey miasma he saw that three of the capsules, including Jun's, were no longer there. He stepped from the capsule - it had done its work well, protecting him from the impact and flying wreckage. A steady rain was falling as he carefully felt his way from the remains of the pod and into the swamp. The boggy ground swallowed his feet up to his shins making his progress difficult, but he forced himself on in the gloom, along the path of the wreckage, to where he hoped he would find Jun still alive.

He managed about two hundred metres before a stark, bright light appeared overhead. He looked up into it just as a thumping pulse hit him and knocked him to the ground. He hit the soft mud with a splat and the light came closer. He felt himself grabbed by something hard and metallic that pulled him out of the mud and high into the air. He tried to move his limbs but the pulse had completely paralyzed him and he was hauled into the craft like a rag doll.

He felt hands on him and muffled words entered his scrambled brain. Words like 'spy' and 'enemy'. He tried to say something but his mouth would not function and all he could hear was his own blubbering. They hit him with another pulse; he sank away from the world and everything stopped.

II

When Bru returned to the world he found himself stripped naked and seated in a room. The room was dimly lit but he could see the bare walls of stone and a small table in front of him. On the table were his mud-soiled clothes in a pile; Gong Lat's knife and a small box containing his remaining supply of survival pills. It was everything he owned. The cold of the room penetrated his flesh and made him shiver. He tried to move but found himself shackled at his ankles and arms. The shackles were tight and bit into his skin. Instinctively he knew that he was probably going to die in this room and it would not be a good death, not an easy death. The room had the smell of the dead about it, echoes of tortured bodies and unspeakable horrors. He gritted his teeth against the cold and waited.

They left him there for four hours and then he heard the door behind him open. Three men entered, two stood behind him so that he couldn't see them and one stood before him. He was in his late twenties, dapper and well dressed in a military uniform. He smiled down at Bru, a chill smile that instilled fear. It was the smile of a man who enjoyed his work.

"I am Captain Fallon and you and I are going to go on a journey. How far we go on this journey depends on you." His voice was soft and a little effeminate. "Now, we shall begin with something simple. Your name."

"Solon Bru."

"Solon Bru; that will do for the time being. I will call you Solon; we will get to know each other very well."

"I am cold, I want to get dressed."

"Solon, we know you are a spy. Who is your contact here?"

"I don't know anything about spying, I crashed here."

"Correction, we shot you down. Now, who is your contact?"

"I have no contact, I am not a…"

The first blow knocked his head sideways; the second knocked the chair over. His head banged on the stone floor. Hands from behind righted him. He peered fuzzily at Captain Fallon who was now holding a truncheon. He could taste blood in his mouth

"Shall we start again, Solon? We know you are from Rion, who is your contact?"

"Don't hit me again, I'll tell you everything you want to know. I swear I'm telling you the truth. I am a Suran; I came here on a freighter."

Captain Fallon laughed. "A Suran?" He deftly flicked Bru's genitals with the truncheon. Bru yelped in pain. "What's that then? Your story is ludicrous; you are quite obviously not a Suran."

"I swear I am a Suran."

The Captain clenched his fist and swung at Bru's face. It hit him in the eye and rocked his head back.

"We know about the freighter, full of arms, is it going to Rion, so our enemies can kill more of us? What was on board?"

"Weapons."

"What type?"

"I don't know."

The truncheon came down on the side of his head again. He tried to lose consciousness but he couldn't. His brain swam with pain. He felt himself unshackled and cuffed. The chair was kicked away and he was hauled upwards by the wrists and suspended from the ceiling. The first whack landed on his thigh. He screamed. The second and third fell on his buttocks; the fourth on his back bringing forth howls of agony. He thought he was going to pass out, but he didn't. He wanted to die, as quickly as possible, but Captain Fallon was good at his game. Two more blows brought him to the edge of his endurance.

The Captain slapped him gently on his swelling cheek. "Are you ready for the truth?"

Bru saw the smiling face through half closed eyes. "Yes," he said. "I am a spy for Rion. I came here with the freighter."

"See, that wasn't so difficult, was it? Take him down."

Bru's cuffs were released and he collapsed to the floor. Captain Fallon's smiling face loomed over him. "Would you like a drink, Solon?"

Bru was in no position to answer so Fallon did the job. "I think he said yes, didn't he? He would like a drink. Hold him down and hold his mouth open, I will give him his drink."

The guards held Bru's head still and forced his jaw open while the Captain dropped his pants and took careful aim. Bru choked and struggled as the Captain's piss filled his mouth.

"There's no quality to the men they're sending now," he remarked, as he shook the last drips from his manhood and pulled his pants up. "We will come back and get what we want from him later, give him a bit more time to think. Hang him up again."

The guards suspended the broken body of Solon Bru from the ceiling while Captain Fallon left the room to make his way to other, more challenging, interviewees. This time Bru's feet could touch the floor so that he could relieve the weight of his body. His head lolled forward and one of the guards grabbed his hair and spat in his face. Then he reached down and grabbed Bru's testicles, squeezing them hard.

"You're going to die, you Rion shit. We're going to cut off your balls and feed them to you one by one." He released his grip and punched Bru in the stomach, causing him to moan and his legs to jerk. Then they left, the door banged and there was silence.

By this time Bru had drawn into himself. He had tasted the warm piss in his mouth but hardly knew what it was; he felt the pain in his groin, his legs, back and the throbbing of his swollen face. He sensed the guard's breath and the wetness of the spit, running down his cheek, but he didn't care anymore. All he wanted in the world was to die.

III

Corhaden had always been a scavenger. Even as a toddler he had scoured the ruined streets of the city for any scrap of detritus that could be sold. Fifty-two years later, he was still at it and so the bonanza of a crashed vessel was like a magnet to him.

Corhaden was stealthy and cunning and knew enough of the world in which he lived to keep away while the military poured over the site of the crash. He watched them from afar, as did dozens of others, and when the soldiers left, Corhaden and his fellow scavengers moved in. The main parts of the craft had been removed, but there were plenty of pieces of wreckage left for them to scrape together and they spent the remains of the day squelching through the marsh in search of scraps.

The short day of Tarnus was nearly over and all but a couple of scavengers remained. Corhaden was searching a little away from the impact site when he saw it, buried in the mud of a marsh pool next to the stump of a dead tree. He looked around him to make sure nobody was watching, then waded into the pool to make certain of what he had seen. There was no doubt; it was a stasis capsule from the crash. He waited until he was the last one at the sight, marked the spot carefully then made his way home with joy in his heart.

The discovery of the stasis capsule was not the first piece of luck from which Corhaden had recently benefited. Just over a year ago he had found a young woman wandering about in an apparent daze in the rain-soaked ruins. He took her back to his cellar on the edge of the city and there discovered that he had stumbled upon a foreigner of astounding beauty. Her name was Matty Saronaga and she told him that she was from Ennepp, a world some distance from Tarnus. But Corhaden didn't care where she was from, his purpose was to benefit from his luck and so he went into the gratification business. Matty was surprisingly willing and soon his cellar resounded to the sweaty grunts of soldiers and miners and anyone with money to spend, while the proprietor observed proceedings through a small hole in the wall.

That night, when Corhaden returned from the marsh, he heard the distinct sound of Matty at work behind the soiled, ragged curtain. Soon there was a grunt and a sigh and the curtain swung back to reveal a solid-looking naked man still swollen with lust. He gave Corhaden a cursory glance and strolled over to where he had left his uniform.

Corhaden watched him dress. "She should charge you double for a thing that size; you're damaging my property."

The soldier grinned and waved the enlarged member towards his host. "Biggest one in Trant, so the ladies tell me."

Corhaden scowled at his guest's proud asset as it disappeared into his uniform and came to a decision. For a soldier, Corporal Beck seemed a decent sort. He had been several times to the cellar and had always paid without quibble. He would take a chance.

"Corporal, can you get hold of a military tractor?'

Beck pulled on his jacket and gave him a quizzical look. "And why would you be wanting that?"

"I have an item I want to recover from the marsh."

"What sort of item?"

"Can you get a tractor?"

"Probably, it would cost me though. What are you up to?"

"I will give you the money. Bring it tonight."

"Not until you tell me what you want it for."

Corhaden was not so sure now; he had not expected this dumb, brutish soldier to ask him so many questions. But it was too late. "I have found something of value at the crash site."

Beck's demeanour suddenly hardened and he narrowed his eyes on the old man. "Something of value? What exactly?" He advanced threateningly forcing the old man to take a couple of steps back. Corhaden now had serious doubts about his choice of partner.

"It doesn't matter," he stammered. "Nothing really to interest an important man like you."

Beck ground his teeth and took a step closer, backing Corhaden against a wall. "You miserly old scrotum; what have you found?"

Corhaden's futile resistance crumbled instantly. "A stasis unit," he whispered dejectedly.

Beck's eyes widened; he took a step back. "They searched the site thoroughly; are you sure?"

"It's buried in mud, under water, away from the main field of the wreckage. We will need some ropes to free it."

The soldier began to pace the room while the limited brain in his bullet-like cranium calculated. "I can get the tractor and the ropes but I will take half."

Corhaden was surprised that he had only asked for an equal share; perhaps Beck had little understanding of fractions; perhaps he really intended to take it all. As he watched the soldier pacing he had already worked out that he would probably have to kill the man and had begun to speculate on the method.

"Alright, a half then," he conceded.

They haggled some more about the cost of the bribe that Beck would need for the tractor and the soldier went off with much more of Corhaden's money than was deemed necessary or desirable. He turned to Matty who had been listening intently.

"And you keep your mouth shut too. If you're lucky I'll get you a new dress. Now get me some food."

IV

Three and a half hours later Beck came back with the tractor and the two men set off into the grey night.

"You didn't tell anyone what you wanted this for."

"Yeah, told the whole camp. What do you think?"

"Keep the lights off. Turn left up there."

Beck steered them to the spot just over three kilometres from the edge of the ruined city. It started to rain as they found the small pool near the stump of the dead tree.

"This is it," said Corhaden. "Down there, can you see it?"

Beck dismounted and shone a light into the dark water. The faint, grey outline of the top of the capsule was just visible through the murk.

"I see it," he said stripping off for the second time that night. He waded into the muddy pool and felt for a cleat and found one at the top of the capsule. "Throw me that rope."

Corhaden tossed him the rope and he secured it to the cleat while the older man tied the other end to the tractor. Beck waded out and climbed onto the tractor and eased it forward. The rope went taught and the capsule came out of the mud with an ugly sucking sound. Corhaden grinned as he cleaned off the foul mud with his hands while Beck, still wet and stinking from the ooze, dressed himself. Then the two men manhandled the heavy capsule on to the back of the tractor and lashed it down.

As they trundled back towards the city, the capsule, sensing that the exterior was now safe for life, began to revive its contents. Jun opened his eyes, he could sense he was being shaken but could see nothing through the small, mud-smeared window. He tried to open the capsule, but something was preventing it, so he remained inside, wondering what was happening and why Bru had not released him.

Eventually the movement stopped and he could see faint shadows moving outside. He felt himself being moved again and the capsule indicated that it could now be opened, but he did not open it. Water splashed on the window and the face of someone he did not recognize peered in. The face suddenly looked shocked and was saying something quite animated to someone else. Another face appeared at the window, an older person this time, and also spoke. Then they started to bang on the window and Jun realized that he had to open the capsule.

He activated it and the doors parted. Three people were standing in front of him, the two who had peered in and a third, a young one, who was looking at him in wide-eyed amazement. Jun could see that two of them were male but the third was different, softer looking with long, lustrous black hair and dark eyes that shone even in the dim light.

"Who are you?" said the older one.

"She could be a spy," said the other.

"Don't be daft, Beck, Rion doesn't send women to spy. Anyway, she's too young. What's your name love?"

"Jun Siu. Where's my teacher?"

"Why don't you step out darlin', we won't hurt you," said Beck.

Jun stepped from the capsule a little unsteadily; the effects of the stasis had not entirely worn off. Of the three people watching him, only Matty realized what they were looking at and she was in awe. She thought he looked like an angel.

Corhaden turned to Matty. "Get her a drink, hurry up, girl."

Matty hurried off to get some wine, while Corhaden, his mind calculating, perused his new prize. "She's quite pretty but shame about the hair; still I can get her a wig until it grows. Sit down darling."

Beck stared at Jun thoughtfully as he took a seat at the grubby table. "She's got no tits, but I grant you, she ain't bad." He pulled the older man to one side and they began to whisper. "You claiming her as your property?"

"I found her, she is mine."

"That's fine, you can have her. Consider her as your half of the deal."

"What do you mean 'my half'? We had an agreement."

"Dead right, we agreed to share half each. She counts as your half, I'm taking the capsule."

Corhaden"s mouth twisted in anger. It was just as he had suspected; the soldier could not be trusted. He brooded. It would be a huge thing, killing a soldier; they would search everywhere the man was known to frequent and summarily execute anyone involved. He began to doubt; perhaps he could reason with him.

"That's not what we agreed."

Beck's eyes flared and he violently grabbed the older man's neck and began to squeeze. "You need to watch your mouth you scrawny fucker. I'll take anything I want, including a free go on that new whore, and there's nothing you can do about it."

He thrust Corhaden away, sending him crashing into the table and grabbed Jun by the arm, propelling him on to the bed behind the curtain. He hurriedly kicked off his pants and bore down on the boy, easily holding him down while he savagely ripped open the ornate gown of Doyen Lim.

Jun was still groggy from the effects of the stasis. He sensed he was being attacked in some way, but having never experienced physical violence before, he did not understand anything that was happening to him. He tried to struggle but he was too weak and his attacker too strong and heavy. The stench of the man's body and clothes, still putrid from the marsh, filled his nostrils. He felt a rough hand grab at his groin.

Suddenly the man roared. "What's this? You dirty…"

Jun heard a thud and the man roared again, this time in pain. Cursing, Beck spun around just in time to fend off the second blow of a large iron bar. Corhaden realized too late that he had not hit the soldier's thick skull hard enough. He dropped the iron bar and tried to run, but Beck was too quick and he caught the older man by his sleeve and pulled him back. Beck's muscular strength was now augmented by blind rage and he clamped his big hands around the older man's scrawny neck and began to squeeze with all his might. Corhaden kicked and clawed at his attacker in vain as Beck throttled the life out of him. When he was done he threw the body down and with his eyes flaring with anger, turned on Jun.

"You filthy…"

Those were the last words that Beck spoke in his life, for Matty's aim was superior to her manager's. The iron bar came down on the back of the Corporal's head with all the strength she could muster. This time his skull cracked and he dropped to the floor near the cellar stairs.

Matty and Jun stared at each other for some moments. The horror of what had just taken place had sobered his condition, but had stunned him into a trance. Matty was shaking, rooted to the spot with the bloodstained iron bar in her hand. Finally she recovered her wits enough to speak.

"We have to get out of here. I've killed a soldier, we will be executed."

Jun did not move; he was now staring down at Beck's body with a strange look on his face. It was neither horror nor fright as might be expected in that situation. It was curiosity.

"Quickly, we have to go."

Matty disappeared into the next room, came back with some of Corhaden's clothes and pushed them urgently at the boy. "Put those on, you are about the same size as him."

Jun looked up at her uncomprehendingly.

"Your clothes are ripped, you can't go out in that fancy gown; you'll get us into trouble."

It occurred to Jun that they were already in trouble and that this creature was quite mad. "Are they clean?" he asked.

"Clean?" she said. "I don't know."

"I couldn't possibly put them on then."

She was taken aback. What sort of person was this? "Yes, they're clean," she said.

Jun took them from her and sniffed them. "They are not clean."

She grabbed them back off him with an expletive and went back to the next room to get him some more. This time she chose more carefully and returned with fresh clothes. Jun sniffed them again and kept them.

"Quickly," she said.

He frowned at her. "Do you expect me to disrobe while you are watching?"
She gave him a look of incomprehension as she drew the curtain. "Hurry up."

Jun emerged from behind the curtain in the late Corhaden's best pants and shirt, looking more masculine, but nothing like the brutish soldiers and miners of Tarnus. She could see that, like her, he was not from this brutal world and she experienced a strong protective urge towards him.

"We have to go into the city," she said. "I know someone that will help us."

Jun nodded and followed her across the room. At the base of the stairs he looked down at the lifeless body of Corporal Beck and pointed to his genitals.

"Is everybody here made like this?"

Matty looked down at what the strange boy was pointing at. "What are you talking about?"

"The genitals of this male are unusually large."

"What does that matter? What an odd thing to say."

She gave him a look of incomprehension and noticed the play of a faint smile touch his lips. With every moment he was becoming stranger, more alien.

She climbed the stairs of the cellar and emerged into the stark night. Jun took a last look at the inert appendage and followed her up. For the first time in his life he realized that he wasn't a freak after all.

V

Commander Elan observed the man across her desk. Their interview had not started well for he had made it plain to her that he resented speaking to a woman.

"I have free passage from General Rey, you are directed to cooperate."

The Commander held her temper. "I assure you Brother Dax, all is being done. You say there are two Suran heretics in the city. It would assist me if you could tell me their names."

The Evangelist regarded this jumped up female with undisguised contempt. She did not seem frightened of him and he was not used to that. He inwardly cursed this benighted planet. "Their names are Solon Bru and Jun Siu."

"And they are guilty of heresy?"

"I have already said so."

'What, specifically, have they done?"

"That is not your concern. They are heretics and will be taken to Kagan, tried and executed. You will locate them and hand them over to me."

"I merely wish to know if they are dangerous."

"The older one, Bru, is dangerous; the other is of less significance."

"I am sure we will find them, Brother Dax, have patience."

"Do you know who I am, Commander?"

"You have made it abundantly clear to me already."

"Do you realize what I could do to you and your despicable, little army?"

"Believe me, Brother Dax, I am well aware of your power. "

"You will deliver the heretics to me within two hours or you will find yourself questioned for heresy. You understand what that means Commander?"

"I assure you, Brother Dax, I am a daughter of the Faith."

"You had better prove it. Failure will not be tolerated."

The Evangelist treated her to a soul-freezing glare, rose and strode out of the office. Elan watched the grey clad figure disappear. He represented everything she hated, the repression and subjugation of women; the bigotry; the wealth and power of the temples. She sat back in her chair and began to think. She recognised Dax from her past on Kagan. He was DeCorrone from the same family as she, and he was a powerful figure in the Brotherhood of Mercy. But why was he here? Why had such an important man been sent, in a specially commissioned cruiser, to find two Surans? And what were Surans doing on Tarnus anyway? What was going on?

Commander Elan realised that something extremely odd was happening and she meant to find out exactly what it was. She called her adjutant.

"The Rion spy from the crash. Is he still alive?"

"Yes Commander, Captain Fallon is questioning him now."

"Tell the Captain he is to cease questioning him immediately. I want him cleaned up and brought to me now."

"Yes, Commander, right away."

VI

Captain Fallon sat casually on the corner of the table on which were placed Solon Bru's clothes and meagre possessions. He studied the unconscious, naked figure hanging in front of him and wondered what to do. Bru's body sagged from the ceiling irons that held his wrists; ugly bruises from the beating had appeared and blood had dripped from his head wound and dried in the matted hair of his chest. He was a sorry, pathetic specimen of a man, thought Fallon; a most unsatisfactory subject. The man seemed to have no resistance to pain, but Fallon was not fooled by that. His victim had capitulated much too soon and the Captain knew, from a wealth of experience, that Bru had a whole lot more to tell him before he would allow him the luxury of death. He inspected his spotless hands and noticed a fleck of dirt beneath one of his fingernails. He reached into his pocket for an instrument he kept for such emergencies and cleaned away the offensive speck. Satisfied, he replaced the instrument just as Bru started to come to. The man was moaning pathetically and Fallon experienced a feeling of disgust towards him. He decided on electricity and called one of the guards to bring the equipment.

Bru saw Fallon through a haze of pain. His left eye was completely closed and his right eye afforded him a blurred image of his tormentor. He had been hanging there for hours, drifting in and out of consciousness, but the death he had hoped for had not come. Fallon was close to him; he could feel his breath on his swollen face. He heard the man speak.

"Solon, it is time. Now you will tell me everything and then this will all be over."

The electrical equipment was brought in and Fallon dismissed the guard. He liked to do these things alone; it made the experience more personal. He carefully attached a conductor to each of Bru's feet and one to his penis.

"Now Solon, we will start with your real name."

Bru tried to speak, but all he could hear was his own rasping voice, choking something out. It was unintelligible, certainly not his name. He heard Captain Fallon's soft, effeminate voice in the distance, he was saying something but Bru could not unscramble the words in his mind. He sensed that he was soon going to be in more pain, more pain than he could stand. Why couldn't he die? Why?

The Captain pressed a switch and observed as the body before him twitched and contorted. There was a satisfying scream of agony; sputum trickled from his open mouth. It was quite a mild shock, but it seemed to have done the trick. Now the man would tell him everything.

He was about to speak when he was interrupted by the unannounced entry of his sergeant.

"Captain, Sir, the Commander has ordered that this prisoner is to be brought to her immediately."

"I have not finished questioning him."

"Those are my orders Sir. 'Immediately', she said."

"Very well, take him." He grabbed Bru's hair and whispered in his ear, "I haven't finished with you."

Bru felt himself taken down and dragged between two guards. They took him into a room and dropped him. A jet of cold water hit him causing him to flinch and cringe into a ball. Then he was taken and dressed in a rough, army uniform and dragged along more corridors and through a door. The two guards sat him down and left.

The room was silent but he could sense he was not alone. With an effort he raised his head. Through what was left of his good eye, he could see a shape moving in front of him. When it finally spoke, the shape had a female voice.

"Which one are you? Solon Bru or Jun Siu?"

He did not know whether he was getting deeper into this nightmare, but he was broken and any resistance was long gone. "I am Bru," he whispered.

"And you are a Suran?"

"Yes."

"What are you doing on Tarnus?"

"Accident... Stowaways."

"You were running from your own world?"

"Yes."

"Why?"

"Evangelists."

"Why are they after you?"

Even now Bru found it hard to utter the words. He coughed and some blood trickled down his chin. "It... can... destroy... them."

Commander Elan went cold. "What can destroy them? What do you mean?"

"Lim... has it."

"Has what? Speak."

"Can't... can't."

Bru's head flopped forward; she could see she was losing him. She hurried to the door. The adjutant outside stood to attention. "Get me a medic here, now. How many did they find at that crash?"

"Just one, Ma'am."

"Idiots. There were two. Get back to that crash site and scour the city, I want the other one brought here unharmed."

The adjutant called the medics and gave the orders to find Jun while Commander Elan paced up and down thinking. Had she really heard him right? 'It can destroy them'. That was what he had said and the arrival of Dax certainly gave him credence. Was this what she had been waiting for? Ever since her shame and forced marriage on Kagan to a man who was so inferior to her; to a man who beat her every day as a demonstration of his religious fervour; a man who degraded her because she could not have his children. A priest of the Faith.

The medics arrived and went into her office. She remained outside; she would at least give him that dignity. Bru felt himself pushed and prodded. He cried out a couple of times as they pushed at his cracked ribs. They bandaged him up and salved his bruises and gave him a pain-killing sedative.

"He'll be okay Commander, Ma'am. We have patched him up and sedated him."

"Sedated! I did not tell you to sedate him."

"Sorry Ma'am, we thought that you wanted him helped."

"Idiots. Get out of my sight before I have you shot."

Elan returned to her office to find Bru fast asleep in the chair. She cursed the medics roundly; there was no chance of waking him up now. She needed to find out more and that meant finding the other Suran.

VII

Jun followed Matty out of the cellar in which such strange events had happened, and up into the rainy night. They struck towards the centre of the city, through the bombed-out streets, over rubble and mud and the occasional unburied body. The smell of decay was everywhere, causing Jun to gag and cough as he tried to get his breath. Twice she had offered him her hand, but the strange boy had refused. He looked utterly bewildered.

After an hour they stopped and sought refuge from the rain in what was left of a warehouse. They found a dry area and sat down against a crumbling wall. Jun could barely take his eyes from her long, black hair that fell onto her shoulders and breasts. He had never seen anything like it.

"Where are we going?" he asked.

"To Corhaden's sister, she will help us find your teacher."

"Was that old person your teacher?"

She laughed. "No, he was my manager."

"Your manager?"

"Yes, I worked for him, he protected me."

"I see. And the younger male, the one who attacked me, who was that?"

"Nobody, just a client."

"And you shared a dwelling with them?"

"With the older one."

"That must be very inconvenient."

"Sometimes it is."

"I would not like it. Your dwellings have no parks, they are all crammed together."

"That is how we live here. What are you called?"

"Jun Siu."

"What a strange name. You don't come from this world do you?"

Jun shook his head. "I am from Suran."

"I don't know where that is."

Jun pointed up into the dark, cloudy sky. "It's up there."

Matty smiled. "I'm from up there too, from Ennepp. Do you know it?"

"Yes, I have heard of it."

"Why did you come to Tarnus?"

"We didn't mean to; it just happened. Some people are chasing us, they tried to kill us."

"Really? Why?"

"We had something of great value, they wanted it."

Matty's eyes widened. "You mean like treasure?"

"Sort of. Shall we go on? I have to find my teacher and the rain is easing."

They pressed on, heading towards the centre of the city, Matty's head filled with romantic notions of alien treasure. As they clambered on she noticed there was an unusual number of soldiers about and once they nearly came face-to-face with a patrol and she had to drag Jun into the shadows. He got angry and told her not to touch him again. Matty assumed that they were looking for her because they had found the body of Corporal Beck. She was desperate to reach Corhaden's sister, but she had only been there once and now she realized they were lost. She began to search for somewhere she knew, leading them aimlessly through the ruined alleys and yards. Finally she gave up and led him into a dark alley where she sat down on a pile of rubble.

"We are lost," she said dejectedly.

Jun observed her. It was obvious to him that they were getting nowhere. He looked about him and noticed the dark outline of a person at the end of the alley. He hailed the person; it was time ask somebody else where his teacher was.

Matty looked up and her heart lept in fear. Jun was approaching a soldier. They had been seen; it was too late.

VIII

Commander Elan sat behind her desk and coolly observed the two soaked individuals before her. At first she thought they were two females, but looking closer it appeared the shorthaired one might not be. The longhaired one appeared frightened; the shorthaired one just looked utterly confused. It was obvious that neither were from Tarnus.

She addressed herself to the one who was obviously the Suran. "You are Jun Siu."

Jun looked at the uniformed figure behind the desk, the cropped, grey hair and stern aspect of the lined face. The voice was hard and clear, but not deep like that of a mature male. "Where is my teacher?"

She caught the pitch of Jun's voice and correctly discerned that he was male.

"You are the Suran. Who is this?"

"I don't know."

Matty spoke up nervously. "I am Matty, I found him."

Elan appeared to ignore her. "What does she know about this?"

"About what?"

"About what you are doing here, what you have."

"I don't know what you mean."

Matty could see that the woman was going to get angry and Jun was going to tell her about Beck. She decided to speak up. "Tell her about the treasure."

Elan's eyes searched the faces of the two. "Treasure?"

"Yes," said Matty, "he knows where there's treasure."

Elan's gaze rested on Jun. "Do you? Well, speak up."

Jun held her intense gaze. "Where's my teacher? I will only speak with the permission of my teacher."

Elan considered. Clearly the Suran knew something, but she did not have the time or the inclination to torture it out of him. "Very well, I will have him brought in."

Two soldiers brought Bru into the room and dropped him into a chair. He was still groggy from the sedative but some of the facial swelling had already begun to ease. Even so, Jun was shocked at what he saw.

"He got hurt in the crash," explained Elan. "We have treated him and he will be fine."

Jun went up to him. "Can you hear me, Doctor?"

"Yes," whispered Bru with a slight movement of the head.

"This person wishes to know why we are here."

"Tell her."

"Are you sure?"

"Yes."

Jun was not sure, but Bru had said he should speak, so he did. "When Doctor Bru was on Agon, he found an artefact of human origin, a sheet of material with markings on it. It was a fragment of something that had been made over one hundred and twenty thousand years ago."

Commander Elan's self-control was momentarily lost. Her eyes widened and her jaw dropped. She instantly realized the implication. "Where is it?'

Jun turned to Bru. "Shall I say?"

"Yes."

"We left it on Suran with our doyen, Doyen Lim."

Now the pieces were starting to fall into place. Jun had just confirmed what Bru had told her. "And does your doyen still have it?"

"We don't know."

No, she thought, *but that Evangelist would know.* "Where did it come from?"

Jun looked at Bru who nodded his assent.

"Star sector KT153 in the Orestean Arm."

"That is a huge distance from here, well beyond any charted region." She turned to Bru and addressed him directly. "What do you think is out there?"

He looked up and tried to focus on her; his voice was almost inaudible as he forced out the words. "I don't know. Maybe nothing, maybe everything."

Commander Elan pursed her lips and abruptly left them. It was clear to her what she had to do. The adjutant stood up. "Send for Captain Fallon and twelve troopers. Also, send for Brother Dax."

IX

Dax entered the Commander's office and his cold, grey eyes surveyed the situation. Both the heretics were there and he was forced to stifle a smile. The woman had done her job well, he had to concede that, and now he had the heretics at last.

"You are fortunate, Sister, you have succeeded. I would have destroyed you had you failed."

Elan bowed. "I am a loyal daughter of the Faith, Brother Dax."

Dax turned to Bru and grabbing his hair, he brought his face unpleasantly close. Bru stared into the piercing, hate-filled eyes.

"Doctor Bru, you have been a worthy adversary. You eluded me on Agon, but now I have you. Your public trial and death will bring many people joy."

Jun now realized who and what this stranger was. He turned angrily on Elan. "You have betrayed us."

"Silence!" she hissed.

Dax turned his attention on Jun. "And you, you are just a child, so you will be beheaded. We are merciful to children. Your death, Doctor, will be different, it will be long and slow and agonizing, I assure you. Who is this?"

Dax's gaze suddenly lighted on Matty, who had been shrinking by the wall. She felt that something evil had come into the room; she could practically feel the temperature drop. She had been frightened before the man had entered; now she was terrified.

"She came with the heretic Jun Siu," replied Elan.

"She has associated with heretics; she will share their fate."

Matty was too frightened to reply, but realized what he had just said. She sank down and began to sob.

Dax ignored her and addressed himself to Elan. "Why is Doctor Bru injured? Has he been questioned by one of your degenerates? "

"No Brother, but I would very much like to question them, with your permission, of course."

"You will not question them, these are now my prisoners."

"Of course, Brother, if that is your will."

Bru heard this last exchange with rising hope. The Commander had lied to Dax about his interrogation. Was she distancing herself from any association with them for self-protection, or was she playing some other game?

"It is my will," replied Dax.

"I have sent for the guard to escort the prisoners to your vessel. They will hand them over to your own crew."

"I travel alone; I do not require a crew."

Elan noted this with an inward smile and summoned the guard. Captain Fallon entered with six soldiers. He gave Bru a look of disgust, but said nothing.

Bru went cold at the sight of him. "I will walk," he said, and rose unsteadily to his feet. The painkiller was wearing off and his body and legs had begun to throb uncomfortably, but he found he was able to walk by himself.

Dax spoke as he passed. "The journey to Kagan is short, Doctor Bru, but I look forward to conversing with you. Perhaps you will recant your heresy and be saved."

The troops left with the three prisoners, but when Elan tried to follow, Dax stayed her with an outstretched hand. "Commander, your presence is not necessary."

"Brother Dax, my presence is very necessary. These prisoners are still technically mine and until they are safely aboard your vessel, I intend to carry out my duty."

"Very well, Commander, your diligence is noted."

Dax allowed her to follow her troops. He was not entirely sure that she had been truthful and had already decided her fate. Women, after all, were not to be trusted.

X

The troop transport rose above the drab ruins of the city and headed towards what was left of the port where the cruiser belonging to Brother Dax was waiting. It was still dark and the rain lashed against the body of the craft where the two rows of troops and prisoners sat facing each other. Dax took the seat next to Bru, in a place slightly separated from the others. Jun and Matty sat opposite, further down the craft; Matty was still sobbing quietly but Jun had a look of stoic indignation on his face because he was forced to sit in close confinement with so many people. Commander Elan and Captain Fallon sat separately at the back. They were deep in whispered conversation.

Bru glanced at Dax's gaunt profile. He was in his mid-forties, but a life of self-denial had lined and aged his face. He had a prominent nose, unusually large ears and full lips drawn into a permanent sneer of disapproval. He was entirely hairless, like a Suran, in the tradition of Evangelists who eschewed any physical adornments that might tempt vanity. Carnal knowledge was also forbidden and Bru also knew this was insured by a particularly gruesome initiation practice that the Brotherhood required of their young novices who, at puberty, were induced, during a frenzied ceremony, to relieve themselves of their own manhood. In this way they could be tortured by desire but lack the means to gratify it. It might have guaranteed their abstinence but it also explained why Evangelists were so angry and vengeful.

Just sitting next to the man, Bru could feel the cold power he exuded. Dax was intimidating, but Bru wanted the answers to some questions and if his hunch was right he might not get another chance. They were far enough away from the others to have a private conversation. "Why were you on Agon?" he asked.

The Evangelist turned piercing, grey eyes on his prisoner. "By the grace of the Prophet, I was worshipping at the Shrine of Imbar."

"How convenient."

"Did you think that we would forget your heresy? We have been waiting for you; we knew you would not be able to resist further blasphemy. Your own father-in-law betrayed you."

"I did nothing wrong."

"Was it not you that sent your assistant, Engin Par, to retrieve the casket?"

Bru went cold. "I am interested in ancient artefacts; I do not see why that should arouse suspicion."

"We have the casket, Doctor Bru, we know what it is."

"It was you who murdered Par wasn't it?"

"I showed him the true path."

"An interesting euphemism, presumably his path was straight down. Did you analyse the casket? Do you know how old it is?"

"The Prophet tests our faith in many ways. What was inside the casket?"

"Nothing, it was empty."

"I do not believe you, but you will tell us the truth during your confession period. I am also keen to know how you eluded me on Agon, but perhaps we'll leave that for the confessional too."

"How did you know I was on Tarnus?"

"That was simple, a life pod missing on an unmanned craft which had come from Suran. It could only have been you. I simply diverted on my way back to Kagan from Suran."

"You were on Suran too!"

"I was obliged to go there after our agent had, so spectacularly, messed up. The Council was asking awkward questions about the small nuclear explosion that destroyed the residence of your co-conspirator and our agent could not complete his task and destroy this blasphemy for once and for all time. It was not until I arrived on Suran that the task could be completed and the foul stench of heresy expunged."

"You murdered a doyen of Suran and a High Council Member?"

"I assume you refer to the heretic Lim? We have been watching that individual for many years; we thought that you might dare to return even though you were exiled; it was one of the eventualities we covered."

"I assume Lim is now dead then."

"You may assume what you wish; if Doyen Lim is dead it was not by my hand. The Heretic was not there."

"Lim had gone!"

"Yes, I searched the premises thoroughly."

"How did you get in?"

"It was not difficult, but there was an unexpected problem."

Bru could not help a smile, even though it hurt his swollen face. The undignified vision of this self-important fanatic being stripped naked by Lim's security system was something to treasure in the midst of this misery.

"I see you are amused by something, Doctor Bru. Go ahead, be merry; it will be the last thing in your life that will amuse you. Now tell me something, did you tell them anything when they tortured you?"

"No." Even as he said it Bru knew he had fallen into a trap. His mind was not sharp any more.

"So you were tortured. I thought so. I do not blame Commander Elan for being disingenuous. She is a woman and lying comes naturally to her kind. Do not worry, Doctor Bru, on Kagan we are not like these savages, we will make an exception for you and preserve your Suran dignity. You will not be stripped naked during your execution."

Dax had neatly returned the compliment and Bru glanced at him to see if he was smiling. If he was, he did not show it.

XI

The interplanetary port had long been out of commission and lay dormant on the edge of the city. A large crater bore witness to a massive explosion that had destroyed everything in the area two years before. The authorities put it down to a Rion attack knowing full well that the Division of Rion did not have such capabilities. They made the best of the disaster by using it to stoke the enmity of the indigenous population towards their neighbours and thereby to justify the continued state of war. Dax's fine cruiser was incongruous amid the dilapidated assortment of military vehicles surrounding it at the edge of the crater. A troop of soldiers excersised unenthusiastically in a dusty field under a forlorn sky as they landed close by; others milled about aimlessly amid the vehicles and low sheds. A few looked up at the landing, counted it nothing unusual and continued their mundane business. As they filed out of the troop carrier Bru made a special study of Captain Fallon, wondering what Elan had told him. The man looked distinctly nervous. As they approached the cruiser, it recognized its owner and a ramp door opened in its belly. Dax stopped them at the base of the ramp.

"The prisoners will enter unaccompanied; there will be no further need for the guard."

Bru, Jun and Matty were thrust forward by the soldiers who then withdrew. Dax and Commander Elan stood together at the base of the ramp. Bru lost hope; she was going to do nothing to help them after all.

"Your duty has been done well Commander, it will be noted."

"Thank you, Brother Dax."

Commander Elan didn't see the weapon; it flashed into Dax's hand and was at her head before she knew it. He grabbed her round the neck and used her body to shield himself from the surprised guards.

"Tell them to drop their weapons."

Elan felt the easy power of his arm about her throat, choking her. She smelled the warm masculinity imbued in the rough cloth of his habit. "Drop them," she said.

The guards let their weapons fall to the ground.

"Did you really expect me to trust a woman?" he said as he began to back into the ship with her. "You three follow us in."

"We are going nowhere," said Bru. "Kill us now if you like. Better that than being taken to Kagan."

Dax took the weapon from Elan's head and pointed it at Bru, as he did, there was a sudden pulse of energy from Commander Elan's torso and the two of them were thrown apart like two repelling magnets. The weapon clattered on to the ramp followed by its owner. Elan picked herself up and went over to the sprawled Evangelist and planted a well-aimed, vicious kick to his ribs.

"Did you think you could get the better of me? You didn't recognise me, did you? I am not one of these Tarnus peasants, I am a daughter of Kagan, you arrogant, misogynistic fucker."

Dax tried to speak but he was totally paralyzed. He wanted to tell her how she would burn in the eternal fire of retribution but his mouth would not move. His hate-filled eyes glared up at her.

Captain Fallon arrived next to her and viewed his next victim with relish. "You were right to be prepared Ma'am; the filthy spy will pay dearly for this."

"I'm sure you will do your duty Captain, now get those prisoners on the ship."

The Captain barked his orders and Matty, Jun and Bru were escorted on to the vessel while Elan followed. When they were all on board she addressed Fallon again.

"Take your guard back to headquarters, you are in command until I return. You have your orders; the spy is to be liquidated."

The Captain bowed and the troops began to file off the ship while four of them picked up the prostrate body of the Evangelist.

"He will not die easily at the hands of Captain Fallon," said Elan, as they disappeared from view.

XII

Dax's ship, *The Antares,* was a vessel commensurate with the high status of a man operating at the centre of an organisation greater in wealth and power than any other in the human diaspora. It was built on Barta Magnus to the latest and most sophisticated Suran design that made full use of the recent advances in propulsion. Few such vessels yet existed as they were built to commission and were well beyond the means of any but a tiny minority of corporations and goverments. And so to find themselves in command of such a vessel was most fortunate indeed. There was only one problem and that was how to dismantle the complex security system that protected the ship.

"You're supposed to be the genius here; can't you override it?"

Bru squinted through his good eye at Commander Elan who had assumed an air of impatience. "It will only respond to the command of Brother Dax and he is not here."

"Why didn't you inform me of this before?"

"The opportunity did not present itself."

"I'll tell Fallon to bring him back."

"I prefer you didn't; anyway he would never cooperate."

"What are you proposing then? I assume you have a plan."

Bru sighed. "Not really."

"Brilliant. We're stuck in the middle of General Rey's headquarters in a ship that can't go anywhere."

"So it would seem," replied Bru. He was tired and dispirited; the beating and torture had taken its toll on both his mind and body. "I have no suggestions to make."

"In that case I'm going to bring Dax back."

"It would only make matters worse," replied Bru.

"How could they be worse? It won't be long before General Rey realises there's something wrong. We can't close the ship; we can't stop them boarding."

"Dax might be able to order it to self-destruct; it would destroy everything for a thousand kilometres."

"Nonsense, these ships are immune. They are guaranteed by treaty."

"That's as maybe, but when did you hear that Evagelists adhere to international treaties? It is theoretically possible to overload the propulsion system and it wouldn't surprise me if Dax knew exactly how to do it."

"Perhaps we could convince him to join us," put in Jun.

Elan rounded on him. "Don't be stupid, boy; I know these people; they are beyond fanatical. They are consumed by hatred and Dax is one of the worst. I know him well and true," she added vehemently, "it is fortunate that he did not recognise me. Damn him; damn him to Hell."

She subsided into bitter silence and began to pace about while she plotted her way out of the mire into which she had fallen. One thing was for certain; they wouldn't take her back to Kagan alive; she would make sure of that at least.

"How does it know?"

They turned towards the source of the question. It was Matty.

"Be quiet, girl," snapped Elan.

"Know what?" asked Jun.

"How does it know who Brother Dax is?" she replied timidly. It seemed to her that she had passed from one nightmare to another.

"Live D.N.A. analysis," replied Bru. "We are all unique in that."

Matty did not understand the answer, but little suspected that she had asked the right question. Jun caught Bru's eye; they had both seen the answer at the same time.

"Search the ship; find me anything; blood, saliva, anything," said Bru with sudden animation.

"What are you doing?" said Elan as Jun ran off.

"If we can culture a small quantity of Dax's D.N.A...."

"What do you need?"

"The medical kit from one of the life pods."

She was gone almost before he had finished what he was saying.

The ship was designed for a compliment of twenty, with twenty cabins and two life pods containing ten stasis units. Dax had occupied two cabins; one served as his sleeping quarters, the other served as a chapel. Jun came upon the chapel first and glanced over the meagre contents carefully arranged upon a golden cloth covering a side table; a ceremonial knife, a golden cup for libation, a small incense burner, a scourge and an ancient copy of the Book of Minnar, resting opened on a bejewelled lectern. There were numerous other theological books stacked neatly to one side. Jun took up the scourge and inspected it; its many tails were caked with blood. It was exactly what they needed.

By the time he returned Elan and Bru were already setting out the contents of the medical pack with Bru indicating the items he needed. Jun placed the scourge on the table.

"Perfect," announced Bru and he took it up and cut a small section from one of the tails and placed it into a beaker. He then added the contents of two phials, shook it before decanting it carefully into another vessel into which he introduced a thermometer.

As he worked Jun noticed Bru's hands shaking. "Shall I do it?"

Bru shook his head. "I can manage. Give me your weapon, Commander."

"What for?"

"Just give it to me."

She reluctantly offered the sidearm. Bru took it and set it to the lowest level before pointing it at the beaker. He delivered a pulse of energy into the liquid while watching the thermometer.

"That should do it," he declared, returning the weapon to its owner.

Elan holstered the sidearm. "Do what?"

"Rejuvenate the blood molecules. Now we wait."

"How long?"

"Thirty minutes should do it, then it will have to introduced into a host bloodstream otherwise the ship will not recognise it."

"And that renders command? Even that small amount?"

Bru nodded. "It should be sufficient to fool the system."

"We'll use the girl," said Elan.

"The recipient will command the ship," replied Bru. "At least until it can be legitimately transferred."

"Very well, the boy will receive it; he is under your influence."

"I won't allow it," replied Bru. "It must be you or me. You choose."

Commander Elan eyed him suspiciously; she didn't trust him and had no idea how much resentment he harboured for the rough treatment he had received. "I will have no part of that man in my body; you receive it but you will cede command to me at the earliest oportunity and know that I will be watching."

It was fortunate that Bru's swollen face hid his expression of relief; he would give her the illusion of command but keep true power for himself.

The craft rose into the air with the ease of its almost limitless power and soon they were free of the pull of Tarnus and blasting towards the depths of space. As they watched the receding planet, Bru remarked that he thought he was going to die down there.

"It is an easy place to die," said Elan, "and a hard place to live. Lay in our course Doctor Bru, we have a long journey ahead."

Bru laid in the course and the ship began to gather speed towards their distant destination. Tarnus rapidly disappeared and its sun became just another star in the bright arc of the galaxy. Bru turned to Elan and indicated that he wanted a private word. They spoke out of earshot of the other two.

"Why didn't you kill the Evangelist?"

She looked at him in some surprise. "I promised Fallon that he would get his chance. I did not want Dax to get off lightly."

"What will happen when Fallon strips him and discovers that he actually is an Evangelist? Is the Captain a devout subject?"

Bru could see in her eyes that she had not foreseen this possibility.

"I don't know; I never discussed matters of faith with any of my command."

"If Fallon spares him how quickly could he leave Tarnus?"

She thought for a moment. "Quite quickly, the Brothers have influence in the higher command."

"Do they have vessels like this?"

She shook her head. "No, he will have to go back to Kagan to obtain something capable of following us."

"That, at least, will buy us time."

"Perhaps Fallon will do his duty; he was practically salivating at the thought of interviewing Dax."

"If he kills an Evangelist, he will know they will come looking for him. I have an awful premonition that we have not seen the last of Brother Dax."

XIII

Dax's journey back to headquarters was a strange one. He knew he was being manhandled, but could feel nothing. He saw himself lying on the floor of the troop carrier, looking up the noses of the guards; he saw himself being dragged along dim corridors and into the interview room that Bru had so recently occupied; he saw himself being stripped to his loincloth and hung up. It was as though he was watching all of this from afar and none of it was actually happening to him.

Dax knew that he was going to be tortured and he welcomed it. It was the judgement of the Prophet for his failure and it was well merited. He tried to remain awake while the paralysis eased, but after five hours he shut his eyes and slept. When he awoke, Captain Fallon was in front of him minutely inspecting his fingernails.

"Ah, Mister Dax, I will call you that for the moment, just until we discover your real name. I am glad you have joined us, I trust the effects of the stun have worn off, it will make our discussion so much more fulfilling."

Dax drew himself up and hissed with all the venom he could muster, "I curse you to burn in the fires of eternity."

Fallon looked at the lean, muscular torso and smiled. *This one will be hard to crack,* he thought. "Your curses mean nothing; you are not a Brother of Mercy as you claimed, but a common spy. We will start with your real name."

He picked up his truncheon and went to work.

He beat the man until he passed out, but Dax said nothing, he did not even scream in pain, not once. Towards the end he just grunted as the blows rained down on his hairless skin. Fallon left him hanging there to recover for four hours, and then returned to renew his efforts. The spy's resistance was phenomenal, not a word of a confession passed his lips and the Captain was beginning to get a little frustrated. The Commander had said he would be hard to crack, but she expected results on her return. She had said that the imposter was not to be spared anything and she did not expect to see him alive again.

Fallon had been surprised at what she had told him in the troop carrier. Bru really was a Suran who had come to Tarnus to trade arms and that Dax had been sent from Rion to kill Bru and stop the arms sale. It now made sense; Bru's weakness under mild questioning; Dax's treachery at his vessel. And it was brilliant of the Commander to use the spy's own ship to retrieve the arms from the freighter. Soon she would return with them and they would renew their attack on Rion and give that scum something to think about.

Captain Fallon's admiration of his Commander, spurred him to greater efforts. It was time to make the spy talk. He called the guards for the generator.

The guard appeared with the machine and Fallon ordered him to cut the bloodied loincloth from the victim. Dax watched them impassively; their methods were crude and distasteful. The guard removed the loincloth and took an involuntary step back.

"Fuck! What's this?"

Fallon pushed him aside and stared in disbelief at the missing member and the scar tissue of the devotional chevrons above it. "I don't believe it, it can't be."

Dax pulled himself up. "You now see that you have been duped by the woman you call Commander."

Fallon fell on his knees. "Brother, forgive me."

"Release me and I will forgive you."

Fallon rose and hurriedly released the Evangelist who told him to kneel before him for forgiveness. He kneeled obediently while the man gently placed his powerful hands either side of his head. Even after the beating and deprivation, Fallon could still feel the raw power in those hands.

"I forgive you my son," he said.

The Captain's eyes fixed on the hairless scrotum and penile stump that only a Brother of Mercy would have. He felt the grip on his head tighten. There was a sudden twist and the sound of snapping bone in his ear. That ugly stump was the last thing he ever saw.

The guard watched his Captain's body slump to the floor and took a step back, pulling his weapon and aiming it at the powerful Evangelist. Dax ignored him and strode to the table and wrapped his bruised body in his rough habit. "How long have I been in this shit-hole?"

"About fourteen hours, sir."

Dax made the calculation. The time it would take him to get another vehicle plus the time he had wasted here. He would be about six or seven days behind them. The private signal that *The Antares* would be sending would still be active if the fiend, Bru, had not discovered and stopped it. He would be able to pick it up and it would guide him to them, wherever they were. They would not escape him, even if he had to follow them to the edge of the universe. Praise to the Lord Minnar!

XIV

Life aboard *The Antares* soon settled into a regular pattern. They agreed that they should run clear of inhabited space before going into stasis for the five year journey to KT153. This would take about twelve days. Bru resumed Jun's lessons but otherwise he sought solitude, much as he had always done. His injuries were healing well and with a certain amount of mental fortitude, he had begun to leave the nightmare memories of Tarnus behind. He and Jun spoke little of their experiences; Bru mentioned that he had been tortured but did not go into detail and Jun told him that he had been attacked by a soldier and that Matty had saved him.

After her initial bewilderment, Matty soon grew used to the small company of fellow travellers. She tried to attach herself to Jun but he was distant and just as strange as ever. She fared little better with Bru and he was obliged to explain to her what it meant to be a Suran. She was incredulous but at least now she began to understand Jun and why he was so odd.

"Will he ever have sex with me?" she asked of him, quite unexpectedly. "I would like it if he did."

Bru raised his eyebrows. "Jun is capable, but it is unlikely."

"Perhaps he doesn't like me."

"Surans tolerate rather than like or dislike. It is a question of inclination."

Matty did not fully understand the answer, but she decided that it would be better if she did not pursue Jun for sex. She turned to Elan for company, but the older woman was not gregarious and did not seem to require a great deal of human companionship. She felt she was tolerated, but nothing would develop between them by way of friendship and so Matty became quite lonely and started to hunger for the squalid life she had left on Tarnus.

For Elan the two Surans were ideal companions. They were emotionally undemanding and intelligent and this suited her very well. She had had enough of men and, although the Surans were certainly male, they were unlike any she had ever met before. She found Jun strange and uncommunicative, but Bru was easier and on the fourth day of their journey together she found herself alone in his company. She decided to ask him something that had played on her mind for a while.

"Do you resent me for what happened to you on Kagan?"

Bru considered. "You were not wielding the stick."

"True, but I was responsible, ultimately."

"Torture is rarely successful, unless it is used as an instrument of revenge. I would have told the Captain anything he wanted to hear. I confessed to being a spy even though I wasn't."

"Our resources are limited and we are at war; we have to make the best of what we have."

"Shouldn't you be speaking in the past tense? You are Kagan, like Dax, I overheard you telling him so. What is a Kagan doing on Tarnus and why did you help us? This is not about treasure is it?"

"No, Doctor, it's not about treasure. I suppose I am tired of war and of the men who wage it."

"That is a commendable reason, but that is not the whole truth is it?"

She pursed her lips and thought for a moment. "When I was fifteen I was given, in marriage, to a man who was much older. I come from a high family and it was a union of advantage to both sides. My husband abused me and beat me for seventeen years. He was a priest who recited scripture even as he thrashed and raped me. Three times I ran away and three times I was taken back to him to be punished. I still bear the scars. Finally, one night, I could stand it no longer and I stabbed him through the heart and killed him. I cannot tell you that I found the experience of taking a man's life shocking. I didn't, I enjoyed it. It was as though I was striking back for all the women who have been subjugated by the doctrine of the Faith.

"Of course, I would have been put to death had they caught me, but I escaped and found my way to Tarnus, where their interminable war has weakened the machinery of war. On Tarnus I found a place where I need not be a man's chattel, his property, a place where I could be somebody."

"I see. You wish to destroy the Faith. I cannot promise you that what awaits us will fulfil your ambition."

"Isn't that what you want?"

"I want to know the truth, that's all. If the Faith stands in the way of that, I will try to destroy it, but it is not my principal desire."

"The Faith does stand in your way, so we are at one, I trust."

"I hope so, for neither of us needs any more enemies."

She smiled ruefully. "What do you really think we will find?"

"I do not know. I have listened to that region of the galaxy, but there is only silence. Perhaps there is nothing there after all."

"You don't believe that, do you?"

"No."

XV

Dax sat, cross-legged, on the raised, stone slab that served as his bed in the dark cell below the palace of the DeCorrone on Kagan. He was naked, save for a bloodstained loincloth to preserve what remained of his modesty, having been ceremonially divested of his fraternal gown. A small gap in the stonework of the wall behind him afforded a drizzle of light that played on the thick, metal door before him and the small plate of uneaten food at its base. He had failed in his endeavour and to take food, even the mean and plain ration that had been supplied, was to deny himself the full measure of self-sacrificial punishment.

His journey back to Kagan had been a bitter one and he had scourged himself until his flesh screamed and he thought he would pass out. Every waking thought was devoted to the Surans who had slipped through his fingers and to the she-devil who had assisted them. He had plotted and planned and castigated himself, but no amount of self-flagellation could atone for his failure. He knew that he must stand before the Grand Master of the Brotherhood and receive the full measure of his punishment and that the punishment would be severe. He expected to be stripped and flogged until he was near to death, but it was not this grim prospect that concerned him most; indeed, he welcomed it as fitting and fully justified. What concerned Dax, in fact consumed him with fear, was the possibility that he would be expelled from the Brotherhood of Mercy.

The Grand Master of the Brotherhood was also the head of the DeCorrone Clan. He held the title of Arkon DeCorrone and was, at that time, the most powerful man on Kagan. The Arkon was known for his vituperative nature and Dax had received the full measure of his spleen. Surprisingly, the fiasco of his failure to extinguish the heretics was only mentioned in passing, for what had most angered the old man was the loss of an extremely expensive cruiser. Dax, with his forehead pressed firmly to the stone floor, had heard the tirade as the words fizzed in his ears and echoed from the walls of the Hall of the Throne. A few elders were present and looked on in keen expectation of the event to come; and come it duly did.

"Stand up, you son of a whore," the Arkon had screamed and Dax had stood while his gown was cut in half, torn from his body and burned in front of him. Then two Brothers had stepped forward and the whipping had begun. They had started with his legs and soon weals appeared and blood had trickled down his legs and moistened the floor beneath his bare feet. He had stared stoically ahead, focusing on nothing, gritting his teeth but making no sound. Then they had gone to work on his torso and as the blows rained down, stripping the flesh from the muscle, Dax's only thought was the welcome justice of the punishment. And when he had finally collapsed to the floor, they had dragged him out and down to the cells below the palace.

He had languished in his cell for two days, taking neither water nor sustenance and seeking no respite with sleep. For two days he sat, straight-backed and unmoving, gritting his teeth against the pain that racked his body and concentrating his mind on the deep shame of his failure. He had not even attempted to clean the wounds that had darkened on his body, as the blood had congealed and dried. And in all this time of agony, his all-consuming concern had been the preservation of his membership of the Brotherhood of Mercy.

As the light that touched the door began to fade with the coming of the night, the door opened and there stood the Arkon himself, with another man behind him. Dax immediately slipped from the stone slab and fell to his knees. Pressing his forehead to the floor, he awaited his fate, his heart pounding lest he heard the awful pronouncement of his expulsion. The Arkon stared impassively down at the lacerated back; the other man stared too and the sight of the disgraced Brother, brought so low, quickened his pulse. He had seen Dax before and judged him to be an over-proud individual.

"Raise yourself and stand before me, Brother Dax."

Dax stood and although the pain of movement stabbed him to the core, his expression betrayed nothing. He drew himself up to face his Arkon and Master and to hear his fate."

The Arkon DeCorrone was ninety-three years old with an erect wiry frame and a vigorous, lined countenance. His blood-shot, green eyes stared unblinkingly from deep sockets accentuating his large, high-ridged nose. His mouth was a permanent slit of displeasure, for nobody had ever seen him smile. His head was hairless, in the correct manner of an Evangelist.

"You are my brother's grandson," he began in a rasping whisper, "and on you I rested my hopes for the future of our clan."

This was news to Dax, for it had never before been mentioned.

"Your failure to carry out your duty and expunge these heretics from the universe has cost me great anguish and distress."

Dax met the stony, glazed stare of the Arkon with a resigned steadiness, but, eventually, he could not help allowing his eyes to flicker towards the figure behind. Even in the paltry light of his cell, he recognized the man, another Evangelist, but not one of his clan. This man was Aurex DeRhogai, a high born from a rival clan. Dax was inwardly appalled that this man should see him naked and hear of his shame. He wondered what purpose the Arkon had in bringing him here.

"This heresy runs deep," continued the Arkon. "I have just received news from Brother Aurex that has disturbed me greatly. The conspiracy has spread even to Kagan itself. He suspects that a Doyen of Suran may have penetrated the very heart of our society and, even as we speak, is polluting our sacred soil. What did the Heretic, Solon Bru, tell you during your conversation with him? You may speak."

"Most Noble Master, I did not have the full opportunity to interview the Heretic, before the woman who called herself 'Elan' double-crossed me."

The Arkon drew his face nearer. "The woman who called herself 'Elan' is your second cousin. She is Magred DeCorrone. You did not recognize her?"

Dax was visibly shocked. The name was well known to him for the murder of her husband, a highborn priest from another clan. She was also wanted for the even greater crime of apostasy. A great deal of time and effort had been spent looking for her. "I did not recognize her, Master; I am truly sorry."

The Arkon nodded imperceptibly. "That is of minor importance now. The casket you retrieved from Doctor Bru's assistant, was it utterly destroyed as I directed?"

"Yes, Master, utterly."

"And Doctor Bru gave you no indication of what it contained or where he had placed the contents?"

"He said the casket was empty, but I knew it was a lie. I would have got the truth had I been allowed, but I suspect whatever was in the casket was left with Doyen Lim."

"You searched the premises of Doyen Lim?"

"Most thoroughly, Master, but not for fifteen days after the explosion that destroyed the dwelling of Jun Siu. There was nothing to be found and no sign of the Doyen."

Here, the Arkon turned and addressed himself to the man behind him. "Do you have any questions for this unworthy subject, Brother Aurex?"

The other man stepped forward and Dax watched his face emerge from the shadow into the failing light of the cell. He was about ten years older than Dax and, in common with all devout Brothers, wore a cadaverous expression of self-denial. His dark eyes studied the bloody torso of the disgraced man, openly gloating over his fall and his power over him. He wore a tightly fitting cowl on his head to cover a crop of short, grey hair, which, as Dax surmised, was evidence of DeRhogai vanity. Dax knew him by reputation; he was ambitious and had manoeuvred himself into position to inherit the DeRhogai throne. He was a dangerous and powerful man but it still cut Dax to the quick that a member of a rival clan should be allowed to question him, particularly in this state of undress.

"Why did you not pursue the Heretic Bru to Suran?"

Dax noted that his inquisitor had not addressed him with any degree of respect but saw that this was not an occasion for protest. "Doctor Bru disappeared unexpectedly and I was unable to locate him. I assumed he had left Agon and gone to Barta Magnus. That is where I went."

"He eluded you, even with all the resources you had at your command."

"Yes, Brother; Doctor Bru proved to be more resourceful than I anticipated."

"'Than you anticipated'," echoed Aurex sarcastically. "Your dereliction, your incompetence has endangered our sacred communion. I am astounded at the leniency of your punishment. And what of the Doyen; what steps did you take to locate that infidel?"

Dax glanced enquiringly towards the Arkon who gestured an assent. "Our agent on Suran, a member of the High Council, made discreet enquiries but found nothing. Doyen Lim just disappeared without trace."

Aurex's eyes widened in surprise; he turned to the Arkon. "We have an asset in the High Council!"

The Arkon nodded. "You will not speak of it to anyone."

"Of course not, Master," replied Aurex quickly. "It is strange that a Doyen should be allowed to disappear so completely. They are slippery, these Suran devils."

"Not as slippery as they think," announced the Arkon. "*The Antares* was detected passing through sector 38 two days ago. The fiends had obviously tried to disguise its signature, but our analysis revealed its true nature. We may not know where they are going but we will be able to follow them and you, Brother Dax, will be the pursuer."

Dax immediately fell to his knees and kissed the feet of the Arkon. "Thank you Master."

The Arkon scowled at the ugly lacerations on the back of his grovelling subject. "You will follow these infidels, even to the dark, extremities of the galaxy and you will destroy them and any blasphemous evidence you may find. Do not communicate with another soul lest it leads others to the source of this wickedness. When you have completed your task, I will allow you a martyr's death. I need not describe your fate if you fail again, Brother Dax.

XVI

By the tenth day of their journey Bru had begun to notice a change in Jun's character. The normally attentive boy had become distracted and agitated and even more withdrawn than usual. During one lesson Bru got so frustrated that he stopped what he was saying, mid-sentence and asked. "Do you wish to discontinue your instruction?"

Jun returned from a reverie and looked up surprised. "No, I wish to continue."

"You demonstrate every sign of the opposite."

"I'm sorry; I will concentrate more in future."

But Jun did not concentrate and some minutes later Bru abruptly ended the lesson. Jun was crestfallen but he knew Bru was right. He had let his teacher down because his mind was elsewhere. It had been going missing for some time and the cause of it was Matty.

He hardly knew when it had started. It had crept up on him like a thief, robbing him of his equilibrium. Had it been on the ship, or on Tarnus that he had first experienced this strange feeling in his gut? He did not know, but now he was beginning to think that it was the first moment he saw her in Corhaden's dingy room. It jarred every fibre in him, but now he could not stop thinking about her. He would furtively observe her whenever they were in each other's company, looking away if she so much as glanced at him. He would hurry away if there was a remote chance of them being alone together. He did not know why, but he equated it with some fault in himself, some weakness that had to be overcome. But the worst thing was the increasingly frequent and repulsive swelling of his manhood that seemed to occur when he thought of her and this he could not overcome.

Following his aborted lesson, Jun dejectedly made his way to the common area. Matty was sitting alone and he instinctively turned to retreat to his cabin, but this time something stopped him and he advanced towards her. He could see that she had been crying; her beautiful, dark, melting eyes were slightly red. She saw him and looked away.

He approached tentatively. "Why are you crying?"

She had not expected him to speak to her; she looked a little startled. "I don't know," she replied.

"That is peculiar, you cry without knowing the reason."

"I suppose so. I'm sad, I feel alone and empty."

"You are not alone, there are three others here."

She forced a smile. "You do not understand; I am used to company, you are not. Elan is distant, Doctor Bru little better and you are unfriendly."

"I don't mean to be, I'm sorry, I am confused, that's all."

"It's alright, I don't blame you. Doctor Bru has explained to me about Suran, I do not expect you to be friendly."

"I want to be, though."

"Do you?" His open, innocent face betrayed him, her heart filled with sudden joy. Was it possible that everything Bru had said about him was wrong? Was it possible he could really feel something for her?

"I have never had a friend," he said, "I don't know what it will be like."

"Perhaps we could find out together."

"I would like that. How shall we go about it?"

"Well, we could start by telling each other about ourselves. Why don't you go first?"

Jun smiled sheepishly. "There is not much to tell."

"I'm sure that's not true."

"I'm afraid it is. On Suran we do not lead dynamic lives. Our lives are planned and regimented and I thought mine was perfect, now I'm not so sure."

Jun told her of his young life and about Lim. He even told her about the awful incident when he first met Bru. She laughed mischievously and said she wished she'd been there. He coloured and said he was glad she had not been. He told her about their flight and the explosion and getting into Dolon Export and about the journey to Tarnus and the crash that had brought him to Corhaden's door. But as he told the tale, it struck him that he had more to tell about the last eighty days of his life than in the rest of it put together. This gave him pause, for although his recent experiences had been far from ideal, they were at least evidence of a life lived rather than a mere existence, however ideal.

Matty listened intently, asking frequent questions, especially about his strange parentless upbringing and enforced solitude. It seemed to her quite bizarre that anyone would choose such a life and although she could see that there was something to admire about the affluence and education of Suran, she did not envy him in the least.

"Your world is a strange place," she said when Jun finished his story. "I do not think I would like it."

"Perhaps it is strange," he replied, "but is it any stranger than a world where men attack each other and destroy each other's dwellings?"

"Men are always fighting; they can't help it."

"It is a waste, I shall never understand it. Now it is your turn, tell me about yourself."

'We will sleep first and when we wake up I will tell you my story."

Later, in his cabin, Jun found that he could not sleep. He rose from his bed and stole into her cabin. She was asleep and didn't wake up when he entered. For ages he stood looking down at her, knowing that he had never encountered anything so wonderful.

Sensing he was there, she opened her eyes and saw him caught in the starlight. "I am glad you have come to me," she whispered.

"I don't know what to do."

"Would you like me to teach you?"

"Yes," he said.

Their lovemaking was awkward and gentle. Several times she had to assure him that what was happening was completely natural and that he was in no way a freak or grotesque. He did not believe her until the electric bolt of ecstasy seized him when she touched him intimately and then nothing mattered for he was completely immersed by her.

When they were spent, she held him and told him he was wonderful. He let her hold him, her skin was warm and fragrant and now it seemed the most natural thing to him. He did not want to move, not ever. He only wanted to stay in the dreamy, starlit repose in that quiet place.

"I don't want to sleep," he said.

"I don't either."

"We will sleep for a long time soon enough. In ten hours we will go into stasis."

"Will we dream?"

"No, our bodies become living corpses."

"I don't think I'm going to like that."

"Don't be afraid, you just shut your eyes and sleep. It is easy. Will you tell me about yourself now?"

She leaned over and kissed him on the ear. "I will tell you everything you want to know."

PART FIVE

ENNEPP

I

The oceanic world of Ennepp was unlike any other place where human beings had settled. The principal constituent of its surface was water which enshrouded the planet with a continuous, deep, acidic ocean where storms and powerful eddies carried away any person foolish enough to brave the waters. Only one place afforded Men a chance to survive on Ennepp, for in one segment, between the equator and the southern polar region, the crust had heaved a long, continental island above the toxic waves.

The island was unequally divided by a lofty, impenetrable range of mountains that, for over two thousand years, separated the inhabitants and caused them to divide into two distinct races. To the north of the Great Divide, under oppressive, tropical skies, lived a primitive people who called themselves the Pal, but became known to others as Natives. To the temperate south lived the Bhasi who were dark-skinned folk with curly hair and sharp features. They were industrious and prospered in their fertile lands where the sun shone kindly and soft breezes caressed the endless fields of crops. Towns and cities sprang from the fertile soil and a civilization advanced that soon looked for fresh opportunities. They turned their eyes to the north and eventually found their way across the Great Divide.

In the north they discovered the Pal, people with lighter skins, straight, black hair and soft, attractive faces. They called them 'Natives' because they lived primitive lives in the verdant forest under permanently leaden skies that deluged, dripped and drizzled into the deep valleys and gorges. In the tropics sunlight filtered through the grey gauze of heavy cloud and never touched the land.

The Bhasi despaired at the plight of their fellow men and built them towns and showed them the fruits of civilization. But the Natives were too dull to grasp the advantage and would not be civilized so the Bhasi killed them, or enslaved them and made them into a resource. The Bhasi were farmers and so they did what came naturally to them. They farmed the Natives.

II

Born into the mud and squalor of Faloon Pal, a town built on the proceeds of human depravity, Matty Saronaga came squealing into the world, one grey afternoon. She was the tenth child of a prostitute called Fantasy, whose faded delights had long banished her to the outer reaches of her trade.

Fantasy had once been a great beauty and had communed with clients from many worlds in the salubrious brothels of Faloon Pal, where all manner of depravity could be purchased at little trouble to the pocket. A place where human life was held so cheap, the right consideration could bring forth any gratification, no matter how base. A place where youth was prized but soon lost, so that at twenty, already addled with cheap drugs and alcohol, Fantasy slipped into the shadowy, backstreet world of the fallen and was permitted to breed. Her first two children were stillborn; her third, a boy, was sacrificed for a small sum of money before his first birthday; the forth, Cristo and the fifth, Benni, both boys, survived. Her sixth child, an albino, was destroyed at birth and the seventh lived eighty days until it was dashed against a wall by an angry client who could not stand its constant bawling.

By now Fantasy's addiction had reduced her to a pallet under a flimsy lean-to near the edge of town. There she would lie for days at a time, unmoving under the dripping roof of her home. Benni and Cristo disappeared into the muddy back streets and were rarely seen. She did not mind their absence, or even notice it; she was not maternal and thought, with some justice, they would do better without her. Now she was only visited by the meanest of her race and fell pregnant again with her eighth child who succumbed to the cocktail of drugs that she had pumped into her womb. The death of her eighth child sobered Fantasy and she resolved to temper her habits. She cleaned herself up and moved into a rude shack rented from the local gang master. Here she conceived her ninth child as the result of a drunken dare by a group of Bhasi soldiers from the town's garrison. The boy was born later that year and she named him Jodi.

Fantasy was now twenty-nine years old and, although a distance from her former allure, was still able to ply her trade and provide for herself and her new son. She had at last become sober and sensible enough to care for him. Jodi was different from any of her other children. She saw, straight away, that he was of mixed race and took pains to hide the fact. Natives were not allowed to breed outside their race and she knew that if discovered, both she and her son would be killed. She kept his hair short so that its natural curl would not be seen and she never allowed him to run around naked.

When he was barely one year old, Jodi received a sister, courtesy of Fantasy's landlord who had taken to occasionally receiving the rent in kind. Matty was Fantasy's tenth and last child and the only female. Fantasy loved and cared for her daughter, discovering for the first time in her life a true maternal instinct. Girls were rare in the eugenically governed society of the Natives, and Fantasy had to protect her by dressing her as a boy so that she would not be taken for the sex trade as she herself had been many years ago.

When she was old enough to walk, Matty scoured the muddy streets of the shanty with her brother, scrounging and stealing wherever they could, and ranging further and further from their mother's side. They soon came across the local gang of urchins and Jodi was regularly beaten for straying onto their patch. At five, Jodi was precocious and tried to give as good as he got, but he always returned to his mother bloodied and ragged from the scrap. She would tell him off, bathe his wounds and put him to bed in their shabby, little cabin on the edge of town.

One day, when he was nearly six, Jodi and Matty returned to the cabin after one bloody encounter with the gang. Jodi was bruised and badly cut on the head, but when they returned their mother wasn't there. They waited in the cabin for three days until hunger finally drove them back into the streets. They spent many days searching for their mother. No one could tell them where she'd gone or why she'd left. Finally they gave up and began life on the streets. They never saw their mother again.

After a few more scraps Jodi was finally accepted into the urchin gang. The gang was run by Cristo, Jodi's half-brother, a wild, vicious individual who took out his frustrations on the other members of the gang. The older kids steered clear of him, but Jodi always faced him down which earned him plenty of beatings. Jodi was resilient and spirited and by the time he was eight even Cristo preferred to leave him alone.

Jodi's protection of Matty was fanatical and he would take any punishment in her defence. They had struggled together through adversity and their relationship was tight because of it. Unfortunately, it didn't stop the older boys picking on her, until one day, a boy slapped her and Jodi took an iron bar to his head and nearly killed him. After that they left her alone too.

The gang survived and even prospered in the back streets of Faloon Pal, living among the mud and detritus of intense poverty. They combed the dank alleys for opportunities to steal and cadge, flouting the curfew that cleared the streets at night, and dodging the garrison soldiers who sometimes killed the children for fun, throwing their battered, twisted bodies into the river or the open sewers that meandered through the foul streets. Sometimes the children just disappeared and no trace of them ever came to light. It was rumoured that the soldiers ate them alive, although no bones were ever found to give this credence. In fact, the truth was less macabre; they were taken to be slaves on the Bhasi estates to the south.

When Jodi was eleven, Cristo was killed in a knife fight with a rival gang leader and, although there were several boys older in the gang, it was to Jodi that they naturally turned for instructions. He was fast, cunning and skilful with a knife and it was not long before Cristo's death was avenged and Jodi's gang increased in size and range. This brought him into contact with numerous other feral gangs that roamed the streets of Faloon Pal and small wars were in constant progress. When the streets were too dangerous for her, Jodi made Matty stay in the crude hovel that five of the gang shared. After the fights he would come back to her, bloodied and bruised and she would clean his wounds whilst he watched her with impassive, dark eyes. It was the only intimacy they shared, but it was enough. She knew he loved her, just as she loved him.

Sometimes, when there were traders in town, Matty would help the gang with their work, providing them with a decoy to distract the traders while the boys flitted like ghosts, snatching whatever they could from the hard-pressed tinkers. They were relatively easy targets; lethargic forest dwellers, troglodytes who gathered fruit in the lush valleys outside the town. The Garrison took their share of their meagre profits, extorting from them in return for protection which was usually conspicuously absent, but on one occasion a soldier did his duty by the traders, and it was a day that would change the lives of Jodi and Matty forever.

Jodi had been head of the gang for just over a year. He was twelve years old and his cunning and experience had kept him out of the hands of the garrison soldiers, although in his short life there had been many narrow escapes. But this day was different.

They awoke to the usual grey, sultry embrace of a day that melted into the dank poverty of the town and seemed to coat it to the core with decay. It was the day the traders were in town and that meant the gang would be in action. At the edge of the square Jodi split the gang into four and each went their way, dodging amongst the traders and the grubby, jostling crowd. Matty went with Jodi, as usual, and they targeted a fruit seller with a pile of ripe gourds laid out on a mat in the mud. As usual, Matty approached the trader and picked up one of the fruits, pretending to inspect it.

The old man eyed her suspiciously. "You buy it, or put it down," he shouted.

"I got money, Mister," she replied, producing a coin from her pocket whilst allowing the delicate fruit to fall from her hands. The trader watched in horror as the precious gourd fell and split open, spilling its sweet, white flesh into the mud. He screamed an expletive as Matty ran, but a bystander had seen what was happening and grabbed her before she could get away. The trader caught her and slapped her, while the gang helped themselves to his goods and disappeared into the shadows. But Jodi, always watchful of his sister, saw that she had been caught, drew his knife and plunged it into the right buttock of the trader. The man yelped in agony, released Matty and turned his attention to Jodi, flailing wildly at him. Matty ran as Jodi easily dodged the blows but did not see the heavy lump of wood wielded by the bystander. It sent him flying into the mud and knocked the wind from him. He felt the jolt of a well-aimed kick to his ribs but he was soon on all fours ready to spring and knife anyone who was trying to stop him.

Suddenly he felt a weight on his back that splayed him and pinned him to the ground. He tasted the foul mud in his mouth as he tried to struggle. He was easily flipped over and a large boot descended on to his chest and he found himself looking up into the sour face of a Bhasi soldier.

A small crowed surrounded them and began to chant 'kill him'. He felt for his knife but it was gone. He tried to squirm free but he was held fast in the mud. The soldier smiled grimly and he felt a jolt to the side of his head. His struggle was over.

Matty saw them take his body away and knew that she was now alone in the world. The rain began to fall heavily, washing the tears from her face, as she ran back to the hovel where they had lived. Three of the boys had returned with their hoard and were already eating it.

"They killed Jodi," she said.

They looked at her impassively; she had cost them some beatings at her brother's hands. "So what?" said one of them.

"Good riddance," said another.

Matty sensed the mood and backed out into the rain. She turned and fled. For the first time in her life she was alone, utterly alone. Drained and empty, she splashed aimlessly through the sodden alleys while the warm rain soaked the ragged clothes to her thin, childish form. Her only thoughts were of Jodi; of the last moment she saw him, dragged lifeless out of the square between two soldiers. He was at peace now, away from this soiled world and she would never be able to feel him, smell him, taste his wounds on her lips and look into his dark eyes again. He was gone and she wanted to die.

She wandered until darkness fell and the curfew sounded. She found herself back in the rubbish-strewn square where she had last seen her brother and sat down in the mud to weep. The square was deserted now, lit only by the weak, flickering lamplight that stole through gaps in the shuttered windows. Only soldiers would be on the streets now, languidly patrolling their forlorn beat. Only soldiers and shadowy individuals like Ezil Ganneh, a Bhasi slave trader from the south.

Ezil did not walk the night-time streets of Faloon Pal because he enjoyed the scenic pleasures of the place. He was not like other traders who would lazily buy the stock on offer at the garrison fort. Ezil liked something for nothing and anything on the streets after curfew was fair game. If he could get it before the soldiers, it became his property. And so when Ezil strode easily into the square that night and saw the ragged, forlorn figure of Matty, he praised his luck. But then, he did not know how lucky he was about to become.

He was surprised that it did not try to escape as he approached. It did not seem to notice him. Even when he stood before it, it did not stir and he began to suspect that it was a dullard, and practically worthless. He tapped it on the head with his gloved hand and it looked up at him. A shock ran through his cold heart. He was looking down into the most perfect, beautiful eyes he had ever seen. It was dressed as a male, but surely no male could do that to a man.

"Stand up," he commanded and it rose obediently to its feet. It watched him impassively as he pulled off his glove and thrust his hand inside the ragged shorts. He was right. It was a female. His usual, dour expression broke into a smile, females commanded a considerable premium and this one was special.

"You gonna kill me, Mister?" it asked.

"No, I'm going to take you somewhere nice," he replied and snapped a metal handcuff over the slender wrist and led Matty out of the dank, muddy square.

III

Jodi woke up to a throbbing pain in his head. He knew his eyes were open but he was surrounded by an impenetrable darkness that made him fear that he had gone blind. He tried to sit up and became aware of the tight, metal manacle that was cutting into his wrist. He moved his arm and the chain that held him to the wall jangled taught. He sensed that there were others surrounding him, softly sobbing in the dark. The reek of stale urine and blood assailed him and the fearsome smell of the sweat of many bodies. He knew he was in the hell of the garrison fort and he would not have long to live. He shut his eyes again and tried to sleep.

When he awoke, his body ached. He didn't know how long he had slept, but the room was almost quiet now with only soft pitched moans occasionally breaking the silence. The pungency of excrement was now in the air, it made him feel nauseous so he placed his free arm over his mouth and nose and tried to breathe through the thin, ragged sleeve of his shirt, but he could not keep out the thick, foul atmosphere of the dungeon. Time passed slowly in that place and it became impossible to tell how long he had been there.

He thought of Matty. How would she be able to manage without him? The gang would not help her; he knew that. She would be cast out alone on the streets. He began to weep for her and the tears ran down his swollen face and into the bloody rags that covered his bruised body.

After some hours, a harsh light suddenly flooded the room. Jodi winced against the starkness as his eyes quickly adjusted. The room was about ten metres by three with walls of undressed stone. The floor was smooth stone and sloped towards three drains that ran down the centre. Along each long wall seven iron cleats were evenly spaced. Attached to each cleat was a short chain at the end of which was a boy. Some were lying down and did not stir when the light came on; others sat up blinking and rubbing their eyes. Three were naked, youngsters no more than eight, the rest were dressed in shanty rags. Jodi recognized a couple of them from a rival gang; they were good fighters, but they weren't fighting now.

The door at the end of the room opened with a loud, echoing clang and five soldiers walked in, covering their noses against the stench. Behind them Jodi could see a pair of long shiny boots with a pair of powerful, stocky legs inserted into them. The legs belonged to a large man of about forty, with a high forehead and piercing blue eyes; a handsome man with an air of easy authority about him; a man intolerant of dissent. The guards watched as the man walked slowly along the rows of boys. He came to one boy who had not raised himself and kicked him hard. The boy did not stir.

"This one's dead,' he announced, then made his selection from the rest. Nine of the boys were chosen, but not Jodi or the boy next to him who had obviously taken a severe beating.

"That's only nine," complained the Sergeant.

Ezil Ganneh gave him a withering look. "I told you before; I don't want them if they're too damaged."

"What about this one?" persisted the Sergeant, grabbing at the hair of a boy with a badly cut face.

"That cut's infected. You think my clients are nurse maids?"

The Sergeant pointed at Jodi. "This one isn't cut; it's just a little bruising."

The trader peered sourly at Jodi. "Alright, I'll take it, but that's it. Cull the others; I don't want you slipping them into my batch."

The Sergeant nodded to the soldiers who quickly stepped forward and drew their knives. They slit the throats of the three unselected boys including the lad next to Jodi. He heard the gurgled gasp as the blood pumped from the squirming body and splashed Jodi's legs. The room was quiet except for that terrible noise.

Ezil Ganneh and the Sergeant left the room and the soldiers unshackled the remaining ten boys and herded them into an adjoining room where there was a deep, stone bath full of grey water sunk into the floor. The boys were told to strip and get into it. This really frightened Jodi for his mother had drilled into him that he should not be seen naked; it would betray his mixed-race parentage and he would be killed. But he had no choice so he quickly peeled off the blood soaked rags of his old life and covering his private parts with his hand, jumped into the bath. The guards forced them to duck their heads right under the water that smelled of strong chemical and stung their skin. They stayed in the bath for several minutes and then they were ordered to climb out and form a line. Jodi got close to the boy in front of him so that his genitals could not be seen. One of the guards casually sized up the children and handed them a rough woven shirt and a pair of long pants. Jodi quickly put his on. They were a little large for him and he had never before worn long pants, but they were the best clothes he had ever worn in his life.

Damp and smelling of the chemical bath, the children trooped out into the large courtyard of the garrison where Ezil's transport waited. It was still night but the first hint of dawn was in the air. The curfew would soon be lifted and the daily grind of life in Faloon Pal would begin again. As they crossed the yard, Jodi furtively looked about, reckoning his chances of getting away, but the garrison walls were high and the guard was well armed and he could see it was hopeless. Ezil was waiting for them as they were ushered aboard the transport and shackled to a bulkhead. They settled down on the floor and waited, some crying, all afraid of the unknown and what was about to become of them.

The guards left and Ezil closed the door. "Anyone who makes a noise will be killed," he announced gruffly and strode to the flight deck beyond the forward bulkhead. Presently he returned with a small child. Jodi's heart leapt to his throat, he could not help himself. He shouted out, "Matty!"

She saw him at the other end of the transport and the world that had been dead to her suddenly sprang to life. He was not dead; he was alive, and here with her. "Jodi," she screamed and tried to run to him, but Ezil easily held on to her and shackled her to the bulkhead. Then he stormed down the line toward Jodi and pulled out his weapon. Jodi cringed and covered his head as Ezil put the weapon to it. It would have been so easy to pull the trigger, to make an example. The native wasn't likely to fetch much in that condition anyway; it was almost ballast. He was ready to pull the trigger, blast the thing's life away, but something stopped him. He looked toward the front and caught sight of the frightened, pleading eyes of the female and he did not pull the trigger.

"I told you silence," he growled and strode back to the flight deck, turning angrily on them. "Any more noise and I will kill the lot of you."

The trader disappeared through the flight deck door leaving the frightened children to stifle their sobs while Jodi and Matty beamed at each other from opposite ends of the craft. The transport shuddered and began to rise into the air. There was a muffled gasp from the children as it magically cleared the high wall of the garrison fort and climbed above the meagre lights of the town. They gaped through the windows of the craft at the dark, receding panorama of Faloon Pal, a place that none of them would ever see again.

They flew over the dank forest and into the dense cloud that constantly enveloped it, on toward the high, jagged peaks of the sierra that separated their old, familiar world from the strange and alien one for which they were destined. At last they broke through the cloud and, for the first time in their lives, the children saw the two jagged moons of Ennepp and the dwindling array of stars. In the distance they could see the white fangs of the sierra, pushing through a silver sea of cloud. The tips of the peaks were tinged with pink by a mysterious light that seemed to come from below the land. It was the most beautiful sight they had ever seen. But soon their wonder turned to fear, for, as they drew near to the mountain range, they caught sight of the first, dawn segment of the sun rising from behind the land. It flooded the cabin with gorgeous light and the tops of the clouds seemed to be on fire. They had never before seen the naked sun of Ennepp and thought it would surely burn them alive.

The craft rose over the snowy peaks and the sun rose too and the awestruck children thought it must be the lantern of a giant. Their eyes gradually became accustomed to the intense light and they learned that they should not look at the face of the giant's lantern.

Jodi was also frightened. He could see that they were travelling a great distance and that they would never be able to get back. The awesome views of this strange world drew him and he could not tear his eyes away from the scenery passing far below them. He even forgot about Matty who was staring at him intensely, hoping that he would turn and give her one of his reassuring smiles. Eventually he looked her way and smiled and pointed out of the window so that she should look too, and she knew everything would be fine.

Eventually, they left the snow-capped peaks behind and began to descend. Now the land below became flat and a patchwork of green and gold stretched to an endless horizon. The sky above was an intense, startling cobalt with not even the hint of a cloud. The air seemed to sparkle in the morning light and Jodi thought they must have arrived in paradise.

After an hour the craft began to descend and now they could pick out tiny, moving specks of people in the fields. There were houses too and to the children they looked like fabled palaces; great mansions of white stone, surrounded by fragrant gardens. They landed close to one such palace and Ezil emerged from the cockpit. He walked down the line and unshackled three boys and led them out. Jodi strained to see what was going on. He saw Ezil touch hands with a well-dressed stranger who spoke with him a while. Another man, a poorly dressed Native came forward and bowed to them then led the three boys away. Jodi could not see what happened to them, but he did not sense anything bad.

Presently, Ezil touched hands with the well-dressed man once again and returned to the craft. He gave the remaining children a warning scowl and disappeared into the cockpit. Soon they were on their way again, climbing into the impossibly blue sky and heading south.

They stopped twice more. The first time four boys were taken, the second just one. While Ezil was outside speaking to the final owner, Jodi grinned at Matty. "I think he will keep us together."

"Don't speak, he will know and he will kill you."

"No he won't, he's getting money for us."

"Do you think this is a good place, Jodi?"

"Yes, I think so; I think we'll be fine here."

"I think he is a good man, he will keep us together."

Jodi remembered the savage cull of the unwanted boys and forced a smile. "Yes he will," he said.

The return of Ezil cut their conversation short. He climbed in and grimly looked from one to the other. "Are you two related?"

"Matty is my sister, Sir," replied Jodi, keeping his head bowed. He did not want to meet the trader's eyes; he did not want to know what he was thinking.

Ezil nodded imperceptibly and vanished into the cockpit.

For the final time, the transport climbed into the air and headed south. It was now late in the afternoon and the sun was beginning to lose its strength. They passed over rolling hills and woodland. The farms grew sparser in the landscape and in the distance they could see the sparkling horizon of an inland sea. Soon they were over water, pressing further and further into the cool southern air. At last they saw the far shore and the craft began to descend.

They landed in a courtyard of rough-hewn stone that glowed red in the slanting light of the failing sun. At one end stood a large house, drab and forbidding, a world away from the sparkling palaces of the north. The stark, dusty courtyard was flanked on the other three sides by lower buildings of a meaner quality, some of wood, some of rough stone like the house. Opposite the house stood a great, arch with gates of heavy iron, lending a penal aspect to the place. This was the Doah Farm and it was to be their home.

Ezil left the craft and strode toward the house. A man emerged from the portico and approached him. He was short and stout and about fifty years old. The skin of his rotund face was the colour of brown mud, darker than most Bhasi, and pockmarked from too much sun. He wore a moustache that, like his curly receding hair, was greying. He was dressed casually in a brown full-length coat against the cold. They touched hands and the stout man's round face creased into a smile.

"Ezil Ganneh, I am happy to see you."

"Gore, I am glad to be here, it has been a long day."

"Have you brought it?"

"I have. Are we alone?"

"Do not concern yourself, my wife is visiting her sister in the city, we will not be disturbed."

"Then come, you will see for yourself, I have not been false with you."

Ezil led Gore Doah back to the craft and pointed to Matty who was curled up in the corner of the cabin. She felt his eyes on her and it made her flesh creep.

"You say it is intact?" he asked casually.

"Indeed," replied Ezil.

"It is passable, I suppose."

Ezil laughed. "Come, we will discuss the price over dinner, like civilized men."

"When were you ever civilized, Ezil?" Replied Gore, giving a snorting laugh and followed the trader out of the craft.

Across a table groaning with food the two men passed the time in easy conversation. There were few visitors to the remote Doah Farm and Gore was glad of the company. Ezil was a study in false bonhomie. He did not care for Gore very much and would sooner have been on his way home. But business was business and the effort had to be made. Having eaten, they began to haggle over the price of Matty.

"Have you ever seen such a specimen? Ten times better than the last one I brought you."

Gore pursed his full lips and poured some more wine into Ezil's goblet. He noticed the man had hardly drunk anything. "You exaggerate, Ezil, but I grant you it has something about it."

Ezil named his price and Gore stared at him in disbelief.

"That's ridiculous, you can't possibly be serious."

"Do you realize that if I'm caught transporting a female I will lose my licence?"

"Of course, but even so, your price is way too high. I can't afford it, I just can't."

"You had a good harvest this year."

Gore's beady eyes narrowed on the trader. "What is that to do with it? I have expenses, not to mention a wife who watches the money."

"Are you not the master in your own home?" chided Ezil, knowing full well that he wasn't.

"Of course I am, but that has nothing to do with this. Anyway, if I don't take it what will you do? You won't be able to sell it anywhere else."

"I would rather throw it into the sea than sell it cheap, I've done it before and I'll do it again, if I have to."

The two men haggled on for some time, Ezil eventually allowing Gore to beat him down to the maximum he thought he was going to get anyway. He topped up his wine and took a good, long swig. "I tell you what, Gore, even though you have practically robbed me, I'll make you a gift. I have a spare male; you can have it for nothing."

"I don't need any more, I have enough."

"It's good and strong, very healthy."

"Just another mouth to feed."

"Suit yourself; I'll throw it out over the sea."

Gore treated the trader to a sour look. He had just agreed to part with over half the year's income and was wondering how he was going to hide that from his wife. He was also wondering how he was going to keep her from finding out about the female. There had been a terrible scene when she found out about the last one; it had nearly cost him his marriage. Gore could not afford to lose his marriage because his wife owned the farm. He was taking an enormous risk but when he thought of the exquisite gem he had just seen in Ezil's transport, it all made sense to him.

Having created a problem for himself, Gore drowned it with alcohol. By the time Ezil eased himself out of his chair, Gore was fast asleep, his head lolling to one side, snoring open-mouthed through stained teeth. Ezil smiled down evilly at him; the farmer's weakness had given him a rare bonanza. He would make more from this trip than from the last ten put together. He stole out and made his way to the old overseer's quarters. Without knocking he entered and the old man dozing in the chair woke up startled and peered at him in the flickering lamplight.

"Come, your master has bought some stock."

The old man struggled to his feet and bowed obsequiously. Ezil ignored him and strode out of the mean cabin. On the transport he found Matty asleep in the corner. Jodi was wide awake, waiting for what was going to happen to him, he watched intently as Ezil woke Matty and unshackled her.

He pushed her out of the craft. "Go with this person, you now belong here."

The old man grabbed her with his bony hand and pulled her. She sensed that Jodi wasn't coming and began to struggle, calling for him. The old man slapped her and pulled her while she tried to get away. Ezil turned to Jodi and met his pleading eyes.

"Let me go with her, Sir," he said as calmly as he could.

Ezil glanced out to the courtyard at the small, struggling figure with the old man and cursed his soft heart. He called to the old man to wait, unshackled the boy and led him out.

Matty saw him through her tears of desperation and broke free of the old man's grasp. She ran to Jodi and threw her arms around him, sobbing tears of joy. He held her close and told her to be calm and that they would never be parted again.

"A gift for your Master," said Ezil, "but keep it hidden for a while. Better he doesn't know."

The old man bowed defferentially as Ezil abruptly turned and strode back to the transport. As the craft rose into the night sky, he saw the brother and sister embracing while the overseer stood by and thought smugly how foolish and magnanimous he had been.

IV

Mister Minogi, the old overseer of the Doah Farm, watched Ezil Ganneh's vehicle rise into the chilly, night and disappear to the north, while the two children clung to one another in the darkened courtyard. He had little time for these brats his master purchased from Ganneh; most of them were half-starved or damaged and could not do a decent day's work. Some died after a few days, exhausted by the cold and the shock of having to work in the fields for long hours. Those that survived the initial shock fared little better, for they could expect a short life of drudgery in a place where joy was in very short supply. The small boy, clinging unnaturally to his older companion, would not survive long.

The overseer placed his gnarled hand on Jodi's shoulder. "That's enough," he said tersely. "Follow me."

Hand-in-hand they followed him to the corner of the courtyard while the frosty air cut them to the bone. The night sky above was filled with strange and beautiful lights such as they had never seen before. The myriad points of light bathed the buildings surrounding them in a soft, silvery glow that belied the true nature of that forlorn place.

They reached the corner of the courtyard and stopped before a low, windowless stone building with a rough, ill-fitting, wooden door.

The overseer turned. "I am Mister Minogi and you will do as I tell you. These are your quarters. You are now the property of the Master and Mistress who own this farm. Obey and work hard and you will not be punished. Try to escape and you will be executed. You will be fed in the morning."

He unlocked the door and pushed them in. The lock turned behind them and they found themselves in a low-beamed room with mud plaster walls. Several sleeping pallets were pushed against the walls with piles of threadbare blankets upon them. The air was cold and musty with the pungent odour of unwashed bodies and dirty rags. A feeble lamp burned from one of the beams and illuminated a group of ten skinny, hungry-looking boys who were huddled below it. They were engaged in a game involving stones and a pattern etched into the dusty, earthen floor. Large sunken eyes in sallow cheeks turned their way.

"What's this?" said one boy, standing up. "Two more jungle brats."

He was older than Jodi and a head taller and Jodi immediately knew what was going to happen. The other boys stood up and the group moved toward them behind the oldest boy. Jodi pushed Matty behind him and steeled himself. He did not wait for them to attack; he sprang straight at the leader, surprising him and knocking him to the ground. He got several good punches to the face of the boy before the others overpowered him and pinned him to the ground while the leader furiously laid into him with offended vigour. Jodi curled up against the blows, covering his bruised face with his arms. It was no worse than he had had many times before.

At length, one of the boys stepped forward. "That's enough, Matori, you've beaten him."

The oldest boy swung round and glared at him with savage eyes. "I say when he's had enough. You want some too, Garron?"

The younger lad backed off. "No."

Matori kicked Jodi in the ribs a couple of times more then turned his attention to Matty who was cowering against the locked door. "Come here you."

Matty did not move; her eyes were fixed on Jodi, who was lying still.

"Leave him," said Garron. "You've beaten that one enough for two of them."

"You telling me what to do?"

"No, but if he can't work you know what will happen? We'll all get a lashing."

This staunched Matori's anger. "Fucking jungle brats," he said and spat on Jodi. The group of boys returned to their game and were soon absorbed. Matty helped Jodi to an empty pallet and lay down with him. He was crying; great tears of frustration and hurt ran down his face. He knew he could not protect her any more. He knew that their fates were no longer in their own hands and his helplessness made him angry.

Matty had not seen Jodi cry since they were small children together and she was overcome with tenderness for her brother. She cradled his head and rocked him to sleep.

Presently a gong sounded outside and the game broke up. The boys sullenly took to their pallets, some in pairs to ward away the cold. Matty was shivering now; her thin tropical clothes were useless in this place but she was too frightened to move. Garron picked up one of his blankets and brought it over. He knelt down beside her pallet and offered it. He was about thirteen, sunken eyed but with regular features and an honest, open countenance. She took it gladly and spread it over them both.

Garron peered at her and his eyes suddenly widened. "Are you a girl?" he whispered.

"Yes," she replied.

"Shit! There's going to be trouble again."

"What is this place? Why is it so cold here?"

"You'll get used to it. Is this your brother?"

"Yes."

"He's a good fighter."

The flickering lamp waned and died and left them in darkness. Garron crept back to his pallet and wrapped himself up in his blanket. He knew Matori's reign over the boys would soon be at an end.

Later that night Jodi woke in the still darkness. Matty was still holding him and she felt warm. He had never slept this close to her before; there had been no need in the warmth of their distant home. But now, in this intimate darkness, he felt the full urgency of his love for her. He kissed her and he could feel her unseen smile. He was hers and she was his, and it had always been that way between them. His bruised body ached but it didn't matter. Silently they explored each other and, in the stillness of the cold night, they made love.

V

The cold woke Matty early the next day and she lay still, not wanting to wake Jodi, watching the first hint of light creep under the door. It was so quiet here, no sound of rain on the roof, or the incessant splash of dripping water. She knew they had come to a very strange place, a place unlike anything she had ever known; a place without trees or mountains where the endless sky was filled with light. She did not know whether this was better than the close, oppressive tropics, but it didn't matter. She had him now, she had all of him and that was everything she had ever wanted.

The light through the cracks in the door gradually gained strength and she began to hear the sound of people moving about outside. Shuffling feet and the low murmur of men's voices filtered in. She heard the grinding complaint of the great iron gates of the courtyard as they were opened and then there was silence. A moment later the lock of the hut door was turned and Minogi entered. He banged a small gong and left. The boys wearily hauled themselves from their pallets and began to file out. Matty tried to rouse Jodi but he would not stir. Garron came over to them.

"Get him up, quickly or you will miss your food and he'll get a lashing."

"He won't get up," said Matty

"He must, I'll help you."

Together they got Jodi to his feet and helped him out into the harsh, morning light of the courtyard. The other boys had already disappeared into a nearby hut and they followed, latching on to the back of the line of boys. Ahead a man wearing a metallic collar was dishing out meal into bowls while Minogi stood by and watched the portions carefully. Each boy was given a bowl, which he took away and consumed greedily.

"Stand up straight, don't let him see you're injured," whispered Garron to Jodi as Minogi's eyes narrowed on him. Jodi took his bowl of brownish meal and withdrew without meeting his eye. Minogi noticed the bruised face and arms and knew he'd got a good kicking last night. *Tough little sod,* he thought.

Matty was last to get her meal and now Minogi's old eyes widened. He had not seen properly in last night's darkness, but he could see now. His heart sunk. What had the Master bought?

"You, put that down and come with me," he said and led her out of the hut. "You're a female," he said accusingly.

"Yes Sir," she replied.

Minogi cursed under his breath. "Did any of those filthy brats touch you last night?"

"No Sir, they didn't hit me."

"I'm not talking about that," replied Minogi angrily. "Did they fuck you?"

"No Sir, I slept with my brother."

"Your brother?"

"Yes Sir, Jodi."

"And he doesn't fuck you?"

"Oh no Sir. He's my brother."

Matty's innocent assurance visibly relieved Minogi. "Listen and listen good," he said, "you are not to ever tell the Master where you slept last night. Now come with me."

"I am hungry, Sir."

"Food will be brought to you."

He led her to his own quarters, a dingy room next to the great iron gates with a raised pallet in the corner, a large trunk, a table and chair and some shelves on which were arranged a number of books and a sparse assortment of personal items. He went to the trunk and pulled out some clothes. "I will send water, wash yourself thoroughly and put on these clothes. When the Master comes, you will do whatever he tells you. If you do not please him, he will send you away and you will never see your brother again. Do not leave this room."

He turned abruptly and left her on her own. Cursing the name of his master, he crossed the yard back to the chow hut. The last girl his master had bought from Ganneh had nearly cost him his life when the Mistress had found out about her. The Master had hidden her in the old overseer's quarters and there he visited her for three years until the stupid girl tried to run away. That was when the Mistress had found out and hell descended on the farm.

How could he be so stupid and weak? thought Minogi, knowing that, once again, it would be his job to hide the female, and his fault when it all went wrong.

He found the chow man. "Take some water and food to my quarters. Do not speak of what you see there." Some hope; it would be all round the farm by sunset. He then returned to the boys' hut and led them out through the iron gates.

They went into the fields where vast, level swaths of a green root crop had been recently harvested. Here they were to grub for roots that had been missed and fill panniers that were to be sent back to the farm store. The sun climbed above the flat horizon and began to warm them. The work was hard and, to Jodi, quite alien. His body ached and he wanted to stop, but Garron and the other kids kept him going with the news that he would be whipped if he stopped without permission. Minogi watched him carefully. The boy looked particularly resentful and a little wild, he saw that he would have to flog him into submission.

In Minogi's quarters Matty ate the bowl of meal that had been brought by the man with the metal collar. He had given her a strange look and left without speaking before she could ask any questions. The food was not nice but she was hungry so she ate it all. After she had finished she washed herself with the water he had brought. The water was cold and made her skin tingle and shiver in a way she had never known before. She dried herself with a rough cloth and put on the clothes that Minogi had got out of the trunk. It was a white dress and almost fitted her. Then she sat down to wait.

About three hours later, the door opened and there stood the old man who had looked at her last night with such intense strangeness. Now he looked angry, his face contorted into a resentful sneer. She stood up alarmed.

"You disgusting, little whore," he spat, and before she could move he grabbed her and forced her onto the table. He slapped her hard across the face as she tried to struggle from his grasp. He smelled of perfume and alcohol was on his breath.

"Keep still, I'm going to teach you a lesson," he hissed as he yanked at her white dress. She stopped struggling and shut her eyes while he fumbled at his pants. He thrust himself into her with a grunt and then, just a few moments later, a guttural cry of ecstasy and it was all over. The whole thing had lasted less than three minutes and Gore Doah was on his way out of the cabin leaving her looking up at the beamed ceiling. She did not cry; except for the violation, he had not really hurt her. She had taken far worse slaps and his manhood was of such modest proportions that it did not trouble her physically. He was smaller than Jodi, who was still just a boy, and she reflected how strange that the same act could be so different; the one, loving and wonderful; the other, sordid and disgusting.

She stayed still for some time. Tears came to her eyes and trickled gently down her cheeks and onto the table. She could still smell him on her, that strong, soapy perfume and the alcohol of his breath. She rose and washed herself thoroughly, trying to expunge all trace of him from her insides. But she could not and finally she broke down and wept again.

She was still crying when Minogi returned with the boys from the field. The sun was almost touching the horizon when he appeared at the door, framed in the slanting golden light.

"The Master has come to you," he said.

"Yes," she murmured.

Minogi was conditioned by his years of servitude and his heart had become hardened to the cruel life of the farm. It was a requirement for his own survival that he should not allow himself the luxury of emotion, but something in him melted when he saw the exquisite girl crying in his cabin and he stepped forward and held her to him. She clung to him like the child she was and in that silent moment a bond was forged between them.

Minogi had been bought by the father of the Mistress nearly fifty years ago. As a small child he worked in the house, scrubbing and cleaning and carrying out various menial duties. The house workers invariably fared better than the land workers, living in the cellar of the house, which was warmed by the large kitchen above it. Minogi remembered the birth of Parn, the Mistress, forty-seven years ago and the early death of her mother twelve years later. He also remembered the old Master's death and Parn's marriage soon after to Gore, a small, poor excuse of a man, who took his wife's name since his own had no great value. From the outset, Gore proved himself indolent and dissolute and the farm soon began to decline, as did their marriage, so that now both institutions existed without enthusiasm, on the edge of viability.

Parn Doah's return to the farm, from a visit to her sister in a city to the north, filled Gore with justified consternation. He anxiously watched her vehicle approach over the great sea and heartily began to wish he had not purchased the female. She was very fine, but not intact as Ezil had assured him, and she had cost a great deal of money, a fact that he would find difficult to conceal.

The craft landed and Parn emerged alone. She was almost a head taller than Gore, sharp featured with darting, accusative eyes.

Gore ambled up and pecked her on the cheek. "Good trip, my love? How was your sister? I hope you remembered me to her."

"I did no such thing." His unctuous solicitude immediately aroused her suspicion. He had done something prohibited; she recognized the all too obvious signs. She swept past him and toward the house knowing that it would not long be concealed.

VI

Jodi's first few days were characterized with aches and sharp stabbing of the night-time cold. He missed Matty but Minogi had told him that she was staying with him and that she was better off then he was. Jodi accepted this with the naivety of youth; Minogi was strict but he was not evil and could probably look after her better than he could. On the second night, Garron crept over to his pallet and tried to sleep with him but Jodi rejected him. He was so cold that he was sorry and on the following night accepted Garron as his sleeping partner. Matori repeatedly goaded Jodi, calling him 'Garron's new bum friend'. Jodi ignored him for two days and then, one evening just after they returned from the field, Jodi pounced, without warning. The struggle was brief for even though Matori was bigger, he could not match Jodi's ferocity. He was soon curled up in a ball on the floor, trying to protect his face from Jodi's quick fists. This time the other boys did not intervene and Matori's reign was over.

The following day, out in the shimmering, flat fields, Minogi saw the change. Matori's beaten, sullen face was the evidence and the boys were now looking to Jodi as their leader. Minogi was pleased to see it; he had never liked Matori, but chose never to intervene in the internal politics of the hut unless things got too serious. *Let them sort themselves out,* was his philosophy. Minogi sensed that there was something different about Jodi, but he could not quite fathom what it was.

The next morning Jodi woke up early and heard the shuffling of many feet and low, muffled voices outside the hut. Garron was still sleeping soundly beside him as he eased himself off the pallet and placed his eye at the crack in the door. On the far side of the quadrangle he could just about make out a sorry group of ragged men in the dim morning light. Another man, a Bhasi, tall and upright and well-dressed against the cold, marshalled them into line and they trooped out of the great, iron gates. Jodi crept back to his pallet with a sense of foreboding. Even though he had seen nothing untoward, he was struck by a sense of raw brutality pervading the men. Later, in the fields, as they worked together he asked Garron about the men.

"I saw the men go out this morning."

"Better you don't look."

"I saw one man, not like the rest, one of their race."

"That's Gollik, the Workmaster, he's a bastard. He does bad things to the men if they do not work hard enough."

"What sort of things?"

"Terrible things, things that hurt them. And they make them wear those collars, so they won't get away or hurt the Masters."

"You seen this?"

"Two seasons ago one man tried to get away, I don't know how. They caught him and put him on a rack in the middle of the yard. He was up there screaming for three days before he died, kept us all awake at night."

"Shit!"

"They left him up there for many days, stinking and rotting, to remind us, they said."

"They are always killing us," said Jodi, reflectively. "Even in the warm lands they killed plenty of us. It is no different here."

VII

The return of Gore Doah's wife withered his ardour and Matty was not troubled for the next few days. She spent the time in apprehension and tried to occupy herself with small tasks that she judged the old man might appreciate. One day she cleaned and arranged his shelves and then took down one of the ragged books and began to look through it. It was full of meaningless squiggles that said things, clever things; things way beyond her understanding. She was still looking at the book when Minogi returned and asked the question he always asked.

"Has the Master been to you today?"

"No, Sir."

Minogi got himself a drink of water and set himself tiredly down on to the stool next to the rough table. "I see you have found my books."

"They weren't hidden Sir. I'm sorry, I didn't think…"

"Do not be concerned, child. It must be hard to stay within this room all day. Yet you must stay here, in case the Master comes for you."

"Do you know how to read, Sir?"

"Yes, I was taught long ago by the man who was overseer before me."

"I have never known anyone who could read words."

"Not many of our race can. It is quite hard, Matty."

"Have you ever shown anyone how to do it?"

Minogi sighed, "Once, long ago."

"Did he learn the words?"

"Yes, he learned and it got him killed."

"What happened?"

"I don't want to speak about it."

"Sorry."

Minogi lit the lamp and shared some bread with her. He seemed pensive and as they ate he said, "Would you like to learn to read, Matty?"

"Yes, Sir, very much." Her smile disarmed him and stripped him to his bones. He smiled back and thought himself blessed that this bewitching girl had come here to lighten his old age.

They began the lessons there and then; the old man patiently showing the young girl the different letters and how they sounded together and separately. Matty was not a quick learner, but she tried hard and gradually mastered the rudiments. By the time they climbed into their pallets to sleep, she had an unceasing whirl of letters going round in her head.

The next day, Gore Doah sneaked into the cabin like a thief and carried out his business in the same manner as before. When Minogi returned he found her quiet and subdued.

"Has the Master been to you?"

"Yes, Sir."

"Did he hurt you, Matty?"

"Not really, he slapped me, but nothing more."

"I'm sorry he slapped you."

"Do not be, Sir, it doesn't hurt me really and his cock is so small I hardly notice it."

Minogi roared with laughter. "Do not repeat that Matty, not to anyone."

"Who would I tell? I never see anyone. It is very lonely here."

"I know, child, it is difficult for you, imprisoned here. But if you are seen by the Mistress there will be a lot of trouble and you will be sent away."

"I know, but I miss Jodi so much."

Minogi heard this with a jolt that took him back to the embrace he had seen outside Ezil Ganneh's transport. A resolution formed in his mind and led him to do something he would never have contemplated before. It was against the rules and would mean severe punishment if he was caught, but Matty had melted him without even knowing it, and pleasing her was a greater temptation than the fear of punishment.

The next night the boys were at play with the game of stones when they heard the door unlock. Minogi entered and pointed his bony finger at Jodi. "You, come with me."

Jodi got up and left the hut with the old man. The door locked behind them and Matori grinned and drew his hand across his throat. "He's fucked; they'll rack him and leave him to die. Good riddance."

"Why don't you shut your mouth?" Said Garron.

"Hark at his little bum friend. Missing his cock already?"

"Shut it, you prick. I can't wait 'till you get taken to the barracks. They'll fuck you up good over there."

Matori's eyes flared and he thought about thrashing Garron, but his beating at the hands of Jodi was still fresh in his mind and on his body and there was no real reason why Jodi wouldn't return. He contented himself with a few well-chosen expletives and moodily flung himself back on to his pallet.

In the dark shadows of the quadrangle, Jodi followed Minogi to his hut. The old man opened the door and pushed him in. Never had he seen such a vision of light and happiness as Matty's face when she saw Jodi at the door. She threw herself at him and they embraced without words for a long time. They sat down on the floor, holding hands and chatting while he watched and listened. They were like young lovers, this bewitching girl and her fine-looking brother. So intense and obvious was their mutual attraction that he began to suspect that more than sibling affection ran between them. Incest was not uncommon in a race so starved of females and if it was so, he did not particularly disapprove. Anyway, there could be nothing physical between them while he was there.

After an hour or so, he got up and told Jodi it was time to go. The children kissed each other and he took Jodi outside.

"Do not speak to anyone about where you have been tonight. Say that I gave you extra chores as a punishment."

"Yes, Sir. Thank you, Sir."

Minogi unlocked the door of the boy's hut and pushed Jodi in with his foot, sending him sprawling. He scowled at the rest of the boys and withdrew, locking the door behind him.

"What happened?" asked Garron anxiously.

"Nothing," said Jodi. "He just made me do some extra work, that's all."

The other boys complained on Jodi's behalf except Matori who eyed him suspiciously. Jodi ignored him; he didn't care what Matori thought. He had seen and held Matty in his arms and that was all that mattered.

When the old man returned, Matty threw her arms about him and hugged him, weeping tears of joy. He too wept, glad that he had made her happy.

VIII

The southern plains of Ennepp were bathed in days of cool sunlight, interrupted by vicious electrical storms that occasionally raged across the landscape. During the storms no one stayed outside for many had lost their lives to the searing lightening that smashed into the ground and tore at the lonely trees standing like gory sentinels, waving their feeble arms against the rage. When Jodi woke on the seventh day of his imprisonment he heard the familiar, metallic thwack of water on the roof and the less familiar sound of thunder shaking the drab timbers of the hut. He got out and peeped through the gap in the door. Already the men were assembling in the quadrangle, looking up to the early, grey of the sky and pointing at the forbidding clouds. Mister Gollik led them out of the iron gates and then Minogi was at the door.

"Hurry up, you runts. We will be going to the packing shed."

They ate quickly and followed him out through the gates and down a route to the side of the farm that Jodi had not yet seen. The rough road ran between two high banks of golden-headed crops that obscured the vast, squat building beyond. The clouds were rising in an angry tumult above their heads and the rain gathered pace towards the deluge to come. A huge bolt of lightning cracked over the farm and they began to run for their lives. They got to the shed just as another mighty fork burst from the black heart of the clouds and lit up the farm behind.

Minogi led the wet boys into the dark interior where various gangs of men were working under the watchful eye and eager whip of Mister Gollik. Minogi went up to him and bowed and they had a brief conversation during which Gollik pointed to the far end of the shed with his whip. Jodi had never seen this august gentleman at close hand and took his chance to look. The Workmaster, as he was known, was tall and well-built, with tightly curled black receding hair, greying at the temples, and a dark complexion with taught skin drawn into a haughty, superior expression. He was about forty and reminded Jodi of the garrison soldiers in Faloon Pal. He glanced Jodi's way and his penetrating, blue eyes rested on the boy.

"Who is that?"

"A new worker, Sir," said Minogi, bowing again. "Master Ganneh brought him here as a gift for the Mistress and the Master."

Gollik raised a sceptical eyebrow; Ezil Ganneh and gifts were never mentioned in the same sentence. "Ganneh has been here has he?"

"Yes, Sir, ten days ago."

"During the Mistress's absence?"

"I think she was away, Sir." Minogi was beginning to grow uncomfortable; he did not know how much Gollik knew of Matty. He dreaded the next question but Gollik just twisted his mouth into a faint smile and dropped the subject.

"You have your orders, Overseer," he said peremptorily.

Minogi bowed and sloped off to lead the boys down to the far end of the shed where they started packing cobs into boxes and loading them onto the railed carts that ran down the middle of the building. The rain slammed against the metal roof of the shed and almost deafened them. Outside they could see the fields yielding under the deluge and turning to lakes under brilliant flashes that wheeled across the landscape. Jodi had seen many tropical storms but nothing to compare with the violence of this.

"Does it rain like this often here?" He asked Garron.

"About every so often," replied Garron unhelpfully.

As he worked Jodi noticed some of the men working near them. They were thin and ragged, just like the boys and went about their business in sullen silence. Occasionally, when Mister Gollik wasn't looking, one or another would glance over at the boys, point at Matori and make a graphically obscene gesture.

"What's the matter with them?" asked Jodi.

"Nothing," replied Garron, "give them no mind."

"They're pointing you out, Matori. Why?"

Matori scowled. "Mind your own business."

Jodi could see that Matori was visibly upset by the behaviour of the men and decided that he would find out what was going on.

The storm passed in the late afternoon and the sun poured life into the earth once again. As they trudged back along the swamped path that evening, Jodi asked Garron again.

"Do the men always do that to Matori?"

"Lately. He's next."

"Next for what?"

"To go into the barracks."

"So it's a sort of joke."

"A joke? Here? Look around, do you see anything funny?"

"No, nothing."

"Wake up, Jodi, there are no women here. The new ones get used instead."

Jodi was shocked; he had not expected to hear anything like this. "What happens?"

"For fuck's sake Jodi, do you want me to draw you a picture?"

"They won't do that to me when it's my turn, I'll kill them all first."

"Well, good luck with that," replied Garron and they trudged on with this new information a dark stain on a distant horizon.

IX

Two nights after the storm, Minogi came for Jodi again. As they chatted, Matty told him that she was learning to read. Jodi seized on it immediately.

"Please teach me the words too," he said to Minogi.

The old man considered. "I will teach you, but you must never tell anyone."

"I never will. Can we start now?"

Minogi got up and pulled a large book off the shelf. "We will start with this. It is called the Book of Minnar and it was written a long time ago by a man who came from a different world. It tells us how we should live."

Jodi was voracious for knowledge and his brain was sharp. Minogi was surprised at how quickly and easily he learned. Jodi started to visit his cabin once in every three nights and was soon reading whole sentences, outstripping his sister who was much slower. For Minogi, the coming of these two children into his life had brought him a hint of what family life could have been. He knew it was dangerous to drop his emotional defences, but he was hopelessly out-gunned and he didn't care anymore. At long last he had found joy and he meant to hold on to it as long as possible.

The boys in the hut learned to accept Jodi's absences for 'chores', especially as he started bringing back pieces of bread and even extra blankets. Matori sneered at the bounty and said that Jodi was now Minogi's bum friend, but took his fair share all the same. Garron said that Matori should not get any extra bread but Jodi insisted that all of them should share equally. He did not like Matori but to Jodi's generous spirit, that was no reason to deny him.

X

The first season of their life on the farm wore on, punctuated by little moments of joy and despair. Gore came to Matty less and less frequently, his stuttering, conjugal visits only characterized by their brevity. It was as though he was looking over his shoulder during the business, which of course, he was. His wife was rarely seen; she confined herself to the house and to visits with her limited circle of rural friends. There were strong rumours that Parn Doah was seeing rather too much of Workmaster Gollik's 'whip', but nobody ever saw them together.

For Matty, time wore heavily. Except for the evenings with Minogi and the special ones with Jodi, she was left to herself in the confines of the dingy hut. She knew that she had no right to complain, that the old man had done more for her than she could have ever hoped, but she missed the outside, the air and light and the space. She did not say anything but Minogi saw this and his love for her made him reckless. One day, on a day following one of the Master's visits, when they were working in one of the furthest fields, Minogi bade her put on some boy's clothes and took her out, through the iron gates with the others. She held Jodi's hand as they walked between high banks of rustling crops in the morning sunshine, and thought that it would not be possible to be happier. The other boys viewed her with great interest, especially the older ones. Minogi realized that the short time she had been on the farm had brought a change in her. She was nearly thirteen years old and the woman she would become was beginning to emerge. She was careless of their attention, only Jodi existed for her on that bright day, but Minogi watched them all carefully and never let her out of his sight.

Other excursions followed and in each case, Minogi was lucky. Gore Doah was a man of habit and never visited Matty on consecutive days, so she went out into the fields and picked and packed the golden cobs in the sunlight.

At the end of the first season an accident occurred in the packing shed. One of the men fell and trapped his arm under one of the railed trucks. Mister Gollik inspected the badly smashed arm and decided that the man could no longer work. He took him away and shot him in the head. Two other men buried him in the ground reserved for the Natives behind the packing shed.

The next day, the door to the boy's hut was unlocked early and the grim aspect of Mister Gollik appeared. He pointed at Matori and wordlessly beckoned him out. Matori shuffled out after the Workmaster, his head bowed. He was crying. They saw him in the fields several days later. Even from a distance they could see he was badly beaten. He had suffered the same brutal violence that seemed to pervade the farm, not constant, but intimidating and more than enough to blight their degraded lives. Within the men a hierarchy of brutality governed their society, which suited the indolent bosses as long as the men didn't actually damage each other beyond their capacity to work. It gave the work force a natural structure and discipline that found an expression in the unnatural state of the gender imbalance that existed in the Native population. The principle tool of subjugation was sodomy.

The passing of Matori brought the dark cloud on the horizon a little closer to Jodi. He vowed anew that he would never go into the barracks.

XI

Soon after Matori's departure the farm received another visit from Ezil Ganneh. This time he brought just one boy and under Parn Doah's more rigorous negotiation had to part with him for less than he would have liked.

"I was not expecting the pleasure of seeing your wife," he said to Gore as they chatted next to Ezil's transport.

"Her sister is unwell, she had to defer her visit," replied Gore, unaware of the trader's agitation at having to deal with Parn. "Are you sure you won't stay for supper?"

"Better not," replied the trader, stepping into his vehicle. He did not relish an evening at the mercy of Madam Doah's barbed tongue. "By the way, how's that female I brought you coming on?"

"Well enough," said Gore shortly.

Ezil grinned slyly. "Parn doesn't know yet does she?"

"She knows what I tell her. I run this farm."

Ezil laughed contemptuously. "Just as you say Gore. Good day to you."

The craft rose into the evening sky leaving behind the farmer and a frightened ten-year-old boy called Pallas.

When the boys returned from the fields that evening, they found the new boy sitting on a pallet, shivering and crying. They started the traditional hut welcome, but before they could hit him, Jodi stepped in and stopped them. He sat down next to the child and put his arm around him. "'Look through the eyes of another man and there you will find wisdom'," he quoted from the Book of Minnar.

The boys looked at him dumbfounded. "Sometimes you really talk funny," observed Garron.

Under Jodi's protection Pallas soon settled in. He was a scrawny specimen who had managed to stay with his father until they were separated during a food riot in a jungle town. He got picked up by soldiers and never knew what happened to his father. Jodi felt sorry for him because he was not a street kid and was not tough like the rest of them.

"You'll ruin that kid," said Minogi one day as they walked to the fields. "He's soft and useless and you're making him worse."

"'Compassion is my father and my brother,'" replied Jodi.

"Merciful Prophet! I have created a book weed," said Minogi, with a toothless grin and Jodi put his arm around the old man and laughed. He had just turned fourteen and was the same height as the overseer. Imperceptibly, without either knowing it, they had become as father and son.

XII

Midway through their second season on the farm, the occasion of Parn Doah's birthday was celebrated by the gift of half a day's holiday. There had been holidays before and on such occasions Minogi had simply locked the boys in their hut, leaving them to their own devices. But this time he approached Mister Gollik and asked if they could go to the sea. Gollik regarded him with ill-disguised distaste and began to wonder if the overseer had not lost his wits.

"To the sea. What for?"

"Your pardon Master, I just thought, for the air."

"There is enough air in their hut; they don't need to be sucking it in by the sea."

"No, Master, I'm sorry to have troubled you." Minogi bowed and went to leave but Gollik detained him.

"Wait. To the sea, you say?"

"Yes Sir."

"The Mistress and the Master will be away for the day. You may go."

"Thank you, Sir."

Gollik ignored Minogi's bow and strode off toward his dwelling which lay at some distance, beyond the perimeter walls. He suspected that the change in Minogi's demeanour had something to do with that female that the fool Gore Doah had bought. He knew she was hiding in the Overseer's accommodation and suspected that she was sending the old man soft. It concerned him that Minogi might not be getting the full measure of work from the brats and he decided to keep a close eye on things in future.

The day was unusually hot when they returned from the fields and set out toward the sea. They walked between high, rustling banks of golden stems while the sun beat down upon them. They had been given extra bread and they ate as they passed through parts of the farm they had never seen before. High avenues of rustling cane dwarfed them under the brilliant light that touched the day with magic and darkened their bronze skins.

At last they turned a corner and there, at the end of the cloistered crop, was the sea. It sparkled impossibly blue in the early afternoon and the boys ran towards it. By the time Minogi and Matty arrived at the white, sandy shore, the boys were in the water, stripped naked, splashing, and screaming. Matty and the old man sat down upon the soft, white sand and watched the battles and the antics. Jodi hoisted Pallas upon his shoulders and they fought off the others who had paired off, eventually getting ducked themselves amid hoots of laughter. Jodi was a strong swimmer - he had learned in the muddy, polluted river that ran through Faloon Pal - but here the water was like crystal and he could see right to the bottom. He swam out further than the others and dived down to the sea-bed and looked up at the shimmering surface above. It suddenly struck him how wonderful it would be to stay down there forever, in the peace and light of the sea. This is where he would do it, when the time came for him to go to the barracks. He would swim out and sink into the cold depths of the sea and he would never come up.

His lungs were bursting as he broke the surface, gasping for air. Far to shore he could hear the screams of the boys playing tag on the beach. He swam back in and ran to join them. Matty watched him with admiration. He was lean and fine and becoming a man, faster and stronger than the rest. Even Garron, who was older, couldn't keep up with Jodi.

Minogi was also watching. In his joyful exuberance, Jodi had forgotten his mother's injunction and when the old man saw him naked he realized why Jodi was different. Later as they walked back, tired and happy in the last slanting rays of the day, he held Jodi back.

"You're a half-breed," he said.

Jodi was suddenly alarmed. "No Sir, I swear I'm not."

"You can swear all you want, your mouth can lie, but your cock can't. It's ten shades darker than the rest of you."

Jodi knew he was discovered. "It's true, my father was a soldier. Are you going to tell anyone, Sir?"

"How would it profit me to do that? You have become a son to me, Jodi, losing you would be like cutting off my own arm. You will have to be very careful from now on, if the Masters learn of it, you will be done for."

"I know, my mother always warned me never to let myself be seen."

"She did well to warn you. Fortunately none of these runts will have recognized it, you are safe for the time being, but there will come a time…"

"I can't go to the barracks, you know that."

"Yes, you would be exposed. Gollik would surely kill you."

"I know; I have made my plan. I will go to the sea and swim out as far as I can, and then I will sink to the bottom and never come up."

"You will do no such thing. We still have at least a season, I will think of something and, with the Prophets' help, I will get you away from here and safe."

They caught up with the others and made their way back to the farm. The shining day had turned dark for Minogi for, although he always knew that he would lose Jodi to the barracks, it was only now that the prospect of it filled him with foreboding. The thought of Jodi in the barracks was bad enough, but at least the boy would live. Now, things had changed for in that depraved environment, the evidence of his mixed parentage would soon be discovered. He would not survive long.

XIII

The year turned and another harvest ripened. Matty approached fourteen and she too ripened into a young woman of astonishing beauty. Oddly, as she matured, Gore Doah visited her less and less, finally ceasing altogether. It crossed his mind several times that he should sell her but he was indolent and concerned that his wife would discover his secret if he disturbed the arrangement, so nothing was done and Matty stayed in Minogi's hut and worked out in the fields almost every day.

Neither Jodi nor Minogi told Matty of their plans but Jodi spent more and more evenings in the hut learning writing and reading and numbers. His education had left Matty far behind and he could now read as well as Minogi himself. The old man was pleased but he was also getting worried. Jodi was half Bhasi and it was becoming increasingly obvious. He was bigger than any of the others and once or twice Minogi noticed Gollik looking curiously at the boy during their regular inspections. He was going to take him to the barracks soon; he could feel it.

"You are almost a man now, Jodi," he said as they walked in from the fields together. "I have noticed Gollik looking at you."

"Yes, I have noticed too, the time is coming."

"The time is now Jodi. Tomorrow you will take my best clothes and I will get bread for you to take. The crop is high and will hide you. Go along the sea-shore in the direction of the sun rise, but stay in amongst the crops. You must not be seen, not by anyone. If we are lucky they will not notice you are gone for a few days. There is a large city on the shore; I have seen pictures of it. In four or five days you will come to it and there you will be able to hide and find others like yourself."

"They will be hard on you, my father."

"I am old, what can they do to me now?"

"And Matty, what will become of her?"

"The Master no longer comes to her. There is a change coming, she will be taken away whatever you do; you cannot stop that. They took the last girl when the Mistress found out about her. Do not worry, Matty is valuable; she will not be harmed. You are the one in danger and you must think of yourself now."

Jodi knew this was true but his heart was heavy. He knew that once he struck into the high stems tomorrow he would never see any of them again.

The next day was bright but there was a familiar change in the air. A storm was coming. Minogi packed bread into a satchel lined with his best clothes and led the children out through the iron gates. As they passed through the main gates Gollik suddenly appeared before them. He had been waiting for them behind the wall. Minogi's heart sank; he knew instinctively what the Workmaster wanted. They were too late.

"Hold there, Overseer," Gollik's voice seemed to shake the air.

"Sir."

"I see you take the female."

"The Master has no use for her; she should earn her bread in the field."

"That is commendable, Overseer."

Gollik's eyes rested on Jodi and he was about to speak again but Minogi interjected. "Sir, there is a large storm coming, we have much work to do if we are to gather the ripe crop before it. I will have to keep them out late today."

Gollik looked at the sky and sniffed the air. "Daresay you're right Overseer. Get on with it."

Minogi led them off into the high crop, his heart pounding. They had got away with it. He led them to the far field where the crop was high and ripe and set the boys to work, and then he took Jodi and Matty off into a clearing in the stems. He unpacked his clothes from the satchel.

"Put them on quickly, at least you won't look like a worker from a distance."

"What's going on?" asked Matty, alarmed.

"Jodi is leaving," said Minogi.

"No!"

Minogi held her while Jodi quickly stripped off his soiled and ragged clothes and put on the old man's best. They were a little small for him, but he looked handsome in them.

"Jodi's half-breed, Matty, you know that and you know what they will do to him if they find out."

Matty nodded heavily.

"Gollik nearly took him just now. He has to go, there's no choice."

"I know," she whispered, tears started from her eyes and began to stream down her cheeks.

Jodi came over to her and held her in his arms. "Don't worry, wherever you go I will find you. They won't keep us apart."

He held her close as she sobbed and then he kissed her. She looked up into his eyes shining with tears. "Go and be free," she said, "and do not think of me."

"I will always think of you; I will never forget you," he said.

Minogi picked up the satchel of bread and gave it to him. "Go now, the storm will help you. Remember; keep to the coast in the direction of the rising sun. The Prophet keep you, my son."

"And you too, father."

Jodi kissed the old man on the forehead and with one last look at Matty, disappeared into the wall of ripening golden stems.

XIV

The storm was slow in coming, but that was because it was gathering its might to blast their world away. When it finally arrived, two nights after Jodi left, its black heart tore into the farm with a fury that had never been known before. It tore the roof off the packing shed and spoiled the harvest; it stripped away the flimsy roof of the barracks and killed five of the men and injured a dozen more; it hammered at the doors and roof of the children's hut, like a furious monster, as they cowered inside.

When they emerged into the dazed morning the world had changed for all of them.

Mister Gollik strode from the ruined barracks with Gore and Parn Doah in tow. He had just shot three of the men, judging their injuries to be beyond economic repair and given orders that the dead should be buried behind the packing shed. The scattered and sheared sheets of the barracks roofing should be gathered to make repairs. They headed for the relatively undamaged huts on the other side of the quadrangle and were met by the sight of the Overseer and the boys straggling out into the blustery morning.

"Any injuries, Overseer?" Gollik's voice boomed above the wind.

"No Sir."

"Where is the tall one? Get him out, there is work to do."

"He is not here, Sir."

"Not here!"

"He must have left in the night, during the storm."

Gollik's withering eyes turned on the old overseer. A weak lie. He roughly grabbed one of the boys. "Where is the missing brat?"

The boy spluttered, "Gone Sir."

"Gone! When? Speak up."

"Two days ago, Sir."

Gollik dropped the boy and grabbed Minogi by the hair with his huge hands. "Speak up, Overseer."

Minogi grinned. "He's out of your murdering clutches, Gollik."

The Workmaster furiously threw him to the floor and drew his weapon.

"Stop," commanded Parn. She walked up to the crumpled old man. "You were my father's overseer, I trusted you, gave you everything you have and this is how you repay me?"

"Yes," replied Minogi, "I worked for your father and for you and not a day passed that I didn't loathe you and your father and all your kind for what you have done to my people. I let the boy go because he is a half-breed and you would have killed him, but he is the future, the only hope for the future and getting him out of this hell-hole is the best thing I have ever done in my whole, sorry life."

Parn's eyes flared. "Give me that," she hissed, grabbing the weapon from Gollik.

Minogi smiled defiantly as she took aim and fired, killing the old man instantly. Matty, who had been watching anxiously, through a gap in the hut door, burst forth and threw herself on to the lifeless body, holding it up and wailing. Parn looked down in shock and disbelief, and then slowly turned on her unfortunate husband.

"You… you filthy, squirming lazy lump of dirt. You disgusting turd."

Gore began to back away, his wife advanced on him, weapon in hand, her face determined and grim.

"Darling, don't do anything…"

"Do anything? I should have done this years ago." She raised the weapon and pointed it at her cowering husband.

"Madam," said Gollik, placing his hand firmly on the weapon, "you should go inside the house."

Parn looked up at him and then at the gallery of frightened and bewildered boys watching her. She realized that her anger had momentarily robbed her of her self-control and the thought of it instantly sobered her. "Of course, you're right Mister Gollik."

"Take your husband inside and I will attend to things here."

She stalked off with Gore, still pleading, in her wake and Gollik turned darkly on the boys. "Get inside and stay there. From now on you will wear collars, like the men and you will work with the men."

He locked them in their hut then roughly grabbed Matty and pushed her into the overseer's hut. "Get in there and stay there," he said and locked her in.

He made his way out of the old iron gates and down toward the packing shed. From the path he could see the devastated fields all around where the maturing crop was flattened and useless. Ahead he saw the packing shed, or rather what was left of it. The roof was off and one end had collapsed. The packed crop inside was waterlogged and ruined. He trudged back to the house to report.

Inside he found Parn and Gore sitting in glacial silence in the salon.

"We've lost the packing shed and at least fifty percent of the crop," he announced.

Parn regarded him moodily. "The insurance will pay for the crop and the workers can rebuild the packing shed."

"Actually, my love,' said Gore, "there may be a slight problem."

Gollik turned on him. "What?"

"The insurance," continued Gore sheepishly, "I'm not sure that I…"

Gollik hoisted the old farmer up by his collar. "You didn't insure? You limp-brained fucker; how're you going to pay me? You owe me a year's salary."

"I'll pay you, I swear I will."

"How?"

"We'll get a loan, like always."

"You useless fool," said Parn. "The farm is already mortgaged to the roof."

Gollik let his boss slump back into his chair. Gore remained still, shrivelled and dejected. "We're ruined," he said.

"At last, reality dawns," said Parn, sarcastically. "Well done, after thirty years of marriage, you finally uttered something that is actually true."

"Is there really nothing left, Ma'am?" said Gollik.

"Nothing. The sale of the farm will not cover the debt, not now." She laughed mirthlessly. "The only thing of value is that contraband female in the hut down there."

"I'll take that then," said Gollik.

She looked up at him in surprise. "What will you do with it?"

"Sell it."

"You'll get good money for that, it's very fine," said Gore, instantly shrinking under his wife's reproachful stare.

Gollik ignored him. "What will you do, Ma'am?"

"The creditors will soon be here to seize the farm, they'll soon sniff blood. I'll go to my sister in the north. We never really got on but she'll take me in. I suggest you take what's yours before they get their hands on it. Goodbye, Mister Gollik, thank you for your hard work. I am sorry it has ended like this."

Gollik took her hand and bowed. "Goodbye Ma'am and good luck."

Ignoring Gore, he left them and crossed the quadrangle to the old overseer's hut. He found Matty sitting at the table.

"Stand up. Where are the clothes you wore for your master?"

"In the chest, Sir."

"Put them on."

Matty took the white dress from the chest and turning her back on the man, slipped off her ragged clothes.

"Wait, turn around, I want to see what I own."

She turned slowly and Gollik's eyes roasted her. Out of the boy's ragged clothing he could see her true form; the pert, girlish breasts; the developing curve of her body; the inviting, dark wispy triangle at her crotch. He felt a flood of urgency in his loins.

"Get dressed," he snapped, angry that he had succumbed to such feelings towards a Native female.

He watched her squeeze into the white dress she wore for Gore's visits and pulled her out of the hut. Matty went in numbed silence; she didn't care what happened to her now. Jodi was gone, Minogi was dead, there was nothing left in her life. She took one last look at the lifeless body of the old man as Gollik pulled her across the quadrangle and out of the iron gates and felt a sickening, hollow emptiness in her stomach. He took her to a part of the farm she had never seen where a squat, single storied house nestled in a clearing next to a gnarled tree. Outside the house a small vehicle stood on the rough ground. He opened it and pushed her in.

"Sit there and don't move," he ordered and went into the house. Presently he emerged with a bundle of clothes and a box of miscellaneous objects. He threw them into the back of the vehicle and took his seat at the front. The long-dormant craft sprung to life and rose into the grey, blustery sky. Matty saw the receding patchwork of the farm through the dusty window and remembered the time she had arrived nearly three years ago, with Jodi in Ezil Ganneh's craft. Tears came into her eyes as she thought of Jodi. Where was he? A long way away by now.

They headed out over the inland sea, to the north. Most of the way Gollik was speaking to various people; arguing, cajoling, begging. Matty took no notice; she drew her knees up to her chin and folded into her own world. Eventually Gollik found the friend of a second cousin who knew someone who might be interested. They crossed the northern shore of the sea and flew over the land for a long time, finally coming to rest in a remote forest clearing. Gollik broke out something to eat and began absently to chew while time drifted by and the billowing edge of the storm fell away to the east.

It was almost dark when the light appeared in the sky and approached the clearing. Gollik sat up, suddenly attentive and very nervous. The craft landed nearby and a man got out. Matty could see that he was tall and lean, but nothing more as his features were hidden beneath a large hood. He wore a full coat the colour of sand and long, black boots. Gollik had good reason to be apprehensive; this man was a Moontrader, a member of a notorious brotherhood of inter-planetary pirates.

Gollik got out of the craft and bowed and greeted the Moontrader but the man remained still and silent.

"I have brought what we spoke of," said Gollik and pulled Matty from his vehicle. "I assure you it is everything I said it is."

He thrust Matty forward.

The Moontrader allowed the intimidating silence to gather. Finally he spoke in a whisper that carried clearly on the air. "This is a child. I do not like this trade."

"It is nearly full grown, really, you can see, I'll let you see." He began to reach for Matty's dress.

"Stop," commanded the Moontrader. "Come here, child."

Gollik pushed her forward. "That's right, have a closer look at it."

Matty went toward the tall, sinister figure.

"Has this man harmed you, child?'

"No, Sir."

"Has he forced himself upon you?"

"Not this one, Sir."

The Moontrader rested his gaze on Gollik who seemed to wither visibly. "This girl has saved you. I would have killed you if you had harmed her. Now go and do not trade in people again."

"But it's mine, I own it."

Suddenly, with alarming speed, a large firearm appeared in the Moontrader's hand. It seemed to come from nowhere. "I do not usually give second chances."

"Wait... okay, I understand. I wasn't going to ask for much. Maybe we could come to an understanding..."

A searing blast of heat hit the ground next to Gollik's feet and singed his boots. He jumped in fright as the Moontrader glared at him and levelled the firearm at his middle.

"Don't shoot, I'm going," he spluttered and hurriedly climbed back into his vehicle and closed the door.

As it ascended into the darkness the Moontrader allowed himself a furtive grin and turned to the girl. "What is your name child?"

"Matty Saronaga, Sir."

"I am Sevarius DeRhogai and you belong to me now."

XV

Laon Cour Son took a delicate sip of the sweet, syrupy wine in the fine goblet before him and smiled. "And what would I want with a Native girl of that age?"

Sevarius grinned wickedly showing a full set of perfect teeth. "We both know your boss's tastes, Laon. Why pretend? You've seen her image; she's perfect and, from what I can gather, not greatly used."

"I grant you, she is a gem. Where did you get her?"

Sevarius's grin faded. "You'd hardly expect me to tell you that."

"It's not like you to go dipping around in the north. She must have been brought down here illegally."

"I dare say, but since when did that concern you?"

"I have to tread carefully these days; the Commissioner has come under scrutiny recently. There are several jurisdictions that would like to snip his balls off and get a piece of his fortune for themselves."

Sevarius considered for a moment, keeping his gaze on the man across the table. Laon Cour Son was in his late thirties. Slight in stature, he was obviously of mixed race, the sharpness of his Bhasi features being tempered with a softness from an undetermined off-world source. His skin was light brown below tightly curled black hair that he wore short and neatly trimmed around extraordinary ears that stuck out like two small jug handles. He had soft, expressive, dark brown eyes that belied a steely determination to get what he wanted. Sevarius had dealt with Laon a number of times before; he was one of the few people that he actually liked.

"I am a trader, I have no interest in betraying the Commissioner's trust," said Sevarius.

"You are a pirate, who knows where your interests lie?"

Sevarius laughed and several nearby drinkers in the lounge turned and looked. "Fair point, Mister Secretary, but take my hand and I will make a trader's bond with you. Nobody will learn of this from me."

Laon was surprised; he was being offered an unbreakable agreement by the Moontrader, normally only a pledge that could exist between two of their own kind; a pledge of death rather than betrayal. Tentatively, he took Sevarius' arm in a clench. "I don't know whether to be honoured or horrified."

"Both would be appropriate, Brother."

Laon smiled. "Let's get out of here."

In the park of the discreet bar where Laon always conducted his more shady business, they climbed into the Moontrader's vehicle. Matty was asleep in one of the seats, she did not wake up when they entered.

"What did I tell you? The image did not lie," said Sevarius. "A girl like that could turn a man straight."

Laon laughed. "Not in my case. What's her name?"

"Matty Saronaga. She keeps going on about her brother, something about him running away from the farm they were on."

"A runaway worker, he'll most likely be dead by now."

"Most likely. Well, wake her up, she's all yours now."

Laon shook the sleeping girl's shoulder; she opened her eyes and the innocent perfection of them stunned him.

The Moontrader stepped forward and gently raised her to her feet. "Matty, you belong to this man now, go with him, he will look after you."

"Is he going to fuck me?" she asked.

Laon smiled. "No Matty, your virtue is safe with me."

Matty didn't quite understand the reply, but got the gist. This new man had a nice, slightly comical face that put her at ease. Sevarius nodded for her to go with him and she followed him out of the Moontrader's craft.

Outside the two men clasped arms. "Where are you heading for now, Sevarius?"

"Tarnus, then probably Crixus."

Laon grinned. "Good luck, Brother."

"Death before betrayal," replied Sevarius and he climbed into his vehicle and was off.

Laon took Matty to his own vehicle and soon they too were speeding through the night sky.

XVI

The Commissioner for Culture and Trade for Lamon Utile was a massive bulk of a man in his early sixties. His broad, jocular face and exceedingly pronounced eyebrows leant him an approachable mien that often deceived his many enemies. The Commissioner was a study in excess; his body had too much fat; too much skin; and way too much hair. His voice was too loud, his temper too quick and his libido, for a man of his age, too pervasive. The Commissioner was, also, far too wealthy.

Lamon Utile was a sparsely populated moon colony in a star system in the Suran region. As such, its obscurity should have been preserved had it not been for the trade sanctions that existed between the despised Bhasi on Ennepp and the rest of the human race. Embargos, of course, are little more than political tokens and are created to be broken. And so it was with Ennepp. Through the good offices of the Commissioner, goods and services poured into and out of Ennepp and the good people of Lamon Utile, taking their rightful percentage, became inordinately wealthy.

The Commissioner, not being the retiring type, celebrated his wealth and position in the only way he knew. He built a massive, vulgar palace in a large park on the edge of Gom, Ennepp's principal city. It had porticoes of highly polished stone from far-off worlds; it had fantastical turrets twisting into the sky, with crowns of precious metal that shone like torches; it had lakes and islands in the lakes on which primitive buildings were represented in idyllic decay; it had gorgeous boats on the lakes, lit at night with the fire from a thousand torches. It was, in short, like the Commissioner himself, a study in excess and the consequences of resting too much wealth in the hands of an individual ill equipped in the facility of moral judgement.

It was late at night when Laon's transport descended into the park and landed in the private place reserved for his use. He ushered Matty out of the craft and she emerged into the fantasy world of the palace and its garden. Laon procured women for the Commissioner on a regular basis. They lived in the palace in what could only be described as a harem. Some stayed for a few years and were then retired with a small but adequate pension; some were sold on and fared worse, each according to the great man's whim. It was to the harem that Laon was going to take Matty, but no one saw them enter the palace together and for some reason, that he did not even understand himself, he did not take her to the harem but, instead, took her to his own, private apartment.

Matty walked through the place open-mouthed; she had never seen such things or imagined they could exist. The golden statues; the polished, stone floors; the high, ornate ceilings of endless corridors all conspired to reduce her to silent awe. When, at last, they entered Laon's apartment, the restraint and simplicity was like a tonic to her mind.

"Your house is very big and grand."

"It is not my house, Matty; this place belongs to a very important man, a very rich man. I work for him."

"Does he own you?"

"No, I am free to go any time."

"But he owns me now, doesn't he?"

"Yes, he does."

"I don't mind."

"You must be tired; I will show you where you will sleep."

He led her into one of the many rooms in the apartment and showed her where she should sleep. She looked at the soft, white bed in confusion.

"I have never slept on something like this."

"You just lie on it. I'm sorry; I don't have any night-clothes for you."

She looked more confused, then, by way of a revelation, she unfastened her dress and let it drop to the floor. "Would you like to fuck me?" she asked with disarming innocence.

Laon could not help staring at her nubile body. "How old are you, Matty?"

"Ten and three years, I think. Maybe ten and four."

"You are too young for sex."

"No, I have done sex many times, with my master."

"I am sorry to hear it. I do not require it. Go to sleep and we will speak again in the morning."

Abruptly, he turned and left, leaving the naked, bemused girl alone in the room. She climbed into the bed and pulled the soft, billowing sheets about her. They smelled wonderful, like fragrant moss, and the bed was so soft she seemed to float in its folds. It seemed impossible to her that such comfort could exist and she shut her eyes and thought of Jodi. If only he was with her, she would be the happiest person alive.

Unlike Matty, Laon did not sleep well. His mind was in turmoil about what he had done, or rather, what he intended to do. And in truth, he could not entirely explain his actions to himself. It could not be sexual attraction that led him to take Matty into his private apartment, there was no question of that, but there was something about this girl, something different that made him want to protect her and look after her. She had a particular quality of innocence about her that instilled in those with the sympathy to recognize it, an overwhelming desire to possess her. The thought of the grotesque and bloated body of his employer smothering this wonderful being with his flesh, made Laon feel quite nauseous.

She would not be violated, he would not allow it, but it would not be easy to keep her hidden from his enemies. And Laon Cour Son had many enemies in the palace.

XVII

His Excellency, the Commissioner of Culture and Trade for Lamon Utile was seated at the head of his table, at his breakfast when Laon walked in. The Curator of His Excellency's Establishment, an elderly Bhasi by the name of Murgh Perglin, was already there, standing on one side of the great long table that dominated the gaudy breakfast room of the palace. The Commissioner was speaking to him whilst cramming food into his jowly face, causing small pieces of half-masticated food to fly out and form a spray pattern on the table.

"…And secondly, Curator, I want you to double the guard in the grounds, not simulants mind, I want real people. I've heard rumours… Ah, Secretary, you are late."

Laon bowed imperceptibly and took up his position on the opposite side of the long table to the Curator. Neither acknowledged the other. "My apologies Excellency, I was detained by nature."

"What was I saying?"

"You've heard rumours, Excellency," said Murgh Perglin in his slow, nasal drawl.

"Yes, rumours, ugly rumours, so double the guard."

The Commissioner was always hearing rumours for there were many acquaintances happy to stoke his neurosis.

"Later today I am leaving for Barta Magnus and I do not know when I will be back. Secretary, you have the list of forthcoming trades. Be sure that you receive the full commission from each, no discounts. And I'm putting trades from Tarnus and its colonies up to three percent. I don't trust those fanatics. You're going to be busy, Secretary, so I am handing the procurement of my female staff over to the Curator. I have been disappointed in the last two purchases, Secretary. You lack an eye for women."

"Native women of quality are not easy to get, Excellency."

"Rubbish, we will see if the Curator can do better. Get rid of the older ones, it is time for new flesh."

"Yes Excellency," said Perglin, "I will not disappoint you."

"See that you don't, Curator. That is all."

The two men bowed simultaneously and withdrew. Perglin maintained his usual, impassive face, but Laon knew he was laughing inside. The Curator had just wrested another slice of power from him and diminished his influence at the palace. It was a small but significant victory and they both knew it.

Laon hurried back to his apartment and found Matty still in bed asleep. He prepared some food and placed it on the table then he went back to her and gently woke her.

"You must have been very tired Matty, you have slept a long time."

"I was Sir, and I have never been in a place like this."

"It is where you will stay for the time being. You must come and have some food and then I will show you how things work and where things are.

Matty sat at the polished table in Laon's kitchen and observed the overwhelming selection before her. She had never in her life witnessed such bounty and didn't know where to start. She looked questioningly at the smiling man opposite.

"What's the matter? Are you not hungry?"

"I am hungry, Sir. Is this all food?"

"Yes. Try some and see what you like."

Tentatively she took a small bread from the ornate plate in front of her. It was sweet and delicious, like nothing she had ever tasted before. Laon laughed at her wide-eyed reaction to the flavour of the bread. She was so open and uncomplicated, a delight to behold and a delight to be with. She ate hungrily, using her hands and he patiently showed her how to use the utensils before her.

"Do people eat this food all the time?"

"This is not special food, Matty, it is quite ordinary."

"It's lovely, I could eat it all."

"Well don't eat too much, it's not good for you and you'll get fat."

"Oh, no I won't, I don't like fat. My master was fat and I didn't like it at all."

"Did your master mistreat you?"

"No, not really. He used to hit me and call me names when he fucked me, but it didn't really hurt."

"Well, no one is going to mistreat you here, Matty, or call you names." He rose from the table. "I must go, I have work to do. I will come back soon."

He left her still munching at the various, unfamiliar delights he had provided and made his way to his office in another wing of the palace. His staff of six looked up in surprise when he entered; Laon was always there before them. He ignored them and went straight into his private office. There he ordered some female clothes to be delivered to his office, making sure that the source of the order could not be traced back to him, and then he went out to give his staff their instructions for the day.

XVIII

The Commissioner organized his establishment at the palace in such a way as to guarantee conflict and ill-feeling. Two rival departments, the Secretariat and the Household, vied for dominance over His Excellency's affairs, which he encouraged by deliberately overlapping their respective spheres of duty. In this way, he reasoned that each would act as a check on the other and neither would be able to cheat him out of his vast wealth. When he left for Barta Magnus, later that day, he was confident that each faction would carry out their duties with scrupulous diligence, since each could easily observe the other's activities.

Matty was now caught and became an unwitting central character in the web of palace intrigue that constantly dominated the lives of those within. Laon kept her secreted in his apartment, enjoying her company more and more as each day passed. Her innocence and simplicity were refreshing after the stultifying machinations of the palace and he enjoyed her undisguised wonder at the new things he had to teach her. She did not once complain about her confinement, she understood her position very well. She was entirely reliant on this man and his kindness and, although she was well aware of the inequality of the situation, she quickly developed a genuine affection towards him that was not primarily a function of her own self-interest.

Laon's pleasure at seeing her in his apartment was augmented by, what became for him, a consuming interest. Matty talked constantly about Jodi and about their history in the tropics and their time on the farm. Laon began to document her story and pressed her with increasing industry to confide every detail to him. In this way he became intimate with Jodi without ever having met him and he even made some cautious enquiries as to the boy's fate. Matty was understandably sketchy about the location of the farm, She knew that it was across some water, that it was cold there and the land was flat. Laon discovered the most likely location of the farm, but found that it had been wound up and sold off in parcels by its creditors and the records had disappeared. He did not press the matter any further and did not tell Matty he had made enquiries lest it raised her hopes unjustifiably.

The Commissioner was away for one hundred and twenty three days; this was not unusual for he was habitually absent from the palace for long periods. His interplanetary stature and prodigious appetite took him to far more exotic places than the unsophisticated backwater that was Ennepp. Whilst he was absent Murgh Perglin, the Curator, diligently carried out his new responsibility by personally making a trip to the tropical north and selecting three Native females for the Commissioner's collection. He brought them back and installed them in the harem with great satisfaction for they were both experienced and very young. Laon watched the process with interest. He suspected the Curator had made a serious mistake and he plotted a way to take full advantage of it.

But unfortunately, Laon had made a mistake himself. The procurement budget had been removed from his department before he was able to properly conceal the large sum he had paid to the Moontrader for Matty. He had secreted the payment in another account and three days before the return of the Commissioner, one of the Curator's meticulous bookkeepers discovered the discrepancy.

Perglin's cool exterior was almost breached at the joyful news and he began to dig deep into the affair. He found the original purchase from the procurement account but not a record of what was purchased. He found several orders for female clothing that did not go to the harem. He found out that Laon's consumption of food had more than doubled over the last one hundred and twenty days and reasoned that only one thing was possible, that the Secretary had bought a female and was keeping it in his private quarters. This surprised Perglin, for he was well aware that the Secretary's sexual proclivities did not lie in that direction and he searched his mind for some motivation that would cause his enemy to do such a thing. But, try as he might, he could find none and so resolved to bring the whole thing to light on the return of the Commissioner. The upstart, half-breed,

Laon Cour Son would be finally exposed and defeated and he, Murgh Perglin, would assume his rightful role as the head of the entire palace staff.

The Commissioner returned and the meeting in the grand breakfast room took place the next morning. As Laon reported the various trades that had taken place in His Excellency's absence, the great carcass sat impassively eating and swilling, taking in information on profits and food with greedy relentlessness. The Curator spoke next, reporting his success in the procurement of three new girls and giving various accounts of the activities of the palace. When he had finished the Commissioner nodded and waved them out of his presence. He was keen to see what the Curator had obtained for the harem, but Perglin forestalled him.

"Excellency, during your absence a serious discrepancy in the accounts has come to my attention."

The words 'discrepancy' and 'accounts' caused the Commissioner to stop eating and give his whole attention to the Curator. Laon felt the blood drain out of his face as he listened to his enemy begin his denouncement.

"A procurement was made just before you left, which was subsequently carefully buried in the accounts. I believe a female was purchased but not added to Your Excellency's staff."

The Commissioner turned his accusative gaze on Laon. "Secretary, explain."

Laon struggled for calm. "The Curator is right Excellency. I did purchase a female on your behalf, an exquisite creature, but very wild and quite untrained. I felt it necessary to keep her back until I had trained her…"

The Commissioner's face went dark red with rage; his temples began to throb visibly. "Where is she?" he bellowed.

"In my quarters," replied Laon weakly.

The Commissioner skewered him with a look of furious contempt. "Guard!" Two liveried heavies entered. "Take the Secretary's pass and go to his chambers. Bring me the female you find in there."

The guards rushed out, their heavy boots clattering on the polished, stone floor.

"Excellency, let me explain," started Laon, but the Commissioner was in no mood for explanations.

"I trusted you, Secretary, promoted you beyond your deserts and you repay me by keeping to yourself something of mine."

"Excellency, you know that I would not use your property for myself."

"Be quiet. Hell's gate knows what you had in mind. Training you say? You were training a native girl to do the very thing she was born to do. Do not insult me, Secretary. Do you take me for a cuckold?"

"No, Excellency, I thought I was acting in your best interests."

The Commissioner's great, fat fist thumped the table and made the breakfast plates jump into the air. "You don't decide what is in my best interest, Secretary, I do. And now I'm going to tell you something. It's in my best interest to bust you. You will work for the Curator here as his number three until the end of your contract, which I am holding you to, and you will move out of your fancy chambers and into accommodation befitting your post. Is that understood?"

Laon bowed unsteadily. "Yes Excellency."

"Curator, you will assume command of the Secretariat until further notice."

Perglin bowed stiffly, not daring to betray his triumph. "I will do my duty, Excellency."

The Commissioner was about to speak again when the great doors of the breakfast chamber opened and in walked Matty between two guards. She looked terrified but when she saw Laon she forced a smile. He did not smile back, but barely met her eye. She knew there was something very wrong.

The Commissioner stared at her in disbelief; even he had never seen anything quite so perfect. He turned angrily on Laon. "How much did she cost?"

Laon told him.

"Get out, all of you, leave the girl here."

Laon, Perglin and the two guards bowed and rapidly left the chamber leaving Matty standing bewildered and frightened, in the august presence of her owner. Laon caught her beseeching look but stared stonily ahead. His power was gone and he could do nothing for her now.

"I will allocate you quarters in the basement," said Perglin as the great doors closed behind them. "I believe there is a room free next to the generators. It is a little warm, but quite suitable."

Laon swallowed his bitterness. "Thank you Curator."

"No, from now on you will address me as 'Sir'."

XIX

The guards bursting through the doors to Laon's chambers gave Matty considerable alarm. She had not seen a soul other than Laon for over a hundred days and the sudden appearance of uniformed strangers meant only one thing to her. She was in deep trouble. She went with them meekly, along the bedecked corridors and into the presence of the man they called His Excellency, her new owner.

Laon was there too and another older man. She could see that His Excellency was cross with Laon and she felt sorry for him. She wanted to speak to him, to tell him not to worry about her, but His Excellency looked too angry she did not dare. Suddenly Laon and the older man and the two guards who had brought her, left the room and she was alone with the huge man at the table.

"Come closer," he commanded.

Tentatively she stepped one pace forward.

"Take off that dress," he said, drawing his mouth into an ugly leer.

She undid the dress and let it slip to the floor. His greedy eyes probed her young body.

"Has the man Laon Cour Son had sex with you?"

"No Sir."

The Commissioner visibly relaxed. "I thought not. He is not a true man."

"He was very kind to me, Sir."

"Kind!" The Commissioner spat the word as though it was a blasphemy. "It is not for the likes of you to receive kindness." He rose to his feet and allowed his ornate, saffron robe to part. Matty could not disguise horror at what she saw. The Commissioner's huge, bloated body was covered in thick, black hair to such a degree that hardly any of his pallid flesh was visible. His large, flabby genitals emerged like a grotesque stalactite from the folds of skin below his belly and dangled between his improbably skinny legs.

"What's the matter? Have you never seen a proper man before?" he said as he advanced on her, divesting himself of his gown.

Matty wanted to run, but she was frozen with fear and surprise at the sudden and unexpected advance. The mountain of flesh and hair bore down on her and she found herself pinned to the breakfast table, then hoisted on to it with her legs forced apart. A scream escaped her and she received a hard slap across the face and then the flesh began to envelope her, swallowing her into its folds. Her head swam and above her she could see the huge leering head of the Commissioner as he attempted to insert himself into her. In panic she tried to wriggle free but his weight crushed her, squeezing the breath from her. He was speaking to her but she could not make out what he was saying. Some saliva dropped from his lips on to her neck as he hauled himself up on to the table, pinning her down with his full weight, descending on her like a massive, deflating balloon. Desperately she tried to struggle as she felt the life being crushed from her body. He grabbed her hair and banged her head on the table. The remains of the breakfast danced and began to topple over, staining the polished surface with sugary fruit.

"Keep still, damn you," he bellowed as he grabbed her slender neck with one hand and reached down to insert himself into her with the other. But Matty hardly heard him; she was as at the edge of consciousness. Her arms flailed in panic until her hand found the cold metal of a two-pronged fork. She grabbed it and blindly swung it toward the jowly head of the Commissioner. The fork pierced clean through his cheek and buried itself into his tongue. He let out a great roar of pain as blood filled his mouth and began to dribble down his chin. In a paroxysm of surprised anger he grabbed Matty's head and banged it repeatedly on the table. She lost consciousness after the second blow, but he kept going until waves of pain overtook him and he lurched, naked, out of the breakfast chamber and into the corridor, holding the fork to his cheek and screaming at the shocked guard.

A physician was called and the Commissioner's cheek and tongue were repaired. Matty's unconscious body was removed and locked into a room in the palace basement to await her fate.

XX

"What will you do with the female, Sir?" Laon eyed his new boss furtively; he had been made to stand waiting while the Curator issued various orders to his staff.

Perglin shot him a dismissive glance. "That is no concern of yours, Cour Son."

"I brought her here Sir; I am responsible for what she did."

"I am glad you think so; it is the very thing I intend to press upon the Commissioner."

"Have a care Sir; the Commissioner may recall that it was you that brought her to his attention."

The Chief of the Household narrowed his wary eyes on his former adversary. "The Commissioner will not hold me responsible for this in any way."

"I am glad you are confident of that, Sir," replied Laon stiffly, knowing that he had sown the seed of doubt in the other man's mind. "Is the female badly damaged?"

"Concussed, nothing more."

"Has the Commissioner issued any orders regarding her?"

"None".

"Perhaps he believes he killed her."

"What are you driving at Man? I have no time for your nonsense or to worry about the fate of a Native whore."

"You are quite right Sir, I am sorry to have wasted your time. It's just that the Commissioner may believe he killed the female, a valuable commodity."

Perglin suddenly realized what Laon was intimating. "Do not try your tricks on me Cour Son, I am not a fool."

"Excuse me Sir, I did not mean to suggest anything, it's just that opportunities like this fall to the likes of us so rarely, perhaps never again. You have won our little battle, I freely acknowledge that, but think about it, you have worked for the Commissioner faithfully for over thirty years and what have you received for your loyalty and effort? All this time you have been surrounded by great wealth, but how much of it comes your way? Your salary, like mine is small, and your pension, when he has done with you, will not allow you even a small fraction of the life you have been used to here."

"Silence! You are a traitor. I have always known it."

"Maybe so, but consider this, you would have to work more than ten years to realize what that female could get you if you sold her in the right market. And I know where to sell her to get the most."

The Curator glared at him, "Get out, now."

Laon bowed and withdrew knowing that he had laid the fertile germ of an idea in Perglin's mind. He would be hearing from him again on the subject of Matty.

XXI

After two days' recuperation the Commissioner was recovered enough to visit his harem where he sampled the delights offered by the three new girls that the Curator had procured for him in the north. He was very pleased with them for they were polite and obliging and did not recoil at the sight of him. At their daily meeting the Curator, by way of a reminder of the former secretary's transgression, could not resist asking if he had experienced the girls and was he satisfied with the acquisition.

"They are acceptable, but not special," was the Commissioner's non-committal reply, but knowing that he never passed compliments, Perglin was satisfied with this. Since the meeting was at an end, he bowed and went to take his leave, but the Commissioner forestalled him with another question.

"The vicious whore that attacked me, where is she?"

The Curator hesitated imperceptibly, his heart beat rose and he plunged into deception that Laon had suggested two days before. "Her skull was broken Excellency, she died soon afterwards. I disposed of the body discreetly."

"It is as well. You may go now, Curator."

While this conversation was taking place, its subject was sitting on the floor of a dark, windowless room in the basement of the palace. She had been brought down to the room, naked and unconscious, two days earlier, but she had no idea how long she had been unconscious or how long she had been in the room. She lost all sense of time as she lay curled up on the hard floor awaiting her fate. She expected to die; it was only natural after what she had done to the Master. Now she just wished they would come for her and get it over with.

She was asleep when the door eventually opened and a dim light crept into the room from the corridor outside. She opened her eyes and saw Laon in the doorway. He stepped forward and took her naked form in his arms.

"Are you alright, my dear child? I am sorry I could not protect you."

"I am alright," she replied weakly, clutching on to him. "Am I to die now?"

"No child, you are not to die, you are going to be taken away from this place."

Matty noticed another man standing in the light of the doorway. It was the same man she had seen in the room before His Excellency attacked her. He was old but he was staring at her in a lascivious way.

"Put these on quickly," said Laon, producing a small, white dress and some slippers from a bag slung across his back. She obeyed and soon the three of them were hurrying down deserted corridors from which the guards had been dismissed for the night byPerglin. It was a balmy night in the fragrant palace garden where Laon's vehicle rested in the secluded spot he had once enjoyed. Now it was at the disposal of the Curator and it was in that that they rose above the thousands of burning torches floating on the lakes, the gaudy turrets of the palace, aglow in the golden fire and the vast, ornate park and Matty saw them for the last time.

They flew south east, over an arm of the Great Sea and headed toward Zurat, a town on the coast about five hundred kilometres away, where they were to meet the contact that Laon had arranged, an intimidating Moontrader who he had dealt with before. Perglin had expressed misgivings about the rendezvous; Zurat was a run-down place, notorious for all manner of illicit and violent activity, but Laon had simply told him that it was the Moontrader's choice of venue, take it or leave it.

"You know, of course, that I don't trust you, Cour Son. I should warn you that I have made provisions against any treachery you may envisage."

"I would expect nothing less, Sir. We are enemies, but in this matter we share a mutual benefit. You will gain financially and with the ten percent we agreed, so will I and I will have the satisfaction of seeing Matty moved on rather than killed. We all benefit."

"I am intrigued by your obsession with this female. You are a homosexual, so it could not be a matter of lust and yet you risked everything to keep her to yourself."

Laon turned and looked at Matty who was sitting at the back of the transport, staring distractedly out of the window. "I can't answer that, I am not sure what prompted me to do it. Perhaps there is something in us that makes us protective of children."

"A Native and hardly a child."

"She is fourteen and whatever her race, she is still a child."

"You bleeding heart compassionates, you will never rule."

"Perhaps not, but we sleep better at night."

"I assure you, I sleep well enough."

They landed in a large dusty square on the edge of the town where bedraggled, low mansions spoke of glories long since passed. Meagre lamps lit a few shrivelled trees that clung to the soil with gnarled, searching roots. A fine drizzle had just started to fall. Laon and the Curator secured Matty in the vehicle and made their way through the dark streets to the rendezvous.

"I do not like this place," complained the older man, his eyes darting nervously into the shadows.

Laon was not comfortable himself but he kept his face stony calm. A few unsavoury-looking locals gave them curious glances, discomforting the Curator even more. He was in a cold sweat by the time they turned into a low, dingy bar where a few patrons lounged in various states of intoxication. Laon ordered two strong wines and they took their seats in a dark corner of the room.

"Why here?" whispered Perglin. "He could have chosen a thousand places better than this."

Laon observed the obvious discomfort of his enemy with quiet pleasure. He was about to become a lot more discomforted. "I told you, they dictate the place of meeting, it is always so."

"And you know this man?"

"I have dealt with him before. He is the only Moontrader on Ennepp at this moment. We cannot be too fussy."

"I don't like it; I don't like it at all."

"Do you wish to renege?"

"No... No, of course not. And remember, I will do the talking."

"As you wish, Sir."

They fell into an uneasy silence, feeling the eyes of the other patrons upon them. The Moontrader was late and as the minutes passed Perglin became more and more agitated. He pulled out his ornate timepiece and consulted it.

"Put that away," hissed Laon. "Are you trying to get us killed?"

The Curator stuffed it away quickly, but a heavy, unshaven man rose from a chair nearby and sauntered over.

"Strangers," he mumbled.

"We meet with Salex Contran," said Laon.

The man's eyes widened and he nodded resignedly and returned to his chair but continued to stare. After some moments more a man entered the bar. He was of average height but heavily muscled beneath a loose drapery of white cloth. His head was entirely obscured with more wound cloth except for a slit from which two dark, murderous eyes stared. He walked directly to their table and sat down abruptly.

"Where is the merchandise?" His voice was like a rasp.

The Curator was so alarmed at the sight of the man that he could hardly speak. "It... it is in my vehicle... quite near."

"What use is that to me? Are you wasting my time?"

"I have a picture..."

The Curator fumbled in his pocket and instantly found that a large weapon had appeared from nowhere and was levelled on a spot between his eyes.

He quietly wet himself. "It's just a picture," he stammered and offered it to the Moontrader with a shaking hand.

The man lowered his weapon, took it and glanced briefly at it. It was an image of Matty, naked. He narrowed his eyes on the old man. "This is a child."

"No... No, she is at least fourteen."

"And does she show naked pictures of you around?"

Perglin was now both confused and frightened; the conversation had taken a potentially unpleasant turn. "No," he whispered hoarsely.

The Moontrader crumpled the image in his large hand and handed it back to the Curator. Then he took out a tablet and scribbled a figure on it. "This is what I will pay," he said.

The Curator looked at the figure, it was less than a tenth of what they were expecting but he was in no condition to bargain with this man. "Agreed," he stammered dejectedly.

XXII

While the one-sided deal was being struck, Matty sat in the transport wondering what was to befall her now. She trusted Laon but it was clear that he had lost his power to protect her and she was now in the hands of the older man. She was being traded again, that much she understood, and she was powerless to command her own destiny. She had to accept whatever was coming her way.

She stared out of the window at the bleak, rain-soaked square. The hour was late but a few stragglers were about. An old man entered the square some distance away, shuffling slowly from one side to the other. He was ill-kempt and stooping and trailed from his hand a long length of chain which was attached to a collar around the neck of a figure that followed him at some distance. The second figure was a boy, emaciated and ragged and carrying a heavy load. As she watched their slow progress, a strong sense of familiarity stirred in her. She gazed more intently, her eyes straining against the darkness and rain, until they passed below one of the meagre lights. And then she saw the face of the boy at the end of the rope. The boy was Jodi.

XXIII

When the three men returned to the vehicle they found Matty curled on the floor, still crying inconsolably. She had banged on the window and tried to get out of the locked vehicle to no avail and the man and boy had passed out of the square only fifty metres from her.

"What is the matter with that whore now?" said Perglin angrily. He was still smarting from a very real sense of shame at the price he had just agreed with the Moontrader. He suspected that Laon and the man had come to a private arrangement, but he did not dare suggest it in front of the Trader.

Laon knelt and took Matty in his arms, listening as she spluttered and told him that she had just seen Jodi and how terrible he looked.

"You must have been deceived, Matty," said Laon gently. "The night is dark and it is raining; it is easy to make mistakes."

"No," she insisted, "it was him. He looked so thin and ill. You must help him, say you will help him."

"I will do my best to find him. I promise. Now you must go with this man, he is your new master."

Through tear-blurred eyes Matty beheld the figure of the man who now possessed her. He looked rather frightening. "No, I want to stay with you, I want to find Jodi. Please don't send me away."

"Do not be afraid, Matty. You will be better off with this man, I assure you."

Salex Contran quietly observed the weeping girl in the arms of his co-conspirator. Laon had not played him false, she was stunning and the promise that Laon had extracted from him would not be hard to keep. He stepped forward and shot a tranquilliser into her. She instantly went limp and he bent down, picked her up and slung her limp body over his shoulder as though she was weightless. With a barely perceptible nod to Laon, he was gone into the night.

The moment he was gone, the Curator rounded on Laon. "You have deceived me for the last time, I will not forget this."

"You are a fool. You allowed the man to intimidate you into a ludicrous deal, which has cost us both dear. You should have allowed me to negotiate, you are not competent."

"Do not try to bluster your way out. I know what you did. You are the fool, getting sentimental over a Native whore."

"It was you who made the deal, not I. You were free to say no, nobody forced you."

The Curator treated him to a murderous scowl and climbed into his seat. The journey back to the palace was conducted in resentful silence.

XXIV

Ten days after the sale of Matty to the Moontrader, His Excellency the Commissioner for Trade and Culture to Lamon Utile, was preparing to leave for another extended absence, when he became giddy and had to take to his bed. The physician was called and the hulk examined whereupon a small irregular lump was found on the underside of his penis. After extensive tests the doctor delivered his verdict.

"I regret to tell you, you have contracted the tropical strain of Croman's Syndrome, Excellency."

"What! You're lying, that is not possible."

"I'm sorry, the tests are positive, there is no doubt."

The Commissioner let out an enormous, guttural wail. "How is it possible?"

"It is endemic in the Native population where it is passed through the females during anal intercourse. You have come into contact with a carrier."

A grim realization now hit the Commissioner. His face twisted into a vision of fury. "Guard," he screamed, quite alarming the doctor. A liveried man rushed in. "Get the Curator up here." He then turned to the doctor. "Is there no cure?"

"None, it is a Native disease; no research has been done to my knowledge."

The Commissioner's jowly head bowed and he studied his enormous girth resignedly. "And what is the prognosis? How soon am I to die?"

"In men, the genitals and brain are attacked. You will gradually loose higher brain function. Your genitals will blacken and rot and will have to be removed, the sooner the better."

"How long before this kills me?"

"It varies; the average is about two years."

The Commissioner seemed calm when the Curator entered the room. Perglin was visibly shocked at the sight of his boss lying on his bed entirely naked. He exchanged a nervous glance with the physician.

"Come in Curator," said the Commissioner. "I want you to come here and look at this."

Perglin advanced tentatively. "Excellency."

"Take a look at my cock, Curator."

"Excellency, I..."

"Look at it," snapped the Commissioner.

The Curator reluctantly peered down at the oversized member.

"What do you see?"

"Your... your thingy, Excellency."

"Lift it up."

"Sir?"

"Lift it up, I tell you."

Gingerly, Perglin took the copious foreskin between his forefinger and thumb and lifted the thing. Straight away he saw the irregular, black growth that had appeared on the underside.

"Do you see it, Curator? Your handiwork."

"I don't understand."

"Well perhaps you understand this." With surprising speed and sudden ferocity the Commissioner kicked his employee in the stomach with the ball of his foot. The old man was sent sprawling and sliding across the polished stone floor. "Guard," bellowed the Commissioner. Two guards rushed in, "Get this man out of my house. Escort him to the gate now. He is to take nothing with him, nothing, do you hear me?"

The Curator was picked up and practically dragged from the room. He was set outside the gate with nothing but the clothes he was wearing. His savings and small pension were seized and confiscated. In a moment, everything he had worked over thirty years for was stripped from him. He was left with nothing and it was going to be a long walk to town.

When he had recovered some semblance of equilibrium the Commissioner sent for Laon. By the time he arrived in the state bedchamber, the doctor had left and the Commissioner was sitting in his bed beneath a finely worked cover.

"Secretary, I have decided to reinstate you with all your former privileges."

"Your Excellency is most gracious," said Laon, somewhat surprised.

"You are an able man and I always intended to reinstate you. Your demotion was to teach you a lesson. I trust you have learned it well."

"Your Excellency is quite correct and you were justified in what you did."

"I know. Now a situation has arisen. The Curator has been dismissed."

Laon raised his eyebrows in surprise. His heart leapt. "I see."

"The whores he procured were not screened and now I have Croman's Syndrome."

Laon realized instantly what that meant. He also knew that the mistake he suspected the Curator had made during the purchase of the three new Native women, had worked to his advantage sooner than he expected. He suspected the Curator had neglected to screen the women he had bought, foolishly relying on the word of a trader as to their health. Croman's Syndrome was just one of a large number of infections carried by Native women, but it was the only one that was fatal. "I am sorry to hear that, Excellency."

"No you are not. We are both men, let us be frank. You do not like me and I have little time for you, but you do your job well and I recognize that. You are cunning and ambitious and those are attributes I can use. You will take charge of the Household as well as your own department."

"Thank you, but Your Excellency will require more of me as time goes on."

"You are ambitious, Cour Son, what are you proposing?"

"You will need a deputy, Sir."

The Commissioner stared at him malignly and Laon realized he had gone too far. Then the man's face suddenly relaxed into a resigned scowl. "Very well, the appointment will be ratified in the next dispatch to Lamon Utile."

"Thank you Excellency."

"Now get out, I wish to be alone now."

Laon gave a low bow and with the greatest of difficulty stopped himself from skipping and dancing out of the room. He had everything he wanted now, except Matty, whom he could not get back while the Commissioner was still sensible. He could not risk another confrontation with his boss over Matty, but, as for her brother, that was a different matter. Had she really seen him crossing that drab square in Zurat? Or was it just her vivid imagination and the darkness playing tricks on her eyes? Before he closed the door to the Commissioner's bedchamber he had resolved to find out.

XXV

Salex Contran took Matty to his ship and placed her in a stasis pod while she was still unconscious. Thus she left Ennepp for good without seeing the bright, blue curve of the planet disappear into the black distance of space. It was Salex's intention to put her up for auction at an obscure moon base in the region controlled by Barta Magnus where he knew he would realize the maximum return. His promise to Laon, that she would not be sold into depravity, had not been sworn, so he felt himself free to seek the best price he could, regardless of the girl's fate. But, before attending to the sale of Matty, he first had an arms trade to complete on Tarnus.

Salex knew full well that he was heading into a war zone but he was young and confident of his ability and the potential for profit was considerable. He had an acute sense of danger and had always been able to assess the potential of a situation before his opponents and thus, avoid trouble by reacting first. Now, seated across the desk from the smiling General and surrounded by five guards, he could sense that he had walked into a trap.

"Of course we will have to see the merchandize before we part with any money," said the General.

"I am a Moontrader, my word is good enough," replied Salex.

"This is Tarnus, Comrade; we do things a little differently here. I know you are a man of your word, but I answer to my superiors. I have to personally verify that the weapons are as described." The General was still smiling, but his eyes were glazed with hate.

"You know that I cannot allow access to them until they are paid for."

"That is very unfortunate because I'm afraid I'm going to insist."

Salex cursed himself; he had always known that selling into a war zone was likely to be dangerous, but the profit had tempted him. He had rashly landed his craft and now he realized that this man wasn't going to let him go. He let a silence fall as he steeled himself. Seemingly without moving a muscle, he initiated a predetermined instruction to his ship and then he acted.

He killed the General first, then he got three of the guards before the last two brought him down in their cross fire. He killed four people in that war bunker, but they were not the last people Salex Contran killed for he left behind a token of his revenge.

XXVI

When the soldiers arrived to strip Salex's ship of its cargo and anything else they could find, they were being watched. They quickly found the large stash of arms on the vessel and made ready to carry them off while impassive lenses looked on. Salex's last instruction had been specific and when the first box of weapons was lifted from its housing, a chain reaction began in the heart of the vessel. The life pod containing Matty in stasis was launched and sprang from the craft with sudden force. It travelled for over ten kilometres and came to rest on a tract of wasteland on the far side of the city. Moments later the sky above the city lit up as though a new sun had been created. Nothing within three kilometres of Salex's vessel survived.

XXVII

Matty left the life pod and wandered toward the city in a daze. She had no idea where she was, but she saw lights in the distance and knew that was the way she should go. The place was unfamiliar and the air smelled strange, but, in her singular mind, it had to be the town where she had seen Jodi. She pressed on and soon came to the war-torn city where she began to search for her brother.

She met Corhaden two days later. She was hungry and wet from wandering the streets and combing the ruins. He found her sleeping while he was scavenging in a recently damaged building. He took one look at her and saw, under the grime, what he had found. He praised his luck and took her home.

There, in his dingy basement he fed her and laid out his plans, telling her they would be partners and that he could get her plenty of business. She listened to the man too tired to care what he was saying. He bought her a nice new dress and tidied up the dingy basement in anticipation of 'the guests', as he called them. It was Corhaden who explained to her where she was; that she was a long way from Jodi, on a different world entirely. At first she had refused to accept his word but finally he persuaded her of its truth and cajoled her to cooperating with his plan.

Her first client was a young soldier, no more than eighteen. His body was slim and muscular, like Jodi's had been on the shore of the inland sea on that wonderful day by the water. He smelled of the barracks, of stale sweat and oil, but she didn't mind for he did not stay long on top of her or inside her. When he had finished he grinned shyly and gave her money. She took it and held it in her hand, staring down at it as though it was something alien and marvellous at the same time. Money could buy anything. Money could get her back to Ennepp, back to Jodi.

She looked up at the soldier and her eyes suddenly filled with joy. And then she began to laugh.

PART SIX

HYPERION

I

The drab, basaltic mass of the volcanic plain loomed in the darkness. In this remote part of the galaxy there were fewer stars to light the sky and the distant sun was yet to crest the craggy horizon. The cruiser had come to rest finally, after almost five years, at the base of a bulbous nose of solidified magma, about sixty metres in height, which formed the stark edge of the flow that had covered the chamber and destroyed the mineralogical mission over one hundred and twenty thousand years ago. At the base of the cliff was a small opening, just large enough for a man to crawl into. This was the entrance to a shaft that struck into the cliff and tunnelled below the magma field, to where the ancient chamber had remained hidden for thousands of years.

A ramp was lowered from the belly of the cruiser and two figures emerged. They were swaddled in suits and cowls that clung to their bodies and a dark mask that obscured their features. Each figure glowed with the aura generated by the survival belt around their waists. The thin atmosphere on the fourth planet of the star KT153/2739 was toxic and the temperature outside the ship was minus one hundred and fifty three degrees.

Bru and Jun moved slowly towards the shaft entrance, their bodies working hard against the elevated gravitational pull of the planet. The conditions were extremely hostile to life; quite apart from the freezing temperature and absence of air, there was the presence of a lethal degree of radiation seeping from the rocks below and around them. This made communication almost impossible unless the subjects were in close proximity. Elan and Matty observed them from the bridge of the cruiser as Bru led the way, followed by the slighter figure of Jun.

At the entrance of the tunnel, they knelt down and Bru shone a lantern into the darkness. The circular shaft was smooth sided and struck down into the basalt at a shallow angle. About fifty metres in they could just make out the entrance to the chamber that had held the casket safe for so many millennia.

"I'll go first," said Jun.

Bru nodded; it was going to be a tight squeeze for someone of his size. He watched as Jun pushed the lantern into the tunnel and began to crawl in after it. He let the boy gain a few metres then followed him.

His progress was uncomfortable and slow as his shoulders rubbed along the wall of the tunnel. He experienced the rising panic of claustrophobia as he edged deeper and deeper into the rock and he was seized by the urgent need to back up and get out of there. He stopped and quelled the impulse and concentrated on the rear end of his student disappearing into the gloom. The thought of being bested by Jun spurred him and he pressed on.

Jun had changed. Even an individual as emotionally obtuse as Bru could not mistake that. In the six days since they had emerged from stasis he had become furtive and secretive and even more reticent than usual. He seemed to be spending a great deal of time in the company of Matty, a fact that somewhat mystified Bru as he could not ascribe any sensible reason to it. Matty and Jun were poles apart in character and intellect; what could they possibly have to discuss? Very little, he had concluded, but it was nevertheless interesting that a Suran was able to tolerate company to such a degree.

Up ahead the progress of Jun's rear end suddenly stopped and he let out an expletive that would have embarrassed a Tarnus soldier.

Bru froze; he had never heard such language from a Suran. "What's the matter?"

Jun choked out the words, they crackled into Bru's ear. "Bodies… in there."

"Bodies! How many?"

"I don't know, a few."

"You have to go in Jun, I can't back up. Go ahead, I'm right behind."

He emerged from the tunnel and into a precisely fashioned chamber about seven metres by five. The walls, ceiling and floor were like polished obsidian, where the rock had been melted to form the shape of the tomb. In the ceiling the circular remains of the original entrance was blocked with a magma plug and on the floor beneath a small stalagmite of solidified rock had formed. He found Jun standing near one wall staring at the macabre sight of five human beings in various contorted poses, lying on the floor of the chamber. Their bodies were twisted with the final, brief agony as death had claimed them, one by one, as their survival belts failed and their bodies had frozen as they had suffocated.

Bru and Jun exchanged glances.

"Attor never mentioned his crew," said Bru at length.

"Why did he leave them here?"

"I don't know."

"How long do you think they survived?"

"For as long as they chose to live. They would have died of thirst a long time before their belts failed."

"That's terrible; inhuman. He just left them here to die."

Bru nodded. "So it would seem." He stepped over one of the corpses and began to examine the chamber wall.

"He just left them here," repeated Jun; he was staring intensely at the corpses, fixated by them. Bru turned and noticed the look on his face; it was a strange confluence of revulsion and fascination. The boy had seen death before, the soldier and Corhaden on Tarnus, but he had never seen the evidence of prolonged death throes and the sight seemed to be having a profound effect on him. Bru quickly realized that he would be ineffective in any objective investigation of the site and interrupted his view by standing in front of him.

"Go back to the ship Jun, tell them what we have found. I don't think there is anything more for you to do here, but I will take a look around."

"You shouldn't be here alone, something might happen. You won't be able to communicate."

"I'll be alright. I won't be long; just give me an hour."

"What are you going to do with them?"

"There's nothing we can do. We would have to dismember them to get them out of here and then what would we do with them? No, let them stay here; it is a fitting tomb."

Jun took a last look at the ghastly sight and climbed back into the tunnel. Bru watched as his feet disappeared into the blackness; then he turned his attention to the five bodies arrayed on the floor of the chamber. They were clad in the grey, protective suits normally worn in hostile environments and the name of the wearer was etched on the chest of each. They were all male; all about thirty years old and fair-skinned. He noted the name of each man as he inspected the corpses; he would eventually have to inform the authorities of their deaths. He recalled his former student, Attor, bright-eyed and eager to learn and thought ruefully of what he had become. What sort of monster would leave men to die like this? It occurred to Bru that he might have had something to do with it. After all, it was he who had influenced the young man and sown in him the seeds of an obsession that would eventually drive him to madness. But Bru was not an individual much given to flights of self-doubt; he dismissed the idea from his mind and turned his attention to an inspection of the chamber itself.

In the wall opposite the tunnel entrance he found what he was looking for; the outline of the door to the cavity that had housed the casket, almost invisible in the reflective blackness of the rock. He took a tool from his belt and prised at the wall. The door eased forward and out of its snug housing to reveal the small niche that had been so carefully hewn into the rock. He stared into the empty blackness, imagining the thoughts of his former student on beholding the casket for the first time. Was it that which had finally sent him over the edge of sanity? Was it the realization that his obsession had finally born fruit and was, at last, vindicated?

Bru stared into the cavity and gave himself over to long reflection.

II

Brother Dax emerged from the stasis pod and walked stiffly to the bridge of his small vessel. He had set it to follow the signature of his cruiser and to only revive him when the vessel finally stopped moving. On four occasions during his long journey he had been revived only to see the vessel still moving away from the home region. As it passed into ever more remote space he had begun to doubt his reason and to wonder what manner of enemy he had encountered. He found it necessary to ask the Prophet for guidance, and each time the Prophet had spoken to him and commanded that the infidels must be pursued and destroyed.

Now he knew, after all this time and all this distance, that his prayers had been answered. The vessel had finally stopped moving and he was closing in on his quarry. He focused on his instruments and was shocked. He had been in stasis for almost five years and was now in a region of the galaxy far beyond the reach of civilization.

He checked the tracker. The cruiser was orbiting the fourth planet of a star designated KT153/2739 and he was now less than a day behind them. He forced a thin smile to his lips as he thought of the fate of the infidels and the revenge he would bring down upon their unworthy heads.

He rose unsteadily and made his way from the bridge to the small cabin furnished with an altar. Here he gave thanks for his deliverance and made libation. Then he disrobed and, taking up the ornate knife that lay cushioned on a pillow before him, he drew a new chevron into his flesh above the others, starting at the base of his penile stump and carving up to his waist on both sides. Blood seeped from the wound, ran down to his groin and flowed from the stump. It dripped into a bowl he had placed between his legs, while he closed his eyes, recited incantations and avowed his faith. He staunched the flow of blood with a tincture that burned his skin and made him grit his teeth in agony; then he picked up the bowl and drank the blood.

This time he was sure that the Prophet was on his side. The infidels would soon be burning in the fires of retribution.

III

Commander Elan had little expectation of what they would find on the fourth planet of star KT153/2739. She had enough sense to realize that Bru's former pupil would have removed anything valuable to their cause and that they were likely to find very little that would assist them. But, as Bru had pointed out, they had to start their search somewhere and this was as good a place as any. Also, he was anxious to see the original hiding place of the casket for academic reasons and to document the site in a proper scientific way. She acquiesced in this, allowing him to dictate the agenda whilst, at the same time, making it clear that she would make the final decisions. Bru had deferred graciously and she knew that there would be no trouble between them as long as they had an agreed purpose.

Elan was a woman of strong opinions who had escaped a loathed servitude at the hands of men. As a young woman her sexuality had been subverted by the mistreatment she had received at the hands of her husband and now, as she approached middle age, her waning libido diminished her suppressed needs to almost nothing. With his Suran manners and intelligence she had found in Bru a perfect soulmate and with every encounter she was allowing herself to be more impressed. Towards her he seemed civil and, for a Suran, quite gregarious. He did not even seem resentful of the way he had been treated on Tarnus and had been diplomatic on the one occasion she had brought up the subject.

Toward Jun she maintained a careful distance. There was something unfathomably odd about him. He was silent and secretive and she could not read him at all. At first she put it down to his androgynous characteristics but when she had mentioned this to Bru he had raised an eyebrow and said, "Jun is not androgynous, he is male," and then added enigmatically, "he is not typical and has quite a lot to be secretive about."

Elan's relationship with Matty was non-existent. During their journey she had hardly exchanged a word with the girl. She regarded her as a simpleton and assessed that they would have little in common. But lately, she had noticed that Matty and Jun were spending time in each other's company and her curiosity was piqued.

As they sat together on the bridge watching the two figures disappear into the tunnel, she addressed herself to the young girl.

"You seem to be spending a lot of time with that young Suran."

"I like him," replied Matty with innocent simplicity.

"'Him'? How do you know that Jun is male?"

Colour rose in Matty's cheeks as she searched for a reply. "He told me he was."

"Surans don't discuss their gender."

"What do you mean?"

"I mean that Surans are ideally neither male nor female, it is a subject that they do not talk about."

"Doctor Bru is male, isn't he?"

"Yes, Doctor Bru is male, but he is not a typical Suran. Jun, on the other hand, looks like a Suran. I don't believe he would have told you what gender he was. Have you been spying on him Matty?"

"No," she replied with some warmth.

"Then you have still not answered my question."

"Do I have to answer? I don't think you should be asking me these things."

"As your commander I should know everything that occurs on this ship. Are you in love with that Suran?"

Matty bowed her head and whispered her reply. "Yes."

"Foolish girl, he cannot return your love."

"That's not true," she protested. "He does."

Elan fixed her with a look of surprise. "Do you mean he has actually, physically joined with you?"

"Yes, he has."

"Good Lord! That is a surprise. You are to be congratulated Matty, you are probably the only human being in the universe to have seduced a Suran."

With that, Elan burst into laughter. Matty had never seen her so much as smile and the howls of laughter coming from the older woman seemed a little incongruous. She giggled nervously at the prospect, aware that she had betrayed Jun and their secret.

Commander Elan's eyes were watering with mirth and she did not perceive that they had been joined on the bridge by a third person until a man's voice cut her short.

"I am happy to find you in a state of gladness."

She swung around and was confronted by the blood-draining sight of Brother Dax. She heard Matty scream, but she found herself struck dumb with shock and surprise.

"Did you think you could best me, Magred DeCorrone? Oh yes, I know your name. You told me yourself you are a daughter of Kagan, how ironic that we are cousins from the same noble clan. You, however, chose to murder your husband, a priest, and flee to a life of dissolution and corruption. You are an apostate."

Elan found her tongue. "How did you find us?"

"Simple enough, by the grace of Minnar, the Great Prophet, I was guided here."

"There is a tracker in this vessel?"

Dax nodded solemnly. "It seems the great Doctor Bru does not think of everything."

She glanced past him toward the entrance to the bridge.

A shadowy smile touched his face. "Do not concern yourself, I know where the Suran infidels are, they will soon be burning in Hell."

"I should have killed you myself, not left it to Fallon."

"The Captain, it turns out, was a believer; unlike you, Magred DeCorrone."

Elan held his intense gaze, her brain desperately searching for any means of defence. She knew that he had come to kill them all and, like some monstrous automaton, no quantity of reasoning would deter him. "I am a daughter of Kagan," she said rising slowly.

"You are no more than the most despised speck of dust."

He drew his ornate sword from his gown and advanced towards Elan. Matty screamed and with the consummate skill of an advanced practitioner, Dax silenced her with a blow that slashed across her body, slicing her open across the midriff. Matty began to fall, clutching at the wound while blood spurted between her fingers. Elan seized the moment of distraction and launched herself at the Evangelist, digging her nails into his cheek. But Dax was too swift and his blade too sharp. He brought the sword up sharply, almost severing her right arm just below the elbow. She reeled back with a gasp, clutching her arm as Dax advanced on her. She slipped and fell to the floor as she retreated and then he was upon her, pinning her down with his foot.

"Curse you and your kind," she screamed as he slowly drove the point of the sword into her throat, filling her last words with blood that gushed from her mouth and from the wound. He held himself over her, his eyes boring into hers as life deserted them. He did not speak; there was nothing that he could say to save the soul of an apostate such as she. She was on her way to Hell and the first part of his work was done.

He became aware of moaning. The young whore was not yet dead. She was bleeding badly from the deep gash across her body and would not last long. *Let her suffer*, he thought. The ghost of a smile passed across his face and he reached into his gown and withdrew the small, grey cube he had obtained on Agon. It had been reinstructed to obey only him now. It was the only device capable of defeating the complex safety mechanisms of the deep space cruiser and the irony of the use of their own technology against the infidel Surans gave him an unworthy shiver of pleasure. He was about to initiate the sequence when it occurred to him that Doctor Bru had not suffered long enough down in the black hole and so the sequence should be delayed. This pause led him to another revelation; one that he had not expected to discover. He did not want to die!

As he hesitated he reasoned that the Prophet must have other work for him and although he could never go back to Kagan, he could still be His servant in the struggle against iniquitous lies and devilry. Four hours would be enough to get clear and what was four hours in the span of everlasting life? He set the sequence and the clock began to run down. Finally, with one last glance at the body of the apostate, Elan and the bleeding, prone figure of the Whore, he left the bridge and headed for the air lock. Soon the Suran devils would be destroyed and the whole site would be dust.

IV

Jun emerged from the blackness of the tunnel just as the distant sun crested the horizon. Its weak light flooded the land with a brutal, angular luminescence that danced on the smooth hulk of the nearby ship. He was glad to be out in the open again, away from the ghoulish scene in the claustrophobic chamber. He made his way across the dusty ground and soon reached the ship, ascending the ramp that gave access to the belly of the vessel. Inside the airlock he removed the survival belt and opened the inner door. Once inside he made his way to his own quarters and stripped off the uncomfortable, close-fitting suit and cap that had protected his skin from the high levels of radiation in the rocks. He placed the suit in the decontaminator and stepped in after it, staying there for longer than was normal to make sure he was not irradiated. He noticed his naked form in the reflective walls of the unit and smiled. How foolish he had been to regard himself as a freak. All those years of misery and shame were wasted years; a time before the happiness he now felt; a different life.

Finally he emerged from the unit and dressed himself in the clothes that he had inherited from Corhaden on Tarnus and then, anticipating the pleasure of seeing her, he set off for the bridge.

No manner of event and no stretch of time would ever wipe from his memory the vision that awaited him there. At first he could not comprehend what lay before him, and then he heard the faint murmur issue from the mouth of the dying girl. He ran over and, gently raising her, cradled her in his arms while her blood-soaked clothes stained his.

"Matty… Matty," he implored her to come back to him, but she had lost too much blood and was barely conscious.

He kissed her face and his tears soaked her soft, olive skin and he heard the faint sound of the last words she spoke.

"Jodi, is that you?"

V

Solon Bru was still minutely inspecting the chamber wall opposite the tunnel entrance when he sensed that he was no longer alone. He turned, expecting to see that Jun had returned for some reason, but it was not the figure of his student that confronted him.

"Where is the other infidel? I saw you both enter here."

Bru was so surprised that he did not properly register the immediate danger. He stood still, regarding Dax believing his eyes had deceived him.

"Speak up, where is the other Suran?"

Bru noticed the weapon aimed at his midriff and gathered his wits. He pointed to the body of Attor's crewmember lying nearest him.

Dax glanced down. "Lies; who are these infidels?"

"Seekers of truth; like myself."

"They are fools. Where is the other Suran?"

"As you see, he is not here."

"No matter, I will deal with that devil later. You seem surprised; did I not warn you that you cannot escape judgement? Did you not realize that the Prophet watches over his disciples? The Lord Minnar will not be denied."

Bru noticed that Dax was wearing the crude cloth of the Brotherhood and had neglected to protect himself from the high levels of radiation present in the chamber. He was a walking corpse. "I am surprised; I did not expect to see you. I did not expect Sergeant Fallon to be so inefficient."

"That person is addressing himself to his unworthy ancestors."

"What have you done with the women?"

"The Apostate Elan DeCorrone is dead by my sword and the Whore soon will be."

"This is monstrous."

"They will suffer an eternity of torment and you will soon join them."

"And all this hatred and carnage is done in the name of the Prophet and to protect the words of a man whose testament was written over two thousand years ago."

"Do not speak of Him. Your lips are the lips of a devil."

"Look about you, Brother Dax; open your eyes. You are standing in a place created over one hundred and twenty thousand years ago by men like us."

"Fool; can you not see how our faith is tested?"

"I see only superstition and blindness."

"Then I pity you. You Surans will never know the glory of His truth."

"I prefer the glories of science and reason."

Dax smiled. "That is your loss. You have been a worthy adversary, Doctor Bru. I never expected you to recant your blasphemy. Soon this place will be dust and truth will be restored."

The smile faded and the weapon was levelled at his head. Bru knew he was going to die at that moment. He braced himself and closed his eyes. But the scorching, searing pain hit him in the top of his left leg. He screamed and collapsed to the floor.

Dax advanced and stood over him. "You will take a long time to die, Doctor Bru, and you will die knowing exquisite agony as is befitting your offence. I know you will not remove your survival belt as Surans cannot destroy life, most particularly not their own, so you will be trapped here in this perfidious place until it becomes dust by my hand and with the grace of the Prophet."

Through pain-watered eyes Bru saw the look of triumph in Dax's eyes and then the Evangelist abruptly turned and climbed back into the tunnel. He looked down at the shattered flesh of his leg. The wound was extensive and ugly but not fatal as the blast had sterilized and sealed his arteries. But the suit was breached and now radiation would begin its attack and for that, he had no defence and no answer.

Presently a swirl of dust particles entered the chamber from the tunnel and he realized that Dax had sealed the chamber with a blast of energy from his sidearm.

He pulled himself up and leaned his back against the wall of the chamber. He was going to die here, another corpse to be discovered in the distant future, or perhaps never to be discovered at all.

What had Dax said? 'This place will become dust by my hand'. He meant to destroy the site, the only evidence that might have pointed humanity to the truth of its origin. Tears welled up in his eyes; tears of pain, frustration and regret. Elan was dead, Matty would soon follow and Jun. What of Jun? He would stand little chance against the likes of Dax. Jun would soon be dead. He had failed the boy; he had failed them all; he had failed humanity and that was a heavy burden for a dying man.

VI

Jun held Matty in his arms while the last life drained out of her and she was no more. He sat cradling and rocking her lifeless body in the silent coffin of the bridge. He didn't care what happened to him now; all that was precious in his life, all that meant something was gone and would never come back. Bitter tears ran down his cheeks and moistened Matty's sweet face. He would never feel alive again.

In the blackness of his grief, after he cradled her body until he looked up and saw in the monitor the image of a gowned figure emerging from the tunnel. The figure turned and fired a sidearm at the entrance of the tunnel and it collapsed as the shattered rock fell and sealed the entrance. He watched the figure as it made its heavy way toward the ship while an overwhelming seizure of hate welled within his soul. He gently laid the girl down and made his way to Elan's cabin. There, he soon found what he was looking for and picked up her weapon. Holding it with both hands, he calmly waited for his quarry.

By the time Dax reached the ramp of the cruiser he was already beginning to feel the effects of the radiation he had received in the chamber and on the toxic surface of the planet. He felt sick and quite dizzy and his head felt as though it would soon burst. He staggered into the air lock and entered the ship, drawing his weapon. The Infidel must be here; he would not be able to hide for long. He reached the bridge and saw the blood soaked bodies of the two women. The Whore had obviously expired and was lying prone, near the corpse of the Apostate. He felt anew the rush of pleasure and satisfaction at the sight.

Suddenly, he sensed a movement to his left, just beyond his field of vision. He swung round and fired. A metallic crackle filled the air and then he was thrown off his feet and propelled through the air and slammed into a bulkhead. The smell of burning flesh filled his nostrils; he felt his legs collapse from beneath him and he slumped to the floor. Blindly he felt for his weapon but it was out of reach. He fumbled for his sword, but it was too heavy. A figure loomed over him.

He spat the words through clenched teeth. "You will burn in the everlasting flames of Hell."

"Maybe," whispered Jun as he fired the weapon, "but not before you."

VII

Had he been on Suran or any other reasonably civilized planet, Solon Bru knew that he would have survived the weapon blast and even the radiation. But here, where there was nothing but barren waste, he realized that he was condemned to die. As he sat, leaning against the wall of the chamber, he reflected on the rush of events that had brought him to this lonely place and people that had played their parts so well. He thought sorrowfully of Attor, his former student; of his researcher Engin Par; of Lim who had first set him on the path that had led him here. He thought of Rhell, his wife to whom he had shown little consideration; of Gong Lat, the boy who had made him laugh in the desert on Agon; of Elan and Matty who had shared his journey; and he thought of Jun, the sensitive, prickly boy who had changed out of all recognition and had blossomed and matured into a complex human being. In the gloomy, macabre surroundings of his tomb, he waited for the release of death.

It was probable now that Jun would have shared the same fate as the rest of the party and he hoped that the boy had not suffered too much. Of all of them it was to Jun that he felt the deepest responsibility. He had taken him from the comfort and security of his home and dragged him halfway across the galaxy, only to meet a grizzly end at the hands of a madman. He thought of Dax, the fanatic who had sacrificed himself in the name of ignorance. He would be dying now, ravaged by the radiation that he failed to notice in his headlong thirst for revenge. The readings on his belt were so high, especially in the chamber, where no man could survive long without protection. He would have been sickening even as they spoke. This thought gave Bru a kernel of hope. He activated the communicator on his belt, causing it to transmit static in regular pulses; then he listened.

After some time he tried again. Still there was no response. After the fourth attempt his signal was returned by several faint pulses. Jun was still alive!

He gritted his teeth and dragged himself towards the tunnel entrance, trailing his damaged leg behind him. He pushed himself into the tunnel and began to claw his way along it, his face contorted with pain. He propelled the lantern towards the entrance and up ahead saw the tumble of rocks that blocked the way out.

By the time he had dragged himself to the rockfall he was exhausted. His body was beginning to shut down and the pain in his leg seared through his entire being. He forced himself on, clawing at the rocks and throwing them down the tunnel behind him. Eventually he could continue no more and he slumped with his hand wrapped around a rock beyond his head, and lost consciousness.

He did not know how long he had been unconscious; it might have been moments; it might have been an hour; but when he awoke he heard the distinct sound of laboured breath in his communicator. And then a rock was moved and a gloved hand thrust into the small gap ahead. He grabbed the hand and clasped it so tightly that he almost crushed the delicate bones.

"Let go," said Jun, "I need both hands."

Together they cleared a hole just large enough for Bru to escape and Jun began pull him out of the tunnel by his arms. He could hear the boy grunting as he strained with the dead weight of his teacher against the dense pull of the planet. He pushed with his good leg to help him and at last he emerged from the tunnel and they both lay sprawled on the dusty ground under the stars and the light of the distant sun.

Jun supported his teacher as they struggled back to the ship and up to the bridge. Even through tears of pain and distress, the scene they came upon shocked Bru. The blasted corpse of the Evangelist lay splayed on the floor, his grim features burned and melted into a grotesque mask. Elan's body was lying near the control interface. Matty was near her; the ugly gash that had ended her short life, clearly the source of the blood that covered her. He staggered to a seat and slumped while Jun knelt down and took Matty in his arms and held her body close to his and with sudden clarity Bru saw what his pupil had become.

"Jun," he whispered, "I need drugs." But the boy did not seem to hear; he had not spoken a word since he had rescued Bru from the tunnel.

"Jun," repeated Bru, "please, I need pain relief now."

Jun looked up at his teacher as though he had just realized the presence of another. Slowly he lowered the girl's body and regarded Bru through dead, unseeing eyes.

"The locker," encouraged Bru.

Jun rose mechanically and retrievced the medical supply and brought it back to Bru, placing it next to him; then, without a word, he returned to Matty and took her in his arms once again. Bru found what he was looking for and shot it into his leg. The pain relief flooded into his body almost instantly, numbing the nerve paths to the damaged leg. He quickly sterilized the wound and sealed it with new skin. Finally he bound the wound tightly. He pushed himself up onto his good leg and limped over to the control interface. He recalled Dax's words in the chamber, 'soon all this will be dust', and he knew what he was going to find. And he found it; the disrupter; Dax had not bothered to hide it; it had already started the irreversible, fatal sequence. His stomach turned. Had they minutes to live? Hours? He could not tell. There was but one slim chance; if Dax had set a delay long enough for him to get back to his ship and away from the planet they might just have time themselves. He considered the life pod, but it was doubtful that it would get them far enough away. There seemed to be only one option. Dax's ship.

Dax had arrived on foot, so the ship had to be near and the only possible place was that he could have approached unseen was the other side of the giant nose of solidified magma. Assuming he had not sent his ship back into orbit, that was where it would be found.

He stuffed the remaining phials from the medical supply into his suit and looked down at the pathetic, forlorn figure of his pupil, still cradling the dead girl. "Jun... Jun, we have to leave this ship now."

The boy looked up at him. "I'm not going anywhere."

"The cruiser's going to blow up, we must leave."

"You go, I'm staying here."

"It's our only chance. Do you want to die?"

"Yes," replied Jun flatly.

"That's insane."

"Is it? This whole thing has been insane."

"I'm going to die; you're the last hope. You must go on."

"What for? What is it all for?"

"'What is it for'?" echoed Bru, angrily. "It's for Humanity, you idiot!"

"I don't care; I didn't want this; I never wanted it."

Bru held the boy's gaze. "I know," he said calmly, "I'm sorry."

He watched as Jun wept over the dead girl. Realising his own emotional inadequacy he did not feel what Jun felt; he had never experienced such feelings with any human being, but he did not despise it as before. At least now he understood and it was sorrow that he felt as he gently placed his hand on Jun's shoulder.

"You go ahead," said Bru. "I have a last duty to perform."

He watched Jun rise and trudge slowly from the bridge before going over to Dax's corpse. He opened the medical kit and selected the instrument he required. Leaning over the body, he extracted a measure of the Evangelist's blood and introduced it into his own veins. Then, with one last look at the bodies of his companions, he left the cruiser to its fate.

VIII

They made their way along the base of the massive headland of congealed magma, leaving behind the cruiser and the three dead people within. Jun supported Bru, but even so, their progress was slow and he knew they were running out of time. Silently Bru cursed Jun's newly acquired emotions; they had cost them valuable moments. He wished he could send the boy on alone; he would have a better chance of making it in time, but he didn't have Dax's blood in his veins. No D.N.A. trace; no take-off. Grimly he pressed on, hoping that his hunch was right and they would find Dax's craft on the other side of the headland.

The tongue of magma had not seemed so large when they had flown above it when coming in to land, but now it seemed interminable. Finally, they rounded the last craggy outcrop at the base of the cliff and saw the broad, flat, boulder-strewn plain beyond. The basalt massif fell away to the right and there, at the base of the cliff, stood Dax's vessel. They saw in the feeble light that bathed the basalt surface of the planet that the access ramp was down. With renewed hope Bru realized that they might just make it and struck determinedly onward.

Time had almost run out by the time they reached the ship. They staggered up the ramp and into the opened airlock chamber.

Jun smiled weakly at his teacher "I'm going back," he said. "I helped you to get here because I owed it to you as my Doyen, but I should never have left her alone."

Bru had been expecting something like this; he had recognised the disturbed state of Jun's mind and had already decided what to do. He smiled resignedly and nodded his assent then, with sudden brutality, he punched Jun on the jaw, sending his head jerking back. He caught the boy as he fell and dragged him into the ship and commanded an emergency take-off. The ramp snapped shut; the ship shuddered and began to climb. Bru saw the dwindling aspect of the basaltic promontory and the glint of their old ship against the blackness of the planet. Against all the odds they had made it! They had actually got away.

The blinding pulse of light almost knocked him over. He covered his eyes and braced while the surface of the planet beneath imploded and then exploded with the power of a million volcanoes. A second later the blast front reached the ship and he was thrown violently against a bulkhead, cracking his head open and knocking him unconscious. The ship was propelled upwards towards space within a bubble of super-heated gas, as though it had been caught in the flare of a star. The dense hull was bombarded with particles of debris travelling at near light speed; it began to fail and soon the propulsion system was compromised and it began to shut down.

When Jun opened his eyes he found himself in almost total darkness. Beyond the faint glow of his lifebelt, a feeble light source drifted somewhere above his head and for some moments he had no idea where he was. His head was sore and, his jaw ached and his body felt as though he had fallen into some infernal pummelling machine. He also realised that he was completely weightless. He reached out, grasped at a bulkhead and propelled himself towards the light at the end of the passageway. As he drifted into the bridge-space, the memory of where he was returned and through the transparency of viewing portal he saw the great, curving horizon of the planet and the distant star beyond. Slowly the horizon disappeared as the ship tumbled and all he could see was the, stark, black surface of the planet beneath the ship. Bru's body had drifted on to the bridge and was floating near a bulkhead; the wispy halo of light from his lifebelt still clung to his form. He was still alive but tiny globules of blood were issuing from a cut across his forehead. Jun vaguely recalled standing by the airlock door and then nothing. He knew he had not wanted to board Dax's ship, and yet here he was, still alive and still in pain.

The ship continued its slow-motion somersault across the black sky of the planet and now Jun could see the massive debris cloud they had outrun billowing into space above the horizon. Matty was in that cloud, now just atoms in the dust. An impossible sadness oppressed him; why hadn't he died?

When Bru eventually opened his eyes, it was not to look upon any scene of joy. As the ship had yawed and pitched in the maelstrom of the blast cloud, he had been propelled along the corridor and through the open door leading to the bridge. Now his body was bruised and his head felt as though his brain had been exposed to the elements. He gingerly put his hand to his forehead and felt the sickly, wetness of blood as it escaped his body. And then he realised that he was weightless and the ship was dark and there was Jun, staring through the viewport at the world and the huge cloud of dust above the horizon.

He pushed himself over to the boy. "We've lost the drive."

Jun did not acknowledge him.

Bru expected resentment. "Are you hurt?"

"We're going to crash," said Jun flatly.

Bru looked through the port; Jun was right, they were nowhere near orbit velocity. "Have you checked the life pod?"

"Why would I do that?"

"It might still be functional. We could use it to land."

"And then what?"

"Or we can achieve a stable orbit."

"And then what?" repeated Jun.

"We can at least try to survive a little longer."

"You're dying, and when you're dead I'll be here alone."

"You can go into stasis; someone might come."

"No one is coming."

"You don't know that; our Doyen knows we are here."

"Doyen Lim is dead; you pointed out the disease yourself."

"Yes but would have imparted the mission to a trustee."

Jun turned and met the eyes of his teacher. "We were the trustees and we failed. It was all for nothing, and how many people got killed? Think about it."

Bru held his gaze and now saw clearly what had changed the boy. "It must have been terrible to kill a man."

Jun turned away tight lipped.

"I'm sorry Jun, I wasn't thinking."

"You don't understand," replied the boy, "I'd have killed him a thousand times over."

"I'm sorry for you," said Bru heavily.

"You don't have to pity me," replied Jun in a voice empty and devoid of emotion. "I am not a Suran any more; perhaps I never was."

IX

Bru now saw that Jun was right. Their mission had ended. After several orbits the ship would lose altitude and begin to fall into the crust of the planet and they would become part of this remote world. In truth, he was resigned to it; he was hurt and he was tired and when the phials of analgesic ran out, he would be in serious pain. Better to go this way.

As for Jun, he seemed ready for his fate and, although he might be able to cling to life in the survival pod, there was always the possibility that he would be found by Evangelists and that would not be a suitable fate for a Suran. He smiled at the impending prospect of death and a euphoric feeling of calm crept into his brain.

The sparse void above the curve of the world was strange and beautiful; it would be the last thing he would see before closing his eyes and letting the sleeping draught take its course. He stared out intently, trying to see the part of the heavens that they had come from, where he had come into being and where he had lived, but he could not identify the region. As he peered resignedly, at peace with himself at last, he became aware of an almost imperceptible disturbance in the great sweep of stars above the planet. An object was passing overhead. At first he dismissed it as a meteor or a large chunk of debris that had been blown upwards from the planet's surface, but as he watched the object, he became increasingly aware that it could be neither. This odd phenomenon was reflecting light with an intensity that precluded either explanation; moreover the light was varying in intensity in a regular way. He stared at it in fascination for a while until, finally, drawing Jun's attention to it.

"Do you see that object over there?"

Jun followed the direction of his teacher's pointed finger. "A meteor," he offered.

"I don't think so," returned Bru. "The light is too intense; it is more reflective than a meteor or any other natural thing."

Jun shook his head sadly. "You see what you want to see; it is desperation. Why do you not accept what is happening?"

"Because, unlike you, I am not content to accept failure. We haven't finished what we started and while there is some hope I mean to continue. You have younger eyes; now look again and tell me what you see."

To humour his teacher Jun concentrated on the object for some time.

"Well?" prompted Bru after a pregnant silence.

Now Jun wasn't so sure. Bru was right; it did not look natural. "I don't know," he said reluctantly; he had no further interest in their quest. He wanted to die. He needed to die.

"It's a vessel, isn't it?" said Bru.

Jun made no reply.

"Damn, you, Jun; it's a ship of some sort."

"It might be," conceded the boy imperceptibly. His fears were realised; he knew what was coming.

""We have to try for it," announced Bru in a voice that carried in it the hope of survival.

"What for?" replied Jun angrily. "You're dying and I no longer wish to live."

Bru's eyes were alive with a luminous intensity. "It's our duty," he said.

Jun secured himself in the launch seat and observed as Bru pushed the last of the provisions into the life pod. Cocooned in its housing, the vessel seemed to have escaped the ravages of the explosion; it was intact and all the systems were functioning. He recalled his former experience of a life pod launch as the cargo ship they had ridden together from Suran, soared through the upper atmosphere of Tarnus. It had not been a pleasant experience, but it had brought him to the girl who would change his life. He thought of her now, as they prepared to launch, and wondered what she would have wanted him to do. He knew the answer straight away; she would want him to survive.

Bru glanced at him as he secured himself. "Are you ready, Jun?"

Jun nodded. "Ready."

Bru initated the emergency launch sequence. The peppered outer doors of the housing blew into space, the engines engaged and they were hurled clear of the doomed hulk of Dax's ship. The pod stabilised and its limited thrust pushed them towards the distant object.

"What are you going to do if it's just a shiny rock?" said Jun.

"I don't know; you can decide."

Jun smiled at the irony; for the first time in his life he was to be permitted autonomy; just at the very moment it no longer mattered. "Are you releasing me?"

Bru looked confused. "We are a long way from Suran and any other civilisation. Do such things matter any more? I have not thought of you as my charge for a long time."

This was news to Jun; it made him feel a little uncomfortable. "I didn't know," he said.

"I can formally release you if you wish."

"No, we will leave things as they are."

Bru arched an eyebrow; he had not expected to still be held in such grace. He suspected that Jun didn't know he had knocked him out cold in the airlock of Dax's ship. The incident had certainly not been mentioned so far. "I am content, if that is what...."

Bru was silenced before he could finish his sentence. The magnified image of the object they were heading towards had just appeared on the navigation screen. The sight shocked them both into silence until Bru uttered, "May the Prophet save us!"

They approached the object slowly and, it began to grow in their field of vision. As the shape revealed itself against the black backdrop of space, the extraordinary, alien nature of it became apparent. It was truly massive and shaped like an elongated pod with a wide middle and two ends which tapered markedly. It was at least three kilometres long, turning slowly end over end and catching the stark rays of the distant sun in its reflective surface.

The sight of it silenced them both and, as they approached, features and detail began to gain focus. Towards one end the otherwise solid surface was interrupted by a gap in the skin. Beyond that, some regular markings were etched into the surface. Bru manoeuvred the craft into a vector that matched that of the enormous hulk and approached. The hair on his head stood on end as the inscription came into range. It was in the form of the ancient script, written in upper case lettering. It said *'HYPERION'*.

X

"What do you think?" said Jun, breaking a long silence. "It's not Evangelists, is it?"

"No, I don't think it is, but they would understand what is written on the hull. It is the same as the script used in The Book of Minnar."

"How do you know?"

"I studied the ancient form in order to read The Book in its original text."

"What does it say?"

"It says 'Hyperion'."

"Does that mean anything?"

"Nothing that I can understand; it is probably the name of the vessel or its owner. It is also an incontrovertible link between whatever built this and our own early culture."

"Do you think it's ancient, I mean as old as the fragment?"

"Yes, at least from the same era."

They continued in silence as Bru carefully manoeuvred the life pod towards the gap in the ship's skin that was located near one end of the vessel. As they approached the great hulk loomed above them, obscuring the field of stars behind. As they neared, they could see that the gap in the hull was an open bay, one of two in that region of the ship. It was much larger than they expected and it was able to accommodate their tiny vessel with ease. Bru switched on the lights as they entered and the blackness of the ships belly was thrown into sharp relief by the stark navigation lights of the life pod.

Once inside, Bru set the pod down on what appeared to be a landing area, locked it into place by means of the powerful magnets on the feet of the craft and killed the main motors. An eerie silence descended as they peered out at the large, cavernous hangar now enclosing them. The hangar must have once housed one or two smaller vessels, but it was now deserted. The bulkheads were of ribbed metal and largely devoid of feature save for some unintelligible markings that appeared to be a combination of words and numbers. Towards the end of the hangar a small door was open to the dark heart of the vessel.

Bru rose from the pilot's seat and found the medical kit that he had brought from Dax's ship. He opened it and took out a phial to restore the purity of his blood together with another dose of analgesic and delivered them both into his leg. The throbbing that was beginning to divert his attention instantly ceased and he shut his eyes as the soft flush of wellbeing passed through his body. He counted the remaining phials; there were twenty four, sufficient to last him long enough to investigate what they had found and to deliver the overdose that would end his life when the pain became too much to endure. He shut the container and turned his attention to Jun, who hadn't moved from his seat.

"Are you coming?" he asked.

Jun nodded and sullenly joined him.

They put on their survival belts and picked up two lanterns from the emergency stores. They took some rations and Bru also retrieved some new skin from the medical kit before they moved to the small airlock chamber at the back of the craft. Crammed in together in the tight chamber, they waited for the air to be expelled. Bru had never before been in such close personal contact with Jun. He looked down at the young, sad face of his companion and wondered what he was thinking. He did not seem in any way affected by what they had found; he was reticent and uncommitted and preoccupied elsewhere. It was as though the very essence of the boy had been ripped out, leaving only the shell of the person who had once been there.

Bru raised his arm and touched him on the shoulder. "You do realize what we have found, don't you?"

Jun nodded slowly.

"She won't have died in vain," he added. "This will bring light to many worlds."

XI

The outer door slid open and they floated free of the craft and activated the small thrusters on their belts. They drifted down to the open door at the end of the hangar and Bru sent one of the lanterns ahead to light the way. They passed through the door and found themselves in a long passage with openings to the left and right. A light introduced into the first opening revealed a chamber about ten metres by five that appeared to be some sort of storage area. It was completely empty.

They passed along the passage and found several more identical chambers, all of which were also empty. At the end of the passage they passed through another open door and came to a junction where the passage split with one leading to the right and the other to the left. Bru shone the lantern down both passages and saw that they were identical, each with openings to further chambers and an open door at the end. Through both doors he could see another junction where the passage split once again. They were surely heading into a labyrinth so he took out the new skin from his belt and sprayed a rough arrow on the bulkhead indicating the way back to the hangar. He chose the right hand passage and they moved deeper into the heart of the ship.

They advanced through several more sterile passages, each identical to the last. Every time they altered their direction Bru marked the way they had come with the new skin. In the eighth passage, they came across something new. The door to one of the chambers was closed. Bru inspected the area around the door and noticed a slight indentation to the right. He pushed at it and it slid forward and unfolded into a handle as if it had been made yesterday. He smiled at the fine engineering; it was a testament to those that fashioned it all those years ago. He took the handle and began to wind it. The door slid in and to one side with the same easy mechanism.

Inside the chamber a number of containers floated aimlessly about. Each container was about one metre cubed and each was sealed shut. On every surface was written a word that Bru could not translate and a series of numbers. Underneath was the characterization of a human skull and an 'X' drawn in red.

"Let's get out of here," he said. Although he did not know what the containers held, the symbol had done its work.

"What do you think they contained?" asked Jun, it was the first time he had spoken since they had arrived.

"Nothing good," replied Bru as he re-sealed the door.

They passed on through numerous passages, plunging deeper and deeper into the labyrinthine interior of the ship. Had he not had the presence of mind to mark their route, they would have been hopelessly lost and might never have found their way back. Eventually they turned into a passage which appeared to be a dead end, but as they approached, it became evident that the bulkhead at the end was, in fact, a door, different in character to those that sealed the chambers. Bru searched the perimeter for a mechanism and found it to the right of the door. He pushed at it and it unfolded in the same fashion as the handle to the storage chamber. His heartbeat increased, he sensed they had come to the core of the vessel. He took the handle and began to turn.

XII

The door split down the middle and began to part, each side sliding into a gap between two bulkheads. When it was fully open, Bru sent in a lantern and in the harsh light they saw the heart of the ship for the first time. It was a large, almost ovoid space at least thirty metres long and twenty wide. The ceiling arched gracefully overhead, coming to a point in the centre like a flattened dome. The area was furnished with numerous chairs and tables, arranged in groups and locked to the floor. At the far end stood a strange construct which appeared to be some sort of controlling device. An odd shoe floated near the apex of the ceiling and an assortment of what appeared to be eating implements and flat platters were suspended nearby; the remains of a last meal, taken so long ago.

They moved into the area and saw that theirs was just one of a number of doors that gave on to what must have been the common room. Bru floated up towards the ceiling and grabbed the shoe. It was made of soft material with a harder sole and had been well used. He let it go and reached for one of the platters. Particles of food were still stuck to its hard, creamy surface. He wondered if there was any food on board and if there was, in what condition would it be? The thought of eating such alien food excited him, especially as he had lived off survival rations for such a long time. He let the plate go and drifted back towards the door where Jun was waiting, watching him impassively.

There were seven doors in total arranged at regular intervals around the common space. All were shut except for the one they had used. He chose the one to the right of it and wound it open using the standard mechanism. It parted in the same way as the first to reveal an oblong vestibule entirely void save the presence of seven further doors. He opened the first and sent the lantern before him. It was a room, about five metres square, with a fixed bed to one side. Various items floated freely within the space; a chair; a small table; items of clothing and other accoutrements of a personal nature. A small, framed image of a young woman with two older people to either side came to hand. He looked at it and handed it to Jun without comment. The boy studied it for some time then let it go.

Opposite the bed the wall was interrupted by the presence of a number of recessed shapes. Bru pressed one and it slid forward to reveal a drawer filled with brightly patterned clothing. He closed it and opened another to its left. This proved to be a disposal unit for human waste. Another unit contained more clothing and personal items.

They moved on and opened the other cabins, each in turn. They were all identical to the first, differing only in the nature of the personal items they contained. There was no sign of the individuals that once lived their lives in this remote outpost of humanity.

They returned to the common space and tried the next door; it proved to be further crew quarters and was essentially identical to the first except that two of the cabins were entirely empty of personal items.

The third door they opened gave on to more passages, identical to those that led to the hangar deck. The fourth door was at the far end of the common space, it gave on to a short corridor at the end of which was another open door. A weak natural light enticed them and they found themselves in another common area, smaller than the first but having instead of blank walls, a transparent material that afforded them a panoramic view of the ship's exterior. Above them they saw the great curve of the planet drift slowly into range, bathed in the weak gleam of its distant star. A small dot of light hung above the horizon; the failing orbit of Dax's ship.

The fifth door revealed only more passages; but the sixth opened on to a suite of laboratories. Samples of rock and equipment floated aimlessly in the harsh light of the lantern. It was a place of learning and it detained Bru for some time so Jun moved off and opened the last door.

Inside the final door he found a space of an entirely different nature. The room was oblong, about twenty metres in length and seven wide. Along each of the long walls transparent faced coffin-like structures stood on end; fourteen each side. For some reason his heartbeat rose and he felt the hair of his head stand on end. He advanced into the room, peering into each of the units. In the fourth one he discovered a grizzly sight; the half decomposed remains of a human being. The skull was almost devoid of flesh save a small patch that incongruously clung to the cranium and supported a few meagre tufts of blond hair. Both eyes were still in their sockets and stared blankly out at him, making his skin crawl. The cadaver was clad in a single piece suit of pale blue that was scarcely supported by the wasted body. On the breast was a pocket with something inscribed in two parts.

When Bru finally entered the room Jun was still staring at the remains.

"Alex Johansen," Said Bru, annunciating each syllable slowly. "What stories will this person tell us? Is this the only one?"

"I don't know," replied Jun.

Bru inspected the other units in turn. They were all empty.

"These are the only remains here," said Bru, returning, "I wonder what happened to all the others."

"They left," said Jun, "the same way as we came."

"Perhaps," replied Bru. "This looks like some sort of stasis unit."

Jun nodded. "I wonder if it's a male or a female."

"The bone structure looks male, but there's only one way to be sure."

"I don't think you should try and open it."

"Why not?"

"It seems wrong, it should be preserved."

"It is a specimen Jun, no more, no less, and there is nothing here to contaminate it; no atmosphere; and our belts will insulate us from it."

"It still seems wrong."

"If not us then who? There's a good chance we might be the only human beings ever to see this."

"It feels like a violation."

Bru glanced at the boy and wondered at the extent of his corruption. He seemed to have entirely cast off his Suran rationality. "It's an inert object that was once the corporal shell of a human being. It has no spirit and no existence other than as a collection of atoms and molecules."

Jun's eyes widened at the admonishment. "Open it then," he said.

Bru searched the unit for some sort of lever or mechanism, eventually locating four small locking arrangements that secured the transparent cover to the unit. By turning each one ninety degrees he released the cover and it floated free of the unit. Alex Johansen stared accusingly back at him and a shiver ran up his spine as he carefully attempted to remove the pale blue overall. A piece of the ancient material snapped off in his hand. It was frozen solid and could not be removed without destroying it.

"It's no good," said Bru, "it will have to be thawed out before we can inspect it."

"Leave it where it is," replied Jun. "I think you should replace the lid."

"Alright," replied Bru, "we will come back to it later."

He reached for the cover and was about to fasten it back down when he noticed a small bump in the breast pocket of the overall. He let go of the cover and pulled at the material. It snapped away to reveal an object shaped like a flattened lozenge about four centimetres long. It was featureless and gave no indication as to what its use might be. He passed it to Jun and retrieved the transparent cover and locked it back into place.

When he finally turned around to speak to Jun he found the boy studying the lozenge intently. Suddenly he let out a cry and let it go. It floated out of his hand and as it turned Bru could see that the thing had changed colour and had started to glow with a dull light. As they watched the light faded and the object resumed its original condition.

"What is it?" said Jun.

Bru reached out and carefully took the object in his palm. Immediately it resumed its transformation. "It's probably responding to heat or something metabolic." He let go and the lozenge, once again, began to fade. "Whatever it is," he said, "it still works."

He took it up for a second time, this time holding it firmly in the palm of his hand. The device began to glow more intensely until there was a sudden flash of brilliance that almost caused him to drop it again. They gasped as a three dimensional projection burst from the object and hung before them. It was a numbered list with one hundred and fifty two items arranged in three rows. It appeared solid for nothing could be seen beyond it, and as Jun placed his hand into the beam, so his hand was represented in the image.

Without meaning to he placed his finger on item thirty-one and immediately the list disappeared and was replaced by a title page with writing that Bru could not decipher. The title page dissolved and they found themselves amongst a large gathering of seated people dressed in strange garb. In front of them a raised platform contained about a hundred people dressed even more outlandishly. The people on the platform were clutching objects of various shapes and sizes and appeared to be waiting for something. Presently two individuals appeared; an old, grey-haired man preceded by a statuesque woman in a gorgeous, flowing gown and a turban of brilliant blue. Her skin was as black as jet; blacker than they had ever seen and her eyes shone like jewels. A sound came to their ears; Bru heard it directly; Jun received it through their communicator; it was the sound of the crowd banging their hands together repeatedly. The two people bowed and the noise died. The old, grey man raised his hands and a sweet and mellifluous sound came to their ears; a sound such as they had never before heard. And then the woman began to sing three words in rising tones; "Asie... Asie... Asie."

As she sang the final note her image began to disappear along with the rest of the auditorium, evolving, like liquid, into a procession of astonishing scenes of wilderness and desert. The music poured into them and they were surrounded by steaming, emerald forests, then snow covered mountains, then a shining ocean burnished with a golden sun. And then people flooded the scene, people more diverse than any they had ever seen, clad in gorgeous cloth, in exotic, teeming cities, their eyes flashing with the joy of life in that ancient world. And then they saw something that really astonished them; living creatures that were not men; huge, unwieldy, with men riding them and leading them under yolk. They saw creatures flying through the air, immense and black; they saw creatures leaping from azure seas by vessels with billowing white sails. They saw a man beheaded before a baying crowd and many other astonishing sights illuminated with extraordinary colour and light and unfettered opulence and over it all the pure sound of a human voice, soaring above the instruments that seemed to form a unity which, although strange to their ears, was yet, distantly familiar. It was the unmistakable hand of human genius, reaching out and touching their souls across an aeon of silence.

The piece finished and the gorgeous images faded as the music tailed off into silence. The lozenge returned to the list and waited for the next selection. Bru regarded Jun and saw that tears had started from his eyes. They floated away like tiny orbs of glass.

"I wonder," said Bru quietly, "where it is."

"It is a world that no longer exists," said Jun.

XIII

Item 152
This is the personal record of First Officer Alex Johansen.

I leave this record and testament to the events that occurred on the survey vessel *Hyperion* during the period forty one dash twenty five seven and forty eight dash twenty five seven. All previous records are to be found in the standard log according to proper practice. As a preliminary, I will state that the mission to the surface of Vega Delta was not wholly successful. For the record this was entirely my responsibility, I did not calculate correctly the magnitude of the volcanic eruption that we had come here to observe and measure; also I delayed take-off for personal reasons endangering my colleagues in the surface party. This was unprofessional and against company policy. As a result one of the landers was damaged by the blast wave and I was stranded on the planet's surface necessitating a rescue and further endangerment of the crew and company property. Captain Kumar would have been well within her rights to demote me and suspend pay, however circumstances have become difficult and she has prioritised crew participation over punishment.

41-2507
It is now 6 days since the last communion with the On Board Intelligence. It is functioning but gives us no indication what is wrong. It has now shut down both the core and its auxiliary and now there is no prospect of regaining sufficient impulse to take us out of orbit. It has also shut down the communication system, so we are now unable to send or receive any further dispatches. In short it has effectively stranded us in the Vega System and isolated us from the rest of humanity. Since it's primary directive is to protect the crew and company property, I am forced to wonder from what it believes it is protecting us. And why the silence? Is it acting on a Company directive unknown to the crew, or has the situation on Earth become critical? We just don't know.

42-2507
I have conferred with Captain Kumar and the other senior officers and since there is no prospect of *Hyperion* returning to occupied space, the captain has proposed that the majority of the crew should make the attempt in the remaining lander. She has convinced herself that the 'Obi' has malfunctioned in some way and she is determined to attempt the return to civilisation. The station at Argentu is the nearest relief and the navigator has calculated that, using Vega as a slingshot, the traverse time will be almost fifty-six years. We have one operational lander with twelve stasis units so the journey is possible for twelve of us. The captain has insisted on remaining on board but I feel strongly that she should go as the active officer on the lander. I suppose the others will have to be drawn by lot.

42-2507 (supplementary).
Second Officer Clark has suggested that stasis units from lander one could be adapted into lander two. I have looked into this and calculated that a total of ten units could be supported without too much loss of potential. This means that twenty-two of our number will be able to leave and four will remain. The captain has proposed that instead of drawing lots, four volunteers might come forward. As I have no family or relatives to return to I have decided to remain.

43-2507
Work has started on the transfer of the stasis units to lander two. We have also started to supply it with all the necessary accoutrements for such an extended journey. Landers were not designed to undertake such journeys and there will, no doubt, be difficulties. My calculation is that they have little better than a fifty percent chance of success. Clark has announced that she wishes to remain on

board *Hyperion*, I agree with her decision; she is a geologist and would not be able to make a meaningful contribution to their efforts. I admire her courage. The other two positions will have to be drawn by lot.

45-2507

The two crew members who are to remain are West and Chin Sen. Neither were exactly pleased, but as I pointed out to them, they have almost as much prospect of surviving here as in the lander. The work of transferring the stasis units and other supplies is almost complete. It has lately occurred to me that both landers should be taken with lander one in tow. In the event of a system failure it could be cannibalized and would, in any case, provide extra storage. I don't know why it has not occurred to any of us before, perhaps we were not thinking rationally. The captain has agreed to my suggestion and ordered lander one to be prepared.

47-2507

The preparations have been completed and Captain Kumar and the rest of the crew will be leaving in four hours' time. Clark has been industrious in working for the success of the landers but West has been obstructive and Chin Sen remote. I can't help thinking that we should have left the drawing of lots until the last moment. I do not look forward to keeping company with either of them.

In one hour we are to share a final meal together. The captain has sanctioned a modicum of alcohol to make us merry.

48-2507

Captain Kumar and the rest of the crew have left. I believe she had tears in her eyes as she hugged me. I wished her luck; she will certainly need it.

West is still under sedation following his lewd and drunken antics during the final meal. He seems to have lost all self-control and I will not embarrass his ancestors by describing his behaviour. Michaels eventually managed to tranquillise him. Suffice it to say we all saw more of him than any of us ever expected or hoped to.

I have calculated that there is sufficient reserve for seventy-six years on minimum so the sooner we get to stasis the better. I have restricted the gravity field to the crew accommodation and have set its removal when we achieve stasis. This will save the reserve and extend our period of survival. In the event of an emergency I expect the 'Obi' to revive either Clark or myself, whoever shows the stronger vital signs. This ends the report.

75-2577

I have been revived after seventy years in stasis. I discover that the reason for my revival is the termination of Clark, West and Chin Sen approximately twenty hours ago. There are no reports of contact so I must assume that Captain Kumar failed to reach Station Argentu. I now face the unpalatable truth that I am the only survivor of this mission. I have decided to remove their bodies and place them in storage in the hope they can be disposed of with the correct ceremony at a future date.

There is no doubt that the 'Obi' terminated these individuals and I do not propose to take issue with that decision or to pontificate on the wisdom of allowing the on-board intelligence to make such decisions. We all sign up to such a thing when we come aboard. I presume the cold calculation was that one could survive longer than four and that I was to be the chosen one. I take solace in the fact that none of them would have known anything or felt anything. I propose to take one last meal and then I will resume stasis. At present power consumption there is provision for my stasis unit to continue for another ninety-six years, however I hope I am not revived again unless rescue is certain, which I have to say, seems unlikely.

I have one last thing to add and it is a confession regarding a matter that has troubled me. Some time ago I took possession of a valuable object which I was not entitled to own. It is the last surviving fragment of a first century papyrus of Aristolian literature, his treatise on the Constitution of Athens to be exact. It lies in the escape chamber that is now below the basaltic flow at a grid reference that can be obtained by consulting the ship's log. The object belongs in a public museum and, since it cannot now be returned to Earth, I leave it to those who discover this record to carry out my last wishes.

I conclude this log.

XIV

The revelations contained in Alex Johansen's personal account were translated by Solon Bru as he and Jun observed them in the relative comfort of the life pod on the hangar deck. They spent many hours in the company of Johansen's singular tastes in both literature and art and were most particularly introduced to early twentieth century romantic composers. In item one, they discovered a large number of images of Johansen as a child with one female adult, presumably his mother. There were other images of places, both urban and rural, some with movement, some without. There was one arresting image of an entire planet, an exquisite place of blue oceans and white clouds with land masses of green and ochre. It appeared to tie in with the images of Johansen's youth and they surmised that this was his place of birth. This was a particularly interesting image to Bru who speculated that it could be the place of human origin, given the copious amounts of water and vegetation. But even more interesting was the presence of another image they discovered in the same folio. It was the picture of a leafless tree, a gnarled old specimen that stood on the crest of a hill, captured at night. The tree itself was remarkable but it was not the principal source of Bru's interest, for above it he could see a panorama of stars caught in exquisite detail.

"If we had the right equipment we could pinpoint the place where you would have got that aspect one-hundred-and-twenty-thousand years ago."

"Do you think this is the place of origin?"

"It could be; it has the right attributes. Perhaps it is the 'Earth' that Johansen refers to."

"We will never see it."

"I won't," replied Bru, "you might."

"If it still exists."

Bru smiled weakly, "I think it still exists, somewhere."

Jun regarded his teacher. Bru's condition had deteriorated markedly. He had ceased any further excursions into the labyrinthine belly of *Hyperion* and now confined himself to the life pod where he occupied himself with Johansen's personal records. There was much to see and much to hear as the lozenge contained the sum of the man's lifetime of experiences as well as a large number of entertainments. At first he found the spoken language difficult to follow. The pronunciations of the words were not as those he had heard spoken by the scholar priests of Agon. But, as he persevered, his ear gradually attuned to the language and meanings began to be revealed.

There were sequences of Johansen's life; of friends and women he had known although apparently none of offspring. There were lengthy sequences of on board life, casual moments of celebration and disappointment. He had much to say about his fellow travellers, some of it mildly vitriolic and castigating. Of Captain Leila Kumar he said very little except to praise her leadership of the mission. It was essentially the record of a man who could have lived in their era; his frailties and strengths at one with men who lived in another age.

As Bru's condition eventually confined him to the life pod, so Jun took to increasingly longer excursions into the intricate interior of *Hyperion*. He explored the endless passages that formed the structure of the ship and the countless chambers that they contained. He found many strange things, alien objects that defied logical analysis. He would sometimes take them back to Bru and they would discuss them at length, sometimes arriving at a probable truth, sometimes not. He found food, but it was in a form so concentrated that it was completely unpalatable. He found the bodies of Clark, West and Chin Sen, placed in containers and floating about in one of the chambers close to the common area. They were intact, frozen to the core; their eyes shut in peaceful sleep. He checked their overalls for personal items and discovered the image of a man in Clark's breast pocket but nothing else. He returned the image to its place. He brought Bru to see them, but it was obvious that any movement was becoming difficult for his teacher and that was the last time Bru ventured into the interior of *Hyperion*.

Jun observed his companion with a distant compassion. Bru was his teacher and mentor and he had come to respect his intellect and even his sardonic character. But the fact was that he had learned very little of academic quality from the man; not since their long journey from Suran to Tarnus had there been anything like a sustained period of instruction and after Tarnus his once-receptive mind had been dishevelled by Matty. He knew Bru was going to die and the time was not far off. The thought of it disturbed him badly enough, but the thought of what he expected Bru to ask him to do actually frightened him.

As he wandered the endless passages Matty was his constant companion. He would speak to her, ask her what she thought of various things; laugh at her naïve jokes. He would feel her skin next to his, smell her, touch her. He would shut his eyes and tears would escape from below the lids and float into the void spaces of the ship and he would ache for her. To Jun, who had never before known such mental torment, the pain was endless.

They had been on *Hyperion* for forty-three days when Jun returned from a particularly long excursion to find his teacher in some distress. Bru grimaced in pain as he helped him to the cot they had rigged up in the pod.

As he settled, his eyes closing with the pain, Bru said, "The time is near Jun, you know what you have to do."

"I won't do it," replied the boy. "You'll have to do it yourself."

"You know I can't. The drugs have nearly finished; would you see me die in agony, screaming for mercy?"

"I don't care, I won't do it."

Bru turned his head and looked into the boy's face. "I will tell you when," he said.

XV

At the end of his life Solon Bru gave himself over to reflection on what he had achieved. He had discovered the beginnings of the truth of human origin and was now able to prove that the early scriptures were wrong. But in that certainty was a kernel of doubt and he began to wonder at the subtleties of human belief. Did it really matter that the tenets of the Faith were based on false constructs? Was it not the act of believing that was important? Was it absolutely essential to base one's existence on cold logic and scientific proof, or was it reasonable, even desirable to temper that hard approach with the softer character of simple faith? Even faith in a lie.

He turned the matter over in his mind and wondered if the drugs that coursed through his veins had dulled his brain or whether it was the imminence of death that had caused him to doubt. He recalled the faces of those he had known and whose deaths he had caused. Most particularly, he recalled the severed head of Rhell, his wife; the innocent, simple woman who had trusted him and whom he had betrayed with his arrogant certainty. He shut his eyes and he knew it was now time.

Jun returned and Bru could see that the boy had been crying.

"I am sorry," he said, 'to burden you in this way."

Jun nodded and Bru handed him the phials that would end his suffering. His hands were shaking as he took them and Bru steadied them with him own. "I didn't want to leave you in solitude," he said. Jun bowed his head and waited.

"I am ready," whispered Bru.

XVI

Jun stared at the body of his teacher. Bru's face was in repose, his eyes shut. A human being who, just moments before, had been a living, thinking organism, now lay before him, lifeless. It struck him as odd that such a thing should occur;

that the very essence of a person should simply dissolve and disappear, leaving behind just flesh, bone, various tissues and elements that would themselves become something else; something quite foreign to that which had existed before. Solon Bru was gone and he was now entirely alone.

He cancelled the gravity and pulled the body by its arm. It was still warm and he could feel the flesh and muscle under the pseudo-military tunic Bru had worn since leaving Tarnus. The sensation did not revolt him, not simply because his teacher was no longer alive, but because Matty had taught him a new philosophy. He had learned to touch people.

He guided the body out through the airlock and felt it stiffen as it quickly froze. At the hangar entrance he looked out at the vast crescent of the planet below and the distant star that hung just above the craggy horizon and touched the peaks with its thin, stark light. And as *Hyperion* slowly turned, so the myriad of galactic stars came into view and he looked back towards Suran, lost among countless points of light, he knew he would never see his home again.

He took one last look at his teacher and pushed the body out into the void. It floated slowly away from the ship and began a graceful tumble against the backdrop of stars. He watched as the familiar features of the man who had changed his life were lost to the darkness and distance. He watched as the body drifted away, until it was no more than a faint glimmer of light. And as the bulk of the ship turned to obscure his view, the man who had been Solon Bru was nothing more than a speck on the face of the galaxy.

Jun returned to the life pod and sat down. For a long time he stayed motionless in the oppressive silence, sometimes closing his eyes, sometimes staring blankly out towards the gaping hangar entrance. He was a Suran and thus should have been able to tolerate solitude, but this was a quality of solitude so deep and remote that despair invaded his soul and he began to weep. Nobody would comfort him or tell him what to do and his only solace was the memory of those he had known and she whom he had loved.

Through glazed eyes he noticed the ship's record that Bru had left next to the cot on which he had spent his last hours. It was in the form of a thin, flat tablet and he took it up and began to read. It contained an account of their quest, written in Bru's dry, precise style. It was detailed and well crafted but it lacked any form of humanity. He cast his mind back to the beautiful dawn of his own emotions and that moment when he had first made love to Matty and he remembered, in every particular, the story that she had told him of her life on Ennepp. He was seized by the realization that, with him, the memory of her would die and that was something he could not bear. He began to write and as the words formed beneath his fingers, she began to return from the dead and take form as though actually in his company, standing behind him, watching as he wrote. He was moved to ask her if she approved of the composition and the silent reply was, "Yes".

He wrote without pause, stopping for nothing, as the words flooded from him and found indelible form on the face of the tablet. He wrote for hours and hours, not heeding time or any need for rest and sustenance. He wrote down everything she had told him during that wonderful time on the journey and when he had finished he put down the tablet and smiled and Matty smiled too. Then she faded and was gone.

He ate some rations and put on a lifebelt, and then he took up the tablet and the lozenge and left the pod. He made his way along the familiar maze of passages in the belly of *Hyperion* until he came into the command space at its heart. He placed the two items in a locker and closed the door. Maybe they would be found in a thousand years and travellers in distant times would read them and they would live once more in the imaginations of future beings.

He went into the accommodation and found a sharp, pointed knife. Bringing it back to the locker he scratched four words into its dull, metallic surface. It was a simple message, just sufficient for the guidance of those who might follow. It said; 'Look at the stars'.

His task complete, he made his way back to the life pod. He unlocked the anchor and eased the small craft out into the void beyond the slowly tumbling bulk of *Hyperion*. Above the ancient ship, above the remote, stark world where a fragment of a lost civilization had lain for thousands of years, he paused. Then he turned the vessel towards the sun.

HYPERION

BOOK TWO

PART ONE

LODAN

I

Lodan DeRhogai opened his eyes and tried to remember where he was.

Above him, a stone ceiling began to resolve as his eyes slowly adjusted to the harsh, morning light streaming through the closely spaced bars of a high window. The ceiling was grimy and cracked and for some moments he thought himself in a cell; it would not, by any means, be the first time Lodan had awoken in custody with little recollection of how he came to be there. The interiors of the prison cells of the city were almost as familiar as his home. But this was not a cell; there was no reek of stale urine or vomit, nor the echo of screaming prisoners and orders being barked from the mouths of tired and angry officers; this place was somewhere different; somewhere low and unsavoury where the sickly smell of stale perfume and sweat mingled with the dry, dusty heat of the tired air. He tried to focus but the ceiling would not stay still, it swayed gently to and fro above him and induced an unpleasant, queasy sensation in his stomach. He felt sick and his head felt like it had shrunk so that his brain seemed to be trying to burst from the sockets of his eyes. Attempting to move his limbs was futile, he knew they would be too heavy to command; it was as though his body and his mind had separated during the night and all he was left with was an aching shell of flesh. He shut his eyes and waited.

What had he taken? Perhaps, more accurately, what had been slipped into the normally harmless cocktail of narcotics he had ingested to heighten his pleasure? Now he began to recall that he was in a 'night-house', but it was not the sort of classy establishment he normally frequented; this place was a foul and sleazy dump way out in the desert, well away from respectable civilisation. He vaguely remembered his cousin's insistence as they exercised together in the gymnasium.

"You must go there," he had said; "the women are truly remarkable; very dirty, very experienced." Two adjectives he knew would excite Lodan's curiosity. He would be having words with his cousin if he could ever get his body to move.

He opened his eyes again and waited for the ceiling above to stop swaying around. Without lifting his head he could see a broken ceiling fan lethargically disturbing the fetid air of the room. A threadbare rag of a curtain hung limply across the door; a large, gilded mirror adorned the wall opposite the high window. There was nothing else in the room other than the bed on which he was lying. He gathered a good measure of determination and tried to raise his body.

Fireworks went off in his head. He gritted his teeth and managed to ease himself up against the wall behind the bed. Breathing heavily he awaited the passing of the pain and the churning sickness in his stomach. Looking down he saw that he was naked; nothing unexpected in that, but this morning, unusually, all below was serene and calm; no engorged flesh greeted him with its morning salute and endless demands.

To his left a woman sprawled carelessly in slumber. A mature female of ample proportion, just the way he liked his women. She had dark green hair and a plain, rounded face beneath copious layers of cosmetics applied to suggest an expression of permanently surprised pleasure. Her ample breasts dangled pendulously into hairy armpits and were the only parts of her torso spared the adornment of indelible illustrations depicting all manner of sexual expression. Seeing them again he now vaguely remembered studying them at close quarters as they danced across her skin in animated scenes; they were extremely graphic and well executed.

Beyond the illustrated female slept another. She was slight and her skin was unadorned, which usually meant that she was a novice. Her long, black hair tumbled among the soiled cushions that lay scattered beneath her. He had no recollection of her at all; she was far too young for his tastes; her breasts were small, as yet undeveloped and there was no more than a hint of soft, pubescent down at her crotch. He guessed that she was no more than fourteen years old. She was not someone he would have ordered for his own use and was obviously a placement to increase the charge. He would refuse to pay, of course.

He remained still for some time. The young girl sighed and turned in her sleep. He wondered if, in his oblivious state, he might have dallied with her. It would have been most unconsciously done, but anything could have happened last night; literally anything. He needed a piss; he needed to get out of there. He gently eased his legs to the floor and sat up on the edge of the bed. More fireworks crackled in his head.

Finally he stood, swaying like a drunk wearing a pair of lead boots. Now he could see himself in the large, gilded mirror; it was not an edifying sight for he appeared to have lost control of the muscles in his face. Lodan was not a handsome man; at best he could be described as rugged. His face was scarred from fighting, his nose had been broken in three places and was rather flattened; he had small ears that stuck out like jug handles beneath severely cropped blond hair. He was a man careless of his appearance but even he was shocked at the palsied face confronting him. He tried to move his lips and achieved little more than the faintest twitch. A smile, had he been so inclined, would have been way beyond his present ability. It was as though a grotesque mask had been applied to the front of his head during the night and as he stared at the strange image so it stared right back, as though mocking him for his naïve stupidity.

On the floor by the bed, cast aside in haste, his clothes formed an untidy pile. His underwear of white cloth, wound loosely in the tradition of Kagan, had been ripped from his body and cast aside and there was no sign of the expensive shoes he had worn which, no doubt, had been purloined by one of the low-life types that frequented such places. He ignored his underwear and gingerly picked up his britches and shirt and slowly dressed. By the time he had finished a measure of sensation was beginning to return. He looked into the mirror again and detected a small increase of animation in the mask. At least the damage wasn't permanent.

He set his eyes on the rag that covered the door and began to make his way towards it. His feet dragged on the dusty, stone floor as he slowly progressed. His head was beginning to clear a little and the pain induced by the effort of moving had begun to subside, but now he discovered that the paralysis, pain and memory loss were little more than small inconveniences compared to the troubles that were about to head in his direction, for, at the foot of the bed, he was arrested by the sight of another naked figure lying curled up, asleep on the floor.

He stared in disbelief as the true horror of his situation began to dawn on him. He was looking at the sleeping figure of a pre-pubescent boy.

His stomach churned, his head burned and he was sick, violently sick. He began to fall and stumbled against the wall, hitting it hard. He couldn't think straight; all he could do was stare at the child sleeping quietly with his thumb in his mouth. He desperately searched his memory for any shadow of recollection of what he had done. He could find none and such a thing was entirely against his nature and yet the child was there, in this place where no child should ever be. He knew the law and agreed with it; there was no mercy for homosexuals on Kagan, anyone physically indulging in such activity was summarily put to death, but the molesters of male children faced a fate too gruesome for even the most avid sadist. His highborn status would not save him; nothing would save him.

It was clear to him that he must be the victim of some sort of elaborate trap; there could be no other explanation for the presence of a male child in such a place as this. No doubt there would be images; all manner of condemnatory evidence. He had a long list of enemies; cuckolded husbands, jilted women, victims of his violence or those he had casually insulted, but none, surely, angry enough to do anything this dishonourable? Kagan was a well-ordered society where certain proprieties were always observed; among the elite there was formality, perhaps even chivalry; among the governed there was total obedience. This was not the Kagan way of revenge; it simply wasn't the done thing.

He sat down heavily on the end of the bed and began to arrange his mind. Now it occurred to him that this might be an innocent mistake on behalf of the owner and he had assumed too much to believe it a conspiracy against himself. No doubt it would cost him dear but he could buy the images (if there were any), and all would be well. He could buy silence: he had done it before and it was a thread of hope to which he could cling for a moment. But the moment soon passed; he knew in his soul that something sinister had come his way; something that could not be bought off. He rose stiffly and walked unsteadily from the room.

Outside the room the narrow corridor was lit by the remnants of light escaping from the various curtained rooms either side. The hour was too early for the likes of the clientele and staff of the night-house and no one was astir. He stepped over the unconscious body of a man so careless of his modesty that the peasant had failed to cover himself decently. Lodan scowled in disgust at the sight and found his way back to the large reception room where he vaguely recalled plying himself with narcotics and choosing the illustrated woman. The room was empty now, devoid of the numerous painted females that had previously decorated its worn couches. A flickering night-light burned in the corner and cast shadows on the rough-stone walls; a beam of natural light shone dimly into the room from the arched opening opposite. He headed towards the natural light hoping he would not come across the owner of the establishment; he did not want to have any difficulties in his present condition.

Beyond the opening another narrow corridor terminated in a harsh curtain of light and the open air of the desert. He lunged forward, yearning to fill his lungs with the untainted, clean desert air where he could clear his head and think. Concealed behind a screen a pair of dark, smiling eyes observed; it had been an exceptionally lucrative night; the images had been sent; images so explicit that nothing could save the jumped-up fool. He would scream as he was roasted and gradually dismembered and the whole of Kagan would watch. It had been a very good night indeed.

Kagan, an arid world where no surface water ran, shone in the brilliance of the rising sun climbing into the perpetually cloudless sky. Lodan dropped his britches and pissed long and hard against the wall of the night-house. His brain still thumped inside his skull but at least he had recovered a large measure of his movement. He walked slowly towards his craft some fifty metres away among a few less sophisticated models. At his approach it opened and he entered the welcome coolness of the well-fashioned interior. He swallowed two measures of a general antidote he kept handy and ordered the craft to transport him to his home. It rose into the clear air above the wind-blown desert plain and headed towards the naked, craggy peaks that guarded its western extremity.

As the antidote began to take effect and his mind cleared he revisited the dilemma of his present situation. The consequences of last night's activities became ever more vivid and he cast around in his memory for any instances of indiscretions that might have involved a member of the nine ruling families of Kagan. He had favoured many women in his short life, but none of them, (as far as he knew), were high born. He had been careful in that respect, especially since his last appearance before the Arkon at which he had had to answer for an illicit affair with the wife of one of the palace undersecretaries. On that occasion he had got away with a flogging but the Arkon had warned him that any further indiscretions would be punished 'in extremis', a euphemism for death much favoured by the head of his clan.

The old man's stern words began to resound in his head and he knew that he could not defend himself. A clearer head brought him to greater pessimism and he now had no doubt that the evidence against him existed and would be irrefutable. By the time his craft had reached the craggy peaks that guarded the desert plateau he had worked out that his only chance of survival was immediate flight; he had to leave Kagan straight away. He had to disappear.

The slow advance of the sun had not yet reached the high mountain range and the boulder-strewn, undulating plain beyond was still in semi-darkness. On the horizon before him he could see the finger of light from the city extend its bony reach into the pre-dawn sky. His mouth was dry as he approached the familiar metropolis and watched its complex pattern of luminous towers, temples and palaces begin to paint the darkness of the wide landscape below. The lights of a few other vehicles danced above the regimented plan of the city. He would have to be quick, not even time to clean himself. Everything had to be done before the dawn light roused his accusers. He would have to transfer his assets to another jurisdiction and take the next interplanetary flight to anywhere; anywhere away from the planet of his birth. He would never be able to return to Kagan.

He approached the DeRhogai Tower where all the direct descendants of the Arkon had a right to live. The antidote had done its work quickly and his body and face had returned to health. He stood in readiness as the door of a vehicle port slid aside and his craft disappeared into the thirty-second level of the vast edifice. He hurried to his accommodation and quickly accessed his personal interface and began the process of transferring his assets to a private account his father had arranged for him on his thirteenth birthday. That had been nine years ago and it was the last time he had seen his father. The account was on Suran, well away from the clutches of the Family, and now he fully appreciated his father's wisdom and forethought.

The transfer would take a little while so he made use of the time by throwing some clothes and personal possessions, including an image of his parents, into a bag. Moments later the system indicated the completion of the transfer. His personal assets were not great, but they were sufficient for him to live modestly on Barta Magnus for some time. He decided against using his own craft because it would be too easily traced, so he took one last quick look around his accommodation and advanced towards the door that led to the common areas of the building and to the emergency exit. The first hint of dawn was creeping into the room, but it was still too early for people to be about so he imagined he would not be seen.

As he approached the door it slid silently open to reveal the person of his great uncle.

"Where is it to be, Lodan? Agon? Barta Magnus? You would certainly do well enough there with your philandering ways."

Lodan clenched his teeth and took a step back. His great uncle advanced into the room and sniffed the air disapprovingly. "It smells of cheap whores in here."

"This is an unexpected honour, Uncle," replied Lodan, as steadily as he could. There was a chance the man had not yet heard of last night's activities and the unusual visit was for something more mundane.

Great Uncle Aurex threw him a disdainful glance. He was taller than most of the DeRhogai and had a stately gait. His close-cropped, silver hair was hidden below a tight-fitting skullcap worn in deference to the sect to which his entire life had been devoted. He was a Brother of Mercy, an Evangelist and vain adornments like hair were not appropriate for his kind. His gown, though of a finer weave than was normal was, nevertheless, sufficiently abrasive to the skin to allow him the satisfaction of discomfort.

"You were warned in plain language by the Arkon himself. You chose to ignore the wise and fatherly advice of your supreme Lord and respected head of our family. You have transgressed for the last time and will go before the Arkon. I am here to escort you. You will cleanse yourself and dress in something appropriate."

'Transgressed', thought Lodan; hardly the manner of expression his uncle would use to describe his alleged crime. The man didn't know why he was being summoned. "Uncle, I have done nothing to dishonour this house."

Aurex almost laughed at such a preposterous assertion. "You, you Lodan, from the moment you were born you have brought dishonour to this house and dismay to all who have the misfortune to know you."

"What I mean, Uncle is that I have done nothing recently," replied Lodan rather despairingly.

Aurex shot him a look that would have soured the sweetest wine. "That is for the Arkon to determine; I am commanded to bring you before him within the hour."

Lodan bowed his head; there would be no escape. He was a dead man. "Yes Uncle," he replied tamely.

He put down the bag of personal items and walked heavily towards the part of his accommodation that contained the facility for ablution and sleeping. As he disrobed he was aware that Aurex had followed him and was watching. This was a deliberate insult to a member of a race that practised modesty; only the condemned were stripped to augment their disgrace and Aurex was making a point by such an intrusion. Lodan was angered by the insult but there was nothing he could do about it; if he was very lucky and the Arkon showed him mercy, this man would be his executioner and there was no point in antagonising him. Aurex had been known to blunt his sword for individuals he particularly despised.

"What happened to you Lodan? You were a conscientious student; you mastered the ancient scripts at a young age; you did well in all your studies. I would have taken you into the Brotherhood had your foolish father not forbidden it. But you chose the path of dissolution and corruption over the joys of self-discipline, sacrifice and prayer. I am sorry for you."

As the particle bombardment cleansed his body Lodan thought of the gruesome sacrificial rite that all young Evangelists had to perform and gave silent thanks that his great uncle had not prevailed over his father's wishes. He listened resentfully with his back to the man as the censure continued.

"Pride and vanity have led you astray; all this fruitless exercise and physicality has addled your senses. Are you not ashamed when you look at yourself? Instead of penance and contemplation you waste your time in the gymnasium and degrade yourself with fighting and whoring."

Lodan turned off the particle shower, walked past his great uncle and back into his sleeping quarters. He remained silent as he pulled on his finest shirt and britches.

"You have too much of your mother in your constitution," continued Aurex pointedly. "She was dissolute and free with her morals, just like you; your father should have allowed the natural course of punishment to descend on her unworthy head instead of his foolish and headstrong act of self-sacrifice. She was a whore and deserved to die like a whore. Now, come with me."

Lodan had heard this condemnation before from his great uncle's lips and resented it no less in his present circumstances. He wanted so much to speak; to tell this man, this usurper, that his father was a better man than he and would have been the Arkon's natural heir had he not been unjustly banished. Now Aurex was the heir to the throne of the DeRhogai but it was not an ascendency Lodan was ever going to witness. He was trapped and now he had to face his fate. He grimly pressed his lips together and followed Aurex from the accommodation.

They descended to the ground in stony silence and walked out beyond the gleaming façade of the tower. The world had turned and the harsh light of dawn touched the fabulous towers, temples and palaces of the City of Kagan-Minnar. Normally it was a sight that Lodan loved to see as he returned after a night of feasting and careless love, but now it just seemed stifling.

Beyond the polished, stone base of the tower lay an extensive, vertiginous park decorated with finely sculptured fountains served by water extracted from rocks buried deep below the surface. The frivolous use of water, an extremely valuable commodity, was a sign of great wealth and ostentation; a testament to the importance of the owner. Rare and exotic plants augmented the point and were arranged in grounds surrounding the white-stone palace of the Arkon. A pleasant path wound through the impeccable, incongruous garden towards the palace where no vehicles other than those of the Arkon himself were permitted.

Lodan had trodden this path too many times before on the occasions of his audiences with the Arkon. Sometimes his transgressions were for impiety and usually resulted in physical punishments that did not particularly bother him. Other occasions for inappropriate dalliances invited more severe censure such as the payment of compensation to offended husbands and a period of detention in the family jail. Lodan was not terribly bothered by the pain of a flogging, but days of boredom and enforced prayer really did inconvenience him, particularly as it meant a period of enforced celibacy. However, on these occasions, he was not nearly as inconvenienced as the ladies involved who usually lost their heads.

Lodan had not appeared before the Arkon since the middle of the previous year, when he had been discovered in flagrante with the wife of one of the under-secretaries of the palace. On that occasion he had got away with no more than a mild thrashing, but the Arkon had warned him that he would tolerate no more transgressions of any sort. This had alarmed Lodan sufficiently to encourage him to restrict himself to whoring rather than chasing married women and he had even eschewed several juicy fights that he could have enjoyed. Indeed, until last night, his record was exemplary and the Arkon would have found nothing to reproach him for.

As they mounted the wide steps of the palace, Aurex spoke again. "I do not need to remind you of the procedure, you have done this before."

"I remember, Uncle," replied Lodan.

They passed through a great door and into the cool interior of the building. A great vaulted reception area announced the importance of the occupant to any visitor. Unusually it was totally devoid of its usual compliment of secretaries and lackeys. A looming silence prevailed and accentuated their footsteps on the highly polished stone floor. A generous flight of steps issued from the middle of the hall and ascended almost twenty metres in a continuous flight. At the top of the flight was a massive, finely wrought pair of doors. This was the entrance to the Sanctum of The Arkon.

Lodan's heartbeat rose with each step and he wondered how many days he would be permitted to put his affairs in order before his execution. At the top of the great flight they paused and Aurex opened the doors and stood aside to allow Lodan to pass inside.

Lodan entered, steeling himself for the ordeal to come. A Condemnation was an intimidating, degrading experience and he had heard of men weeping and begging for mercy during the ceremony. He would show no weakness of that sort; he was a DeRhogai, a direct descendant of the Arkon and he was determined to maintain his dignity, even in these circumstances. The long hall was elegantly vaulted and decorated with images of DeRhogai achievements going back centuries. Images taken from the life of the Prophet Minnar, executed in mosaics of coloured stone, adorned the ceiling. A large, pure white stone statue of the Prophet holding a sword in one hand and a book in the other loomed over a low, stone dais on which stood the only piece of furniture in the hall, a throne of intricately carved granite. On this great seat of power sat the Arkon.

Immediately Lodan noticed that the circumstances of the Condemnation were not as others. Where were the councillors; the secretaries; the hangers-on and the piously self-satisfied sadists looking for a good show of contrition? Where were the guards? The hall was entirely empty save for the presence of the Arkon himself. As he performed the obeisance, genuflecting and pressing his head to the polished stone floor, Lodan could hear his great uncle muttering in surprise behind him. He counted to ten, then rose, advanced ten paces and repeated the traditional obeisance. He did it five times more until he reached an inlaid line in the floor six metres from the Arkon and there he stayed, his forehead pressed firmly to the stone. His great uncle advanced beside him, bowed but remained standing.

"Cedum Cedanus, you may go." The Arkon's voice, hardly more than a whisper, echoed around the empty chamber. He pointedly always used Aurex's given name rather than the one he had assumed on induction to the Brotherhood of Mercy.

Aurex's surprise was augmented and he could not prevent disappointment from colouring his tone. "You are without guards, Arkon. And where are the Councillors of Judgement and the Recording Secretaries?"

The Arkon had anticipated his descendant's disquiet. "Be not alarmed, Cedum Cedanus, I have judged this man's offence so heinous that I do not believe it can be heard by others; not even by your own ears. On my shoulders and mine alone must it rest. I do not expect him to murder me, but if he does you will come to this office sooner than you expected."

"I have always prayed for your longevity, Arkon. My loyalty and service to you is surely beyond question."

The Arkon nodded slowly. "Beyond question."

"I… I merely wished to verify the punishment, so that I may prepare myself for my duty."

"I assure you, my loyal kinsman, the punishment will be more severe than any you can devise. Now leave us."

Aurex bowed low and withdrew, his footsteps echoed around the polished walls. The Arkon waited until the door had closed behind him before he spoke.

"Raise your head, Lodan Sevarius. I do not wish to address the back of your neck."

Lodan raised himself but remained kneeling. His eyes flickered towards the august person before him then back to the floor. The Arkon was one hundred and fifty eight years old and had been in office for over eighty years; longer than any previous incumbent. The responsibilities of office did not seem to have diminished him; his lively grey eyes betrayed no sign of lethargy as they darted about the chamber, picking up on the smallest nuance of behaviour. His memory was legendary and his understanding undiminished by age, which is more than can be said for his exterior which was crumpled and crushed by the passing of too many years. His robe of finely decorated scarlet and blue hung loosely from his shrivelled body and flowed over the elegant lattice of his throne.

"This is the seventeenth time you have come before me, is it not, Lodan Sevarius?"

"Yes, Arkon."

"You may look at me, if my appearance does not revolt you."

"No Arkon, it does not."

Lodan raised his eyes and beheld the old man.

"The last time you came before me, having disgraced the family name, I recall warning you that I would tolerate no further indiscretions, and yet, less than a year has passed and you appear before me again, this time with an offence almost beyond credence. I had hoped for better. Your studies were more than satisfactory and I believe your great uncle was ready to induct you into the mysteries of the Brotherhood. It is a pity that your foolish father prevented the Sacrificial Rite for it would have deprived you of the organ that has got you into this trouble and you would have been spared the fate that awaits you. I had hoped for an atavistic tendency to prevail and you would follow the example of your excellent paternal grandfather, but sadly you have inherited the libidinous habits of your mother and the wilful stubbornness of your father. You are a libertine and a degenerate. Whoring among the detritus of our society is bad enough, but with your activities of last night, you passed into an entirely new realm of degradation."

"I did not order the boy; I have been set up."

"Be quiet, I did not give you permission to speak. I am dismayed that the clear warning I delivered to you during your last audience before me has achieved nothing. You are an incorrigible philanderer and you leave me no choice on this occasion. Lodan Severius DeRhogai, I condemn you to public dismemberment; may the Prophet have mercy on you."

The words fell like stone from the mouth of the Arkon and Lodan felt the blood drain from him. He considered a plea of mitigation but it would not be thought manly or befitting the pride of a DeRhogai. He felt weak, empty and powerless to avoid his fate.

"What do you say to this judgement? Do you plead for your life, Lodan Severius? Do you plead for your uncle's blunted sword?"

"No Arkon, but I am not a pederast; I swear it in the name of my father; I do not deserve this."

The old man shook his head sadly and reached into his gown and pulled from it a small device. A graphic and explicit image appeared between them. "Is this not you then?" asked the Arkon in an ironic tone.

Lodan glanced at it and hung his head; it was much as he had suspected. "I was insensible; I had no conscious knowledge of this."

"And yet here it is," replied the Arkon, "the inevitable fruit of your dissipation."

The image disappeared and the Arkon sat back in his throne and perused his subject as if in deep thought. "Did you know the boy was a DeCorrone?"

Lodan's eyes widened and he dumbly stared at the Arkon in confusion.

"The thrice-great nephew of the Arkon DeCorrone, to be exact."

Lodan remained dumbstruck; his mouth fell open, but no sound emerged.

"I see from your reaction you have grasped the seriousness of the situation. I have already received a demand for your extradition; our cousins the DeCoronne are most efficient are they not? Should I give you up? The punishment they will devise will doubtless make public dismemberment seem like a blessed mercy. It is unlikely that they would kill you; at least not for a long, long time."

"Arkon, I beg of you, you cannot give me up to them."

"For once you have grasped the truth, Lodan Severius; I cannot render you to their justice; no DeRhogai will ever be subjected to the justice of another ruling house. To allow it would set a dangerous president and enable our enemies to demean us by broadcasting your fate."

Lodan breathed again. "I will submit to dismemberment and bear it as best I can."

"You will do what I tell you to do," replied the old man with sudden animation.

"Yes Arkon."

The Arkon remained silent, staring at the pale, cropped hair on the top of his subject's bowed head. He had a soft spot for Lodan, his grandson of the fifth generation, perhaps because he saw echoes of the rebelliousness of his own youth. Lodan was physical and possessed a disdain for authority and convention that attracted his great ancestor. He was well read and intelligent, but not mendacious or devious in any way. He would do as well as any other for the task ahead.

Eventually the Arkon spoke again. "I have some questions to put to you and you will answer them candidly."

Lodan raised his eyes to the old man's craggy face. "Yes Arkon."

"When your father prevented your induction to the Brotherhood, were you relieved?"

Lodan considered avoiding the question; it occurred to him that he was being drawn ever deeper into a trap. But if he lied he knew the old man would soon find him out, so he replied, "Yes Arkon, I was relieved."

"Why was that?"

"I had already known pleasure of fornication and knew I would not live easily without it. Also, I feared I would fail in piety."

The Arkon's eyes narrowed on his subject. "You defied the sacred edict of the Prophet with an act of illegal fornication? At what age did you transgress?"

"I was thirteen, Arkon."

The Arkon stared at his descendent in disbelief. "Thirteen," he repeated slowly.

"Yes, Arkon."

"It seems that your degeneration began early. Had I known I would have confined you and ordered the Rite of the Sacrifice to proceed in spite of your father's wishes. Your amorous adventures would have been curtailed and you would have gone into the Brotherhood. But this is idle reflection; you say you were afraid that would fail in piety. Is your faith truly so weak?"

Lodan was now seriously alarmed; he did not wish to die an apostate. "I am of the faith, truly I am," he protested.

"Come, come, Lodan, we are being candid with each other, are we not? Look around you; do you see any witnesses? You are already condemned to die so you may open your heart without fear."

"I am ready to die, if that is your command, but do not excommunicate me, I do not wish to suffer eternal agonies in the After-world."

The Arkon smiled faintly at his naïve subject. "Lodan, be assured I will not condemn you to such a fate, but I have been watching you. Your attendance at the Temple is no more than the minimum and when you are there you show obvious signs of distraction. Now, you will tell me the truth. Look behind me, what do you see?"

Lodan raised his eyes to the serene face of the enormous statue that loomed over the throne. "The Prophet who is the Lord of All Men."

The Arkon regarded him as one addressing a foolish child. "Really? I'll tell you what I see. I see a large slab of rock that has been hewn and expertly fashioned into the imagined image of an ordinary man who lived on Agon many generations ago."

Lodan was shocked; he had never heard such blasphemy. It was extraordinary considering it was coming from the lips of the spiritual leader of the DeRhogai, a man of the most assiduous piety. "I don't know what to say, Arkon."

"You are surprised, no doubt, to hear such a view expressed?"

"Yes, I am most surprised."

"And to discover that you are not alone in your doubt of the Credo."

"I do not doubt; I have never doubted, Arkon."

"Do not be alarmed, Lodan, there have been many men throughout history who have doubted. The notion that Man was fashioned from the waters of the Sea of Creation by the will of Minnar himself is difficult to reconcile with what we now know of the Universe. It requires faith and discipline to maintain such an unnatural notion in the face of scientific reason. Once you lose that faith your mind may be opened to other possibilities."

At this point the Arkon again reached into his gown and produced a thin tablet of a design not used for over a hundred years. "You may rise and take this object from my hand."

Lodan stood thankfully; the pressure on his knees had become quite painful. He advanced and received the tablet. He had never been so close to the Arkon; the man smelled strongly of incense. He stepped back quickly.

"On this tablet lies the Book of Minnar, the most sacred text of our faith. It is in the ancient form as written by the Prophet Himself on Agon. You have studied the book in this form and, I was led to believe, prospered in the endeavour."

"My efforts were acceptable, Arkon."

"Commendable modesty, Lodan Sevarius. But that is not all that is written on that tablet, for hidden in the matrix of the visible text lies another document. This document is a scientific treatise on the true origin of Man and must not be seen by anyone other than yourself. Do I make myself perfectly understood?"

"Yes, Arkon."

"You will study this document and commit the essence of it to your memory: then you will destroy the tablet."

"Yes Arkon. How will I access the hidden document?"

"It will know you and only you. Now kneel and kiss my foot and swear on your eternal soul that you will never divulge what has been said here to anyone."

Lodan knelt and touched the old man's gnarled foot with his lips. "I swear it," he said.

"You will go to your chambers; you will speak to no one; you will gather a small parcel of essentials and board the next liner to Barta Magnus. There you will be met by one of my agents who will instruct you further. You will desist from any fornication whatsoever. There will be no more whoring for you; you are entering my direct service. Do you understand?"

"I am to be spared!"

"You are, but you may have occasion to curse me and wish you were dead before my business with you is finished. I have placed on your unworthy shoulders the responsibility of the future prosperity of this family. You will go to Barta Magnus and there you will receive instructions that are to be followed exactly. You will never attempt to contact me or any other individual on Kagan and you are never to return. Do not fail me, Lodan Sevarius, I have a long reach and I will not hesitate to initiate your sentence of death should you falter or stray from the path I have designed for you. Now go and send in your uncle who doubtless lurks beyond that door preparing his sword for your unworthy neck."

Lodan bowed and retreated. He could hardly take in what had just happened; one moment he was condemned to an hideous and degrading death, the next he was spared and charged with mysterious errand for the Arkon, himself; a man who appeared to have lost his faith. The whole business was extraordinary, quite bizarre. He opened the heavy, ornate doors to the hall and discovered his great uncle, as expected, just outside.

"The old man wants to see you, Cedum."

Aurex visibly bristled at the casual insult; only the Arkon ever used his given name. "Wait here," he snapped, "I will deal with you shortly."

Lodan smiled, waited until his uncle had entered the audience chamber and then ran down the steps of the grand staircase two at a time.

"I will dull my blade for that boy's neck," uttered Aurex, bowing.

"When you are Arkon you may cut off the heads of as many of this family as you please, but the head of Lodan Sevarius will not be one of them."

"You have not condemned him? Replied Aurex incredulously.

"Oh yes, I have condemned him, that much I will grant you. He is to be banished, he is to disappear."

"I don't understand."

"Do you not? His offence is against the DeCorrone, would you hand him over to them to make a public spectacle of him?"

Aurex frowned. "What did he do, Arkon?"

"My respected kinsman, I will not sully your ears with the details; let us say his offence was against natural law and concerned a young, male member of the DeCorrone."

The Evangelist's face twisted in shock. He began to pace. "I knew he was dissolute but this… this is way beyond anything I could have imagined. He must be punished, surely our laws demand it."

"Would you give our enemies that satisfaction?"

Aurex stopped pacing and looked up sharply. "What do you mean?"

The Arkon held his gaze steadily. "You would sacrifice one of my blood-line to satisfy their demands?"

"I would not punish him according to their demands."

"Maybe not, but that is how it would look. It would show weakness; it would hand the DeCorrone family a propaganda victory over us."

Aurex was, by no means, in favour of handing anyone a victory of any sort, but the Arkon's logic eluded him. It was yet another example of the recent strange behaviour of his leader, who had lately stood down his personal guard and sealed his private chambers against any intrusion. Aurex had become convinced that there was someone or something in the Arkon's chambers that warranted investigation, but he did not dare to embark on such a hazardous course. "And where is Lodan Sevarius to be sent?"

"That does not concern you. You are not to pursue this matter any further."

Aurex was about to protest, but his disquiet stayed him. He bowed and whispered, "Of course, Arkon."

The old man nodded imperceptibly and waved him away. He watched the Evangelist retreat and waited until the doors had closed behind him, then he slipped off the throne and limped around the back of the great statue of Minnar and through a concealed door that led to his private chambers.

The Arkon's private quarters were in direct contrast to the austere, unfurnished throne room. The furnishings and decorations were of the finest quality, gem encrusted antiques and gorgeous rugs of natural fibre were tastefully arranged around a flaming brazier to form an intimate space in the middle of the room. Since all natural light was excluded, the brazier formed the principal source of illumination, its flames cast subtle, flickering shadows on to the likenesses of previous Arkons, who's stern features adorned the walls.

The Arkon limped over to his favourite chair and slumped into its folds. As he stared thoughtfully into the mesmerizing flames of the brazier a barely perceptible whirring came from the other side of the fire and a chair hovered out of the shadows and claimed a position nearby.

"You think this person capable?" The voice was scarcely more than a whisper.

The Arkon sighed. "There are many faults of character but Lodan is intelligent and has an independence of thought that is unusual on Kagan. There is also knowledge of early scripture and learning that may prove useful."

"I detected a distracted nature, are you sure of loyalty and discretion? Are you sure that he is open to the denial of his faith?"

The Arkon considered. "I do not know, but we have little choice, honoured Doyen. Time is short; the DeCorrone agent Dax has returned to Kagan and, by now, the Serene Master of the Brotherhood must be entertaining a suspicion that this is not a normal conspiracy. He is bound to send out another agent and we must assume the worst."

"The casket is the key. Do you think they have it?"

The Arkon shook his head. "It is normal practice to destroy anything that hints of any contradiction of doctrine, lest it fall into the wrong hands. I doubt they would have had it analyzed. We may assume the casket was destroyed on Agon when Doctor Bru's unfortunate assistant was murdered. Without the casket they would have no physical evidence so how could they know? My spies in the DeCorrone Palace tell me that Brother Dax has been punished severely for his failure. Fortunately I am in a position to intercept any communication that may come from that quarter."

Lim glanced at the ancient alumnus whose crumpled features danced in the flames. "Do you regret our association, Juran?"

"Sometimes; it has forced me to live a lie my whole life. I am the spiritual head of this family, I have prayed to a false prophet knowing my prayers echoed upon nothing greater than well-fashioned stone and I have obliged others to do the same. And what was the reason for all this false devotion? Money and power, Herton; money and power."

"They have their uses; we have both had occasion to discover that."

The Arkon nodded slowly, thoughtfully. His old teacher, Doyen Herton Lim was staring into the flames of the brazier, apparently on some deep, personal mental journey. The Arkon contemplated confiding his true motive to his ancient teacher but dismissed the idea almost instantly. What purpose would be served by it? Lim would be disappointed in him and his old doyen's disapprobation was something that he was unwilling to experience. It was as though, on their meeting, the years had dissolved and their former relationship of respect and supplication had somehow re-established itself. This was strange because Lim was now reliant on his protection and, in effect, their roles were now reversed. When his frail teacher had arrived following a recent flight from Suran, it was clear that the journey had taken its toll and Lim was dreadfully weakened by the ordeal. His teacher had lost the ability to walk in the process and the voice was no more than hoarse whisper.

He observed the ancient pedant, bent double in the chair, creased and crumpled like a pile of discarded rags, so physically reduced that life was scarcely clinging to the yellowed flesh. He tried to recall the haughty, proud person he had met so long ago. "I never asked you, Herton, do you regret our collaboration on the Fourth Proposition?"

Lim looked up, suddenly animated. "We were both young and our thoughts were fresh and perhaps, rash; we should have seen the terrible consequences. We should not have published."

"But we did and now we are here."

"Now we are here," echoed Lim. "and now we owe it to those who sacrificed their lives so many years ago to see this business finished."

The Arkon took his eyes from his teacher and directed them towards the flames of the brazier. He had never shared Lim's terrible anguish over the pogroms that resulted from the publication of the blasphemous Fourth Proposition; his principal concern had always been self-preservation and the consequent fear that the identity of the authors would be discovered. But regardless of how many were murdered in the purges that swept their civilization, they were never exposed. "You are right, Herton; there has been great loss of life and I fear there will be more to come."

Lim turned back to the flames, eyes closed. "In the name of all those who have perished, I hope you are wrong, Juran."

II

Aurex was not surprised to discover that Lodan had already gone when he passed through the great doors of the throne room and out into the high, vaulted vestibule beyond. He was in a severe state of conflict, torn between, on one side, his natural loyalty for the head of his family and, on the other, his calling as an Evangelist. He agonized for some time before deciding on his next course of action, for he knew there was no turning back once it had been embarked upon. In the end, he saw that the nagging suspicion that he harboured in his breast had to be assuaged and that meant crossing a forbidden line.

He armed himself and went directly to the residence of the one man who could enlighten him; the one man who he knew had recently visited the Arkon in his private chambers; the Physician to the Throne.

The Arkon's personal physician was a mild, gentle soul who had attended exclusively to his patient's medical requirements for over forty years. He was seventy-two and lived in some comfort in a villa in the DeRhogai Park. Aurex had been to the villa twice before, each time on the rare occasion of a reception that the man had given. He was unmarried and lived a reclusive life, devoting himself to the study of medicine and other virtuous occupations.

Aurex strode to the villa through the sunlit, fragrant park and applied for an audience. The simulant that met him at the entrance to the residence, bowed, and said that it would enquire. It came back directly and informed him that the physician was indisposed. At this point Aurex crossed the line. He pulled out his sidearm and fired it at the simulant. There was a peculiar scream and the sound of escaping air as the thing clattered to the floor and began to melt from within. Aurex watched its death throes disinterestedly and walked past the smoking heap into the villa. Physician Sokolom was sitting on his terrace in the morning sunshine studying a large display tablet when Aurex strode into his presence. On seeing him there, the physician stood and angrily challenged him. Two simulants rushed on to the terrace and Aurex disabled them both in quick succession. They stumbled and clattered to the polished, stone floor where one began to burn with an acrid stench. Another simulant appeared with an extinguisher and doused the flames. When the fire was out the simulant looked at Aurex with fear in its eyes.

"Return to your post," commanded Aurex, levelling the firearm at it. It scuttled off with obvious relief.

Sokolom observed the destruction of his domestics with alarm; no one had ever dared to threaten him before; he was an important man; a man under the direct protection of the Arkon himself.

"Sit down, Physician," said Aurex, carelessly waving the sidearm in his direction.

Sokolom lowered himself into his seat and stared up at Aurex with fear in his gentle face. "What do you mean by this intrusion?" he stammered.

Aurex took a seat opposite the man and pointed his sidearm in the direction of his head. "You attended the Arkon four days ago. What was the purpose of your visit?"

Sokolom's eyes bulged at the effrontery of the question. "You well know, that is confidential; I could not possibly divulge such information."

"That's as maybe, but I mean to have it out of you all the same."

"Go away now and I will not report this disgraceful offence to the Arkon."

Aurex moved closer and brought the sidearm close to the man's forehead. "Before I leave here, you will tell me what I wish to know."

The physician shut his eyes. "Go ahead, kill me; I will not break my oath; not for you, not for anyone."

"I am not going to kill you, Sokolom; I'm going to dismember you very gradually, until you judge that you have suffered enough pain and lost enough of your extremities to speak."

"You are a despicable thug; I have always known it."

"I am an instrument of the Prophet; that is all. You have a choice, Physician; you are elderly and the agony will not go well for you. If you speak freely, I guarantee that the Arkon will not discover your broken oath, unless you choose to confess it yourself. Now, who is in the Arkon's private chambers?"

Sokolom scowled and considered his situation. He knew Aurex's reputation well and little doubted that he would carry out his barbaric threat; there seemed little point in suffering needlessly. "I don't know; I never saw... the person before."

Aurex lowered his sidearm and leaned back in his chair. "'Person'?"

"Yes, I could not determine the gender of the Arkon's guest."

Aurex frowned. "I take it you were not there for a social visit."

Sokolom nodded. "I was called to administer to the guest."

"You conducted an examination and you could not establish the gender of your patient!"

"I was not permitted to physically examine the patient; he or she remained fully clothed throughout my visit. I was not permitted to touch or go too close."

"Not permitted to touch them! What did this person look like?"

"Extremely old and confined to a chair."

"What was wrong with... this individual?"

"Basically, he or she was dying; mainly from exhaustion but there were other contributing factors, one of which was extremely unusual. I confess I had to do research for my diagnosis, for I have never seen it before."

"And what was that?"

"Crome's disease, an affliction of extreme age."

"Crome's disease; I have never heard of it."

"That is not surprising; it is almost entirely restricted to the population of Suran."

"Suran!"

"Yes. There have been isolated instances on other worlds, but the vast majority of cases appear on Suran. They are a very long lived race."

"Was this person a Suran?"

The physician arched his brow. "I have never seen a Suran in the flesh, but, I am sure that the Arkon would never tolerate the presence of such a devil anywhere near his person. It is a most unlikely scenario."

Aurex stood up suddenly; he had heard enough. "Did you not know that the Arkon's father was Kagan's ambassador to Suran?"

Sokolom shook his head thoughtfully. "No I did not."

"I apologize for the manner of this intrusion. I will, of course, have the damaged simulants replaced. Be assured that this conversation will remain entirely confidential."

Aurex strode quickly out of the residence and into the park leaving the elderly physician shaking his head in confusion.

On leaving the physician's villa Aurex went straight to his quarters. He was extremely alarmed at what he had just heard for he entertained no doubts that the Arkon had not only admitted a Suran to his presence, but that this devil was actually living in the palace. It was almost impossible to believe, but if it was true, it meant that the Arkon had been corrupted. Furthermore, his behaviour towards Lodan Sevarius had been inexplicable and Aurex had convinced himself that the libertine, Lodan Sevarius' banishment was somehow connected to the presence of the Suran devil. He contacted one of his minions and issued some instructions; then he changed into a fresh robe and boarded his private craft for the short journey across the city.

The Palace of the DeCorrone was larger than that of the DeRhogai although it lacked the architectural integrity of its rival. It was older than any other building in the city, having started its long existence as a fort in less harmonious times. To the south of its extensive grounds rose a massive ziggurat on which stood the Temple of Mercy, a giant, forbidding edifice of polished basalt, where the Brothers of the order prayed and scourged themselves in the name of the Prophet. Aurex entered the temple and some cursory enquiries led him to the presence of His Eminence, the Serene Master of the Brotherhood of Mercy, who was strolling in the cloisters with a small cohort of young devotees, pontificating on the joys of devotion and obedience. On Aurex's approach he suddenly ceased his oration; this visit was unusual and most unexpected. Aurex, though high born and well respected in the Brotherhood, was of a rival family and not in the confidence of His Eminence.

Aurex bowed and waited for his leader to initiate the audience.

"Brother Aurex, welcome. We are pleased to see you."

"Thank you, Serene Master. I must request an immediate private audience."

His Eminence drew his lined face into a frown; it was obvious from his body language that Aurex had a matter of some importance to convey. He dismissed the young prospects and invited Aurex to walk with him among the stark, basalt columns. "What troubles you, Brother?"

Aurex assumed a position to the left and slightly behind the wiry frame of his spiritual leader. "Master, I come here in great conflict. I am a DeRhogai and not of your clan, but I am also a Brother and that must be the greater allegiance."

"You are correct, my Brother; our devotion over-rides any temporal claims on our loyalties."

"You will understand my difficulty when I report to you what I have learned today. I believe our Arkon, The DeRhogai, has committed a heinous and foolhardy act, the nature of which I can barely credit."

At this His Eminence's pointed ears pricked up and he turned his beady, green eyes on his subject. Was it possible that this man was about to hand him a victory over his long-time enemy, Juran DeRhogai? "Let us sit together and you will relate to me the nature of this act."

They took a seat on a worn block of stone out of the direct rays of the slanting sun. The cloister was silent and empty save the presence of the two men. "I have very strong evidence that the Arkon of my family is harbouring a Suran."

His Eminence's eyes bulged in their deep-set sockets and he sat bolt upright. "A Suran!"

"Yes. He has not allowed any private audiences in his quarters these past five days, other than his physician. I coerced the man into telling me what he saw. A person of great age, who he was not allowed to properly examine; a person who had an affliction almost entirely confined to the cursed population of Suran."

His Eminence was visibly stunned; he had certainly not expected to hear this. He considered at great length before he spoke again. "Did you obtain a description of this individual?"

"A person of indeterminate gender, as one would expect from that degenerate race and, apparently of very great age. The fiend was confined to a chair."

"I see." His Eminence stroked his chin and disappeared into an envelope of thought. He was considering the propriety of his next move, for it seemed that certain disturbing events had begun to conspire into a potentially devastating plot against the very heart of the Faith. Could this person hiding in the DeRhogai Palace actually be Doyen Lim?"

"There is something else, Master," said Aurex, disturbing the older man's reverie. "Early today, my great nephew, Lodan Sevarius, a man of degraded character, was unaccountably spared my sword and banished. I do not know the details but the offence was apparently against a member of your own family."

"I know nothing of it."

"I thought as much. The whole thing was a ruse, designed to engineer an order of banishment. I have no proof but I sense that there is some connection between this and the presence of the Suran."

The Arkon stood with sudden resolution. "I am the Arkon of the DeCorrone and I would know if any transgression had taken place concerning my family. I am indebted to you, Brother Aurex, for bringing me this information and I well realise the anguish it must have cost you. By your action you have demonstrated your loyalty to our just cause and I will repay that loyalty with trust. You are in direct line to become the next DeRhogai; as the head of your family you will be able to bury the onerous and destructive rivalry between our two great and ancient houses; we will be able to work together for the greater glory of the Faith and those who would protect it with their lives. But first, I must tell you, I believe we are in great danger; there are strong forces ranged against us; forces that have lain hidden for many years and have now turned their mendacious faces towards us. Come with me, Brother, it is time for you to know the true nature of this danger."

He led his fellow Evangelist into the temple and down into a subterranean, low-vaulted cavern below the body of the building where few men now passed. At the end of the cavern an ancient door slid to one side on their approach and they entered a downward sloping passage that wound into the heart of the ziggurat on which the later temple stood. This was a precinct of history that few ever saw; its ancient stone-paved floor was worn with the steps of long-dead pilgrims and the block-stone walls were pitted and crumbling with the action of damp and mould. The air was cold and musty and exuded the odour of neglect. As they moved through the passage, lights flickered into life at their approach and died at their passing, creating a short burst of life in that dead, dark place.

They descended the slope until the gradient gave way to a flight of crude, winding steps. Aurex estimated that they had penetrated over a hundred metres below the temple when they finally entered a large chamber at the base of the staircase. This hall had been the chapel of the DeCorrone and was once richly adorned with the sacred images of the Faith. But now it was long abandoned to the darkness and was without feature save the presence of a large, metal door set into one of its walls.

"This is the chapel of my ancestors which now serves us as a vault for the most precious relics of Our Glorious Faith," announced His Eminence. "Get down on your knees, Brother Aurex."

Aurex knelt before him.

"Now, you will swear to me, in the sacred name of the Prophet, that you will never divulge what you are about to see."

Aurex so swore and the Serene Master allowed him to rise. He then loosened his gown and removed a gold chain from around his neck. Attached to the chain was a small metal key. He took up the key and placed into a hole to the side of the door. There was a loud echoing sound of multiple bolts being withdrawn from their housings and the door opened inwards. "Come," said His Eminence, and they entered the vault.

Inside the vault was an arrangement of shelves on which rested various objects of antiquity. There were scrolls, tightly bound, on which the words of the Prophet were written by ancient hands; there were fragments of bone, the remains of revered ancestors of the Faith; there were crudely fashioned icons, clearly the work of men who had lived millennia ago; there was, in one corner, a complete skeleton, which His Eminence attested were the remains of Mithra, one of the Prophet's many disciples. At one end of the vault there was a gap in the shelves where a small door had been set into the dressed stone lining of the vault. The door was not contemporary with the rest of the vault, for it was obviously of more modern construction and designed to withstand any assault. The Master approached it and a panel to the side of the door lit up. He placed his hand upon the panel three times and recited a brief incantation. The door opened, sliding into the wall and disappearing from view. The master turned to Aurex. "What you are about to see may cause you distress, but you must remember, above all, to have faith."

He ducked into the chamber and, stooping low, Aurex followed with a pounding heart. Inside the chamber was a small table on which was placed a single object. A book.

"Just over four centuries ago," began His Eminence, "a devotee was walking by the shore of the Sea of Creation on Agon. A storm suddenly blew up and the man took refuge for the night in one of the many caves that line the cliffs around the Sea. In the morning, he noticed the tip of an object protruding from the sandy floor of the cave. He dug and brought this object into the light of day. He was not an educated man and could not read what was in the book; however, he knew that it was in the ancient language of our forefathers. He took it to the priests in the Temple of Imbar who were very perplexed by it and confiscated it. Look at it and you will see why."

Aurex stepped forward and looked down at the book. It had a dark-brown, plain cover and was in surprisingly good condition for a volume that had supposedly been buried in the ground. He opened it and noticed that his hand shook as he did so. He had convinced himself that he was about to look upon a relic with a direct association with Minnar, the Prophet himself. He noticed the material from which the book was made was of a strange quality, robust and yet smooth and delicate. He looked down at the first page and read the title. It read:

INSTRUCTIONS FOR PLANTING CROPS. (FIRST ROTATION)

It was written in the ancient form, but uniquely, was not the work of a scribe.

He looked up from the book and turned to the Master, his face betraying the disappointment and confusion he felt.

"I see you have immediately discerned the conundrum, Brother Aurex. This book, a mundane volume describing the planting method to be used when laying out initial crop rotations, is of no great significance in what it contains. The significance of this small volume is that it was obviously produced by a machine a thousand years before such things existed."

"I don't understand," replied Aurex.

"No, neither did the priests at the Temple of Imbar. They took it as a hoax and buried it in their library. Then, just over two hundred years ago, the volume was discovered in a forgotten corner of the library and some assiduous individual decided to test its age. It turned out to be over one-hundred-and-twenty-thousand years old."

Aurex reeled and had to support himself on the table. "That can't be possible."

The Master placed a comforting hand on his shoulder. "Do you not understand, Brother? Our faith is being tested and this volume must have been buried by the Prophet himself, to test our fealty. In his wisdom he knew that it would be discovered and analysed and those who doubt would be exposed."

Aurex shook his head in sorrow and tears came into his eyes. "And now you are testing my faith, Serene Master."

"I know you are strong in your belief; that is why I have shown you this."

Aurex knelt. "I do believe, Master, with all my being."

"I know, Brother, I know."

"But who else knows of this?"

"Very few; no more than can be counted on a single hand."

"But, why have you shown me?"

"Stand up, Brother. Do you know of a certain individual called Solon Bru?"

"No, Serene Master, I have never heard of him."

"He is a Suran devil who was banished from his world forty-seven years ago. He sought to re-awaken a most foul and heinous lie that should have remained buried for all time. He was banished to Agon, but we knew that, sooner or later, he would commit blasphemy and we watched him closely. Not long ago, the fiend started behaving erratically and sent his associate to procure some objects from a reclaimed deep-space cruiser on Station Two-Eleven. We alerted my kinsman, Dax, who happened to be on Agon with two other pilgrims of the Brotherhood.

"Two others went to Station Two-Eleven to discover what had been purchased. It was a casket of a strange design. Of course they destroyed the Station and all who might have come into contact with these devils, but on Agon, Dax failed. He destroyed the casket and Doctor Bru's associate, but allowed the Suran to escape. Dax reasoned that he would go to Barta Magnus and betray those with any sympathy to his foul cause. But Bru did not go to Barta Magnus; he went to Suran and to the home of his former teacher, a creature by the name of Herton Lim, an extremely ancient Doyen. Fortunately, we had already sent an agent to Suran, but the fool allowed Doctor Bru to escape once again. Soon afterwards Doyen Lim also disappeared."

"So that is who the Arkon harbours."

"From what you tell me I am now sure of it. And now I see we are in greater danger than I previously suspected. You are, of course, aware that the Arkon DeRhogai's father was the Kagan ambassador to Suran?"

"Yes, I was aware."

"There must have been some sort of link established during that time. As far as I know, there is no record of a doyen ever having left Suran and to induce such an action would require a momentous reason. I think that the Surans may have something in their possession, something like this," he pointed to the book on the table, "and they plan to use it to destroy us."

"The Arkon must be denounced; this is the opportunity I have been waiting for."

"Have a care, Brother, no one has ever unseated a presiding Arkon, but I agree with you entirely, this conspiracy must be ripped out at the heart."

"Indeed it must," replied Aurex grimly, "and it is my onerous duty to usurp the throne and restore our ancient house to its proper, righteous path."

"That is your destiny, Brother. The Prophet wills it."

Aurex took some moments of silent thought during which he visualised himself sitting on the throne in the DeRhogai Palace wearing the stately vestments. His Eminence observed his fellow devotee, knowing exactly what he was thinking. He smiled inwardly in the knowledge that he would use this man's ambition to destroy his enemy. The moment of reflection passed and Aurex returned to the matter in hand.

"But what of Doctor Bru? Surely the Blasphemer must be caught and executed?"

"Doctor Bru and another Suran devil recently came to light on Tarnus. Brother Dax diverted his ship to that benighted world and apprehended them, but was betrayed by a she-devil, a Kagan fugitive. The Surans escaped once again, this time in a deep-space cruiser, one of our finest crafts. We do not know where they intend to go, but just this morning, I received news of the craft heading through one of the remote outer sectors. It is clear to me now that our priority must be to pursue and destroy them at all costs."

"I agree, the entire resources of the Brotherhood must be mobilized."

"That is precisely what must *not* happen, Brother. It is vital that knowledge this blasphemy must be contained to as few people as possible. We cannot allow an opportunity for those less committed in their faith to come into contact with this calumny. I will send one person, the very person that has the greatest motivation. Come with me, you will meet the instrument of the Prophet's will."

He followed the Serene Master out of the chamber and the door closed behind them sealing in the strange object once more. They ascended to the level of the temple and took the Serene Master's private car to the nearby palace.

Aurex had never before set foot in the DeCorrone Palace and he was struck by the ancient gloominess of the place. A few minions passed him a curious look, but he was with the Arkon and so they kept a respectful distance. He followed the man down into the underbelly of the palace and there, in the chamber of cells he was brought into the presence of Brother Dax. Even Aurex, a man well used to gore, was shocked at what he saw. The man had been flayed until no part of his torso and upper legs resembled flesh. It was as though something had turned his skin inside out, exposing all the rudiments of the vessels and capillaries that contained the human being inside. Even so, Dax was stoically sitting in his cell, seemingly heedless of the agony he must have been enduring. Aurex, who had encountered the man before and judged him over-proud, could not help a pang of admiration for his brother Evangelist.

When they had finished questioning the prisoner and the Serene Master had given Dax his commission, they withdrew. Outside the cell the Master spoke. "Brother Dax will pursue these devils to the end of the universe, if necessary. They will not escape him again. You must discover what your kinsman, Lodan Sevarius, is up to. We will destroy him when we have discovered the extent of this foul conspiracy. You will be my eyes and ears in the DeRhogai Palace; report everything you see and hear to me and me alone. If the Prophet wills it, we will be successful and our beloved faith will prevail until the end of the universe."

III

Lodan, unaware of the machinations that would conspire to confound and endanger him, stood on the open terrace that served his dwelling. The sun was high now and seared the city with relentless heat. His head was alive with the prospect that lay before him. In an instant he had gone from condemnation and certain death to the joyous escape and temptations offered by a trip to Barta Magnus, a place oft denounced by the Arkon himself as the very essence of vacuous wickedness. In his elation he had placed the strange and disturbing business of the Arkon's apparent blasphemy to the back of his mind; it was something to be considered later, when he was of a more tranquil temperament.

He entered his quarters and removed the fine clothes that an audience with The Arkon required and stood naked in the centre of his sleeping chamber. He put his hands on his head and began to laugh, slumping on to the wide divan as his mirth resounded about the room. He reached down and animated his favourite appendage like a puppet. "We're going on a little trip, you and me. What do you think about that?"

"Pretty, fucking good," came the reply in the squeaky voice Lodan reserved for such conversations, for they had both already forgotten the Arkon's injunction.

A few hours later Lodan boarded the liner to Barta Magnus. He had followed The Arkon's instruction and not spoken to a soul before leaving. He had no expectation of ever returning to Kagan and it had troubled him that he had not had the opportunity to say goodbye to his mother who was cloistered with an order of devotees in a temple to the south. He had only seen her twice since her retreat to the Order and on both occasions she had been distant and reserved in his presence. He had never really known whether this was because she was frightened or that she didn't care for him. He knew (because his great uncle had taken pains to tell him), that his father had saved her life after she was discovered in an adulterous relationship. His father had invoked an obscure privilege and had placed himself at the disposal of the executioner in lieu of his wife, but the Arkon had stepped in, forbidding the execution of his nominated heir and thereby, preventing a wide dissemination of the scandal. Instead the Arkon had banished him forever, thereby sparing the blushes of the Family. This unfortunate event had occurred nine years ago, when Lodan was thirteen and he had not seen his father since, nor been allowed to enquire after him. He had lost both parents at that age, an age when their guidance and love might have fashioned his character differently, for even he had to admit that he became exceptionally rebellious and wild after their loss.

Now, that innate wildness had led him to an effective banishment, following in the footsteps of his excellent father. Kagan was his home, but he had no particular love for it; its strict traditions and stifling morality and its interminable demands for overt demonstrations of faith. He was a devout as the next man, but was it really necessary to attend the temple four times a day? Stepping on to that liner bound for Barta Magnus Lodan felt a release, like a man freed from a lifelong, sunless prison who suddenly saw the sunlight for the first time. He could not stifle a grin as he stepped across its threshold and knew that his feet would never again touch the sacred soil of his home world.

"Do you require anything else Sir?" enquired the dour simulant as it placed his small valise on to the receptacle in his sparse cabin.

"No, you may go," replied Lodan, well aware that the thing would report any inappropriate actions or comments.

The simulant withdrew mechanically and Lodan sat down on the unforgiving bed. It was only now that his joy sobered enough to reflect fully on the events of that day and as he thought about them the realization gradually overtook him that he had been the victim of a deception. It was not even subtle, for it could only have been the Arkon himself who had arranged everything, right down to the DeCorrone boy in the night-house. The Arkon had maneuvered him into a box and then offered him the key to escape, but in exchange for what? His mind churned with many questions, none of which he could resolve. He opened his bag and picked up the small tablet containing the Book of Minnar that the Arkon had given him. The familiar title page of the Book appeared. He scanned the first few pages of the work; all seemed familiar, just as he remembered it in the long hours of study during his time of apprenticeship to the Brotherhood of Mercy. Then he noticed an unfamiliar phrase at the bottom of the second page. It said, 'speak the name of the Prophet'. Lodan knew this was not in the original text and so he said the sacred name out loud. Immediately the face of the tablet reconfigured and the words 'The Fourth Proposition' appeared. Lodan had heard of the first three Propositions, but never The Fourth.

Intrigued, he began to read. The script was dense and technical and he could immediately see that it would require long hours of study. He had plenty of time to perform that duty, so he put down the tablet and turned his mind to other things.

Less than thirty years ago the journey to Barta Magnus would have taken almost a year, but now took just over six days. Six days in which Lodan would have ample time to reflect. He had never left Kagan before and was keen to observe the departure, so he made his way to the social lounge where a large observation window afforded a view of the international port and its immediate, desolate surroundings. There were about forty people milling around or sitting on the occasional furniture. All were men and most were natives of Kagan, with only about five being obviously citizens of Barta Magnus, distinguished by their informal, colourful dress and lighter skin tone. If there were any women on board, they would be either restricted to their cabins or in a separate lounge hidden away in the belly of the ship.

A few eyes strayed disinterestedly in his direction as he entered, then, seeing nothing remarkable, resumed their previous preoccupations. This was a Kagan ship and poorly patronized, being hardly more than ten percent full. It lacked the amenities of the more commercial liners of Barta Magnus; there would be no gambling or inappropriate entertainments; there would be no women; there would be no artificial stimulants, other than the mild wine fermented from the bitter sap of a desert plant. There would be plenty of time for reflection and for prayer and the four daily assemblies of obeisance that must be attended by everyone aboard.

Lodan approached the attendant simulant and ordered a goblet of wine. The simulant produced it with expressionless efficiency. Lodan took it and moved to the observation area. They would be leaving very soon.

"Your first time?"

A man had sidled up to him and was addressing him in a confidential tone. Lodan turned and beheld a Kagan of moderate height, probably in his mid-twenties. He had prematurely thinning, dark hair and large hook shaped nose and small, penetrating eyes which were set a little too close together. His open mouth revealed white, uneven teeth behind thick, dark lips drawn into a rather unconvincing smile.

"Yes, is it obvious?"

"Only to one such as myself; I am an astute observer of human behaviour."

"Is that so?" Lodan did not particularly wish to engage this person or any other at this time, but the man possessed a persistent quality that was hard to ignore.

"It is. You will no doubt be curious to know how I was able to discern this fact." The question was rhetorical and the man did not trouble to pause for an answer. "You see, seasoned travellers know that the initial phase of the take-off is not interesting; the spectacular views only occur when we reach the upper atmosphere so most people stay in their seats and do not stand by the observation port. Also I noticed you were gazing intently out at a scene of no particular interest. This is a classic sign of first flight nerves."

Lodan, who was not nervous, held his tongue, but the man was not discouraged by his silence.

"Now that we have had a conversation you must permit me to introduce myself. My name is Morg Perswant."

"Lodan Sevarius," replied Lodan, deliberately omitting his family name.

"Sevarius? That is an unusual familiar."

"Is it?"

"Indeed, I have never come across another of that name."

"There is a first time for any experience."

"That is true. Is your trip to Barta for business or pleasure?"

Lodan bristled imperceptibly at the increasingly intrusive nature of the conversation. "You'll forgive me, I believe we are about to take off."

"Yes indeed we are. I see that I have intruded on you at a private moment. Perhaps we will talk again when you are feeling more relaxed."

Morg Perswant bowed slightly and made his way over to engage a more receptive subject. Lodan watched him from the corner of his eye; it was a long trip and he was going to be a nuisance. Shortly after a slight shudder rippled through the ship and ground began to slowly slip away. Soon he could see the entire expanse of the spaceport and the city beyond. The jagged mountain chain to the east of the city shrunk as the liner rose higher into the clear sky and began to climb towards the edges of the atmosphere. The magnificent sweep of the horizon shone in the intense light of the afternoon as they rose ever higher and soon he could see the edge of space and the curve of the world on which he had spent his whole life. He would not miss it or anyone on it. So many women; so many perfumed bodies had touched his but none had claimed a place in his heart. He had lusted but he had never loved and he now realized, as he watched the glowing curve of his world, that he was quite alone.

IV

The exhilaration of take-off was soon replaced by the tedium of a long journey devoid of entertainment. Lodan kept to his cabin for the first day, taking his meals there and spending his time reading the Fourth Proposition. He found it extremely difficult to read, not only because of its highly technical content, but also because its basic argument contradicted everything he had been brought up to believe. The

Arkon had chosen him for some purpose related to this document, but he had chosen ill, for despite Lodan's lax devotions, he was, fundamentally, a true believer. He persevered but the relentless intensity of technical data eventually drove him from his studies and into the common areas, but as soon as he set foot in the one of the passenger lounges, Morg Perswant invariably materialized next to him and resumed their one-sided conversation as if no time had passed since the end of the previous one.

"Lodan Sevarius, I am gratified to see you; I was beginning to think you would not be socializing at all today. What is it that detains you in your accommodation for such a time?"

"I am not gregarious."

"Me neither, I have to make an effort. What about a game?"

Lodan contemplated an instant refusal, but heard himself agreeing to the proposal. Morg grinned widely and conducted him to a free table. The favoured game of Strategy materialized between them and they began to play. Lodan was an infrequent but proficient player but Morg Perswant turned out to be an expert and had him beaten in less than half an hour. They played a second game during which neither spoke, devoting all their mental resources to the moves. Eventually Morg prevailed, though not so easily as the first time and he sat back smiling in suppressed triumph.

"You learn quickly, Lodan Sevarius. I am not sure that I should accept a third challenge."

"I am not sure that I should make one."

Morg observed him thoughtfully with his beady, dark eyes. "Perhaps a drink?"

Lodan nodded and watched the man stroll over to the simulant and procure two drinks. When he returned with them Lodan noticed his was alcoholic and his companion's was not. He wondered, as he casually studied the man, at his motivation. He had certainly not encouraged the association; quite the reverse, in fact and yet the man had doggedly persisted when there were clearly more receptive passengers aboard.

"What is your reason for this trip?"

Morg seemed slightly thrown by the sudden interest. "I...I am visiting family."

"You have family on Barta Magnus? That's quite unusual."

"I know. My second cousin is in need of a husband and I am to do her the honour."

"Was she born on Barta?"

"Yes, she is fourteen."

"And you are to marry her and take her back to Kagan?"

"That is her father's wish. He fears for her soul if she remains on Barta where women are allowed far too much latitude for their own interests. Did you know that they are permitted to leave their dwellings without a chaperone and that they are even allowed to choose their own husbands?" He shook his head at the wonder of it. "Who knows what might happen? There are many distractions that will turn a young woman's head."

"No doubt. And what does the young lady think about your suit?" added Lodan mischievously.

Morg looked at him as if he had just blasphemed. "She does not know I am coming, of course."

"You are a brave man, taking a wife who has been raised in such a liberal society. Do you not expect trouble?"

Morg increased his expression of incredulity. "Trouble? What sort of trouble?"

"Perhaps willfulness; independence of thought?"

Morg's face broke into a grin. "She will be thrashed," he replied simply.

Lodan made no reply other than to nod noncommittally; he had no knowledge of the girl but felt sorry for her all the same. Conjugal bliss with Morg Perswant seemed an unlikely prospect.

"And what of your purpose on Barta?" he rejoined after a mouthful of his drink.

"Business," replied Lodan flatly.

'In what line?"

"I cannot tell you."

Morg leaned forward and whispered. "Now I am intrigued. I will have it out of you by the end of our journey."

Lodan straightened and looked his companion in the eye. "It is possible for a man to know too much." He stood. "I believe I will retire now."

Morg stood quickly and lightly touched his arm. "Forgive me; I fear I have offended you. I did not mean to pry."

Lodan nodded and strode off with his erstwhile companion looking after him. In the corner of the room another passenger was apparently deep in conversation with a small group of others, but this particular passenger was not listening to his companions' ill-judged observations. He was watching Lodan and had been doing so since embarkation.

Lodan left the lounge and waited out of sight to make sure he was not followed, and then he made his way to the purser's office. As he entered a simulant stood up and bowed obsequiously.

"I delight in assisting you," it said.

"I want to see the purser," replied Lodan looking past it to the open door beyond.

"I will make you an appointment."

"I don't want an appointment; I wish to see him now."

"I don't think it will be poss-…"

"You in there," interrupted Lodan, "I don't want to speak to a tin box. Show yourself."

The simulant looked quite shocked. "We have feelings too."

"Shut up," snapped Lodan just as an elderly gentleman in a slightly shabby uniform appeared at the door of the inner office. He was of average build and, unusually for a Kagan, sported a moustache. He wore a skullcap to conceal his head of threadbare, grey hair. Incongruously his eyebrows were black as jet and sprouted luxuriantly from his furrowed brow. Lodan assessed him instantly as a journeyman, plodding through his little life behind his little desk, hoping not to be too noticed.

"Can I help?" he was instantly defensive, as if expecting a strong complaint.

"I want to speak to you privately. My name is Lodan DeRhogai."

The purser bowed. "It is always an honour to have a DeRhogai on board. Please come in."

"Turn this off first," he said pointing to the offended simulant. "I don't want this damn tin box listening through the wall. What I have to discuss is very private."

The purser looked intrigued. "My staff-man is very discrete, but if you insist."

He switched off the simulant using a control that he kept in his pocket and led the way into a small office that contained two chairs either side of an information table on which rested a primitive clay model of a person.

"My daughter made an effigy of me when she was four years old," explained the purser, sitting and indicating a seat for his guest. "She's married with her own children now. What can I do for you?"

"I require access to the passenger manifest."

The purser treated him to a look of indignation. "I would lose my job. It's impossible."

Without replying Lodan removed a small tablet from his pocket and placed it in front of the man. The purser glanced at the figure on the tablet but kept his countenance. Lodan waited; it was a large amount for a man such as this, he knew he would crack soon enough.

"Perhaps if sir had a specific question," said the purser at length.

"The passenger Morg Perswant, when did he book passage on this vessel?"

The purser nodded. "I can allow that information." He animated the table and brought up the information. His bushy eyebrows danced upwards as he read. "That's very odd; the passage was booked only half an hour before departure."

Lodan's face darkened, so much for the story of Perswant's marriage plans. "I want access to his cabin."

"I couldn't possibly allow it."

Lodan speared him with such a dangerous glare that the man was obliged to shrink away from his own desk. "This fucker is threatening my life. You will give me access."

"What are you going to do? We can't have any murders on board."

"Don't worry; I'm not going to murder anybody. It won't come back on you; I give you my word on it."

The purser swallowed hard, he was used to dealing with the trivial and mild complaints of travellers, not dangerous and aggressive psychos. He contemplated informing the captain, but dismissed the idea immediately; he had already embarked on the path of corruption by giving this man confidential information. It would not take the captain long to discover the indiscretion. Besides, he was looking at two year's salary on the table in front of him. "You're not going to kill this man?"

Lodan shook his head. "I just want to find out why he's following me, that's all."

"Alright, double that and I'll do it," he said, pointing to the tablet.

Lodan smiled mirthlessly, it was small change to him. "Very well." He changed the figure and verified it by placing the minute device concealed beneath the skin of his palm on the appropriate part. The purser touched the tablet and the amount peeled from Lodan's fat account and floated off into the ether to swell the property of the recipient.

The purser overrode the lock. "Cabin 512."

Lodan rose and strode out past the inert simulant.

Morg Perswant's accommodation was identical to his own, consisting of a bed, a place for ablutions, a locker and one or two occasional pieces of furniture to lend it a modicum of comfort. Lodan searched it thoroughly, rifling through the man's possessions and clothing. He found nothing that could give him the information he wanted so he settled down to wait for the occupant. He waited for just under an hour before the door slid to one side and Morg Perswant entered. He did not see Lodan who had taken up a hiding place in the ablution unit and was listening to the fellow as he mumbled a complaint to himself. After a brief moment Morg entered the ablution chamber, still mumbling, and came face to face with Lodan. His gasp of surprise was truncated by blow to the side of his head from Lodan's fist that knocked him sideways. Then he felt himself grabbed around the neck and propelled backwards until the two of them tumbled on to the bed. He started to flail and punch his attacker but Lodan twisted him easily and caught him from behind in a headlock and began to squeeze tighter and tighter.

"Keep still, or I'll break your neck."

Morg stopped struggling and lay still, face up, on top of his attacker.

"Who sent you to follow me?"

Morg's brain raced, he concentrated on the ceiling and choked out some words. "I don't know what you mean."

"It's a simple question; who instructed you to board this ship and spy on me."

"No one; I swear it. I am just..."

Lodan tightened his grip choking off the man's words. Perswant started to struggle again; his face had turned quite red. "I... can't... breathe."

Lodan eased his grip again. "Pull your britches down."

"No, for the love of the Prophet, don't do this."

"Pull them down, or I'll snap your neck right now. I'm not going to fuck you."

Morg hesitated and felt the grip tighten constricting his windpipe again. He was close to passing out. "Alright." He raised himself and reached down and lowered his britches.

"Remove the under-cloth."

"Am I to be left no dignity? To be treated as a low criminal?"

"I will not ask you again."

"Very well."

Perswant's hands shook as he slowly removed the white under-cloth. The vice around his neck eased a little as his attacker looked at what had been exposed.

"Getting married are you? You're going to fuck her with that are you?" Lodan freed his left arm and reaching down flicked Morg's genital stump viciously. The man yelped with pain and cursed through clenched teeth. Then his body went limp and he began to sob.

Lodan released him and climbed out from under. He stood and looked down at the pathetic figure splayed on the bed with his britches at half-mast and his arm over his face. He sat down in one of the chairs and waited. Morg eventually sat up and stared at him with red-eyed hatred.

"Why don't you dress yourself? I don't want to look at that sorry abortion any more."

Morg pulled his britches up and wiped his eyes.

"Some fucking Evangelist you'd make," said Lodan, smiling thinly, "crying like a lost child as soon as you're touched."

"What do you know of it?"

"Quite a bit, I did all the training, but I wasn't stupid enough to cut off my own cock."

"You didn't have the guts."

"You're right there; I thought I might need it one day. And sure enough I did."

"You're a disgrace to your family. I know all about you."

Lodan raised an eyebrow. "Who told you about me?"

"No one," replied Morg defensively, he realized his mistake immediately and tried to cover it. "Your activities are well known."

"No they're not." Lodan leaned forward forcing the smaller man to shrink back. "Do you think I don't know who sent you? What did my uncle tell you to do?"

"I don't know what you're talking about."

Lodan sat back and observed the man. "I see you have no chevron scar at your groin; you have not bled; you have not been accepted yet. How old are you? Twenty-five? Twenty-six?"

"Twenty-five."

"What did my uncle promise you? Full membership of the Brotherhood?"

Morg nodded resignedly.

"The average age for induction is nineteen and they never take anyone over twenty-two. You have been deceived and used. They only take about ten percent of the applicants, those who demonstrate mindless obedience, stoicism and the skill and inclination to murder those who have the temerity to disagree with them. There are many thousands of unfortunates caught in the half-world between the Brotherhood and normality. They have made the physical sacrifice but they have been judged insufficient in the qualities demanded of a true Brother. They creep around cockless and lost, haunted by their failure and useless sacrifice; some become monks; many kill themselves; a few readjust and even marry. I have seen quite a few in my time. What are *you* going to become, Morg?"

Morg bowed his head. "He promised, he said he would cut my first mark himself."

"The only mark he's going to cut on you will be the one across your throat when he discovers you have failed."

Morg suddenly looked up; it was obvious that this danger had not occurred to him. Lodan watched the expression on his face as the realization gradually penetrated.

"I repeat my question, what did my uncle tell you to do?"

Morg shook his head in dejection and mumbled, "I was to befriend you and find out why you have been sent to Barta."

"Is that all?"

"Yes. I swear it. He didn't tell me why he wanted to know. He said you are a fornicator and a disgrace to the Family."

Lodan stood. "On that subject he is correct. We will resume our games of Strategy after sleeping time. I look forward to the challenge."

Morg stared at him. "You still wish to play?"

"Why not? Now we know each other better there need be no impediment; besides your life may depend on maintaining the façade of companionship. I would suggest you devote some thought to what you are going to tell my Uncle Aurex. If you follow me once we get to Barta, I will kill you." Lodan passed him a mirthless smile and left the forlorn agent to his meditation.

Back in his cabin he slumped on the bed and tried to work out what was going on. The Arkon had forbidden any contact so he couldn't inform him that Aurex had place an agent to follow him? What was his uncle's purpose? Why had the Arkon inquired about his faith and revealed himself as faithless? To these questions and many others he could find no solution but he felt sure that he would find the answers he sought within the text of the Fourth Proposition. During the remaining days of the journey he studied the document with renewed interest. He waded through the dense, technical argument with limited understanding until he came to the final section, which was the part of the treatise composed by Juran DeRhogai, his own Arkon. Here the argument became theological and the meaning of it clearer and clearer. The more he read the more he was shocked that such a document could exist for it brought into doubt the very essence of the One True Faith. His mind became conflicted and deeply troubled and as he destroyed the document he realised what was to be his role.

He had become the agent of a heretic!

During social times on the journey his intercourse with Morg continued, but now the man seemed to be in a perpetual state of nervous distraction. Lodan was able to beat him several times at Strategy, but now Morg didn't seem to care and barely noticed the defeats. On the final day, as the sun of Barta Magnus began to shine with increasing intensity through the observation portal, Lodan won every match.

"Have you decided what you are going to do?" asked Lodan as he completed his closing move.

Morg glumly resigned his position and looked up. "I'm going to stay on Barta. I'm going to disappear."

"Do you have any money?"

Morg shook his head. "Not much."

"It will not be easy for you; Barta is no place for the bereft and the Authorities will deport you if they catch you."

"I know, but what you said was right, Aurex will kill me for having failed him. He was never going to accept me into the Brotherhood; I was deluded and weak. I see that now."

"He may send a Brother to find you, he does not forgive betrayal."

"I'll have to take that chance, what choice have I got?"

"Very little."

Morg shot him a brittle grin. "Perhaps it will work out for the good; there must be plenty of illegal Kagans on Barta."

"No doubt." Lodan stood abruptly. "We won't meet again." He strode out without looking back.

From the corner of the room another passenger watched him leave.

Morg Perswant enjoyed the liberal air of Barta Magnus for several hours. His torso, minus hands and feet was discovered in a remote forest twenty-six days later. The post mortem investigation confirmed that his extremities had been removed while he was still alive. His head was never found. The post mortem also revealed that a small section of trachea, close to the point of severance, had been removed. The investigator was experienced enough to know that this was the result of the extraction of a minute, ingested recording device. The investigation was immediately shut down; the remains were atomised and all traces of the investigation were removed from the record.

V

Barta Magnus was, both in dimension and population, the largest planet in the human diaspora. The principal constituent of its surface was water but splayed across the equatorial region on one side of the planet was a large continent of varied topography from low, fertile plains in the south to snowcapped mountain ranges in the north. To the east of the continent lay two large volcanic islands where, for almost a thousand years, the population had maintained an independent existence from the continental nation. Now the occupants of Barta Magnus had homogenized into a single nation of just over one-and-a-half billion.

The first settlers of the planet discovered an environment well suited to human occupation and of the five ancient worlds it was Barta Magnus that first forged a path of wealth and technology. It was the intrepid technologists of this planet who were the first to establish contact with the other occupied worlds and to travel the vast distances between them. They exported technology and imported superstition and mysticism. The Faith of The Prophet Minnar became an unlikely import, quickly supplanting a more believable but banal explanation of human creation and while the excesses of devotion practiced in less developed societies were largely, but not exclusively, avoided, there was on Barta, a prevailing and sizeable rump of devotional fanatics.

Fanatical devotion notwithstanding, Barta was known to be a place of liberal and freethinking individuals. A place where shallow entertainments mesmerized a shallow population; a place where good teeth and hair were valued over mental acuity and good character; a place where the anything-goes culture had largely curtailed the more extreme strictures of the One True Faith. It was into this world that Lodan walked as he disembarked from the stolid and stultifying atmosphere of the liner that had transported him from his home world. It was still dark when the ship landed and as it slowly descended through the atmosphere, he was treated to the breathtaking sight of a wealthy capital, with its spines of light like luminous crystal, stretching far across the southern plain of the continent. The night was warm and a sweet fragrance perfumed the air as he walked through the terminal ahead of a simulant luggage porter. Even at this early hour there was a bustle and vibrancy about the place which would have been quite alien on Kagan. But, even though he had been forewarned, the aspect of Barta that astonished him beyond all others was the women. The bright colours of their clothing; the provocative style of dress that, in many cases, left almost nothing to the imagination; the freedom with which they were permitted to go about and socialise; all was shock and revelation and he found himself unable to take his eyes from their alluring forms as they crossed the concourse in front of him. He quickly became aroused even as he walked towards the local transport, and was obliged to discreetly adjust his dress lest it be noticed. The skin of the women was fairer than those of his native planet and the majority of them had blonde hair that hung straight and long. It was as though he had wandered into an enormous and fabulous whorehouse in which the stock paraded provocatively for his personal delight.

As he reached the exit one of the women stood in front of him and blocked his way. She was also blonde with long straight hair and her skin was pale, but her true origin was betrayed by the deep, brown hue of her large eyes. She was wearing a shift of vibrant blue and green that clung to the form of her well-shaped breasts. Her legs were exposed to the thigh, above which rested a sash tightly wound about her hips so that it required very little imagination to assemble in the mind what was not exposed. It took Lodan only a second to picture her wide mouth and full lips in conference with his intimate parts.

"Lodan Sevarius." She spoke with the easy drawl of a native of Barta.

"Yes,' he replied.

"Welcome to Barta. Please come with me."

He followed her mesmerizing buttocks out into the balmy air. It was a cloudless night and the stars spangled the sky even through the glare of the port lights.

"Who are you?" he asked as they headed towards a line of stationary vehicles.

"Do not speak," she replied curtly.

They found a large, waiting transport and entered it. It was well appointed inside and of a type used by the wealthier elements of society. She commanded it to take off and it rose easily into the sky and headed east over the dazzling lights of the city.

"Take off your clothes," she commanded.

"This is quick, isn't it customary to…"

"Shut up and do as I tell you."

He began to strip as she went to a locker and pulled out a small instrument. She returned and watched him impassively as he removed his boots, shirt and britches and stood facing her dressed only in his wound under-cloth.

"Everything," she said.

Lodan hesitated. He had never before experience any form of awkwardness in the presence of a woman, but now he felt uneasy and distinctly intimidated. In an odd form of role reversal he was experiencing a distinct sense of vulnerability.

"Quickly," she snapped.

Hesitantly he unfastened the under-cloth and, covering his vitals with his hands, let it drop to the floor. She smirked faintly at his typical Kagan embarrassment and directed the instrument towards him. Suddenly a frown replaced the smirk.

"Your left palm; your I.D.; were you not instructed to have it removed?"

"No, there wasn't time, I suppose."

"Have you used it?"

"Yes."

"Stupid, stupid, stupid," she declared vehemently. "They will have tracked it; it will have to be removed immediately."

"Who will have tracked it?" replied Lodan.

"Be quiet," she replied as she continued to scan his body thoroughly.

"You haven't been tagged," she declared when she finished. "Put on those clothes," she added, pointing to neatly folded pile on one of the seats of the transport.

Lodan was never so glad to dress himself in the presence of an alluring woman. The clothes were lurid and in the fashion of Barta. As he was dressing she picked up his old clothes and put them into a disposal unit and switched it on. It instantly atomized them and ejected them into the night air. Then she picked up his bag and pushed that into the unit.

"Wait," he said, but he was too late, she activated the machine and the last vestiges of his life on Kagan fluttered into the atmosphere of Barta.

"What did you do that for?" he demanded warmly.

"They have tags that can't be detected now. They can make them mimic the atomic structures of inert objects. They haven't found a way of mimicking living tissue yet, that's why I made you strip."

"Very interesting, but why would anyone want to tag me?"

"I don't know, I'm just doing what I've been told to do. Sit down and put your left hand here."

Lodan placed his hand on the surface she provided while she delved into her bag of supplies for another instrument. This turned out to be a sharp knife.

"Keep still," she commanded as she made a small cut in the palm of his had near the base of his thumb. She expertly extracted the minute, subcutaneous device and threw it into the atomizer then stemmed the flow of blood with coagulant and sealed the wound.

"You're an efficient surgeon," observed Lodan.

"You should have removed it before you came here," she replied tersely as she stowed the instruments.

Lodan sat and watched her take a place opposite. He noticed that she kept her legs tightly together but he could not prevent his eyes flickering towards her crotch and upper thigh. She was wearing under garments that had assumed the colour of her flesh.

'You know who I am, so who are you?"

"I am Gerrin DeRhogai, your third cousin on my father's side."

"So we are related."

"Yes. Perhaps I should have told you earlier; had you known we were related it might have saved you the embarrassment."

"I doubt it. Anyway, who says I was embarrassed?"

"I do. Kagan males are prudes; you were not comfortable being subjected to a personal search by a woman."

"You speak your mind very plainly for a female."

"Be careful, Lodan Sevarius, you are on Barta now. We are the equal of men and do as we please, whatever the Prophet said."

"The Prophet never denigrated women; that was done by His followers."

"Perhaps so, but the result has been the same where the fanatics rule."

She held his gaze during a moment of silence, something that no Kagan woman would have done. He found himself fascinated and shocked at the same time. Then she said something that shocked him even more.

"I expect you are wondering what I thought of your body." She did not trouble to wait for his reply before continuing. "You are well muscled and have obviously looked after yourself, perhaps through vanity, perhaps not. Your penis is large for a Kagan male, although I confess I do not find such things particularly attractive." She grinned at his shocked expression. "Your attempt at modesty was to no avail; the machine sees all. Your face has character; I would say that you had been in too many fights and you have nice ears, small and neat, except for the damaged one although they do stick out too much. Your teeth…"

"Have you quite finished?" interrupted Lodan, forestalling any further personal observations.

She laughed for the first time, revealing her own perfect teeth. "Are you offended?"

"Wasn't that the intention?"

"Perhaps; I am used to speaking my mind"

"Maybe I should tell you what I think of you."

She smiled archly, "I already know that."

"You flatter yourself."

She laughed again. "I doubt it; I have been informed of your character."

"You shouldn't believe everything you hear."

"You assume I have heard ill of you."

"That's usually the case."

"I was born on Barta and brought up here, I am difficult to shock." She smiled again and rose. "I expect you are hungry, I'm afraid I only have wafers." She took a pack from a locker and handed it to him. He took it and began to eat; it was several hours since his last meal on the liner.

"Are you going to tell me where we are going now that we can't be overheard?"

"South Island, my father keeps a villa there."

"And who is your father?"

She raised a delicate eyebrow in surprise. "You don't know? My father is the trade envoy. He licenses and controls all the commercial exchanges between here and Kagan."

"That must present him with many opportunities."

"If you mean he is corrupt and rich, you are quite correct."

"And what is your relationship with the Arkon?"

"I met him once three years ago; he came to my marriage feast on Kagan."

"You're married! ...To a Kagan!"

"Yes, Daddy insisted; it was a good connection."

"And what does your husband think of you? Your liberality?"

"Oh, he was soon educated. He works under my father and money can acclimatize a man to almost anything."

"And what did you think of our illustrious leader?"

"I liked him. I found him witty and irreverent and he treated me as an equal. We had quite a long, private chat."

"A private chat with the Arkon!"

She became suddenly serious, leaned towards him and levelled her dark eyes on his. "I am his eyes and ears on Barta; not even my father knows of my association with the Arkon. He has chosen to expose my position to you. Why?"

"I don't know, he hasn't informed me."

"He's told you nothing?"

"Nothing specific. I suspect that he set me up and arranged my banishment from Kagan, but I do not know his reason for doing it."

She leaned back and stared at him for some moments. "You really don't know, do you?"

He shook his head.

VI

By the time the craft landed in the grounds the villa, the largest of the three moons of Barta had risen and spread its dusty red luminescence across the wide expanse of the ocean. The villa was perched on a rocky promontory about a hundred metres above the water that swirled and hissed among the rocks below. A simulant let them in and Lodan found himself in a world of impressive but restrained luxury and quality. She showed him to a room containing an enormous bed and tasteful items of an artistic nature, with a large terrace overlooking the ocean.

"Get some rest," she said, "tomorrow you will meet someone here."

"Who?"

"I don't know."

She left the room and the door slid shut behind her. Lodan walked out on to the terrace and stared at the ocean. He had seen pictures of oceans before but had never actually experienced them in reality. The infinite expanse of it disturbed, almost frightened him and he was filled with awe at the abundance of something so rare on his home world. It moved the air with a sound so elemental that he fancied, for a moment, that he could hear the voice of the Prophet calling him from the depths. The warm, sultry air wrapped itself about him and a soft breeze blew up from the waters below carrying with it the fragrant, salty trace of the ocean. In the vibrant, ruddy-hued starlight he could see across the bay to the next promontory where the lights of another cliff-top villa shone into the night. He smiled to himself at the glory of the view and the fact that here he was, in a place of his dreams, in a world free of stultifying conventions where you could be judged and condemned for the merest infraction. He stood on the terrace for a long time, drinking in his freedom and the glorious view of the ocean until fatigue drove him inside. Still smiling, he slowly removed the strange garments he had been given went to clean his body in the opulent unit of the room. Finally he slumped on to the large bed and shut his eyes.

An hour later he had still not slept. He could not shake from his mind the vision of Gerrin, her dark eyes, her full breasts and the flash of underwear he had discerned beneath her sash. He wanted to go to her, but realized, with a rare self-command, that she was beyond him. She was not a whore or a servant or anything like the low-class women he was used to. She was his equal and although the thought intimidated him, it also excited him. Never in his life had he experienced a real relationship with a woman and, until now, had never troubled himself over the fact. Thinking about it, he could not recall one occasion when he had not paid for his pleasure or imposed himself upon a woman of lesser status, without any thought to what it might mean to her. In such matters he had never had to consult anyone but himself and it had never occurred to him to consider the feelings of anyone else.

He rose and walked out on to the terrace once again. The barren, dull surface of the moon blanched the water with a rusty glow and drowned the light of all but the nearest stars. The air seemed warmer now, as if the sun had reached a finger around the globe and touched that place. He looked down at himself; he had an arousal that showed no intention of subsiding. "Why don't you leave me alone?" he said, whacking it with the palm of his hand.

"I can if you insist."

He modestly covered himself with his arms and turned his head to look at her. She was standing in the door to the terrace, completely naked. He gazed at her not knowing what to say.

"Although it looks as though you're expecting me. Seven days on a Kagan liner, you must be ready to burst."

She advanced on him with a confidence he had never before witnessed in a woman. He felt like a naughty schoolboy caught with his pants down, confused and rather intimidated.

She reached him and pulled his arms to one side. "I thought so," she said and pressed herself against him, enfolding his eager manhood against her belly. She didn't kiss him or offer him her lips, she just took his shoulders and pressed him down so that he descended close to her and could take in all the intimate sights she offered and the perfumes she wore. She did not allow him to linger though, but kept pressing until she had him pinned to the hard floor of the terrace. She used him as though he was a subject of hers, under her complete command. She knew exactly what to do to prolong her pleasure and, consequently his. He had never before known such an experience and when he was finally released from the dizzy elevation that had invaded his brain; she touched his lips with hers and released him from her body.

She stood, panting quietly and looked down at his splayed form. He raised his head and looked up at her. "Are you not going to offer a judgement; say, points out of ten?" he asked.

She grinned. "It was adequate, but I believe you can do better."

She pulled him to his feet and he tried to embrace her but she turned away and strolled back into the room and climbed on to the bed and covered herself. He followed and took his place next to her. This time she allowed him to caress her and lay still as he explored her body with his mouth. Their second intimacy soon followed, but this time she allowed him to take the lead, impressed by his youthful powers of recovery. Gerrin had many sexual encounters outside her marriage, her husband was usually too busy or tired to attend to her needs, but she had always chosen older men, committed men who would not fall for her and become a nuisance. Lodan was, by far, the youngest man she had encountered sexually and his vigour and passion pleased her. With him, though, she knew she was safe; they would not see each other again after this night.

She watched him sleeping next to her, like a child at peace and thought of her husband lying in his solitary bed. Her man was slighter and better looking than Lodan, but there was something so raw and masculine about this man that she felt herself in some danger of attachment. Physically he had satisfied her more completely than her husband or any other she could recall and she knew that it was not simply because he was more generously endowed than her spouse. Such shallow considerations had nothing to do with it. Instead, she decided that it was an innate sense of power that she had tamed and made gentle that pleased her the most. She slipped away and stole out quietly lest that power be aroused again.

In the morning, as they took their first meal of the day on the terrace, she had returned to her brusque, impersonal manner and, taking his cue from her, no mention of their intimacy passed their lips. They made small talk as they ate the well-prepared food that the simulant brought, while the sun climbed above the watery horizon. He asked her about her husband and father and when she expected to start a family. "In about twenty years," she replied.

"That seems a little late," he observed diplomatically.

She gave a brief laugh. "Wealthy Barta women do not carry their own; they pay others to do that, or have it done artificially, if they have the money. That is, by far, the best method as the whole process is monitored and controlled for the best results. That is why the population is generally, attractive. I expect you noticed at the port."

"Yes, especially the females."

"Fifty is a normal age to start a family on Barta; it ensures mature, thoughtful parents who are financially secure and able to provide the best conditions for their offspring. It also allows women to fulfil their potential."

They spoke at length of the differences in their two cultures and she seemed particularly interested in his training for the Brotherhood and the privations and sacrifices that it entailed. She smiled when Lodan explained that his father had interceded to prevent his own Sacrifice and accession and asked him about his own parents.

"I have not seen my father for nine years He left Kagan and I do not know where he is or what he does. My mother keeps herself in penance at a place of pilgrimage. I have only seen her twice since my father left."

"Do you miss them?"

He frowned and considered for some moments. "I don't know," he concluded.

The morning was still fresh when they observed a metallic speck glinting near the horizon. The simulant came forward and announced that the occupant of a craft was requesting permission to land.

"Allow it," she replied and they watched as the craft skimmed over the sea towards them until it landed on a terrace to the side of the villa. A door sprung open and a small figure emerged into the sunlight. The visitor was clad in a suit of purple and gold and wore an elaborate headpiece of golden, wound cloth. At first, Lodan thought it was a child, but when the visitor turned to face them, he saw that this was a man of about sixty. He had a jolly face that broke into a wide grin as he saw them on the terrace above him. He waved at them with unnecessary vigour as he climbed the winding steps that led up to their level.

"Has the Arkon sent us a circus act?" remarked Lodan

Gerrin touched his arm. "Be careful Lodan; knowing the Arkon, things are probably not what they seem to be."

They watched as the diminutive figure approached and performed an elaborate bow. "I am Jinzy," he announced, straightening to his full height, which, even with the elaborate cloth headpiece, barely reached Lodan's chest. Up close they saw that he had unusually small arms and hands, stubby, thick legs and barrel-like torso that joined with his head without the separating benefit of a neck, so that he was obliged to turn his whole form to face in one direction or another. He had thick, prominent eyebrows above mischievously twinkling eyes; a small, turned-up nose and a singularly wide mouth that appeared to be drawn into a permanent expression of merriment.

It was not the custom to bow on Barta, but Lodan and Gerrin both essayed a slight gesture in return. "Our names are……"

The man instantly raised his arm to stay any further conversation. "I have not given you my real name, of course and I do not want to know either of your names," he announced forcefully. "Although, I do know them," he added in a theatrical aside.

"We cannot be overheard here," replied Gerrin.

The visitor pointed a small finger to the sky and whispered, "There is always somebody listening."

Gerrin smiled indulgently. "We have a shield over this property."

"Is that so? Well, I am pleased to hear it. You can't be too careful; never know who's got eyes and ears on you."

"Will you sit down and have a drink of wine?"

The small man stayed her with a look of false horror." Wine! It gives me dreadful wind; I can practically take off on my own after half a cup."

"Perhaps some cob-nut juice then?"

The dwarf pulled himself on to a chair, in the manner of a small child and declared that cob-nut juice would be acceptable. Gerrin left them to find the simulant and Lodan took a seat opposite their guest.

Jinzy fixed his gaze on her receding behind. "Was she a good fuck?"

"What?"

He turned to Lodan with a lecherous grin. "Don't tell me you didn't nail that one down."

"I don't see what it has to do with you."

"Describe it. I bet it was full on; no quarter given. I bet she smells lovely down there. Is it clean-shaven or bushy? I must know."

"What?" repeated Lodan, astonished.

"Come on, don't be coy, I need to get the full picture here. Quickly, before she comes back."

"Clean-shaven," said Lodan, caving in to the insistent dwarf.

"Ooooh," he shut his eyes and leaned back in his chair. "Now I can see it."

Lodan watched as the fellow luxuriated in his own lecherous thoughts and wondered what manner of clown had been sent to them.

After some moments Jinzy opened his eyes and grinned. "Just because I am deformed, it doesn't mean that I am without needs. I don't see many real women in my line; I have to take any chance I can get."

"I see."

"Fact is," he added, pointing to his groin, "it's perfectly normal; about the only part of me that is. Would you like to see it?"

"No thank you, I think I'll pass."

"I bet you've got a big one. You look the type."

Lodan shifted uncomfortably, he was not accustomed to discussing his anatomy with another man. "It's adequate," he said defensively.

"I thought so, you lucky sod. Mine's not big, but it is perfect. Guess what, my testicles hang evenly; I've had compliments about them."

"Congratulations."

"In most men, the left hangs lower than the right; did you know that?"

"No."

"It is so. Did you know also that… "

Mercifully, the return of Gerrin, followed by the simulant, forestalled any further genital observations.

"Not a bad little shed," observed Jinzy with an encompassing gesture as the simulant placed a drink on the table before him.

"It's my father's," replied Gerrin taking a seat next to Lodan.

"I know." He took a delicate sip of the cob-nut juice. "I love Barta; the women are so… so interesting."

Lodan smiled as Jinzy lecherous eyes flitted between Gerrin's face and other more southerly points of her anatomy. She must have noticed, but seemed quite relaxed about it.

"I think I will apply for residency when I retire; perhaps I will get a place by the sea, like this."

"You are not from Barta then?"

"Gracious me, no. You think they would allow a deformed specimen like me to survive here? I would never have seen the sunshine of this planet, that's for sure."

Gerrin smiled awkwardly; the man was quite right, he would have been terminated long before birth.

"I am from the Galaxy," he declared with a sweeping gesture of his shrivelled arm. "I'm from anywhere and everywhere."

"You are well travelled then," she replied.

"Indeed, you are quite right about that. And speaking of travelling, it is high time we were on our way; there is no time to lose."

"On our way to where?" said Lodan.

"To where we are going," replied Jinzy, slipping from his chair to the ground. "Madam," he said, taking her hand and pressing it to his lips, "I am pleased to have made your intimate acquaintance."

Gerrin passed an enquiring look to Lodan over the head of her admirer. Lodan shrugged.

"Perhaps when I return to Barta, we can renew our acquaintance."

Gerrin extracted her hand with some difficulty and noticed that the man was not addressing her face at all. She stepped back, suddenly aware that her morning attire was revealing more than modesty allowed. I'll look forward to it," she replied with forced politeness.

The dwarf grinned wickedly and tripped off towards his craft.

Lodan stood and came to her side. "What do you think of him?"

"The Arkon must know what he's doing. I think our lecherous little friend is not all he seems; I think he might be a Moontrader."

"A Moontrader!"

"Yes, they are not all swashbuckling murderers."

"The Arkon wouldn't have dealings with a Moontrader."

"No, not normally, but this situation is not normal, is it?"

"I don't know, Gerrin. I feel I'm caught in some great, devious plot, without a clue as to why and what I am supposed to do."

"No doubt all will be revealed in good time. You'd better go; the dwarf is waiting for you."

"Thanks for last night," he said, taking her hand.

She grinned. "Thanks yourself. Keep safe, Lodan, and good luck; something tells me you will need it and don't trust this man; there's something not quite right about him; I can't quite work out what it is, but there is definitely something wrong here."

"I'll keep it in mind." He released her hand and walked to the steps that led to the landing level. He had never in his life felt such a pang at leaving another human being, but he did not look back. She watched him board the dwarf's craft and take off and then she walked back into the villa and sat on the bed where they had made love. It still smelled of him and she smiled at the memory of their passion. Perhaps in other circumstances she would have foresworn her self-imposed rule and taken up with him, but he was gone now and she would never see him again.

VII

The dwarf's ship was a riot of disorder and an unequalled example of how not to run a vessel. It had once done service as a military patroller belonging to one of the new, outer republics, but its glory days were well behind it. The passages, storerooms and even the basic living quarters were crammed with cargo; crates of varying sizes had overtaken all available accommodation, forcing their owner into an ever smaller, ever more cramped space. Lodan followed the dwarf along the passage that connected the living quarters to the crammed hangar where the shuttle had squeezed into what remained of its docking-space. Passing awkwardly between high banks of diverse stock with their identifying markings consisting of a complex arrangement of numbers and letters, they eventually came to a central area consisting of a small galley, a dining area and an old-fashioned control panel. These islands of normality were surrounded by yet more stock, piled floor to ceiling in crates of various sizes. Formed among the crates were seven passages leading to seven doors, only one of which was open. Lodan followed his host down one of the passages towards the open door and found himself in a small cabin, made smaller still by the presence of yet more stock. Here, squeezed between the piled crates was a crude cot.

"This is where you will sleep," announced the dwarf unapologetically, and then adding as a placatory afterthought, "I am not used to passengers."

"So I gather," replied Lodan. "What is all this stuff?"

"You mind your own business," snapped the dwarf, suddenly losing his fixed grin. "And don't touch any of it." He pushed past Lodan and shuffled to the door, where he turned. "We will eat in two hours, get settled; we have a long journey ahead."

"Where are we going?"

The dwarf passed him a slightly contemptuous smirk and the door closed, leaving Lodan alone in the narrow, claustrophobic space. He stretched out on the cot that only just accommodated his height and put his hand behind his head. The dwarf had told him the journey was to be a long one but had pointedly not told him where he was to be taken. Lodan began to ruminate on the various possibilities, but it did him no good; he could not even begin to imagine where they were headed, but he had an uncomfortable premonition about it. He shut his eyes and drifted off to sleep.

When he opened his eyes he discovered the dwarf standing next to his cot peering at him.

"I have prepared some food," he announced and turned abruptly and left.

Lodan swung his feet to the floor and followed him to the dining area where he discovered a large plate of hot food of an indistinct nature. The dwarf hauled himself up into a seat and began to greedily consume the unappetizing concoction. Lodan sat opposite and sampled the food that tasted much as it looked, indistinct and bland. Clearly it was not to be a journey for gourmandizing.

"I asked you where we are headed," he began.

His host stopped eating and looked up sharply. "I do hope you aren't going to be difficult."

"I merely asked; it is a natural question."

"I'll tell you when I'm good and ready and not before."

He resumed eating, shovelling the gruel into his mouth and swallowing it without tasting. Lodan observed him furtively whilst picking over his own food; the fellow possessed neither grace nor any trace of social etiquette; perhaps the result of too much time in isolation on his vessel.

"Are you a Moontrader?"

Again the dwarf paused and delivered a stabbing look with his dark, glinting eyes. "What makes you say that?"

"All this stuff," replied Lodan with a wave of his hand. "You always travel alone, I presume."

"Maybe I am a member of the Fraternity. What of it?"

"It wasn't an accusation, just a question."

"Questions can lead to trouble," he replied, resuming the incessant shovelling until all the food had been crammed in and he sat back in his seat in apparent relief.

"How long is the journey to be? A passenger has a right to know."

Jinzy considered. "Eight or nine days."

Lodan recalled his knowledge of the local region, but without knowing their speed or direction he was none the wiser. He decided not to pursue the subject. "Do you have a library on board?"

"Of course, I am an educated man. I have a first class doctorate in human biology."

This surprised Lodan; he had not so far detected any trace of learning in the man. "You have a first class doctorate and yet you chose this life?"

"This life is not so bad; it has compensations. A man like me is always subject to prejudice and discrimination. I prefer to be where these things do not matter."

"You mean in isolation."

The dwarf nodded.

"It is a lonely existence."

"Loneliness is a state of mind. I have not always been solitary; I have been married four times."

Lodan regarded him quizzically. "What happened to your wives?"

"None of your business," Jinzy snapped defensively.

"Sorry, I didn't mean to pry into your private life."

The dwarf treated him to a dark, penetrating stare that momentarily revealed the ruthless, dark character of a Moontrader, then he slipped off his seat. "Come, I will show you where you can clean yourself and perform your biological functions."

He led Lodan down another passage formed between high stacks of crates to a second door that opened to reveal another room crammed with crates with very little free floor space. In one corner two low crates formed a base on which a lay a mattress and some dishevelled bedding which served as a sleeping place for the dwarf; a gap between other stacks led to a place of ablution, mercifully clear of stock.

"You can use this one, all the others are unavailable."

"Thanks, I'll try not to disturb you."

"You won't; I rarely sleep."

They squeezed their way out into the makeshift sleeping quarters and Jinzy picked up an object that had lain hidden below his bedding. "You asked for a library, try reading this."

He handed Lodan a book of printed pages made from a tough carbon compound. "Have you ever seen a volume like that before?"

"Only in the temples; the Book of The Prophet and other early works of the Faith."

"I had that one specially made, a weakness of intellectual vanity I suppose."

Lodan read the title. "'Pubescent Labial Development by Horan Jinzeraskhan'. Is that you?"

Jinzy nodded. "You may find it a bit dry and technical, but the subject matter should interest you. It was the subject of my final doctorate thesis."

"Thanks," said Lodan, "I'll give it a try."

"How are you getting on with the book?" enquired the dwarf at their next meal after Lodan had witnessed the man's all-consuming greed for the second time.

"It is difficult, but interesting," replied his guest.

"Not to everyone's taste, but the result of much close study."

"That is evident.'

Jinzy allowed himself a faint grin as he recalled the detailed fieldwork, then he slipped to the floor and repaired to the galley. Presently he returned with a flask and two goblets and placed them on the table. "I have a small stock of corn wine of the finest quality. It is the only wine my constitution permits me." He poured a generous measure into each of the two goblets and sat back in his seat. Lodan tasted it; it was a revelation; he had never tasted wine so smooth and refined.

"It's delicious," he declared.

The dwarf seemed pleased at his approval and visibly relaxed. "I picked it up on Ennepp as part of a debt. It's over thirty years old."

Lodan took another sip and felt the atmosphere of suspicion begin to ease. He decided to venture a question. "What is behind the other doors I see here?"

The dwarf bristled and he instantly regretted his boldness. "Why do you want to know that?"

"I'm sorry, but I couldn't help wondering."

"You stay away from those doors. What's behind them is no concern of yours." And then he seemed to consider in the awkward silence that followed. "Perhaps I will show you what's behind one door towards the end of the journey."

"Why not now? There is little enough to divert me on this ship."

The dwarf pursed his lips and turned his frame slowly towards his guest fixing him with a sly, sneering glare that made Lodan shiver internally. "Are you quite sure you want to see?"

Lodan paused and was about to withdraw his request, but something in his cavalier nature forestalled him and he said, "Yes, I would like to see."

"Very well," replied Jinzy, sliding from his seat.

Lodan followed him down another passage in the crates and watched him open the door at the end. It slid back to reveal a room, about four metres square, mercifully devoid of crates. Instead, the room was filled with books; hundreds and hundreds of volumes the like of which Lodan had never seen; not even in the most magnificent temples of Kagan. They were arranged on shelves about the room and piled waist high upon the floor so that it was barely possible to enter.

"You asked if I have a library; well, now you see it."

"It's astonishing," pronounced Lodan, "I have never seen so many ancient volumes in one place. They must be worth a fortune." He picked up one from the top of a nearby pile; it was an ancient work by a known disciple of the Prophet himself.

"Do you read the ancient form of Agon?"

"Yes, we were obliged to learn it in training school."

"Training school?" replied Jinzy, instantly on guard.

"Yes, I trained for the Brotherhood of Mercy, but did not join."

"I was not told of this," muttered the dwarf angrily.

"I assure you, I am not an Evangelist," declared Lodan, turning to face his host.

Jinzy grunted. "Pick a book, or even two."

"Thank you," replied Lodan and began to explore the titles. It did not take him long to discover a macabre theme dominating the titles for although there were many religious scripts, most seemed to concern various forms of violence. There were books on war; books on torture and ancient human experiments that usually resulted in maiming or excruciating death; there were books about gouging and impalement, about murder and rape, about combat and all manner of viciousness.

"You have a singular taste in literature," remarked Lodan at length.

"Does it disturb you?"

"Not really, it is a remarkable collection."

"Have you made a selection?"

Lodan picked up a volume of ancient and macabre fables in its original form. "This will do for the moment."

The dwarf peered at it. "It's light reading. Take care of it, it is very old."

Lodan followed him out of the library and repaired to his cramped quarters to read. He had always enjoyed reading, ever since he was a young student in the school of the Brotherhood and he would never again have such an opportunity. He settled down in his cot and ruminated on the sight he had just seen and began to wonder what was beyond the other forbidden doors.

He slept for some time and upon awakening noticed that he was beginning to ripen; he had not cleaned himself since his stay at the villa on Barta two days ago. He got up and made his way to the dwarf's cabin. Its occupant was nowhere to be seen. Lodan surmised that he was probably in one of his secret rooms doing who knows what. He undressed and placed his soiled garments in the non-organic cleaner then stepped into the unit. The particle bombardment made his skin tingle as it rid him of the minute bacteria that had developed since his last ablution. The process always gave him pleasure and he stayed in the unit for the maximum time allowed. When he turned around to step out of the unit he discovered his host standing silently in the door, unashamedly staring at him.

"I wanted to make sure you were not an Evangelist," he said.

"You might have surmised that by my activities on Barta."

"It might have been all talk; I can't be too careful."

"Well, as you can clearly see, I am not an Evangelist," replied Lodan, grabbing a cloth and wrapping it around himself as quickly as he could. There was something depraved and menacing about the way the man was looking at him.

"No you are not; at least in your physical appearance."

"What is that supposed to mean?"

"You are from Kagan and all Kagans are zealots."

"I am of the Faith, if that's what you mean. Do you say you are not? Have you denied the Prophet?"

Jinzy dealt him a hard-edged glare. "Am I to give praises to the Prophet for receiving this deformed and corrupted body? I would sooner pluck out my own eyes than offer up one prayer to your glorious Prophet." His face twisted into an ugly sneer as he spat out the last words then he turned abruptly and disappeared into one of his forbidden rooms.

Lodan watched him go with some relief; he had no desire to keep company with an apostate. He finished dressing and repaired to his cabin to read.

The following hours brought only more tedium. He saw nothing of Jinzy until they came together for their single meal but, in the absence of occupation, the question of what was behind the remaining doors had begun to gnaw at him and he formed a determination to ask for another to be opened. He waited until his host was mellowed with wine before he broached the subject. "When we finish this journey we will never encounter one another again."

The dwarf shot him one of his piercing, quizzical looks. "That is undoubtedly true."

"And what you know of me... I mean, do you think you can trust me?"

"I trust no one. All men have hidden motives for the things they do."

"I don't; I am a straightforward person."

Jinzy frowned. "Then you are unusual. What is this leading to?"

Lodan shrugged. "I am puzzled that you imagine what you keep behind those locked doors would shock me. What can be so terrible?"

The dwarf drew himself up and peered into Lodan's eyes across the table. "A man's soul," he said. "A man's soul."

"I don't believe you are as terrible as you think yourself. I think too much time spent alone has depressed you."

Jinzy twisted his lips into a grim smile. "Do you really think that, Lodan?" Are you sure you want to find out more?"

"Open the next door, I assure you I will not judge you or baulk at its contents."

The dwarf stared at him for some time and Lodan saw in his eyes a depth of hard cruelty that almost made him shiver. "Very well, I will open one more door, but ask no more of me."

He led Lodan down another passage of high-stacked crates and unlocked the door at the end. It slid aside to reveal a darkened room roughly the same size as the library. Lodan stepped inside and as his eyes adjusted to the dim light, so emerged an array of implements and machines. At first he could not make out what they were but as he began to inspect them he began to understand.

"Yes," said Jinzy, "they are all instruments of torture and death. See, they still bear the marks of their last victims. Look at them, look at the dark congealed blood on the blades and skewers and think of the suffering that they have caused; the contortions of agony; the screams."

Lodan slowly walked around the exhibition, inspecting many of the items. He indicated a particularly gruesome device that was designed to slowly impale its victims. "I have seen this in use."

The dwarf was immediately aroused. "You have actually seen such an execution?"

"As part of our Evangelist training we are required to witness many things."

"Describe it to me; leave nothing out."

Lodan smiled grimly; he had got a hook into the man. Let him stew for a bit. "Perhaps later."

"Why not now?" insisted the dwarf.

"I am tired and the memory of the event still fills me with horror."

"Do these objects horrify you?"

"They are just objects; it is their use that brings the horror. Have you ever used them?"

Jinzy's deformed silhouette did not move from the frame of light cast by the open door. His face was in darkness and Lodan could not see the hard, chilling expression on it. It was the face of a murderer weighing up his victim. Abruptly the man turned and left the room without another word.

Two more days of boredom followed in which Lodan saw even less of his host. The dwarf had taken to eating in his room alone, leaving a meal for Lodan on the table. Lodan had seen the blackness of his soul and now the dwarf wished to avoid all contact. Finally Lodan encountered his host as he emerged from his place of ablution.

"Have I offended you?" asked Lodan as the man tried to push past him.

Jinzy looked up at him furtively. "No," he replied.

"You have been avoiding me."

"Yes."

"Why?"

"Because I know you will ask me to open the remaining doors."

"You could always refuse."

"Yes, I could."

"But you are afraid that you won't. You want to show me what is behind them."

The dwarf cast his eyes to the floor.

"What harm can be done now? I am sure I have seen the worst of your character and I have not judged you."

Jinzy sneered. "You know nothing about my character. You judge other men by your shallow, self-serving standard. Your brain is lodged firmly at the end of your cock; you cannot empathize and care nothing of the emotional pain you might cause."

Lodan was momentarily stunned by his host's raw criticism and, for a moment, was lost for words; then he sank down and sat himself on the floor and nodded slowly. "You are right. On Kagan I spent my time seeking pleasure; women, strong drink and mind altering experiences. I studied hard at the school of the Brotherhood and afterwards in a more liberal institution, but when I left there I soon discovered that my life was not going to mean anything; that it would have no real purpose. I sank down; I see that now. Men are occupied by war, religion, the pursuit of wealth or goodness, even employment and drudgery, but I had none of those. There is no war on Kagan and I had all the money I needed. My devotion to the Faith was suppressed by indolence and base desires and I had not the character for acts of altruism. All I had was a void that I filled with the pursuit of pleasure, physical pleasure. I am twenty-two years old and I have never loved another human being. What does that tell you about me?"

"It tells me that you are pathetic; full of self-pity," replied the dwarf scornfully. "If it was not for the money I am to receive…" He stopped abruptly and the two men gazed at one another as if each had suddenly been stripped of his shell of respectability to reveal the putrefaction within.

"Tell me what you saw done by the Brotherhood," said Jinzy in a low, dead voice.

"Show me what is behind two more doors and I will tell you everything."

Jinzy nodded slowly. "Very well, I will open two more, but I will never reveal what is behind the final door. Never; never; never."

The third door slid to one side and Lodan entered a brightly lit chamber. It was stacked from floor to ceiling with jewels, precious metal and fine objects of incalculable value. They glittered and sparkled with impossible radiance in the harsh light of the chamber.

"I have never seen such fine things," declared Lodan, picking up and inspecting a huge lump of polished crystal.

"I come in here often to look at them. They are the result of many trades on many worlds. They have been paid for by the misery of many."

Lodan frowned and put down the crystal.

"That gem cost the lives of a thousand people. Others you see here cost even more. The weapons I have traded have caused hell and degradation on many worlds and all of it distilled into this one place. There is blood on every object you see here."

Lodan shook his head sadly. "You are rich beyond measure, why continue? You could retire and live the life of a potentate."

"You said it yourself; a man must have something to live for. I live for money; I hoard money; I exist for it because I have nothing else now."

"That is sad, but I understand it."

The dwarf hardened suddenly. "Are you offering me pity?"

"Pity? No, I don't think so. I just think that with all this wealth you could achieve something, perhaps something that would fill you with more purpose; something that would help others."

Jinzy stared at him with hard, dispassionate eyes as if Lodan had uttered something so incomprehensible and sacrilegious that it could hardly be credited. Then he turned away. "Come, I will show you what is behind the final door, for it is the last I am prepared to open."

Lodan followed him and soon they stood together in front of the fourth door. The dwarf drew the key from his belt and it slid to one side to reveal a larger chamber than the others. The walls, floor and ceiling were entirely without colour, they were uniformly covered with a material of the deepest black; a black so profound that it was such as may be seen in the starless reaches of the universe. In the centre of the chamber stood one single object; a large, ornate canopied bed of ancient design and manufacture. The bed was dressed in linen of the finest quality, all black as the darkest night.

"This is my marriage chamber," whispered the dwarf in reverential tones. "This is where I brought each of my wives in turn and took them to this bed and made them love me."

Lodan walked around the strange chamber. It was like a macabre shrine. An involuntary shiver ran down his spine as he imagined the women lying with the dwarf in this loveless place. "Were they virgins?" he ventured.

"All were virgins of the most pure flesh. They were unblemished, each and every one."

"What happened to them?"

Jinzy's face subsided into an expression of impossible sadness; he stared longingly at the bed, the place of past joys. He opened his mouth as if to speak but something, some terrible memory prevented him. Instead, he just grunted, turned away and slowly trudged out of the room.

Now Lodan knew that he had to find out what was behind the fifth and last door and he laid his plan to do it. He quickly followed Jinzy as he squeezed between the crates that formed the narrow passage to the marriage chamber.

"Thank you for showing me your treasures, I know that it must have been difficult for you."

"No other man has seen them, only my wives have stood inside those places before you. Ask me no more questions about these chambers and what they contain. We will be parting soon for the journey is nearly over. You must promise me you will never divulge what you have seen on my ship; not to anyone."

"I do so freely."

"Now you will tell me what you have seen done by the Brotherhood and nothing is to be left out."

Lodan nodded resignedly. "I will tell you everything."

Lodan spent the next four hours reliving the experiences of his time in the seminary of the Brotherhood of Mercy. The exercise brought back many memories he thought he had buried for good. The punishments, the deprivations, the exposure to the most depraved and revolting methods of execution ever devised; all details eagerly consumed by the dwarf as he listened, occasionally soliciting more detail where he felt he had been underserved. He was especially attentive when Lodan described the Sacrifice, a ceremony few outside the Brotherhood had witnessed.

"Do any fail in resolve?" he asked.

"I have never seen it; the penalty would be harsh."

"And what is done with the severed part?"

"It is burned in a dish in front of its owner."

"And the boys do not pass out?"

"It happens occasionally, if they are not strong enough."

Jinzy smiled and nestled into his seat. "But you escaped the seminary intact."

"On the eve of my own ceremony my father stepped in and prevented it."

"That must have pissed off the Brothers."

"I believe so. It was probably a contributing factor to his banishment although other reasons were cited."

"And so you were thrown out of the seminary."

Lodan shook his head. "Not immediately; I was allowed to continue my studies there in the hope that my father would change his mind. He didn't and eventually I was expelled for having knowledge of a woman."

The dwarf's laugh clattered in the air between them. "I hope it was worth it."

"It was not the first time; I was bound to be caught eventually."

"It's a pity, you would have made a fine Brother of Mercy; you are self-absorbed and careless of others."

Lodan pressed his lips together and said nothing; having his character so mercilessly exposed had cost him no small amount of self-regard.

Jinzy smiled, he seemed happier now than he had ever been and his demeanour had now returned to that of their first encounter on Barta. "We will soon go our separate ways; I am hungry, we will take one last meal together."

"Will you now tell me where you have taken me?"

"I will tell you later."

The final meal was a repeat of its predecessors. Jinzy slurped up the gruel-like substance with no concession to manners or taste. When he had finished and licked the last morsel from the metal, he repaired to the galley and brought back a flask of his fine wine. Lodan rejoiced, it was exactly what he had wanted to see and now he would test the man's capacity for alcohol.

"I drink to your former wives," he said and downed his goblet in one go.

Jinzy looked at him with sudden suspicion. "That wine should be savoured, not guzzled like that."

"You're right, no doubt, but I do not know when I will ever taste its like again. I do not even know where I am going."

"You will know soon enough and I suppose the fee I will receive will run to a flask of wine."

"Have you ever carried passengers before?"

"Never, you are the first and the last."

"I feel honoured. I hope I have not caused you too much trouble."

"Not too much. You did not complain about the food or accommodation as others might have. You are used to luxury I suppose."

"The food was edible and the accommodation adequate. I think we rubbed along well enough."

Jinzy grunted and Lodan topped up his host's goblet and then his own.

"I found your library fascinating and your own work on labial development was very interesting."

The dwarf was suddenly animated, as if a switch had been pressed in his brain. "You read it!"

"I did. I confess I did not understand all of it, particularly in respect of the molecular biological analyses, but I think I got most of it."

"What did you not understand? I will explain it."

Lodan smiled inwardly, he had hooked him. He began to ask the dwarf questions about the workings of the female anatomy and listened as Jinzy answered, illuminating his expositions with examples. Lodan encouraged with his own personal observations and they conversed were like two old lechers comparing notes. All the while Lodan plied the dwarf with drink while sparingly sipping his own.

As time wore on Jinzy became freer with his comments and their discussion ranged into more general directions. The dwarf talked of his young life, of his education and subsequent employment. He spoke bitterly of the prejudice and taunts he had endured at the hands of those who should have known better. He spoke of the places he had been and of the women he had met. But in all this, he never once mentioned his wives.

The second flask of wine was drained and at last, came the onset of debilitation. His speech started to slur and his eyes shut with increasing frequency. Finally his head slumped, as far as it could, on to his chest and Jinzy drifted into a drunken slumber. Lodan held his place, watching the dwarf carefully. He was snorting loudly as his laboured breath passed between his pale lips.

When he was certain the man was in a deep, inebriated sleep, Lodan slipped stealthily from his seat and moved around the table. He carefully lifted the key from the dwarf's belt and unfastened it. Its owner exhaled heavily and smacked his lips, but showed no sign of consciousness. Grasping the key in his hand, he approached the forbidden door, pointed the key at its lock and watched as the door quietly slid to one side.

Lodan had a vague suspicion of what he would find behind the door; he suspected that the dwarf had acquired some form of banned weaponry; some sort of biological or chemical doomsday device, but as he entered it was obvious that he was totally mistaken. The room was the largest yet; about twenty metres in length by about six wide. It was dimly lit with stealthy lights set into the walls. The lights illuminated four transparent, conical containers arranged on ornate plinths along one wall. Each container appeared to be full of some sort of gel-like substance and inside each container was an object. At first the nature of these objects was indistinct, but as he approached the containers the dim light afforded a better view of what they held. Inside each was the naked form of a human being.

Lodan approached the first container. Inside it was the body of a young woman of exquisite beauty. She had been caught, standing erect and proud, her arms flat by her side as if to attention. She had long, flowing red hair that waved gently in the eddies of the gel. Her skin was fair and without blemish; her breasts young and firm. Her intense, blue eyes were open, staring blankly into the room. Lodan peered into them and a shock wave stunned his body and sent him cold. The eyes were looking back at him.

He reeled back in horror. The sad, pleading eyes followed him and a small bubble of air escaped the mouth and travelled slowly up through the gel to the top of the container. Here, inside this prison was a living, breathing person, trapped, as if in amber, for all time.

"I see you have found my wives."

Lodan twisted around to discover the dwarf watching him from the door. His eyes were dark and dead and no emotion passed across his face. There was no trace of his recent inebriation.

"This girl is alive," spluttered Lodan. "This is monstrous."

The dwarf advanced. "This is my first wife. I met her one morning on Tarnus, when the red sun shot flames into the high clouds and lit her hair. She was the daughter of a soldier and I traded weapons for her hand. She married me out of duty."

He passed Lodan and stood in front of the next cylinder. It contained the naked body of another beautiful woman; this time with long, blonde hair wafting in the gentle eddies of the gel. This one was posed with both hands held out in front of her in supplication.

"This is my second wife. I met her at noon on Barta Magnus, when the blazing, golden sun warms the land and grants it vibrant life. She was the daughter of a usurer. She married me for my wealth. Look at her, Lodan, is she not fine?"

Lodan stepped forward tentatively and peered into the container. Once again the eyes responded, angry and resentful. "She is alive too," he whispered in disgust.

The dwarf moved on. "This is my third wife. I met her at dusk on Kagan. She was the daughter of a priest. She married me out of pity."

In the third cylinder Lodan discovered a woman of his own race. Her hair was short and the colour of the dark-brown dust of the desert. Her arms were placed in front of her, palms down, as if patting the head of a child. She was not as handsome as the previous two but she was voluptuous with the full breast and large nipples so typical of the women of Kagan. He looked into her face and there he saw incomprehension and hurt.

"A woman of your own race," said Jinzy, "a religious woman who tried to make me good."

"And you repaid her with this appalling captivity."

The dwarf ignored his remonstration and moved along to the last cylinder. "And this is my fourth wife. Her name is Santora and I met her on Ennepp at midnight when the stars cast a silver spell over the land. She was the property of a Bhasi merchant who kept her locked in a sunless cellar under his house. I paid him with gold and jewels that she might see the glories of the starlit sky. She, the finest of all my wives, married me for love; and, in return, I loved her best of all."

Lodan approached the final cylinder. It contained the naked form of a Native girl, more beautiful than any he had ever seen. Her long, black hair shone as it waved gracefully in the thick preservation; her beckoning hands welcomed advance. She could not have been more than fifteen for her face had not yet matured into the woman she might have become and her breasts were not yet fully formed. Her large, dark eyes were filled with the sadness of betrayal and the agony of her fate.

"You loved her best and yet you did this. Why?"

Jinzy nodded his head. "I loved her and she loved me and that is how it must remain. It could never have been more perfect than our marriage night and that is how it must stay, for all time."

"This cannot be; it is a violation of everything that a human being should be. You can't stop time, no matter how you try. This is horrible, horrible beyond words."

"Horrible!" repeated the dwarf mockingly. "Their beauty is preserved, it will never diminish."

"Beauty preserved in a living death; it is inhuman. You must release them."

"They are mine; they are my brightest jewels; my lovers. I will never give them up. I told you not to enter this chamber, but you could not control your curiosity. Your presence on my ship must end." A sidearm appeared in the dwarf's hand and pointed at Lodan. "Leave this chamber now."

Lodan stepped back. He had gone too far and it seemed he would die here. "Are you going to kill me?"

"Leave the chamber, you are disturbing them."

"Disturbing them! You are truly a monster. Your twisted body has twisted your mind. You have lost your humanity; you have lost your sanity."

Jinzy's face darkened and Lodan knew it was the end of him. The dwarf spat through clenched teeth. "They are mine; nobody shall take them from me."

Lodan felt the pulse rattle his brain and his legs collapsed from under him. He fell heavily to the floor and lay there while his body shook with violent spasms. At last the convulsions stopped and his body was still. His bulging eyes were paralyzed open and staring up at the ceiling. He was unable to move any part of himself as the pulse had disrupted his nervous system. The dwarf appeared in his field of vision and he heard him speak.

"Only your value to me has saved you from death. You will not be able to speak or move for several hours, at least until we get to where we are going. By the way, you are going to Rion on Tarnus. Now you know why I didn't want to tell you. You would not have consented to go there; of that I have no doubt."

Lodan felt himself dragged along the floor by his feet. The dwarf was strong despite his size and he was pulled out of the chamber of the wives and deposited in the main area, by the dining table. The last words of the dwarf shot through his brain filled him with horror. May the Prophet preserve him; he was going to Tarnus.

VIII

Where the institutions of democracy and reason fail there emerges the opportunity for corruption and determined ambition to flourish, for men require leadership and in the absence of consent, imposition is always the final resort. Thus it is that the scourge of tyrants have afflicted human society since the dawn of civilisation and whether they name themselves King, President, Chairman or any other title, the maintenance of power inevitably becomes the principal thrust of their policies; policies usually characterised by the wiping out of all opposition and the pilfering of state coffers. As their crimes are compounded the stakes become higher; dissenters must be crushed at all costs for no one can be allowed to question the authority of the leader and to bring his crimes to judgement.

One such leader was Umbert Strellic, who stood in the glorious sunshine of his own importance on a high balcony in front of his palace. His gaudy military uniform glinted and dazzled the retinue of lackeys surrounding him as he watched impassively as three thousand impeccably turned out soldiers marched past with clockwork unison and comically exaggerated steps to the thwack of an incessant drumbeat. Beyond the ranks of soldiers stood a large crowd of well-dressed peasants, waving enthusiastic banners with the face and name of Umbert Strellic, the Beloved Leader, emblazoned on each one. The crowd, although large, did not fill the stone-paved square that was dominated by a fifty metre tall statue of Strellic as a young officer, striding majestically forward. The vast, indulgent palace was one of the few undamaged buildings in Salom Gul, the capital city of Rion; it occupied one entire side of the central square which was formed, on the other three sides, by the bombed-out ministries of long dead democracy, for in Strellic's empire ther was no room for discussion. The ruined land and devastated population were invisible to him, for here, in front of him, was the army and there the people who loved him, who would die for him, waving and shouting their adulation over the thwack of the drum.

Strellic was seventy-two years of age and had wielded power in Rion for just over forty of those years. He had come to power through violence and maintained his authority in the same way, ruthlessly murdering anyone who might have possibly posed a slight threat to his authority. Anyone with a sniff of talent or initiative was put on trial for his life and executed without mercy. The population received an education, if that is what it might be called, consisting of interminable repetitions of the random thoughts of the Beloved Leader and the certainty that he would deliver them from their poverty and spare them the ignominy of defeat by the many enemies of Rion. Thus the people waving the emblazoned banners beyond the army really did think that the Marshal of Rion was infallible, had no personal odour; survived on a daily diet consisting of a small square of plain bread and a small cup of water; swam five kilometres per day in freezing water; and never slept but only rested by meditating on the glory of his own people. In short they believed that sunlight streamed from the fundament of Umbert Strellic.

"You see, General, how much my people love me," remarked Strellic to General Arkuna, who had taken a position to the side but behind his leader. Arkuna had heard this rhetorical pronouncement countless times and always responded appropriately.

"You are the very sunlight to them, Marshal."

Strellic, who never caught the faint irony in Akruna's voice replied, "It's true, I know, but I always feel inadequate of their love."

Akuna swallowed the butchery of the language that characterized the Beloved Leader's written and spoken pronouncements. He was a distinguished, soldierly fellow of seventy-three who possessed a full head of steel-grey hair above a stern, deeply lined face. "You could never be judged inadequate in any endeavour, Marshal."

Strellic waved to the troops and turned to face his only trusted general. "I know, but sometimes my modesty gets the better of me."

Arkuna bowed and smiled at the Marshal of Rion. Strellic was a portly fellow with dark, bulging eyes and sagging chins that waggled when he spoke. He had a small nose and a dainty mouth above which perched a thin, pencil moustache. His hair, under the grand military cap, was improbably black and thinly plastered across his balding head like sparsely sown grass beaten down by a strong wind. When not wearing his cap, he had taken to donning a small toupee, which he insisted was his real hair. Since no one had summoned the gumption to contradict him, he continued in the belief that he had successfully fooled his subjects.

At last the final squadron of troops filed past and the crowd were encouraged to surge forward to gain a better view of the Beloved Leader. Not too close, lest they might be overwhelmed by the aura of greatness that surrounded the man. Strellic waved dismissively and turned away and strode into his palace followed by Arkuna and the rest of the entourage.

"These weekly parades are such a trial, but it is my duty to attend them, I suppose."

"You are a martyr to duty, Marshal," replied Arkuna. "And now, with your permission, I have a number of matters that require attention."

"Oh, must you go and leave me here with this riff-raff?" whispered Strellic.

Arkuna bowed. "I'm afraid the army will not govern itself, Marshal."

"Very well, of course you must attend to matters. You are my right hand, General; and my left," he added after considering further.

Arkuna smiled and left the gaggle of hangers-on to their buffet feast. Strellic had always been inconsistent and quixotic but in recent years he had become increasingly ridiculous and self-deluded to a degree that might compromise the safety of Rion. But Strellic had two ambitious sons, both of whom had designs on power and the thought of the internecine blood-bath that would inevitably follow their father's demise turned him cold for he would be dragged in and have to choose sides. It was the general's considered advice that tempered his leader's increasingly deranged ambition; his ridiculous, ill-considered plans for the invasion of his neighbours and eventual world domination. Strellic listened to his general as he listened to nobody else and, while Strellic lived, the general knew he was safe; free to carry on his business, for, with the Beloved Leader's trust, came the control of the only thing that mattered in Rion, the military budget.

He took his craft and flew ninety kilometres to the south where he enjoyed direct command of a military camp. His home inside the perimeter was a conspicuously modest place, nothing that would excite alarm or jealousy, with a deep bunker for protection. It was here that, in a few hours' time, he would meet Jinzeraskhan, the dwarf Moontrader, and conclude a very lucrative deal.

Ever since he had become Strellic's right hand, he had cautiously augmented his wealth by striking deals with illicit arms traders. On assuming responsibility for the military budget of Rion, Arkuna had quickly realized that the army could not be adequately supplied from this source. Strellic and his extended family purloined the majority of Rion's dwindling wealth for their own personal use and aggrandizement and any request for those funds would have brought accusations of treason and financial incompetence upon his head so Arkuna set up a network of contacts and made procurements through them, allowing himself a small percentage from each deal. In this way he had kept the army supplied and his leader happy. But with Strellic's apparent lack of interest in recent times, he had grown bolder and sold arms to anyone who wanted them, even to Rion's enemies on Tarnus. Mostly it was field weapons and military vehicles, but lately he had started to trade in space-going vehicles of an altogether more deadly nature.

In short, General Arkuna had become one of the most influential but least known traders in the entire galaxy. Had Strellic known that his most trusted and favoured general could obtain vehicles of such power, he would have demanded their use on his enemies and dangerously escalated the war. For on Tarnus, war was maintained and contained by sanctions that limited the capabilities of the five competing powers. Arkuna knew that if this happened his money-spinning venture would be at an end for no trader nations would ever deal with him again.

He strode past the permanent guard that protected his dwelling and entered his home and called for his daughter. There was no reply so he called in the guard.

"Where is she?"

"I think she's gone to the water-hole, Sir."

"Alone?"

"I don't think so, Sir. Lieutenant Norgu left with her."

Arkuna scowled. "That will be all."

The soldier left and the general began to pace up and down. Lorel was spending far too much time with that young officer; he would have to have a word with them both.

IX

Strellic sat in the ornate chair in the centre of the echoing hall of his palace and brooded. He had eaten his fill and now watched the undignified squabble of his entourage as they gathered up the scraps. He had commanded his sons to be at the parade, but as usual, neither had appeared. They were a diverse and deeply flawed brace, but they were his and in his uniquely skewed way, in he had real affection for them. He was sorry that Arkuna had not stayed, the only true friend he had;

the only man who he could really trust. Their relationship went all the way back to the early days in the army, when Arkuna and he had risen through the ranks together.

A distant sound, like a roll of thunder, shuddered through the open window and brought a pause to the gluttonous activities at the table. They looked up briefly, at each other and then resumed as if nothing had occurred. Somewhere in the city yet another building had been destroyed and more lives lost. Soon afterwards a junior officer entered the hall and bowed before his leader.

"Report," said Strellic showing no real inclination to hear what the man said.

"Most Beloved Leader, two dwellings destroyed in sector six. Eight fatalities."

Strellic waved him away; it was nothing of great importance. *If only*, he thought, *he could get his hands on some real weapons, not the pathetic pop-guns they allowed through the embargo, he would show his enemies what he could do; he would destroy them and rule over their lands and peoples with magnanimous justice, just as he ruled over his own dominion.* He imagined himself as the ruler of all Tarnus, not just this pathetic little corner; he imagined himself fated and revered as the bringer of peace to a world that had known nothing but conflict; he pictured himself attending inter-planetary conferences where his opinion would be sought by all manner of dignitaries and men of power. Strellic was frequently wafted into these flights of reverie by an intense dissatisfaction with his present condition. His small, dainty mouth drew itself into a pout and his large, bulging eyes turned disgustedly upon the undignified rabble at his table. He was about to scream at them to get out when his drift was interrupted by the entrance of his favourite son.

Sarlat was the closest of Strellic's offspring to his father's image. He was portly but not yet obese and had the same dainty mouth and bulging eyes. He was also extremely artful and sly; qualities much appreciated by his father.

"Hello Dadda," he chirruped with false bonhomie.

Strellic scowled. "I've told you not to call me that when I'm on duty."

Sarlat smiled; it amused him when his father was in a bad mood, it meant someone usually got hurt. "There's someone here who you should meet."

"Who is it?"

"Can't say; he won't give me his name; says he has important information that he will impart only to you."

Strellic's curiosity was piqued. "What does he look like? Has he been checked for arms?"

"He is unarmed and not from Tarnus."

Strellic looked incredulous. "How did he get in? I have not been informed of any incursions; I will personally twist off someone's balls for this."

Sarlat grinned in the knowledge that he was about to launch a missile. "He says he has information about a traitor."

"A traitor!" bellowed Strellic in alarm. The diners at the other end of the hall stopped eating and looked up in consternation. Strellic stared at them accusingly, wondering which of them was guilty.

"That is what he says."

"Well, what are you waiting for? Bring him here immediately."

"As I said, he will not see you publicly; he is in my apartment."

Strellic bristled. "I am Umbert Strellic, the Marshal of Rion; I do not see people in apartments."

"Very well, clear this lot out and I will bring him here."

"You lot," Strellic bellowed, "clear out."

The generals and pseudo dignitaries at the other end of the hall, looked at each other in dismay; there was still plenty of food on the table.

"Now," screamed Strellic and they snatched what they could and filed out, muttering quiet protests. The Beloved Leader observed them with unconcealed contempt. They were the dross that remained after many a cull had withered all initiative and talent from his immediate staff. Up to now, the only comfort he could derive from their presence was that they were all loyal to him. The notion that one of these ingrates could be a traitor turned his stomach to jelly.

"Go and get him," commanded Strellic.

Sarlat performed an exaggeratedly ornate bow and left. Strellic watched him leave with a twinge of pride. Sarlat was rude, cruel, manipulative and cunning; he was the perfect successor. He pulled his gold-plated sidearm from its bejewelled holster and checked its charge to make certain. There had been several assassination attempts during his long reign and he had learned to sense danger. He was sensing it now in these unusual circumstances. He put the sidearm down beside him, ready and primed.

A tall, gaunt man entered the hall from the far door; he was alone and dressed in the drab robes of an Evangelist. Strellic sat up and his hand grasped the sidearm. Long ago, at the outset of his rule, he had proscribed the Faith and all its adherents. He wanted no rival for the affection of his people and so the Faith had been driven from the land of Rion. He knew there were a few underground pockets of adherents, but they were weak and of no consequence. Evangelists had tried to kill him before; he had been declared a heretic and an enemy of the Faith, they had tried to resist his New Dawn, his Glorious Revolution, and he knew they still helped his enemies. And now, here was one of them, here before him, no doubt ready to deal in more trickery and falsehood.

As the man approached, Strellic brought the sidearm into view and levelled it on his chest. The Evangelist stopped and insolently pierced him with a haughty gaze.

"That is near enough," uttered Strellic, his words echoing in the curious silence. It was as if the man had brought an atmosphere of malevolent chill into the room.

"I am Aurex DeRhogai, chief secretary to the Arkon DeRhogai of Kagan. Thank you for granting me this audience, Marshal Strellic."

Strellic eyed him and kept his weapon steadily aimed. "What is your business with me?"

"I have information that will be of benefit to you."

Strellic pursed his dainty mouth. "Why should I trust anything that comes from the lying mouth of an Evangelist?"

"Because you will see the truth of it with your own eyes."

"And why have you decided to part with this information? To a heretic," he added sarcastically.

"It is of mutual benefit. You will be in a position to do us a service."

Strellic leaned back in his ornate chair, but kept the weapon firmly aimed at the Evangelist. "I am not in the habit of doing favours for my enemies. Evangelists have tried to assassinate me in the past; how do I know that you're not just another assassin? I ought to have you put to death."

Aurex regarded him steadily, concealing his loathing of this murderous cretin. "If you do that you will never know how I could have helped you; and you would bring down on your head retribution of considerable force."

Strellic bristled. "I am Strellic, Marshal of Rion, I am not afraid of your pathetic threats."

"Marshal Strellic, I am not making a threat, I am simply stating a fact."

Strellic eyed him contemptuously. "What is your information?"

"An enemy of the Brotherhood, a low heretic, is coming to your region with a Moontrader. I believe his purpose is to obtain a military deep-space cruiser."

Strellic laughed. "Everybody knows there are no deep-space cruisers on Tarnus; the international embargo has seen to that. Your story is ridiculous."

Aurex gave a thin, indulgent smile. "There are ways around the embargo for those who know whose palms to grease."

"That's ludicrous; I have tried for years to run the embargo, without success and anyway, no individual in the Division of Rion could finance such a trade."

"You are mistaken, Marshal Strellic. The individual is none other than your own minister, General Arkuna."

Strellic went cold and the ruddiness of his face drained. The notion that his long-time friend, confidant and advisor, the leader of his army, was in possession of a weapon that could wipe out his enemies in an instant was impossible to believe. If it was true the betrayal was monstrous. "You are lying, Evangelist, Arkuna would never betray me. Anyway, he could never have amassed the finances necessary, it is impossible."

"That is what we thought, but when we realized the heretic was coming to Tarnus, we began to investigate. Our investigations eventually led us to General Arkuna, although the path was torturous and well concealed. There is no doubt that your general has betrayed you."

Strellic lowered his weapon and brooded, rearranging his thoughts in the light of what he had just learned of his trusted friend and confidant. The suspicious and vindictive nature of the man needed only a moment to transport his trusted general from a friend into the most hated and loathed enemy he had ever known. "And how will you benefit, Evangelist?"

"The heretic is high-born; we do not want a fuss."

"You want me to do your dirty work for you? You want me to kill him?"

Aurex frowned and recalled the insult Lodan had dealt him outside the Arkon's door. "No, we do not want him killed, you have other means at your disposal; he is fit and strong and I'm sure he will prove useful to you."

Strellic narrowed his protruding eyes on the man. "You would want this for a high-born of Kagan?"

Aurex nodded.

"I want the cruiser."

The Evangelist smiled indulgently. "We have no idea where it is; it is unlikely to be here."

"How do you know that?"

"It would not be easy to conceal a deep-space cruiser in Rion, even for your general."

Strellic regarded him sceptically and paused for thought. He was not particularly familiar with the geography of his lands but had to admit it was an unlikely scenario."

"Very well, I will arrest the general and question him about this. Your kinsman will be dealt with also."

The Evangelist bowed slightly. "I ask nothing more."

X

Lieutenant Norgu stretched himself on the warm, sun-bleached rock above the deep pool and shut his eyes. His army uniform, neatly folded lay in a pile beneath his head next to Lorel's more casually arranged pile. Below him he could hear the splash of her strokes as she swam repeatedly up and down the length of the waterhole. Beyond that lazy splash there was no other sound in the world and the contentment of peace and quiet overtook him as he began to drift. They had been friends since he had come to the garrison as a young cadet of fourteen. She had been thirteen then, just budding with the promise of maturity, watched over by parents jealous of her innocence. He had liked her instantly, but as they grew and matured, she had always made it clear to him that their relationship could never be more than platonic. Now, at twenty-three, she was a fully-grown woman with a fine body and nothing could prevent him from desiring her.

The splashing stopped and he looked over the edge of the rock and saw her climbing back towards him. He turned over on to his front so that she would not see the evidence of his lust.

"Don't you want to swim?" she asked as she approached, breathless from her exertions.

"No," he replied without looking at her. She always swam naked and he did not want to further stoke the flame of longing within him.

She was natural with him and careless of her modesty in his presence; she did not give much consideration to the effect she was having on his anatomy; she had seen it before and just laughed and told him not to be so silly.

"We should be getting back soon," she added, "come on, Vannic, one last swim."

"No thanks," he replied, "you go, I'll get dressed."

She stood over him and he felt the shadow she cast fall on his back. "Come on, it'll cool you off." She lifted her foot and pushed her toes between his buttocks.

"Don't do that, I've told you before," he protested angrily.

"I thought you liked it," she replied casually as she removed her toes

"It's not fair, Lorel; it's not a way to treat a man."

"Oh dear," she replied mockingly, "have you got a little bonus going on down there? Has your twig become a branch?"

"Piss off," he replied warmly.

"It's not like I haven't seen it before, in all its modest glory."

"What would you know? You've never been fucked." He twisted his head and was treated to a frontal view of her framed in the sunlight that streamed through her pale, blonde hair, roughly cropped in the military style. The outline of her well-muscled body moved against the sun so that he could see the point of her firm breast as she leaned towards him. "You know one day, Lorel, you'll push it too far and someone will hold you down and screw the arse off you and it'll be your own fault."

She smiled and brought her face close to his. Her eyes were of an intense blue; quite unlike any he had ever seen. "Not while my father is alive."

She straightened and strolled to the edge of the rock. He watched her dive into the pool, catching the brief, intimate flash of her anatomy as her parted legs disappeared over the edge. He shook his head; she really was totally shameless.

XI

Jinzeraskhan pitched his shuttle inside the vast compound walls of the garrison and turned to his silent passenger. "My debt to the Arkon of your clan will soon be discharged. I have delivered you according to the agreement we made. Our paths will soon divide and we will never see one another again. It is a pity that your persistent inquisitiveness has led you to reveal an aspect of my character that I would have preferred to have kept hidden for, I confess, I like you Lodan and I think under different circumstances we could have become more closely acquainted. But that is, of course, impossible now. It is my duty, under contract, to deliver you into the hands of General Arkuna and this I will now do."

He unfettered Lodan's feet and helped him to rise. His hands were still bound behind his back and he nearly overbalanced on his unsteady legs. He went before the dwarf with laboured steps, like a man having to learn the art of walking anew. Outside the craft two soldiers were waiting to conduct them to the general's quarters; they gave Lodan a quizzical look as he struggled from the shuttle to the door of the general's residence.

General Arkuna had never seen Jinzeraskhan in person, although he had dealt with him on numerous occasions. The meeting was risky for them both, but it took place on the insistence of their paymaster, the Arkon, who would have no intermediaries or communications that could be compromised. The general dismissed the soldiers and greeted the dwarf affably. Jinzy returned the greeting with spare courtesy, his eyes suspiciously darting about the small, sparse room.

"Why is this man bound?" inquired the general, turning his attention to Lodan.

"We had a slight difference of opinion," replied the dwarf. "He did not want to come here and I had to stun him."

The general peered at Lodan. "I do not blame you; my homeland has not enjoyed a good reputation of late. Will you please release him?"

"Gladly, he's your responsibility now."

The dwarf severed the ties that had bound Lodan's wrists and stepped away rapidly. Lodan rubbed his wrists where the tight bindings had left a ruddy mark.

"I was expecting something a little more opulent," observed Jinzy.

"I do not need or desire such things," replied Arkuna. "Shall we complete our business?"

"Best done soonest," replied Jinzy and pulled a small, black casket from his pocket. He handed it to the general. "It's all there, your percentage as agreed."

Arkuna opened the casket and inspected the contents closely. It contained five, multifaceted stones that emitted a luminescent glow. The glow lit his deeply lined face for a moment before he closed the casket. "It is as agreed," he announced satisfied.

"Very well, I will be on my way."

He turned and stalked out of the room without further ceremony or word, darting Lodan a contemptuous glance as he went.

Arkuna watched him go then turned his attention to Lodan. "An unpleasant fellow, but he has his uses."

Lodan nodded. "He kee-...; he keeps w... wom... men." He forced the words from his frozen lips.

Arkuna gave him a look of incomprehension. "Sit down, my boy; I will get you a drink."

"No...; no...; you ha... have t... t... to sto... stop... him."

Arkuna shook his head and strolled off to get Lodan a drink of water. Lodan seethed at his inability to communicate; he felt himself trapped in his own, useless body. The general returned with a beaker of water and offered it to him. Lodan waved it away angrily and tried to speak again, but the results were no more comprehensible to his host than his previous efforts.

"You had better rest," he said. "You have been stunned badly and it will take a while for your senses to return. Your Arkon commissioned me to procure a military, deep-space cruiser for your use. His instructions were specific and I have met them in full. I am bound to say though, that this business has intrigued me greatly; I have never before had the honour of dealing with an Arkon."

Lodan gave up his efforts and tried to take in what he had just been told. A military, deep-space cruiser for his personal use! What could the Arkon intend for him? Huge sums would have been exchanged to make such an unusual purchase; a single, private individual in possession of a powerful, military craft; it was unheard of.

As Lodan ruminated in silence, the door opened and a soldier dressed in fatigues entered the room, approached the general in a most familiar way and kissed him on the cheek, all the while looking quizzically at Lodan.

"You've been to the water-hole?"

"Yes, Dad,"

"With the lieutenant, I presume."

"Yes."

"I've told you before; I don't want you going there alone with him."

"Don't worry, Dad, he's like a brother to me; nothing's ever going to happen. Who's this and who was in that shuttle?"

Lodan observed the newcomer with interest; it was obvious that, despite the fatigues, this was a woman and natural curiosity was aroused. She was young, in her early twenties with the strong features of her father; pale skinned, with alarmingly blue eyes. Her face was interesting and full of character, but could not be described as attractive in the conventional sense.

"This is my daughter, Lorel," said Arkuna, placing a paternal arm around her. "This man will be our guest for a short while."

She smiled, revealing even, white teeth. "A guest! That's something new. Why is he here?"

"Business, my dear. Just business."

"Does he not speak? Is he dumb?"

"He has been stunned."

"Stunned! Did you do it?"

Arkuna smiled and shook his head. "No, my dear, it was done by another."

"One of the guards?"

"No, by the man who brought him here."

She grinned impishly at him. "I got stunned once, by accident. It's not nice is it?"

"No," whispered Lodan.

"I mean anyone could get hold of you and do anything they liked and you couldn't do a thing to stop them."

"Lorel; that's enough. Go and get changed; what have I told you about wearing mens' clothes? You look more like a boy than a young woman."

"Well, thank you Dad, for that," she replied laughing.

They watched her trip out of the room. "She spends too much time around soldiers," observed Arkuna.

Lodan did not attempt a reply, but the woman had made an instant impression on him. She seemed to be a woman of no artifice, the complete opposite of the whores that he had known and quite different from the mannered and socially stunted females of his home world.

"She is all I have now," said the general. "My wife died nine years ago; she was a victim of this endless war. Are you married, Lodan?"

Lodan shook his head. "No."

"I suppose these things are arranged on Kagan."

"S... some."

The general smiled and took a sip of wine. There was a silence before he posed his next question. "Why does Arkon DeRhogai want a deep-space cruiser?"

"I... d... don't... know."

"Stupid question; you wouldn't tell me if you did and anyway, it's none of my business. He is a Minister of Kagan though, so I would have thought he could procure such a ship through ordinary channels. I conclude that you are acting in a private and secret matter."

Lodan shrugged. "Yes; b... but I... don't know."

The two men were interrupted by the arrival of a soldier at the door. Arkuna rose and strolled over. It opened to reveal one of the garrison's senior officers.

"Sir, Minister Sarlat Strellic is approaching and demands access to the garrison."

Arkuna frowned. What would Strellic's son be doing here? "Tell him he is welcome," he replied and closed the door on the officer. He walked quickly across the room and disappeared into his office. There he secured in a hidden safe the small casket containing the payment Jinzeraskhan had given him. He returned to Lodan. "Stay here, the marshal's son is coming, it is better that you are not seen."

He disappeared through the door and strode on to the large parade ground to receive his guest. Lodan could see the worried strain on his face as he left. He sensed danger. Something was definitely wrong.

A contingent of the Elite Guard disgorged from the craft and formed a cohort of arms on the dusty ground. Sarlat stepped out of the craft and sniffed the air. He walked boldly from the protection of his own soldiers and scowled at the hastily assembled guard of honour that shuffled into order. He strode past them towards the general, stopping a few paces short so that the two stood face to face, then he haughtily raised his arm and pointed his finger at Arkuna. "This man is a traitor," he announced in a high, reedy voice. "He has betrayed our wise and beloved leader in a most foul and despicable way."

A ripple of confusion and concern began to spread among the guard of honour. To a man they looked toward the general to see what he would do. One word from him and they would defend him to the death. Sarlat's elite guard levelled their weapons on the soldiers.

Arkuna met the accuser with a steady gaze. "This is a false accusation; the Marshal has my full loyalty. How do you intend to prove this allegation?"

Sarlat twisted his face into a leering smile. "The proof is in your own house. You entertain an enemy of our Glorious Republic."

"It is true, I have a guest but he is not an enemy of the state. He is a private citizen from Kagan."

"See… See," screamed Sarlat, "he condemns himself from his own lips. The zealots of Kagan are all enemies of Rion. Guards, bring out the spy, let the men see him for themselves."

Four of Sarlat's guards marched into the General's dwelling and emerged with Lodan held between two of them. His feet described two ruts in the dust of the parade ground as they dragged uselessly behind him.

Sarlat stepped forward and peered menacingly into his face. "A filthy Kagan spy. See men, what did I tell you? A spy kept right under your noses by this traitor." He pointed triumphantly at Arkuna who stared contemptuously back at him. He knew that he could command his men to overpower Sarlat and his guard, but if he did, it would be the start of a war that would split the army and cost the lives of many of his loyal troops. He stayed silent and waited for Sarlat's next move.

He pointed at Lodan. "Put him in the troop carrier; he will be questioned at headquarters. General, you will be questioned too. You will come with me by order of the Beloved Leader."

At that moment, Lorel ran from the dwelling and grabbed her father's arm. "What does he want, Dad?"

Sarlat glared at her. She had rejected his advances in no uncertain terms two years ago, after Strellic had suggested that she would be a good match for him. Now, he was going to avenge the slight. "Bring her too," he shouted. "She will tell us what she knows."

This was too much for Arkuna. "You will leave her be," he growled.

A ripple of disturbance jostled the guard of honour. They outnumbered the Elite Guard by over five to one. The Elite Guard readied their weapons. The air crackled with tension. Sarlat pulled out his sidearm and aimed it at Lorel. "One wrong move and I will shoot this whore in front of you. Now, get into the troop carrier."

Arkuna knew that he would do exactly what he said. He separated himself from his daughter and walked slowly to the carrier. Sarlat, his face running with sweat, grinned in triumph, Arkuna had often treated him with condescension and he carried a long-harboured grudge against the man, not improved by his daughter's flat dismissal of his suit. Now, he could get even with her too and he pointed his sidearm at her head. "You too; you will also be charged."

Lorel made him no reply; without looking at him, she simply walked into the craft behind her father.

At the barrack window, Lieutenant Norgu trained his weapon on Sarlat's head, his shaking finger poised above the trigger. He would have gladly sacrificed his life to protect her, but he didn't know what to do. In the end he did nothing and Sarlat and his Elite Guard filed back into the troop carrier while Norgu sank to the floor and banged his head against the wall in frustration.

Lodan recalled little of the journey to Salom Gul. He was bound at the wrists and wedged between two soldiers, one of whom had fetched him a generous whack across the face with his weapon. He now realized that whatever the Arkon had planned for him was not going to be possible. He also realized that he was in serious trouble.

He remembered looking at the loathsome Sarlat who was leering at Lorel, while she sat next to her father in stoic silence, pointedly ignoring him during the entire journey.

He vaguely recalled the shudder of the landing and being dragged between soldiers, down various passages reeking of chemicals and boiled vegetables, until he was thrown into a pitch-black cell where not even the meagre light of the passage could filter beneath the heavy door. He was given no food or water and lost track of time in that dark place and in his forlorn state he turned to the only real source of inner strength he possessed. He began to pray. And as the prayers fell from his dry lips he began to realise that the Prophet had decided to punish his blasphemous thoughts and past misdeeds. Tears of regret came into his eyes and he began to quietly implore forgiveness. But the Prophet was hardened to his supplications and did not heed him, for when they finally came for him, the real horror started.

The door of his cell flew open and a harsh light pierced his eyes.

"Stand up, prisoner," commanded a voice behind the light.

Lodan struggled to his feet. "I am the grandson of an Arkon of Kagan," he said with all the bravado he could summon.

The guard laughed. "You could be the grandson of your precious Prophet, himself; it won't help you here." He stepped forward and went to deal Lodan a blow to the head with a truncheon, but Lodan, with the agility of practice and sudden adrenalin, dodged the blow and crunched his fist into the man's unprotected cheek. He reeled and crashed to the floor while two more guards rushed in. Lodan could now see and skilfully dealt with the next two, but the fourth guard caught him a blow to the back of the head and he went down. They kicked his torso and head until he was senseless then they dragged him out of the cell.

They took him down more foul smelling passages and delivered him into a large room of beams and pulleys that reeked of blood and urine. Here they pushed him to the floor, face down, while steel manacles were attached to his ankles. Then, they hoisted him aloft until he was suspended upside down from one of the high beams. A man entered the room. He could not see him, but he smelt him. It was a pungent chemical smell, a smell he would remember for the rest of his days. He spoke only one sentence. "This is what we do to the enemies of the Beloved Leader."

And then the beating started.

Lodan's screams of agony echoed down the passages, just as the screams of many before him had echoed in that hellish place. They thrashed him with sticks of split cane on his torso, buttocks and legs until blood soaked his clothes and drizzled from his hair on to the floor. When he passed out, they stopped and threw water on him and started again. Eventually, mercy granted him oblivion and he was dragged back and thrown back into the dark cell where he stayed, blood-soaked and flayed, his face swollen from the blows of the angry soldiers.

Terrible though it was, Lodan's torture at the hands of the guards was mild when compared to the agonies suffered by General Arkuna who was questioned by Sarlat who exposed himself as dull-witted, brutish and sadistic during the process. The general was strung up by his wrists and repeatedly thrashed while Sarlat screamed into his face. His right ear was cut off and then his left and a hot wire plunged into his left eye. His bloody clothes were cut from him and electrical currents attached to his extremities. Through all these agonies Arkuna screamed and howled but did not divulge the vital information that Sarlat sought. The general knew that he had to endure whatever extremity of pain and degradation rather than give up the location of the deep-space cruiser. He knew that, with that weapon, Strellic or his son would lay waste to the entire planet in conquest and no one would be able to prevent it. It would cost the lives of millions and his conscience would not permit such an atrocity.

Eventually Sarlat tired of his victim's agonies and his attention turned towards the general's daughter. Lorel had heard the awful screams of her father along the echoing passage and was in no illusion as to what was in store for her. She was brought into the chamber where she saw her father, hanging by his wrists, almost unrecognisable in his state. She called out to him and heard him mumble, "Be strong my darling."

Sarlat approached her and grabbed her hair, bringing his face close to hers. "Look at your pathetic father," he said, "I want to know where it is and one of you will tell me before I leave this room."

She gathered a generous amount of sputum in her mouth and spat it into his face.

He recoiled and angrily punched her in the eye. "Strip her, let the traitor watch while his daughter is degraded."

The clothes were torn from her body and she was strapped by her legs and arms to a table in front of her father. He nodded to a guard who had a certain reputation. "Fuck the bitch," he commanded.

The fellow regarded him quizzically.

"Fuck her, I said!" bellowed Sarlat.

The guard approached the victim with obvious reluctance.

"Get on with it," screamed Sarlat impatiently. "Haven't you ever seen a cunt before? Don't you know what to do?"

"Yes, Sir," replied the soldier.

Sarlat suddenly produced his sidearm and put it to the man's head. "Then do it," he said with sudden quiet menace.

The soldier quickly dropped his pants and began to encourage himself while Lorel clenched her teeth and waited for the first pain. She was determined not to cry out, not to give any satisfaction to her enemy, but the man was large and the pain acute as he entered her and she could not prevent a brief cry from escaping her lips. The general watched the defilement of his beloved daughter and tears salted his blood-caked eye.

Sarlat turned to him. "Speak and it will stop," but the general only moaned and whispered through his bloody lips, "I have told you everything... everything."

"Then you will watch this bitch die," he replied.

"She knows nothing; she can tell you nothing," he whispered.

Sarlat sneered at him; frustration and anger had conquered his fragile reason. He turned his attention back to Lorel and pushed the soldier away from her. A trickle of blood had escaped and gathered on the table below her buttocks. Sarlat grabbed an energised prod and rammed it into her vagina. She screamed with pain at the unnatural intrusion but when he activated the instrument her body arched and shook in silence.

She saw his face above hers, he was speaking, spitting as his words were formed. She could barely make them out. "Where is it, you whore? Where is it?"

Another bolt shot through her; it seemed to fire every nerve in her body. She tried to speak and he drew near to hear her. She formed the words with difficulty. "Fuck you."

Sarlat's limited patience snapped. He banged her head on the table screaming insanely into her face until one of the soldiers stayed his arm, saying, "I believe, Sir, that she is dead."

Lodan did not know how long he had spent in the blackness of the cell. He tried to sleep but the pain of his injuries allowed him no rest. He remained curled up on the cell floor, shaking and uttering supplications to the Prophet who had deserted him. At last, the door opened once more and he was pulled from the cell by four burley guards. They took him to a room where a large bath of grey water was sunk into the floor and cut his clothes from his body. As they pulled at the blood congealed cloth his wounds began to bleed afresh and he gritted his teeth against the pain.

When he was naked a soldier with an ugly looking black eye kicked him in the groin causing Lodan to double up in pain. "Want to have another go?" he screamed and propelled his victim into the grey water with the sole of his foot. Lodan tumbled head first into the bath. The water stung like fire and the pungent chemical in it burned its way into his wounds. It got into his nostrils, his eyes and mouth and burned them too. Then they pulled him out and doused him with a powder that sealed his seeping wounds. He was forced to kneel while his head was shaved then a guard threw him a bright-red jumpsuit. "Get dressed, your trial and execution is now."

XII

Lodan was the last of the accused to arrive. They chained his hands and brought him, without further physical abuse, into a large chamber in which about fifty uniformed officers sat in total silence. In the centre of the chamber was a raised platform on which stood his two fellow accused, in manacles. They were both dressed in the bright red jumpsuits of prisoners, but were almost unrecognizable from the man and the woman he had met two days earlier. Lorel had not died at the hands of Sarlat Strellic; the soldier who had stayed his arm had saved her from death. After Sarlat had left the torture room they had discovered that she was still breathing and called him back. He was about to order them to finish her off when it occurred to him that he could condemn her to a far worse fate than an easy death. She was revived and brought to trial and with her face swollen and bruised, her head shorn; she stood stone-faced, staring contemptuously before her. Her father, his steel-grey hair removed, stood beside her locked in an iron frame for support. His injuries were terrible. He had lost both ears and his left eye and what remained of his face could hardly be recognized as human. He exhaled blood from his mouth, indicating that his lung was punctured. As Lodan was placed in the dock, he heard the general whispering to his daughter.

"My darling, do you remember that trip we took to the north? The last trip we were all together, you, your mother and me. Be strong and always remember it. Say you remember it."

Her eyes moist with pity turned to the broken man by her side. "Yes, I remember it Father."

"Good, it is vital you remember." Flecks of blood issued from the General's mouth and spattered the front of the red suit. "Now I believe we are about to be judged by our inferiors. Goodbye my darling."

Three officers of high rank and wearing full ceremonial regalia entered the chamber from a hidden door behind three raised thrones, above which a ludicrously flattering portrait of the Beloved Leader impassively surveyed the proceedings. The company stood in military unison and the three officers took their seats.

The officer on the central throne, the President of the Court, spoke first. "These are the accused who stand before you; Rembat Arkuna, traitor; Lorel Arkuna, traitor; Lodan Sevarius DeRhogai, a citizen of Kagan, spy. Who speaks against them?"

An officer rose and stepped before the three thrones. "I do, your Eminences."

"Who speaks for them?"

Another officer stepped forward and bowed to the trio.

"Very well, the Accuser will present."

The Accusing Officer bowed. "The prisoner Arkuna, a once esteemed and trusted general of our glorious army, has, for many years, conducted illicit trade with enemies of the state." He picked up from a table the small casket of crystals that the dwarf had given the general and held it up. "I have here the evidence of a payment that the accused received only two days ago. This was payment for arms that were sold to our enemies; a fact admitted by the accused under examination."

The Accusing Officer handed the casket to the President of the Court, who opened it and peered at the glowing contents. He then offered it to his colleagues to verify.

The Accusing Officer waited until the President had placed the evidence on the table before him and continued. "I now call my witness, the dwarf, Horan Jinzeraskhan."

The announcement of the name shocked Lodan. He watched as the dwarf waddled into the court from a side door and took his position before the President. As he passed the dock of the accused he threw them a shifty smirk.

"You are Horan Jinzeraskhan, a man of no fixed origin?"

"I am."

"And your business is the illegal trading of arms?"

"Amongst other things."

"Tell this hearing what you have traded with the accused."

"Weapons of all description, military vehicles amongst other things."

A ripple of surprise went around the court.

"Silence!" bellowed the President.

"What was your business with the spy, Lodan Sevarius DeRhogai?"

"I brought him from Barta Magnus to Rion. My commission was to deliver him to the general."

"The Accused," corrected the President.

"Sorry Sir, the Accused."

"And what was your impression of DeRhogai?'

"He was objectionable and intrusive. I had to stun him and restrain him."

"A typical spy then?"

"Yes, I would say so."

"Did the spy, DeRhogai say what his business was with the traitor Arkuna?"

"No, he did not."

"That is all; you are dismissed."

Jinzy essayed a stiff bow toward the President and shuffled out. Lodan followed him with his eyes but the dwarf never returned his gaze. *They caught him and he cut a deal,* thought Lodan. *He will get away and the torment of his wives will continue.*

The defending officer now rose. "Clearly the accused are guilty, it is my duty to ask the court for clemency."

"Thank you," said the President, "your duty is noted. The accused may now speak before I pronounce judgement." He pointed to Lodan.

"I am the grandson of an Arkon of Kagan. I am not a spy. I was brought here against my will by the lying Moontrader on whose evidence you are relying."

"Silence," called out the President. "You may not traduce a witness for the State. Is there a confession?"

"Yes, by his own lips," replied the Accuser.

"Very well, that will do. You next," he said pointing at Lorel.

She glared at him with all the contempt she could summon and stolidly pressed her lips together.

"Lorel Arkuna is condemned by silence. Rembat Arkuna will now speak."

The general gathered all the resources at his command and began falteringly. "For many years I have been the loyal servant of our Beloved Leader, Umbert Strellic and for many years he has trusted me with the government of his noble army. I have done this duty, even through the difficulties of sanction and privation. I have no personal fortune; there is no money and none will be found because it has all been spent on the army. All of you in this place who now sit in judgement on me, have benefited from the soiling of my own hands by the trades I have done on your behalves. The exchequer of the state was long ago emptied by profligate behaviour and bad management of our affairs. My daughter is innocent and knows nothing of what I have done; I ask the court for clemency for her."

The stunned silence of the court was at that moment shattered as the Beloved Leader, himself burst in. "Treason!" he screamed. His wild eyes bulged; his face was purple with rage as he approached Arkuna. He pulled out his golden sidearm and raised it to the general's head. "You are a liar and a traitor."

Arkuna drew his swollen lips into a smile. "And you are a fool."

Strellic fired and the general's body crackled and his head slumped in death. The whole courtroom froze in terror as Strellic rounded on the President. "You... you allowed him to spout his lies."

The President looked as if he had wet himself, which he probably had. "But... but Marshal, it is the law."

"I am the law," screamed Strellic. "You had your instructions."

"Sorry, Marshal, I did not know what filthy lies he would speak."

"You are all incompetent and a disgrace to your uniforms. You are all reduced to the lowest rank; get out, all of you."

The trio scrambled from the thrones with undignified haste and Strellic swung round to face the two remaining prisoners. He raised the golden sidearm and pointed it at Lorel's head. "It makes me sick to think that I once hoped you would become my daughter-in-law; now I see you are nothing but a lying whore and the offspring of a filthy traitor. Death is too good for you; I will not spare you as I have done your traitor father. You will rot in the mine and that spy will rot with you. Take them both away," he bellowed and strode from the chamber, his face still livid and twisted with rage.

XIII

The principal economic asset of Rion was located about one hundred and fifty kilometres north of the capital. The Mine of Kusk was a deep mine of extraordinary character yielding vast quantities of precious minerals trapped in ancient volcanic seams within deep strata. In more enlightened times the workings were done by robots whose uncomplaining labours had tunnelled a maze of passages and caverns deep into the crust of Tarnus. But over time, the lack of investment in the technology of mining had robbed the place of its productivity and, during the time of Strellic, the efficient robots were gradually replaced by an army of some thirty thousand beings who laboured in the heat, dust and human filth that now characterized the workings. These unfortunates, who had the temerity to inconvenience the Beloved Leader by their constant need for food and other commodities, slept, ate, drank and defecated where they worked. Once swallowed up by the mine, they would never again see the light of day but were reduced to troglodytes, scratching at the unyielding rock while overseers flogged and harried them to their deaths. It was estimated that the average life expectancy of the workers was no more than one hundred days. They died from disease, maltreatment and hunger, but most of all from hunger, for the mean sustenance that trickled into the mine through corrupt fingers was insufficient to sustain them in their hard and dusty labours.

Lodan and Lorel journeyed to the Mine of Kusk in a primitive, wheeled transporter. They were carried along bumpy, unmade tracks in a convoy of prisoners, packed so tightly that all were obliged to stand. These damned souls were stripped of everything that had once made them individuals. They were stripped of clothing; their heads were shorn and every last possession removed so that they were reduced to the condition of empty vessels whose only purpose was to work for the state until overtaken by exhaustion and death. Many bore the marks of recent torture; many were still bleeding from ugly wounds on their bodies and faces. Those sent to the mine were mostly male, men whose transgressions, both real and imagined had condemned them; but some women also ended up there, mostly the sick and elderly who were of no further use to the state. On the prison transport both sexes were carried to the mine without segregation. Any condemned person convicted of political dissent also condemned their family who were separated from them and buried in the mine. Even children tainted by their parent's treachery and judged to be of use, were taken and put to labour, but these unfortunates rarely lasted more than a few days.

Lorel had not spoken since the traumatic drama of their trial and her father's death. Lodan managed to jostle her to the open grill at the side of the transport to get some of the dusty air, but she remained stone-faced, her dead eyes glaring sightlessly out of the wagon upon the treeless, barren landscape. Her body and face still bore the signs of her recent ordeal. Her face was swollen and there was an ugly cut at the back of her skull where her head had come into violent contact with the table. Her body was bruised but not as badly cut from repeated flogging as his was. He noticed also that there was blood at her crotch and guessed that she had been abused during her questioning.

Since their first meeting in Arkuna's house they had hardly spoken to one another, but, even so, he felt a strong affinity towards her. They had shared the horror of torture and now they were to share the horror of the Mine of Kusk and by assuming some sort of responsibility for her welfare he sought to deflect from himself the true consequence of what they were both about to face. In his mind it bound them together and they would face the future as one.

In the wagon the naked, skeletal cargo jostled, moaned and cried with anguish at what they faced. But there was one fellow who was different, standing against the opposite side of the truck from Lodan. This man was exceptionally muscular and well built, with huge shoulders and arms and a pair of legs like two solid, stone columns. He stood impassively with his back to Lodan, looking out over the passing landscape. His back and buttocks were covered with a lattice of lash marks that were still bleeding from a recent flogging. Lodan watched him for a while, but the man didn't turn around, he just kept staring out as though taking in as much as he could of the last sky and land he would ever see.

After two hours of bumpy, dusty travel, they came upon a collection of squat, mean building nestling at the base of an escarpment. The buildings housed workers whose business was to serve the mine. Beyond the village, set into the face of the escarpment, was the gaping entrance to the workings, above which was an enormous, full-length portrait of the Beloved Leader, smiling with fatherly severity upon those who were seeing the last daylight of their lives. To the left of the entrance was a small collection of huts that served as barracks for soldiers whose unlucky duty it was to govern the mine. Around the portrait of Strellic was an array of formidable looking defences; weapons protruding ominously from slits hewn into the rock face.

The convoy passed through the village and disappeared into the gaping mouth of the mine. The daylight dwindled and finally died and the last of the natural light was finally gone. They travelled deeper and deeper into the heart of the workings, down a wide tunnel, scoured from the rock by robots and generations of men long dead. As they descended the sloping road the air began to warm. The temperature rose inexorably until it felt as though one had entered an oven where dust and the stench of human waste clawed at the skin and nostrils of the prisoners. It became difficult to breathe and many in the transport began to cough and choke and gasp for air.

After about three kilometres they came upon two massive, steel gates over which straddled a metal enclosure where the guards peered moodily from dusty windows. The convoy stopped before the gates and the doors of the wagons swung aside. The wagons disgorged, leaving behind the corpses of four children and an elderly woman. The children had been strangled by their fathers to spare them the horrors of what was to come. The old woman had simply died of despair. Guards, wearing filthy, pale-blue shorts, came down from the guardhouse and flung the bodies out on to the ground while the prisoners were herded into a corral next to the steel gates. There was the crack a weapon discharging as one elderly male prisoner did not move fast enough. He went down and was dragged away to the incinerator.

From the corral each naked prisoner passed through a narrowing passage into a room where their orifices were searched with the use of probes. Lodan endured the indignity with gritted teeth, but Lorel, who was next in line, began to get agitated and pushed the guard away. He angrily pulled a small electric rod from his belt and was about to discharge it when a superior officer stopped him.

"Stop," he commanded. "Don't you know who this is?"

"I don't care who it is, I got to search them," replied the guard defensively.

"Let this one pass; that is an order, trooper."

The guard reluctantly waved Lorel through and resumed his search of the next prisoner. The sergeant observed the daughter of his one-time commander; there was little he could do for her now, but at least he had spared her that indignity. Very little of any consequence was ever found during these searches, they were primarily designed to re-enforce the total loss of humanity that these unfortunates were now to suffer. They had become nothing more than meat and bone and all semblance of what each person had once been was now lost. They were without gender, age, personality, or any other aspect of individuality; they had become units, expendable units, cast into a pit of hell in the service of the state.

After the search, each prisoner was fitted with a collar placed around the neck. With these instruments, the guards now had absolute control over their subjects, with the power of life and death through a transmitter located in the guardroom and a personal instrument they carried on a belt around their waists. The prisoners now passed through a small, steel gate located to the side of the main gates. They were now subjects of the mine.

When they were all assembled an officer appeared on the balcony of the guardroom. "Welcome to Kusk," he declaimed. "You are now the proud guest workers of Umbert Strellic, our Beloved Leader. Work hard and you will be rewarded, but if you slack, you will be punished. The collars you are now wearing have been fitted for your protection. They will prevent you from disgracing yourselves by attacking the glorious and triumphant soldiers who now command you. I will now demonstrate what will happen if you attempt to attack one of my soldiers."

A guard switched off his device and approached the group of prisoners. He pulled out a skinny youth and led him to the front of the group, below the guardhouse. The captain looked down impassively and nodded. The boy looked wild with fear as the guard reactivated his device and approached. He was less than half a metre away when the boy screamed and grabbed desperately at the collar. Steam issued from his eye sockets as his brain boiled in his head. By the time his body hit the ground he was already dead; his limbs twitched in spasm for a few seconds then he was still.

The captain watched the spectacle with the boredom of familiarity as two of the guards dragged the youth away. "These collars will remain on your necks while you are the guest workers of our Beloved Leader. I know that you will remember what you have just seen. That is all." He nodded to the guard detail and strolled back into the guardroom.

The sergeant who had spared Lorel went up to the well-built man who Lodan had seen in the wagon and whispered something to him. The fellow looked over at Lorel and nodded then the guards split the group up into six details and led them into the mine through a set of iron-barred gates that were controlled from the guardhouse. The well-built man took his place just ahead of Lorel, while Lodan walked beside her. The fellow seemed to be up to something and as Lodan observed his broad, lacerated back, he began to suspect that he would have to deal with this fellow and it was not an inviting prospect. As they penetrated ever deeper, breathing the scorching, fetid air, heavy with the odour of sweat and defecation, became increasingly difficult. The heat and dust clung to their bodies that ran with sweat. The sounds of metal on rock and occasional screams of pain echoed up from the depths.

They walked for more than two kilometres, growing ever deeper, until they came to a vast cavern where tunnels issued from galleries at every level. Here, the guards split the party in two with one group going to a tunnel on the second level and the other entering a tunnel on the third. Here the labyrinthine workings were no more than two metres high with many offshoots descending into deeper seams. Lodan, who was taller than the other prisoners, had to duck sharp protuberances in the roof as they came across other workers, naked, skeletal shadows in the flickering light. They were carrying spoil out of the tunnels in crude baskets slung across their backs. They paid no heed to the newcomers as they trudged mechanically by.

Further individuals were separated off and disappeared into tunnels until just five of the original prison transport remained; Lodan, Lorel, the well-built man and two others, an elderly, stick-like fellow and a bewildered looking youth of about sixteen. They followed the guard into a working and came to a stop. A thin specimen came forward; he was collared, but carried a short stick capable of delivering a painful but temporarily debilitating charge. He was probably in his forties but had the stoop and face of a very old man.

"This is your foreman; he tells you where to work, where to sleep, where and when to eat, shit and piss. You will obey him without any question. If I have to come in here to sort out any trouble, you will all die."

He hawked and spat on the ground then trudged away.

"Come with me," said the foreman in a dusty, broken voice and led them down the tunnel. They walked further into the labyrinth until they came to the face working where about twenty other dust-covered individuals were hacking at the rock and carrying it away. The foreman pointed a crooked, grubby finger at Lodan and the three other males.

"This is where you will work," he rasped. There will be no talking, or contact of any kind between workers. The pick workers will not leave their station; if you need to shit or piss you do it where you stand. There will be a break for water of twenty seconds every hour."

He picked out three of the exhausted workers. "You three, take over the picks from this, this and this man."

Lodan and the two older males stepped forward and took the tools from the exhausted, skeletal miners. The men handed them over with obvious relief and began to pick up the spoil and load it into the baskets. But Lodan did not swing the pick soon enough for the foreman's taste and he shot a bolt from his prod into his back. He screamed with pain as the electricity shot through his nervous system and made his whole body shake for ten seconds.

"That was just a taste, you fucker, now work."

And so, Lodan joined the workforce at the face of the mine workings. He threw the pick at the unyielding rock until it splintered away and was gathered into baskets by those who were too young or too weak to swing the pick. Lorel and the boy joined those picking up and loading the spoil. Lodan wanted to see what happened to her but did not dare risk another taste of the foreman's stick so he just kept working. He now saw that his chivalrous notion of protecting her was completely at odds with his situation; he could not even protect himself anymore.

The heat soon began to take its toll. Sweat poured from him as he worked the pick and a raging thirst soon came upon him. At last, two workers trundled a cart with a large water butt on it into the workings and the miners were allowed to visit the cart in twos. Lodan found himself opposite the water butt with the well-built man and as they drank and doused themselves with the dusty water, they eyed each other up. Lodan saw that the fellow was shorter than he and his grim, stoic face bore the scars of a recent beating. His nose was broken and had lost its original shape some time before his recent punishment and there were marks on his cheeks and forehead where old scars had not properly healed. As he drank, Lodan could see that some of his teeth were missing, which together with his solid, square jaw, suggested that the man was no stranger to fighting. But with all his fighting assets and obvious past, what struck Lodan most about him were his eyes, which, in stark contrast to his rugged exterior, were dark, soft and expressive, as though affording a window on to the true character of the man. As they doused themselves he gave Lodan an imperceptible nod, as though in recognition of a kindred spirit, but Lodan did not respond; he was far from trusting anyone in this hell.

The foreman called time and they returned to their labours, giving way to two more thirsty miners. Lodan cast a furtive look eye about for Lorel, but he did not see her.

After six hours of grinding labour a klaxon sounded and they were all told to down tools. Lodan's muscles ached from the unaccustomed work. Each worker filed past the water cart, gulping its polluted contents and dousing himself. As each finished the foreman handed out a thick, dry biscuit and the workers disappeared into nooks and tunnels of abandoned workings about the place. Lodan took his biscuit and waited for Lorel a little way from the cart. Eventually he saw her join the queue for water. She was between two skeletal prisoners who seemed to be assisting her. They made her drink and take her biscuit then they took her down a nearby tunnel. Lodan followed and found the two sharing Lorel's biscuit while she watched impassively.

"You fuckers are stealing her food."

They looked up in alarm as he approached and scuttled down the unlit tunnel like the trolls they had become. Lodan did not waste his time chasing them into the labyrinth of passages, he gently took her arm and led her out of the tunnel and further away from the other workers. As they passed the end of another tunnel a voice hailed him.

"Hey, in here."

Lodan instinctively knew who it was and hesitated.

"There's plenty of room," the voice persisted.

Lodan turned and saw the face of his water partner in the gloom. He steered Lorel into the tunnel and gently pressed her to the floor then took his place by her side opposite the man. He halved his biscuit and tried to encourage her to eat but she turned her mouth away from the offered food and did not speak.

"I know who that is; is she your woman?" the man enquired as he observed her intently.

"No," replied Lodan as he slowly chewed on the tasteless, dry biscuit.

"I thought not; they never keep couples together. Are you claiming her?"

"I aim to protect her."

The big man smiled mirthlessly, displaying his broken teeth. "Protect her from what? Death?"

"Maybe from you," replied Lodan, feeling the onset of an adrenaline rush; if they were going to fight, better to get it over with.

Now the man laughed, genuinely amused. "You really think you can protect her from me?"

"If I have to," replied Lodan rising to his feet.

"Sit down, my friend, I mean you no harm; or her for that matter. The sergeant asked me to watch out for her; there aren't many young women in the mine. He didn't want the general's daughter tinkered with. What's your name, friend?"

"Lodan DeRhogai," replied Lodan sinking back to the floor, somewhat relieved; he really didn't fancy himself against this brute.

"You're not from Tarnus, are you?"

"No, I'm from Kagan."

The man raised an eyebrow in surprise. "A Kagan! What are you doing on Tarnus?"

"I was brought here, against my will, by a Moontrader and branded a spy."

"Shit, that's tough. Looks as though they thrashed you pretty thoroughly."

Lodan nodded. "You too."

He grinned. "I deserved it. I'm Allrik Tonovic." He stretched out his huge right arm in greeting and Lodan took it. Lodan had big hands but they grasped less than half of the circumference of the man's forearm.

"What was your sin?"

"I was in the army; I murdered my sergeant. They don't take too kindly to that."

"Why did you kill him?"

"He got jealous, there was a fight; it was sort of accidental."

"What do you mean, jealous?"

Allrik shrugged. "Strellic banned marriage for army staff, except for officers over thirty. Instead the men are supplied with women from the prison population; that's why there aren't any young women here, only old crones that nobody wants. There aren't enough young women to go round so some guys go strange."

"Oh," replied Lodan, taken aback by the casual frankness. "Have you killed many men?"

"A few," replied the ex-soldier, taking another chunk out of the biscuit, "but only in regimental bouts. I was the champion of our regiment, I fought many contests." He gave Lodan an arch look. "You're going to try and escape, aren't you?"

"If we stay here we'll die."

"It's never been done."

"That doesn't mean it can't be done."

"You could kill the foreman, that would be easy, but then you'd be fucked. We can't get these collars off and one touch of a switch and they could just burn your head off, just like that poor sod outside the guardroom. You can't get near the guards; that's for sure."

"You don't necessarily have to get near a man to kill him." He picked up a sharp piece of spoil and tossed it to Allrik. "There are plenty of weapons here."

"Fuck! You really do mean it don't you?"

"Yes. Are you in?"

Allrik grinned. "Yes, we're all going to die down here; we might as well take a few with us."

"You will fail."

The two men turned to Lorel. It was the first time Lodan had heard her speak since they were separated and tortured.

"There is a central control; they can kill every prisoner with one instruction."

"How do you know?"

"I am a general's daughter; you pick up on such things."

"What else do you know about this place?"

"Enough to know that you will never escape. You will die here; we will all die here."

Her voice was bitter and she hung her head between her raised knees and covered it with her arms.

He tried to put a comforting arm about her but she shied away. "No man will ever touch me," she whispered vehemently.

Lodan watched her pensively. She had mistaken him, for his only motive was to protect her and comfort her. Under normal circumstances he would not have been able to control himself in such proximity to a naked young woman, but here, in this immodest community, he had no desires in him for there was nothing about her nakedness that aroused him. It was as though his libido had been torn from him when the guards stripped him for transportation. Down here, in this hell, all these naked souls were nothing more than walking flesh and bone.

A distant klaxon sounded and a few seconds later the lights went out. At first it appeared that they had been plunged into the blackest night, but as his eyes became accustomed to the darkness, he began to see that there was still light. It was a ghostly glow emanating from the rocks themselves; more specifically from the quartzite seams that ran through the strata. He could see the veins of luminescence running through the black surfaces of the tunnel and, under other circumstances, he might have thought them beautiful; but here, they only cast a light on misery. He looked over at Lorel, she had lain down and he could make out the whiteness of her buttocks and the gentle rise and fall of her body as she breathed. She seemed to be asleep and he listened awhile to her regular breathing and thought bitterly of what she must have suffered at the hands of her torturers. She was the daughter of a soldier, used to being around rough men, but now she had been damaged by them and she would have to carry those scars with her for the rest of her life. His heart bled for her.

Opposite him he noticed Allrik looking at her intently. The soldier noticed Lodan staring and faced him in the half-light.

"Don't worry, I won't touch her," he said and stretched out with his hands behind his head. "I reckon she's wrong though. There must be a way out of here, it's just a question of finding it."

Lodan stretched out in the dust that formed the floor of the tunnel and shut his eyes. He did not attempt to implore the mercy of the Prophet for he was now certain that he had been totally abandoned. His body ached from the grinding work of the day but Allrik's words turned in his brain until fatigue took him into a deep sleep.

It seemed that he had been asleep but a moment, when he became aware of a hand on his shoulder. He opened his eyes and saw that it was Allrik, squatting next to him and shaking him awake.

"Something is going on," whispered the man.

Lodan sat up and heard blood-freezing screams that stopped abruptly at that moment. Then they heard the sound of a commotion that sounded like a brief scuffle and footsteps coming.

Lorel had not woken so they stepped over her and went to the end of the tunnel where it joined the main gallery. In the gloom they saw four figures approaching at speed carrying something between them. Another figure stumbled after them crying out for help. As the quartet passed them they could see that they carried another human being, held by each limb while the head dangled and bumped along in the dust. One of the carriers glanced at the two of them as they passed; his eyes, fired with triumph, shone in his dark, dusty face. The four men were bearded and their long hair hung lankly about their shoulders; they had been in the mine for a long time. They ran on into the gloom of the gallery while their pursuer stumbled up to the two men. Lodan recognized him as the thin, elderly fellow who had arrived with them.

He saw them and stopped and grabbing Allrik's arm pulled him forward. "They've got the boy," he panted. "Please, they will kill him, you must get him back."

Allrik needed no encouragement at the prospect of a fight and he set off in pursuit of the kidnappers. Lodan followed but Allrik was surprisingly swift for a big man and was soon well ahead. He caught up with the kidnappers as they were about to disappear into another tunnel. They heard his footsteps behind so they dropped their quarry and turned to face him. He piled straight into them, knocking two aside and crunching his fist into a third. When Lodan arrived they saw, if they did not know it already, that they were out-matched and three of them scurried away while the fourth, the one that Allrik had downed, growled and bared his rotten teeth at them and swayed into a tunnel holding his head. Lodan and Allrik let him go; there was no point in killing a man who was running away. Even so, Lodan noticed that these individuals were different. They were not skeletal, starved specimens, they all showed signs of moderate nutrition.

The elderly man arrived, panting and wheezing and knelt beside the victim, cradling his head. Now they could see it was the young boy who had arrived with them. He was groggy and a wound to his head seeped blood into the dust. Allrik pushed the man aside and easily took the boy up into his arms and they started to make their way back.

Lorel woke up as they arrived. Allrik stepped over her and laid the lad on the ground and checked his head wound. Lodan and the man sat down and watched as Allrik took the boys head in his hands and licked the gash until it was clean and the blood had stopped flowing. Lodan glanced at Lorel in surprise. "It's army," she explained, "if there is nothing to clean a wound and you can't reach it for yourself."

When the bleeding had stopped the boy reached up and clung to Allrik like a baby.

"He's a simpleton," said the old man.

"Who were those people? What did they want with him?" asked Lodan.

The old man shook his head sorrowfully. "It is horrible; inhuman. They are flesh-eaters."

The others looked at him in disbelief.

"It is not possible," said Lorel.

"That is what I thought," replied the man, "but I have been told a different truth."

"You must be mistaken," said Lodan. "It is physically impossible to eat flesh in any form."

"I heard rumours," said Allrik. "Barrack talk mostly, but I never believed them."

The elderly man looked in his direction. The boy had fallen asleep still clinging to the soldier. He now had a more robust protector and the fellow was glad to be relieved of that duty. "Did you not notice that those men were not starving?"

"Yes, I did," replied Lodan.

"Well, the biscuits are strictly rationed; they are getting more protein from somewhere."

"But flesh cannot be digested," said Lorel

"That is what everyone believes," replied the old man. "It is written into every cannon of human ethics. We learn it from the moment we can receive instruction. But the truth is we can digest flesh. At first the stomach rejects it violently, but if one persists, gradually it can be taken down and digested. It is highly nutritious if one can tolerate it. They take the old and the weak, any less able to resist; but they especially prize the young ones. They keep them alive as long as possible, so that the flesh does not putrefy in this heat. First they hang the bodies up and drink the blood until the victim is barely alive, then they take sharpened stones and begin to cut until the victim mercifully dies, which if they are skilful, can take two or three days. Finally, they cut through the flesh and gorge on the organs. The marrow, liver and brain are particularly prized."

His account silenced them until Lodan spoke.

"How do you know this?"

"It is common knowledge in the mine."

"I wish I'd killed them all," said Allrik.

"Are there many flesh-eaters?" asked Lorel.

"I don't know, I don't think so. I think most prisoners would rather die than eat flesh."

"And the guards do nothing?" said Lodan.

The old man shook his head. "There are few guards and they don't come into the mine during sleep time. As long as not too many are taken, they do not concern themselves."

"You had better stay here with us," said Lodan.

"I thank you for that and for saving the boy. My name is Candar Lun; I have not yet found out the boy's name, he is traumatized and does not seem to know it. He speaks very little and what he does say is unintelligible; just noises mostly."

The other three introduced themselves to the newcomer and then they settled down to sleep. But Lodan did not sleep straight away; despite the fatigue in his body, his mind was racing. It was something that Candar had said that occupied him, 'there are few guards'. It encouraged him in the belief that there had to be a way out.

He slept, it seemed for but a moment and the next thing he heard was the klaxon sounding the assembly.

"Quickly," said Candar, "we have to assemble. The foreman will punish any who are late."

They struggled to their feet and made their way to the work-face. They were the last to arrive and the foreman glared at them angrily. "You are new, so I will not punish you all."

He stepped forward and shot a bolt into the boy who was still holding on to Allrik. He dropped to the floor and began shaking, his eyes rolled and his bladder released. Lodan felt Allrik tense beside him. *He's going for the foreman,* he thought. He grabbed Allrik's arm and stopped him.

"He's a simpleton," objected Lodan.

The foreman glared at them. "I don't care what he is. You got something else to say?"

"No, Sir," replied Lodan quickly.

"Then get to work, all of you."

They filed past the now stilled child and the foreman kicked him in the ribs. "Get up, you useless fucker."

The boy tried to rise but could not find his feet. He tried to crawl away so the foreman kicked him on the buttocks. The boy yelped in pain and crawled faster but the swung his bare foot and kicked him again. Lodan kept hold of Allrik as they filed away; he could feel the man's anger and feared he might do something impetuous.

"Not now," he hissed urgently.

The foreman kicked the boy a few times more and left him to moan on the ground. Then he gave his orders and detailed the company to their chores. They were allowed a few seconds at the water station then the grind started.

They worked as before, Lodan, Allrik and Candar hacking at the rock face and Lorel carrying the spoil. They saw the boy, further down the line, his head down, mechanically loading the baskets with spoil. He was bruised but the foreman was weak and barefooted, so he was not too badly injured. The foreman had separated Lodan and Allrik so they did not see each other at the water station during the brief respites of the shift. At last the klaxon went and they filed past the water station and received their daily ration of biscuit.

Lorel brought the boy back to their tunnel with her. He saw Allrik and immediately nestled down beside him, holding on to his arm.

"He won't last long," said Lorel, setting herself down next to Lodan.

"None of us will," replied Candar. "You two guys are strong, but you will waste away and die just like the rest of us."

"Wonder what his foul crime was,' said Lodan, nodding towards the boy.

Candar cast his eyes over the boy. "He probably lost his guardian and had no one to protect him any more. In Rion there is no place for the abnormal. He's done nothing; he's just an innocent swept up by this brutal regime."

"Are you innocent too, old man?" asked Allrik.

Candar forced a weak smile. "Is forty eight old these days?"

Lodan was more surprised than the other two who had often seen the ravages of poor diet and hard work that prevailed in the population of Rion. Candar looked about seventy, but his body, though gaunt, was more in keeping with his age.

"No, I am not innocent. I was a teacher; I taught history at the university in Salom Gul. I was convicted of treason because I did not lie about the state of things before the rule of Strellic. I was reported by a student for 'exaggerating' the utopian history of Rion before our Beloved Leader's era."

"You did not adhere to the official line," said Lorel.

Candar nodded. "There is no learning in Rion. Academia is dead here."

"It is a pity you chose history instead of science," said Lodan. "You might have been able to tell us how to get rid of these collars."

"There is no way," said Lorel, "not without killing the wearer."

Lodan turned to her; she was sitting pensively chewing her rusk. "How do they take them off when a prisoner dies?"

"There is a device that neutralizes the charge; only then can they be unclipped."

"Who has them?"

"All the guards. The same device protects them from us; they just use a different frequency to unlock them."

"How close can we get to them?"

"Depends on the setting. In these confines it would be very close otherwise they'd be killing anyone near them. I would imagine you'd have to practically touch them."

"You might be able to kill one or even two but you wouldn't be able to get at the device; not without some sort of tool," said Allrik.

"Like a pick axe?" replied Lodan.

Candaric held up his hand. "This is all academic. Even in the extremely unlikely event that you could detach a collar and get out of the mine, there is nothing around here, not for a hundred kilometres in any direction. You wouldn't survive for long."

"They brought us here by truck," observed Lorel. "That would be our way out."

The klaxon sounded and the lights went out. Once again the ghostly glow of the rocks illuminated them. They lay down and exhaustion saw them soon asleep.

During the next shift two workers dropped and would not be revived. The foreman went and got a guard who inspected them and then activated their collars. Lodan watched from the corner of his eye as their heads fried briefly as their bodies writhed and the mine chamber filled with the sickening reek of burning flesh. A cart came down the main gallery and two skeletons loaded the bodies on to it and pulled them away to the furnace. The stench of the cooked flesh seemed to hang about the working like a pall; it was a salutary reminder of what was going to happen to all of them eventually.

After the third day, hunger pangs began to gnaw at them. Candar and the boy were less affected, for they were used to the near starvation diet of the civilian population, but the other three were troubled. Lodan felt himself losing weight and getting weaker. He knew that if they did not do something soon, he would not have the strength to carry out any plan.

For the next three days, after every shift, they sat and discussed their plans for escape. But in every case the discussions ended in stalemate for they did not possess the ingenuity to get around the problem of the collars. At the end of the seventh day, they were too tired to talk about anything; they ate their rusks and curled up in the dust to sleep. They had finally been consumed by the mine and stripped of all hope.

Now the drudgery of long working days and steady decline began. They ceased to talk or even dream about escape and only strove for survival. As the interminable days of filth and drudgery passed, workers died and were replaced by newcomers who, already weakened by the harshness and deprivation of life in Rion, soon adapted to this new, starker reality. They worked and waited to die.

On the twenty-fifth day of their incarceration three workers died in quick succession and three more arrived to replace them. Lodan paid them little heed for he had received a punishment from the foreman's baton the day before, for taking too long at the water station. The newcomers were all male, but all civilians, already half-starved and included a pre-pubescent boy. His father had not managed to kill him in the wagon that brought them here and now they had become separated. They had not seen the flesh-eaters since they had tried to kidnap the simpleton, but that night they came again and carried off the newly arrived boy. This time only Allrik heard them and he rose and stole out of their tunnel and followed.

Later, towards the end of that sleep time, Lodan awoke to the sound of retching. Allrik was missing from the place he usually slept. He pretended sleep and when the ex-soldier returned to his place and saw the dark stain of blood around the man's mouth. His heart sank; Allrik had become a flesh eater.

The following night he managed to stave off sleep and wait. When he thought the others were asleep, Allrik stole from the tunnel and disappeared into the main gallery. Lodan rose silently and followed. Allrik led him into the network of tunnels, deeper and deeper into the heartless pit of the mine. As he followed he took note of his direction for these were places where few now trod. Finally

Allrik turned to his right and disappeared down a low, dark tunnel where the rocks did not cast their luminescent glow. Lodan peered into the darkness and could see the familiar glow coming from a chamber at its end. The heat was even more stifling here and the putrid stench of the place almost drove him back. He crept forward, his eyes straining in the gloom. He heard voices, muted whispers and another sound that could not quite identify. It sounded like mud, slopping around in a bowl.

He went on all fours and crawled to the mouth of the dark tunnel. In the gloom he beheld a sight that would never leave him; he had come to the very mouth of hell. Corpses, five or six in number, strung to rock protuberances by their feet from rope made of human hair. One body was that of the small boy who had been taken from them the night before. He was covered in wounds where blood had been drained, but his eyes were open and he was still alive. Below the hanging corpses about a dozen individuals were squatting, or tearing at the corpses with sharpened rocks. They were all eating flesh and their mouths were stained dark with blood.

One of them noticed Lodan; his half-mad, haunted eyes watched as he chewed the raw flesh. Lodan entered the chamber and slowly walked towards Allrik who was tearing at a piece of liver with his teeth. The soldier noticed him and stopped eating. Their eyes met and Lodan saw the same haunted glaze in the eyes of his friend. The other cannibals stopped eating and turned their attention to the newcomer, waiting to see if he would become one of them.

Lodan bent down and picked up a shard of rock. He approached the hanging child. "I'm going to take him back," he said, keeping his eyes on Allrik.

A cannibal to his right sprang to his feet. His long beard was caked with blood and his hair, matted and filthy, covered his shoulders. He had been in the mine a long time. "He is ours now," he growled. Others got up and waited for the longhaired man to make a move. "You are not one of us," he said and picked up a large, pointed shard of rock.

With sudden speed Lodan ripped the shard of rock he had picked up across neck of the child. Blood sprang from the severed artery and sprayed the floor. There was a collective moan of anguish at the waste of food and then they came for him.

The longhaired man lunged at him with the pointed shard. Lodan forgot his weakness and hunger and the years of training returned with a burst of adrenalin. He grabbed the shard, parried the lunge and broke the man's arm before the others got near. The man's roar of agony was truncated as Lodan slammed his fist into his face. He sliced across the neck of another and buried the shard in the stomach of the third. But he was not the man he was and two more pulled him down and began to punch him while others held his arms and buried their teeth into his flesh.

And then the attack stopped and bodies were flying to one side of him and then another. He looked up at the back of Allrik as the man flung another, sending him crashing against the rock wall. Lodan sprung to his feet and the two of them faced the remaining attackers. But the cannibals now hesitated. Four of them were dead and would provide new flesh for those who survived. Lodan and Allrik stood side by side, breathing heavily, their bodies tensed for a fight to the death.

The cannibals glared at them but did not advance. The two men began to back slowly towards the tunnel, watchful of any fresh attack, but their blood-smeared attackers offered no further combat; they had new flesh to consume and fewer to share it with. Lodan and Allrik backed into the dark tunnel then turned and crawled out of that ghastly place.

When they reached the gallery Allrik suddenly bent double and retched. A pile of gore issued from his mouth and splashed to the ground. He staggered on then slumped to his haunches his head in his hands. "I'm sorry… I'm sorry. I was so hungry, Lodan; so hungry. I couldn't stand it anymore." He looked up at his friend; tears started from his eyes and trickled down his cheeks.

Lodan squatted down in front of him and put his hand on the man's shoulder. "We're all hungry, Allrik. Our stomachs are empty and our bodies are dying; I would be lying if I said I didn't think about… about that." He pointed towards the dark tunnel.

"But you didn't do it, did you?"

"We all make our own judgements. I am of the Faith and I think it is better to die than to live with that shame. You have no such doctrine to guide you."

Allrik looked into his friend's eyes; his own eyes were haunted by guilt and shame. "I could have saved that child but instead of saving him I drank his blood. I don't want to go on, Lodan; I want to die."

"You saved my life in there; you made that choice."

"You are my friend and I love you but there is nothing you can say to diminish my guilt. The only thing I can ask you is not to tell the others."

"We will never speak of this again."

Allrik nodded resignedly, his broken, craggy face a study of misery. "Where is your Prophet now, Lodan?"

Lodan considered for a brief moment; it had been some time since he had privately tried to commune with his Lord. "He has abandoned me; He has abandoned everyone down here. It's time to end this; we'll fight and take as many as we can with us. Let's go back now."

The two men stood and began to make their way back. Each had saved the other's life but in two different ways; Allrik had saved Lodan's skin and Lodan had saved Allrik's soul. They knew from that moment that they were soon going to die together and the thought of it warmed and supported them both.

Lorel and Candar were still fast asleep on their return, but the boy was awake, fretting at the absence of his friend. He grabbed Allrik and clutched on to him and the ex-soldier patted his head affectionately. They settled down and spoke in whispered tones.

"When shall we do it?" asked Allrik.

"Tomorrow, before the shift; we'll kill the foreman and arm ourselves with rocks. Guards will come when he doesn't report in; with any luck we'll get them too. They won't take us alive, that's for certain."

"If we could just get these fucking collars off," replied Allrik, pulling at the thing.

The boy, who had been listening, was suddenly alert. He let go of Allrik and started to wave his fists out in front of him. His face screwed up as if in some super-human effort to express himself. Suddenly his lips parted and he spoke.

"Break them... break them." The words came to him with difficulty, blurting incomprehensively from his lips. "Break them," he repeated, waving his bony fists before him.

The two men regarded each other in surprise. They watched the boy trying to form the words that seemed trapped in his mouth.

"Allrik... can't... die. Must break this." He pulled at Allrik's collar. "Use stick of bad man who hurt me."

"He's talking rubbish," declared Lodan.

"No... no, listen to him," insisted Allrik.

The boy seemed to be gathering himself and reaching into some forgotten corner of his brain. He grabbed insistently at Allrik's collar and suddenly became lucid as if a dam had just broken in his brain and released the waters of knowledge. He began to describe the constituent parts of the collar and its method of manufacture. He was like an automaton spouting some pre-recorded message until he finally came to the nub of the matter when he became more animated. "Basic... basic. Easy... Easy to disrupt with high charge of static like stick."

"What the hell is he saying?" said Lodan and he roused the other two from their sleep. "Listen to this," he said as they sat up.

The boy repeated himself exactly, word for word. Lorel stared in surprise but Candar was the only one of them who realized what was happening.

"Goodness me!" he exclaimed. "He's a low-order savant."

"What's that?" said Lodan.

"His higher brain functions are scrambled, the synaptic connections aren't firing properly except in limited parts of his brain where they fire with excessive vivacity. It causes peculiar behaviour, but brilliance in specific, limited capacities. It's like a house where every room is a shambles except one where all the treasure is kept. It's usually some trauma that unlocks the room; what happened to him?"

"We were planning to kill ourselves," said Allrik. "We've had enough."

"That would have panicked him well enough," replied Candar.

"So, we can rely on what he is saying?" said Lorel.

"If I'm right; I have not seen one before; they don't normally survive in Rion."

The boy stood up and started a disjointed animation. Allrik gently pulled him down, cupped his hands around his head and looked into his eyes to calm him. "Tell us how to do it."

The boy stared unblinking into his friend's eyes and reached into his mind. "You take the stick from the bad man and hold it against here." He pointed to the clasp in the collar. "You hit... You hit hard to break here. Keep stick on collar, full charge; don't take away. Collar will break and Allrik won't die. Allrik mustn't die. Allrik can't die."

"It can't be that easy," said Lodan.

"It isn't," said Candar. "A full charge of the baton anywhere on the body will kill you, let alone on the neck."

Lodan slumped back; it seemed they had arrived at the end of another blind alley. He put his head between his knees and gnashed his teeth.

"Unless we can insulate the body from the charge," said Lorel. "What can we use?"

"The water butt," announced Candar. "It's a compound of carbon, it won't conduct a charge."

"Yes," said Lorel, "If we cut a section we can use it as a shield between the collar and the skin."

The boy started to wave his arms. "No water… no water."

"He's right," said Lodan. "It'll have to be completely dry."

The boy picked up a handful of dust. "Put this on Allrik."

Lodan laughed and hugged him and the others did too. The boy beamed; it was the first time any of them had seen him smile.

"Of course," said Lorel, "when we break the lock there will be an alarm in the guardhouse and they will come."

"I'm counting on it," replied Lodan and they grinned at each other for the first time and, in that moment of hope, Lodan knew that he loved her; that he had always loved her from the first moment they had met and throughout all the meaningless encounters with the women he had known, it was she that he was destined to be with.

Even though exhaustion wracked his body, Lodan could not get to sleep that night. His mind turned with thoughts of Lorel and of what had to be done upon the hated sound of the klaxon. He had not dwelt upon the Prophet for many days, but now thoughts of devotion suddenly returned and, almost as a revelation, he knew he had not been abandoned as he had thought; he had been punished; punished so absolutely for his past sins that he had foolishly imagined that the Prophet had abandoned him. He had been plunged to the depths of despair and he had survived and now salvation must surely be at hand. He rose silently and walked further into the tunnel to a place where no one else could hear or see him and here he fell to his knees, pressed his forehead to the dusty, rock floor and gave thanks.

"If your will is to spare and deliver me, I will be forever your servant," he intoned quietly, now prostrating himself upon the dusty ground as he repeated the mantras that he had often mindlessly rehearsed in the Temple of the DeRhogai.

And this time, for the first time in his life he heard the voice of the Prophet in his head and a warm lightness invaded his body and he felt as though he was gently floating above a beautiful lake of golden water and the Prophet said; "You will be saved for you are my true servant."

He opened his eyes and the moment of ecstasy vanished and he was back in the Mine of Kusk with all its stifling misery and filth. He raised himself from his prostration, kneeled and intoned some more devotions, but the Prophet had left his body and would not now return. He looked down at his own dust-encrusted flesh and was disgusted. His foolish vanity meant nothing now and the instrument of pleasure that had once proudly served him was now nothing more than a useless appendage of skin and gristle dangling grotesquely at his groin. No more would it taunt him with its incessant demands; no more would it drive him into the wild, grasping dens of iniquity, for it had succumbed at last; it was dead. The Prophet had made him an Evangelist!

He rose, stole back to the others and slept the sleep of dreamless contentment.

They awoke before the klaxon called them to work and discussed their plan and who would do what. It was agreed, after objections from Lodan, that Allrik would be the first to be released from the collar and Lodan would kill the foreman. Allrik acceded to this arrangement in mind of what he had seen Lodan do to the cannibals. His friend was an efficient killer. Lorel also insisted on being released. Lodan was reluctant but she overruled him, declaring that she could fight as well as any man. He could see that she was intent and lustful for revenge and hoped that she would not be too reckless.

The klaxon sounded and they walked to the assembly point. Allrik hung back and arrived after all the others. The foreman cursed him for his lateness and rushed forward with raised baton, eager to teach the insolent fellow a lesson he would never forget; but as he passed Lodan, he felt a large hand clamp over his scrawny arm and his sun-starved, brittle bone was snapped over Lodan's knee. A fraction of a second later he felt his head twisted around with a snap so, as he died, his killer's face was the last thing he saw. He dropped where he stood and the boy rushed forward and began to kick the inert body of the hated foreman. The other miners gasped in dismay as Allrik gently pulled the boy away. Everyone started shouting at once.

A skeletal individual screamed, "You fools, they will kill us all."

Lorel picked up the baton of the dead foreman and advanced on them menacingly. "You're already dead, you pricks; you just haven't realized it yet."

The melee continued until Lodan shouted at them. "Shut the fuck up, all of you. We're busting out of here." He pushed his way through the crowd of flesh and bone to the water cart and kicked it over. The foul contents splashed into the dust amid groans from the miners, but no one dared interrupt him. He picked up a shard of rock from the ground and began to hack at the water butt. It did not cut easily or cleanly, but eventually he managed to separate two pieces of the flexible material about the right size and shape. He bathed them in the dust until they were dry then he turned to Allrik.

"Are you ready for this?"

Allrik nodded gravely and spread himself on the ground, face down. Lodan picked up handfuls of dust and used it to drive the moisture of sweat from his back and head. He placed the larger shield on Allrik's back, feeding the narrow part under the collar and then the smaller piece over the back of his head and under the collar for extra protection.

"You four," he called, indicating four recently arrived prisoners. "Get over here."

They hesitated and got another bellowed invitation.

"You two hold his arms and you two hold his legs. Hold him down hard or I'll kill you."

The miners took up position and Lodan crouched down and met Allrik's eye. "You ready?"

"Do it," he whispered.

Lodan went and retrieved a pick from the work-face and beckoned to Lorel. She came forward with the baton and placed it by the collar where it joined. She nodded to Lodan who straddled Allrik's torso and took aim.

"Now," he shouted and he swung the pick at the collar just as Lorel delivered the maximum charge into the thing. It broke apart at the first blow and the four miners were thrown off with the electrical discharge. Lorel quickly removed the baton and Lodan turned him over and snatched away the collar. Allrik's body shook violently, his eyes rolled and his bladder emptied as the residual shock racked his body. Then he was still.

"He's not breathing," shouted Lorel. She pounced on him and frantically began to pump his chest. She pumped for about thirty seconds before he spluttered back to life.

He opened his eyes and groggily focused on her. "Did it work?' he gasped.

Lodan took his hand and grinned at his friend. "It worked fine." He pulled Allrik to his feet. "Are you alright?"

Allrik blinked and swayed a little, "I'll be fine. Give me a moment; you get ready."

The miners stared open mouthed; they had just seen a miracle. Lodan spread himself on the ground and Lorel rubbed him thoroughly with fine dust, then she fitted the shields behind his collar. Allrik took the pick into his hands and straddled Lodan. The four miners held him down as he took careful aim and raised the pick. Lorel readied the baton. "Now," he said and he swung the pick at the collar. But he only caught it a glancing blow and the clasp did not break. Lorel removed the baton as the four miners were thrown clear. Lodan began to shake. "Again," screamed Allrik, jumping on Lodan's back to still him. He quickly swung again as Lorel delivered another bolt into the collar. This time his aim was truer and the clasp broke. Lorel threw the baton down and they turned him over and Allrik yanked off the collar. His eyes were rolling wildly and his whole body was shaking uncontrollably. He pissed himself as his limbs flailed at the air. And then he was still as the trickle of urine ran down his thigh into the dust.

Allrik stared. "Is he dead?"

Lorel put her ear to Lodan's chest. "His heart is beating." She slapped his face.

Lodan opened his eyes suddenly and gasped. For a moment it seemed he didn't know where he was; then his eyes focused on Lorel. "What are you slapping me for?" he said drowsily.

Allrik smiled. "You've pissed yourself, Lodan."

Lodan looked up at his friend. "So did you, you arsehole."

"Now me," said Lorel, rising.

"No," replied Allrik. "It's too dangerous and we haven't time."

She began to protest but she knew he was right. The guards would soon be arriving and they had to be ready. Lorel was not officially in the army, but she had seen her father directing men and now she took charge of the cohort of prisoners. "You and you," she commanded, pointing to two of the miners, "get that water cart righted. You, take this baton, you are now foreman. You three, get rid of this body, I want it out of sight. The rest of you, get to work, everything must look normal."

Allrik helped Lodan to his feet and the boy ran up and hugged him.

"I'm right," he said. "No collar and Allrik not dead."

Allrik grinned and kissed the top of his head. "You're a genius."

Candar gently pulled him away. "Leave Allrik, he has more work to do and we must do our part." He led him away to the mine face where the detail had just started under Lorel's command.

Allrik watched after him affectionately then turned to Lodan. "Are you good to do this? I could do it alone if you're not."

"And let you have all the glory?" said Lodan, rubbing his neck.

XIV

Such was the confidence in the safety of the security system of the mine that only four guards manned the night shift. The foremen, elevated prisoners, would sort out any troublemakers and even if there was a disturbance, the prisoners could not get out of the mine workings without killing themselves. Three privates and a corporal, barefooted and naked save the standard issue, loose fitting shorts, lounged in airless heat of the guardroom. Two watched a pornographic performance involving three women; while the third, a green recruit, sat in a corner reading. The fourth strolled back into room having spent some time in the toilet.

The corporal glanced at him. "Had a good wank in there, Private?"

The man slumped in a chair. "Mind your own business."

The corporal laughed. "Why didn't you do it here? We wouldn't mind, would we, Flogger?"

The man next to him shook his head absently. He was absorbed in the performance.

The corporal then addressed himself to the new man in the corner. "Oi! Twig-dick, would you mind if Storric here had a wank in front of you? You'd like that, I bet?"

"Don't call me Twig-dick," replied the lad without looking up.

"I thought that was your name, Twig-dick. See Storric, Twig-dick wouldn't mind."

"I'm not wanking in front of you homos," protested the private.

The corporal sniggered. "You were pulling your todger in there, you dirty fucker. Oi, Twig-dick, come and watch these tarts, you're missing the good part."

The green recruit looked up from his book and wondered, for the umpteenth time, what had possessed him to join the army; an occupation for which he was eminently ill suited. The privations of civilian life that had driven him into the arms of the military were still vivid in his mind, but even so, he was still mightily sorry for himself.

He was excused any further invitations by the sounding of an alarm. The corporal swore and dragged himself away from the display of flesh and ambled over to the control panel. It showed an unspecified alarm in one of the tunnels, deep in the mine.

"It's probably a faulty collar. Storric, get a chariot and take Twig-dick here and check it out. Kill the prisoner and make sure you bring the collar back."

Storric scowled. "Why don't you send Dasric? He likes killing these fuckers."

"Flogger's busy and I told you to go. Now piss off and do as you're told. Take a couple of sidearms, you may have to use one if the collar's fucked."

The two soldiers buckled their combat belts around their waists and ambled out. As they descended the steps to the guardroom, Storric muttered an array of colourful complaints against his superior. They mounted one of the two-seater open chariots that were used in the tunnels and set off in the direction of the fault. After they left another alarm went off in the guardroom; the corporal swore at it and ignored it.

"This your first time in the tunnels, Twig?"

The new recruit ignored the taunt and replied that it was.

"You never get used to the stench," observed Storric.

"It's truly shocking," replied his partner.

They turned into another gallery and the lights from the vehicle swept along the craggy walls.

"I wasn't wanking in there, by the way. I was just having a good, long shit."

Neither image excited any admiration from his companion who remained silent.

"You're a strange one, Twig."

"What do you mean?"

"Reading books and all that crap. What is it you're reading?"

"It's a permitted book," replied the new recruit quickly.

Storric smiled. "I couldn't give a fuck what it is. Read what you like as long as it isn't the nuggets of wisdom written by our Beloved Leader."

The new recruit was shocked, he had never heard such opinions freely expressed.

"Have I shocked you?" continued Storric. "No one gives a fuck what we think. Here we are stuck in this arse-end of an arse's-end; the only good thing about this shit-hole is we're not gonna get killed here."

They turned into another gallery; they were nearing their destination.

"Cheer up, Twig. You're about to see your first extermination."

This information did not cheer the new recruit; he was not looking forward to it at all.

Allrik and Lodan listened to the hum of the approaching vehicle as they lurked in the shadowy darkness of a side working. Further down the tunnel the familiar clunk of pick on rock was evidence that Lorel had got the miners organized. They waited until the chariot passed them then set out behind it, running swiftly and silently. The chariot pulled into the working chamber and stopped. The driver got out and pulled his sidearm as the two men emerged from the tunnel behind.

The new recruit was watching his partner with mounting apprehension. He had no desire to witness the extermination, let alone carry one out himself. Storric approached the foreman and was about to speak when, suddenly, a naked figure flashed past the chariot. The new recruit was astonished when the naked man caught Storric and brought a rock down on his skull with a sickening crack of bone. He instantly forgot all his newly formed soldierly instincts and stared with incomprehension at the amazing sight. He became aware of the presence of another standing beside him. Instantly he knew what was going to happen; he shut his eyes and waited.

The miners heard the second crack, dropped their tools and came running. Their eyes were alive with mindless revenge and they wanted the corpses. Lodan stepped up and shouted for them to get back. They stopped and Lorel snatched the baton from the makeshift foreman and waved it at them. "You people calm down; there is more work to do."

They backed off while Lodan and Allrik pulled the recruit's body from the chariot and stripped the shorts and belts from both soldiers. They pulled on the shorts and swung the weapon belts around their waists. Allrik jumped into the driver's side of the chariot and turned it around.

Lodan took Lorel to one side. "Be careful, don't let them come out before we have neutralized the guards and killed the transmitter. We don't know how many there are up there."

"Good luck," she said and squeezed his shoulder. She had not touched him before like that and for a moment, he thought he saw a spark of desire in her eyes; but in an instant she had turned away and got back to the business of controlling the exited miners. He climbed into the chariot next to Allrik and they set off.

In the sweltering guardroom the two indolent soldiers watched the exciting conclusion of the absorbing entertainment. Such things were one of the few compensations of the mine posting as the Beloved Leader had declared pornography to be morally corrupting and had proscribed it. Citizens caught with such material were harshly dealt with, many ending their days in the Mine of Kusk. Soldiers who found themselves unable to resist such depravity were flogged and demoted. Only at the mine, a forgotten and degraded posting, did they turn a blind eye, for, as long as it produced a sufficient income for the ruler, no one could be bothered to find out what was going on there.

Dasric, momentarily sated with breasts and pubic regions, rose and sloped away for a drink.

His corporal cocked an eye at him and observed the distended bump in his shorts. "Doesn't that thing ever rest, Flogger?"

"Not if I can help it Corp. You jealous 'cause you can't get it up any more?"

"Bollocks."

Dasric pulled a drink from the ice machine; it was warm. "Shit, this piece of crap is knackered again." He took a swig and noticed the chariot emerging from the tunnel. "Those two arseholes are back," he said, as he slumped back into his chair.

The corporal frowned. "That was quick; those lazy twats had better have done the job right." He got up and pressed a switch on the control panel and waited while the metal barred gate slid open and the vehicle came out; then he closed the gate and went back to his seat.

A few moments later the door to the guardroom opened. Neither soldier looked up as two men entered. The corporal opened his mouth to deliver his admonishment but the words never left his lips. Allrik fired his sidearm and the man was dead.

Dasric looked up, his face a study of confusion and surprise. "Fuck!" he exclaimed.

Lodan walked coolly up to him. "Get up."

The soldier rose unsteadily to his feet. "You killed the corp," he uttered.

"And I'll kill you, if you don't do exactly what you're told."

"Who are you?"

"Shut your mouth and listen," growled Allrik.

Lodan pushed the weapon into the soldier's face. "Turn off the transmitter, the one that controls the collars."

"But they'll all be able to get out."

Lodan pushed his grim face nearer. "That's the general idea."

Dasric, his terrified eyes fixed on Lodan, sidled over to the ancient control panel. He pulled down a heavy, metallic lever and a harsh, red light started flashing. Then he pulled down another lever and the flashing stopped. "That's it," his voice shook as he spoke. "You don't know what they'll do."

"Oh, I think I do," replied Lodan. "Now open the main gates."

Dasric went further along the panel and pressed a large knob with the palm of his shaking hand. A klaxon sounded and there was a clunk of metal as the massive gates slowly opened.

"Thank you very much," whispered Lodan in his ear, just before he fired the weapon.

"Let's go," said Allrik.

Lodan stepped over Dasric's body and held up his hand. "Wait, you'd better take off those shorts and that belt, we don't want to be taken for guards."

Allrik nodded. "Good point."

They stripped and gathered up the sidearms of the two dead guards. At the door Allrik turned to him; he had tears of joy in his eyes. "We did it Lodan, we did it."

Lodan beamed back at his friend. "Let get some fresh air into our lungs."

By the time they had descended the guardroom steps, Lorel was emerging from tunnel that they had entered twenty-six days earlier. She was leading a large group of miners who, at first disbelieving, eventually began shouting and cheering at the sight of the open gates. She saw the two men at the base of the steps in front of the gates and her heart leapt. She ran across the gallery floor and hugged them both while miners ran past them and through the gates, into the wide tunnel that led to the air and sky.

Lodan gave her a sidearm and they began to run with the increasing crowd. The word had gone through the tunnels like a bush fire in a gale and miners were emerging from tunnels and pouring into the cavern and out through the gates. A tidal wave of humanity was soon moving up the wide entrance tunnel, at once joyous and grim and ready for revenge. Recently incarcerated, healthy prisoners soon gained the front leaving the weak and feeble in their wake. Lodan ran with Lorel, but Allrik, who was faster than either of them, soon gained the head of the advancing swarm of miners.

Lodan could see the gaping entrance ahead and the first light of the breaking dawn when one individual ran past him. Lodan noticed him straight away; there was something about him that separated him from all the others. He was young and lithe with powerful legs and haunches propelling him forward with the graceful ease of an accomplished athlete. He was average in height and his shaven head together with the fresh wounds on his back bore witness to the fact that his incarceration was very recent. His skin tone was darker than was common on Tarnus, but his origin was indistinct. But that was not what struck Lodan. He had caught sight of the man's face as he ran past; a handsome face, but a face twisted with a grim fury so intense that no amount of blood would sate it. This youngster was obviously not of a pure breed but he was a purebred warrior.

The youth passed Allric at the entrance of the tunnel and tore towards the barracks with Allrik and other miners in his wake. The sleeping, unsuspecting soldiers didn't stand a chance. The warrior, Allrik and the miners burst into the undefended barracks and killed everyone inside.

Lodan and Lorel arrived at the mouth of the tunnel and looked out on the glorious spectacle of the pre-dawn sky. They had seen skies like this many times before but never in their lives had either of them seen anything so beautiful as that first dawn of their freedom. They stopped running and embraced as the miners poured out of the tunnel and into the fresh air. Some, thirsting for revenge, descended on the village and pillaged it, killing every worker and his family with their bare hands. Others fell on the ground and kissed it and held their hands up to the dawn. The bodies of the guards were carried out of the barracks and ripped to pieces by the frenzied prisoners. Their limbs and other parts held aloft in triumph. Some prisoners had detached the head of an officer and were kicking it about in the dust.

Allrik, his hands and torso covered in blood, found them as they observed the macabre spectacle. "I think they got a message out; the army will be coming."

"I know," replied Lodan.

Allrik smiled ruefully. "I'm going to find Candar and the boy genius," He gave them both a kiss and disappeared into the crowd.

"He's right," said Lorel, "We don't have much time. This mine is the only thing Strellic has got, he won't let it go."

Lodan nodded gravely. He was distracted by sight of the dust and blood-caked warrior. He had seen them and was striding purposefully through the crowd towards them with a large field weapon slung across his shoulder. Lorel noticed him too and was transfixed; never had she seen another human being of such physical perfection. Beneath the blood and dust his form was a copy of the idealised statues of ancient gods that had once adorned the palaces of Salom Gul. She could not discern his age; he might have been fourteen or twenty-four; hairless save for a dark, pubescent crescent at his groin and yet an adult, carrying himself with the easy authority of a man.

She had seen many naked men in her life; the soldiers at the garrison had always treated her as one of their number and took no account of her presence when they bathed and in the last twenty-six days she had seen more flesh than she had ever wanted to see. It was her opinion that nudity rarely flattered men; their ugly genitals and hairy bodies were not things of beauty and without the imperative of sexual attraction, they became positively repellent. But this young man was different. Savage and graceful, he moved with the ease of an athlete and focused on Lodan and Lodan alone.

He broke through the crowd and stood in front of them, fixing his quarry with dark, unblinking eyes. When he spoke his voice was flat and emotionless.

"You are Lodan DeRhogai."

It sounded more like an accusation than a statement.

Lodan nodded. "I am."

"I am Jodi Saronaga; your father sent me to find you."

PART TWO

JODI

I

The storms that swept across the southern plains of Ennepp were a regular inconvenience to the sparse population that tilled the flat, stony fields and coaxed from them hardy root crops and cob-nuts on high canes that swayed and rustled in the cool breezes. But, about once in a generation, a storm would gather over the southern pole and twist itself into a furious giant that would lay waste to the hard-won produce of the population.

As Jodi ran through the high canes, one such storm approached.

The day before he had kissed his sister, Matty, for the last time and hugged his mentor, the old overseer, Minogi and plunged into the high canes in a determined effort to escape the bondage and degradation of the Doah Farm, an estate on the southern shore of the great inland sea that lay at the heart of the single continent on Ennepp. He had run, keeping the shore to his left as the old overseer had told him, through adjacent estates and seemingly endless fields of maturing canes, until exhaustion had forced him to rest and eat the meagre ration that Minogi had spared him. On his road he had several times been forced to make long detours around settlements or farms where he knew there were men who would kill him and claim a reward for his corpse. He was ever wary of any movement or the sound of a voice in the fields and would crouch low and be still, sometimes for hours, until he was sure of a safe path.

On the second night of his escape, the starlight that had guided his way disappeared behind a gathering mass of black cloud. The storm had caught up with him and the first drops of rain began to splash the parched soil of the surrounding fields. The canes rustled and jostled in the gathering wind and the drops of rain congealed and tumbled to the ground with increasing velocity. Ice formed in the heart of the clouds and was buffeted and tossed high into the atmosphere, gathering weight until it plummeted through the maelstrom to the surface. A stone of ice hit Jodi hard on his shoulder and then another, stinging him with icy blows, then a sudden, blinding light thwacked the ground in front of him and threw him off his feet. The very air about him shook as thunder rolled across the sky. He curled himself up into a ball and put his arms over his head to block out the terrifying noise. All about him he heard the awful crack of lightning hitting the ground. The icy wind blew like a furious monster and began to flatten the cane fields under the increasing deluge. He gathered the broken canes over him against the fury and there he stayed until, at last, the black heart of the storm passed away to the north leaving in its wake debt and ruin for many farms.

The storm had raged all night and when Jodi rose, shivering from the ruined land, the dawn was just about to break. He looked around him at the flattened crop and saw that he was the only thing standing as far as the eye could see. He was exposed in this flat, featureless landscape; anyone venturing out to view the devastation would see him instantly. He hunkered down and began to scratch at the muddy soil until he had made a depression large enough to lie in. He was wet and cold and needed to run for warmth but he did not dare. Instead he nestled in the depression and covered himself as best he could with the damp soil and the soaking debris that had once been a valuable crop. He lay there shivering uncontrollably as the sun came up and warmed the devastated land. He had caught a chill and even as his body warmed he could not prevent himself from shaking.

In the distance he heard the sound of voices and tried desperately to keep still. It sounded like two men talking but they soon went away and he heard nothing more. He finished the last of his bread as it had become soaked and would soon be of no use, then he shut his eyes and tried to sleep.

He woke up as the late sun was drawing towards the long horizon. It had warmed and dried his cocoon as he slept and he had stopped shivering. He waited until the last vestiges of sunlight had left the sky and rose from his hide. He felt weak and a little feverish, but he knew he had to go on. Somehow he had to get to the city to the north where he might find other runaways like himself and some measure of protection. Now he had to be even more wary. He had lost the cover provided by the standing crop of canes and, in the glow of the starlight, he might be seen. He ran onward, constantly scanning the horizon for lights or other potential signs of life.

About midnight exhaustion forced him to rest and he sat down against the trunk of a broken tree. He drank the last of the water from his flask and refilled it with water from a nearby pool that had formed after the rain. He picked up a few of the immature cob-nuts that lay scattered about and bit into one. It was fibrous and almost impossible to digest. He chewed it for some time to extract what nutrients it could offer and spat out the flesh. Then he dragged himself to his feet and struck on.

As the stars faded with the coming day, he found himself a slight depression near a gnarled tree and scraped out a hollow in its centre. Just as he had done on the previous dawn, he covered himself as best he could with soil and broken canes and settled down to sleep. He was exhausted and sleep came quickly, but some hours later he was awoken by the sound of nearby voices. Field workers had come out to start to clear the land and several were quite close. They were gathering the ruined crop into the great piles and burning it.

Jodi peeped out from beneath his hide. Pyres dotted the landscape and sent wisps of grey smoke into the clear afternoon air. About a hundred metres away a man was shouting at the workers, berating them and directing them with a stick. Jodi quickly ducked back below his canopy of canes. His heartbeat rose and his mouth went dry at the thought of what would happen to him if he were caught. He shrunk back into his hide as far as he could, cursing the weakness that had prevented him from excavating it to a sufficient depth. He could see the clear, blue sky through the canes above his head as he listened to the voices of men getting nearer. Soon he heard the sound of a man's foot right next to him. He froze. A shadow passed over and suddenly he was looking into the eyes of another. The eyes peered back. They belonged to wizened, Native fellow whose face bore the scar of great sorrow and long suffering. Jodi braced himself knowing that it was the end of his escape for he was discovered and would soon be killed. But instead of pulling him from his lair and exposing him to his fate, the wizened Native just smiled and moved away. For the rest of the day that wizened old guardian angel kept the other workers away from Jodi's hiding place and he was not discovered.

Once again, as the night pushed the day below the horizon, Jodi travelled on. Hunger pangs were beginning to insist he take in food and he found some rotting root-crop tubers in one field that afforded him some sustenance. But the water he had gathered in the rain pool, on the second night of his escape, now began to take its toll. His legs weakened and his stomach churned. He had contracted dysentery. The meagre contents of his digestive system soon poured out of him, leaving him weak and barely able to walk. He staggered on until he could go no further, too weak to cover himself, too weak to care anymore. And there he stayed, lying exposed in the flat landscape, for the rest of the night.

The sun rose and found him curled up in the middle of a vast estate. But now, fortune lent him a hand for he had come to rest on a part of the estate that had already been cleared of ruined crop and nobody was about. He stayed in that place, unmoving and drained of energy, all through that day and halfway through the following night. Finally, as energy gradually returned to his wasted body, he dragged himself to his feet and staggered on like a drunk.

For two more days and nights he dragged himself onward, keeping the sea to his left as the old overseer had directed. Now he came upon parts of the land that the storm had only sideswiped and the crop had survived. Here he found that he was able to hide in the high canes once again. On the sixth night of his escape his lack of food and weakness left by sickness brought him to the final limit of his endurance. He sunk down among the canes and prepared to die.

But Jodi did not die, he merely slept until dreams of food stirred him and he returned to harsh reality. In the distance he could hear the sound of laughter and a gentle breeze that was blowing off the sea brought with it the unmistakable aroma of cooking. He looked up at the vast mantel of stars above him and saw that there was no sign of the dawn so he stealthily crawled towards the sound of the voices and that wonderful smell. As he drew near he saw the flickering light of a fire through the vegetation. He edged nearer until he could see the outline of three men sitting on the ground in a clearing around the fire over which was set an iron pot. He caught sight of their features as the flames danced and crackled in the peaceful night. They were all Native men.

Jodi's experience of adult males belonging to his race was not auspicious. Apart from Minogi, he had experienced very little good of them. He recalled the brutalized people of his hometown in the north and the savage behaviour of the farm labourers towards the young and weaker workers and the thought of those practices gave him pause. But he was starving, exhausted and desperate and it seemed like providence had come to his rescue. Even if they would not share their food with him, they might be able to tell him of the city he sought and if there was haven for others like him in that place. He stood up and walked out of the canes and into the clearing.

All three men sprang up and drew their knives, staring at him in surprise.

"I'm one of your kind," said Jodi quickly.

They peered at his face, caught in the flickering light of the campfire. They were all mature males but not old. Their appearance was ragged but they were obviously not starving or emaciated. Their fearful, darting eyes searched him and the darkness behind him, as if they expected an army to descend on them.

"Are you alone?" asked one fellow who appeared to have lost all his teeth.

"Yes," replied Jodi.

"How did you find us?"

"I saw the fire."

"There's nobody hereabouts, where you from?"

Jodi pointed behind him. "Back there."

"You're a runner," said another, a rough-looking specimen with one ear missing and a large burn scar on his cheek. "Are you being followed?"

"No."

The men visibly relaxed and sat down. "Come in then, we have to look after our own."

Jodi gratefully took up a place by the fire. The smell of the pot overwhelmed his senses.

"You hungry, boy?"

"Yes, sir."

The toothless man laughed and took a battered, metal bowl and a spoon from his sack. He filled it with the bubbling stew from the pot and handed it to Jodi. He tried to eat it, but it was too hot and burned his lips.

"You have to wait a while, boy. Tell us where you're from."

Jodi held the bowl under his nose and let the fragrant steam feed his senses. "I don't know, I have been travelling for six days, I think."

"You come up from the south, I reckon. What's it look like down there?"

"The storm has ruined the crops, they're all flattened."

The men passed each other a significant look. "Reckon there'll no work for us down there," said One-ear.

Jodi began to eat the cooling stew. It was delicious.

"You like that, Kid?"

Jodi nodded, he did not want to waste a moment's eating time.

"Eat it slow, Kid, there's plenty more," said Toothless.

One restless eye secretly caught another as they watched Jodi finish the bowl; each knew exactly what the other was thinking. Jodi saw nothing beyond the contents of the bowl which Toothless refilled for him. As he was waiting for it to cool, Jodi began to question them.

"Is the city far?"

One-ear waved a hand to the north. "Zurat's about two, maybe three day's walk from here. That where you're headed?"

"I think so. Are there many like me there?"

"You mean runners? A few."

"Are you runners?"

"No, we're Freelancers. We go about the farms and do repairs that the Bhasi owners don't want to pay workers of their own race for. We're skilled and we work cheap, very cheap so it suits them to leave us be, as long as there aren't too many of us and we keep to ourselves."

"So they don't keep you on the estates?"

"No, Kid, as I said, we are Freelancers."

The man next to him issued a guttural grunt and nodded sagely.

"Pay no mind to Yuki, he's lost his tongue; had it cut out of his head some years back."

The man opened his mouth and showed Jodi where the organ used to be.

"He wagged it once too often," observed One-ear.

Jodi began to eat his second bowl of stew as he listened to the two men chat while the dumb one observed him with a disturbing, furtive grin on his face. The food filled his aching stomach and the heat of it made him glow inside. He had only two days to go and knew, for the first time, that he was going to make it to the city.

He finished the bowl and Toothless took it back and stuffed it into his sack. One-ear stood up and smiled down at him. "We have to be on our way now, Kid. So, now you gonna pay us for the food you just ate."

Jodi frowned, he had a sudden sense of foreboding. "I haven't got any money."

"That's too bad. Food doesn't come free, Kid; not in these parts."

The other two men suddenly stood and surrounded him; their friendly mood had changed in an instant. Too late Jodi realized that he was in serious trouble; there would be a price on his head, he would be killed and the money would be claimed. But what Jodi didn't know was that these Freelancers could not hand him in even if they wanted to; they would receive no payment or gratitude for presenting his severed head to the authorities. These men meant him an entirely different harm; a harm that resulted from the genetically engineered breeding programme that the Bhasi overlords had initiated in which very few females were born. They fell on him and dealt him a couple of blows to the head. He struggled and flailed furiously but they were all bigger and more powerful than he. He was turned over and his face was pushed down into the soil; he got the taste of it in his mouth as he struggled in vain. Knees pinned him down as his cord of his pants was cut and they were yanked off him. He felt the coldness of a knife blade against his neck and One-ear's voice was in his ear.

"Stop struggling or I'll slit your miserable throat."

He lay still for a moment, breathing heavily with the fear of a condemned man about to meet his end and then a weight descended on him and the pain started. He screamed through his gritted teeth as the violation began. He tried to struggle but he was so weak and they were all heavier and held him down easily. Soon he stopped struggling and shut his mind to the horror while all three took their turn. Tears of pain, anger and frustration fell from his eyes into the dust as the awful violation took its toll on his flesh and on his character, for after this he would never be the same again.

Finally it was over and the rancid stink of the last of them left his nostrils and his arms were released. He curled up into a ball and wept broken tears as the three Freelancers gathered their belongings and kicked out the fire.

They looked down at the pathetic figure and laughed. "You should have stayed where you were, boy," said Toothless. "This is no country for little boys."

There was a rustle of cane and then silence.

II

Dawn broke and Jodi did not move. A trickle of blood ran from his buttocks and into the soil beneath his groin. Tears of anger and frustration welled in his eyes and dampened the ground below his head. His whole body shook with the trauma of what had just happened to him. The sun rose and spread light and warmth on the land, but the warm glow of generosity in Jodi's soul had been extinguished that night and it would never be lit again.

The day was half gone when he picked up his sack and torn pants and walked unsteadily to the sea. He crossed the white, sandy beach and waded out into the cold water, trying to wash any trace of his assailants from his clothing and body. He stayed in the water until the cold drove him out. He found a place in the wind-blown sand-hills beyond the beach and took off his clothes. He laid them out on the fine sand to dry and spread himself to let the sun dry his skin. As he lay there in the sand-hills, an unquenchable rage burned within him as the memory of the violation pressed repeatedly into the front of his mind. Why hadn't he killed them all? Why had he let them do it to him? His powerlessness angered him beyond measure and he vowed to himself that, from that moment on, that he would rather die than be so defiled again.

The sun climbed in the clean blue of the sky and Jodi rubbed the sand from his body and dressed. The bleeding had stopped now but his internal injury was painful and sore. He walked slowly back into the high canes and turned north.

He walked for three more days and nights, moving slowly and cautiously, avoiding any place where other human beings might be found. He ate the immature cob-nuts and rotting tubers where he could find them and drank from the numerous streams and shallow rivers that meandered into the sea. There was no sign of the city that he knew must be close and, by the third night following the assault he had reached the limit of his endurance. A light rain presaged the coming of another storm and soaked him to the skin. By sheer force of will he dragged himself on, but he caught another chill and hunger, damp and cold and the hopelessness of his situation drained him to the core and he knew he was beaten. He would never get to the city. He stumbled out of the high crop and saw, through the rain, the dark outline of a small huddle of buildings. He staggered towards them, now uncaring of the consequences of being discovered.

Through the increasing rain he could see a low dwelling surrounded by some outbuildings. He approached the building furthest from the dwelling, a rude, structure of wood and iron and tried the door; it was locked and chained shut. A brief inspection of the perimeter brought success for he found a loose weatherboard that he was able to push to one side affording a narrow opening that he could squeeze through. The darkness inside was intense and it smelled musty, but there was no sign of human occupation. He felt his way inside and bumped into something hard and metallic. Feeling his way carefully, he rounded the object and came upon something soft lying on the ground. He knelt down. The musty smell was coming from the soft material, some type of sacking. He lay down on it and pulled it over him for warmth while the rain thwacked noisily on the roof above. Moments later he was asleep.

When he next opened his eyes he could see shafts of daylight streaming through the gaps between the timber cladding of the shed. The light fell upon the rudimentary tilling machine he had bumped into, an assortment of other tools and containers and piles of storage sacks. He tried to raise himself but he was too weak and feverish to stir. He pulled a few more sacks over himself and shut his eyes.

He remained under the sacks for the rest of the day and all through the next night.

When he next awoke the fever had subsided and he was able to raise his head a little. The morning sun was slanting through the gaps in the cladding and he could see the tilling machine standing in the middle of the shed. Sitting on the machine was a small boy, watching him with a curious expression on his face.

"What's your name?"

Jodi observed the child who was pretending to drive the machine.

The boy repeated his question. "What's your name?"

"Jodi," he replied in a hoarse whisper.

The boy dismounted and approached. "Mine's Parkel; I'm six."

Jodi hauled himself up and pitched his back against the shed wall. In the half-light he could see that the boy was pure Bhasi with black, tightly curled hair, a dark complexion and sharp features.

The lad peered at him. "You look funny, all dirty. Why are you sleeping in our shed?"

"It was raining."

"Don't you have your own house?"

"No, I was travelling."

"Where to?"

"The city."

"I've been there; I don't like it."

"Is it far?"

"Oh yes. It's a long, long way off. Long, long, long, long. Do you want to play a game, Jodi?"

"I'm not very well."

"When you get better then?"

"Yes, I'll play with you, but you mustn't tell anyone I'm here."

"Oh, I won't; I won't tell Mammy and Daddy's not here."

Jodi shut his eyes, he just needed to rest a bit longer then he could be on his way. "Good lad," he whispered.

When he woke the sun had crossed the sky and dark-amber slants of evening light stole through the gaps in the timber cladding. He looked down and saw that a large chunk of bread and a tumbler of water had been left by his side. He grabbed the bread and ate it so quickly he almost choked, then he drank the soft, clear water; it was the best he'd ever had. The fever had left his body now, but he was still weak. He decided to risk staying one more night before moving on.

When he awoke the next morning, the child was back, watching him curiously. Another plate of bread was by his side, this time with some fruit of a variety he had never seen before.

"Thank you for the food," he said as he bit into the soft pith. It tasted wonderful, sweet and fragrant.

"It's your breakfast; everyone has to have breakfast; it's the law, Mammy says."

"Not where I come from."

"Where is that?"

"A long way from here."

"Jodi, you smell funny."

Jodi forced a weak smile; he had to admit the boy was right.

"Mammy would make you have a bath."

"You haven't told her about me, have you?"

"Oh no, I would never do that. You're my friend. Can we play now?"

"Not just yet, but soon, I promise."

"But you said you would play with me; you must keep your promise."

"I will, don't worry."

They heard the sound of a woman's voice, calling for her son.

Jodi stiffened. "You'd better go, we don't want your Mammy coming in here and finding me, she won't let me play with you."

Parkel's face twisted with alarm at such news and he ran to the place where the loose board was. "I will bring you something at lunch time and then we will play."

"Yes," replied Jodi.

The boy disappeared through the gap and ran off, calling to his Mother. Jodi pulled himself to his feet and walked about the shed unsteadily. He found a rusty knife and slipped it into the string belt that held up his pants but nothing else of use. He was still weak but he had stayed here too long; it was time to move on. He returned to his makeshift bed of sacking and picked up his sack. Inside were the grubby, rotting tubers he had picked up from the field two nights ago. He looked at them and recalled with longing the delicious bread and fruit the boy had brought him. There would be more of that to come if he just stayed a little longer. He knew it was a risk, but the thought of that wonderful food over-rode his better instincts. He sat down and waited.

III

Rea Tuvah was a woman who had been passed by. She had been abandoned by the muses of beauty and good fortune; she had been excused the love of her parents and the friendship of siblings and contemporaries. Even love, which had visited her heart in the early years of her marriage to Forn Tuvah, had now moved on and all she had left now was her son, Parkel.

She had married Forn sixteen years before at the age of twenty-five. Forn was a man of modest means and even temper, twenty-eight years older than she. He brought her back to the smallholding by the sea that his dead parents had bequeathed him and soon furnished her with a child, a boy who they named Calah. But the smallholding was not fertile and Forn was obliged to seek employment in Zurat, a city thirty kilometres to the north, leaving his wife to till the land and coax a crop from the sandy soil. But when the child was two, while her husband was away, tragedy struck. While Rea was inside the house preparing for her husband's return, Calah climbed on to the tilling machine and fell, hitting his head on one of the sharp blades that turned the soil. Her husband returned and found her cradling the bloodied, dead child on the ground by the machine. He never forgave her.

The death of their son soured their marriage and Forn found an increasing need to stay away. But in Bhasi society, the dissolution of a marriage was extremely rare, and so Rea stayed on the farm, sinking deeper and deeper into depression and despondency. As the years passed her relationship with her husband settled into a routine tolerance that rarely expressed itself in any physical way, however, on one occasion, when Forn returned to his home after a particularly long absence, alcohol loosened their inhibitions and Rea conceived once again.

The birth of their second son brought a thaw in their frosty relationship and Forn found occasion to return to the farm more often. Rea's depression lifted and she devoted her entire existence to her son, teaching, nurturing and protecting him from danger, whether real or imagined. The tilling machine had always remained locked in the shed since the death of Calah; she could not stand the sight of it and never used it, but she did not know that the abandoned shed had become her son's secret hideaway.

Parkel finished his lunch quickly and waited until her back was turned before grabbing the rest of the bread and some fruit and running out into the yard to play. She turned and noticed that some of the food on the table had disappeared and peered out of the window. She caught sight of her son rounding the corner of the house at a run and an alarm went off in her brain. She followed quickly and saw, with horror, his leg disappearing through a narrow gap in the wall of the machine shed. With a beating heart, she rushed back into the house and found the key where it had hung, undisturbed, for thirteen years. She took it down and ran back to the machine shed and unlocked the bolt and chain. She opened the complaining door and froze at what she saw inside; her precious son with a filthy looking Native with a mouth full of bread.

She caught the hunted, desperate look in the Native boy's eyes as he stood and reached for her son, taking him by the hand. She saw the rusty knife in the string belt and the grim look on the boy's face. She clasped her hand over her mouth and stifled a scream. She knew she had to keep calm.

"Let him go," she uttered as calmly as her voice would allow. "Parkel, come here, darling."

Parkel held on the Jodi's hand. "He's my friend, Mammy, he's going to play with me."

"Just come here, Darling."

Jodi gazed into the frightened, pleading eyes of the woman and realized that, for once, he had the upper hand; he could dictate terms. He held on to the boy and placed his hand on the hilt of the knife. "I want food." he said.

"You can have all the food you need, just let him go," she replied as tears moistened her eyes.

"Get the food," replied Jodi, steadily. "Plenty of food; do it now." He half drew the knife in warning.

"Don't hurt him; please don't hurt him," she pleaded and ran to the house.

Jodi smiled down at Parkel. "This game is called 'scare the Mammy'. It's a good game, isn't it?"

Parkel frowned. "I don't think I like it much."

"It's a grown-up's game, but we won't play it any more if you don't like it."

"I know what we can play," replied the boy in a brighter vein.

"Tell me later," replied Jodi, hearing the hurried footsteps of the boy's mother.

Rea rushed back into the shed carrying a hastily packed bundle of food and placed it on the floor between them. Jodi picked it up, watching her all the time, but knowing that she was too frightened to try anything. He let go of the boy's hand. "Go to your Mammy, Parkel."

The boy looked up at him then slowly walked to his mother. Rea knelt, grabbed him and hugged him to her so hard that Parkel squealed.

"Now take your food and get out," she said.

Jodi picked up his sack. "I wouldn't have harmed him," he said as he walked towards the door. "I just want to get to the city. You don't have to tell anyone I was here."

She stood up; tears glistened on her cheeks and her eyes were still full of fear. "Just go," she uttered weakly.

As Jodi turned to leave, Parkel slipped his mother's grasp and ran to Jodi, shouting, "No!" He fastened his arms around the top of Jodi's right leg. "You promised to play with me. You promised."

Rea gasped and froze as Jodi lifted his hand, but all he did was tousle the child's hair and then he knelt and smiled at the boy.

"Parkel, your mother wants me to go and we must always do what Mammy says."

Parkel flung his arms around Jodi and hugged him. "No, I want you to stay, Jodi." He began to sob. "Why won't you stay? Make him stay, Mammy. Please, please, please, Mammy."

Jodi gently detached himself from the boy's embrace and stood up. "Thank you for the food," he said and smiled. For the first time she saw how fine his features were under the grime of travel and she realized that neither she nor her son had ever been in any danger. This was just a half-starved Native youth trying to get somewhere where he could be safe. She knew of the harsh conditions that Natives endured on the estates, especially those in the south and his gentleness with her son awakened her compassion. As he was about to disappear through the door, she found herself asking him to wait for a moment.

Jodi stopped and rested his dark eyes on her.

"Zurat is not a safe place for a Native boy."

"It is where I was told to go."

"You're a runner, aren't you?"

"Yes, Ma'am."

"Where have you come from?"

"The south."

"How long have you been on the run?"

"Don't know; maybe eight or nine days, Ma'am."

She considered. Nobody would be looking for him now; not after eight days; he was no one's property.

"You can stay here for a while, if you are willing to work for your food."

Parkel ran to his mother and hugged her. "Thank you Mammy," he cried.

Jodi looked undecided; he was by no means certain of his safety.

"Don't worry," she said. "You will be safe; no one ever comes here. You can stay in here if you like."

Jodi thought of the journey ahead and the uncertainty of his destination; he was still weak and he was tired of travelling. He made his decision. "Thank you Ma'am, I would like to stay."

She nodded. "That's settled then. Give me back that bundle of food and I will bring you something hot to eat."

He handed her the bundle he was holding and she took the child away and left him alone in the machine shed. He contemplated his situation; he was wary and not at all sure that he was doing the right thing. Was it a trap, or had his luck really turned and had he really found some sanctuary? He sat down on the sacks and waited. Presently she returned with a bowl of hot stew and some bread and placed it on the tilling machine.

"Thank you Ma'am," said Jodi.

She nodded and withdrew without speaking.

Jodi tasted the stew. It was like nothing he had ever come across. Thick and filling and so wonderful he thought he was imagining the experience. He put the bread in his satchel in case he had to get away quickly, but as he finished the delicious bowl, the mother came back with a bundle of clothes and a small phial of an oil-like substance.

"I have found you some of my husband's old clothes. He is bigger than you, but I think they would be better than the ones you have on. There is a pool behind the house where you can wash. I have brought you a cloth for drying and some lathering fluid."

Jodi did not know what to say, this unexpected kindness was not normal for one of her race. He had only the model of the brutal garrison soldiers in his hometown in the north, the trader who had brought him south and the owners of the Doah Estate to provide him with the character of the Bhasi and how they treated the Natives. Hitherto they had been uniformly hostile but now this woman seemed to recognize that he was also a human being in desperate need and it made him wonder if he had misjudged the people of the south.

He waited until she had gone and gathered up the bundle of clothing and the drying cloth and phial. He found the pond behind the house; a pleasant pool, fed by a stream, surrounded by ornamental bushes and a large, gnarled, old tree at one end. The afternoon sun dappled the clear water through the foliage of the tree with a brilliant light that shone into his face and made him smile.

He removed his clothes and sniffed them; they were quite disgusting. He cast them aside and waded into the cool water. He washed himself, noticing anew how thin he had got. He could see every rib of his torso sticking through smooth, stretched skin and his legs and arms had lost much of the developing muscle-tone of his emerging maturity.

He looked up and noticed the phial on the shore by the drying cloth. He waded over, picked it up and opened it. The container released a sweet fragrance that reminded him of the luxuriant blooms in the forests of his homeland. He tipped some on to his hand and lather the colour of a morning sky sprang to life in his palm. He had never seen its like. He tentatively rubbed some on to his arm; it felt smooth and delicate and immediately removed the ingrained soiling of his skin. He smiled at it and began to rub the liquid over himself, he rubbed it into his scalp, his face and everywhere that he could get it and the accumulated layers of grime fell away and left his skin tingling and soft like that of a new baby. He stepped out of the pool and dried himself on the soft cloth and pulled on the thick-lined pants that belonged to the woman's husband. They were loose on him and too long in the leg, so he tied them up at the waste and turned up the legs. Then he put on the thick shirt that was a nearer fit and picked up his old clothes and washed them as best he could in the pool. Then he walked back towards the house.

Inside the machine shed Rea and Parkel were waiting for him. She had brought an old mat for him to sleep on and a neatly folded pile of thick blankets that she had laid on the floor behind the tilling machine.

She smiled at the clean, fragrant boy in her husband's clothes and observed anew how handsome he was. "You can sleep here for another night. My husband will return this evening and we will speak about you."

This news disturbed Jodi and a frown creased his brow; Bhasi men were not renowned for tolerance or compassion.

"Don't worry, my husband is a good man; I am sure everything will be fine."

"I can't go back, Ma'am."

"Nobody is going to send you back. I will ask my husband if you can stay and help with the farm. Would you like that?"

"I would like that very much Ma'am. I'm a good worker, I'll work hard."

"Good, that's settled then."

Parkel ran over to Jodi and hugged his legs. "Can I play with Jodi now, Mammy?"

She smiled. "Go and get your games then."

The child ran off gleefully and for the rest of the day he taught Jodi how to play various games in the sunshine of the front yard while Rea watched them through the window as she cooked her husband's homecoming meal. She had rarely seen her son so happy and the Native boy was so gentle and patient with him. She also noticed that Jodi played a simple word game with her son without any apparent difficulty. This surprised her because, although her contact with Natives had been minimal, she had always understood them to be ignorant savages, incapable of learning. Jodi was the first Native she had ever spoken to and his one example disproved the prejudice.

When the light began to fail and the wide, red sun of Ennepp shot the sky with a myriad of colours that danced in the high atmosphere, she brought them out some food and her son and Jodi ate it sitting on the front porch of the house. She noticed that Jodi slipped some bread into the pocket of her husband's pants but said nothing. After the meal she gave him a lantern and said good night. Jodi thanked her and Parkel ran up to him and demanded a kiss. Jodi dutifully kissed her son on his head and walked around the house to the machine shed.

"I love Jodi," said her son as she coaxed him back into the house. "Do you love him Mammy?"

Rea smiled down at him. "He seems very nice," she conceded.

IV

The sound of a land vehicle interrupted his nightmare. One-ear was on him again and all the pain and degradation of the assault was replayed, stark and vivid as he struggled in vain beneath the foul-smelling flesh. He woke up and remembered where he was and listened to the sound of the land-cart approaching. Light briefly penetrated his sanctuary and then the sound of voices and the closing of a door and then silence. Jodi listened attentively and a little while later he heard the sound of a man's voice raised in anger.

Moments later the door of the machine shed swung open and an elderly man entered with a lantern. He looked grimly at Jodi as he sat up. His tightly curled hair was grey and he wore a moustache above full lips. His sharp, green eyes narrowed on Jodi. "Where're you from, boy?"

"From the south, Sir."

"Whose estate?"

"The Doah Estate, Sir."

"I thought so; a runner."

Now Jodi saw the sidearm in the man's hand.

"Stand up, boy."

Jodi obeyed with his eyes fixed steadily on the weapon.

"Come with me," said the man menacingly.

He backed out and Jodi followed, calculating the odds of getting away before he was killed, but the man was wary and kept his eyes constantly on him as he ushered him round to the front of the house. He stopped by his vehicle and reached in and took out a communicator.

"Central files."

"Central files," repeated a flat, mechanical voice.

"Bounties," said the man.

The machine echoed his command.

"I have a runner from the Doah Estate; what is the registered bounty?"

"There is no registered bounty from that estate."

"No bounty?"

"The Doah Estate was liquidated two days ago; there is no registered bounty or any record of missing personnel."

Forn Tuvah stared at Jodi. Rea came out with Parkel, they were both crying.

"I told you to stay inside," said Forn angrily.

Parkel pleaded between sobs. "Daddy, please let him stay."

"Be quiet, son," commanded his father.

Rea went to her husband and took his arm. "Please, Forn, let the boy stay, I need help with the farm; you know that."

"Rea, you don't know these people. They're ignorant savages; they can't be trusted. Besides we don't have a license to keep them and I certainly can't afford to buy one."

"No one ever comes here, not from one year to the next. Who would ever find out? It's lonely here when you're away and the farm needs another hand; we could produce so much more for ourselves, maybe even sell the surplus."

This last revelation caused Forn to consider. "It'll be another mouth to feed."

"I don't eat much, Sir," said Jodi.

"Be quiet, boy," snapped the old man.

"He'll soon earn his food," said Rea. "He knows farm work."

Parkel tugged at his father's leg. "Please let him stay; please, please."

Forn lowered the sidearm and glared at Jodi. There was something about the boy's open countenance that persuaded him, against his better judgement, to accede to his family's wishes. "Very well, we will give him a trial period."

Rea kissed her husband on the cheek. "Thank you Forn."

Parkel ran to Jodi and hugged him while his father looked on aghast. "Parkel," he shouted, "go back into the house."

The child let go of Jodi and ran off obediently.

"I don't want my son mixing with your kind," said Forn. "You stay away from him."

"Yes, Sir," replied Jodi quickly.

The old man nodded. "Work hard and don't give any trouble, boy. Now, go back to your bed; I will speak to you in the morning."

"Thank you, Sir," said Jodi and returned to his bed in the machine shed.

Rea kissed her husband and took his arm and they walked back into the house. "Thank you Husband."

"I just hope I won't regret this."

"You won't; he's not a savage. He could have killed us both; he had the chance. He's just a frightened boy on the run."

"Maybe so, but they are savages and ignorant too."

"The way we treat them is it not surprising that they are hostile to us? Wouldn't you want revenge if you were treated like we treat them? Jodi didn't think of harming us, I don't think it even occurred to him. I wonder if we would be so mild if the roles were reversed."

"We are a superior race; the roles could never be reversed. The Natives will always be ignorant."

"Jodi can read."

"What!"

"He can read, I witnessed it myself."

This silenced Forn; his suspicion that there was something different about the boy had just been confirmed.

V

The next morning, Jodi rose before the sunrise and washed himself in the pool behind the house. Then he stood where he could be seen at the front of the house and waited. Forn also rose early and saw the boy through the window, standing patiently in the front yard. He let him wait while he took his breakfast, then he strode out of the house.

"Come with me, Boy."

He led Jodi to one of the six small fields that surrounded the homestead. "This field needs tilling and planting. You will find the hand tiller and the tubers in the green shed. They are to be planted this deep and one pace wide, like so. Do you understand?"

"Yes, Sir. I have done this before."

"Good. My wife tells me you can read. Is that true?"

"Yes, Sir."

"Who taught you?"

"The old overseer on the estate, Sir."

Forn scowled disapprovingly. "And you can write too?"

"Yes, Sir."

"What else have you learned?"

"Numbers, Sir, and some philosophy."

Forn glared at him in surprise. "What is twenty-seven plus fifty-two?"

"Seventy-nine," replied Jodi immediately.

Forn shook his head; he had never come across anything quite like this. "Learning can be dangerous for your kind. You should try to be more discreet."

"Yes, Sir; I will."

"Come, I will show you the crop you are to plant."

He took Jodi to the green shed to the left of the house and opened it. Inside were piles of tubers of different varieties and a hand-drawn tilling instrument. Forn pointed to one of the piles. "These are the ones you are to plant. Do you know how to work this instrument?"

"Yes, Sir, it is like the ones we used on the estate."

Forn looked puzzled. "This type was used on a large estate?"

"For some fields, yes Sir."

Forn reflected on the fact that human beings were cheaper to run and maintain than machines; they required little fuel and were easily replaced when worn out. He had seen enough of this type of estate on his travels, especially in the more impoverished south. "Well, let's see you work, boy."

He watched Jodi pull the machine from its place in the shed and wheel it to the field. He primed it using the large handle on the side of the machine and set off, ploughing a deep furrow in a perfect line. When he had gone ten metres, he re-primed the machine and set off again. Forn had seen enough; the boy obviously knew what he was doing. He watched while Jodi turned the machine at the far end of the field and ploughed a perfect line a metre away from the first.

"That is acceptable work," he said as Jodi finished the second line. "You will find a cart in the store-shed. Load it with the crop and plant them as I directed. My wife will bring you food presently. You will receive two meals a day, one in the morning before work and one after work when the light has failed. There is a waterspout behind the house for drinking and washing; I expect you to keep yourself clean. Dig yourself a deep hole in the corner of this field which you will use as your lavatory; I don't want you messing all over the place like most of your kind. Out of sight of the house, mind; I don't want my family to be able to see anything of that sort."

"Yes, Sir."

Forn gave him a hard-eyed stare of disapproval. "I'm letting you stay here against my better judgement. You better not disappoint me, boy."

The old man stomped off to the house; he was due in Zurat to start another five-day tour of the western farms where he was to supply seeds and other agricultural essentials for his employer. He kissed his wife and son and gave her the firearm he was carrying. "Keep this handy and lock yourself in at night. Promise me."

Rea smiled. "I promise."

Forn nodded solemnly and walked to his land-cart. "And don't over-feed the boy; they can be greedy sods, believe me."

With that parting shot, he engaged the motor of the cart and swerved away down the long track that took him to the next estate and out of the farmlands towards Zurat.

Jodi watched him go as he pulled the first cart of tubers towards the field; he was not sorry to see the back of Forn Tuvah.

By the time he'd planted and covered half of the first row, Rea came out to the field with his breakfast. She gave him a bowl of hot porridge with vegetables and watched him eat it. When he handed her back the bowl, she gave him some bread wrapped in a cloth.

"For later," she said, "in case you get hungry."

"Thank you Ma'am."

He watched her walk back to the house as he resumed planting. Her attitude towards him slightly mystified him; she was over-solicitous and smiled constantly in his presence. She was quite unlike any other Bhasi he had seen.

He worked through the day, stopping only to dig a latrine in the corner of the field, out of sight of the house. In Faloon Pal, his home before he was taken, the population just went anywhere they fancied and had no care if anyone saw them, but the Bhasi were more particular and preferred to undertake bodily functions in private. When he had finished digging the hole, he squatted down and emptied his bowels. It still hurt him, but at least he had stopped bleeding when he went.

The sun climbed and shone on his efforts. He removed his shirt and put it on a bush by the side of the field. It felt so good to be out in the sun and safe, with food in his belly and a shelter at night. He would work hard for the Tuvah Smallholding, but, as he told himself, they didn't own him, he was not their chattel as he had been on the Doah Estate. He wondered what had happened to his sister, Matty and to his surrogate father, Minogi. The estate had been 'liquidated', a word he understood to mean 'ended'. He took solace in the wise words of Minogi, the old overseer, who told him that Matty was too valuable to be harmed. He hoped she would be safe until he could find her and take her away to a new life together; away from the Bhasi and back to the north; back to the deep forested valleys where the soldiers never went.

The sun was almost below the horizon when Rea called Jodi in. He had ploughed and planted almost a quarter of the field with neat, straight rows of sandy soil attesting to his skill with the tilling machine. The work had been hard, especially as he had not regained his former strength and he was weary as he returned the tools to the shed for the night. He trudged to his place and found a raised cot had been placed there instead of the floor mat and the sacks had been stacked away to one side. A book had been placed below the lantern. He picked it up and read the title page. 'The Word of the Prophet'. It was a book he knew well. He put it down and noticed that a fresh cloth and a number of lathering phials had been placed on the cot, together with some more clothes belonging to Forn Tuvah. He was beginning to suspect he had arrived in some sort of paradise. He picked up the cloth and a phial and made his way to the pool at the back of the house.

That evening he ate his food on the porch step as the last vestiges of the sunlight shrank from the sky.

Rea came out as he finished and sat in a chair, watching him. "How old are you, Jodi?" she asked.

"I don't exactly know, Ma'am," he replied as he mopped up the last of the stew with his bread.

"You have no idea?"

He considered. "More than twelve and less than twenty, I think."

"Didn't your parents ever tell you?"

He shook his head. "I never had a father and my mother went when I was small."

"How did you survive?"

He shrugged. "Just did; stealing and scrounging until I got taken by the garrison and brought to this country."

How sad, she thought, and another measure of compassion entered her heart.

"Thank you for the book and the clothes, Ma'am."

"You're welcome to them; my husband never wears them now. Have you seen that book before?"

"Yes, I have read it three times."

"Three times! I will get you another."

She went into the house and came out with another volume. Jodi took it and read the title. It said, 'Stories of Mystery'.

"My son loves that book. You must be tired and it's getting dark."

Jodi rose and handed the bowl back to her. "Thank you Ma'am; that was the best thing I've ever eaten. And thank you for the book."

"Do you have enough blankets? It gets quite cold at night."

"Oh, yes, Ma'am. I am used to the cold."

She watched him disappear behind the house and a feeling of sadness crept up on her. It was good to have someone else to talk to; someone other than her son. Even though he was of an inferior race, the boy was, nevertheless, company in that lonely place. That night she lay awake for a long time thinking about him.

For the next five days Jodi furrowed and planted the field until it was all finished. When Forn Tuvah arrived in the late afternoon of the fifth day, Jodi was engaged in repairing the timber walls of the machine shed with spare planks he had found behind the house. Without greeting his wife, Forn dismounted from his cart and walked over to the field to inspect the boy's work. He was shocked to see that the work had been finished and, it had to be said, secretly disappointed that he would have no reason to berate the boy. The furrowing was incredibly neat and straight and, despite himself, he was impressed.

He strode into the house and immediately noticed how neat and clean it was. "You have been busy," he said.

Rea kissed him. "I have had time," she observed with some emphasis.

Forn grunted and Parkel ran in and hugged his father. "I see the boy has finished the west field."

"He finished about mid-day; he's repairing the machine shed now."

"Good, keep him working."

"I didn't tell him, he just did it."

"I don't trust him."

Rea took her husband's hand. "Forn, he is a gift from the Prophet; why don't you just accept it?"

"A gift from the Prophet? We shall see."

Before he left the following morning on his next tour, Forn took Jodi into the east field where the crop was maturing.

"Do you know how to select this beet, boy?"

"Yes Sir, the ones where the tips of the leaves are turning yellow."

"That is correct. Raise them and sack them and put them in the dry shed, the one next to the green shed. Is that clear?"

"Yes, Sir."

Forn scowled and looked him up and down. "I see you are wearing clothes from my wardrobe."

"Yes, Sir, your wife was kind enough to allow it. Mine were damaged when…"

"When what?"

"When I was on the road, Sir."

"You may keep them, I wouldn't wear them after they had touched your skin." He dealt Jodi a disdainful glare and turned and strode off. Moments later Jodi saw the land cart disappearing down the long track. This time Forn wouldn't return for six days.

Over the next days, Jodi raised the crop and stored it in the dry shed in open weave sacks. He worked shirtless and the sun darkened the skin of his face and torso. Parkel badgered his mother to let Jodi play with him and she eventually relented, defying her husband's injunction and allowing them to socialize after their evening meal.

She watched them with the affection of a mother; at least that was how she deluded herself. In Jodi's company, Parkel was bright and inordinately happy; his studies improved for he caught from the older boy the habit of enquiry. It seemed to her that Jodi wanted to know everything. He asked her about the world and she showed him books on the geography of Ennepp. He asked her about other worlds; about what they were like and what type of people lived on them. She started taking her meals with them and often, after Parkel had gone to bed, she and Jodi would talk into the night on the front porch.

Forn's brief visits came and went and on each return he discovered a marked improvement in the smallholding. When Forn was there, Jodi kept his distance and, when not working on the farm, stayed in the machine shed and read books. But as soon as Forn's cart disappeared down the track, they resumed their easy intimacy. As time passed, Rea and Parkel took to coming out to the field at midday with a basket of food. Jodi would stop work and they would sit down under a tree and eat and talk.

Good, wholesome food, hard work and the passage of time had wrought a change in the waif-like creature that had arrived on the smallholding that rainy night thirty odd days before. Jodi had gained weight quickly and his face had filled out and, as they ate and chatted, Rea saw that he was physically nearer a man than a boy. She congratulated herself on the transformation; her son was a fine looking chap. *Her son?* She caught herself in the delusion. Her dead son would have been Jodi's age, fine and upstanding, just like this boy. She now realized that the Prophet had sent him to her to replace the boy she had lost and she praised His mercy. This revelation changed her view of Jodi, for it now disposed her to love him as she would her own offspring.

That evening her maternal affection took her to the pool behind the house at the time she knew he would be bathing. She carried with her some newly altered clothes of her husband's meaning to leave them for him so that he could wear them that evening. Her heart was light as she rounded the house and approached the pool, but then she saw that Jodi had already left the water and was drying himself at the water's edge. She stopped but he had heard her steps and he turned around to face her. He looked at her with impassive, dark eyes, making no attempt to cover himself as he dried his back with the cloth. She uttered an apology and withdrew in confusion for the sight of him had shattered her delusion. She had convinced herself that her feelings for Jodi were pure and maternal, but that evening, as she watched him while he ate, she saw the smoothness of his young skin and the defining muscle of his arms in a new light. Later, as they sat on the porch together, she asked him if he would like to sleep in the house.

He looked at her in surprise. "Yes, Ma'am, I would like that very much, but I can't. Your husband would find out and send me away."

This reply brought her up short. She wasn't thinking straight. Jodi was obviously right and, for the first time, she resented her husband and his unnatural prejudice towards this boy. "You are right, Jodi, but I wish it was not so."

That evening, as she lay in bed, she could not expunge the sight of the naked boy drying himself by the pool and the obsession that had gradually stolen into her soul could no longer be endured. She crept from her bed and went out into the cool night and walked round the house to the machine shed. Her heart was pounding as she paused outside the door where a small light from the lantern escaped on to the dusty ground. She knew that once she entered that place there would be no return to the woman she thought she was. She knew she would be degraded forever and that it was a one-way trip to nowhere good. But these certainties did not stop her. She opened the door and went in.

Jodi was lying in his cot reading. He sat up in surprise as she came in. "What is it Ma'am? Is anything wrong?"

She approached unsteadily. "Have you ever had a woman, Jodi?"

He looked confused and stood up to face her. "No, Ma'am."

"You are a man now, I can see that. You must have thoughts about such things."

Jodi swallowed hard. "Yes, Ma'am, sometimes."

She undid her gown and let it slip to the ground so the she stood before him naked. He had never seen a mature, naked woman before and he was wide-eyed at the sight of her full figure and large breasts. He was shocked and fascinated at the same time.

"Ma'am, I think this is wrong," he whispered.

"Don't be afraid, Jodi," she said stepping forward. "No one will find out." She took his calloused hands and placed them on her breasts, guiding them over the hard nipples as she shut her eyes. "That's right, touch them, they're all yours, my darling."

Jodi felt her soft, supple skin and smelled her perfume, heady and sweet like blossom in the rain. She opened her eyes and kissed him on the forehead, nose and ears then she pulled his shirt off and kissed his shoulder, armpit and belly, descending until she was kneeling before him. She undid his pants and they slipped to his ankles, while she teased him into a full state of passion with her tongue. He watched the top of her head as she took him into her mouth and saw the surreal, craziness of it even through his pleasure. He saw the supplication of her act and knew that, from this moment, this woman had become his slave and he could make her do anything he wanted. He pulled himself away and allowed his base instincts to take form. He pulled her up by her hair and twisted her around and pushed her up against the tilling machine while he tried to push himself into her from behind.

It was the way he thought it should be done, the way of all Native men, but he floundered and she was obliged to take him and guide him to the right place. She moaned at the penetration, it was more vigorous than her husband had ever managed and it spread into her belly like fire. And then it was over and only her shame was left.

She reached down and hurriedly gathered up her gown and placed it around herself. She did not want to look at him; to see her guilt and shame reflected on his face. But she could not prevent herself and as she glanced at him she saw him standing still, watching her, a look of quiet triumph on his face as the evidence of physical passion drained away. He was not shamed by what they had just done and there was no sheepish modesty in his attitude, indeed, it was brazen, as if to say, look at me, for now I own you.

She hurried from the shed and back into the house and wept at her weakness and the betrayal of her marriage. For days she had deluded herself that Jodi was a child just like her dead son, but this night had taught her the real truth; Jodi had deceived her, for he was a man in all respects, hard-edged, knowing and cruel.

When she had gone Jodi dressed and climbed back into his cot. Lying on his back with his hands behind his head, he stared at the dull, metallic ceiling of the shed and ruminated. What had just occurred had changed everything and now he would have to be very careful indeed if he were to stay on the Tuvah Farmstead.

The following morning he found his breakfast on the step of the front porch and Rea nowhere to be seen. He took it away and ate it by the pool, before going to work in the middle field. She didn't bring him his midday meal and in the evening he found his food left on the tilling machine in the shed. It saddened him that she should feel so much shame that she couldn't even face him; he understood that she had betrayed her husband, but Jodi was from a society that rarely considered such social niceties. In the north possession was a thing of moment that rarely lasted beyond the ecstatic rush of intercourse.

The following day Jodi saw nothing of her and that evening Forn came home for one of his visits. It concerned Jodi that she might tell her husband to get rid of him, but the next morning, after giving Jodi his chores, the old man took off down the long path just as he had always done. That evening he found his meal on the tilling machine once more, but this time he picked it up and took it around to the porch, put it on the step and waited. He knew she was watching him through the window, but he waited as the last of the sun faded across the sky and all light was lost. Eventually she came out holding a lantern so that her angst-torn face was illuminated in its soft glow.

"Don't you want your food tonight?" she whispered.

"I want to eat with you."

"I have already eaten."

A silence fell before Jodi spoke again. "I am not ashamed of what happened."

"You have nothing to be ashamed of; the fault was all mine. I took advantage of you, it was very wrong of me."

"I didn't mind."

"That is not the point. I am old enough to be your mother and you are just a boy."

"You know I am not a boy. Was I not enough for you? I have seen other men and they are much the same as me."

"That is hardly the point."

"Did I not do it properly? I know I have much to learn about the ways of sex."

"No, no, it was… perfectly done."

"I don't understand. Why don't you want to see me?"

She put down the lantern and sat down on the porch step. Tears formed in her eyes and glinted on her cheeks in the golden light. She put her head in her hands.

"You don't understand. I didn't want to see you because I can think of nothing but you. I love you, Jodi."

He sat down next to her so that his skin lightly touched hers. "I am glad," he said.

And now the dam in her conscience was fatally breached and she gave herself to him. No moment of the day passed without her thinking of him or watching him work in the sun-lit fields and when the evenings came and he had bathed and Parkel had been put to bed, she would go to him in the machine shed and teach him all the ways a man could make love to a woman. Her husband had now become an obstacle to her true passion and she began to resent him even more, not least because of his brusque and brutish attitude towards the boy.... the man she loved. But she was not so foolish as to betray any sign of her new, forbidden passion; they had not conducted any of their affair in the house and were never close to one another when Parkel was about and so Forn suspected nothing. Indeed, even if they had been less discreet he would have never suspected, for it would have been impossible for him to believe that his wife could be intimate with a filthy Native, especially one so young.

For his part, Jodi was not so love-struck for there was no room in his heart for anyone but his sister, Matty. For him their intimacy was a means of improving his lot, not just by the physical comfort he now enjoyed or even the sexual education he now received. Rea had books, plenty of them; books he had never read about things he could never have imagined and Jodi meant to read them all. Their moments of intimacy meant little to him beyond the immediate, physical pleasure. He liked the woman for her kindness and generosity in the face of normal prejudice, but that was all it ever would be for him.

And so it was that the routine of the farmstead drifted through the season. Jodi worked hard and all the fields were planted and the outbuildings repaired. In the evenings she would watch him play with Parkel like a child and then, later in the quiet of the shed where he slept, he would become a man for her. Forn punctuated their routine with increasingly frequent homecomings as his tours became more local. His attitude towards Jodi softened slightly as the farmstead improved in appearance and prosperity, only becoming angry when Jodi suggested using the tilling machine in the shed. But when Jodi had been on the farm just over sixty days, fate turned a page in his life and set it on a new and dangerous compass.

On the evening of the sixty-third day of Jodi's stay on the farm, Rea kissed her son and but him to bed. Forn was due home later that evening and so Jodi had gone back to the machine shed to read. She began to prepare her husband's food, resenting the labour for a man she didn't love and aching to be with the man she did. She looked out of the window and noticed a slight drizzle had moistened the ground and a cool wind had suddenly struck up from the south. Perhaps a storm was coming and her husband would be obliged to stay until it passed. She could not bear the thought of two days without the touch of her lover, so she hurriedly doused the fire and ran from the house, into the shed where Jodi lay in his cot, reading.

"Go back," he said, "your husband is coming soon."

"No, we have time," she insisted and she pulled him from his cot and kissed him on the lips.

"No," he said, but she was not to be denied and she pushed her hand down into his pants so that he could not refuse her.

"We can be quick," she uttered breathlessly as he responded to her touch. He pulled off her dress and urgently pushed himself inside her.

Inside the house the fire she had hurriedly doused was coaxed back to life by the wind and a spark leapt on to a pool of oil she had spilled on the wooden floor of the homestead. A fire was started. It caught slowly at first, but with gathering energy, it spread to the woven mat on the floor and soon into the furniture. By the time the smell of smoke drifted under the door of the machine shed, the house was well ablaze.

Jodi noticed it first and stopped their lovemaking.

"What's the matter?" she whispered.

"Smoke," he replied as he pulled away from her.

She screamed in alarm and they ran naked from the shed. Outside, the flickering glow of the fire was already lighting the yard. They rounded the corner of the house, ran to the porch and burst in; a wall of fire blew them back through the door, as the sudden rush of oxygen fed the flames. Jodi picked himself up and tore around the house to window of the room where Parkel slept. The flames were already licking the night through the melted window. He ran back. Rea was inside the house; he could see her flailing about amongst the burning timber. He rushed in and grabbed her and pulled her out, dousing her hair and skin on the ground before the house. Then he tried to get into the house again, but the heat and the smoke drove him back. He staggered out through the burning frame of the door, and collapsed on all fours, choking and coughing up black sputum.

It was this scene that greeted Forn Tuvah. He had seen the glow in the distant sky and rushed his vehicle to his home. He saw his wife, naked and prostrate on the ground and the Native boy, also naked choking nearby; but he did not see his son. He leapt down from the cart and ran to the burning house, staggering backward as the searing heat hit him. He grabbed Jodi and pulled him to his feet by his arms. "Where's Parkel? Where's my son?" he screamed into the boy's face.

Jodi pointed a soot-blackened finger towards the house and Forn let out a terrible roar and threw him to the ground. He ran to his wife who was moaning with the pains of her burned flesh, knelt and took her in his arms. "What have you done?" he bellowed above the rush of the fiery wind.

She looked up at him and through blistered lips uttered one word. "Jodi."

It was now that he noticed that she was naked too and the impossible horror of what had occurred at his home finally dawned on him. He dropped his wife and swung around, but the boy was gone. A white-hot rage descended on him and he raced around the burning house and burst into the machine shed. The filthy Native had fled and all he found was his wife's discarded dress. He picked it up and shook as he ripped the dress to pieces. His face was a mask of blind, unquenchable fury as he ran to his cart and drove it out into the field. Its lights blazed into the darkness while the building behind him spat glittering embers into the night sky.

"Boy, I'm going to kill you," he screamed, over and over again as he swung the cart about in ever more erratic circles. Beams of light swung wildly about as the ripening crop was flattened and destroyed under its wheels. But the boy had disappeared into the night and Forn eventually saw the hopelessness of the search and stopped the cart. He sat still, breathing heavily while his boiling rage found a new direction and a deadly resolve. He ran back to the burning house and found an old spade that Jodi had stowed neatly in the tool shed. He picked it up and went around to the front yard where his wife lay moaning on the ground. She looked up at him impassively as he raised the shovel over his head and brought it down on to her skull three times until he was certain she was dead. He threw the shovel down by her smashed head and walked into the flames of his burning home.

Jodi had heard the awful bellowing of the man in the distance while he ran as hard and fast as he could, across the north field and through a gap in the boundary hedge. He ran until his lungs nearly burst, until the fire was just a faint glow on the horizon. He stopped and coughed up some black soot and stood up and looked back at the wispy, red glow in the night. He had managed to gather up his clothes but everything else was left there; his satchel and water carrier, his old clothes; the books and gifts that Rea had given him to keep. Amid the embers of the burning house he had left the sad, lonely woman who had loved him; the young boy who had saved and befriended him; safety and the only homely comfort he had ever known. But he could not think about that now; now he had to go on; he had to survive to save his sister and to get her away from this hateful land. He dressed quickly, turned his back on the place and ran.

VI

Just as it had been when Jodi took flight from the Doah Estate, so it was as he ran from the Tuvah Farmstead, for a storm was coming. Black clouds massed in the dark sky above him as he ran before it. In the early morning, before the sun turned the high atmosphere pale pink, the storm caught up with him and he was forced to take refuge in a clump of low bushes while lightning fired bolts across the sky and thunder shook the ground. The cold rain penetrated his lair and chilled him to the marrow. The rain persisted until the middle of the next day and then gave way to the sun as the storm hauled its lumbering carcass away to the north.

He looked out from his hiding place and found himself in a pleasant, green landscape of low rolling hills. Ahead he could see a ridge of forest-capped upland that ran from east to west, terminating at the Great Sea where the soft rock had been eroded into cliffs. The isolated copses of wind-blown trees of the Southlands had now given way to substantial tracts of dense, upland forest interspersed with pleasant valleys populated by more productive farmsteads. He saw that his shelter lay on the edge of one such farmstead and he scanned the countryside about him for any signs of life. In the far distance he could see the outline of a low building from which a thin column of smoke curled lazily into the cool air.

There was no other sign of human activity so he cautiously crawled out of his lair and struck in the direction the uplands. He came across a brook and stopped to drink before moving on. Soon his path began to ascend towards the dark, forest-crested hill and the welcome cover afforded by the dense trees. He crossed one last field and reached the edge of the forest and plunged in.

Inside the forest, the high canopy of needle-like leaves smothered the light, dappling the mossy floor with shafts of sunshine. The air was sweet with the damp, heady smell of foliage and the dying wind sang through the high branches like a distant choir. He walked on stealthily, constantly listening for any unusual sounds that would betray the presence of others. As he crested the first rise, he caught sight of the glistening waters of the Great Sea in the far distance to his left and knew that his path was good and true. As he plunged into the valley he heard the ripple of water and came upon a brook running through a small but pleasant clearing. He listened carefully for any signs of life, then, drank from the brook. The afternoon sun was still warm and he was tired and still wet from the rainfall, so he stripped off his wet clothes and washed them in the brook. He laid them out on a rock in the sun to dry and then washed himself from head to foot and settled down next to the rock to rest for a moment.

When he awoke the sun had already set and the sky was darkening. He shivered at the descending air of the night and dressed himself in his damp clothes. He was hungry now, but that didn't matter, all that mattered now was to get to the city. He took his bearings and started into the gloom of the forest.

He walked through the night, finding his way through the temple-like columns of tree trunks and checking his direction by glimpses of the brightest stars through the canopy. The forest floor was almost sterile and little grew under the smothering roof of branches and greenery. There was nothing to eat in these uplands and so he knew he could not stay hidden in them for long for he would soon starve. He sensed the city could not be too far away as he had travelled for many days towards it and remembered it on the map Rea had shown him.

The next day he rested in a valley clearing where a sweet water stream had cut a gorge into the gentle folds of the land. It was better to sleep during the day when the sun could warm him and to travel by night when he was sure that no one was about and he could keep the cold out of his bones. He set off again that evening; hunger was now gnawing at his stomach but he ignored the feeling and walked until dawn where he found a large clearing of felled trees in a shallow valley with a pool fed by a streamlet. He slept but was awoken by the sound of cracking timber not far off. The buzz of a machine and men's voices echoed through the nearby forest and made him scramble in alarm to the nearest thicket. He listened and tried to discern from which direction the sound was coming. It was to the east and quite close. He stole away from it and back into the safety of the trees.

The sound of those voices was the only evidence of humanity that he came across during his journey through the forest. He was becoming increasingly tired and hungry as he trudged up yet another incline towards the crest of a ridge. It was the end of his fourth night in the forest and the dawning sun was beginning to touch the high clouds with an early glow. He reached the summit and sat down on a stone and looked through the trees towards the next, interminable summit.

But the next summit was not there. Instead of a dense, green barrier he could see light. He found an accommodating tree nearby and climbed until he could see through the thinning canopy. Stretched out before him was a great plain with a large river meandering into the distance. The river discharged into the Great Sea and, as the first segment of the sun crested the horizon, he saw the city.

VII

It would be generous to describe Zurat as a city. It was, in fact, a sprawling agglomeration of low, mud-brick buildings infesting the southern bank of the wide, marshy mouth of the river. It was a rude and makeshift place where farmers traded and loggers drank and few cared for the niceties of the law; a wild place, full of bars and dives of any variety where murder and assault were committed apparently without witnesses. It was a frequent of Moontraders and bootleggers and any who preferred their undertakings to be conducted beyond the scrutiny of the Bhasi authorities.

Jodi waited until dusk and made his way down through the last of the forest and out on to the open plain. It was night when he stole into the city. He moved cautiously, avoiding the sparse lights that spilled through ill-fitting doors and windows. Apart from the temperature, it reminded him of Faloon Pal, the squalid town in the north where he was born and had grown up until his abduction into slavery. There were the same smells of human waste and detritus; there were smells of boiling pots that made his raw stomach turn with desire. There were sounds of drunken voices and laughter coming from squalid, low hovels of wood and mud and the occasional raised voice of argument or protest and the sound of fists on flesh and howls of pain.

As he moved among the shadows deeper into the city, he saw people on the street, mostly drunk or the worse for narcotics. They were all Bhasi, but low Bhasi, disenfranchised and raucous. A group of men staggered towards him, singing. He dived into an alleyway, but one peeled off and came in after him. With a pounding heart he hid behind a pile of steaming rubbish and waited, but all he heard was the sound of urine splashing on the dusty ground and a loud fart. The man rejoined his companions and they lurched off to another drinking hole.

Somewhere in this forsaken place there would have to be others like himself, other Natives; freed men as Minogi, the old overseer on the Doah Estate had told him. He recalled the last time he had come across freed men and shuddered at the bitter memory of the assault. He would never let that happen again and he would kill anyone who tried.

He penetrated deep into the darkness of the narrow alleys that ran between the low hovels, stopping and listening all the time for any danger. He passed an open door where a dim light shone on a table on which sat the remains of a meal. He crouched down and peered in. He could see bread and bowls of half-eaten gruel and a variety of fruits, left in plain sight for anyone with the nerve to snatch them.

He listened carefully and heard no sound from within. Reckless with hunger, he darted in, grabbed the bread and stuffed it into his pockets. He turned to run, but found the door barred by a huge Bhasi with a shovel. Before he could dodge to one side, the flat of the blade crashed down on his upraised arm and knocked him flying. He hit his head on the corner of the table as he fell senseless to the floor.

The huge logger stared down at his unconscious quarry. It was not what he had expected. Goraf Bah had been anticipating a visit from his neighbour who, he was convinced, was stealing food from him. He had set his trap and meant to teach the thief a damn good lesson. But this wasn't his neighbour; it was a young Native. Goraf smiled, there was a reward for Natives caught abroad in Zurat after sunset. He reached down and grabbed the collar of the unconscious youth and pulled him out of the hovel like a sack of cob-nuts, down the dark alleyway while Jodi's trailing feet scored two shallow grooves in the dust behind him.

VIII

The Garrison at Zurat consisted of six men whose principal occupations were survival and extortion. This outpost of the law was, in fact, nothing more than a faint token of authority for Zurat was a wild place and even a garrison of six thousand would have struggled to tame it. The Garrison of Zurat was so enfeebled that its only official function was the issuing of licenses to the traders; no officers patrolled the streets, or intervened in the occasional riots that broke out among the drunken populace; no officers investigated the frequent murders that ravaged the dark, barren alleys behind the squalid houses; indeed, no officers braved the streets after dusk for they would certainly would not have survived long; instead they barricaded themselves into their quarters and passed the nights in apprehensive tranquillity.

During the daylight hours the garrison functioned as a sort of clearing house for Natives caught without their owners. A reward was paid according to the condition of the individual and they were accommodated in small cages until somebody came to buy them. This was not a particularly lucrative trade for most of the Natives were in poor condition by the time they arrived at the garrison, having either suffered traumas when being captured or having been weakened by starvation. But the garrison performed a function of keeping the streets of Zurat relatively free of 'this human pollution'.

That evening two guards lounged in the metal-clad sanctuary of the garrison house as Goraf Bah hammered urgently on the thick, metal door. The officer of the watch, a stocky, ill-kempt individual removed his booted feet from his desk and sauntered over to the door and drew the small, hatch-cover aside.

"What?" he enquired with an air of anger at having his boredom disturbed.

Goraf's brutish face appeared at the window. "Got a Native brat for you."

"Come back in the morning; you know the rules."

"I won't be here in the morning; I got an early start."

"Too bad," replied the officer.

"Come on guys; do me a favour, just this once. I'm totally skint."

"Tough."

"Who is it?" called his colleague, emerging from one of the cells where he had been asleep.

"Just some logger with a brat," replied the officer.

"Let's have a look," said the guard. "We don't have any stock at the moment."

He approached the hatch and Goraf lifted Jodi's inert body up for a viewing.

"It looks dead," said the guard.

"'Course it's not dead, I hardly touched it." He slapped Jodi's face and coaxed a slight response. "See."

The guard closed the hatch flap and turned to his disinterested superior. "Curah was in today, he's looking. This one will do him."

"That fucking old miser; what the hell does he do with them?" replied the officer. "Seems like he's always buying."

"So what; it's nothing to do with us what he does with them. It'll be dead by morning if we don't take it now."

The officer of the watch thought about it for a moment then pulled his sidearm. "Alright, tell that logger to step well away from the door."

The guard opened the flap and ordered Goraf to get back. The logger grinned, dropped the boy and stepped back into the street. The guard unlocked the numerous security bolts and opened the door. He quickly grabbed the boy's inert body and pulled him in while the officer re-secured the door as quickly as possible. The guard dragged Jodi across the room and into a holding cage while his officer handed Goraf's reward through the hatch. The brutish logger scowled and stomped off into the night to get thoroughly drunk.

"Looks like a young, healthy one," commented the guard as he rejoined his superior. "Reckon we might get a bit extra."

"From that old miser? You must be pissed."

IX

If parsimony had been a subject for academic study, Culas Culah would have been considered its greatest student. Over his sixty-six years he had practiced and honed his subject to such a degree that no one on the benighted world of Ennepp could claim to be a greater proficient. Culas Culah calculated the cost of his daily activities and weighed each against the potential benefit. He applied this principle to every aspect of his existence, so that he would not heat the grubby room in which he lived, nor would he cause a light to be struck unless it served to illuminate the gold he kept hidden in a safe buried in the stone floor of his home. When he was forty-seven, he worked out that his wife and child no longer represented good value, so he threw them out on to the street to fend for themselves and rejoiced in the saving he accrued as a result.

Culah was a market trader whose principal commodity was cob-nuts which he bought cheap and kept locked in a store behind his house. He bought crops at the end of season when their musty odour betrayed the final stage of their nutritious value. He took the cob-nuts to the central market every day; or rather his Native slave took them, pulled along on a chain which was attached to a choker around the neck of the unfortunate employee. When not employed in this commercial endeavour, the slave was kept chained to a metal post in leaky lean-to next to the storeroom behind the shack. Culas Culah despised his fellow men, but he reserved a special hatred for Natives, regarding them as lazy, filthy degenerates without morals of any kind. Like many of his race he had come to the conclusion that they were not human beings at all, but some sub-race, to be worked and discarded when of no further use.

It was this gentleman that walked into the garrison a few hours after Jodi had arrived. The officer of the watch swung his feet off the table where they habitually resided and ambled over to the heavy, metal door.

The old miser muttered through his grizzled beard. "Any pick-ups today?"

The officer perused the despicable creature, his bald head crowned with a grubby skull-cap, his grey, shifty eyes, hard and alert to any chance of profit and pointed over his shoulder to the cages. "Got one in. A young one, strong and healthy."

"I'll look," announced Culah, "but I ain't paying a premium, if that's what you're thinking."

The officer unbolted the door and the old miser shuffled in and followed him to the back room where the cages were kept. Only one cage was currently occupied; it contained a resentful looking specimen with an ugly bruise on the side of its head. It was sitting with its chin on its knees, brooding within the confines of the cage.

"It's the only one in at the moment but it's strong and healthy."

"Its head's damaged."

"It's nothing, just a bruise. You can soon fix that," he added by way of a straight-faced joke, knowing all too well his customer's unsympathetic disposition.

The old miser passed him a withering look. "Make it remove its shirt; I don't want any like the last one."

"Take off your shirt," commanded the officer.

Jodi didn't move; he could not understand why the garrison soldiers hadn't killed him.

The officer brought out his sidearm. "You heard me, brat."

"Go ahead, kill me; I don't care."

The officer laughed. "I'm not going to kill you; I'm going to hurt you; hurt you so bad you'd wish I had killed you."

"He's a feisty one," said Culas. "He wants taming."

"And you're just the man for the job. I should put up the price."

The miser recoiled visibly. "You'll get nothing more than the standard fee."

The officer laughed again; he enjoyed goading the old fool. "Do you want it or not?"

Culas made a study of considering but, in fact, he was desperate to purchase the Native. It was young, strong and healthy which would make the observation of its long demise all the more interesting. "Alright, it seems healthy enough; the standard fee, mind."

"Agreed," replied the officer laconically. "The collar and chain will be extra, of course."

"I have my own, as well you know."

The officer shook his head in mock sadness. "That won't do; we have to issue a new one, for safety reasons."

"That's a lie; you're just trying to cheat me as usual; you soldiers are all the same; nothing but lazy, greedy, money-grabbers."

The officer arched a brow. "Please yourself, there's plenty of others who will want it."

"Damn you," hissed Culas vehemently. They both knew he needed a slave to do his carrying and he had no choice but to accept the onerous over-charge. He pulled some coins from his belt and counted them into the officer's palm with shaking hands. The man smiled and his colleague brought in the collar and choker-chain while he opened the cage and waved his sidearm at Jodi. "Get out of the cage, brat. You are now the property of this man."

Jodi crawled out of the cramped cage and the guard placed a metallic collar around his neck and locked it. Then, he passed the choker-chain over Jodi's head and handed the other end of the chain to the old miser.

"It's all yours," said the officer with a toothy smile.

Culas tugged on the chain and the choker tightened around Jodi's throat. He walked out behind the old man, glad to get away from the soldiers and their sidearms. He was already calculating how easy it would be to overpower this old fellow who now thought he owned him. He would not stay caught for long.

He followed the old man out into the grey of the early dawn and heard the door of the garrison lock shut behind him. Now would be his chance. He darted for the fellow and a sickening pulse of energy seemed to fry his brain and made his eyes bulge from their sockets as though they would fly out. He slumped to the ground and shook. The soldiers, watching through the barred windows of the garrison house, burst into laughter as the old man turned and stared in disbelief at his latest acquisition shaking in the dust.

"You should have set it to kill," said the officer through his laughter. "Would have served the miserable, old fucker right and it would have done that Native a favour. I thought that little brat had never worn a collar before, it'll know better next time."

The old man stood outside the garrison house scowling at the laughing soldiers. When Jodi stopped shaking he kicked him hard in the ribs and repeatedly yanked on the chain until Jodi staggered to his feet. Culas delivered one last filthy look towards the garrison windows and pulled his latest victim away to his new home.

It did not take long for Jodi to realize that his situation had taken a decided turn for the worse. He suspected that the man who now owned him and controlled him with this infernal contraption locked around his neck, was neither pleasant nor charitable. As the sad, grey fingers of dawn light slid between the narrow alleys of Zurat, he was brought before a sorry looking hovel at the end of a narrow passage and led through a gate and around the back of the building.

"You are to be my carrier," announced Culas. "You will obey my commands and work. If you do not work I will inflict pain on you, a lot more pain than you will be able to stand. If you try and run away, the collar will fry your brain until you are dead. Is that clear?"

"Yes, Sir," replied Jodi, quietly disguising the seething anger he felt inside.

Culas opened the store and filled two strapped panniers with cob-nuts then he directed Jodi to pick them up by slinging the straps over his shoulders. Jodi knelt and lifted them, they were heavy and the hard, bulging husks of the fruits dug into his hips and thighs; but he was able to walk as the old man picked up a rough, woven mat, closed and locked the storehouse doors and pulled him out into the alley.

They twisted and turned along sad, rubbish-strewn alleys where the smell of cooking pots scented the morning air. They were late for the market and Culas hurried as well as his ageing legs would allow. Finally they came into a large square where numerous traders had set up stalls and early buyers were weaving among them, calling out and bargaining in raucous voices. Culas rolled out the mat on the ground and made Jodi empty the panniers on to the mat and the long day's trading started.

Culas was the only trader in the square who refused to buy a full license from the officers at the garrison. This meant that he was not entitled to trade from a cart, but had to carry his stock by hand. He had done his sums and worked out that it was cheaper to use a Native carrier, even if that carrier had to be replaced three or four times a year. The other traders despised and laughed at him, but he cared nothing for their opinions, after all, it was he, not they who kept gold under their floors.

Jodi sat cross-legged and silent as the old miser argued with his customers, and insulted them behind their backs whether they had bought his musty stock or not. He was constantly out of humour and fixed every one with a beady, accusative stare in case they thought of offering a price too low. Jodi's stomach rumbled at the sight and smell of all the food on display and the cooking pots bubbling full of rich, spicy stew. He had managed to eat some of the stolen bread in his pocket while in the pen at the garrison house, but it was too little to sate his hunger. He wondered when the old man was going to feed him, but the man himself had taken no nourishment during the day's trading and Jodi sensed that it would not be wise to test the subject.

By the time the day's trading had ended he felt weak and his head throbbed from the blow he had received from the logger. Culas had sold nearly all of his stock and seemed resentfully pleased with the day. He made Jodi load the panniers with the unsold stock and led him back to the hovel at the end of the alley. It was now that Jodi was introduced to his future for, when the panniers had been unloaded and the storehouse secured, Culas unbolted the shoddy door that guarded the entrance to the wooden lean-to next to the storehouse. The stink of human decay nearly made Jodi retch as the door was opened. In the dark interior he could just make out a human form lying on a pallet. The man was attached by means of a chain around his neck to a sturdy, metal post, set in stone in the middle of the lean-to. That post was the only substantial thing about the place, which everywhere else was rotting and decayed. His owner did not seem to notice the smell as he entered and unlocked the chain from the post and gave it a yank. The man's head jerked awkwardly, but his eyes remained shut and he did not otherwise move. Culas cursed him and kicked him hard in the ribs, but still the man did not move.

Culas turned angrily. "Pull it out," he ordered and stepped aside to let Jodi through.

Jodi came forward into the shack and took the man under his arms and pulled him out into the yard. The man groaned as he was moved, but said nothing. It was hard to tell his age for he was nothing more that bone and skin, with sunken eyes in a head that more resembled a long dead skull than anything living. His ragged clothes, torn and filthy, hanging from the pallid flesh, dragged in the dust as Jodi pulled him to a clear area in the darkening yard.

"Stop," said Culas. "This filthy, lazy bag of bones has cost me plenty. I have not traded for two days because of it." He leaned down and unlocked the collar and removed both it and the chain.

"This is what will happen to you if you don't obey me and work hard," he said as he fetched a nearby container of liquid. He doused the body of his last employee and set it alight. The man suddenly came to life, squirming and screaming as the flames burned the flesh from his bones until, with a last whimper, he was still. Culas watched the agony with an intense look of pleasure that he did not trouble to conceal. His old, grey eyes became animated as he watched the flames reduce the man and the sickening reek of sizzling flesh filled the air.

Jodi covered his mouth and nose with his sleeve as the fire consume the body. Culas watched him disdainfully; over the years he had become well used to the smell of burning Native and it didn't bother him in the least.

When the body was almost entirely consumed Culas ushered his new charge into his accommodation and attached the chain to the post in the middle of the lean-to. Then, without any further word, he left and bolted the door. Jodi sat down on the wooden pallet and looked about him. The foul odour of the last occupant began to ease as fresher air blew through the many gaps in the shell of the crude structure. He looked about him despondently and saw a hole dug in the corner that served as a latrine and a container of water that filled with rainfall by means of a hole in the roof above it. There was nothing else in the shed, nothing he could use to escape; nothing he could use to attack and kill the old man from a distance. He was trapped, caged; with only the fate of his predecessor to look forward to. He considered whether it would be better to get it over with quickly, attack the old man and in so doing, kill himself, but that would be giving up on life and any prospect of seeing his sister again and this he could not do. He would survive somehow; he *must* survive somehow and get back to her, wherever she may be. He gritted his teeth against the gnawing emptiness in his stomach and lay down to sleep.

The sound of the bolts of the lean-to door being drawn aside woke him and the old man shuffled in and unlocked the chain from the post. He passed Jodi an ill-humoured glance and jerked on the chain. Jodi followed him out into the yard where the first hints of a fine day cast early morning shadows on the dusty ground. A charred pile of bones described the shape of a man on the ground; the accelerant had consumed everything else. Rags, flesh and organs and all that remained of the man was a blackened pile in the dust.

Culas kicked the remains to the edge of the yard where they rested against the charred bones of others who had gone before; he then directed Jodi to load the panniers, pointing out the individual nuts he wanted to dispose of. And so, the long day started, just as many would in the future, with a heavy-laden walk to the market, a day's trading when Jodi would sit behind the old man, still and cross-legged on the ground and watch the activity of the market, its bustling, rude people, shouting and squabbling over trifles; its noon-day heat and the welcome shadow of the afternoon; and then the late evening return, after all the other traders had left, when the old man would throw some stale bread into the lean-to if he was pleased enough with the day.

As the days passed Jodi's dream of escape faded and died. He knew that this would be his last place; the final chapter in his short life and he no longer had the strength or the ambition to change that prospect. Once again, his body began to waste and his clothes and skin took on the smell of decay. He lost track of time, for every day was the same as the last; sometimes he would be fed and sometimes not, according to the old man's disposition. He spoke to no one and no one spoke to him other than the old man to order or berate him. And so the days of his life melted away, just as the life force within him melted, withering his indomitable spirit until it disappeared without trace.

Only on one occasion was the monotony of his existence broken. The stock of cob-nuts had become depleted and the old man was obliged to receive a delivery from a smallholder who farmed a spread on the outskirts of Zurat. The delivery arrived very early one morning, well before sunrise, on a cart pulled by a young Native man. Culas woke Jodi up and ordered him to help the Native unload the stock while he took the farmer inside his house to haggle over the price. Jodi rose stiffly and went into the yard to help with the unloading and storing of the new stock. When the young Native beheld him he was so shocked he stopped working and stared at Jodi.

'You look like shit and you stink like it too," he declared.

Jodi ignored him and started to mechanically unload and store the crop.

They worked together in silence until the young man spoke again. "My boss hates that old man; calls him the Fucking Miser. He reckons he's got plenty 'cause he never spends any; keeps it hidden in a box somewhere in there."

"Ask your boss to buy me off him. I'll work hard; I won't be any trouble."

"He won't do that. Look at the state of you; you're fucked. You'll soon be over there with them," he added, pointing to the charred pile of bones by the yard wall. "I won't be seeing you again."

With this salutary truth ringing in his ears, Jodi continued unloading the cart until Culas appeared with the farmer. The farmer regarded Jodi with undisguised distaste. "Why don't you feed them properly, you old miser?"

"Mind your own business; it's mine, I'll do what I like with it."

"It must cost you, having to replace them all the time."

"That's my affair, food isn't cheap; you farmers make sure of that."

"I think you like watching them die, that's what I think."

The farmer saw by the twisted expression on the old miser's face that he had hit on a truth. They observed the last of the unloading in silence and then the farmer and his boy were gone into the darkness. Jodi saw the expression too and now it made sense to him; Culas was watching him die and the process was giving him pleasure. He exchanged the briefest of glances with the old man and Culas saw that Jodi had seen right into the black void of his soul. His face twisted in anger and he would have killed him there and then if it had not been a cost to him.

"Get loading, we'll go early today," he spat the words angrily and shuffled inside to re-count his money.

A few days later, another small event punctured the monotony of Jodi's slow death. As they were crossing one of the squares between the market and the miser's home, Jodi noticed the unusual presence of a fine craft at its centre. The craft was lit inside and he could see through one of its windows the figure of a young girl, clearly distressed, banging on the window as if trying to get out. Even through the rain there was a vague familiarity about the girl, but he could not place her. *She has her problems and I have mine,* he thought, and ambled out of the square behind his master.

That evening, as he lay on his pallet, he was reminded of Matty and tears came into his eyes and rolled into his dusty hair. He was near the end and he knew it. Every day the panniers got harder and harder to lift and his bones became ever more prominent; he was becoming the man he had pulled from the pallet and out into the yard to be burned alive. He wondered at the brief agony of dying in that way; what would it feel like? It was coming soon; about that there was no doubt.

Jodi lasted fifteen more days and then his time was up. He lay on his pallet barely conscious one morning when Culas entered the lean-to. The old man kicked him hard several times, breaking two of his ribs, but Jodi did not respond. Culas spat on him in anger and stalked out towards the garrison to see if they had picked up any Native strays. Jodi drifted in and out of consciousness as he lay unmoving on the filthy pallet. His time was near and soon he would burn and become just another addition to the charred collection of bones in the corner of the yard. He awaited the final release of death when all this pain would be over and his last living thought would be of his beloved sister, Matty.

X

The Commissioner of Trade for Lamon Utile sat at his breakfast table and moodily observed his newly promoted deputy. He was leaving Ennepp later that day and had many instructions to deliver. The meeting had lasted for over an hour, during which the corpulent baggage ate while he spoke, careless of propriety, or the odd morsel of half-chewed food that occasionally landed on his employee.

"While I am gone you may stand down half the guard and get rid of those expensive auxiliaries that your predecessor employed. And get rid of the harem, there will be no use for them when I return."

Laon Cour Son raised an eyebrow in surprise. "Are you sure, Sir?"

"Do it," replied his boss emphatically, spraying out more of the half-eaten contents of his mouth in his deputy's direction.

"As you wish, Sir. How long will you be away?"

The Commissioner scowled. "I don't know. I will have the operation done immediately after I arrive on Barta Magnus. It's not every day a man has to have his genitals cut off and I don't trust my palace physician or any of these Ennepp quacks."

"Very wise, Sir."

The Commissioner nodded thoughtfully. "You may go now, Secretary."

Laon bowed slightly. "I have a request, Sir."

"What is it?"

"I would like to appoint a new head of the palace guard."

The Commissioner narrowed suspicious eyes on his employee. "Why?"

"The present head is my predecessor's man; an appointee of Perglin. I am not certain of his loyalty."

The huge man sat back from the ornate table and drew his copious jowls into the hint of a smile. "You make a good point, Secretary; do you have anyone in mind?"

"Yes, Sir, Murgan Doh."

"Doh? The man Perglin fired for brawling in the palace?"

"Yes, Sir. He is intelligent and efficient and I believe I can control him."

"Is he one of your sexual partners, Secretary?"

"No, Sir and he would not thank you for suggesting it."

"I don't care what any member of my staff thinks, as well you know. Very well, Murgan Doh it is, but mark me, Secretary, if there's any problem it'll come down on your head."

Laon bowed and withdrew. He had a mission for Murgan Doh that he would have to complete before his new appointment and he knew just where to find the man.

Murgan Doh had only two great interests in life; women and fighting. He was a huge, barrel-chested man with arms the size of most people's legs and a scarred and grizzled face that would have better suited a man of fifty instead of one of thirty-two. He was a Bhasi but had been relieved of his race's myopic prejudices by an off-world education. He had joined the palace guard just a year ago and had shown himself to be a capable leader, respected by his fellows for his strength and keen wit. He had risen quickly to the position of squad leader, when, shortly after his appointment, he found himself in dispute with six of his fellow leaders and sought to carry his point by means of his fists. Three of them ended up in the infirmary and Murgan ended up on the track outside the palace walls with his kitbag. Laon had always liked Murgan Doh, respecting his strength and fighting skills, two traits he, himself decidedly lacked.

On leaving the Commissioner's breakfast interview, he repaired to his apartment and headed for the ablution unit. He disrobed and discarded the bespattered clothing then cleaned himself lest any of the Commissioner's breakfast remained on his person. He dressed in fresh clothing and took his personal vehicle to the city. A few well-placed enquiries soon brought him to a shambolic room above a cheap brothel. Lying spread-eagled on a pallet amongst a pile of filthy linen was his quarry. Murgan was snoring so loudly that it made the dingy shutters on the window rattle. Laon cast about the room and found an ewer of water. He picked it up and poured some of its contents over the man's face.

Murgan spluttered and opened his eyes drowsily, trying to focus on the source of the annoyance. "Cour Son, what the fuck are you doing here?"

Laon replaced the ewer. "I've come to offer you your job back."

Murgan stretched luxuriously then reached under the sheet to scratch his testicles. "Not interested."

"Really? You like living here do you?"

"Plenty of women on tap; what's not to like? Anyway, that old fart, Perglin, would never have me back."

"Perglin's gone; I'm Head of Household now."

Murgan stopped scratching and sat up. "Perglin's gone? How'd you manage that? I thought you were busted after that business with that little Native girl."

"Perglin made a mistake and the Commissioner re-instated me. I'm now his deputy."

"Well done, Cour Son; that fat plonker finally seen some sense?"

"That fat plonker's got Croman's Syndrome. He's off to Barta for the chop today."

Murgan suddenly burst out laughing. "Well, hail to the Prophet, never was a disease better deserved or a knife more justly wielded."

"Well, what do you say? You must be running short by now; even a dump like this costs money."

The huge man grunted. "You're right there, Cour Son, Things are getting a bit tight." He swung his massive legs off the bed. "What did you have in mind?"

"Head of the Palace Guard."

Murgan's bloodshot eyes bulged in disbelief. "What have I got to do? Give you a blow-job?"

Laon smiled. "That won't be necessary, especially when I think of where your mouth has been. But I do want you to do a job of another sort for me."

Murgan stood suddenly and began to search among his hastily discarded clothing for his underwear. "And what would that be?"

Laon quickly turned away; Murgan was still sporting a morning erection. "I want you to go to Zurat and find someone for me."

"Zurat? That shit-hole. What would you want with anyone from down there?"

The huge man found his underwear and covered himself, much to Laon's relief; the sight of Murgan Doh's engorgement made him feel quite awkward.

"I made a promise to somebody, to Matty, the Native girl I was trying to protect. I failed her and now she is dead, blown to pieces on Tarnus. She has a half-brother, a half-breed in fact, called Jodi. He's a runaway and she was convinced she saw him in Zurat when Perglin sold her to the Moontrader. I want you to find him."

Murgan regarded him sceptically. "A half-breed and a runaway. He's bound to be dead. She must have been mistaken."

"Probably, but I intend to keep my promise."

Murgan shrugged. "Alright, you're the boss."

Laon handed him an image of Matty. "Jodi would be about sixteen years old, or maybe fifteen. That image of his sister should give you some idea of what he might look like; she always said they looked alike. Also, Jodi has a birth mark; a diamond shaped discolouration on his left thigh."

Murgan studied the image. "She was a lovely looking girl. A real sweetie."

"Yes, she was. Start with the garrison down there; they may have had dealings with the boy. Don't mention that he's half Bhasi; if he's still alive they'll kill him for sure if they find out. If you locate him let me know, I'll come and get him myself."

Murgan smiled. "Don't worry, Boss, if he's down there I'll find him."

XI

It would be inaccurate to say that cheating his new boss by spending all his time in bars and whorehouses instead of looking for the unlikely sight of a half-breed runaway did not cross the mind of Murgan Doh. But he was basically an honourable fellow and so he decided to make the effort. The nervous officers at the garrison were unhelpful and gave him peculiar looks as if he was mad to be making enquiries about a Native boy. He spent three days combing the area around the square where Matty had said she had seen her brother, but nobody would give him any information. He was near to giving up, having at least discharged what he regarded as his duty, when, towards the evening, he wandered into the market square and saw a ragged and starving Native boy, sitting on the ground behind an old trader. The boy was secured to a post by a chain around his neck, not an unusual sight in Zurat, but there was something in the face of this boy that caught him. He pulled out the image of Matty and compared them. It was a distinct possibility. He went over to the old man and bought two cob-nuts while taking a closer look. The old man forced a toothless smile to his face; the big man hadn't even haggled about the price.

"That boy of yours looks half dead," he said as he handed over the coin.

The old man's smile sunk without a trace and he visibly bristled. "What's it to you?"

Murgan shrugged. "Nothing; just doesn't seem right that a sight like that is on display. It might put your customers off. What's his name?"

The old trader regarded him with narrowed, suspicious eyes. "You're not from round here, are you? Who the fuck cares what it's name is?"

"No, I'm not from round here."

"Well, if you were you'd know what filthy, lazy, scum they are. Not one of them is good for anything. It'll get what's coming to it soon enough."

Murgan nodded gravely and moved off. He stayed in the market square until all the traders had packed up and left except the old man. He watched the old trader yank the boy to his feet, and pull him out of the square behind him. The boy could barely walk, shuffling along with an ungainly limp behind the old man. He followed the couple discreetly, through darkening squares and down filthy alleys until he came to the hovel at the end of an alley and saw the old man and the boy disappear into its yard. Then, he contacted Laon.

"I think I have found your boy, Boss."

"Are you sure? Have you checked for the birthmark?"

"Boss, I'm not about to strip him and check that. He's about the right age and looks like the girl as far as I can tell. The kid's in a bad way; starved and beaten. He belongs to a miserable old market trader. What do you want me to do?"

"Nothing just yet. I have some important commodity trades to finalise here, but I should be able to get away early tomorrow. I'll meet you then."

The stars were still casting their ghostly shadows when Laon and Murgan Doh arrived at the hovel of the old trader. Murgan banged loudly on the wooden door with his huge fist but no one emerged and no lamp was lit.

"Try the yard," suggested Laon.

Murgan tested the high gate of the yard to the side of the house, but it was firmly locked.

"Do you want to get in there?" he asked.

Laon considered. "Yes," he replied.

They looked about them but there was no sign of life from any of the surrounding houses in the alley, so Murgan hauled his huge frame over the gate and unbolted it from within. Inside the yard, the pre-dawn half-light cast deep shadows but they could see enough to discern the storehouse and a decrepit lean-to. Murgan tested the door of the storehouse but it was firmly secured with several hefty bolts. The lean-to was less secured with just two bolts on the door. Laon drew them back and opened it. The complaining hinges creaked loudly in the silence as the foul odour within escaped. He covered his nose and mouth with his sleeve and entered.

The boy on the pallet was scarcely breathing and did not notice their presence or stir. His shallow, rasping breaths, irregular and laboured, were the only sound in the place. Laon drew near and tried to look at the lad's face, but the light was not strong enough to properly discern his cadaverous features.

Murgan peered down at the boy from over his shoulder. "He's in a bad way, Boss. Almost dead I'd say."

"Why would anyone do this to a child?"

"Some folks are just mean when it comes to Natives; they can't help themselves."

"Can you pick him up? Let's get him outside; this place stinks."

Murgan knelt and carefully lifted the boy and carried him out into the pre-dawn light. He placed him on the ground and pulled a large knife from his belt and cut away the ragged pants at the left thigh. Even in the poor light they could see the dark stain of a diamond on the drawn flesh.

"That's your boy," said Murgan.

Laon smiled and nodded. "That's Jodi," he whispered. "Let's go."

Murgan picked up the boy but just as they were about to leave and figure slipped in through the gate and they found themselves facing a raised sidearm.

"That's my property, put it down or I'll send you both to the After-world."

Murgan froze, with his arms full he could not defend either of them. Laon stepped forward and the weapon swung towards him.

"You trespass and steal what is mine, I'm going to blast you away, curse you."

Laon puffed himself up and assumed an air of denunciation. "We are government officers, I advise you to moderate yourself. Did you not know this boy is a half-breed?"

"What!"

"A half-breed, Sir. You have been reported. Do you know the penalty for keeping a half-breed? A very large fine and the forfeit of your trading license; and that's just the start of it."

The weapon wavered as the consequences of his transgression dawned on Culas. "I got it from the garrison, legitimately, I swear it; I never knew it wasn't pure-bred."

"It is your duty to check. Holster your weapon and stand aside; we have to carry out our duty, this half-breed must be registered and destroyed immediately. You, Sir will be hearing from us."

Culas fell on his knees and began to sob. "I swear I never knew. I was going to burn it soon I swear; I swear to you, Sir. Do not report me, I am a poor man."

"It is too late for that; your transgression has already been noted."

Laon swept passed the crumpled figure of the old trader, followed by Murgan cradling the boy. As they struck out of the darkness of the alley, Murgan grinned widely. "You did well back there; it's not everyone that can face down a primed weapon."

"Thanks, but I do need to change my underwear. Let's get out of this shit-hole."

By the time they reached the palace, the dawn had broken. Jodi's breathing had become shallower on the journey back and once or twice Laon thought they had lost him. Murgan carried him into the palace through Laon's private entrance and into his apartment where he laid him on the very same bed that his sister had occupied.

"Where's the Physician? I told him to be here."

"I'll bring him, Sir."

Laon noted that Murgan had assumed a less familiar tone now they were back in the palace. "Thank you Chief," he responded.

Moments later the palace physician arrived somewhat out of breath. "What is the emergency?" he wheezed.

Laon rose from the boy's side and pointed. "I want you to save this boy."

The Physician looked down and froze. He was a Bhasi of about sixty, a hypochondriac who, if required to attend anyone other than his boss, usually found himself indisposed with a wide variety of imagined medical complaints. It had always mystified Laon why the Commissioner kept this quack in his service, for he had no particular competence. The man's eyes narrowed on his potential patient and then met Laon's with a look of offended anger. "I have rushed here from my sickbed for this?"

Laon kept his countenance; he had never got on well with the Physician but was determined not to alienate him for Jodi's sake. "Yes, Parah, the boy is dying and I require you to save him."

"It is a Native, what would be the point of saving it? It would be a waste of time and drugs."

Nevertheless, I ask you to help him."

"I will not soil my hands of the likes of that. Good day to you, Cour Son."

The Physician turned to go and now Laon knew he had to impel the man. "I am the Deputy Commissioner and I require you to save this boy's life."

The Physician turned on him angrily. "I am not under your jurisdiction, Cour Son; I am not a member of your staff. I am an appointee of the Commissioner himself. My responsibility is for his health not for the welfare of scum like this."

"A responsibility you singularly failed to carry out."

The Physician's eyes widened. "That is a slur; I have always devoted myself to that man's wellbeing; no one could be more solicitous."

"Really? I believe he thinks so, but you should have warned him of the dangers of having carnal relations with unscreened Native whores."

"That's ridiculous. It is not my place to screen the harem. That was the Curator's job; a function he obviously failed to carry out."

Laon hardened his voice. "A competent physician would have foreseen the danger and taken the appropriate action. Because you did not, the Commissioner is on his way to Barta to have his genitals removed and will die a rather unpleasant death within two years. Do you really think that when I point this out to him he will retain your services? You will lose your over-generous stipend, and the luxury apartment you keep in the palace. Now, you will save this boy or I will carry out my threat; I guarantee it."

The Physician bit his lip in barely suppressed anger. "I have never liked you, Cour Son; you are a man of no morals or principles."

"Maybe so, but I invite you to consider which of us is less principled; me or you, a man who refuses to save another human being's life because of ignorant, blind prejudice?"

The two men stared angrily at each other, but the Physician knew that Laon could and would jeopardize his position at the palace. He was obliged to assist.

"Get those filthy rags off it, I'm not touching them."

Laon fetched some shears and began to cut away the filth-encrusted rags that clung to the cadaverous body of the boy. He cut off the shirt to expose a torso in which the rib-cage was so apparent it was even possible to see the broken ribs sustained from the kicking delivered by his former owner. Then, Laon took the shears to the boy's pants, carefully cutting down the length of each leg and through the ragged waistband. The Physician looked down in horrified disbelief at what was exposed. It was obvious from the dark shade of Jodi's genitals that he was not pure Native.

"A half-breed!" he declared. "I thought there was something wrong about this affair. What is your game, Cour Son? This offence to decency should be destroyed immediately, not saved."

Laon straightened. "Physician, you will save this boy or I will destroy you. And another thing, you will not use an impersonal pronoun to refer to this boy in my presence."

"This is a foul business," replied the man through gritted teeth as he opened his box with studied reluctance. He placed various instruments and probes onto Jodi and began his work. He listed the various ailments and causes that had wasted the body and administered some appropriate remedies. "It is mainly pneumonia complicated by extreme malnutrition. There are two broken ribs, which you can see for yourself. I have stabilized its... *his* condition for the moment. He will have to be given intravenous supplements, I will send for those."

"You should get them yourself. I don't want anyone else to know about this. We have broken the law, after all."

The Physician passed him a look of disdain. "At your insistence; and now you have involve me in your illegal activities."

"In that case, you had better be discreet about what you have seen."

"You need not concern yourself; I am hardly likely to broadcast the fact that I have treated a half-breed. You do realize what you will have to do until the patient is well enough to move for himself? I mean things of a personal nature; I can fit a colostomy to the penis but there will be a small amount of solids to deal with."

"That will not be a problem."

The Physician stood. "I will bring the intravenous substitute and the necessary equipment directly. I suggest you bathe the patient before we are *all* infected." He handed Laon a small phial. "Put that in the water, and make sure he is fully immersed; his skin is probably riddled with disease. Incinerate those rags and anything else he has touched, I don't want to be dealing with any outbreaks amongst the staff, especially when I am feeling so unwell."

He left them with a departing scowl and, in private solitude, Laon looked at his new charge and smiled. He could see enough of Matty in the boy's face to remind him of her and the memory of her brief, stay with him. He picked up his charge and took him through to his private bath of polished stone. The boy was so light in his arms as he waited for the flood of warm water to fill the large, sunken pool then, he descended into the water, fully clothed and washed the lad as one would wash a baby; cradling his head as the water swirled and gently cleaned his hair and skin. And in that intimate act a bond of love was formed just as a man would form towards his own offspring, for Laon was in need of love and commitment and Jodi became the object of that need.

Jodi did not regain his senses for two days. When, at last, he opened his eyes and surveyed the world about him, he fancied that he had arrived in the After-world that he had read about in the Book of Minnar. The air about him smelled sweet and his head was softly pillowed on clean, white cushions that covered him in luxurious, billowing mounds. Above all, he was warm, warmer than he had ever been since leaving his home in the Tropics. Above him he could see a ceiling of soft light and beside him sat an angel, dressed in fine clothes, sleeping. By the quality of his surroundings Jodi knew he must be dead and that what was written of the After-world was true. He pushed the cover away from himself and looked down at his body. It was still the same, skeletal body he had occupied in life, but now there were strange additions, not least among them a strange object attached to him to drain away liquid waste.

The angel woke up and smiled. "Welcome back, Jodi," it said and pulled the cover back over him.

"Am I dead?" whispered the boy.

"No, Jodi, you are not dead. My name is Laon and I took you from that trader and brought you here to get better."

Jodi frowned. "I'm not dead!"

"No, you're alive and you're going to get strong again."

This revelation taxed his understanding and he closed his eyes and went back to sleep.

When he woke again the angel had gone. He pulled off the cover and tried to move, but he could not lift his legs. He lay still and looked about while he waited for the angel to come back. In the After-world there was fine furniture and mysterious images on the walls that constantly changed. Everything was clean and smelled of the rare and gorgeous blossoms of the forests of his youth. The After-world was a remarkable and lovely place.

In a while the angel came back and brought with him another. The first angel had a kindly, open face with two ears that stuck out in a slightly comical way; the other was more serious and scowled prodigiously.

"He has regained consciousness, the danger is passed. Let me look at you, boy."

The older angel waved gadgets over him and poked and prodded his body. He detached the urinary sheath and inspected his water with another machine, then replaced the sheath.

"Remarkable, it's almost normal. I've never seen such powers of recovery."

"When will he be able to walk?" asked Laon.

"At this rate, two days. You can start feeding him normally now; use this supplement instead of the intravenous one; and he will need plenty of liquid."

He pulled a bottle from his box and gave it to Laon. "The broken ribs are knitting, but will need protecting. Keep the analgesics going for the time being, he'll be in pain without them. I shouldn't need to see him again. I hope you know what you're doing, Cour Son."

"I know exactly what I'm doing. Thank you for your help, Physician."

The man turned at the door. "Don't thank me, Cour Son; it should have been destroyed like the rest of them."

Laon watched the door close, relieved that he would not have to deal the unpleasant fellow any more. It seemed to him that racism was ground into the Bhasi from the moment they were born; racism particularly directed against Natives, blinding them to any virtues of those unfortunate people. He pulled the covers back over Jodi and sat on the bed, studying his face.

"This isn't the After-world, is it?" said Jodi.

"No, Jodi, this is Ennepp, the world where you have always lived."

"What is this place?"

"This is my home. My name is Laon Cour Son."

The name sounded familiar, as if he'd heard it in his sleep. "Why am I here?"

"I brought you here to keep you alive."

"Why?"

Laon paused and considered. Jodi must never know the true reason; he must never know how his sister was failed. "You were seen in the market-place in Zurat. I decided to rescue you."

"He wanted to burn me, before I was dead; just like he'd done to the others."

"He can't get you now; he is a long way from here. You are safe and your life will begin again. Now get some rest, you have been very ill and you will need time to recover."

"And when must I leave?"

"You don't have to leave, not ever. This is your home now; it's where you will live."

Jodi looked about at the wonders of the place. The contrast with his last accommodation or indeed anything he had known before could not have been greater; but, if it wasn't the After-world and it wasn't a dream, it must be real. Already his mind began to turn towards the rescue of his sister. This man could help him; he was rich and powerful, that was obvious. He could find her and get her back. He shut his eyes and drifted away with that thought turning in his mind.

The Physician was correct in his prediction, for two days later Jodi was sufficiently recovered to leave his bed. He had put on so much weight that his pelvic bone and ribcage were hardly visible under the skin of his torso and his legs and arms had filled out to something near their former dimensions. Laon seemed overjoyed at his rapid progress and brought him a set of clothes to wear. He helped Jodi up and removed the urinary sheath, then, he introduced him to something called 'underwear', a sort of cloth that wrapped around his waist and between his legs to enclose his genitals. It felt strange and restrictive, but he suffered it for the sake of his benefactor. Then, clad only in this underwear, he stood and, supported by Laon, took a turn around the room.

"How does it feel?" asked Laon as he conducted the boy back to the bed.

"Feels alright, I think I'll try on my own."

He stood and with Laon in close attendance, walked unsteadily around the room.

"Well done Jodi; we can dispense with the urinary sheath now."

"You mean that thing I piss into?"

"Yes; I'll show where to go and what to do."

Laon conducted the boy to the ablution unit and amid much incomprehension, demonstrated the facilities; then, he walked him back to his bed.

"Would you like something to read, Jodi?"

It immediately struck Jodi as odd that this man knew he could read. It aroused suspicion in him but he was careful not to betray it. "Yes," he replied.

"What subject would you like?"

"Something that explains why things are like they are and why the Bhasi hate us so much."

"Nothing explains that, Jodi. I'll bring you a history of Ennepp."

Jodi read and slept for the rest of the day and when he woke up it was evening and the last of the sun was streaming through the high window and casting a ruddy glow upon the ceiling. A huge, uniformed man was standing near the bed, gazing down at him. Jodi's eyes widened in terror, he had seen enough Bhasi soldiers to know that this was not a good thing, but the man's eyes creased into a smile when he saw the boy's fright and he laughed.

"Well, my boy, you certainly smell better than the last time I saw you."

Jodi glared at him, he had never seen a Bhasi soldier smile, let alone laugh. He did not know how to take it.

Laon suddenly appeared from behind the huge man. "Stop alarming the boy, Murgan. Dinner is ready."

"I see you can read, Jodi; what are you reading?"

"A History of Ennepp, Sir."

"Don't call me 'Sir', I am Murgan Doh, Captain of the Palace Guard. 'A History of Ennepp', you say? You won't find much joy in that volume."

He turned and strode past Laon and out of the room.

Laon grinned. "That was the man who found you and carried you out of Zurat, Jodi. He will not harm you."

On the terrace attached to Laon's apartment the two men watched the last of the daylight disappear from the sky and drank fine wine from the palace cellar. They had eaten together and were mellow with alcohol.

"Thank the Prophet we don't have to light those damn torches," remarked Murgan.

Laon surveyed the darkening park. "It makes a welcome change to see it getting dark here. The stars will make a good show tonight."

"That they will."

"Any trouble with the staff?"

"One or two rumblings, I soon dealt with that. They're all as soft as shit; none are properly trained. I don't know what we'd do if the palace was attacked."

"It's not likely to be, is it?"

"You never know. Everyone knows how rich the Commissioner is; some fool outfit might try something one day."

"Why don't you shake things up then? I'll leave it to you."

"When's the Old Baggage coming back? Have you heard?"

Laon shook his head. "Not for a while I would imagine, he'll stay on Barta to recoup. I'm not looking forward to that particular homecoming. I dread to think what he's going to be like."

"You mean 'she'."

Laon laughed. "Be careful, Murgan, the Commissioner won't take kindly to such barracks humour. Make sure the guards don't indulge; it *will* come back on you."

"Noted; speaking of which, that boy of yours; be careful Laon."

"What do you mean?"

"I've seen eyes like that before; they look at you but you see nothing when you look back into them. They are like the eyes of the dead; they're pitiless, murderer's eyes."

"That's harsh and I think you're wrong. He's bound to be scarred by what he's been through; wouldn't you be? You'd be defensive and suspicious, especially when a great, hulking, uniformed brute fetches up in front of you."

"Maybe so, Laon, but take it from me, that boy is damaged. When I was in the army I saw men with eyes like that; they only love war and death; they are incapable of love as you and I would know it."

"I don't require love from Jodi."

"Are you sure?"

Laon took a thoughtful sip of wine. "If I can guide him, educate him; nurture him, perhaps one day he will come to look upon me as a father."

"Perhaps you are right, but I repeat; be careful or he will surely break your heart."

XII

During the following days Jodi's strength gradually returned and he came to know the apartment of Laon Cour Son very well. The supplement that the Physician prescribed together with the copious and astounding array of food that his benefactor plied him with, soon restored him. His face filled out, his ribs healed and his torso and limbs resumed their proper proportions. He revelled in the unaccustomed luxury of keeping himself clean and having fresh clothes to put on whenever he pleased. He enjoyed the taste of foods that he had never before eaten and the library that would magically appear on the astonishing instrument that Laon had given him. He enjoyed all these new things and others, but, through all of it, he never once smiled for his overriding preoccupation was the fate of his sister, Matty.

He had spoken of his sister with Laon on a number of occasions before, but the man had always quickly changed the subject and seemed strangely reticent. When he had asked him if he could find out where she was, he became evasive and said it was impossible. Jodi did not believe him and this was the first strain in their relationship. He was also told that he must not leave the apartment for there were men abroad who meant him ill and would have him destroyed if they could. Jodi knew from experience that this was true, but his desire to find his sister overrode any personal dangers he might have to face.

He had been at the palace for just twenty-four days when the urge to escape became too great to resist. He secreted some food in a sack and waited until nightfall, when most of the palace slept. He found Laon's key where he had seen it kept and let himself out on to the terrace. The stars were bright and he could see his way among the specimen trees of the park. He rounded the lake and ran into the faux wilderness until the grey, turreted outline of the palace disappeared. After two kilometres he came upon a high, fortified wall and began to search along its perimeter for a weakness. He had gone only half a kilometre further when a harsh, white light nailed him against the high wall.

"What are you doing, Jodi?" Laon appeared out of the light and came towards him.

"I'm going to find my sister, you can't stop me,' he shouted.

"Get back in the cart, Jodi," said Laon calmly. "We will look for her tomorrow."

"Do you promise?"

"I do."

Jodi climbed aboard and Laon turned the cart around and headed back to the palace.

"Where did you think you were going, Jodi?"

"To the north, where I am from; that is where they have taken Matty."

"You don't know that and you wouldn't have got very far."

"I got this far. I can read maps; I know how far it is."

"You got as far as Zurat where you nearly died. Didn't that experience teach you anything about this world?"

Jodi made no reply. He knew Laon was right, but he had forced the man's hand and that made him smile in the darkness when no one could see him.

The following day, Laon was true to his word. While Jodi watched he enquired into the fate of the Doah farm and the circumstances of its dissolution. Most of the estate had been bought from the creditors by the adjoining estate and the assets had gone to them. There was no reference to Matty and she was not listed as an asset.

"Of course, that is not surprising," said Laon as they sat together before the image of the Doah Estate, "they wouldn't have had a license to keep a female. I'm sorry, Jodi, it is certain that your sister was killed before the creditors moved in to prevent any prosecution for illegal possession. I'm sorry; I thought this would be the case but I shouldn't have tried to protect you from this information."

Jodi stared at the image of the forlorn place where he had lived for four, long years. Memories of Matty came flooding back and tears welled in his eyes and drizzled down his cheeks. Why had he been so lucky? Why had he been the survivor surrounded by luxury while she had died in the miserable, bleak place? Why couldn't it have been him and not her?

Laon saw the tears and tried to comfort him. It was the first sign of any emotion he had seen in the boy and he tried to put his arm around him; but Jodi pulled away and hurried from the room. Laon felt guilty about the lie he had told about the fate of Matty, but he wasn't at all sure how Jodi would react to the true story of her stay at the palace and his failure to protect her. He was also sure that, had he known the truth, Jodi would not rest until he had gone to Tarnus and seen for himself the place where his sister had actually died. One sibling had perished there already and he did not want to lose the second to that savage world.

Jodi did not mention Matty again and seemed to settle down to his life in the palace. Laon realized that he could not keep the boy confined to his apartment and so started to allow him the freedom of the palace and its park.

This was when Jodi started running. He ran around the sixteen-kilometre perimeter of the park, once in the morning and once in the evening, finishing just before sunset. He timed every run; forcing himself to go faster and faster, as if trying to expunge the bitterness of his youthful experiences with the pain and elation of the effort. He ran barefoot and never wore shoes for any purpose, pointedly ignoring those supplied by his mentor. He also rejected the wearing of underwear, which he found unnatural and uncomfortable, but, ever mindful of his mother's injunction, was always careful never to be seen naked, even in the sole company of Laon who knew of his lineage. He read and exercised prodigiously, as if making up for sixteen years of deprivation; wanting to know everything about his home world and other worlds beyond it. As he began to put on muscle and weight, Laon watched him grow with fatherly pride and increasing, unrequited love.

On one of his runs Jodi came upon Murgan, instructing a group of his elite guards in the art of self-defence. He was teaching them close quarter weapons combat, fighting two of three at a time and sending at least two of them to the physician for medical attention. Jodi watched, fascinated by the skill of the man who was using a stick instead of a sword. He sought out the Chief of the Guards later and asked him to teach him combat.

Murgan frowned. "I will teach you if the Secretary permits it."

"Why should he have a say in it?" protested Jodi.

"Because he is your mentor and you are his ward and that is how it works."

Jodi was not happy with this reply but asked Laon that evening.

Laon rubbed his right ear, as he was wont to do when confronted with a difficult decision. "You wish to learn the art of combat? Why?"

"So that I can kill anybody that gets in my way," replied Jodi with disarming honesty.

"If that is your reason then I refuse to allow it."

Jodi flared. "What right have you got to say what I can and can't do?"

Laon remained calm; he had seen this ugly aspect of the boy before and ascribed it to the brutality of his past. "I claim no rights over you Jodi, except the right to know what is best for you. You are young and you still have a lot to learn. The ability to kill is not something that a child should learn."

"I am not a child, I am a man. I should be able to make my own decisions."

"And on your mature reflection, you have decided that it's a good idea to kill people that get in your way. What if I got in your way, would you kill me?"

"If I had to," replied Jodi flatly.

Laon saw the dearth of emotion in the boy's dark eyes and knew then that Murgan was right. Jodi was angry and always would be and there was nothing he could do to change that. The only hope was that Murgan would teach him discipline and restraint and that a life without pain and suffering would eventually mellow him. "Very well," he said, "you may go to Murgan for instruction."

Jodi strode away victorious. The man was weak; he could always get what he wanted. Laon watched him go and wondered if he was not in the process of creating a monster.

Sixty-three days after his departure, the Commissioner returned. His operation had been a success, but he had convinced himself that that he was now an invalid and so he took to his bed and would not rise for any purpose. This caused considerable consternation within his retinue of male nurses, for the Commissioner despised simulants and would not suffer any to be near him. His only pleasures now were the accumulation of wealth and the increase of his already ample girth, so that instead of their normal breakfast meeting, Laon was required to attend the Commissioner in his bedchamber.

On entering, Laon bowed slightly and approached the recumbent mound. "I trust the operation was successful and you have regained your strength, Excellency."

The Commissioner glared at him and swept back the ornately worked cover to reveal his corpulent, naked body. He spread his legs to expose a slit with a tube issuing from it where his genitals once were. "I have become a woman, Cour Son. Look at what they have done to me."

Laon glanced at the repulsive sight below the bloated stomach. "You are not a woman, Excellency, I assure you."

The Commissioner pointed towards a window in front of which was a large jar sitting on an ornate pedestal. Inside the jar, floating in preservative was the Commissioner's missing parts. "There is the man I was, Cour Son, there in that jar."

"You kept your genitals!"

"Of course; they're mine, why should I not keep them?"

Laon was rather stuck for words. "I... I can't think of any reason, Excellency."

The Commissioner replaced the cover, much to his Secretary's relief. "They are to stay there as a reminder of my magnificence and prowess and I will have them buried with me, I do not wish to go into the After-world incomplete."

"Naturally, Excellency."

The Commissioner eyed him. "I understand you keep a Native boy in your rooms, Cour Son."

Laon was rather taken aback; he had not expected his boss to mention such a trivial personal matter. "At entirely my own expense, Excellency."

"I wouldn't have expected such a thing to be a charge on the palace exchequer."

"No, Excellency."

"Your own proclivities are your own affair, Cour Son; I do not interfere in such personal matters unless they affect me."

"The boy is my ward, Sir; it is not as you have supposed."

The Commissioner studied his secretary with undisguised puzzlement. "Your ward? A Native boy!"

"He shows great promise and I hope one day soon to add him to your staff."

"A Native who shows promise; that is an unusual thing. Speaking of which, you dismissed the ladies, as I instructed?"

"I did, Excellency."

"Good. Now hear this; I will suffer no women to enter the palace, ever. Is that understood?"

"Yes, Excellency."

'You tell those randy guards that if they smuggle one whore into my house, I will have their bollocks for breakfast. If I can't have women, no one else will under my roof."

"I will inform Chief Doh."

"How is your preferred man doing?"

"Very well, Excellency. He is training the men to a high standard of competence and has dismissed any who do not measure up."

The bloated flesh shifted under the cover and some water drizzled down the transparent tube into a receptacle by the bed. A loud fart issued from the Commisioner's glutinous buttocks and reverberated through the fine linen. "I have been reading your dispatches, Cour Son, I see you reduced the percentage for three contracts."

"To encourage more trade in the commodities Ennepp is short of. The volumes have risen significantly. I increased other contracts and overall, our profits are up by twenty-two percent."

"It seems you have things in hand." The Commissioner waved a dismissive arm. "I am tired now; you may go."

Laon bowed and withdrew knowing that the man approved of his adjustments to trade. His Excellency never passed compliments; he merely suspended his habitual disapprobation.

That evening, as they sat watching the rain after their regular evening meal together, Laon informed Murgan of the Commissioner's decision to ban all women from the palace.

"The men won't like it; four of them have wives living in."

"They'll have to move the wives out, tomorrow at the latest."

"I'll see to it. They'll just have to go to the city for their fun."

As he spoke Jodi appeared, soaked through, after his evening run. He barely glanced in their direction as he passed them on the way to his room.

"How's he doing?" asked Laon.

"Too well. I never saw such raw anger. I had to pull him off one of the men yesterday; I thought he was going to kill him."

"I fear Jodi will not rest until he's killed somebody."

"Do you ever regret bringing him here?"

"No and I never will."

Murgan drew near and whispered. "Has it occurred to you he may kill you, especially if he finds out that you lied to him about Matty?"

Laon nodded. "It's a risk I'll have to take. Other than you, no one else knows the connection between them, so assuming your discretion, the risk is low."

"I hope you're right, because you wouldn't stand a chance if he turned on you."

And so, Jodi's first year at the palace of the Commissioner of Trade for Lamon Utile progressed. His physique matured into that of a young adult and his mind expanded with all the learning it had adsorbed under Laon's guidance. Towards his mentor he maintained a cool distance. He knew that Laon had saved his life, but did not know why. He also knew that Laon loved him and this he could not respect for it showed weakness; a weakness that could be exploited when he chose.

The only person in the palace that Jodi actually liked was Murgan. The soldier had taught him everything that he knew about combat, about strategy and how to spot another man's weaknesses and Jodi had been his star pupil; fitter and quicker than any of the guards. Even though he was still young, he could take any of them down and they all knew it; only Murgan could beat him and that was only because he was practically twice his size. Jodi liked the company of the guards and felt easy associating with them and when the first anniversary of his arrival at the palace had come, he had elected to spend it in their company, shunning the planned celebration of his mentor.

"I want to move out of here and into the barracks," he announced abruptly one morning before his run.

Laon had sensed this was coming but hid his disappointment. "I have no objection, but are you sure this is wise? The men down there have no privacy."

Jodi had not thought of this and puckered his forehead. "I could come back here for ablutions."

"Indeed you could, but how long would it be before some rowdy game down there exposed you? Besides, the guards are all Bhasi; what makes you think they would want a Native living amongst them?"

"They are friendly towards me."

"Because they know you are my ward and Murgan likes you. They tolerate you, Jodi, because they have to, that's all. Give any one of them a chance to bring you down and he would do it. If you are denounced as a half-breed I doubt I could protect you; I'd certainly be arrested myself."

This brought Jodi up short and reminded him that he was from a race considered to be inferior. He ran and fought harder that day and after training, when the others had gone, Jodi started a fight with one of the guards he particularly disliked. Murgan heard the fracas and came back and had to pull him off the man. The soldier's face was bruised and cut and his arm was broken by the time that he separated them. He sent the soldier to the Physician to get patched up and turned on Jodi angrily.

"I didn't teach you combat so you could take out your anger on my men."

Jodi made no reply but just glared at him, his eyes alive with the thrill of the fight.

"What's got into you this time?"

"Nothing."

"You got to calm down, boy; this is training, not the real thing."

"He'd be dead if it was."

"You're lucky he's not, now go home and don't come back to training until you can control yourself. And you can go to the barracks and apologize to that man while you're about it."

"Apologize! What for? He doesn't like me anyway."

"What's that got to do with it?"

"They all hate me because I'm Native, not like them. They look down of me; I've seen it in their eyes; they don't say it because of you and Laon."

"Do you think you're inferior to them?"

354

"No, not to them anyway."

"So why do you give a fuck what they think?"

Jodi gave this some thought. "I don't know."

"Of course you don't because it doesn't matter what other, perhaps ignorant people think about you. What matters is what you think of yourself and what those that care for you think of you and that's the only thing that's important. Laon cares for you, he's the only person in this whole universe that loves you, yet you treat him like shit."

"I can't help it, I don't respect him."

"He's a decent man who saved your life and has given you everything you have. You should think about that sometime."

Jodi turned away and kicked the ground. "I do... I do, but can't respect him."

As Murgan observed the tortured boy a flicker of realization came to him. "What happened to you down there in the Southlands?"

"Nothing."

He grabbed the boy by his arm and held him fast. "Don't lie to me, Jodi. Something happened to you on the farm or at Zurat; what was it?"

"I don't want to say, I don't want to think about it." He pulled away and sat heavily on the ground, his head bowed.

"You were raped, weren't you?"

Jodi nodded without looking up at the man. The shame of it crushed him.

Murgan could not see the boy's face but knew he was crying. "What happened?"

"On the way to Zurat I was hungry and weak and they gave me food. Three of my own race; they held me down while they took turns."

Murgan sat down next to the weeping boy and put his huge arm around him. "That is a terrible thing to happen to a man; a degrading thing; but it wasn't your fault; you were young and weak and couldn't fight back. There was nothing you could do, certainly not against three older and stronger men. But you're confusing two completely different things. What those three men did to you has nothing to do with love; it was a brutal sex act brought about by the way the rulers of this world have genetically engineered your race. They have no women so they have to make do with what's available. What Laon feels for you is something quite different; he does not desire you physically. He's never tried to touch you, has he?"

'No, I'd kill him."

"Exactly; you are like a son to him, you are everything he is not, strong, aggressive, brave. He lives part of his life through you. Give him a chance; it will make him happy and you will become a better person for it."

Jodi was lost in thought for a moment, then, he replied that he would try harder with Laon. "I will go and say sorry to the man I hurt now."

"Good. Let's go back."

As they walked together through the manicured parkland and up to the house, Jodi spoke again. "You won't say anything about... about what I just told you."

"Of course not."

In the days following their talk, Murgan noticed a distinct change in Jodi. It was as though by telling him of the rape, some of the poison that was locked in Jodi's soul had drained away and he became calmer and less angry with the world. Although still distant, he was at least more civil towards Laon and even occasionally joined them for one of their regular evening dinners.

It was about this time that Jodi saw, for the first time, the man who, ultimately, had provided him with his home and everything he possessed. Laon had always restricted access to the Commissioner; no soldiers were permitted and only a small retinue of male nurse attendants were allowed into the presence of His Excellency. The hulk had not risen from his bed from the moment he had set himself down following his return from Barta Magnus and as the disease and inactivity gradually took its toll, so the Commissioner descended into a sort of torpor in which he drifted in and out of consciousness. Eventually, the Physician insisted that he be raised from the bed and placed in a tank of gelatinous fluid in which his strained organs could function more naturally.

Since it was not possible for four men to lift the bloated body of the Commissioner, Laon arranged for Murgan and three of his most trusted officers to construct a hoist over the stately bed. On the day of the move, Jodi particularly asked to be present; he was curious as he had never seen the huge man before, but had heard much about him from the guards. Laon was apprehensive, but agreed because the Commissioner would be sedated during the operation. He was brought into the opulent bedchamber in a part of the palace that had always remained locked. Laon and Murgan were there with the nurses, the physician and three other soldiers. On the bed, naked and splayed, was the largest and most grotesque human being he had ever seen. Tubes issues from beneath mountains of flab and curled into various receptacles around the bed. The nurses buzzed around fussing and fiddling while two soldiers strapped the hulk to the hoist.

Laon went and stood by Jodi as the operation began. "Meet the Commissioner of Trade for Lamon Utile, Jodi. What do you think of your benefactor?"

Jodi was still gawping at the revolting sight. "I didn't know a human being could look like that."

Laon nodded. "It is extraordinary how degraded a man can become physically."

The hoisting began and great hulk shuddered and began to rise. As the enormous legs parted Jodi was treated to a view of the man's groin.

"He's got nothing there," he declared with surprise.

"He keeps them over there, in that jar," replied Laon pointing to the pedestal by the window. "He had something called Croman's Syndrome and he had to have them amputated last year."

"Shit! Why don't you just let him die?"

"The Commissioner may not die, Jodi. As long as he lives we are safe in our jobs. When he dies, a new commissioner will be appointed and we will be in uproar, for a new commissioner will want to place his own staff."

"Why won't they give you the job? You're running the place aren't you?"

"Yes, but I am not a natural of Lamon Utile; I cannot inherit the position."

"And so you keep him alive."

Laon nodded. "At all costs."

"How long will he live?"

"About a year, maybe a bit more if we're lucky."

"What will you do when he dies?"

"By then I shall be secure. You and I will leave this world and find somewhere you can be free and equal."

"I thought Natives were not allowed to leave Ennepp."

Laon smiled. "With money you can do anything you want."

They watched as the bed was removed and replaced by a large, transparent vat filled with a gel-like substance. The Commissioner was lowered gently into the vat so that only his head was visible above the glutinous medium. His massive legs and arms swayed like a monstrous baby trying to swim for the first time as the substance gently churned inside the vessel.

They waited while the Physician checked the connections and the readings. Satisfied, he turned to Laon. "That should keep him alive, although I don't think he's going to like it."

"I'm not concerned with what he likes or dislikes," replied Laon. "Our interest is to keep him alive for as long as possible."

The Physician nodded curtly and stared at Jodi. "I see it is prospering. I have had complaints from the guards about its behaviour."

Laon quickly stepped between Jodi and the Physician; he could feel the boy bristling behind him. "I asked you once before not to use that pronoun when referring to my ward. I won't ask again."

"Don't threaten me, Cour Son; you need me as much as I need you and I'll say what I like about that savage."

"Really? You might do well to think about which of us can be more easily replaced, should either of us meet with an unfortunate accident."

The Physician glared at Laon's stone-clad countenance. "You have become as savage as that Native you protect."

"Better a savage than a bigot; and right now it is you I am protecting, not him. Good day to you Physician."

The man's mouth twisted in anger, but he kept silent. As he left he caught sight of Jodi's face; the look in the half-breed's eyes made his blood freeze. But during the long march to the bedchamber door the boiling anger inside him loosened his tongue and as he opened it, he turned and shouted, "I should have killed that filthy half-breed when I had the chance!"

By the time he slammed the great, carved door behind him, Jodi was half way down the room and quite ready for murder. Fortunately Murgan foresaw the trouble and caught Jodi before he could get through the door. He pulled him back and pinned him to the floor while the boy thrashed about beneath him.

"Calm down," he hissed through clenched teeth as he struggled to maintain his grip. "Calm down or I swear I'll knock you out."

Jodi stopped struggling and glared at the big soldier in blind rage.

"I'm going to let you up now; you make a move for that door and I promise you I'll hit you so hard you won't wake up for days."

Murgan climbed off the boy and Jodi rose, breathing heavily.

Laon turned to the stunned assembly of four nurses and three officers. "Any of you speak of what you have heard here, I will personally see your lives made into a living hell. Is that understood?"

"Yes, Sir," they murmured in unison.

"You three officers; get back to your quarters and mark what I have said."

The officers left, having heard an even more impressive threat from their chief. As they left the bedchamber, Murgan added, "Shall I have a word with the Physician?"

"No," replied Laon, "he won't speak; he saved Jodi's life and is just as implicated as any of us."

"You should have let me kill him," said Jodi vehemently. "I would have killed them all."

"I know," replied Laon reflecting how easily the thin veneer of his ward's civility had been lost in a moment of rage. The secret was abroad and he didn't know how long he would be able to protect him; not just from all the wagging tongues, but from himself.

From that moment Laon lived in fear of discovery. He had reinforced his injunction to those present at the Physician's outburst with the promise of a reward if they held their tongues at least until the death of the Commissioner; but even so, he was sure that some drunken indiscretion would expose the secret of Jodi's mixed origin. He considered a plan to evacuate the two of them if necessary, but it was a plan that would cost him plenty. He made contact with an old friend who he hoped was still alive and was pleased to receive a reply. *At least,* he thought, *there would be a way out if things got too difficult on Ennepp.*

Before the passing of another half year, things did, indeed, get difficult.

XIII

Jodi now had the run of the palace, except for the Commissioner's apartments that remained off limits to anyone but Laon and essential staff. He had taken to reading in the magnificent library the Commissioner had kept but never used. It was full of ancient volumes of great value and had an advanced terminus that gave him access to the entire universe of human knowledge. When not training or running, he would spend hours alone in the library and Laon would sometimes not see him for days at a time.

One evening, as he was heading for his ablution unit after his run, he came across Laon who had been working in his private study. Their relationship had eased as Jodi had matured and his innate anger had been suppressed and he now greeted Laon with a measure of friendly familiarity.

"Hello, what are you doing?"

Laon looked up from his work at the handsome, lithe young man he had nurtured and smiled. "Just catching up on some work."

"How's the Old Man?"

"Oh, much the same; he dribbles a lot and talks nonsense."

"Is he going to die soon?"

Laon knew the thrust of the question; Jodi had not forgotten his promise to leave Ennepp when the Commissioner did finally die. "No, not yet. Be patient Jodi; you have your whole life ahead of you. The longer he lives, the richer we will become and then we can do anything we want."

Jodi nodded and suppressed a smile at the man's assumption. He had no intention of staying with Laon once they were free of this degraded world. Once he was free he would travel the entire universe, see it all; experience everything until fate took him to the After-world.

He cleaned himself and made his way to the great library. Outside the ornate doors he paused. He could hear a voice calling in the distance. He followed the sound and it brought him to the door that guarded the Commissioner's apartment. The great doors were slightly ajar and no guards were present, so he entered. As the volume of the calling increased, he realized that it was coming from the Commissioner's bedchamber. He entered and there saw the huge man, suspended in his vat of gel, screaming at the top of his voice. The nurses were nowhere to be seen and the apartment was deserted save the two of them.

As Jodi approached the huge head poking from the gel stopped calling. A pair of bloodshot eyes focused on him. "Who are you?"

Jodi did not reply, but drew nearer, studying the complex web of tubes that issued from the vat. He walked around the vat slowly, trying to calculate which one would be the most vital. The Commissioner's eyes swivelled in his fixed head, trying to see what was going on. He was experiencing an increasingly rare period of lucidity.

"What are you doing?"

Jodi, having completed his tour, stood in front of the vat and looked up into the jowly face of his benefactor.

"You're the Native that Cour Son brought here."

"I am a member of the Pal Race," replied Jodi haughtily.

"You know the name of your race; he's taught you that much."

"And more; much more."

"Natives are dull; I have seen enough of them to know that."

"They are not permitted education, of course they are dull."

"What is your name?"

"Jodi Saronaga."

"That is a familiar name to me."

"Perhaps my mentor spoke of me."

"Cour Son; don't speak to me of him. He has me trapped here in this living death while he robs me of everything. He thinks I don't know, but I do."

"He seeks to keep you alive, I know that."

The Commissioner's eyes grew narrow and his ample eyebrows twitched. "He keeps me alive so he can enrich himself by embezzling my fortune. I was a fool to trust him; I always knew he would cheat me in the end."

The sun shimmered through the high windows and spangled the ornate, gold-encrusted ceiling of the bedchamber. A shaft of gold caught the jar on the pedestal containing His Excellency's defunct equipment.

"Would you like me to kill you?"

The Commissioner's ample eyebrows knitted. "I didn't say that."

"What life have you got for yourself? You're practically dead anyway."

"That's easy for a young man to say. The young do not treasure life like the old and dying. I have memories. Look over to the jar and see the man I once was."

Jodi moved to the window and looked into the jar. The Commissioner's large and flabby genitals still floated within.

"You see, boy? Was I not magnificent?"

"You judge yourself by the size of your genitals?"

"It is alright to be jealous; all were when I was revealed in my full magnificence. Thousands of women were pleasured by me; thousands I tell you and every single one of them grateful for the honour."

It was at this point in his somewhat, generous recollection of his former conquests that the Commissioner was reminded of a particular failure; the beautiful Native girl who had stabbed his cheek with a fork from his own breakfast table. His eyes swivelled towards the young man by his specimen jar and then he saw her, fixed in the features of this Native male who Cour Son had so inexplicably favoured. Saronaga; that was her name; he had heard it mentioned only once but, in this moment of clarity, it emerged into the light.

"You," he said. "You are a kinsman of that whore."

Jodi walked towards the vat; the Commissioner's bloodshot eyes seemed to start from his flabby head.

"What do you mean?"

"I mean you have come to curse me and then to kill me. Admit it."

"I have no idea what you are talking about."

"I see her in you, her face, so sweet and innocent, but so vicious. She stabbed me in the face rather than submit. Her name was Saronaga."

Jodi took a step back; his mouth gaped in surprise as he stared at the Commissioner. "My sister was here!?"

"Long, black hair, the colour of the darkest night, as fine as any and the face of an angel. But she was not an angel, she was a she-devil like none I have ever seen."

Jodi's heartbeat soared; his mouth went dry. "What happened to her?"

The Commissioner pierced him with a look of triumph. "I smashed her head in."

Jodi stared into the repulsive, jowly face of the Commissioner while an uncontrollable, black anger welled up inside him. He started to shake and the expression on his face warped into ugly fury. He cast about and seized a heavy ornate chair while the Commissioner observed his antics with increasing alarm.

With all his might Jodi flung the chair at the vat. It bounced off, sending a shock wave through the glutinous liquid. The Commissioner yelled in alarm but no one heeded him as Jodi retrieved the chair and took another swing. Again the vat resisted and, scarlet with uncontrollable rage, Jodi turned his attention to the more delicate and vulnerable equipment that surrounded the vat. He rampaged through the machinery, smashing it to pieces while the Commissioner bellowed profanities. Then the profanities suddenly stopped and a peculiar sucking noise issued from the vat as the Commissioner was drawn down into the gel while his withered limbs flailed hopelessly. Eventually the flailing ceased and the bulging eyes peered sightlessly out through the transparent wall of the vat. The Commissioner was dead.

Jodi, breathing heavily, stared at it for some moments; then he ran from the room and through the palace bursting into Laon's library with fury and revenge swamping all other thoughts from his mind. He grabbed Laon by his gown and hurled him up against a wall, pinning him to it with his hands around the man's neck.

"You lied to me," he hissed through clenched teeth. "She was here, in this place. You lied all along; I'm going to kill you."

Laon felt the vice-like grip tighten about his neck; he was raised from his feet by the power of Jodi's anger.

"That heap of shit killed her," Jodi continued. "I've finished him and now I'm going to kill you and anyone who gets in my way."

Laon was beginning to turn blue; he managed to choke out some words. "He didn't kill her."

"You're lying, I heard it from him; what he did to her."

"He just thinks he killed her."

The grip eased slightly.

"She didn't die here. Let me go and I will tell you what happened."

There was a moment in the balance and then reason began to return to Jodi. He released Laon who fell to the floor, spluttering and coughing. He rubbed his neck where a livid mark had appeared. "Your sister is dead, but not by his hand or mine; she didn't die on Ennepp."

"What! Where did she die?"

"Help me up, I will tell you what happened."

Jodi was now confused. How could his sister have left Ennepp? It seemed he was about to learn the truth at last. He grabbed Laon's gown and hauled him roughly into his chair. "Speak," he commanded. Laon looked up at him forlornly and began his story.

"I bought Matty from a Moontrader for the Commissioner's collection. At that time it was part of my job to procure women for his pleasure. I usually bought Native women from the North; experienced women who knew how to pleasure a man and who welcomed the opportunity to live in such surroundings. But Matty was different, I saw her quality and vulnerability the moment that I set eyes on her and I decided to keep her from the Commissioner. I couldn't stand the thought of that bloated monster defiling her so I kept her here, in these chambers; she slept in the bed in which you now sleep.

"She had been here some time when I was betrayed and she was discovered. She was taken to the Commissioner but in her fright and confusion, she stabbed him through the cheek with a fork. He knocked her out and later I told him he had broken her skull, but it was not the case. I smuggled her out of the palace one night and took her to Zurat where I was to meet another Moontrader called Salex Contran. Whilst I was away concluding the deal, Matty convinced herself that she had seen you, crossing a square, attached to an old man."

The memory of the girl banging on the window of the craft now came back to Jodi. It had been her, trying to get to him. He turned cold and tears moistened his eyes as he vividly remembered the scene on that forlorn morning before the sun had risen. "I remember seeing her, but I didn't know who it was; I couldn't see properly."

"She saw you, Jodi, and she made me promise to find you and help you."

Jodi wiped his eyes and nodded. The mystery of why Laon had rescued him had now been solved. "So that's why," he muttered.

"Yes, that's why. It was my last promise to your sister and I meant to keep it, even though I could not save her. Salex Contran promised to remove her from Ennepp and to sell her into a respectable house. But he was incautious; he took her to Tarnus where he meant to conduct an arms trade in the Division of Trant. I don't know what went wrong exactly, but his ship blew up and destroyed the port and everything around it. No one survived for kilometres. That was where Matty died, Jodi, on Tarnus, a long way from here."

"Why didn't you tell me this before?"

"Because I know what you're going to do and I didn't want to lose both of you to that world."

"You were wrong not to tell me."

"I did it for your own good."

"It's not for you to decide what is good for me."

"That is true now, but when you first came to me my duty to your sister was to protect you. That is all I did, but you are a man now, you can decide for yourself."

"You don't know she died in that explosion. You can't prove it."

"No, I can't."

"She could be alive, living on Tarnus; trying to survive."

"Believe me; she could not have survived the blast."

"She might not have even been on that ship. She could be anywhere, anywhere at all."

"I knew you would be irrational about this."

"Irrational! It is you who have been irrational and deceitful. I hate the sight of you. You are not a proper man; you are weak and disgusting. Did you really think I would stay with you a moment longer than was necessary? You can burn in Damnation with all your money and this fine palace. You will never see me again. Never!"

His eyes blazed into his mentor's and then he turned and ran from the library leaving Laon to suffer the stinging barbs of his words. Laon collapsed into a chair; his heart was broken, just as Murgan had predicted; he had been destroyed by the monster he had saved and nurtured and he was to shed many sour tears as a consequence.

On leaving Laon, Jodi went to the barracks to seek out Murgan. Now his only thought was to get to Tarnus and he didn't trust Laon to help him. As he approached the barracks he could hear an uproar issuing from it. He entered to discover the entire garrison, the four nurses and a few others cheering on a lewd performance consisting of five naked women and several soldiers who had been coerced by the women into compromising themselves for the entertainment of the others.

Jodi ignored the performance and arrested the attention of a soldier by pulling his hair. "Where's the Chief?" he shouted over the cacophony of baying troops.

"In the city," replied the man.

"Who's on guard?"

The man shrugged and pulled away. Jodi let him go and left them to it. He returned to Laon's chambers and threw some essential items into a sack, then, he ran out into the park and down the long road to the main gates. He discovered the sentry unit deserted, so he opened the gate and ran towards the city.

XIV

High in the snow-covered peaks of the Great Divide, the massive barrier that separated the fertile south from the tropical north on the single continent of Ennepp, a small spring of crystal water flowed from the melting tongue a glacier. It tumbled down the steep, craggy slope of the mountain until it joined other streams issuing from other valleys of the sierra. The augmented waters became a torrent that fell into the Northern Plain and surged across the land until its energy was spent and it meandered docilely to the northern shore of the Great Sea where a large, marshy delta had developed. On this unhealthy marshland the forefathers of the Bhasi had chosen to build their largest city, a conurbation of some four million called Gom.

As with all large cities, Gom retained within its precincts a diversity of citizens; tradesmen; merchants; villains and the idle rich. These social classes separated themselves from one another by means of elevation, with the wealthier occupying the higher ground while the poor endured the unhealthy conditions of the low-lying districts where a network of ancient canals drained the land. Here, in these less salubrious environments, the underbelly of Gom existed; tinkers and robbers, gamblers and drinkers and all manner of low individuals whose only purpose in life was to exist. It was to one such place that Jodi's path was inexorably bound. The city was drawing him in like sponge and he would soon be absorbed into its rotten heart.

Jodi ran easily under the stars towards the bright lights of the city. For the past year and a half he had led a life that few on Ennepp could enjoy; a life of privilege and comfort, his every whim indulged by a man who doted on him. But instead of enjoying the privilege he had come to resent the smothering, stultifying confinement of the palace. Now he was free of all that and a feeling of elation seized him as he ran lightly over the hard ground under a clear sky sparkling with the mist of a billion stars.

He looked up at the stars as he ran; his sister was out there on a planet orbiting one of those suns; he was certain of that; as certain as he had been of anything in his life and now all that mattered to him was to get to her; to save her and keep her safe just as he had promised on the morning he had left her standing with Minogi in the wide fields of the Southlands.

When he came to the outskirts of the city Jodi stopped running and put on the shoes that Laon had given him. He placed a cap over his head and smeared some of the black, alluvial soil from the fields on his face to darken it. He took out a knife from his sack and shoved it into the waistband of his pants, and then, he disappeared into the city.

The hour was late and few were about. Those that saw him paid little heed to a well-dressed young man whose dark face was obscured by shadow. Emboldened, he moved on into the increasingly dense metropolis, keeping away from bright lights as he made his way to the insalubrious heart of the city. No people of quality or wealth lived here for it was given over to nefarious activities in which the authorities took little interest. The centre was divided into a number of fiefdoms presided over by gang-lords who ran empires of entertainment catering for all tastes. There were gaudy drug dens and drinking houses, moneylenders and property traders; there were whorehouses and bathhouses and places of wager where a man's entire worth could be gambled on the toss of a golden coin. There were brilliantly lit houses of entertainment where actors would declaim stories imported from more fortunately talented worlds; there were dark places too, where ill-trained performers could wail illegal chants into smoky, underground rooms to clients too insensible to notice their paucity of talent.

And in the middle of this mélange of depravity sat the Temple of Minnar; a massive, shining beacon of order and wealth, for even the gang-lords paid their dues to the Temple.

Into this low district drifted Jodi on that starlit night. Even in the small hours the place was alive with people; men staggering along in a daze and pissing where they would in full view; women, loud and raucous, also pissing or wetting themselves with the sheer fun of it all. There were children scuttling about amongst the revellers, with apparent urgency, selling promises written on pieces of paper to anyone drunk or foolish enough to part with their money. Jodi lurked in the shadows watching it all and assessing in what way these people could be used for his ends. Suddenly he was approached from behind. He whirled around, his hand to his knife to discover a crippled youth, plain-faced and grubby, not much younger than himself. The lad was holding an orb from which sprang the gyrating image of a naked woman.

"Five hundred, Mister, she'll do anything you want."

Jodi stared at the fascinating image. "Can she get me to Tarnus?"

"Sure she can, she can do anything; I guarantee it. Come on, Mister, she's just down here." He beckoned and sidled off, dragging his crippled left leg along the dusty street behind him.

It seemed to Jodi a little unlikely that either this lame urchin or the woman in the image could fulfil the lad's claims, but he followed him into a dark side alley whereupon two heavy-set men sprang upon him. But the lad had chosen his victim ill and within a second both his assailants had been introduced to Jodi's knife. He sliced the throat of one and stabbed the other in the chest. They reeled away, staggering further into the alley eventually to collapse and draw their last breaths. The lad, suddenly aware that the usual plan had gone awry, turned around and promptly dropped the orb with the shock of what he had just witnessed.

"I wasn't expecting that," said Jodi with an unpleasant grin on his face. These were the first men he had ever killed and he felt a pleasant rush of adrenalin from the business. "Now where's the lady who can get me to Tarnus?"

The lad would have run, even with his gammy leg, but the alley was a dead-end and Jodi was in the way. "You killed them."

Jodi walked up to the inert bodies and kicked each in turn. "It looks like it." He picked up the spilled orb and shook it. There was no trace of the marvellous naked lady. He handed it to the lad. "Make her come back."

The lad took it nervously and the image reappeared.

Jodi studied it for a few moments. "How is she going to get me to Tarnus?"

"She can't," replied the lad nervously. "It's just an image to lure people."

"Lure them to what?"

"So we can rob them," replied the lad.

Jodi scratched his brow. "So it was just a trick. That's disappointing." He turned to go.

"Wait," cried the lad. "You killed my partners; I need a new one."

Jodi stopped. "Do you get much money?"

"Sometimes, but mostly we get gold and jewellery."

"Gold and jewellery? That could be of use to me."

"We split sixty-forty."

"Sixty for me and forty for you; that sounds fair."

The lad now perceived that he was not dealing with a dullard as he had thought. "Alright, fifty-fifty," he conceded quickly.

Jodi grinned. "What's your name?"

"Benobah," replied the lad. "What's yours?"

They caught their first victim less than an hour later. The unfortunate man was intoxicated and was easy prey. Jodi stabbed him through the neck from behind as the man followed his new partner into an alley some distance away from the first.

"Shit! You're not supposed to kill them," hissed the lad.

"Why not?"

"Because Tallon doesn't like bodies on his patch. It's bad for business."

"Who's Tallon?"

"Who's Tallon! He's the boss of this area, of course.

"Of course he is, I'd forgotten."

"Liar; you're not from here, are you?"

"No."

"I thought not; you look different; like some of the whores they get from the North."

"Is that a problem?"

"Shit! No; as long as do your job I don't care where you're from. We'd better call it a night; there's already three bodies thanks to you and there'll likely be Fort-men around, poking their noses into things."

"Where do we go?"

Benobah looked surprised. "You mean you got no place?"

"That's right."

"Better come with me then, 'till you get your own."

They followed a tortuous route between closely built, high tenements until the lad turned into a particularly run down slum and dragged himself up five flights of stairs. At the top of the building he entered an enclosure consisting of several interconnecting rooms. In each room slept one or two individuals, snoring loudly. The atmosphere was close and fetid as they passed through the rooms until they arrived at the furthest where two bedrolls occupied most of the available floor-space. Benobah lit a lantern to reveal the squalor of the room in which there was little beyond a crude table in the corner on which rested two metal plates of food. The lad grabbed a plate and began to eat.

Jodi put down his bag and pulled out some bread and offered it to the lad who took it and pushed some into his mouth. "Whose food is that?" he asked pointing to the spare plate.

"Collip, one of the guys you killed. I guess he won't be needing it; or his bed for that matter. You might as well take it."

Jodi took the dead man's food and began to eat. The taste was rough, but not unpleasant.

"The old girl next door cooks it. She don't charge much."

They finished the meal in silence and Benobah tossed his plate aside and stretched out on his bedroll and yawned. "Might as well get some sleep," he declared, dousing the light. "If you need a piss, it's outside by the stairs."

Jodi stretched out on the dead man's bedroll. It smelled musty and unwashed. Two years ago he would have thought it luxurious, but now it just seemed dirty and squalid. He looked up at the high, barred window and saw the stars and wondered how long it would be before he would be there amongst other suns.

He slept soundly, as he always did and when he awoke the grey light of day was drifting into the room. It was raining heavily and the walls were running with water and swelling a small pond in the corner. Benobah was nowhere to be seen, but soon Jodi heard his voice coming from one of the other rooms in the enclosure. He was pleading with somebody and then there was the sound of an angry man's voice and the sound of slapping and the thump of a body hitting the ground. Jodi sat up and listened. He heard heavy, echoing footsteps and then Benobah appeared at the door holding his face with blood trickling between his fingers.

"What happened to you?" asked Jodi.

Benobah scowled angrily. "Tallon's man; we didn't make enough last night." He opened his other hand to reveal a small amount of coinage. "The bastard's cheated us again."

Jodi looked at the money. "Is that all he gave you for what we got?"

"Bastard," complained the lad.

"Next time we'll take it to someone else."

"There is no one else. You deal with Tallon or nobody."

It now struck Jodi that Benobah's circumstances did not promise great wealth and whatever they stole would, in turn, be stolen from them by the Gang-lord, Tallon. This was something he was going to have to change if he was ever to get to Tarnus.

XV

Had Jodi penetrated the City of Gom a few hundred metres to the north, he might well have bumped into Murgan Doh, coming out of The Pink Emerald with three of his fellow officers. They had spent a great deal of money on the various relaxations provided by that establishment and they headed back to the palace in a land-cart much pleased with themselves. On returning to the palace, however, Murgan was obliged to reassess his mood, for it was evident that things had gone awry in his absence.

He took a sobering preparation that quickly restored his wits and raged about the place, whacking his chief officer clean across a guardroom and bellowing his other officers to their senses. He found the four nurses in the barrack hall splayed insensibly on the stone floor. He kicked each in turn but could get no rational response from any of them.

He rushed upstairs to the Commissioner's apartment and burst into the bedchamber. Laon was sitting on one of the ornate chairs next to the vat. The equipment surrounding it was a tangled mess and inside the vat the Commissioner's bloated body floated inertly, his last moments of terror fixed in bulging eyes.

"He's gone, Murgan," said Laon quietly.

Murgan looked into the dead face of the Commissioner. "I'll kill those nurses," he growled. "I take one night off and the whole, fucking place goes to shit."

"I'm not talking about him," replied Laon disparagingly. "It's Jodi, he's gone, Murgan."

"He did this, didn't he?"

Laon nodded. "He found out about Matty; he won't come back. You must find him. You must go now and find him."

"Let him go."

Laon looked up at his friend, his eyes red with tears. "I can't Murgan; I can't let him go."

Murgan took a turn among the wrecked equipment and considered. "Where will I look? Where would I start?"

"He's gone to the city, for sure."

"There are over four million people there; it's impossible."

"Don't say that. You could go to the fort."

"What do you suggest I ask them? Have you seen any sign of a murderous-looking half-breed?"

"Don't say that; don't call him that."

Murgan placed his large hands on his friend's shoulders. "Let him go, Laon; it's time. You have to move on now; we have business to attend to; we need to clear up this mess."

"I don't care about that any more."

"Well, I do. How long have we got?"

Laon glanced towards the vat. "About a hundred days; maybe a bit more if we keep it quiet."

"I'll see to it that nobody gets in here. You need to get to work; you need to transfer the remaining assets."

Laon nodded dejectedly. "Alright, I will."

"Good; and I need to sort out the barracks and get rid of those useless nurses." He left his boss weeping in the chair next to the dead Commissioner and returned to the barracks to create a few more sore heads.

XVI

During the hours of light Jodi kept himself to the dark, squalid room at the top of the tenement while his new companion went out and secured some items he considered necessary for the success of the new partnership. It had not escaped Benobah's notice that Jodi was probably a Native and, as such, would not be permitted in the city after sunset. Whereas this would not be particularly significant to those they robbed, it might be of interest to those with whom they lived for they would not be slow when it came to imparting information for a reward.

When the lad returned he had with him a wide brimmed hat and a ragged scarf, together with a jar of skin dye. He told Jodi to sit and dressed his face with the dye, darkening his complexion so that it more resembled that of a Bhasi. When he was finished, he stepped back to admire his efforts. A frown came to his face.

"You still don't look like one of us. Your face is all wrong. Put on the hat and wind the scarf around your face like a mask."

Jodi obeyed and the lad reassessed. "I think that will do, but you'll have to stay here during daylight. We'll have to keep the door bolted; I don't want any of those arseholes out there to see you."

"I'll read," replied Jodi.

"You can read? I can't."

This surprised Jodi; he had never before come across a Bhasi who could not read.

That evening Jodi donned his disguise and he and Benobah left the squalid room in the tenement and went about their sordid business. The young lad was increasingly pleased with is new companion for Jodi was far more effective than his two previous partners put together and now he only had to share the booty with one. His appearance was particularly intimidating and, on two occasions, their quivering victims just emptied their pockets without even being threatened. Their haul was particularly good that night and Jodi had managed not to kill anyone so, as they returned to the damp and dingy room in the tenement, in the small hours, Benobah was in a particularly buoyant mood.

"We'll get plenty for this lot," he declared as they climbed the stairs to their room.

"When will Tallon's man come again?"

"Tomorrow, before midday."

"I'll see him this time."

"No, that's not a good idea; he knows me."

"Yes, he knows you alright; he knows he can take the piss out of you."

Benobah stopped climbing the stairs and turned to face his companion. "Jodi, listen to me, you don't know how things work around here. If you make trouble, they'll come after you and me, and they won't stop until they've killed us both."

"I'm not going to make trouble: I'm going to be nice."

"No you won't. I know you."

"You don't know anything about me."

"I've seen you murder three people without even thinking about it and that's enough for me."

Jodi let the subject drop but he was determined that his efforts should not be undervalued. His one aim was to get to Tarnus and he wasn't about to allow any minion of a gang-lord to stand in his way.

Just as the previous night, they stole past the sleeping tenement dwellers and settled in the dingy room at the end. Jodi removed the mask and hat to reveal his incongruous, nut-brown complexion.

Benobah laughed at him. "You look like a freak," he declared.

Jodi peered at himself in a cracked reflector dangling from a rusty cleat. "Does this stuff come off?"

"It wears off eventually; may take a few years."

"I haven't got a few years," replied Jodi pensively.

The next morning Jodi awoke to discover Benobah gone. It wasn't long before he heard the sound of the lad's voice mingled with a deeper, gruffer voice outside the door. He rose and put on scarf that shielded the lower half of his face and went outside. He found the lad with a large, heavy-set man on the landing; Benobah was pleading with the fellow who had a handful of the lad's hair and was about to rough him up. Jodi came and stood behind his companion and fixed his eyes on the gang-lord's agent.

"Who the fuck is this?" growled the man.

"My new partner," replied Benobah urgently. "Jodi, go back inside."

"Let him go," said Jodi quietly.

"Fuck off and mind your own business," replied the man, jostling the lad roughly.

"This is my business: you're cheating us."

"Oh shit!" wailed the lad as the big man went for his sidearm.

It didn't clear his waistband. The blade flashed through the air and buried itself in the man's neck. His eyes bulged in surprise as blood immediately began to pulse from the wound. He reeled and stumbled down the stairs, clutching at the protruding knife. Jodi watched impassively as the man fell at the next flight and began to tumble down its length. Benobah was not so impassive; he put his head in his hands and began to wail, "Oh shit!" over and over again.

Jodi walked down the two flights and peered at the body lying on the landing of the floor below. He pulled his knife from the man's neck, wiped it on his victim's shirt and placed it back into his waistband.

Benobah came down and joined him. "Is he dead?"

"Of course he's dead."

"Jodi, you don't know what you've done. Tallon will have his whole fucking army out looking for this bastard and if they find us... you have no idea what he'll do to us."

"They won't find us," replied Jodi calmly. "Check his pockets, take everything; I'll go and get our stuff. We're moving."

"Where to?"

"You know the city, where do you suggest?"

Benobah shrugged. "There's only one place left; the riverside."

"That's it then," replied Jodi climbing the stairs. "It sounds good to me."

"That's because you haven't been there."

XVII

"Let me understand you correctly. You want me to go to a city where I would be instantly arrested if discovered; find an individual who does not want to be found and take him to a world on which no sane person would live; stay with him there until he satisfies himself that his sister no longer lives; then smuggle him on to Barta Magnus. Have I assessed your request correctly?"

Laon rubbed his ear and nodded. "I fear you have."

The Moontrader, Sevarius, stretched his long legs and stared out into the empty darkness of the palace park. "You presume on our friendship, Laon."

"I know. It is a lot to ask a man, even one such as you."

"I do not understand your attachment."

"I made a promise to his sister, the young girl you brought to me. I promised her that I would look after him."

"Surely you must feel you discharged that duty to the full. As I understand it you rescued him and nurtured him and he ran away of his own free will. I cannot see why you still feel responsible."

"Do you have any children?"

"I have one son, on Kagan."

"Wouldn't you do anything you could to get him out of trouble?"

The Moontrader took a long swig of his wine. "I have not seen my son for nine years, but, the answer to your question is yes."

"I love Jodi as a son, Sevarius, and there is nothing I wouldn't do to protect him. You are the only man I know with the means to achieve this; I know it's asking a great deal of you, but I beg you to say yes."

Sevarius considered. Laon had offered him a huge sum; a sum that would set him up for the rest of his life. He wasn't getting any younger and the prospect was tempting. "You have the means to honour your promise?"

Laon nodded. "I do."

"I take it you have been embezzling your late employer dry?"

"I have."

Just then Murgan approached the terrace from the darkness of the park. A sidearm instantly appeared in Sevarius's hand.

Murgan froze at the sight of the weapon and its owner. He did not have to be told that he was facing a Moontrader. "You didn't tell me you were expecting company."

"This is my friend Sevarius," said Laon. "Sevarius, this is my Chief of Staff; the weapon won't be necessary."

"A man who walks out of the darkness should be more careful," said Sevarius. "You will disarm yourself."

Murgan glanced at Laon who nodded and, with his thumb and forefinger, he slowly removed his weapon and placed it on the ground.

"Come and have a drink with us," said Laon.

Murgan climbed on to the terrace and sat down while Laon strolled inside for a goblet.

"I guess he's asked you to find Jodi," said Murgan.

Sevarius nodded gravely. "What do you know of the boy?"

"He is fixated with the idea of finding his sister and means to get himself to Tarnus."

"He's a half-breed, is he likely to have survived in Gom?"

"I spent three days searching for him; I didn't find anything. He's resourceful and wily; it's likely he's in there somewhere. You might start by looking anywhere the murder count has increased."

"He's violent?"

"Don't turn your back on him and don't get into a knife fight with him."

"What did you say?" asked Laon, returning with the goblet.

"I was asking your chief about Jodi," said Sevarius.

"The Chief is not a fan," replied Laon, pouring some wine into empty goblet. "He trained Jodi but he is not pleased with his student."

Murgan took a swig. "Jodi is angry with himself, everybody and everything."

"He has plenty to be angry about," replied Laon.

"Maybe so, but he treated you shockingly."

"I betrayed him; I should have told him about Matty being here; I should have been more honest."

"He didn't know his sister was here?" said Sevarius.

Laon shook his head dejectedly. "I thought he would just go after her and I would lose him too."

"And that's exactly what has happened," pointed out Murgan.

Sevarius frowned. "Does he have an unnatural attachment to his sister?"

Laon shrugged. "It's possible; she's was only his half-sister and you saw how lovely she was. Such things are not uncommon in the Pal Race."

"It is a very singular devotion," said Sevarius. "I will go after your boy; I will look for three days and nights in Gom, but no more and if I find him I will take him to Tarnus. May the Prophet have mercy on me."

"How will you go about finding him?" asked Murgan.

"I shall offer him what he most wants in the world and he will find me."

XVIII

Two days after his conversation with Laon, Sevarius sat in the corner of a dingy establishment nursing a drink. It was late and the gentle thump of rain on the metal roof provided a monotonous background noise. A single light flickered timidly above the bar where two women lounged soporifically chatting to the hard-eyed, overweight, sweaty female who owned the place. He had spent two days asking around in all the lowest joints in the city, leaving the message that he was bound for Tarnus and looking for crew. Without fail they'd looked at him as if he was mad to leave this paradise for Tarnus, but the message got out and now all he had to do was wait in the place he said he would be.

They were near the river and Sevarius had heard stories hereabouts of two characters, a cripple and a masked man who had robbed upwards of thirty people in the last six days. Some were killed but survivors spoke of a pathetic cripple begging for money as a distraction before a ghost-like fiend, suddenly appearing from nowhere, with the blackest eyes they had ever seen and a hideous mask covering his lower features. There was quite a posse looking for these two criminals; the officers in the fort were galvanized into action by the complaints of the gang-masters who had begun to lose business as the frightened punters of Gom stayed clear of their establishments. There had even been a meeting of gang-masters who had declared a truce until the felons had been caught and executed. But no one knew where they were and no one had given them up, despite the incentive of a substantial bounty.

He saw the cripple first, glancing in as he passed the door. Their eyes met for the briefest of moments and then he was gone. A second figure lurked in the darkness outside and then disappeared. Sevarius stiffened and his hand close around the sidearm holstered inside his britches. A few moments later a voice came from behind, through a hole in the flimsy, wooden wall of the building.

"There is a charged weapon aimed at your head. Convince me you are not the bait of a trap."

Sevarius smiled to himself; the boy was rightly cautious. "What would you like to hear, my friend?"

"Why are you going to Tarnus?"

"I am a trader, I have business there."

"Nobody goes to Tarnus for trade; I do not believe you."

"I didn't say it was legal trade."

"You are a Moontrader?"

"You may think what you like."

"Moontraders travel alone; I am not convinced."

Sevarius now saw that he would have to reveal himself. "You are right not to be convinced, my friend. I have been sent here to find you by one who loves you."

"I do not want anything from him and I will not go back."

"I do not like speaking through walls; come in and sit with me."

Moments later Sevarius saw his quarry for the first time. His skin and clothes were exceedingly dirty and he carried around with him the unsavoury odour of one who had probably been living in a sewer. Jodi sat down opposite the Moontrader and scrutinised his face. He saw a man in his early fifties, lean and yet muscular, with grey, penetrating eyes.

"I could have easily killed you," said Jodi.

Sevarius nodded. "Perhaps. You have gained yourself quite a reputation. Practically everyone in the city is looking for you."

"They won't catch me."

"I caught you in two days."

"It was I who had the weapon trained on you."

Sevarius smiled frostily. "I have been commissioned to take you to Tarnus."

"I don't need Laon's help."

"Really?" Sevarius sniffed the air. "You live well in the sewers, do you? How long do you think you've got before they catch up with you?"

"They haven't caught me yet and I will soon have enough to get away from here."

"Do you have a death wish, Jodi, or are you just a stupid half-breed?"

He saw a flash of anger in the boy's eyes and his hand tensed on the weapon.

"How much is he paying you?"

"That's none of your business. I'm going to leave now; it's up to you to choose whether you stay here and die in this excremental swamp or come to Tarnus."

He stood and strode to the bar and flicked a coin towards the fat owner. "You know that if you make contact with anyone I will come back and kill you all," he said to the bemused woman.

Jodi followed him out of the dump. "Alright, I'll go with you."

Sevarius nodded and walked around the back of the dive to where Jodi had been standing. As Jodi watched he stooped down and uncovered a small device that he had buried there earlier and put it in his pocket. "A molecular disrupter; had I thought you were really going to shoot, I'd have fried you," he said.

At that moment Jodi understood the nature of the man he was dealing with and the seed of a grudging respect was sown.

"What do I call you?"

"Sevarius."

"I have a request, Sevarius."

The Moontrader raised an eyebrow. "A request?"

"Yes, there is something I want to do before I leave Ennepp. It will be of some advantage to you."

"Very well, but first I want you to tell your companion to take his weapon off me."

Benobah emerged from the deep shadow between two shacks.

"Drop the sidearm," said Jodi.

"You got to take me with you," replied the lad.

Sevarius shook his head. "That is not possible."

Benobah raised the weapon in threat. "I can't stay here without Jodi; they'll kill me."

Jodi went up to him. "No they won't. Take my share and get out of Gom. There's enough to set you up somewhere else. Do something different with your life."

"I don't know nothing else; only robbing."

"You're smart; you can learn."

The lad lowered the weapon and dropped his head. "I'll miss you Jodi."

Jodi roughed his hair. "Yeah, for all of five minutes. Now go; get well away from the city and don't come back."

The lad gave him a mournful look and hugged him. They said their goodbyes and he limped off into the darkness.

"My craft is quite near," said Sevarius, turning away. "I don't mean to remain here one second beyond necessity."

Jodi fell in behind his new companion. "I want to go to Zurat," he said.

XIX

It was still the blackest night when Sevarius landed in the same square in Zurat in which Matty had seen Jodi being led by the old miser over two years before. Very little had passed between the two men as they flew over the Great Sea towards the south; neither were garrulous and Jodi was occupied with the thought of what he was about to do. They landed in the square and an involuntary shiver went up his spine at the sight of it. It threw him back to the horror of his existence at the hands of the miser and reassured him that what he was about to do was right.

"I know why you have asked me to bring you here," said Sevarius. "Do you want me to come with you?"

Jodi stood. "No, I will do this myself."

He left the craft and walked across the square and plunged into the tortuous, narrow alleys of Zurat until he came upon the familiar hovel at the end of the alley. He stood still in the grey light of the stars and the recollection of his decline and suffering flooded back to him in stark detail. He scaled the wall and jumped down into the yard. In the shadowy corner he caught sight of the pile of charred bones and the anger he harboured was further distilled. He went to the lean-to and quietly unbolted it. It was pitch black inside, but the familiar clink of the metal tether informed him that Culas Culah had not foresworn his addiction to the degradation and suffering of his fellow men. He took down the lantern the old miser kept outside the lean-to and lit it. Frightened eyes blinked up at him from the pallet and he beheld a youngster of his own race of about fourteen or fifteen with the sunken, hollow look of starvation on his drawn face.

"Don't be frightened," whispered Jodi, "I am going to set you free."

He took out his sidearm and fired it at the chain, instantly melting the links by the pole that was set into the centre of the floor. Then he melted another section near to the lad's neck and took the free length of chain in his hand.

He doused the lantern and turned to the boy. "When I lock this door, bang on it and call out."

"I can't, he'll come and he'll hurt me again."

Jodi placed his hand on the boy's shoulder. "Do as I tell you; he's never going to hurt you or anybody else ever again."

He shut the boy in and the lad duly started banging and calling out. A light came on in the shack and the door opened and Culas Culah came shuffling out in his nightdress, cursing and threatening. "I'll kill that little…"

His words were choked off by the chain wrapped around his neck from behind and he was propelled inside the shack by someone much stronger that himself, without even a chance to call out for help.

Jodi pressed him to the floor and put his knee in his back as he tightened the chain. "Where is it?" he hissed into the old miser's ear.

Culas spluttered and choked out, "I… I don't know what you mean."

Jodi pulled out his knife and stabbed his victim in the right buttock. He tightened the chain to truncate the scream of pain. "I won't ask again."

"Please, I am a poor man; I have nothing of value."

Jodi stabbed the other buttock and his victim tried to scream again but his larynx could gain no air. Blood flowed from his cuts and stained the dirty mat that covered the stone floor.

"The next cut will be to your throat. Speak and I will let you live," said Jodi, slightly releasing the pressure on the chain.

Culas started to sob pathetically. "Under the table," he rasped.

Jodi dragged the man cross the floor and kicked over the table. The remains of a meal went clattering to the ground. He pulled back the mat to reveal a sophisticated safe set into the stone.

He yanked viciously on the chain. "Open it."

"No, please… Please, I am just a poor peasant."

Jodi yanked on the chain again. "Open it or die."

Sobbing profusely, Culas passed his shaking hand over the sensor and touched a sequence of points on the surface of the safe. The heavy door opened to reveal a hoard of silver coin, some gold and a few poor quality gemstones.

Jodi flipped his victim over and Culas saw his assailant for the first time. His old eyes tried to focus.

"Do you recognize me, old man?"

Culas gurgled. "Please don't take it all; leave a poor man something."

"I am the half-breed you almost starved to death."

"I never starved anyone; I am a good man. Please don't take all of my money. For the love of the Prophet, leave me some."

"You want your money, old man? Well here it is."

Jodi plunged his hand into the safe and pulled out a handful of coin and forced it into the miser's mouth, breaking what remained of his rotten teeth. "Eat it you miserable fucker," he hissed as he continued to cram coins and precious stones into the gaping mouth of his victim. Culas began to gag as the treasure was savagely forced into him. His eyes bulged as he tried to get air into his lungs and then he recognized the face of the man who was murdering him with his own hoard. Jodi pressed his knee into the man's chest, covered his mouth with one hand and held his nose with the other. The old miser flailed and tried to scratch at his assailant but he was no match for Jodi and the struggle was brief. Finally

Culas was still, his mouth wide with coin accumulated from a lifetime of parsimony and the misery of others.

Jodi rose and went outside. He looked up at the stars and a wave of euphoria seized him. He had a taste for killing but none had felt as sweet as this. He unbolted the lean-to and led the frightened occupant into the shack. The lad gawped at what he saw, then he made for the remains of Culas' last meal scattered on the floor and began to crawl about, eating it as fast as he could. Jodi found the keys to the lad's collar and choker and stopped him eating long enough to release him from them. Then he took a sack and filled it with the contents of the safe and what had spilled from the old miser's mouth.

When he stood he noticed the lad watching him from the corner of the room as he chewed greedily. "I am Jodi Saronaga and you are now free to go. Take the coin from this man's mouth and whatever you need and leave Zurat this night. Never come back here in your life."

He slung the sack over his back and walked out of the shack. Years later the lad would tell his children of the night he met Jodi Saronaga, the man who saved his life.

"It is done," said Jodi as he entered the craft. He emptied the sack out onto the deck in front of Sevarius. "This will be my payment to you; I do not wish to be indebted to Laon for this good fortune."

Sevarius glanced at the treasure. "It is a very small fraction of the price he paid me."

"Then I will work for you until it is paid."

Sevarius grinned mirthlessly. "I work alone and ten lifetimes would not be enough to recompense me. Sit down, it is time to leave."

Jodi sat next to his new companion and watched the craft rise into the skies above Zurat. He was leaving Ennepp for good; a world where he could only ever be the lowest form of humanity; a world where he had suffered terrible deprivations, pain and sorrow; but, even so, a pang of melancholy seized his soul. He was leaving behind his carefree childhood in the North and the rare days of happiness on the estate in the Southlands. He was leaving the place where the kind and fatherly overseer, Minogi had protected him and taught him to read and the farm where the Bhasi woman, Rea had shown him compassion and taught him about sex. He was leaving the opulent world of the palace near Gom where his friend Murgan had taught him to fight and kill and where, for a time, he had been able to live like a normal human being.

But most of all, he was leaving behind the world where he and Matty had been brought into existence and grown up as one and he knew then that, whatever the foul abuse and suffering this world had dealt him, he would always be a child of Ennepp.

PART THREE

WAR

I

Aurex's return to Kagan from his successful mission to Tarnus filled him with particular satisfaction. He had stymied the foul blasphemy of his own kinsman, the Arkon of the DeRhogai, and seen the incarceration of Lodan, his libertine great nephew, at the hands of the most despised despot in the galaxy. The journey had afforded him ample time to think about what to do next and it seemed to him that he must ignore the advice of the Serene Master of the Brotherhood, who counselled caution. Aurex saw clearly that the integrity of the DeRhogai clan had been compromised by the actions of the Arkon and it was now necessary to confront the Arkon and depose him for his heretical activities. This, Aurex knew, was a momentous notion, for the deposition of a sitting Arkon had not been attempted for over a thousand years.

Aurex also knew that to achieve his ends he had to have the general support of the elders of the clan and he spent the next fifteen days quietly and secretly soliciting those he knew to be dissatisfied with the Arkon. When he was sure of his ground he chose to make his move at a morning meeting of the elders sixteen days after his return from Tarnus.

The group went into the great audience chamber expectantly and waited for the entrance of the Arkon. When the ancient man came through the door of his private quarters and limped stiffly around the huge, stone image of the Lord Minnar, they fell to their knees and touched the polished floor with their foreheads as respectful tradition required. There was an expectant atmosphere as the Arkon took his throne and invited them all to rise.

Aurex stepped forward. "Lord and Master, we greet you in the respectful spirit of our ancestors. This Council is convened."

The Arkon swept the familiar faces of his kinsmen. Many did not meet his eye and he saw that something was amiss. "Who will speak first?" he said.

Aurex bowed slightly. His heart was beating fast and his palms were clammy with sweat. He knew that what he was about to do was unprecedented in modern times. "Most Respected Lord, there has been disquiet that you have lost your judgement to the extent of harbouring an undesirable alien in the palace."

The Arkon stared at his subject with a look of disdainful incredulity. "Are you challenging my authority, Cedum Cedanus?"

Aurex took a deep, unsteady breath. "I am."

The Arkon allowed an intimidating silence to fall before speaking slowly and deliberately. "You say I have lost my judgement and that I have caused an undesirable alien to be harboured within this palace?"

"In your own chambers, my Lord. A Suran devil, no less."

The Arkon stood and addressed the Council. "Do you understand what is being attempted here? An action that, once done, can never be undone."

These words were greeted by an ominous silence from those behind him and Aurex sensed that their loyalty was shrinking before the intimidating majesty of the Arkon.

"Cedum Cedanus, go into my private chambers and bring out the person you find in there."

Aurex bowed; his mind whirled with doubt as he walked behind the great statue and entered the Arkon's private quarters.

Outside the Arkon re-seated himself on the throne and addressed the Council. "I speak to you with the authority of a hundred generations; an authority granted by the Spirit of the Prophet himself; an infallible authority, for my words come from the ancient heart of the One True Faith; that is why an Arkon cannot be challenged except by the taking of life. Who here will fetch his sword and run it through my heart?"

At this the elders fell on their knees and started wailing. Aurex returned alone and stared at them. He saw that he had lost and that the consequences of his failed challenge would be fatal.

"There was a Suran here," he called out. "I have evidence of it."

The elders looked up.

"The Physician will confirm it," insisted Aurex desperately.

The Arkon shook his head sadly. "My good friend, Doctor Sokolom passed away eighteen days ago. I am surprised you did not hear of it."

"I was away on Tarnus, thwarting your plans," blurted Aurex and instantly knew he had spoken in too much haste.

The Arkon's face seemed to freeze; his eyes narrowed on Aurex. "Clear the hall," he growled ominously.

The elders hurriedly scrambled to their feet and retreated. "Not you," said the Arkon as Aurex tried to follow.

The great doors closed and left the two men alone. The Arkon pointed a bony finger at his clansman. "Cedum Cedanus, what have you done?"

"I have stopped you destroying the faith of your ancestors. Even as we speak, Lodan Sevarius toils in the Mine of Kusk on Tarnus where he will perish. He will not be your salvation."

"You fool, you complete and utter fool; you have no idea what you have done."

"I know exactly what I have done; I know about the Suran devils, Solon Bru and Herton Lim; I know about the Fourth Proposition; I know of the heresy of which you are a part. You have no faith, you are a fraud and you always have been."

"I see that the expectation of your own condemnation has loosened your tongue, but you have misplaced your loyalties. I have always doubted your suitability to succeed me in this office because your principal loyalty is not to the Family; it is to the Brotherhood of Mercy. I know that you dance like a puppet when that charlatan DeCoronne whistles his tune. I bet he counselled you strongly against this challenge, for this would not suit his purpose at all. You aspired to become Arkon of this family, imagining that one day, you would also become the Serene Master of the Brotherhood and the most powerful man on Kagan. Do you really think that DeCoronne would allow the title of Serene Master to leave his own clan? Because of what you have done, Cedum Cedanus, you would have inherited nothing on my death. The family is busted; broke; wiped out. Lodan was our last hope."

Aurex's jaw dropped. But... But that's impossible. The DeRhogai are the wealthiest clan; the whole of Kagan knows it."

"The whole of Kagan *believes* it, and that is the façade I have managed to maintain. But our wealth has been in decline for over a century; it started with my predecessor and I have been unable to halt the decline. In fact I have accelerated it by making some injudicious investments; ironically enough one of them in the very company whose president started this affair by his discovery of an ancient fragment of written material." The Arkon allowed himself a faint smile. "When DeCorronne discovers you are a pauper, how long do you think his support for you will last?"

Aurex bowed his head dejectedly. "How long do we have?"

"About ten years, then the creditors will spook and the whole edifice that I have painstakingly built will come crashing down on our heads. It will affect the entire economy of Kagan and every other world on which bankers and financiers speculate. Because of your rash actions people that once thought themselves wealthy will suddenly find themselves impoverished and those already impoverished will become paupers."

"I don't understand; how could Lodan have prevented this?"

The Arkon dealt him a disdainful look. "You believe that Mankind was created in a mud-pool on Agon three thousand years ago; well, that is your affair, but I know that there were human beings in this galaxy one hundred and twenty thousand years ago. So it is time to throw off superstition and take a good look at what the evidence tells us. Whoever finds the original seat of human civilization will control everything; the knowledge and the unimaginable treasures that must be awaiting discovery. It will alter history and scatter everything we believe to the four points of the compass and we, the DeRhogai could have been at the centre of it all; we could have pulled the strings; we could have controlled the destiny of the entire human race."

Aurex gazed into the bright, crazed eyes of the Arkon. At first he was outraged but then he recalled what he had seen in the vault, deep under the Temple of Minnar and doubt began to oppress him and a profound emptiness crept into his soul. He began to sob and he raised his tearful face to that of the Prophet, serene and sightless in polished stone. "Why do you not send me a sign?" he wailed.

"You are addressing a carved lump of rock," said the Arkon, dryly. "It has no power other that that which you, yourself instil in it. Did you really believe that all this is about the puerile outpourings of a long dead peasant from Agon? You are a fool. This is about power and wealth; that is what the Faith is about; it is what it has always been about; the Arkon of the DeCorrone knows it just as well as I and just as well as anyone with any rational sense. We have our temples and our ceremonies to dupe the people and make them believe in a higher power; we frighten them into obedience with our threats of excommunication and eternal damnation while all the time skinning them of every piece of loose change they possess so that we can build more temples and fine palaces for the those who already have too much. No, Cedum Cedanus, you have not understood the basic truth of the Faith and you have not understood the nature of power. Go now, leave this place; you know what you must do."

II

"Do you feel sorrow?" asked Sevarius.

Jodi gazed through the window at the receding orb of his home world and did not answer.

"It is natural to feel melancholy when one is leaving everything behind," continued Sevarius. "I, myself am an exile; I have not seen my home or family for nine years."

"Do you like being a Moontrader?"

"It is an interesting, if hazardous, life."

"Why did Laon ask you specifically?"

"We are friends and I owed him my duty; he knew I would not refuse."

"Laon has done a lot for me," reflected Jodi, as if speaking to himself.

"Yes he has, more than you know."

"I don't understand him. I never showed him any affection and yet he helped me."

"It was a promise to your sister that he was honouring; he could not save her so he saved you instead."

Ahead of them a distant light grew brighter. Sevarius pointed towards it. "That is my ship."

"Do you have books on it?"

"There is plenty to read, but no books."

"I want to learn about Tarnus."

"I can tell you all you need to know. It is a world in a perpetual state of civil war. There are five states called Divisions and all of the Divisions hate all of the others. They have devastated their world and rendered large parts of it uninhabitable. They are ignorant, brutal people who would cut off your head just for the pleasure of it."

"And this is the place that Matty was brought to."

"By another Moontrader, Salex Contran; a young and reckless fellow."

"Where did he die?"

"Eramon, in the Division of Trant."

"Then that is where I want to go."

"Do you expect to find Matty alive?"

"I don't know; something inside me tells me she is not dead."

"You must love her very much to maintain such a remote hope."

"She is everything to me and always will be."

Sevarius glanced to his side and caught Jodi's sad and thoughtful profile. It was a singular devotion that caused him to wonder at the true nature of their relationship. "Did Laon tell you how Matty came to the palace?"

"Not really."

"It was I who brought her there."

He felt Jodi's gaze upon him but kept his eyes on the approaching outline of his ship. "I obtained her from a man named Gollik."

"He was the workmaster of the estate."

"I do not normally trade in people; I paid him nothing."

"But you received money for her, didn't you?"

"A handsome amount as I recall."

"And you felt happy with that?"

"I am a Moontrader, Jodi; I seek a profit in many areas of dubious morality. Under the circumstances it was the best I could do for her."

"That's alright then; as long as you felt happy about it," returned Jodi sarcastically.

"I am not responsible for the social arrangement of Ennepp."

"But you don't mind profiting from it."

No, I don't mind," returned Sevarius flatly.

The journey from Ennepp to Tarnus was thus begun under something of a strain. Sevarius learned that Jodi was a young man who was quite capable of maintaining a grudge and little passed between them beyond spare and terse snippets of conversation. Sevarius did not mind this state of affairs; he was well used to his own company on board and would have had no objection if he had never seen any trace of his passenger. For his part, Jodi kept to his cabin and read material on the history and geography of Tarnus. He took his meals alone and steered clear of Sevarius when he could.

But, despite their difference of opinion, Jodi had already developed a regard for his host. He recognized in him a kindred spirit with an unemotional single-mindedness that appealed to him despite himself. Sevarius was not trying to be anything other than what he was; a man unburdened with the baggage of scruples. At the end of the third day of their journey, he approached the man with a request.

"Will you teach me about this ship?"

Sevarius raised a sceptical eyebrow. "You understand that you will not be able to control this vessel; it will respond only to my commands."

"I understand that, but I would still like to learn."

Sevarius considered. "Very well, I will teach you the rudiments of navigation."

It was from this point that a mutual regard grew. As they conversed, Sevarius began to understand his passenger and was impressed with the mental acuity of the young man. It seemed to him that Jodi had only to be told or shown something once and it was committed to memory and reproduced at appropriate moments. For his part, Jodi was confirmed in his initial impression of Sevarius and his respect for him increased with every day. They began to take meals together and to enter into philosophical discussions about all manner of subjects upon which Jodi usually found his host well versed and considered.

On the sixth day of the journey Sevarius received a communication that greatly surprised him and he knew would not meet Jodi's approval.

"I have received a summons to go to Kagan," he announced. "I am obliged to divert there directly."

Jodi frowned. "Your contract is to take me to Tarnus."

"You will go to Tarnus, but first I must go to Kagan. I have no choice in the matter."

"Why can't you leave me on Tarnus and then go to Kagan?"

"Normally that is what I would do, but in this case I can't. The nature of the summons is such that I cannot ignore it and must proceed with all haste. I am sorry, Jodi, Tarnus will have to wait."

Sevarius expected a petulant reaction but Jodi was surprisingly sanguine about the alteration. He accepted it without further protest and it did not affect their growing relationship. In truth, the more Jodi read about Tarnus, the more he became convinced that Matty was unlikely to have survived there for any length of time, even if she had survived the destruction of Salex Contran's ship. To delay this confirmation was not particularly unpalatable.

III

Jodi's first impression of Kagan was the heat. It hit him like a stifling wall as he alighted from Sevarius' shuttle. His second impression was the size of the pristine buildings that towered out of a green oasis in the desert. Never before had he seen such structures; great shining walls, reflecting the hard sun like huge mirrors attesting to the wealth of the inhabitants. A contingent of twelve guards approached them as they walked across the landing apron, putting Jodi on his metal. The chief of the guards bowed deferentially before Sevarius. "Are you unarmed, Sir?"

"We are," replied Sevarius, halting and waiting while the guard scanned him and afterwards Jodi.

"Will you take the transportation, Sir?" asked the guard having finished the scan.

"We will walk," replied Sevarius. "It is not a great distance."

"As you wish, Sir," replied the guard respectfully.

Jodi caught the deferential tone and relaxed, looking about him at the shining towers and the verdant, pristine parkland as they progressed. The ceremonially dressed guards marched, in strict order, either side of them as they crossed the private landing area and headed up a wide avenue between two soaring, crystal-like structures. At the end of the avenue they passed through a pair of grand, intricately carved gates, into an even more sublime park where ornate fountains played upon polished stone and well-dressed citizens strolled in casual conversation. As they passed by the conversations stopped and those that knew who they were looking at gawped and whispered to their fellows behind their hands. The park was dominated by a large building of great quality, constructed entirely of opalescent stone that glowed in the stark light of the sun.

"This is the palace of the Arkon; the head of my family," said Sevarius as they approached the great flight of wide steps leading to the huge, arched door.

The guard of honour, now sweating profusely in their heavy uniforms, halted at the door and did not enter the building.

"Thank you," said Sevarius and he and Jodi went into the cool, high vestibule where they were met by a clerk in a flowing, white gown.

"Welcome back, Sir," said the Chief Clerk, bowing slightly and leading them to the impressive staircase that led up to the Hall of the Throne. The Chief Clerk opened the heavy door for them and bowed again as they walked past him into the throne room. The Arkon was seated, quite alone in front of the great statue of the Prophet, his face a stern mask of disapproval. Sevarius approached with Jodi behind him, pointedly paying him no obeisance.

"I see you have forgotten your manners," uttered the Arkon.

"You forget, I am stateless and no longer a DeRhogai - by your authority."

The Arkon scowled and his eyes flickered towards Jodi. "And this is the associate of whom you spoke?"

"This is Jodi Saronaga of Ennepp."

"I am not content with his presence."

Sevarius remained silent, both men knew why Jodi had been brought to the audience; it was a deliberate insult to the Arkon who was not given a choice in the matter.

"No doubt you are anxious to know why I have rescinded the banishment and summoned you here." He slipped from the throne and ambled around the effigy towards the door of his chambers. "Come, we will be more at ease in my private quarters. That young man must stay here."

"Jodi is my family; he is my son; he will go where I go and hear what I hear."

The Arkon turned but the objection died on his lips. He nodded and went into his chambers.

Sevarius and Jodi followed the old man into the more intimate environment of his private apartment. Sevarius had been here twice before, when he was in favour and destined to succeed to the throne. The strong smell of incense pervaded the thick air; the brazier in the centre flickered languidly and cast a sparse, ruddy light upon the vaulted ceiling and the faces of long dead, former incumbents on the walls.

The Arkon sat and indicated a place for Sevarius while Jodi found a stool and seated himself behind and to the right of Sevarius. This was highly unusual for it was not normally permitted to sit in the presence of the Arkon and Sevarius took his seat with a sense of foreboding.

"This will be a difficult conversation," began the Arkon, "both for me to say and for you to hear. It concerns your son, Lodan."

Sevarius visibly stiffened and girded himself for bad news. "Is he dead?"

"I don't know; he presently languishes in the Mine of Kusk, in the Division of Rion on Tarnus."

Sevarius' look of blank horror defied description. "My son is in the Mine of Kusk!" he uttered incredulously.

"He is."

The tremor of rising anger in Sevarius's voice could not be mistaken. "And how did he come to be there?"

"Forgive me, for it was by my design that he went to Tarnus, but I was betrayed by my own kinsman and Lodan Sevarius was taken."

Sevarius stood suddenly. "I should choke the life out of you for this. You sent my son to Tarnus! Knowing his character?"

"My life is near its end, it would be a blessing if it could be ended now, but if you will, let your friend here do it, he looks easily capable; let it not be at the hands of my own descendant."

"You're right, old man; he is capable of wringing your scrawny neck but I would not have him suffer the consequences on my behalf."

"Then sit down and I will explain at length what you should know."

Sevarius sank back into his chair as the flames illuminated the raw anger on his face. "I am prepared to listen," he whispered ominously.

The Arkon produced a torn sheet of material trapped within transparencies from the folds of his white gown and held it up to the light. "This object was discovered on the fourth world of a star designated KT153/2739, in the local spiral arm. It is undoubtedly of human origin and has been dated to more than one hundred and twenty thousand years old." The Arkon leaned forward slightly. "It means that towards the outer edge of our galaxy lies a civilization of great antiquity, yet undiscovered. This evidence fell into the hands of a Suran called Solon Bru who, having twice escaped the murderous attentions of the Brotherhood, fled to Tarnus along with a young Suran student called Jun Siu. On Tarnus Bru was fortunate enough to run into Magred DeCorrone, a fugitive woman of Kagan, who assisted him to escape the agent of the Brotherhood once again. The woman Magred out-smarted the agent, a man called Dax, also of the DeCorrone Clan and seized the deep-space cruiser belonging to the Brotherhood. Forty-one days ago, she, along with the two Surans and another person, left Tarnus bound for the KT region in search of this ancient civilization. You don't need me to tell you of the consequences to the Faith, if they succeed.

"Unfortunately they will not succeed for they were tracked and pursued by Dax who was supplied with another deep-space cruiser. My design was to send Lodan after them, to neutralize Dax and secure the treasures of the civilization for our family. To do this I required the utmost secrecy and so I negotiated with a contact I had established in the military of Rion. This man was to provide the cruiser necessary for Lodan's mission, but he was betrayed. The contact was executed and Lodan was sent to the Mine of Kusk."

Sevarius sat deep in silent thought as the tale unfolded. The reddish light of the brazier flickered on his stern features for a few moments of contemplation. "How long has Lodan been in the mine?'

"Twenty-three days."

"It is very likely he is still alive then."

"You must forget Lodan, he cannot be rescued. I have brought you here because it is you who must go to the KT region; it is you who must secure the treasures of the ancient civilization. The survival of this family depends on it."

"What do you mean?"

The Arkon hesitated then let out a sigh. "We are insolvent, Sevarius. We have relied on a line of credit that matures in about ten years' time. The bond is of an amount that cannot be paid with the means now at our disposal. We need this discovery; it will bring forth untold treasures that will make the DeRhogai the most powerful family in the galaxy."

"And you are prepared to see the destruction of the One True Faith in the process?"

"What does that matter?" replied the Arkon impatiently. "I am speaking of the preservation of the family; of its power and wealth. What is a collection of superstitious, foolish ideas and pronouncements when compared to that?"

Sevarius arched his brow. "These are heretical words indeed."

"Do not banter with me, Sevarius; you have never been a devotee of the Faith."

"I have been raised in its tradition; it is not that easy to throw off years of indoctrination. Have you seriously thought through the consequences to humanity? They will, no doubt, be far reaching, perhaps even devastating."

"Perhaps, to some, for a while."

Sevarius scratched his head and contemplated. "You mentioned that there were four people who escaped Dax. Who was the fourth?"

"A creature of no importance; a young whore, by all accounts."

"A whore! Why would such a person be included?"

"She was involved and had knowledge of the nature of the mission. According to Dax's report she was not a native of Tarnus. He described her as a she-devil temptress of the Pal race."

Sevarius sat up and heard Jodi rise so suddenly from his stool that it tipped over and clattered loudly to the floor behind him.

"What is wrong with that boy?" snapped the Arkon.

Sevarius turned and told Jodi to be seated.

"Jodi is of the Pal race, he was no doubt surprised to hear that one of his own kind was involved."

The Arkon squinted at Jodi and scrutinised his features for the first time. "The whore is of no importance."

Jodi glared at him, picked up his seat and sat down.

"Did Dax give a description of the young lady?"

"Of course not; what is this persistence in a matter of no importance?"

"If I am to undertake any mission, I wish to know all the facts, however trivial."

"You agree to go?"

Sevarius stood up and began to pace about the room. "The first business will be to rescue my son."

The Arkon scowled. "Impossible! No one has ever escaped from that place."

"Then this will be the first time. Where is the deep-space cruiser you purchased?"

"I don't know for certain but I think it is still in Rion; it remained in the possession of General Arkuna, my contact on Tarnus, but the General is dead."

"I have heard that there was a shadowy contact in the Division of Rion responsible for a large volume of weapons trading; until now I did not know the name. It is a pity the man has lost his life; we will require that cruiser."

"It must be in Rion, somewhere. Arkuna has a daughter; she may know where it is."

"Where is she?"

"She was sent to the mine with Lodan."

Sevarius gave out an ironic laugh. "So that's two I have to extract from the mine. How do you know that Strellic hasn't seized it?"

"He hasn't got it, I know that."

"Do you have the means to supply another?"

The Arkon shook his ancient head. "No; that cruiser was the last hope; I managed to raise credit on Suran for it but I could not repeat the process without exposing our financial position. There is no more money for another."

Sevarius stopped pacing and glared at him. "I have always thought you a foolish old man and now you have confirmed my opinion."

The Arkon's face hardened, "you forget yourself, Sevarius."

"I forget nothing. You could have prevented my banishment, but you did not stand up to Aurex as you should have done."

"Your wife was condemned for adultery; you made the choice to stand in her place. I had no other recourse but to condemn you to death or banish you."

"My wife was only accused of adultery, she was not convicted."

"An accusation that carried the weight of truth."

'She was set-up by my uncle and you knew it. He realized that I would inherit the title and so he devised a plan to get rid of me. He knew I would not permit the beheading of my wife and would, therefore, elect to suffer banishment. You were manipulated and you did nothing to challenge him. I hope you are content with your choice and your successor."

"Aurex will not succeed; he is dead by his own hand."

"Well, there's some justice at last," said Sevarius ironically. "Come Jodi, your desire to go to Tarnus will be fulfilled directly."

"Wait, you have not confirmed that you will undertake the mission. The family is relying on you."

"I couldn't care less about the family, but I will go on your sacred mission if I can find the cruiser and survive my visit to Tarnus."

"You are a resourceful man; you will find it."

Sevarius served him up a look of contempt and strode out of the room without another word. He was already thinking how to get Lodan out of the Mine of Kusk, but there was someone he had to see before he left Kagan.

"It's her," said Jodi as they left the presence of the Arkon. "It's Matty, I know it."

"Do not speak," returned Sevarius urgently.

They walked down the wide steps and out into the breathless heat of the afternoon. The park was almost deserted now; just a few hardy souls braved the burning height of the sun. By the time they reached Sevarius' shuttle he had the rudiments of an idea; a very ambitious idea that would test him and his love for his son to the limit.

"It must be her," said Jodi as they climbed into the small craft.

"It would seem so; few of your race ever leave Ennepp and they never end up on Tarnus. I wonder how she survived."

"She had to sell herself," replied Jodi thoughtfully.

"There would have been little alternative. Jodi, you must understand that if this Evangelist, Dax DeCorrone catches up with them they would have little chance of survival. I know of him; he is a fanatic, and a highly trained killer. You must temper your expectations."

"I know Matty; she will survive."

"I hope you are right."

"We must go quickly; they are more than forty days ahead."

"We will not catch them now, and there is something I must do before I leave Kagan."

IV

"It is good to see you, Sevarius."

He placed his fingers on hers through the bars that were set in the small opening in the wall. "It is good to see you too."

Sevarius studied the pale face of his wife; she looked drawn and the harsh regime of the retreat had taken its toll on her soft, delicate skin but her eyes still retained the mischievous sparkle that had first enticed him so many years ago.

"How is it in here?" he asked.

She drew the roughly woven robes about her and smiled. "It is hard but fulfilling; we are given enough to eat and we are occupied."

"It is like a prison."

"No, it is not a prison; I would not leave now even if I could. Have you seen Lodan?"

Sevarius hesitated. "Yes, he is well and has become a fine young man."

"I am glad. Please tell him that I am sorry I could not see him. I have always seen much of you in him and I could not bear to look at what I had lost."

"I will tell him when next I see him. My uncle has a lot to answer for; he has killed himself and so there has been some restitution."

"I forgave him long ago and I am sorry to hear this news. But you have not yet told me why the Arkon has rescinded his order of banishment."

"It is complicated. I have to leave Kagan soon and will be gone a long time."

"May the Prophet go with you."

"Thank you, but I fear he will not be with me on this venture."

A high-pitched wailing song echoed through the hard stone of the cloister.

"I am called to contemplation," she said.

"Then you had better go."

She slipped her slender hand through the closely spaced bars of the small window and he held it in his, feeling the hardened skin of long days of toil in the fields of the retreat.

"Goodbye," she whispered, withdrew her hand, and was gone.

Sevarius was left looking into the grey cloister with the fond memories of her close company filling his mind. Something deep inside told him that he would never see her again.

V

During the six-day journey to Tarnus they made a brief rendezvous with another Moontrader to pick up supplies. These included some weapons and explosives and a number of collars of the type known to be in use in the Mine of Kusk. Jodi saw them as Sevarius brought them on board and a cold sensation gripped him as the memory of his captivity in Zurat came back to him.

"What do you want those for?" he asked as Sevarius unpacked them.

"It's not these infernal things that I require: it's the means to neutralize them. All the prisoners in the mine wear them; it is the only sure means that the soldiers can maintain order. Without these collars they would be overrun in moments."

"And you're planning to attack the mine?"

Sevarius shook his head. "Not directly, it is too well defended from external attack; there are sophisticated weapons located all around the site which can be remotely activated if the garrison is overrun. I plan to attack it from within; that is where the weakness lies. If we can neutralize the guards the prisoners will do the work for us and if Lodan is in there, I know he will be one of the first out."

"You're planning to go into the mine yourself?"

"Yes, getting in is not difficult; it's getting out that always proves to be impossible."

"And what am I to do?"

"You? You are not to be involved; at least until I have successfully flushed the mine out and secured my son, then I will require you to collect us. I will show you what to do."

Jodi picked up a collar and studied it; it was similar to the one he had worn in Zurat. He placed it around his neck and locked it.

"What are you doing?" asked Sevarius.

"Seeing if I could stand it again," he replied.

Sevarius regarded him. "It doesn't suit you; I told you that you are not involved."

"That is clearly not true. I don't have skill with these weapons nor do I have any experience of flying a shuttle. I have, however, worn one of these before and I have starved before; I have plenty of experience there."

"It's a fine and generous offer, Jodi, but I can't permit it. I don't think you know exactly what is involved."

"I will be flogged, stripped naked, searched intimately then set to work in appalling conditions. Have I left anything out?"

"Yes, there is no absolute guarantee that you will not be executed before you set foot in the mine."

"I'll take my chances. All I require from you is that you solemnly promise to go after my sister and to save her and see her to a civilized world where she can be happy."

"That is an easy promise to make and I would do it without the need for any sacrifice from you."

"That is settled then. Each of us will do what we are best suited to do. How do I remove the collar once inside the mine?"

Sevarius produced a tiny device. "This will disrupt the circuit long enough for it to be removed safely. They do not possess sophisticated sensors so if you swallow it just before you are taken, it will pass through you once you are in the mine. Then it will just be a matter of neutralizing the guards that are inside the mine without alerting the garrison. The control point for all the prisoner's collars must be in the mine itself; you will have to neutralize it and then free the prisoners."

Jodi nodded gravely. "I can do that. Do you mind if I ask you something?"

"It depends what you have in mind."

"In the palace, you told the Arkon I was your son."

Sevarius cracked a rare smile. "On Kagan such adoptions are not uncommon. Do you object?"

"No, I have no objection at all."

VI

Captain Jellich strode along the dingy passage that led to his interrogation rooms and burst into large cell that was reserved for his own purposes. The familiar chemical stench filled his nostrils along with undertones of urine and excrement coming from the oubliettes deep in the bowels of the building. The corporal and his assistant stood to attention as the captain entered and scoured the room with closely set, watery eyes.

"Why am I here?" he bellowed, flashing a casual glance at the blood-soaked figure hanging by his wrists from one of the rusting beams that supported the low ceiling.

"Sir, this prisoner is a spy, but he will not admit it. I need your permission to apply more extreme persuasion."

Captain Jellich strolled casually up to the alleged spy and peered at the blood-spattered face. "A spy for whom?"

"We don't know yet, Sir," replied the corporal.

"How was he caught?"

"He was on the liner yesterday; his documents are false."

"How does he explain himself?"

"He says he is a trader, he has an appointment with General Arkuna."

The captain turned angrily on his subordinates. "You called me down for this? Can you not see for yourselves? This man is obviously not from Tarnus. He is obviously an arms-trader who has not heard that the General is dead. Why are you wasting your time and mine with this? Take him down."

"Shall we execute him, Sir?"

The captain cast his eyes over Jodi. "Let him go to the mine."

Jodi felt himself unshackled and dragged along echoing corridors and into a place where what remained of his clothing was cut from his body. He was lifted up and thrown into a bath of stinging, grey water and his head held under until he felt his lungs would burst. When they released him he came up gasping for air and they pulled him out and dragged him to a cell where he was left, wet and cold for a number of hours. When they came for him again he was able to walk for himself and he was shoved into a land wagon, along with about fifty other naked people and so started his journey to the Mine of Kusk.

He elbowed his way to the edge of the truck and looked out at the forlorn scenery passing by. He began to turn his attention to the details of the land, estimating how fast they were going and how long the journey was taking. The landscape beyond the road was desolate with few signs of life. There were no trees and no people to relieve the monotony and he realized that, should he be on his own, he would have a difficult journey back to civilization (a generous description of the Division of Rion under Strellic). His travelling companions were hardly more promising; a collection of malnourished specimens, all male except three elderly women. There were also two children, one male, one female, aged about ten, clinging to their hapless fathers with bewildered, fearful faces. The adults wore expressions of hopeless resignation; they all knew they were going to die in the mine and all seemed to have accepted their fate. There were no hysterics or complaints or belated protestations of innocence; they travelled mostly in tight-lipped silence towards their place of slow, inexorable death.

About an hour into the journey Jodi received a light tap on the shoulder. He turned and beheld a middle aged, skeletal man with a young girl whose arms were wrapped around his thin waist.

"I can't do it myself, friend. You are a soldier; I can see that. I beg of you, do it for me. Make it quick and painless."

"Go away," replied Jodi and turned his back on the man.

The tap on the shoulder persisted. "Please Sir, I beg of you, for the sake of mercy."

"What do you want?" snapped Jodi.

"I want you to kill my daughter, to spare her the horrors that await her. She is only nine; she will be raped by the soldiers and if she is not killed then, she will be worked to death in the mine."

"I can't help you, leave me alone."

Jodi turned resolutely and the man guided his daughter away. Shortly after, there was a commotion and the child began to scream and gurgle as her father tried to strangle her. His efforts were enfeebled by his weakened condition and the gurgling screams went on and on. Other prisoners tried to jostle away and nobody helped. At last Jodi could stand it no more and he barged through the tight throng and took the child's head and twisted it violently. There was a muffled snap, and then silence.

"Thank you," said the man, clutching his dead child to him.

Jodi nodded slightly and made his way back to the edge of the truck. This time the other prisoners made way, a few touching his arm in thanks.

There were no other fatalities on the journey and as the trucks approached the mine, Jodi increased his level of observation. He saw the defensive positions in the cliff-face surrounding the entrance and the garrison buildings outside. He gauged the distance as the truck trundled under the giant picture of the Beloved Leader, into the mine and down the road to the reception area. He watched everything; the position and number of the guards; the working and control of the metal doors; the type of electronic whips they used to encourage the prisoners as they disgorged from the truck and into the reception area.

He was jostled into line and had to take his turn in the cavity search. As he submitted to the indignity and gritted his teeth as the probe entered him, he was briefly thrown back to the moment of his rape. He stifled a shiver and obediently turned and opened his mouth so that another instrument could be inserted. Then he was moved along and the collar fitted to his neck, whereupon he was led into the mine. The chief of the guard delivered his much rehearsed speech and the demonstration of what would happen if the collars were activated was duly performed on one weakened individual. Jodi saw them carry the body away and then he joined the line of prisoners as they were marched into the suffocating bowels of the mine. Inside his gut the key moved a little more towards the end of its journey.

He passed the key very early in the morning of his second day of confinement. He carefully separated it from his excrement and pushed it back inside himself. His plan was very similar to one that, at that very moment, was being carried out in another part of the mine and his intention was to wait until the end of the shift. But that morning, the commotion began and it was clear that something extraordinary was happening. It ran through the tunnels like a bush fire; 'the gates have been opened! We are free!'

Jodi ran, knocking aside any who stood in his way. He ran out of the dark tunnels and through the open, metal gates; he ran up the access road, passing everyone, until he was ahead of a baying crowd of prisoners all bent only on revenge. He ran out of the mine, into the starlit dawn and on into the garrison where he killed and killed until his skin was stained dark with the blood of many men.

The prisoners that followed him into the barracks also had their share of blood, before falling on the galley and ripping it to pieces for every last morsel food to be found. Jodi picked up a large weapon and slung it over his shoulder and left them to it. Outside prisoners were still pouring out of the mine and had begun to rampage through the small settlement of ancillary workers. They found the food store where all of the prisoner's rations were kept and gleefully ripped it apart, gorging on the bounty within. He scanned the scene and there he saw, watching the fruits of his work, Lodan DeRhogai.

VII

Lodan looked in astonishment at the blood-soaked figure before him. "Who are you?"

"I told you already, I am Jodi Saronaga; I am with your father."

"My father is here!"

"He is coming shortly."

"He sent you into the mine to get me out?"

"That is correct, but I see that my efforts were not required. I sincerely wish I had known earlier."

Jodi's eyes flickered towards Lorel who was standing next to Lodan, observing him intently. She could see he was alert and suspicious of anyone he did not know.

"Your father is observing the mine from orbit," continued Jodi in his flat, matter-of-fact delivery. "He will have seen the break-out and will be here shortly. I suggest you prepare yourself for immediate departure. The armed forces of Rion will be here soon."

Lodan frowned and turned to Lorel. "Will you come with me?"

"No," she replied. "These are my people and I will fight and die with them."

"Then I will stay too," announced Lodan decidedly.

She took his arm in her hands. "You should go; it is not your fight."

"The woman is right," said Jodi. "You will die if you stay."

"I will die if I go," replied Lodan looking into her eyes.

Lorel turned away slightly to avoid his ardent gaze. "You must do what you feel is right, but you should not do anything on my account."

At that moment Allrik, approached with Candar and the boy genius clinging to one arm and a large weapon slung over the other. He addressed himself to Lorel who seemed a little relieved at the distraction. "We don't have much time, the army is coming. You are the daughter of General Arkuna, you should lead us. We have weapons and there were some trained soldiers in the mine."

"It won't be enough and we don't have time to organize," replied Lorel. "We need something else, something that will give us an advantage."

"What will they send?" asked Lodan.

"Sky-raiders initially," she replied, "followed by ground troops to mop up. They'll have orders not to damage the mine though."

"What weapons have we got here?" said Lodan.

Allrik shook his head. "Nothing that would bring down a Sky-raider."

"What about the cliff defence weapons?" persisted Lodan.

Lorel gave an ironic laugh. "They haven't worked for over thirty years; they're all just for show. My father told me that Strellic would not release the money to replace them."

Jodi listened to the discussion in silence. It seemed to him that his dream of following Matty was now in some danger. If Lodan would not leave Tarnus, Sevarius would surely not either and he would be stuck on this fractious, destroyed world for an inordinate amount of time. He considered turning his weapon on Lodan and forcing him to leave, but there were too many around him and the soldier with the kid and the gun looked useful. He would have to kill him first. The idea died in his mind and instead he spoke. "Would an S.27 bring down a Sky-raider?"

Allrik laughed. "There are no S.27s on Tarnus; the blockade would never let them through."

Jodi turned to Lodan. "Your father is bringing one, in case I failed; I suggest you get ready to meet him."

VIII

Umbert Strellic, the Beloved Leader of Rion was dozing in his enormous bed of state, waiting for the sun to cast its first rays upon the ornate ceiling above him. He had spent a troubled night fretting at the ingratitude of his army who apparently had not received their wages or any fresh food supplies for fourteen days. When he had summoned the Chancellor of the Public Purse to his presence to explain, the man had blubbered something about a temporary shortness of supply and apologized abjectly for his failure.

"I should have you flogged and sent to the mine for this," Strellic had screamed at the obsequious, bobbing figure, but deep in the recesses of his self-regarding mind, he entertained a slight doubt relating to the state of the Division's finances.

The first beams of the sunrise shot obliquely across the vaulted ceiling as Strellic opened his eyes. Seeing the wonderful sight, the Beloved Leader instantly forgot about the troubles at his exchequer and concentrated on the developing patterns of light above until the fullness of his bladder urged him to consider rising. He pulled back the fluffy, white covers, stepped daintily from the bed and padded barefoot across the soft rug towards his private place of ablution. There, he pulled up his nightdress and allowed his bladder to release itself against the reflective, highly polished wall of his urinal. It had been many years since Strellic had enjoyed a direct view of his own manhood; his stomach had long ago obscured the sight and the member itself was in no way capable of compensating for the mass of flesh above it. In fact it had disappeared quite quickly at the onset of quite a modest paunch and now its owner was forced to rely on a reflection for a view of it.

He waggled his hips to shake off the last few drops of urine and dropped the nightdress back over himself. Two chamberlains awaited his return and he struck a suitably heroic pose as they unfastened his nightdress and made ready to dress him. The first chamberlain was laying out his uniform and the assistant fussing with his underwear when they were disturbed by the onrush of his eldest son, Orgun, who burst through the bedchamber door and into the naked presence of his father.

Orgun, the product of Strellic's second marriage, rather took after his mother too much for his father's taste. He was soft and rather stupid and carried around a rather bewildered expression on his large face. He had his father's dark, narrow-set eyes and dainty nose, but instead of the pert Strellic mouth, he was thick lipped and apt to allow his mouth to gape, reinforcing the impression of mental feebleness. On the demise of his once trusted general, Strellic had appointed him head of the armed forces; a position clearly beyond his capabilities or inclinations.

"Dadda... dadda," he wailed urgently. "They've broken out."

Strellic pursed his lips and wondered what imagined calamity had so disturbed his son. "Who has broken out of what?" he enquired calmly as the second chamberlain fastened underwear around his ample girth.

"The miners... the miners, they've escaped."

Strellic smiled indulgently. "You have been deceived, son. The miners cannot escape."

"Oh!" Orgun scratched his head in confusion. "Only there was an alarm signal sent, apparently."

"Why don't you contact the garrison there and ask them why they sent it?"

Orgun frowned. "I think they have done that already but they couldn't get a response."

Strellic sighed with exaggerated patience and climbed into the britches of his uniform and allowed the first chamberlain to secure them. "It is probably a communication problem; send out a couple of scouts to take a look."

"Good idea, Dadda," replied Orgun, attempting a salute and failing miserably. He turned on his heels and left his father wondering what he had done to deserve such a useless child. The man wasn't worth the considerable effort he had put in to conceive him; he was stupid, lazy and dissolute and not a credit to him at all.

He finished dressing and waddled through to his breakfast that he always took alone. He ate daintily from gold plates and drank from jewel-encrusted goblets, blissfully unaware of the momentous events that were taking place only two hundred kilometres to the north.

IX

The appearance of a bright light in the sky arrested the attention of the freed prisoners and all looked up at the approaching craft sparkling in the violent red of the rising sun. The small town and the desert beyond was awash with filthy, skeletal, naked bodies as the waif-like figures continued to issue from the mouth of the mine and press their predecessors into the dry wastes beyond the town. This vast sea of humanity, having already stripped the town of everything that could be eaten, now set about removing the hated collars by any means they could and sat huddled on the ground in groups or hugged one another at the sheer joy of seeing the sun and the open sky once again.

Lodan and Jodi strode through the throng and out into the desert beyond, well away from the crowd so that Sevarius could clearly see where to land. He brought the craft down close to the two men while the nervous crowd looked on suspiciously. The only flying craft most had ever seen were the type used to kill them and destroy their homes. They watched carefully as a hatch opened in the side of the craft and a man emerged.

Sevarius had not seen his only son since he was a boy of thirteen; now he was looking at a man of twenty-two and the difference was marked. Even so, he would have known his son anywhere.

Lodan stepped forward. "Father."

Tears of joy sprang into the eyes of the Moontrader; a moment he thought never to see had arrived. He advanced and embraced his son. "You have grown well." The words stuck in his throat as he held the soiled body of his only child. "I am sorry I was not there to protect you from this."

"I am glad you were not; I would not have wished these past days on anyone."

Sevarius held his son's head and looked into his eyes. "Well, I'm here now and, from this time on we need not be parted."

The smeared dusty mask of Lodan's face cracked into a smile. "You're here now and I'm starving; I hope you brought some food."

Sevarius released his son. "I have and there is plenty more in the ship." He turned to Jodi, taking him affectionately by the arm. "Thank you for what you did for Lodan."

"You may thank me but I did nothing; Lodan escaped by himself; it had nothing to do with me."

Sevarius regarded his son with a look of surprise.

"It's a long story, perhaps for another time. In the meantime, I would like some food, clothes and the S.27 you have brought with you."

"The S.27? What for? We will be long gone before Strellic's army gets here."

Lodan strode past his father and entered the shuttle. "I'm not going anywhere," he announced abruptly. He ripped open a pack of wafers and began to cram them in his mouth while he looked for a suitable garment.

"What do you mean, son?"

Lodan found a sturdy pair of britches and pulled them on. "I mean that these people will be wiped out if I don't help them, so I'm staying."

Sevarius was speechless with shock; he could not comprehend his son's concern for these peasants. What did it matter if they were massacred? Jodi strolled past him and found his own clothes and began to dress; he chose to remain silent while he waited for Sevarius' next move.

"I won't allow it," announced Sevarius eventually.

"You can't stop me, Father," replied Lodan evenly.

"I take the trouble to get you out of that hell-hole and all you want to do is stay here and help these peasants. It's suicide."

"I have been close to death for a long time; I am used to it."

"We could take the woman," interjected Jodi.

Lodan glanced at him. "She wouldn't come."

"So that's it," said Sevarius. "It's a woman; I might have guessed."

"It's not what you think, Father."

"It *is* what I think; I am not ignorant of your exploits on Kagan."

Lodan bit his lip. "That is in the past. Leave me the weapons and go." He offered his arm to Jodi. "Thank you for coming to get me, Jodi."

Jodi did not take his arm in farewell, but stood still with a look of barely-suppressed anger. He knew full well what Sevarius was going to do and he meant to forestall any decision against his own interests. He quickly produced his weapon and turned it on Lodan. "You're leaving with us whether you like it or not."

Lodan glanced from the weapon to Jodi's face; he had no doubts that this man would shoot him. "What's it to you if I leave or stay?"

"Stop this now," commanded Sevarius, quickly placing himself between the two men. "Lodan, as your father, I beg you to come with us now."

"I'm not going, Father, and that's final. You will have to let Jodi shoot me to stop me."

Sevarius bowed his head and then turned to Jodi. "My son has inherited the DeRhogai stubbornness. You know I can't leave without him."

"I know," replied Jodi flatly.

"I will take you back to my ship."

"Don't bother, I'll stay and fight with you."

Lodan waved dismissively. "It's not your fight, either of you."

"It's not yours either," replied Jodi.

X

The story of the break-out had quickly gone around the community of prisoners and now Lodan was received with reverence as he walked back towards the barracks loaded with the weapons that Sevarius had brought. Jodi and Sevarius followed and the three men discovered Lorel and Allrik in the barracks busy organizing the able-bodied men into a semblance of order. They had both donned military uniforms from the barracks stores and were now engaged in organizing the motley assortment of candidates, thrusting the weapons they had liberated from the arsenal into the hands of anyone who looked likely to be able to use them. Lorel's natural air of authority was augmented by the widely disseminated news that she was General Arkuna's daughter and it was she who had led the breakout. Although only partially true, the miners were disposed to believe this version and this increased her cachet, for there was no doubt who had assumed command at the barracks.

Lorel saw the S.27 slung over Lodan's shoulder and smiled. "So that's what they look like. Do you know how to fire it?"

"No," replied Lodan, "I have never handled one."

"Give it to me," said Jodi. "I know what to do."

"What will they send against us?" asked Sevarius.

Lodan interjected. "Lorel, this is my father, Sevarius DeRhogai. Dad, this is Lorel Arkuna, the daughter of General Arkuna."

Sevarius glanced at her, noting that her face, although characterful possessed no extraordinary beauty. He repeated his question after a curt nod.

"Strellic's options are limited. There are probably no more than twenty attack craft still operating; we have not been able to get the parts to repair them. The army has plenty of land vehicles and about fifty thousand men in eighteen bases."

"The attack craft are our immediate problem then," said Sevarius

"The S.27 should be able to take care of them," observed Lodan.

Sevarius agreed but pointed out that they would have little chance against a large number of trained troops.

"Assuming they're all loyal to Strellic," said Lorel. "My father heavily subsidized the army by trading in weapons. He kept them fed and paid. Since his murder they won't be so well looked after; their loyalty might be called into question."

"Do you think you could turn some of the units?" asked Lodan.

She nodded. "If I can turn one, others will follow, but first we have to fend off the first attack. Jodi, you need to get the gun to a high vantage point. Take Allrik and get to the top of the cliff; you will have a clear line of sight from there."

"I'll go with them," said Lodan.

"No, I want you stay with me; I need someone who can organize the troops. Sevarius, you must take your craft and fly it to where it cannot be seen. They must not know there is such a thing here."

"Very well, I will take it north; there is a canyon about twenty kilometres away." He handed Lodan a small communicator and then embraced him. "Be safe, I do not want to lose you, my son."

"I'll be fine, Father. Now go quickly. The Prophet be with you."

Jodi and Allrik scaled the high metre cliff to the south of the mine entrance together, taking it in turns to carry the awkward S.27 gun. The cliff was difficult and dangerous because the mudstone rock had been shattered by repeated night-frost attack and there was plenty of loose material that their footsteps sent crashing to the floor below. But both men were good climbers and they achieve the summit in reasonable time and took a sheltered position with a clear view to the south. Jodi set up the gun, primed it and they waited.

It was not long before they saw two small dots coming at speed toward them. Jodi activated the aiming device and watched as they got closer. "Why have they only sent two craft?" he asked.

Allrik, peering over his shoulder looked at the enlarged image of the two craft. "They're not attack craft; they're scouts," he announced.

"Are they armed?"

"They have light weapons only."

Jodi took his eyes from the aimer and looked up. "They've come to see what's going on."

"They're in range, shoot them down."

"No, cover the gun, quickly."

Both men stripped off their jackets and laid them over the S.27 so that it could not be seen, then they pulled it behind a rock for good measure. The two craft passed over them and over the sea of miners spilling out on to the plain below, then wheeled in the sky and headed back to the south.

"Why didn't they shoot?" said Lodan angrily as the craft made off unscathed. "Now they have seen everything."

Lorel smiled grimly. "Clever boy, your friend Jodi."

"What?"

"If he'd shot them down, Strellic would know that we are capable of defending ourselves; he wouldn't send in attack craft, and we wouldn't have the chance to shoot them down and weaken him. Strellic won't want to damage the mine so he'll send troops with a few craft for support. We have to get everyone who can't fight back into the mine tunnel."

"We'll never do it; there are too many and most of them won't want to go back."

"They'll go back when they see the troops coming for them and then it'll be pandemonium. Try and get as many back in as you can; I'm going to deploy the armed men in the town; we're going to have to defend our position."

XI

Umbert Strellic sat alone at his breakfast table and moodily prodded at the substantial meal before him. He was feeling dyspeptic and hated it because it denied him one of his chief pleasures, namely consuming large quantities of food. He wondered, with considerable chagrin, at such injustice; that he should have to suffer such agonies of digestion; that he, Umbert Strellic, the Beloved Leader, should be so unfairly afflicted. His dyspepsia increased at the sight of his oldest son, Orgun, bursting in on him for the second time that morning.

"It's true," wailed Orgun breathlessly, "the miners have escaped and the garrison is overrun."

Strellic rose and his face went a peculiar shade of purple. "What do you mean by disturbing me like this? Can't you see I'm out of sorts?"

"But Dadda, what about the mine? What is to be done?"

"Send in troops, you fool, and kill them all; every one of them."

"What, all of them?"

Strellic glowered at his hapless son. "Every last one."

XII

From their elevated position Jodi and Allrik were the first to see the rising column of dust as the long train of vehicles advanced rapidly up the track that led to the mine. In the sky above the column five small points of light kept formation, scouting the terrain and providing cover for the vehicles below. Jodi uncovered the gun and took a bead on the attack craft; he knew he had to shoot all five down before they could get in a response, but he had never handled such a weapon before and was not entirely sure of himself.

Allrik walked back to their position having observed the chaos below. They'll never be ready," he announced.

Jodi rehearsed the shooting down of the attack craft. "If we can get all five before they get us, I'll concentrate fire on the column; that will give them more time."

Allrik knelt down beside him. He felt comfortable with Jodi; they had been the first two into the barracks and Allrik had witnessed, first hand, Jodi's fighting ability, his single-minded bravery and his obvious thirst for killing. He was glad they were on the same side. "Do you think you will be able to get all five?"

"Don't know; I've never actually fired one of these before. We'll just have to see."

They watched as the column of vehicles grew nearer. Now they could see at least a hundred trailing along the un-made track. The attack craft peeled off and began to approach their position rapidly.

"Here we go," said Jodi and he took aim and fired. A bright pencil of light issued from the gun and hit the first craft. There was an intense flash and then the craft exploded, showering white-hot debris onto the vanguard of the column of vehicles below. Three of the advancing land vehicles were hit and caught fire, incinerating their unfortunate occupants. Jodi took aim on the second craft and hit it towards the rear. It veered off and began to spin, eventually breaking up as it hit the desert floor. A third craft suffered the same fate, but the fourth and fifth, now alerted to the danger, began to soar into the sky to avoid attack. Jodi followed the fourth carefully and shot it down as it tried to bank over the column. It wheeled out of the sky and hurtled to the ground, exploding near the middle of the column with such force that it decimated more than thirty troop carriers.

Orgun, leading the attack from the rear, observed the carnage with horror. He had not expected to be placed in such personal danger and alarm seized him. He ordered an immediate retreat and the truncated back of the column wheeled around and began to flee in some disarray.

Having disposed of the fourth craft, Jodi now searched for the last, but it had disappeared. Together they frantically scanned the sky for it and then they spotted it, diving from almost above. Jodi was about to swing the gun on it when Allrik grabbed him and hurled him behind a rock just as a small, intense flash came from the craft. The ground around them exploded with shattering, white heat and the air crackled viciously. The boulder that had partially sheltered them splintered into pieces and buried them as the shards fell back to the ground. The gun had been silenced and now the final remaining attack craft was free to do its grizzly work.

Lorel and Lodan had been watching intensely from their position near the mineral extraction machinery. They had witnessed the short-lived triumph that had brought the demise of four of Strellic's finest craft, but now the remaining craft had silenced the gun and had begun to strafe the miners. A panic ensued and men were scattering into the desert or trying to swarm back into the mine for protection. Weapons were discharged against the attack craft without effect and Lorel screamed at her troops to hold their fire as the deadly pencil beam of super-charged particles scythed the town and its hinterland at random.

Seeing the improvement in the situation, the commander of the vanguard of vehicles, Colonel Doric, resumed the advance. The two sides engaged at just under a kilometre, but it was now an unequal struggle and the superior firepower of the advancing army, together with the murderous strafing from above, quickly sapped the bravado of the defenders.

A shot hit the machinery above them and sent jagged metal fragments into the air, cutting and burning the men below. Some started to run away; they were not soldiers; their first instinct was flight.

"We have to retreat," shouted Lodan above the din.

Lorel shook her head vehemently. "Retreat to where? I'm not going anywhere."

Another shot blistered the metal above them as she finished speaking. A shard pinged from a nearby wall and ricocheted towards them. It struck her a glancing blow on the side of the head and she slumped. Lodan grabbed her head and checked the wound; it was not deep but blood was pouring down her face. He took off his jacket tore off a sleeve and ripped it so he could tie two ends. He wound it roughly around her head and tied it as tightly as he could then he reached into his pocket and took out the communicator Sevarius had given him.

"Dad, we're being ripped apart here."

He just made out his father's voice over the cacophony of battle. "I'm coming in."

"No, you can't do anything. Jodi's dead and I will be soon. Get away; just go; now."

He cut the communication, picked up Lorel and slung her over his shoulder. They were almost the last to leave the ruins of the extraction unit and, seeing Lodan retreat with Lorel unconscious over his shoulder, the last few remaining fighters began to withdraw. They ran across the ground through the sickening smoke of the hundreds of burning bodies of the miners who had not retreated to the safety of the mine tunnel. Above them the attack craft was coming around for another pass when a second craft appeared in the sky. Lodan saw it glint briefly through the pall as it honed in on the final attack craft. There was a terrible flash of intense light as the two craft came together. The attack craft veered off its course and tumbled into the cliff to the north of the mine entrance. There was a sickening heave of screaming metal as the thing broke up as it cartwheeled down the face of the scarp and came to rest at its base. The other vehicle wheeled away to the south and began to spin. Lodan froze and watched in horror as his father wrestled with the guidance system. He could see the small figure in the cockpit as the damaged craft screamed and spun out of control. There was a ground shaking crash as it hit the sand to the west of them, sending up a great plume of dust into the sky. He put Lorel down behind a wall in the barracks and started to run towards the crashed vehicle. The ground in front of him exploded and blew him off his feet. He got up in time to see his father climbing out of the mangled shuttle. A single shot felled him and Lodan saw the figure of his father, Sevarius DeRhogai, fall into the dust of Rion.

With grim determination he turned around and ran back to the place he had left Lorel. He picked her up and began to run, dodging the fire of the advancing troops as he made his way through the barracks to the edge of the settlement. His eyes stung with tears for his dead father as he ran and caught up with the last of the armed stragglers trying to escape into the desert. Several men were fighting over the last vehicle, some shots were fired then the thing trundled away with men running after it. Lodan watched it gather speed as it raced into the empty wastes surrounding the mine. It crossed about three hundred metres before there was a flash and the vehicle exploded and began to burn, forming yet another plume of black smoke in the sky.

Lodan turned around. Now he could hear the roar of the approaching troop carriers. He carried Lorel into a half destroyed dormitory and laid her down onto a dusty bed surrounded by the mutilated, stripped bodies of the garrison soldiers. Lodan sat on the bed and looked about in desperation as the sound of the approaching army grew louder.

XIII

The Beloved Leader was in council with his ministers when Orgun entered the chamber. To his right sat Sarlat, Strellic's younger son, smugly anticipating what was to befall his foolish brother. Orgun approached the great table of state and issued a sort of military salute to his father.

"They had some sort of weapon, Dadda," he began. "We didn't stand a chance."

Strellic smiled ominously and put his forefinger up to his dainty lips to hush his son. He slowly rose and walked around the table, past his silent and fearful ministers.

"So, my son, you didn't stand a chance."

"No, Dadda, honest," replied Orgun, sensing something of a threat in his father's attitude.

"Then how is it that we now have the mine back?"

Orgun frowned in confusion as his father suddenly raised his hand. "You cowardly good-for–nothing," he screamed as he slapped the face of his son.

Orgun tried to defend himself as Strellic laid into him. As he retreated he tripped over his own feet and was soon curled up on the floor begging his father to stop beating him while Sarlat grinned and the ministers bowed their heads to avoid being a party to the awkward domestic scene.

"Now, get out of my sight," shouted the Beloved Leader as he kicked the foetal, cringing form of his first-born. "Get back to the mine and finish the job you were supposed to do. I want every one of them to suffer; not one is to be left alive."

Orgun crawled away from the lashing boot of his father and headed for the door. His two officers bowed hurriedly and ran after him, while Strellic, breathing heavily, marched back to his seat at the head of the table. He shut his eyes and tried to calm himself. "Now, I believe we were talking about the army budget and Minister, you were explaining yourself."

The Minister of the Exchequer shrivelled in his seat. "Marshal, I have searched the public purse and there is no money to pay the army."

Strellic suppressed a volcanic discharge with difficulty. "How is it that these things have been achieved in the past? Has the money disappeared?"

"Marshal, the army has always been paid by a military exchequer, controlled by the late General Arkuna."

Strellic's colour began to rise. "And where is that money now?"

"Marshal, there is nothing left. The last pay round was not even fully covered."

Strellic's eyes bulged even more than usual as he recalled Arkuna's last words before he executed him in the courtroom. He had dismissed it as false boastfulness at the time, but now it seemed there might have been some truth in his words. Had the general really been funding the army from his own arms trading activities? He turned to Sarlat. "You searched the general's premises, what did you find?"

"The crystals, there was nothing else of great value."

"How thorough were you?"

Sarlat shrugged. "Very thorough."

"What about the daughter, did you question her about this?"

Sarlat coloured slightly. "Not exactly."

"Do you mean no?"

"Yes... no, I'm not sure."

Strellic unfastened his gold and jewel encrusted sidearm and placed it slowly on the table in front of him. His entire cabinet tensed; his calm manner was ominous. He stood, picked up the weapon and walked slowly around the table, waving it beside each man's head. "Someone is to blame for this, but who?"

The company remained tight-lipped; even his son, who was reasonably certain of survival.

"I am tired of fixing your cock-ups," whispered the Beloved Leader as he strolled behind them. "I am tired of sorting it out. Minister Brevic, why didn't you tax the people more?"

The Minister of the Exchequer began to dribble. "I... I don't think people can give any more, Marshal."

Strellic slowly came up behind him, bent over and whispered into his ear, "wrong answer."

There was a brief flash of energy and the Minister of the Exchequer slumped in his seat. Strellic walked calmly back to his chair at the head of the table and sat down. "Sarlat, get over to Arkuna's house and search it; question his troops." With sudden animosity Strellic brought his fist down on to the table and screamed, "I want that money!"

XIV

From the moment he opened his eyes, Jodi was aware of the darkness and the crushing weight on his back. It seemed to bear down on him, constricting his chest and making it hard to breathe. He tried to move his arms and legs but found them firmly pinned down by rock and the warm mass above him. He could hear the jagged sound of laboured breathing that wasn't his own and realized that Allrik was alive and on top of him. He tensed and made an effort to wriggle free, but found he could not move beneath the bulk of the man and the constriction of the rock. He tensed again and tried to move his right arm and found that he could just ease it to one side a fraction. He grabbed at some of the splintered rock that had buried them and shifted it a little. Gradually he worked his right arm free until he could pull some of the rock below his body. He continued to clear it from around his head, pushing it under himself and wriggling forward, a centimetre at a time. He worked steadily, methodically, stopping frequently to regain his strength. He gradually worked himself free, slipping gently from under the body of his companion until, after an hour, he could see daylight. The sight spurred him on and he worked harder, eventually scrambling out of the rock tomb and spreading himself, panting, on the ground with his face to the sky.

He regained his breath and dusted himself off then he started to disinter his companion. As he uncovered Allrik's body, it was clear that the soldier had taken the brunt of the blast. His jacket and pants were bloody from various cuts and lacerations and his head was also caked in dried blood. But, incredibly, he was still alive.

Jodi cleared the rest of the rock fragments and tried to pull him up, but the man moaned in pain and he saw that his right arm was broken and the bone had broken the surface of the skin above the elbow. As carefully as he could, he hauled Allrik out of the tomb and laid him out on the ground. The man was moaning and gurgling something unintelligible as Jodi took his knife and cut the sleeve away from the injured arm. Allrik groaned with pain as he pushed the jagged bone back inside the wound. He cut the sleeve into binding and wrapped it tightly around the ugly injury. He then crawled cautiously to the edge of the cliff and looked over.

Down below he could see the army vehicles and the troops among the ruins of what used to be the settlement and barracks. There were bodies strewn everywhere, charred and unrecognizable as human. The naked and fearful miners were being taken from the mine in groups of twenty or so. They were taken beyond the ruins where they were being executed, falling one upon the other in an increasing mound of flesh and bone so that the latest batch were obliged to climb upon the remains of the former in order to meet their end. Beyond this horror, lying at some distance, but clearly visible, was another. Jodi stared at the remains of Sevarius's shuttle and his heart sank further. He had lost his only means of escape and a sensation of bitterness and frustration overtook him. Had he escaped from Ennepp only to die on this degraded and blasted world?

He edged back from the cliff and returned to Allrik. It was clear to him that they had to get away as soon as possible but Allrik was in no condition to walk. Logic dictated that he should leave the man to his fate, but Jodi was not made like that; he gently slapped Allrik's face until he opened his eyes.

"Can you see me?" asked Jodi.

Allrik moaned. "I feel like I've been shot full of nails. Have you got any water?"

Jodi left him and scrambled among the shattered rock of their tomb and there he found the battered remains of the canteen Allrik had brought. Most of the precious water had drained away, but there was mouthful left in the bottom. Jodi took it over to the injured man and carefully poured the contents into his mouth and used the last drips to moisten his own lips.

"They're executing the miners down there, we have to get away."

Allrik grimaced. "I don't think I can move."

"You have to."

Jodi took off his blood-soaked jacket and hacked off the two sleeves with his knife; then he cut Allrik's remaining sleeve from his jacket and tied them all together.

"I'm going to sit you up," he said, easing the man up from behind.

Allrik moaned and gritted his teeth while Jodi eased his arm into a sling and passed it over his head.

"I'm going to help you to stand now."

Jodi grabbed his waste from behind and pulled him to his feet. Allrik shivered with pain but did not cry out.

"Where is the nearest water?"

"Due west," replied Allrik, breathing heavily. "There is a network of narrow canyons containing pools and streams that disappear into the rock."

"How far?"

'I don't' know, maybe twenty kilometres."

"What about any towns?"

Allrik shook his head. "Harlic's Well is the only place; I'm not sure exactly how far it is though, but I'm sure it's less than thirty kilometres beyond the canyons."

Jodi placed Allrik's good arm around his shoulder. "It's going to be a long walk."

XV

"Fucking savages,"

"Bollocks to this, Corp."

The two troopers stood in the remains of the barrack room and surveyed the result of Jodi, Allrik and the other miners' handiwork. Blood-soaked naked bodies were piled upon one another as a witness to the miner's furious revenge. Many had been disembowelled, others had their heads and genitals cut from them and some even displayed signs of cannibalism.

Corporal Dressic stepped gingerly among the piled flesh that had once been his army colleagues. He recognized one soldier from a unit he had joined five years ago. He hadn't been a good trooper, but no one deserved to die like that.

"Let's get out of here," he said, but his private was looking intently at something sticking out from under a pile of flesh. It was a hand, moving very slightly.

"Look Corp, it's moving," said the soldier pointing.

The two men quickly cleared the bodies to reveal the bloody, naked body of Lodan, clearly still breathing. The corporal reached down and read the tag around his neck. "Private Indar Tallic," he uttered. "You are one lucky bastard."

They pulled Lodan free; he had a knife wound to his side that was still bleeding. The corporal undid his water flask and poured some into Lodan's mouth. "Hold on soldier, we'll get you to the medics."

Lodan opened his eyes and tried to speak. He whispered something unintelligible and shut them again.

"Fetch a medic while I check the rest," commanded the corporal.

The Private ran off and Corporal Dressic began his grizzly search. Under another pile of bodies he found a second survivor, a young woman, completely naked and unconscious, but still breathing. He stared at her fine form before kneeling beside her and taking one of her firm breasts into his hand. It had been sometime since Corporal Dressic had been with a woman and the effect on his anatomy was instantaneous. He passed his eyes down to the pale blonde wisps of hair at her crotch and wondered if he had time. But the return of the Private with a medic quickly shrunk his ardour and he called out, "Another one here, a female."

Lodan was carried to the makeshift medical station and placed on the ground along with about a hundred injured soldiers. Lorel was placed next to him and he risked a peek at her when he thought nobody was watching. She was breathing steadily but was still unconscious from the blow to the head. Presently an army doctor and an orderly knelt beside her and checked her.

"Contusion to the side of the head, no other apparent injury. Clean and bind the wound, she should make a full recovery; we'll see when she comes to."

The orderly noted the doctor's instruction and they passed on to Lodan. The doctor frowned. "Superficial wound to the right side of the lower torso." He checked his patient thoroughly and stood up. "No other apparent injury."

Lodan kept his eyes closed; he could feel the doctor was staring at him. "Clean and dress the wound," pronounced the doctor at last and moved on down the line of the injured soldiers.

Presently two orderlies appeared and dressed Lorel's head wound and then his own. A rough blanket was thrown over them and they were left alone. When the orderlies had gone, Lodan tried to rouse Lorel; he shook her arm gently, but she showed no sign of consciousness. He needed her to wake up soon; the doctor had been suspicious and he did not know how long it would be before they were recognized as the enemy.

Colonel Doric was young and ambitious. It was he who had led the attack on the mine as Orgun Strellic retreated with the bulk of the army. Now, Orgun was back, assuming command as though he had personally succeeded in vanquishing the enemy and demoting the captain's efforts to the status of the 'initial skirmish'. Doric was silently offended and resentfully withdrew to the bosom of his comrades, allowing Orgun the glory of slaughtering the unfortunate miners.

Colonel Doric was not used to being sidelined. He was a good-looking man, used to praise, who remained dapper and smart in all circumstances. He was twenty-eight years old and had been promoted young and saw himself rising quickly through the ranks to become an officer long before his time. Now, the captain had hit a problem. He had exposed the incompetence and cowardice of none other than the head of the armed forces, the eldest son of the Beloved Leader and he had enough wit to know that this had not been a particularly good career move. He was sitting on one of his troop carriers brooding on this fact when he noticed the doctor coming towards him.

"How many have we lost, Doc?" he asked.

"Two hundred and thirty one so far."

Doric shook his head sorrowfully. "It was those attack craft, they should not have been anywhere near the troop column."

"You should be careful what you say, Colonel, it may be construed as a criticism."

Doric blinked nervously. "What do you want?"

"There's an injured trooper and a woman that I'm not altogether happy with."

"What do you mean?"

"I can't pin it down; they just don't look like they belong."

"What are their injuries?"

"The man has a superficial wound in the side, a knife wound; the woman is unconscious from a contusion to the head."

"Where were they found?"

"In the barracks; they were the only two left alive."

Doric sprung from the vehicle and followed the doctor back to the medical station.

"The men are hungry,' commented the doctor. "They haven't eaten for two days and the miners took all the rations."

"I know," replied Doric shortly. "We're all hungry."

Lodan saw the doctor and the colonel followed by four troopers coming down the line of injured men and cursed that he had not escaped with Lorel when he had half a chance. Now he had to be brazen, for he could see that they were coming for him. He closed his eyes and feigned sleep.

"What's your name, trooper," asked the colonel abruptly.

Lodan made no reply so the colonel kicked his foot. "Your name, trooper," he repeated threateningly.

Lodan opened his eyes groggily. "Private Indar Tallic, Sir."

Colonel Doric whipped off Lodan's cover and pulled his tag from around his neck. "What is your unit, Tallic?'

"I can't remember, Sir; I was stationed in the mine garrison."

Doric smiled thinly and cast his eyes over Lodan's body. "How come you alone survived with such a slight injury?"

"I don't know, Sir; I suppose I was lucky."

"The woman is also from the barracks," interjected the doctor.

Doric pulled back her cover and perused the bloodstained body.

"She has not regained consciousness," said the doctor.

The colonel turned back to Lodan. "There were no females in the garrison unit; who is this?"

"The cook," replied Lodan.

Doric pulled his sidearm and aimed it at Lodan's head. "Put your hands above your head, trooper."

Lodan raised his arms. "Sir, you're making a mistake."

"Is that right? You two troopers; go and stand on his hands."

The two troopers moved around him and planted their heavy boots on Lodan's hands and the colonel brought his heavy boot down on to Lodan's groin. "I'm going to stamp on your bollocks until you tell me who you are and who this is."

"I am Lorel Arkuna, the daughter of General Arkuna," announced Lorel.

The colonel removed his boot from Lodan's privates and turned his attention to her. He scrutinized her face for a few moments before asking. "Who is this man?"

"His name is Lodan DeRhogai; he is from Kagan."

"I knew there was something wrong with him," said the doctor.

"Guard them," said Doric and he marched off towards the mine.

"Sorry Lodan," said Lorel. "Our time has come."

"It's alright; we failed, the odds were against us."

"I've got an awful headache," she replied.

"You won't have it for long," replied Lodan grimly.

When Colonel Doric set out for the mine, it was his original intention to report the discovery of Lorel Arkuna to Orgun Strellic. He fancied that the information might improve his standing with the son of the ruler and assist in the advancement of his career. But as he approached the killing zone, he reflected on the record and disposition of his commander-in-chief and a strong element of doubt entered his mind. He stopped and observed as the brave son of Strellic ordered the murder of yet another unlucky group of naked, skeletal miners. They included a frightened boy who was clinging to an elderly man and wailing something unintelligible. Candar and the boy genius stood on the rising hill of bodies while the soldiers took aim. Candar held the boy to his bosom as they fell and their flesh mingled with the hundreds who had preceded them.

Doric was in no way a liberal and the element of mercy was not a highly developed part of his constitution, but even he could see that this murder was wrong and futile. He turned around and walked slowly back to the medic station, deep in thought.

The soldiers were still guarding the recumbent insurgents as he approached. "You men are dismissed," he ordered.

The troopers filed away, leaving Doric and the prisoners alone. "Get up," he ordered, producing his sidearm. Lorel and Lodan rose, wrapping themselves in their rough covers. "Now move," he said, jerking the weapon in the direction he wished them to go. He took them down the line towards an empty troop carrier and made them climb inside. The interior was hot and reeked of sweat. Doric waved them to a seat and sat down opposite.

"I saw you with your father," he began. "About six years ago, when you were still a girl. The general was inspecting a guard of honour at our base and he brought you with him. I remember you marching behind him, full of your own importance."

"I was young then."

"We heard that the general was a traitor, that he sold arms to our enemies."

"That's not true; my father was a patriot to the very core. He traded arms to fund the military, but he never traded with the enemies of Rion."

"The army has not been paid for two weeks and the supplies ran out two days ago. My men are hungry. Where has all the money gone?"

"I don't know. Strellic murdered my father, so we'll never know."

Doric narrowed his eyes on his subject. "I think you do know where it is."

"Are you going to torture me, Colonel?"

Doric drew his lips over his even teeth. "Do you think I'd get anything?"

"You could try," she replied provocatively

Doric grinned and turned his attention to Lodan. "And you, what's a Kagan doing on Tarnus?"

"I was brought here against my will and got mixed up in the arrest of the general."

"Why were you brought here?"

"I was kidnapped on Barta Magnus by a Moontrader called Jinzeraskhan, one of the general's contacts."

Doric leaned back in his seat. "None of this adds up, you're not telling me the whole story."

"There is no whole story," replied Lodan. "Why don't you just kill us and get it over with?"

Their conversation was abruptly interrupted by the throwing open of the troop carrier door. Outside, standing slack-jawed in the bright sun was none other than Orgun Strellic with three armed troopers.

"What is this?" he bellowed. "These two are enemies of the state. This is a foul conspiracy."

Doric smothered his surprise and noted that the fool had not armed himself. His hand was forced and now there was only one thing to do. He turned his weapon on Orgun and fired. The stupid mouth gaped and the dull hooded eyes registered a moment of surprise and then the firstborn of Strellic sunk to the ground. The armed guards looked on in confusion as their commander-in-chief crumpled.

Doric sprung from the carrier. "I'm assuming command of this operation," he declared with decisive authority. "Bring these prisoners and find them something to wear."

He marched off with such purpose that the bewildered troopers simply obeyed the last order and conducted Lorel and Lodan back to the dressing station.

"I think we have just started a mutiny," whispered Lorel as they marched together.

Lodan made no reply; he hardly knew what to think.

Colonel Doric marched to the field of execution. The pile of limbs, heads and torsos had grown and more prisoners were scaling the grizzly heap to be mown down by troopers, now exhausted and sickened by the senseless carnage.

"Stop this now," commanded Doric. "Bring those prisoners down and take them back to the mine. That is an order."

The sergeant saluted him. "Sir, General Strellic has given us orders to continue in his absence."

"General Strellic is dead; I am now in command."

"Dead, Sir!"

"That is what I said, Sergeant; dead."

"Yes, Sir." The sergeant grinned and saluted his new commander.

"When you have secured the prisoners, gather up all the bodies and burn them."

A thick pall of smoke curled into the air above the mine as Lodan and Lorel, wearing the uniforms of dead soldiers, were marched into the presence of Colonel Doric and a few of his chief officers. They were having a heated discussion. Doric was speaking. "We have no choice, they'll kill us all anyway now."

"Thanks to you; whatever possessed you?" replied a lieutenant.

"I had no choice."

"You were just saving your own skin; bugger the rest of us. Now what do you propose we do now? March on the capital?"

Doric bit his lip; he had not actually thought that far ahead.

"That's exactly what you should do," said Lorel. "It's the only tactic that makes sense."

"Who is this?" said another officer.

Doric stood up. "This is Lorel Arkuna, the daughter of our late, lamented general."

The company all stared at her.

"You haven't eaten for two days," continued Lorel. "How long can you go before the troops desert? You will find food supplies in Salom Gul and you must strike as quickly as possible, before Strellic knows what is happening."

"What about the Elite Guard?"

"I didn't say it would be easy, but if you take the capital, maybe even capture Strellic, the rest of the army will come over. No one has any great allegiance to Strellic."

"She's right," said Doric. "It's the only way. If we stay here they'll hunt us down or starve us out. We have to go on the offensive."

"We may not be alone," added Lorel. "I think I can get my old unit to come over. It would more than double our strength. I will need to get to my father's old base."

"This is a rebellion," objected one officer.

Lorel rounded on him. "Did you enjoy cutting down those defenceless miners? Do you like going without food and pay? Do you want Strellic's sons to lead you? If you think that our Beloved Leader has led the Division of Rion with wisdom and justice, then stand down, we won't judge you. But I tell you this, if you end up on the wrong side, nothing will save you from the shame. Strellic has destroyed our nation, impoverished the people and turned us into a pariah state and now he doesn't pay you while he sits in his palace surrounded by luxury. Well I say no to that; it is time to end this tyranny."

Colonel Doric stepped forward. "Arkuna is right, let us put an end to Strellic or die trying."

XVI

Sarlat Strellic did not appreciate being duped. He regarded himself as a man of superior intelligence and perspicacity and it irked him that General Arkuna had put one over on him by resisting his 'questioning' and keeping his fortune secret. Judging others by his own character, Sarlat simply could not believe that anyone would accrue wealth only to fritter it away on maintaining the welfare of the army.

He arrived at Arkuna's old base with a large contingent of the feared Elite Guards and ordered that every soldier should parade immediately. The soldiers mustered on the dusty parade ground while the Elite Guards were dispatched to search the barracks and the commander's house. The elderly colonel, who had taken over the premises, objected strongly and was shot dead in front of his men. The troops were stripped of their weapons and locked in their barracks while a select contingent was herded into a corner of the parade ground where they were made to lie face down under the guns of the Elite Guards.

Sarlat personally took charge of the search of General Arkuna's former residence, ripping it to pieces in a frenzied bid to find the missing money. He found no gold or jewels but he did eventually find a record of the military accounts buried in a small wall cavity. Unusually the accounts were committed to paper in the form of a small notebook. He opened it at the last entry and his eyes nearly fell out at what he saw; a huge sum had entered the ledger through a subsidiary account held on Suran. He looked down the page and saw that another entry showed money leaving the account in one large amount to another account held on Suran. It was obviously payment for something the General had bought; but what?

He stomped out of the ruins of the general's residence and approached the prone troops in the corner of the parade ground. "Who is second in command here?" he shouted.

"I am, Sir," called out Lieutenant Norgu.

"Stand up," ordered Sarlat.

Norgu stood to attention and waited.

"General Arkuna purchased an item at great expense just before his impeachment; what was it?"

"I don't know, Sir."

Sarlat strode over to the nearest trooper and shot him in the back of the head. He returned to the lieutenant. "I ask you again, what did the general purchase?"

"Sir, I can't tell you, please believe me; the general did not tell us what he was doing. None of us knew."

Sarlat pursed his dainty lips and walked over to the troopers. He took aim behind another man and shot him in the back of the head. "I will kill every man here until I get the truth," he declared.

Norgu knelt. "Kill me first, Sir, for I swear to you that no man here can answer you."

Sarlat returned to the lieutenant and pressed his weapon against the man's head. The lieutenant shut his eyes and waited to die, but instead Sarlat kicked him with the sole of his boot and strode off.

The troopers watched the craft carrying Sarlat and the Elite Guard rise and head over the craggy hills to the east and their hearts were filled with renewed loathing for the regime of Umbert Strellic. They had been on half rations for over two weeks and supplies were almost exhausted. They were hungry and their mood was black as they took the bodies of the colonel and the two troopers and buried them in the garden of their beloved general's residence.

XVII

Jodi and Allrik's long journey through the unforgiving uplands of Rion began during the full heat of the day. They were covered in dust and blood, not just their own, but the blood of the guards they had killed in the barracks. They were like two soldiers stumbling from a battlefield of carnage. Jodi leant Allrik his shoulder and they staggered about three kilometres until they found a small gulch with an overhanging promontory under which they could hide from the sun and those who might be looking for them.

"We will stay here 'til nightfall," said Jodi, slumping down next to the injured man. Allrik had lost considerable weight in the mine, but he was still heavy and well-built and Jodi had found it difficult going, especially under the full heat of the sun.

"You should have left me back there," whispered Allrik through cracked lips.

"I know," replied Jodi simply. "I'm going for a piss." He got up and began to move away.

"Wait," said Allrik handing him the empty canteen. "Go in this and drink as much of it as you can bear."

Jodi nodded and took the canteen. He went down the gulch a way and urinated into the canteen. Some spilled out of the holes on to his britches and disappeared into the dusty ground, but he managed to save quite a bit. He put it to his lips and drank. It was warm and not particularly strong tasting, but most of all it was liquid.

He emptied the canteen and took it back to Allrik.

"I'm afraid I didn't save you any," he said, forcing a smile.

Allrik grinned. "I prefer my own brand."

Jodi settled himself at a small distance and shut his eyes to sleep.

When he awoke the sun was nearly below the horizon and the sky above had turned a luminous pink. A few wispy clouds followed the sun to the horizon and caught the last of its glow.

Allrik was sitting up and awake when Jodi returned; the pain he was in had robbed him of sleep. "We should get on," he suggested.

Jodi helped him to his feet and the two men stumbled out of the gulch and on to the undulating plateau that formed the uplands. They walked through the night, following the star patterns that Allrik knew well, stopping frequently when the agony of movement became too much for him to bear. Twice he fainted from pain and they were forced to stop until he was recovered enough to continue and they made slow progress over the fractured terrain. As the morning sun rose and painted the sky while the guiding stars faded, they neared their destination.

As the new day's heat gathered they descended into a rocky canyon and heard the sound of trickling water. Both men were exhausted and caked in dust and blood but the sound urged them on. They reached the canyon floor and rounded a rocky outcrop and there beheld the most beautiful sight either man had ever seen; a deep pool of fresh water fed from a waterfall that drizzled from the mouth of a cave hanging ten metres above. The waters were surrounded by a sudden verdant shock of vegetation that seemed incongruous against the starkness of the desert. Cycads dipped their roots into the moist banks and flourished in the shadows; other forms clung to the rocks and fed on the water vapour that rose from the rippling surface. It was an oasis of beauty and life in the dead wastes of the Kusk Uplands.

They stumbled together into the water and allowed its cool, velvet touch to engulf them. They drank greedily as they immersed themselves in its life-saving embrace. When Jodi stripped off his jacket and britches and threw them to the shore, Allrik noticed the still-raw marks of laceration across his back from the beating he had received before his incarceration in the mine. They must have still caused him pain but he had never once mentioned them.

Jodi struck out into the centre of the pool, diving under the water and forcing his way down until he could touch the rocky bottom with his hand. He swam over to the waterfall and floated face up beneath it, allowing the cool water to fall into his open mouth. He spent some time in the water, finally climbing out, hauling himself on to the rock next to his companion.

Allrik sat on a rocky edge dangling his feet in the water. "You swim well," he observed.

"I like the water; there's a lot where I grew up."

"I can't swim," admitted Allrik.

"Not with that arm."

"Even with two good arms, I still can't."

Jodi sat up. "It's simple really; you just do the strokes and breathe in the right places. We need to get that jacket off you, your wounds need cleaning."

He helped Allrik undress, supporting his arm as the jacket was carefully slipped over it. Allrik grimaced with pain during the operation but did not cry out.

"You have quite a few cuts on your back," said Jodi. "I'll get some water and clean them."

He filled up the canteen and poured the cool water over Allrik's back while rubbing carefully with his hand. "Two are quite deep, the rest are superficial. You got lucky. Your pants are bloody; do you want some help to get them off?"

Allrik shook his head. "I can manage."

Jodi moved away and began to wash his own clothes by bashing them on a rock as he had once done in his youth while Allrik removed his britches and waded into the water to clean the wounds on his buttocks and upper legs. When Jodi was satisfied with his laundry he stretched his clothes out on a rock to dry and repeated the process with his companion's clothes.

"Thanks," said Allrik wading out of the water.

Jodi made no reply but stretched himself out on the rock with his hands behind his head.

Allrik sat next to him and stared over the pool. "How old are you, Jodi?"

"About eighteen, I think."

"You don't know?"

"No, not exactly. How old are you?"

"Twenty-four."

"Army, weren't you?"

"Yes, since I was fourteen."

"How come you ended up in the mine?"

"I murdered a superior officer."

"You quite enjoy killing, don't you?"

"No, not really; I'm glad to be rid of the blood of those men we killed."

Jodi shut his eyes. "It didn't seem to bother you at the time."

"Or you."

"Why should it bother me? They deserved to die for what they were doing."

"They were just soldiers following orders; it could have just as easily been me in those barracks."

"They were following the wrong orders. I've seen enough of men following the wrong orders. I'm a Pal, Allrik. On Ennepp people of my race are slaves, just like the miners except they feed us a bit better so we can work longer before we die. That mine was not the first time I was forced into a collar. Before I left Ennepp I killed the man who made me wear one and I'll kill anybody who ever tries to put one on me again."

Allrik glanced down at the other man's face but Jodi had his eyes shut and his flat, matter-of-fact delivery gave away nothing of the passion he must have felt inside.

"Why did you come to Tarnus?"

"To help Sevarius get Lodan out of the mine. We didn't expect to get mixed up in this domestic insurgency."

"Do you think Lodan is dead?"

"Probably, the camp was overrun and the soldiers were executing the miners."

Allrik bowed his head and tried to stifle a bitter tear. "Lodan saved me in the mine. He was a good friend. The best of men."

"I heard he was a playboy of sorts."

"I can't speak of what he was before, but in the mine he was my friend. He saved me from myself. I tasted flesh, Jodi."

Jodi opened his eyes and sat up. "I heard of this but didn't believe it. You actually ate human flesh?"

Allrik nodded sadly. "I was so hungry I sank so low."

"What did it taste of?"

"It was revolting, like blood but worse; I can't describe it; it's like nothing I have ever tasted before; a terrible experience. Lodan came and got me; risked his own life to get me out; that was just before we escaped."

"That was admirable, but I cannot forgive him for causing the death of his own father and trapping me here on this forsaken world."

"Lodan was in love with Lorel; that is why he wouldn't leave."

"Hmmm! But she didn't love him, did she?"

"No, I don't think she did."

"Pity, she was a fine figure of a woman," said Jodi suddenly standing up. He dived from the rock and swum under the water, his head popped up near the centre of the pool and he swum to the other side with easy, powerful strokes. Allrik watched him in admiration; he had always wanted to learn to swim but there was precious little opportunity in Rion, a land deficient in standing water.

He recalled the fury of the man as he killed the soldiers in the barracks and reflected how different his character seemed to be now. Jodi had proved to be a solicitous companion, both gentle and considerate, quite at odds with the man who had passed him in the mine tunnel, entered the barracks and reeked bloody havoc. Allrik suspected that that trait could reappear with little provocation, but even so, was well on the way to liking Jodi very much indeed.

Jodi swam back across the pool and hauled himself back on to the rock. "We'll stay here until sunset then set out for Harlic's Well," he said. "Hopefully there'll be a surgeon there to fix you up."

Allrik nodded and forced a smile. "Mind if I ask you something personal?"

"No," replied Jodi flatly.

Allrik gestured vaguely towards his companion's lower torso. "I couldn't help noticing… it's a different shade from the rest of you."

Jodi grinned and looked down at himself. "I haven't had to worry about that for some time. On Ennepp I could never go naked because my mother was a Pal whore and my father a Bhasi soldier, so I'm half Bhasi. The Bhasi are the rulers of Ennepp; dark-skinned people. Don't ask me why but that's how it comes out when the races mix."

"I don't understand; you are half Bhasi, and yet you were still treated as a slave?"

"I was lucky. On Ennepp our races are not allowed to mix. I shouldn't have survived at all. I should have been culled at birth."

"Killed for not being pure-bred! And you call *this* world 'forsaken'!"

XVIII

The Beloved Leader was taking his lunchtime bath when Sarlat returned from his expedition to the General's old base. He walked in on his father as the two bath attendants were waist-deep, washing Strellic's furry back as he lay prone in a tank of bubbling, scented water. His ample, pink buttocks crested the water like a pair of desert islands in a sunset and offered themselves to the unfortunate attendants who were about to tackle them with a sponge on a stick.

"Look at this, Dadda," said Sarlat, squatting in front of his father with the account book opened at the appropriate entry. "Arkuna made a massive trade just before we arrested him."

Strellic, who objected to having his bath-time disturbed, opened his eyes reluctantly and cast them over the proffered page. He blinked at the enormous figures. So the Evangelist was telling the truth; the traitor had bought a deep-space cruiser. He pushed the attendants away and scrambled to his feet and grabbed the book from his son.

"Where is it?" he bellowed.

Sarlat took a step back and observed his father, seeing, in the flesh, what he would become in a few years' time. It was not an inviting prospect. "Where's what, Dadda?" he asked.

"Where is it?" repeated Strellic with venom. He stepped from the bath and began to walk about, entirely unconscious of his state. Eventually he turned to his attendants and screamed at them to get out. When they had scuttled from his presence he planted his bloodshot eyes on the mystified figure of his son. "The deep-space cruiser, of course."

"Deep-space cruiser!" echoed Sarlat.

"You heard me. I didn't believe the Evangelist; thought it was another of their filthy tricks, but this notebook confirms it. The traitor, Arkuna purchased a deep-space cruiser before he died. The Kagan, DeRhogai, had come here to receive it; it must be here, in Rion. With a weapon like that we could crush any rebellion; I could rule the whole of Tarnus. I must have it. I must have that cruiser. Why haven't you found it?"

"I have questioned the men at the base; I am convinced that they know nothing," said Sarlat defensively.

"Someone must know something. That traitor; that filthy, ungrateful traitor!" He spat the words from his dainty mouth and his eyes levelled on his favourite son. "You questioned him, why did you not get this from him?"

Sarlat coloured. "I… I tried, Dadda. You know I did."

"Obviously you didn't try hard enough. Why am I surrounded by traitors, ingrates and idiots? What have I done to deserve this?"

"Sorry Dadda, but you saw him, I practically killed him and still he said nothing about this."

"You fool; you don't have to torture a man to death to get information. There are many other ways. Why didn't you threaten to kill his daughter in front of him?"

"I did. I don't think she knew anything; she didn't talk either."

Suddenly a spark of hope flashed in Strellic's brain. "She was transported to the mine; she may still be alive."

"You gave orders for them all to be killed."

"I know what I did. Contact your useless brother and tell him to stop the executions immediately. Tell him to find that whore and bring her here."

"Yes, Dadda."

Sarlat hurried off leaving Strellic pacing his bathhouse, deep in thought. Why had Arkuna purchased a deep-space cruiser? Was he planning a coup? And how, in the name of sanity, had he acquired such wealth under the nose of his leader? These vexed questions occupied his mind until Sarlat returned with the news that Orgun could not be contacted.

"Send a scout, then. Must I tell you everything? Blast you!"

XIX

Lieutenant Norgu surveyed the devastation of the interior of General Arkuna's residence and shook his head sadly. The General had always supplied the buffer between army and government, insulating the troops from the greed and stupidity of those who ruled them. Without the General to protect the troops, there was nothing to stop the regime from abusing its power and reducing the army to the state of beggarly compliance. They had not been paid for weeks and the food supplies had virtually expired.

Norgu had just completed the burial of the colonel and the two troopers who had been murdered by Sarlat and his heart was heavy with the unnecessary loss and the prospects for the future. The unfortunate, elderly colonel who had replaced Arkuna as camp commander had not had time to stamp his character on the interior fittings of the modest home and many of the General's old possessions were still there. The lieutenant picked up one of the polished rock samples that Arkuna collected from far and wide and smiled at the memory of his beloved General and the daughter he had always desired.

As he studied the polished strata, a breathless trooper ran into the residence and saluted. "Sir, there is a troop carrier coming."

Norgu strode out into the parade ground. "Tell the guard to fire a warning shot; do not let it approach."

The trooper ran off and soon the sound of a discharge cracked the air above the camp. Norgu mounted the defence wall and peered at the vehicle through a viewfinder. It had come to rest three hundred metres from the camp perimeter.

"Any contact?" he asked his newly promoted second-in-command.

"No, Sir, none as yet."

"Looks like one of ours."

"A troop-carrier, Sir, but what's it doing here? We have nothing scheduled."

"Perhaps they've brought us food," replied Norgu ironically

At that moment a door in the side of the vehicle slid open and a figure emerged and began to walk towards the camp with raised arms.

The lieutenant ordered his troops to hold fast while he peered at the figure through a viewfinder. He could clearly see that it was a woman and she moved in a way familiar to him.

"It's impossible," he declared.

"What is, Sir?" said his second-in-command.

"It's Lorel Arkuna," replied Norgu in astonishment. "Open the gates."

The gates were opened and Lorel marched into that familiar place, a place she had never thought to see again. Lieutenant Norgu saluted her, his eyes moist with tears of joy at the sight of his old flame.

"I heard you had been sent to Kusk," he began.

"Can't you give an old friend a hug?"

"It's not very soldierly," he replied with a wide grin on his face, "but what of that?"

He took her in his arms and squeezed her hard. "Who's with you?"

"Four troopers and Lodan DeRhogai, the Kagan who was arrested with us."

"What are you doing here?"

"We've come for your help. Tell them to come in."

Norgu issued the order and the troop carrier trundled noisily into the camp.

"You got any food here?"

The Lieutenant shook his head. "Supplies are finished; I sent a squad out foraging but they found nothing."

"Same with us. We broke out of the mine."

Norgu's handsome face puckered in confusion. "I thought that was supposed to be impossible."

"We found a way to do it. Strellic sent troops; there was a fight but now the troops he sent have come over to our side."

"A mutiny!"

"A rebellion. It's time to get rid of Strellic and all his cronies. We're marching on Salom Gul."

"Salom Gul! Did you lose your mind in Kusk? What about the Elite Guard?"

"With the troops in this camp we'll have enough to take the palace; after that the rest of Rion will rebel."

Norgu knitted his brow and began to pace. He recalled with bitterness the visit of Sarlat a few hours before and the degrading treatment of the General, a man he worshipped. "You'll have to speak to the troops," he announced. "I have no authority to command them to do something like this. They will have to volunteer."

"I'll speak to them," she replied.

The troop carrier rolled into the camp and the troopers disgorged along with Lodan. He looked around the camp and saw that soldiers were assembling in on the parade ground, emerging from barrack houses, storerooms and arsenal to form a large body of men in the dusty quad.

Lieutenant Norgu climbed on to the troop carrier and waited until the last man had assembled before speaking. "Men of Twenty-Six Company, we all saw the murder of our commander and two of our brethren earlier today. Now hear this."

He jumped to the ground and beckoned to Lorel who mounted the troop carrier and surveyed the sea of soldiers before her. "You all know me," she began in a clear, ringing voice that carried across the silent men. "I was sent to the Mine of Kusk after the unlawful murder of my father by Strellic. Because of my father's murder, you have not been paid and so you have not been able to send money to your families who must now be stricken with hunger and poverty. The food that my father's prudent management supplied has been diverted to the mouths of those who sit in government over you; it is stored in their houses and fine palaces and now feeds their families, their cronies and their cronies' families. I say this food belongs to you and not to them. As soldiers of Rion, it is your sacred right to receive what is your due.

"I broke out of the Mine of Kusk to stop this injustice; to restore your natural rights to you, to bring you food and to restore honour to you and your families and I have already struck the first blow. Orgun, the idiot son of Strellic, had already fallen and lies rotting in the dust of Kusk. Other enemies have fallen and now my victorious army is marching on the capital, marching to destroy the criminal, Strellic, his family and all his fat-laden lackeys and hangers-on. The tide of history is on our side, on the side of justice and right. You, my friends, have the chance to join the swell, to be able to tell your children and grand-children that you were there, right at the beginning, carrying your swords to the very heart of the corrupt monster that dares to call itself your government. You can be there. You can be victorious. Will you join me?"

A sea of noise broke out as Lorel delivered her final words and she punched the air in a triumphant salute at their response. Lodan gazed up at her in admiration; never would he have thought that this was the hurt and naked woman he had first fallen for in the mine. She had grown into a role so naturally that this might have been her hundredth rallying cry, instead of her first.

"We attack tonight!" she yelled, over the din of cheering soldiers.

XX

Colonel Doric's eyes narrowed as he observed the approach of the scout craft. A slight wind had whipped up dust from the floor of the desert and it had clung to the sweat that the heat of the day had produced. He shook it from his moustache and hair and wiped his face on the sleeve of his army jacket. The craft descended and landed outside the encampment and an airman emerged. Doric went forward and the two men saluted each other.

"Sir, I have an urgent message for General Orgun Strellic."

"What is it, Airman?"

"Excuse me, Sir, but I have instructions to deliver the message to General Strellic himself."

"That will not be possible, Airman. General Strellic is in the mine, supervising the clearing out of the insurgent prisoners."

The airman blinked in confusion. "Sir, your communications are inoperative."

"They were damaged in the skirmish. What is the message, Airman? I will see that General Strellic receives it."

The airman glanced over to the still burning pyre of bodies. "He is to immediately stop the execution of the prisoners and locate Lorel Arkuna, the daughter of General Arkuna."

The colonel frowned. "Prisoner Lorel Arkuna led the insurgents, she was killed during the skirmish and her body was one of the first to burn."

Now the airman did not know what to do. Sarlat had not issued instructions to cover this eventuality. "I will have to contact base," he said.

"By all means," replied Doric smiling affably.

The airman climbed back into his craft and contacted his superior officer, presently re-emerging with the news that Marshal Strellic himself wished to speak to the General.

Doric's smile faded slowly. "Airman, tell your superior that the General will be found and brought here but it may take some time."

The airman nodded tentatively, he sensed that something was not quite right. He contacted his base and spoke for some time, when he emerged from the craft he looked pale with fright. "I have just spoken with Marshal Strellic, himself. He has told me to go into the mine and find his son. If I fail he will have me executed."

Doric put a fatherly arm around the fellow. "Perhaps it is time you discovered the truth, Airman."

XXI

The sound of a series of large explosions in the northern outskirts of the city, reached Strellic's ears as he paced about the palace in anger and bewilderment. He ran over to one of the large windows and looked out into the night and saw the angry glow of a fire-cloud rising from the direction of the airfield. He stared at it in disbelief, at first unable to comprehend the significance of what he was seeing. He could not understand why Orgun had defied his direct orders and was leading the army back to the city when the job at the mine was far from finished. A scout craft had reported the approach of the army but no contact had been made. It did not occur to the Beloved Leader that a mutiny was underway; the very thought of it was an impossibility.

Suddenly Sarlat burst through the door, pink with agitation. "Orgun is attacking us," he yelled. "He's attacked the airfield."

Strellic rounded on him. "Don't be ridiculous."

"It's true; he's destroyed all the attack craft and he's just overrun the northern garrison. I never trusted him, Dadda, he's always wanted power."

"Orgun hasn't the wit to scratch him own arse, let alone organize a coup; this is someone else's work. My people love me; they will never allow this. Send the Elite Guards; they will soon wipe them out."

"But the palace will be almost defenceless."

"Do as I tell you," screamed Strellic, turning purple in the face.

Sarlat ran out to organize the defence of the city while his father slumped despondently into his seat at the head of the council table. "My people love me," he opined. "They love me."

Colonel Doric had started the attack before the arrival of the contingent led by Lorel that was approaching the city from the west. The trundling column of troops heard and saw the destruction of Strellic's air power over the horizon and increased their pace.

Now, inside the city, Colonel Doric's troops made easy headway against the ill-prepared and disorganized troops of the city battalion. They surged through the undefended suburbs and in to the central area until they could see the palace itself. But now they came under attack from the well-armed, well drilled Elite Guard under the leadership of Sarlat and were gradually forced back as the crash of buildings being blasted to rubble and the flash of energized beams filled the air above the centre of the city. The terrified citizens cowered in cellars or tried to escape, only to be caught in the deadly crossfire of the opposing forces. The superior weaponry and training of the Elite Guards began to take its toll on the attacking force and the casualties began to mount. They were pushed back into the suburbs and there they held the line until the second wave came into the city from the west.

Lorel and Lodan rode in the vanguard of the attack as they swept into the undefended western suburbs of the city and made straight for the palace. Here they split their forces with Lorel leading the attack on the palace with a small force of troopers and Norgu taking the bulk of the men to attack the Elite Guard from behind.

Strellic stood alone at his high window and watched in disbelief as his personal guard fought a running battle with the insurgents outside the high walls of the palace. A loud flash burst the reinforced window and brought it shattering down on to his head while the air inside the council chamber crackled with energy. He screamed in alarm and ran to the door with as much speed as he could summon. His attendants and staff were already streaming out of the building when one of his loyal officers grabbed him and propelled him into the melee.

"Sir, we have to get you away, out of danger," yelled the officer over the hubbub.

"But my people love me, they love me," wailed Strellic.

Another explosion rocked the building and brought masonry down on to the escaping retainers; there were screams of panic and a stampede began. The officer pulled his leader into the throng, elbowing aside any who blocked his way. The acrid smell of smoke began to fill the air as Strellic was hurried along corridors he never knew existed. At last they were out of the chaos and he was bundled unceremoniously into a waiting carrier. As they set off there was a huge explosion to their right and the fizz of solid rock flying through the air. The ominous patter of shattered rock hitting the troop carrier preceded a pronounced thud that shook the ground around them. Strellic peered in alarm at the sight ahead of him; the surreal prospect of his own dismembered head, cracked from chin to crown, staring straight at him. The huge statue, the symbol of his godlike status, was no more. He grabbed at his wispy hair in anguish as the carrier swerved around the obstacle and sped off to the south.

Lorel and Lodan marshalled their troops outside the high palace wall and blew the heavy gates and rushed in. A few shots were fired by soldiers giving cover to the escaping occupants, but they were mere token efforts. The palace had fallen and Lorel and her small force of insurgents went through the building room by room, clearing it of the last of Strellic's regime. In the basement they discovered stores of exotic food and fine wine on which Lorel ordered a guard, after allowing the soldiers to help themselves. She and Lodan then made their way up to the roof of the building where they could look out over the stricken city. To the north they could see and hear the fires and destruction of urban warfare. The sky was bright with beams of light from the opposing weapons and often there came the rumble of crashing masonry.

"We did it," said Lodan as they gazed over the burning city.

She passed a hand over the dusty velvet of her blonde hair. "Strellic got away; it's not over, not by a long measure. He still has his supporters; he will fight on until he wins or is killed."

"The people will rise, they will support us."

"You may be right, but the people have no weapons."

He put a comforting arm around her and felt the electric charge of her touch course through him. She didn't soften to him, nor did she move to escape; she remained tense and still, watching the battle unfold.

XXII

Jodi and Allrik remained in their pleasant oasis of calm, talking and sleeping until the sun softened at the horizon and the sky turned a florid pink. Jodi dressed himself in the clothes he had washed and dried on the rocks and then helped Allrik to dress.

"You don't remember how far it is to Harlic's Well?" asked Jodi as he eased Allrik's tattered jacket over his broken arm.

Allrik squirmed with pain. "No, I never went there. I can't be sure but I remember it is due east of here."

"You know if we can't find the town we'll have to come back here."

Allrik nodded grimly. "We'll just have to find it."

Jodi filled the canteen with as much water as it could now hold and they set off, climbing out of the canyon and following the familiar eastern star as it rose above the craggy horizon of the plateau. Allrik seemed stronger now and he did not need his companion's shoulder so much, but Jodi could see from his grim face how much pain he was in.

The land undulated away into the darkness as they trudged across its barren surface. Twice they had to make substantial detours around deep cracks in the plateau rock where, a long way below, they could hear the inviting sound of running water. Jodi noted the location just in case they had to return, but did not attempt to climb down into the steep-sided chasms.

After ten kilometres they stopped for a rest and Jodi gave Allrik most of the water from the damaged canteen. He moistened his own lips and saved the rest just in case.

"You can see Ennepp's star from here," said Allrik, pointing to a bright point to the south. "Do you think you'll ever go back?"

"No," replied Jodi flatly. "There is nothing there for me."

"I'd like to travel to other worlds, but I don't suppose I ever will."

"We'll be lucky if we survive on this one."

"That's true, but every day is a bonus for me; I thought I was going to die in the mine. I would have done, but for Lodan. How odd fate is; that I should have met him at all is miraculous in a way. I hope he died fighting, the way a man should die. I will miss him."

Jodi rose abruptly and took a few of steps away from his companion and began to urinate. "Your friend has cost me a great deal; I will probably never leave this planet."

"I am sorry for you; it must be difficult to be trapped on an alien world."

"It is what I can't now achieve that hurts me, Allrik."

He shook away the last drops and turned to his companion. "Come, let us at least get to where we are heading."

The misty arc of the galactic array had risen and spread its pale, grey light upon the land by the time they reached the last ridge in the high plateau. It was not a particularly difficult climb, but Allrik was by now struggling and Jodi had to support him as they climbed over the tumble of boulders. They crested the ridge and now they could see the plateau sloping down to the vast desert plain beyond.

As they squinted into the semi-darkness a small light twinkled and then died in the middle distance.

"That must be the settlement," said Allrik.

Jodi took a bead on it and they headed down the long slope of the plateau and out on to the vast, flat desert plain. As they trudged across the sand, a collection of buildings outlined against the star-field emerged from the darkness. It was a group of low, stone-built dwellings too small to be described as a town. They fetched up to the edge of the settlement and Jodi left Allrik as he went to investigate. He moved stealthily among the closely packed buildings until he found one with a rude, faded plaque nailed to the door. He returned to fetch Allrik and the two men made their way back to the dwelling.

Jodi quietly tried the door, but it was shut fast and the small, barred windows either side of the door were set too high even to look through.

"You could knock," whispered Allrik.

"Unwise," returned Jodi, "they might make a commotion and bring others."

"Try the roof; these buildings usually have vents to let out the heat."

Jodi made a tour of the circumference of the dwelling and returned. "There's no easy way in," he declared.

"That settles it then," replied Allrik and he rapped on the door. Jodi pulled his knife as Allrik rapped again. Finally they heard the muffled sound of a series of expletives coming from within. The door was unbolted and pulled open and there stood the oldest man in the Division of Rion. He was dressed in a long, grey nightshirt that hung from his bent, emaciated form like an old sack. His hair was long and white as new snow and dangled from his skull in tight plaits tied at the ends with random pieces of string. He stared with suspicious, sharp eyes from below abundant brows and turned his head abruptly from one side to the other causing his long, plaited beard to waggle from side to side.

Jodi quickly sheathed his knife before the ancient spied it.

"What?" he barked irascibly, shifting his angry glare from one man to the other.

"Sir, I have an injured man here," said Jodi.

"Come back in the morning," he snapped and tried to close the door.

Jodi stepped forward and jammed the door with his foot. The ancient glared.

"Sir, I'm sorry but I must insist you see my friend."

The old man's eyes narrowed. "You look like a couple of soldiers; soldiers never pay; be gone with you."

Jodi let the old man see his knife. "We're not soldiers, Sir and my friend is in pain."

The doctor noticed the movement of Jodi's hand towards his knife. "You think you can threaten me? I've lived too long to be intimidated by soldiers. Be gone I say."

Jodi took his hand away from the knife and raised his arms. Sir, we are begging you; we are hungry and tired and my friend is in terrible pain. I promise you we are not soldiers, far from it, in fact. Please let us in."

The old man now seemed less certain; he narrowed his eyes and squinted from one man to the other. "You're not soldiers? You're dressed like soldiers; so that's a strange thing isn't it? Can you pay?"

"No, Sir, we have no money."

"Typical, I thought as much."

His ancient eyes lighted in Allrik's injured arm and after a brief struggle, the physician's compassion overcame his natural reticence. "Very well, come in then," he snapped.

They entered the dwelling and the old man pointed them into a room containing an ancient, iron stretcher, a rudimentary desk and stool and some cabinets, mostly empty.

"Sit," commanded the doctor, pointing a bony finger towards the stretcher. Allrik sat and the doctor took up a pair of shears from his desk and cut away the crude binding that Jodi had place around the wound. Jodi watched the operation with his hand close to his knife; he did not trust the old man with the shears.

"You soldiers have got a nerve, waking a man up in the night," he muttered as he pulled the ragged binding from the wound. Allrik grimaced as the doctor prodded at his arm.

"No infection yet," he declared. "I'm going to cut off this jacket and re-set and bind the arm. I have no anaesthetic, haven't had for over four years, so this is going to hurt."

He took the shears to Allrik's tattered jacket, cutting it all the way up so it could be removed without disturbing the arm. As he removed the jacket he caught sight of the injuries, both fresh and old on Allrik's back. He straightened as far as he was able and stepped back, shifting his sharp gaze from the Allrik's injuries to Jodi's face.

"Who are you?" he snapped.

Jodi's grasped the hilt of his knife. "Never mind who we are, old man; just do your job."

"You're from the mine, aren't you?"

"Yes," said Allrik, "we're from the mine."

"I thought so, the old scars on your back give you away; mine dust gets trapped in the wounds as they heal." He called over his shoulder, "It's alright Gran, they're not government men."

A wizened female advanced into the room carrying a sidearm. She was almost bald and toothless but still carried herself in a sprightly way. "What'd you say, Doc? They're not government?"

"That's right Gran, they're from the mine," replied the doctor raising his voice.

"That's quite a walk; you boys must be hungry."

"We are," said Jodi with his eyes fixed on the sidearm waving about in her gnarled hand.

"How about you fix them something to eat while I sort out this fellow's arm?" said the doctor.

"How about I fix you something to eat?" she croaked, evidently not hearing her husband's request.

"Thank you Ma'am," said Jodi, "we would appreciate it."

She squinted at him. "Ain't you pretty; nice manners too. Makes me wish I was fifty years younger."

"You'd still be too old for him, now make yourself busy," chided her husband.

She shuffled away and the doctor shook his head. "Pay her no heed, gents; she gets madder every day. Now bite on this and brace yourself."

He posted an object into Allrik's mouth and eased the arm out of the sling. Allrik began to shake and sweat as the old man turned the arm and re-set the broken bone.

"Hold him still," commanded the doctor and Jodi held Allrik fast as he let out a terrible moan through the bite.

"There," said the doctor, stepping away. "Now I'm going to clean the wound. I've only got pure alcohol so brace again."

He took a swab and poured some clear liquid on to the wound. Allrik moaned again as the alcohol cleaned the wound where the bone had come through the skin. When he was finished the doctor tightly bound Allrik's arm to his body so that it couldn't move then cleaned and dressed the wounds on his back, buttocks and legs, removing the fragments of rock that Jodi had missed.

"That's all I can do for you now, man," he declared as he sutured the last wound. "You'll need to get these dressed again in a few days."

"Thanks Doc," said Allrik, slipping gingerly from the trolley.

"What about your friend here? You injured, son?"

"Not really," replied Jodi.

"Alright, what's your story, gents?"

"We were prisoners in the mine; we broke out but the army came and crushed the escape. We got away."

The doctor raised his bushy eyebrows. "You don't know then."

"Know what?" said Allrik.

"The army at the mine mutinied, turned back to Salom Gul and threw that bastard, Strellic, right out of his own palace."

Jodi and Allrik exchanged confused glances. "But I saw them exterminating the miners," said Jodi.

"I don't know what you saw, but I can tell you the old General's daughter led them right back to Salom Gul and she chased Strellic right out of the city.

"Lorel! Still alive?" exclaimed Allrik.

"You know her?"

"I was with her in the mine; we broke out together. I thought she was killed in the battle."

The doctor regarded his patient with surprise and reverence. "You know the Arkuna!"

"The Arkuna?"

"That is what the soldiers are calling her."

"Is that so? Has there been any mention of a Kagan man?"

"A Kagan man? I don't think so; but this is a cause to celebrate. Gran," he called, "dig up that bottle we've been saving in the cellar. It's time to open it."

"So what's a Kagan doing in the Mine of Kusk?" asked the doctor as they sat around the small, low table in the cooking area of the dwelling while his wife stitched Allrik's jacket back together.

"It's a long story," replied Jodi with his mouth full of the plain and rather tasteless food that the old woman had prepared.

"And you, you're not from these parts are you?"

"I'm from Ennepp."

The doctor shook his head in wonder at such an exotic person in his humble home.

"We have to get to Salom Gul," said Allrik. "Strellic isn't finished yet and we will be needed in the fight."

"You shouldn't be considering fighting," said the old woman. "Look at the state of you."

"I still have one good arm," replied Allrik.

The doctor clapped him on his good shoulder. "That's the spirit."

"Is there any transport in town?" asked Jodi.

The doctor nodded. "The lawman has a cart, that's about it."

"Is he sympathetic?" asked Allrik.

The doctor waved a bony arm and grinned. "He got drunk last night celebrating; the whole village did, except us."

The town sheriff burst in, bleary eyed and reeking of alcohol. He was a skinny fellow in his mid-forties with a large, dark moustache and a very red nose. "Where is he? My darling boy," he bellowed as he proceeded to hug Allrik and smother his reluctant head with kisses. "I can't believe it; you know the Arkuna. What is she like? I must know everything; absolutely everything."

Allrik winced at the enthusiastic embrace and tried to dodge the advancing moustached lips and the powerful alcoholic vapours that issued from them, but the man still managed to plant a wet kiss on his mouth.

"I couldn't believe it when the Doc told me; imagine heroes of the revolution in our little town."

"Mind the fellow's arm," barked the doctor. "I didn't fix him up so you could come and slobber over him."

"Oh! I forget myself," declared the sheriff, in a theatrically horrified manner. He stepped away from the relieved Allrik and grinned at him with an expression of stupid adulation before turning his attention to Jodi. "And a man from another world," he declared, waving an arm to the heavens. "This is truly an auspicious day; a day that will live long in the memory; a day that…"

"Shut up, Samric," shouted the doctor, "you're not making a speech in my house. These men need to get to Salom Gul and you're going to take them."

The exuberant sheriff switched off his wide grin and bowed solemnly. "It will be an honour, gentlemen."

The first threat of dawn hung in the sky as they sped from the village along a dusty track that wound between the plantations surrounding the village. It was clear from the manner of his driving that Sheriff Samric was still the worse for alcohol and twice they nearly left the track and ploughed into a sparse stand of crops, managing to swerve back on to the track at the last moment. Allrik grimaced at the jolting movement as he sat next to the grinning sheriff while Jodi clung on to the back where a temporary seat had been arranged in the goods-well.

They cleared the irrigated plantation and were suddenly thrown back into the stark and beautiful expanse of the desert plain. To their right the massif of the uplands over which they had struggled, loomed in the developing light. The track veered towards the forbidding slope and followed its base for three hours until it sunk away behind them in the shimmering heat of the day. Sheriff Samric talked almost constantly; developing minute details on an array of subjects that principally featured his wife and her annoying habits or her friends and *their* annoying habits. His thirst for knowledge of the battle at the Mine of Kusk seemed to have been forgotten at the convenience of having a captive audience for his domestic complaints.

After six hours of grinding desert travel, they rolled into a village that seemed to spring out of the sand and dust of the barren landscape. Someone had warned the shabby, skeletal population of the approach of the celebrities and a table had been set up in the central square of the settlement and every one of the residents had mustered for the arrival. The 'Liberators of Kusk' were mobbed as they shakily disembarked from the cart. Men clasped at them and tried to touch them and women kissed them and offered favours. They were conveyed to the large table and invited to eat and drink as much as they pleased. Noticing that no others were partaking, Jodi and Allrik ate sparingly while Samric, intent on maximizing his opportunity, consumed the majority of the offering and stuffed a considerable amount into his pockets to the obvious annoyance of the villagers. Ignoring his rudeness, the village sheriff recited a proclamation.

"People of Khom, we are honoured by the presence of the Liberators of Kusk who are known to the Arkuna herself. Few of us can remember the times of plenty before the usurper, Strellic, cast his shadow on this Division and brought us to this mean and low condition. But now Strellic has been ousted from his fat palace and once again, we will know the joys of liberty and plenty. It started with the rebellion at Kusk and it finished at Salom Gul and we thank you from the depths of our hearts for your part in this struggle."

The sheriff whooped and held his fist aloft and the villagers echoed his salute. Allrik and Jodi rose and thanked the villagers for their greeting and their food and declared that they must move on. They dragged Samric away from the remains of the food and the villagers followed them to the cart and cheered as they headed off into the desert.

After three hours of harsh, jolting travel under the relentless sun of Tarnus, they began to come across signs of life. Crude shacks appeared among small patches of scrub-like cultivation and they could see men and women look up from their hard labours as they passed. Since the elevation of the Beloved Leader, mechanical cultivation of the soil had all but died as the machines wore out and could not be replaced or repaired and now the population turned the sod much as their forefathers did a thousand years before.

It was late afternoon when the battle-scarred outline of Salom Gul finally appeared on the horizon. They drove past the burned-out hulks of Strellic's air-arm and approached the city. Down the long, straight road they could see a group of soldiers ahead who were taking a keen interest in them.

"Slow down," said Allrik, tensing. "They'll be nervous and they don't know who we are."

They crawled towards the soldiers until one fired his weapon. The beam whooshed above them and made the air shimmer. The sheriff screamed and slammed the cart into reverse.

"Stop," said Jodi, "I'll get out and speak to them."

"They're trying to kill us," shouted the sheriff, paying him no heed.

Jodi drew his knife and put it to the sheriff's throat. "Stop the damn cart, now."

The sheriff jammed on the break and brought the vehicle to a stop. His white knuckles gripped the steering and his body was shaking quite violently.

"If they'd wanted to kill us they could have done it easily enough," said Allrik. "We'll walk in."

Jodi and Allrik disembarked while the sheriff hurtled off in reverse. They walked slowly towards the wary company of eight men whose weapons were primed and aimed at them. At fifty metres a corporal ordered them to stop.

"We have come to join the revolution," called Jodi.

"Who are you?" shouted the corporal.

"Two men from the Mine of Kusk."

The soldiers discussed this information for a few moments. "Are you armed?"

"No, except a knife."

"Take off your clothes slowly, if you make any sudden moves we'll shoot you."

Jodi and Allrik slowly and deliberately obeyed, placing their clothes on the ground to one side.

"Turn around," commanded the corporal.

They turned and the soldiers saw the tell-tale welts on each man's back. A soldier ran up, picked up his clothes and carried them back to the corporal. He searched them and pulled out the army knife that Jodi was carrying. "We'll it looks like they're telling the truth; he's not armed except this and it looks like they've been in the mine judging from the state of them. Come forward," he called.

Jodi and Allrik approached the soldiers who regarded them suspiciously. The corporal threw them their clothes. "You look like a foreigner, where you from?"

"I'm from Ennepp," replied Jodi as he dressed.

"Ennepp, that's a long way from here."

Jodi nodded. "I came here to look for somebody, a Kagan held in the mine."

The corporal's eyes widened; "do you mean Lodan DeRhogai?"

"Yes, I came with his father. Is Lodan DeRhogai still alive?"

"Very much so; he stormed the palace with the Arkuna."

"I need to see him, and the Arkuna will be glad to see my friend."

The corporal addressed Allrik. "You know her?"

"We were in the mine together; we broke out together."

The corporal's eyes lit up; he was practically in the presence of royalty. "Please forgive the indignity, Sir. There are still elements of Strellic's forces in and around the city. Four men got killed by one of his mad-men wearing a bomb a few hours ago; we have orders to check everyone."

"No need to apologise, we weren't offended," replied Allrik.

The corporal saluted Allrik. "You'll find them at the palace, Sir."

Allrik grinned sheepishly and saluted back; he was not used to being acknowledged by those who out-ranked him.

"Sir, it will be an honour to provide a guard for your safe passage; the city is still dangerous."

Allrik nodded. "Thank you Corporal."

A detail of four was appointed and they set off together into the war-torn city.

Lorel leaned back in Strellic's chair of state and placed her feet on the dusty table. "Are you sure General Gerlic has declared for us?"

Colonel Doric nodded. "I spoke to him personally; he has no reason to support Strellic, the man had his brother and father put to death."

"He brings about ten thousand troops to the cause," said Lieutenant Norgu.

"It's not enough," replied Lorel. "We are still outnumbered by more than two to one. We need more defections." She surveyed the dozen officers seated around the table and Lodan, casually splayed in a seat at the far end. "Any ideas?"

"We need to be able to offer them something," said another officer.

"What about freedom, is that not enough?" replied Lorel.

"Not in this case," said Norgu.

Lorel swung her feet from the table and stood up. "Strellic has fled to Hensk, his place of birth and the seat of his power and we must assume that Sarlat has gone there also with the remains of the Elite Guard. We must also assume they will gather their forces and attack us. In open combat we stand no chance, even with General Gerlic's troops. If only we had air power."

Colonel Doric bristled. "I had to destroy it; it would have been used against us."

Lorel turned to him. "Colonel I wasn't implying a criticism of your tactics; I quite see the point of what you did. It was quite correct tactically."

"What about the Electors of Trant?" said Lodan.

The company stared at him in unified disgust.

"You could offer a share in the mine and a peace deal," he persisted, ignoring their obvious disapprobation.

"Lodan," replied Lorel patiently, "you're a Kagan, you have no idea what you are suggesting. Trant and Rion have been at war for over a hundred years; they are our mortal enemies."

"They're just people, like everyone here. Can anybody remember why you're at war? What's it all about?"

"They want the mine," replied Doric. "They have always laid a bogus claim to it."

"From my personal experience," began Lodan with some warmth, "they could hardly make a worse job of running it. It needs investment, machines, not people who are sent there to work until they die."

"You don't know what you're saying, DeRhogai," said Norgu.

"Really? Consider this; assuming you vanquish Strellic, are you going to preside over the continuation of the mine as it was?"

"Of course not," said Lorel.

"Rion is busted, there is no money for investment in the mine and now there are no air defences to speak of. It is likely that you will be invaded anyway."

"We will fight them to the last," declared Doric.

Lodan shrugged. "It will be the end of Rion and you know it."

The discussion was interrupted by the entrance of a soldier. "Ma'am, I have two men out here who claim to know you. They have been searched and disarmed."

Lorel drew her sidearm; she knew of no one who would make such a claim. "Send them in," she commanded.

The soldier saluted and withdrew and the entire company tensed and turned to towards the door as Allrik walked into the room and saluted.

Lodan was the first to react; he shot to his feet, sending his chair flying and bound over to his friend. He grabbed Allrik and hugged him causing the man to howl with pain. Lodan released him quickly. "I'm sorry, we thought you were dead."

Lorel came up and kissed him, her eyes bright with tears of joy. "We saw the craft attack your position. How did you survive?"

"I nearly didn't," replied Allrik, "Jodi got me through it."

Now Lorel saw Jodi standing near the door; she walked up to him and said, "Thank you for bringing him back to us."

Jodi held her gaze and a flash of understanding passed between them; a brief moment of recognition instantly dissolved by the joy of the occasion. "Allrik saved my life, I could hardly abandon him. Besides, he knew which way to go; I didn't."

"I am glad to see you both," she said.

"I too," added Lodan as he and Allrik joined them.

"I need to speak to you both in private," said Jodi. "It is a matter that concerned your father, Lodan."

Lodan bowed his head. "He should have left when I told him to."

"I agree, but he chose to stay and it cost him his life. Now I have to perform a duty on his behalf. A confidential duty."

Lorel turned to the counsel of officers. "Our friends have returned from the dead. This is a good time to break for a meal. Think about what has been said; we will reconvene in three hours." She turned back to three men. "Get cleaned up, we will discuss this over a meal."

Jodi stepped out of Strellic's large bath and rubbed himself dry on the fluffy, white towels with the embellished monogram *U.S.* on them. He shook out the dust from his clothes and put them on, catching sight, as he dressed, of his image in one of the highly polished reflectors in the ornate room. He was surprised at what he saw; a man much older than he recalled, scarred from recent action, his head still shorn from his internment in the mine. He turned his back to the reflector and looked over his shoulder at the welts on his back. He had not seen them before; they looked angry and it surprised him that they did not trouble him more. A couple of officers disturbed his inspection and he finished dressing while they eyed him curiously as they disrobed and descended into the greyish water of the bath.

Jodi left them to their speculations and made his way along a blast-shattered corridor to a room at the back of the palace. Lorel, Lodan and Allrik were already sitting on heavy cushions around a low table on which sat an array of exotic offerings scoured from the kitchens below. The sun was dwindling and refracted through the shattered window, dappling the room with ruddy luminescence. Outside a distant flash lit the sky for a moment followed by the crackling sound of weapons and collapsing stonework.

"They're still mopping up," said Lorel. "Sit down, Jodi, eat something."

Jodi took a cushion next to Allrik and chose something from the array of food before him. He put it in his mouth and the sweetness of it almost made him gag. He spat it out on to the floor behind him. "What is that?"

"We don't know," replied Allrik with a laugh.

"Our Beloved Leader has strange tastes," added Lorel.

Jodi gulped some wine to expunge the taste. "It's disgusting."

Lodan gazed at Jodi steadily. "I am curious to hear what you have to say, Jodi."

Jodi took another swig and looked into the eyes of each in turn. "I am going to speak of a matter that concerns you, Lodan and because of your late father's involvement, also concerns you, Lorel. Allrik, you have no part in this affair, but I have come to know you and trust you absolutely and I know that you will not betray this confidence so I have no objection to you hearing what I am about to tell you."

His three companions stopped eating and fixed their attention on Jodi.

"A while ago a Suran, by the name of Solon Bru, came across an ancient object of undoubted human origin. It came from a region in the depths of the spiral arm and it proved to be over one hundred and twenty thousand years old."

"That's impossible," said Lodan. A cold shiver ran up his spine in fear of what Jodi was about to say.

"Wrong, it's only too possible; I will explain. About one hundred and fifty years ago a treatise was written predicting exactly this. The authors were a Suran academic called Lim and his pupil, Juran DeRhogai, your present Arkon, Lodan."

Lodan stared at him; he had guessed as much. His own Arkon was the author of the heretical document he had read on the journey to Barta Magnus. "You are referring to the heretical Fourth Proposition," he said quietly.

Jodi nodded. "You know of it?"

"I have read it; a tissue of improbable and blasphemous speculation."

"Your Arkon would hardly agree. The treatise predicted that humanity must have evolved on a world remote from our own civilization, a notion, of course, poisonous to the Faith. The Evangelists came to know about the discovery and Bru was pursued to Tarnus, to the Division of Trant, to be precise, where he came into contact with my sister, Matty. My sister and two others besides went with Bru and they are now on their way to the location where the ancient object was found. Unfortunately they have a pursuer, an Evangelist called Dax. Your original mission, Lodan, was to neutralize the Evangelist and secure whatever lies in the outer reaches for the DeRhogai Family. The Arkon is convinced that a vast fortune in the form of knowledge and artefacts exists somewhere in the outer spiral arm and he was relying on you find and secure this treasure."

Lodan brooded. So the Arkon had tricked him and intended him to be the instrument of the destruction of the Faith. No wonder he kept from him the true nature of the mission.

"In order that you could complete your task, the Arkon purchased a deep-space cruiser. To keep the business secret, he was forced to obtain it in an illicit and obscure way. Your father, Lorel, was to be the provider and we have confirmation that the vehicle was ready. That means that somewhere in Rion sits a deep-space cruiser waiting for its mission."

Lorel furrowed her brow and shook her head. "That isn't possible, how would it run the blockade?"

"The blockade is a sham, a joke. Moontraders run it all the time and anyone with the means to buy off a few petty officials can pass it. I don't think you realize how influential and wealthy your father was. He was one of the few individuals in the galaxy who had the means to buy a deep-space cruiser, and his financial clout opened many doors and blinded many officials and even governments to what he was doing."

Now it was Lorel's turn to be amazed. "My father!" she exclaimed. "I can't believe it; he never said anything to me about this."

"No doubt to protect you should it all be discovered."

"How was the Arkon's plan thwarted?" asked Lodan.

"Your great uncle informed Strellic of the General's extraneous activities. His purpose was to stop your mission."

Lodan's features hardened and his eyes glazed. "So I was sacrificed by my great uncle. I'm going to kill that man."

"You are too late," replied Jodi. "Your great uncle tried to usurp the Arkon; he failed and he died by his own hand."

Lodan glowered. "There is some justice at least. How do you know all this, Jodi?"

"I heard it from the Arkon's own lips."

"You had an audience!"

"I was with your father during his audience."

"That must have inconvenienced the Arkon."

"He was not pleased about it but your father insisted on me being there."

Lodan allowed himself a wry smile. "Typical of Sevarius to insult the old bastard like that."

Jodi turned to Lorel. "I want you to think hard; did your late father ever mention anything about this, even in some oblique way?"

Lorel considered then shook her head slowly. "I don't recall him ever mentioning anything."

"Did he ever go away for any periods without telling you where he was going?"

"Quite often, on army business, he said."

"Did he ever take anyone with him, say a trusted officer for example?"

"No, he always went alone."

Jodi bit his lip and thought for a moment. It seemed that Lorel was not a party to her father's activities, as he had expected and was, therefore, not going to be the means of his escape from Tarnus. He needed to get after Dax and kill him before he could get to Matty, but he had lost too much time and now hope was fading.

"You do realise," said Allrik, "that what we are talking about here is something that will change the entire course of human history."

Jodi nodded solemnly. "Only if we can reach it, otherwise it will be buried by those who want it buried."

"I have never been into space, never even left Rion," uttered Allrik reflectively. "Jodi, if we find the cruiser, I'd like to go with you."

"It's a long trip, a big commitment and it is likely you will never be able to return to Rion and to those you care for."

"The only people I care about are in this room," replied Allrik.

"Then, of course, I would welcome your company."

"We have work to do here before we go chasing after treasure," said Lodan glancing at Lorel to see her reaction, he was in no hurry to embark on this blasphemous quest.

Lorel was deep in thought and betrayed no reaction to what Lodan had just said. He wondered if she was considering abandoning the coming struggle with Strellic in favour of this quest. A silence fell and the echo of firearms drifted through the gaping window as the last vestiges of sunlight drifted away.

After some moments Lorel broke the silence. "What do you think is out there, Jodi?"

"The Arkon is convinced that a great treasure awaits humanity; Sevarius was more sceptical, and doubted whether it could even be found. There are billions of stars out there and most have planetary systems; the odds are not good but he agreed to undertake the mission after releasing you, Lodan. It seems your family's continued prosperity depends on it."

Lodan turned towards Lorel. "You're actually thinking of going on this mad quest?"

Lorel closed her eyes and paused before answering. "My father died because of it; I think he would have wanted me to go. But you are right, Lodan, We do have work to do and I will not abandon my people while they need me."

"Gentlemen, we have all had time to reflect and now we must plot our course."

The eyes of the company were turned on Lorel as she stood at the head of the council table. Darkness had fallen on the city and two flaming lamps lit the room with a flickering bronze glow that seemed to heighten the air of expectation in the room. Jodi stood by the window looking out into the night that was occasionally illuminated with the flash of a discharged weapon. Allrik sat next to Lodan at the other end of the council table; all three had been charged to remain silent during the meeting.

Lieutenant Norgu spoke first, only to ask Lorel what she thought they should do.

"I have given this long thought," she began, "and I have come to the conclusion that we have to approach the Electors of Trant for help."

There was a rising bustle of indignant disagreement from around the table. Colonel Doric stood up. "This is preposterous; I would rather surrender to Strellic than allow the enemy to place his boot on the neck of this Division. They will discover our weakness and we would be humiliated and made subjects of the Electors. Have we not fought these people for over a hundred years, sacrificing the lives of thousands upon thousands? Does this sacrifice mean nothing to you? You would allow this bastard Division to obliterate us and actually invite it? Your father would be ashamed of you."

The colonel sat down with a passionate and furious look on his face. The other officers hummed agreement. Only Norgu remained silent.

"My father," replied Lorel calmly, "is not here to speak. My father, as all of you know, was a practical man who would have looked at the military reality before him and would have come to the best, logical solution. Gentlemen, your passion and patriotism are not things in question here; they are taken as given. My father, since you mention him, would have calmly assessed the military situation and chosen the best course available. Without General Gerlic's forces, which, at this time, show no sign of stirring themselves for battle, we have two and a half thousand troops and Strellic has access to over twenty thousand. He has superior mechanical capabilities, supplies and finances. He will come and re-take the city and we will have no effective means of stopping him."

"I would rather fight and die here than submit to either Strellic or the Electors," said Colonel Doric decisively.

"Is that the opinion of you all?" asked Lorel, casting her eyes over each man.

There was general assent except Lieutenant Norgu. "I agree with Lorel; it is futile to fight and die here."

"Are you afraid to die?" replied Doric sarcastically.

Norgu shot to his feet. "Are you accusing me of cowardice?"

"Do I need to?" replied Doric.

"Stop this immediately," shouted Lorel. "Nobody in this room needs to prove their bravery. We have all fought and many have already died. This needs to be a sane and calm discussion; the decision we come to here will affect the lives of millions of people; not only ourselves but all the citizens of this Division. There must be no bravado or snap judgements, nor must there be any suggestion of suicidal heroism. For the sake of all the people, we need to plot our way out of this mess as best we can."

"I still say, no surrender," said Doric.

"May I say something?" said Lodan.

"You are a foreigner," replied Doric, "your opinions count for nothing here."

"Colonel Doric is right," said Lorel. "And we agreed that you should not contribute."

At this point, Allrik stood up. "I would like to speak."

Doric rose. "You forget yourself soldier; you are a mere trooper and dishonourably discharged at that. You should not even be in this room with real soldiers."

"Allrik is here by my invitation, Colonel," said Lorel with calm but decisive authority. "He may speak."

Allrik, a little nervous in such esteemed company, spoke tentatively. "I was with Lodan DeRhogai for twenty-six days in the Mine of Kusk; he saved my life and I consider him to be a brother and therefore a citizen of Rion. But most of all, he is neutral and may offer an outsider's view. You should hear him speak. That is all I wanted to say."

"Thank you, Allrik," said Lorel, "it cannot harm us to hear what Lodan DeRhogai has to say; if nobody objects that is."

There was a general buzz of assent and Lorel raised an invitational hand to Lodan.

"Allrik is right," he began, "I am not one of you although I have become involved in this struggle. On my home planet of Kagan, we have a unitary government made up of factions who constantly conduct their petty, pseudo wars with each other to nobody's benefit. It debilitates the good government of Kagan, causes stalemate and stands in the way of progress. On Tarnus you have turned your disputes into real wars, destroying your societies and economies and your environments. It has encouraged and allowed the accession of people like Strellic; monsters who usurp power and benefit from the continuation of conflict. I say, why not change this? Why not take this opportunity to break this self-serving spiral of war and sue for peace with your neighbours?"

Colonel Doric banged the table with his fist. "You have no idea what you are suggesting. You don't know these people; they are not interested in peace and co-operation, they are interested in occupation. If we sue for peace they will realise our weakness and we will be invaded; put to the sword, DeRhogai; is that what you want?"

The officers briefly protested their support for Doric. Lodan waited for them to fall silent. "Colonel Doric, gentlemen, I appreciate your fears, they are probably well founded, but don't you think the Elector's spies have not already informed them of the situation here? When you have fought Strellic and the bodies of the soldiers of Rion lie scattered in the ruins of this city, they will come."

It was clear from the reaction of the council of officers that they had not considered this scenario; or, perhaps more accurately, had not wanted to consider it. They all gazed at Lodan, stony–faced, and said nothing. Lorel remained impassive, but she was smiling inside. She, Norgu and Lodan had discussed this very probability earlier and they had decided that he should be the one to bring it to the attention of the Council of Officers. The reaction was just what she had expected and it turned the tide of opinion.

"What do you suggest we do, Mister DeRhogai?" asked one officer.

"An approach to the Electors offering peace and an interest in the mine providing they are willing to invest. That way the mine could be re-mechanized and made more efficient and nobody need suffer in it anymore."

"You think it's that simple?" said Doric moodily.

"It is not simple and there is no guarantee that the Electors of Trant won't take advantage anyway; but as yet, I have not heard a viable alternative."

"Shall we vote on this?" said Lorel.

The vote was taken by a show of hands and all but Doric and one other officer agreed to the approach.

"Colonel Doric, Lieutenant Giric, I am sorry that you do not feel comfortable with this policy; you are both important to the revolution and I had hoped to carry you with us. Will you at least acquiesce?"

Colonel Doric replied, "I believe you are making a mistake, but I am willing to go along with this as long as it looks viable. I do not trust the Electors and neither should anyone in this room, but the only alternative I can offer is blood and sacrifice. By that account I suppose we have nothing to lose."

"Thank you Colonel. Now, we need a delegate. I propose myself."

"No," replied Norgu. "You are the Chairman of the Council and the people now know you; you should not go."

"I agree," said Lodan. "You need a non-military person and someone who might be perceived as neutral; someone who is not from Tarnus."

"Are you proposing yourself?" said Doric.

"I am not proposing myself, but I will go if you wish to appoint me."

"It could be dangerous," put in Lorel. "There is no guarantee that the Electors won't simply arrest and imprison you. They might even execute you."

Lodan shrugged. "I am the descendant of an Arkon of Kagan; unlike Strellic, they might think twice about doing that. Anyway, it's a decent proposal so why would they?"

Lorel smiled. "The chair thanks you Lodan, this is a generous offer. We will take a vote on it."

The vote was taken and a proposal drafted which all members of the council signed. The meeting then disbanded and the various commanders returned to their units leaving Lorel, Lodan, Jodi and Allrik alone in the room. Outside the city had subsided into silence and the residents had clambered into holes below the rubble to take uneasy sleep. In the council room one of the torches died leaving part of the room in deep shadow. Lorel remained seated at the council table, lost in thought; she could feel Jodi watching her from the shadows, but did not look up at him lest she betray herself to him and the others. "Have we done the right thing?" she whispered.

"Do you think it's what your father would have done?" said Lodan.

She frowned thoughtfully. "I don't know; I honestly don't."

Before sunrise the following morning, Lodan stood outside the palace walls with Lorel, a navigator and a driver. The troop carrier had been loaded with necessities and the two men boarded it and waited for their passenger.

"It's normally about two day's journey to the border, but they have instructions to detour well away from any army bases. You will be travelling mostly through uninhabited country so you should be able to remain undercover until you get to the border. Do not try and cross the border, it is riddled with mines and automatic traps. Once you have negotiated the mines on our side of the line wait in no man's land until they come and check on you. You will have to go unarmed. Good luck, Lodan; we will all be thinking of you."

"And I of you," replied Lodan, taking her hand tenderly.

She didn't pull away but he sensed a slight awkwardness in her reaction.

"We have gone through a lot together," he added.

She smiled. "We have indeed."

"We may not see each other again. If I can't persuade the Electors to intervene there will be nothing to stop Strellic; it will be difficult for you here."

"I am ready to die and if it be here at least it will be under the open sky and not in the Mine of Kusk. I will never go back there."

"You know how much I care for you," he uttered hesitantly.

"Yes I do." She held his head and kissed him tenderly on each cheek but he could feel the reserve in her touch. He smiled weakly and turned away. As the troop carrier lumbered away from the palace, he looked back and caught sight of her, arms folded, standing alone below the palace walls.

XXIII

The substantial crowd had been waiting over an hour in the square outside Strellic's southern palace. They were becoming quite restless and the monitors were obliged to strike and make examples of those who displayed overt disloyalty. At last, having judged the expectation to be at its height, Umbert Strellic appeared on the front balcony and began saluting the cheering crowd. Suspiciously well-produced placards were waved in apparent enthusiasm, sporting sentiments such as 'Strellic will live forever' and 'the Beloved Leader will triumph over evil'; there were hats and shirts with similar monograms worn by the gathering that, on the appearance of the Marshal, were ecstatically tossed into the air.

Strellic waved the mace of state nonchalantly at the crowd for a few minutes then disappeared into the relative sanity of his palace.

"You see, gentlemen, they love me; they love me," he asserted as he threw the gold-plated mace on to the table.

The gathering of ministers and generals all concurred enthusiastically, while Sarlat, slumped in a chair in the corner of the room, watched in glum silence.

Outside, the crowd fell silent and disappeared almost immediately, leaving behind trampled placards and discarded hats.

Strellic sat down heavily. "Have we heard from General Gerlic? Has he declared for us?"

"Beloved Marshal, we have not yet heard from the General," replied the newly-appointed minister of arms.

Strellic pursed his lips and drew a sour expression. "He is waiting to see which side of the fence to jump; I will personally twist his balls off when this is over. Have there been any more uprisings?"

Another General replied. "Minor problems caused by malcontents and traitors, Marshal; they will be crushed."

"See that they are; these traitors must be eliminated, without mercy." Strellic banged the table before him with his fist for suitable emphasis. "Now, what of the preparation for the attack?"

The ministers and generals gathered around the chart of Rion and described their strategy. The army was to be split into three factions, each taking a different route north. They were to approach Salom Gul from three directions and co-ordinate the attack in three days' time."

Strellic listened with mounting impatience until, finally, putting an end to their prattling by bellowing, "Rubbish. This is the plan of cowards and diseased minds."

The assembly blinked at him in nervous surprise.

"We will attack tomorrow and we will take the quickest and most direct route, straight up the Gul Valley."

The generals exchanged glances, each waiting for the other to point out the difficulty, but, in the event, none did.

"I suggest you get on with your preparations immediately. I want these bastards wiped out, eradicated; their suffering will be an example to all those who dare to challenge my authority."

The company bowed in turn and filed out leaving Strellic alone with his son. Sarlat was no military genius, but even he could see the folly of his father's plan. He would have gladly let the old fool fall into the error, but self-preservation prompted him to speak.

"Dadda," he began, "I think your plan may be a bit dangerous."

Strellic rounded on him. "Are you still here? Don't call me by that name, you are not my son; I am Marshal Strellic to you from now on."

Duly chastened, Sarlat pouted.

"I wish Orgun was here, instead of you; he was a complete fuck-up but at least he had balls. He wouldn't have lost the city to a rabble."

"We were outnumbered and surrounded; I was lucky to get out alive."

"You should have fought to the death; I never would have taken the fruit of my own flesh for a coward."

"I notice you didn't hang around," replied Sarlat recklessly.

Strellic was so angry that he started to shake; his eyes watered and he looked quite ready to explode. He picked up his mace of office from the table and advanced on Sarlat who was cornered. "No Dadda," screamed Sarlat as Strellic rained blow after blow down on him while he squealed and tried to defend himself with raised arms.

"Don't Dadda; you're hurting me, Dadda," he wailed as another well-aimed volley slipped past his defences.

"If you we're not my own blood, I would have you torn to pieces; now get out," screamed Strellic, stopping for a moment to gather himself.

Sarlat escaped with only one further blow to his back. He ran out through the door leaving his purple-faced father panting on a chair.

XXIV

Lorel spent the day organizing the evacuation of Salom Gul and the defence of the city. Anyone prepared to stay and fight was welcomed and supplied with arms provided they could prove their loyalty to the Revolution. Most of the citizens of Salom Gul bore a grudge towards Strellic; some because they had suffered the loss of relatives to torture and imprisonment in the mine, others because they were so degraded in their circumstances that they simply had nothing left to lose.

In the end, over a million people gathered up whatever they could carry and made their way out into the northern hinterland of the city.

Lieutenant Norgu took a company out into the Gul Valley and left a few surprises for anyone approaching from that direction. Jodi and Allrik went with him and returned to the city that evening hot and exhausted. They did not expect Strellic to commit all his troops to that route, but the general expectation was that some of them would come that way. Leaving Allrik and Norgu to a meal with their troops, Jodi made his way back to the palace and to the private quarters of Umbert Strellic. The palace was practically deserted with only the occasional sound of human occupation echoing down its cracked and dusty halls. The private quarters were empty and the evening was particularly warm and sticky so he entered the bathroom, disrobed and descended into the cool, opaque waters of the polished stone bath. Above him he could see the first, bright stars of evening shining through a large, ragged hole in the ceiling. He shut his eyes and began to review the events of the past few days. How, in the name of the Prophet had he managed to become embroiled in this foreign civil war? It seemed to him now that his time with Laon at the palace on Ennepp constituted the only respite in the constant turmoil of his life.

He ducked under the water and stayed there for almost a minute, holding his breath as Murgan Doh had once taught him. When his head rose above the surface, he knew instinctively he was not alone. He opened his eyes expecting to see another officer, but instead he saw Lorel.

There was a brief moment of awkwardness as neither quite knew how to react. She had not expected to find anyone present and was quite surprised to see his head emerging from the grey water.

"I'm sorry," she said at last, "I thought the place was empty."

"I'll get out," he replied without attempting to move. "I'm sure you'd rather be alone."

She shrugged. "Don't go on my account, we have both seen each other naked."

"Not under these circumstances," he observed quickly.

"Then shut your eyes while I undress and get in."

He shut his eyes and heard the rustle of her clothes and the gentle splash of the water as she lowered herself in as far from him as possible.

"You may open them now," she said.

He opened his eyes. Her head and shoulders protruded above the water level just above the line of her breasts.

"It would be nice to have fresh water, but the plumbing has been destroyed," she began in a conversational tone.

He smiled; a rare thing, she had noticed, and not entirely suited to his general disposition. "I wouldn't recommend drinking it."

"This must be difficult for you, Jodi. This war that has nothing to do with you."

He met her eyes, taking in the alabaster-like whiteness of her long neck and shoulders. "It seems I have been fighting all my life; fighting my own kind; fighting the Bhasi masters; fighting to stay alive; now here, fighting a despot of your race."

"You don't have to fight; you could go, be safe somewhere 'till this is all over. No one would blame you for it."

"Do you really think that?"

"Yes, of course."

'I don't believe you.'

She feigned a look of shock and drew her knees up so that they formed two round islands in the water. "Why should I lie?"

He observed her steadily, imagining what lay beneath the water-line between those two islands, glad that she could not see what was happening below his. "I think you would think less of a man who did not fight."

She arched a delicate, pale brow. "What do you care what I think of you?"

She had trapped him, he struggled mentally for escape. "We are colleagues in arms and, I hope, friends enough to care what each thinks of the other."

She laughed, totally aware that he had narrowly escaped her little mind trap. "Well said."

He coloured a little though she could not see this in the shadowy starlight of the bathroom; he had never before been in the presence of a woman who made him feel so awkward. He changed the subject. "When do you think Strellic will come?"

"Anytime in the next three days."

"Are you frightened?"

She became pensive. "That's an interesting question. I'd say apprehensive rather than frightened. What about you?"

Jodi shrugged. "I have been close to death many times; the thought no longer scares me. I am disappointed that I will not get to see my sister again."

"She means much to you, doesn't she?"

"I made a promise that I would find her when we were forced to part."

"Sometimes promises just can't be kept."

"Sometimes," he replied reflectively.

She gazed at her knees. "You know by this time tomorrow night we might both be dead."

"It's very possible," he agreed barely audibly.

She looked up directly into his eyes. In her short life she had encountered many men, but none as beautiful and complex as he. It seemed to her, at that moment, that some predestined force had brought him from the stars to her and it was the most natural thing that they should be together. Until now she had hardly spoken to him and yet she experienced a feeling of familiarity as if they had known each other for years. It emboldened her and directed her to ask a question that might have shocked her in other circumstances. "Do you have experience with women, Jodi?"

He had not expected the conversation to take such a sudden, personal turn. He considered lying for some reason that he could not quite explain. Other than his juvenile experience with his half-sister, his only real sexual encounter had been with Rea, a much older woman; a woman for whom he held no more feelings than those of simple gratitude. With Lorel he felt something entirely different and now he felt vulnerable and inadequate and certainly inexperienced. His reply was tentative. "I'm not a virgin, if that is what you mean."

440

His reply disappointed her; she had hoped to find him as inexperienced as she and, in truth, she was jealous that other women had known him.

"I suppose we'd better get out," she said after a long silence.

"I suppose," he replied.

"Shut your eyes then."

He closed his eyes and heard the splash of water as she rose from the bath. He was not sure of himself but there was no way he could prevent his eyes from opening. In the half-light he saw her emerge from the water and step on to the stone floor that surrounded the bath. He saw the outline of her breasts and firm body and the exciting shape her buttocks made as she stepped out of the bath. It was too much to endure and he suddenly sprang from the water and grabbed her, violently spinning her around and kissing her hard on the lips as he pushed himself against her. She kissed him back with equal passion as she felt herself carried across the room until her back hit the polished wall of the bathhouse. He picked her up by her buttocks and forced himself between her legs. She reached down and urgently pushed him inside her and they both gasped in unison at the contact as she slowly took his full length and their wet pubic hairs mingled. She ran her hands across the raised welts on his back as they kissed with intense passion and were then still, holding the moment in motionless harmony, entwined figures fashioned from pure, white marble, clinging to one another as if this was the last act of their lives.

Later, in Strellic's bed, they made love again, this time with more care and exploration. He held her afterwards and they talked frankly of their pasts. He was surprised to discover that he was the first man to whom she had made love for she was five or six years older than he and had been in the company of men a great deal. When she told him of her rape at the hands of one of Sarlat's men, he tensed and went silent for some time. When she looked up at his face she could see tears had moistened his dark eyes.

"Do not cry for my sake, Jodi," she implored. "It was horrible and bitter, but you have mended it."

He held her closer and kissed her forehead, but said nothing for some time while the awful memory of his own rape churned inside and forced its way into his present contentment. "I was raped once too," he whispered almost to himself.

She sat up and gazed into his face. "What happened to you?"

He did not meet her gaze, still unable to expunge the shame. "After I escaped from the estate where I was enslaved, I went north towards the city. I got hungry and ill and weak and I came across three men of my own race, camping in the open. They fed me and let me stay near the fire; then they held me down and raped me, one by one. I couldn't fight them; I was weak and just a boy."

She gently took his head and kissed away the tears as he sobbed quietly in the tender, warmth of the night. They felt the intimacy of a shared confidence and it drew them closer together and sealed a bond between them, but neither ever referred to it again.

The next morning she awoke first and watched his face as he slept and the first daylight touched the city through the shattered window of the chamber. The thought of what was to come that day disturbed her tranquillity. She didn't know if she could bear to lose him in the fight and entertained plots to keep him safe. But she had discovered enough about Jodi to know that such an idea was useless and they would have to trust to Fate and whatever it would bring. She wondered if her father would approve of him, this foreigner from a far world, and convinced herself that he would have approved simply because she had chosen him and she loved him. She recalled her father's stern words about men and especially soldiers and smiled. How right he had been.

Her fond thoughts drifted to the dark and traumatic time before his death at the hands of Umbert Strellic and she recalled the oddness of his last words to her; 'Remember the last time the three of us were together in the north. Remember it, darling; always remember it'. She frowned as the words echoed in her mind and the meaning suddenly became clear.

She knew where the deep-space cruiser was.

XXV

The wilderness that occupied a large portion of the northwest sector of the Division of Rion was entirely devoid of population. The Outland, as it was called, lay beyond the Desert of Kusk and extended for over a thousand kilometres until finally being subsumed by the frozen, barren wastes of the Northern Polar Region of Tarnus. On this land no rain had fallen for over a hundred years; no vegetation of any kind clung grimly to life; no rivers ran through it and there were no aquifers to rescue it from universal desolation. The only sign of human presence was the long militarized border between Rion and Trant that ran from the pole in a straight line for fifteen hundred kilometres until it traversed a river in the south, which formed a more natural boundary.

Lodan and his two companions entered this land from the direction of Kusk and began to cross the wide, featureless plain. The troop carrier was rudimentary but well designed for such terrain, having four sets of tracks that rolled over the dust and rock with ease but would jolt its occupants mercilessly as it bumped and pitched over the land. Terrik, the driver, was a young, rather swaggering character who chatted constantly and inconsequentially about every subject that came into his rather vacant head. Fornu, the navigator, was older; a man in his mid-forties, taciturn and laconic in his observations of his colleague. Lodan listened much and spoke little, except to ask pertinent questions about the terrain and the direction of travel.

They travelled through the day without stopping, urinating when required, into funnel-like contraption that had an outlet at the base of the vehicle. When they finally stopped it was almost nightfall.

"There are hidden gullies and ravines," said Terrik, the driver. "It is not safe to go at night. We'll stop here 'til morning light."

Lodan rose from his seat and massaged his spine. He walked down the opening ramp at the back of the vehicle and looked back along the deep-rutted track that the troop carrier had described through the pristine dust. It wound off into the dusk towards the flat horizon where the first the glint of the early evening stars were forming. Fornu walked past him and headed off into the gloom.

"This fucking cart has shook my guts loose; I'm going for a shit," he informed them unnecessarily.

Later that night they sat outside on the ground, leaning against the cool metal of the vehicle and ate their rations. A flask of wine was produced, courtesy of the Beloved Leader's cellar and conversation became easier. Terrik was intrigued to know about Lorel and asked Lodan a number of pointed and personal questions about her. Lodan evaded any compromising answers and concentrated on relating his experiences in the mine.

"I was garrisoned there once," announced Fornu after Lodan's graphic description of the breakout.

Lodan heard this with some surprise. Hitherto he had viewed the mine guards as monsters who had forsaken any degree of humanity. "You were a guard?"

"Yes, I did a stint about four years ago."

"Were you not appalled by what you saw?"

Fornu took a swig of wine and considered his words carefully. "I suppose it was a shock to see it initially, but after a while it just becomes a job; you forget that these are real people you're dealing with, they just become objects. We were brainwashed by those in charge, taught that the prisoners were enemies of the state and could not be regarded as human any more. Once you accept that, nothing affects you."

"But... but you must have known it was wrong; you must have felt something."

"I am a soldier, Lodan; I am trained to do what I'm told and carry out the orders of my superiors. I am not trained to think about the merits or ethics of the orders I'm given."

"But to be given such power over your fellow man; to literally have the power of life and death or to commit any depravity that you wish, without consequence; surely that is a dangerous thing for any man to possess?"

Fornu shrugged. "Certainly there were those who took advantage, many just out of frustration at being in that forsaken place. Personally, I avoided contact as much as possible. The stench and heat were enough to drive a man away from excessive contact with the prisoners."

"I suppose," said Lodan, after some thought, "the mine took away the humanity of everyone, guards and prisoners alike."

Fornu nodded. "I was glad to get away from it when my tour of duty there was over."

They finished the wine and turned in for the night, each folding into a bedroll on the floor of the troop carrier. Lodan fell asleep quickly but was soon awoken by a thunderous noise coming from a source uncomfortably close to his ear. Corporal Fornu had the loudest snore he had ever encountered; its irregular eruptions seemed to make the air in the vehicle vibrate. Lodan listened with increasing despair and then heard the sound of another eruption issuing from the other end of the Corporal's torso. Now, not only his ears but his nostrils were being brutally assaulted and the combined effect was to drive him out of the vehicle and out into the cold night.

But it is a rare evil that brings no benefit and Lodan's self-exile brought him a wonderful sight. The night sky was alight with the most astounding aurora he had ever seen; it flashed and darted above the horizon with a brilliance and energy in an explosive spectrum of vibrant, luminous colours. He spread his bedroll and lay down, watching the performance of nature with transfixed pleasure. He thought of Lorel and wished her with him to see this and to be with him under the glorious canopy of light. She had been awkward and slightly distant at their parting, perhaps, he thought, to spare him emotional trauma. He rationalized her coolness in that way and vowed, when next they met, to tell her how he felt about her. With that resolve, he wrapped himself against the cold and shut his eyes and went to sleep beneath the aurora of the northern sky.

The next thing he knew was Terrik shaking him awake. The aurora had long since vanished to be replaced by the sad hint of dawn. It was still dark but there was just enough light to see the way ahead. He rose stiffly and loped off to perform his morning routine in private. When he had finished he checked that no one could see him and got down on to his knees and delivered his first prayer of the day to the Prophet who had preserved him from death. During the fighting it had not always been possible to keep to the proper recognition of his faith which required four prayer offerings every day, but he knew that his Lord was now keeping him safe for some higher purpose and He would know that his heart was true to the Faith.

"Was I snoring last night?" asked Fornu on Lodan's return.

"A little," replied Lodan.

"You were like a fucking volcano," said Terrik as he got them underway. "We should get there before nightfall, if we don't get any problems."

Lodan took his seat and prepared to be jolted and thrown about for several hours as the vehicle ploughed through the fine dust, whipping it up into billowing clouds in their wake. After three hours of monotonous, featureless boredom, the first hint of the Northern Uplands appeared on the horizon. Terrik adjusted their route to take them through one of the ancient rift gorges that sliced through the wind-worn rocks. At first they appeared to be heading for an unbroken cliff wall, but Fornu was an excellent navigator and as they neared the barrier, so the access to the gorge seemed to materialize in the centre of a seemingly unbroken cliff face.

"There are a lot of these cracks through the Uplands further north," remarked Fornu. "This is the southernmost. Once we are through this it's about four hours to the border."

The sides of the gorge loomed overhead as they picked their way across boulder fields and screed that formed its floor. About half way along the gorge they came upon an unnatural, gaping chasm in the face of the rock wall that reminded Lodan so much of the Mine of Kusk that an involuntary shiver ran down his spine.

"It's an old mine-working," explained Fornu. "There are quite a few in these parts, some go very deep. The last one was abandoned about a hundred years ago, shortly after they discovered the deposits at Kusk. The ore here was very low grade and the working conditions made it uneconomic. They had to bring everything in, even every last drop of water."

"It looks like Kusk," said Lodan as they passed the gaping mouth.

"So it does," agreed Fornu. "It was these mines that started the war between Rion and Trant. Both sides claimed them."

"And Rion won."

"We were stronger then, before Strellic fucked things up. Now, if they wanted to they could just walk in and take them."

A large rock jolted them out of their seats as it passed under the tracks.

Fornu banged his head on a protrusion and swore. "For fucks sake, Terrik, be careful, we don't want to breakdown here."

"I'm doing my best, Corp. This terrain is a total, fucking nightmare."

After two more hours picking their way through the difficult terrain of the narrow gorge floor, they finally emerged on to the High Northern Plateau of Tarnus. Here the polar winds had scoured the dust from the bedrock and worn it flat over millions of years leaving a surface as smooth as a polished table fashioned by the hand of a giant. Here they were able to pick up speed and progress across the endless waste with relative comfort and the Uplands fell away rapidly behind them. About four hours later they saw the first of the line of towers that marked the border.

The towers, which were for observation, were spaced ten kilometres apart and rose fifty metres into the sky. These were ancient structures of latticed metal that guarded the border between Rion and Trant. Beyond the towers, set into the rocky surface, lay a field of deadly, well camouflaged mines, which if triggered would eradicate anything within fifty metres. Beyond the minefield was a narrow no-man's-land giving way to another minefield overlooked by a further set of observation towers under Trant's control. This primitive system had maintained the integrity of the border between these two warring nations for over a century and it had not been breached in living memory.

Terrik halted the vehicle beneath one of the observation towers and opened the door. A cold wind sighed through the metal superstructure and penetrated the warm interior of the cabin. Lodan shivered and climbed out behind his two companions.

"Up you go," said Fornu, pointing to the top of the tower.

Terrik nodded sullenly; he didn't much care for heights, but he began his climb manfully.

"He's going to take out the observation pod; we don't want our lot to see what we're doing."

"Won't they have seen us?"

The corporal shook his head and pointed at the border. "The towers are only looking in one direction. When he's disarmed the equipment we'll have about three hours before one of our scouts gets here to find out what's going on. There will be a way through the minefield; it's just a question of finding it."

Lodan nodded gravely; he had been told about this and wasn't looking forward to it at all. "Say I get through in one piece; what then?"

"When you reach no-man's-land, stand still until they come."

"When will that be?"

"Not long, they'll have seen us and be on their way already."

They looked up as Terrik climbed the structure and disappeared into the small pod at the top. A few minutes later he appeared again and waved.

"That's it," said Fornu and he took an unwieldy contraption from the cab of the vehicle and strapped it to Lodan's back. He placed another contraption over his head so that it covered his eyes, blinding him to normal light rays. He activated the machine and Lodan suddenly found that he could see right through the corporal, right through the troop carrier and into the rocks themselves to a distance of twenty metres. Figures flashed before him as he moved his head from side to side with such information as the density, temperature, composition and distance of whatever he was looking at.

"Remember," said Fornu, "Eight-point-seven is the magic number. If you get closer than eight-point-seven metres to a mine it will trigger and no more Lodan."

"Don't worry; it's seared into my brain."

"Take your time, one step at a time. Check before you move. Good luck."

Lodan took the extended arm of the corporal in farewell and walked towards the minefield.

XXVI

Umbert Strellic stood in the turret of his personal troop carrier and squinted into the morning sun. He had placed himself towards the rear of the force for tactical reasons, and the thrill of seeing his vast, mechanised army rolling into the Gul Valley made his spine tingle with expectation. The rebels would hold his capital for no more than three days and then they would be wiped from the face of Tarnus forever. He had, under his command, over twenty five thousand well-armed troops and they had no more than three thousand. He anticipated a short and bloody resistance culminating in his complete victory.

On a high ridge above the valley, Lieutenant Norgu peered through a viewfinder with a look of puzzlement. "I can't believe anyone could be so stupid," he declared.

"Let me see," said Jodi. He took the viewfinder from Norgu and trained it on the distant, advancing army. "There must be about five hundred troop carriers in the column; plus other vehicles and field weapons."

"It's his entire force, it has to be. We know that General Gerlic hasn't moved and the southern bases have not been co-opted. He's bringing the whole lot through the valley. It's military suicide."

"It certainly appears inept. Could it be some kind of trick?"

"If it is I don't know the nature of it; I can only assume he is prepared to sacrifice his troops to draw us out. He knows he has a huge advantage in men and weapons."

Jodi returned the viewfinder to his companion. "What are you going to do?"

"Stick to the plan; there's nothing else we can do."

They watched and waited while the column slowly advanced up the Gul Valley, sending a broad cloud of dust into the clear sky. It drew level with their position and Norgu waited until the vanguard had passed below them, then he triggered the mines.

The effect on the head of the column was devastating; machines and men were blasted into the air as the ground beneath them erupted, fractured and consumed the vanguard of Strellic's army in a blanket of flame and choking smoke. In that moment over three thousand of Strellic's men died and more yet were to die under the crossfire of field weapons coming from both sides of the valley.

Strellic observed the destruction from the back of the column with disbelief. The air ahead was alive with flashes of energy as the attackers fired on the hapless troops below. Eventually some fire was returned and the rocky crests either side of the valley began to explode and splinter, showering yet more death on to the column as the shattered rock rolled down the steep valley walls on to the troops.

"What are your orders, Sir?" shouted an officer over the din of conflict.

Strellic was paralysed; he had no idea what orders he should issue. He simply waved his arm noncommittally and mumbled, "What is happening? What is happening?"

"Advance or retreat?" shouted the man below him.

Strellic looked down at him like a man in a waking dream. "Perhaps we should have gone another way," he stammered.

"Do you want to retreat?" shouted the officer.

"No," said Strellic. "We go forward."

The battle raged on as the column crept forward, crushing the charred bodies and smashed machines of their comrades beneath them. Eventually the superior firepower of the army began to tell and the weapons of the valley heights began to fall silent. Eventually Norgu judged that they had done as much damage as they could and he sounded the retreat. The weapons were loaded on to tractors and rushed back to Salom Gul with thirty of his men. The engagement had cost the rebellion twenty-one men; Strellic had lost over five thousand.

XXVII

Lodan could feel the moist sweat oozing from beneath the visor and trickling down his face. He was several metres into the minefield and could not see a way through without coming closer than the deadly range of eight-point-seven metres. He turned around carefully and retraced his steps back towards Corporal Fornu.

"I can't get through that way," he shouted to the man who had withdrawn to a reasonably sensible distance.

"Try further to the left," returned the corporal.

Lodan walked ten metres to the left and tried again. This time he got further, but was forced back again. His nerves were now shredded and he was seriously considering giving up. There must be an easier way of getting into Trant. He took off the visor and wiped the sweat from his face with his sleeve.

"Are you sure there's a way through?" he called to Fornu.

"Try again," shouted the corporal encouragingly.

He replaced the visor and tried ten metres further along. As he advanced into the field he could see the deadly devices either side of him, buried in the rock just below the smooth surface. He walked steadily forward and encountered a device dead ahead. He turned to the right and made his way between two mines but once again, found his advance blocked although there was a gap that would take him back towards Rion. He walked into it and found that another gap opened up that would take him parallel to the border. It was much like finding a way through a maze in which it was sometimes necessary to double back. In this way he worked his way through the minefield and could see the way beyond it, but the final gap between the last group of mines was seventeen-point-two metres. He had chosen the wrong route again. He stood still and considered.

In the distance he could see a small speck in the sky over Trant. They were coming. He had run out of time and he now had to make a decision. He uttered a prayer to the Prophet, took off the visor and the backpack and walked between the two final mines with his eyes shut. It was the shortest, and yet the longest, walk of his life, but he finally stepped into no man's land and began to laugh. The mines were ancient; perhaps it had all been for nothing, perhaps none of them worked. He was still smiling broadly when the military craft landed opposite him.

The craft disgorged a platoon of soldiers who aimed their weapons at him. Lodan spread his legs and arms and stood still while an official emerged from the craft.

The official stepped in front of the soldiers and hailed him through an amplifier. "You are in breach of the border line, any further incursion and you will be shot."

Lodan stood still and shouted back. "I am an envoy from the occupiers of Salom Gul. My name is Lodan DeRhogai from Kagan; I wish to speak with the Electors."

"The Electors are busy people; what is your business with the Division of Trant?"

"Peace and reward. I am authorized to propose a treaty beneficial to both Rion and Trant; it is vital that I am granted the opportunity to speak with your government."

The official seemed to consider for a moment, then he disappeared back into the craft. After some time he reemerged and spoke to one of his soldiers, giving him a small, tablet-like device. The soldier nodded and advanced into the minefield on the Trant side, stepping this way and that just as Lodan had done. The soldier moved with confidence and was soon into no man's land. He marched purposefully up to Lodan and ordered him to stand still while he passed a detector over him. Having satisfied himself that his subject was not armed or carrying a communicator, he turned around.

"Put your hand on my shoulder and walk in my footsteps," he ordered.

Lodan did as he was told and was led through the opposing minefield and into Trant.

The official, a small, dapper fellow in his thirties, with a large moustache and black, beady eyes, scanned him warily. "I have been ordered to bring you to Jin; the Electors may grant you an audience."

"Thank you," replied Lodan.

"Do not thank me, Mister DeRhogai; in my opinion you should have been shot on sight."

Lodan followed the man into the craft, took a seat opposite the official and waited for the troops to file in. But instead of entering the craft the troops conducted an engagement. There was a series of flashes outside and the crackling sound of discharging weapons.

"What's going on?" said Lodan, getting to his feet.

"Sit down, Mister DeRhogai," snapped the official. "My troops are dealing with some rubbish that has come too close to us."

Lodan bristled with indignation. "We are on a peace mission."

The official observed him steadily. "There is no peace between Trant and Rion. There never has been and there never will be. Now sit down."

Lodan sat as the troops filed back into the craft. As it took off and swung away towards the west, he saw the smoking bodies of his two companions; Fornu, near the burning carcass of the troop carrier and Terrik at the base of the tower from which he had fallen. "That's just murder," he uttered bitterly.

"No, it's war," corrected the official.

The first part of the journey to Jin, the capital of Trant, was conducted in morose silence. The troops were under orders to be silent and neither Lodan nor the official were in the mood for conversation. Lodan spent the journey observing the landscape as it passed below the craft. At first it was empty of population and desolate, just as it had been on the Rion side of the border. But as they flew south, so he saw small farmsteads and villages dotting the harsh land. Many buildings displayed the signs of conflict, having been wholly or partially destroyed by missile attack. Here, for the first time since his arrival on Tarnus, he saw temples and evidence of the Faith on the landscape. The familiarity of these structures gave him a sensation of comfort, as though he had come home after a long and arduous journey through an heretical wasteland. The one large city they passed over was extensively damaged, being as it was, within the range of Strellic's weapons.

"This is my city," said the official, speaking for the first time. "Destroyed by Rion infidels."

On the outskirts of the city they passed over a large area of marshland. The official pointed out a spot. "Two Suran spies crashed down there earlier this year."

Lodan heard this with a jolt to the brain, but managed to keep his countenance. "Surans? That is very unusual."

The official nodded grimly. "Filthy infidels."

"What happened to them?"

"The people of Trant were betrayed and they escaped true justice."

"How inconvenient."

The official looked up sharply, detecting a note of irony. "You are Kagan and must be of the Faith."

"I am the great grandson of the Arkon of the DeRhogai. My faith has never been questioned."

The official scowled, he did not seem over-impressed. "What were you doing in Rion?"

"I was kidnapped and taken there by a Moontrader. Strellic had me committed to the Mine of Kusk."

Now the official's interest was piqued. "The Mine of Kusk! I have heard many terrible things about that place."

"No doubt they are all true for it is worse than anyone can imagine."

"We have heard of the rebellion at the mine and of the daughter of General Arkuna who led it."

"You are well informed. I speak for her and the Insurgent Council."

"So you say, but who do they speak for?"

"For all those who want freedom and justice in Rion."

The official smirked ironically behind his large, black moustache. "You are a dreamer, Mister DeRhogai; and a dangerous one at that. The Electors will not be fooled by dreams; they have history to guide them."

"That may be true; their bravery and vision will be tested by this moment in history."

The Electors of Trant were an ancient body of men first formed to choose a president who would rule the Division until death or incapacity claimed him. Originally the panel was composed of high priests of the Faith and members of well respected, wealthy families, but as Tarnus descended into conflict, the panel gradually became militarized and reduced in size, the office of president was abandoned and now the panel consisted of fifteen generals who presided over the affairs of Trant.

After several hours' wait, Lodan was finally brought before this august body of gentlemen. His heart was racing as he entered the chamber for what confronted him was an intimidating sight. Fifteen scowling, long-faced men sat behind a semi-circular rostrum, each clad from head to foot in scarlet robes. An elaborate turban of matching scarlet was placed upon the head of each man, imparting the wearer with a certain gravitas.

Lodan was conducted to a rostrum opposite the centre of the semi-circular council and was addressed by an elderly man who sat in a more elaborately featured chair in the centre. This was the Speaker of the Electors.

"State your name and your business with us," he said gruffly.

Lodan's appearances before the Arkon had, to some degree, prepared him for such audiences and he had rehearsed his arguments at length beforehand, but as he stepped on to the rostrum his hands were sweating and his mouth became dry. He stammered his name. "I... I am... My name is Lodan Sevarius DeRhogai of Kagan."

"And your business," prompted the Speaker impatiently.

"I... I have been sent... I come here on behalf of the Rebels who presently occupy the city of Salom Gul."

"And what is such rabble to do with us?" interrupted a man to his right.

Lodan was taken aback by the intense hostility he could feel in the room. He had not made a good start, but he bore on his shoulders the fate of so many people in Salom Gul and in the Division of Rion beyond and he knew that he must not fail. He girded himself and met the eye of each of the men before him.

"What is has it to do with you?" he began with newly found resolve. "Nothing, nothing at all, if the future prosperity and peace of the Division of Trant is nothing to do with you. If that is your judgement then close your ears and minds. If it is not, then open them."

There was a buzz of indignation but Lodan ignored it and pressed on. "I come here as a neutral; I have no affiliation with Trant and certainly none with Rion, whose leader imprisoned me in the foul Mine of Kusk. I come here as a man who sees an opportunity for change, an opportunity the like of which may not be repeated for decades. How many lives and how much treasure will be sacrificed if you are not prepared to even contemplate change?

"Your world exists for conflict. In this faith you have devastated your cities and destroyed your infrastructure and your economies. You have secured the contempt of the community of other worlds who shun you unless it is to sell you arms so that you can continue to cast misery upon your people. I have seen Rion and now I have seen some of Trant and I can tell you that there is no difference between your peoples. You speak the same language; you build your houses and cities the same way; there is no racial difference between you and yet you persist in this illogical antipathy like two squabbling brothers.

"Your enemy is not the people of Rion, it is Umbert Strellic, who has turned the people from the One True Faith and led them down a dark path towards damnation. As a brother nation it is your duty, and your duty in faith, to help rid them of this curse and you may never be in a better position to do it than you are now. Strellic has been weakened; much of his army is in rebellion and more will follow if they can see the way forward. The people I represent are willing to cede fifty percent of the Mine of Kusk to Trant in exchange for military assistance. We require an air attack on Strellic's troops only to equalize the odds between the two factions; the Rebels will do the rest. You should not commit ground troops as this will be seen as an invasion."

The Electors had listened to the nub of Lodan's speech in silence, somewhat nonplussed at being lectured to by this young foreigner. Finally one spoke up.

"You have the authority to offer us half the Mine of Kusk. What is to prevent us from invading and taking it all?"

"Nothing can prevent you, if that is what you intend. Rion is weak now and will be unable to resist. But what you are suggesting is more war; more of the same thing that has brought your world to its knees. You could take over the whole of Rion if you have the mind; but you will never have peace if you do it. Forgive me, gentlemen, I am young and ill equipped to address this respected body, but I have lived long enough to know that force never prevails in the long run. What has brought the factions of other worlds together is mutual respect and co-operation to achieve a mutually beneficial goal. You have before you the opportunity to initiate that process. I beg of you to seize it."

The Electors stared hostilely, apparently not persuaded; they had never been lectured to in such a way and seemed offended. The Speaker addressed himself to Lodan. "Young Kagan, we have listened patiently to your words which have expressed laudable sentiments, but you are a foreigner and you have betrayed a simplistic understanding of the nature of the conflict on Tarnus. It is true that the rebellion in Rion has temporarily upset the balance of power between our two Divisions, but that balance will be restored soon enough and we will continue as before. We have lived separately with Rion and the other Divisions on our far borders for over five hundred years and the war that we now conduct has existed for over one hundred years; it has become the way of life, the expectation of our peoples and we do not consider the alteration of this state without long and grave thought. We thank you for your address and for taking the trouble to come here. You will withdraw while we deliberate; you will be afforded the comforts due to a diplomat during that time."

Lodan heard these words with a sinking heart. It was clear from the expressions on the faces of the Electors that they were not interested in helping the insurgency. It seemed to him that the only thing on their minds was the preservation of the status quo; they had become so accustomed to war that they could not envisage a future without it. He bowed and was conducted from the chamber a disappointed man.

He was taken to a waiting room by a smartly liveried chamberlain and there told to wait upon the decision of the Electors. The room was large and airy and looked out, through a gallery of high arches, upon the compact city of government which lay beyond the walls of the citadel. It was now evening and the warmth of the day was melting away. In the distance a bank of black storm clouds were gathering; *Perhaps*, he thought, *a fitting metaphor for what was going to happen to Salom Gul*. He thought ruefully of Lorel and wondered if he would ever see her alive again. If the Electors refused to help, as seemed most likely, he doubted it and the thought gave him a great deal of disquiet.

After about two hours the chamberlain returned with the news that his audience had been unsuccessful. The darkness of early evening had now descended and the first heavy drops of rain had begun to fall. A jagged fork of lightning briefly illuminated the room with stark whiteness and a roll of thunder followed.

"I am to conduct you to the temporary guest quarters," said the chamberlain, casting a nervous eye through the open window.

"What do they intend to do with me?" asked Lodan as he followed the man into the labyrinthine interior of the citadel.

"I don't know, Sir, but the guest quarters are comfortable and there is another gentleman already there for company."

"Another diplomat?"

"I believe the gentleman in question is a military man from Rion, Sir."

"An army man from Rion!"

"I believe so, Sir."

"Do you get many such visits?"

"To my knowledge we have never had one before, Sir."

Lodan was highly intrigued and pondered this news as he was led into a well-appointed bedchamber in the high wing of the citadel.

"You have had a long journey, Sir; if you would care to bathe there is a facility through that door." The chamberlain indicated an arched door at the other end of the large room. "In Trant the tradition is to bathe communally, but I believe the other guest has already availed himself of the bath, so you will not be disturbed if you wish to be private. A meal will be provided presently; you may take it alone or with the other guest."

"Thank you," replied Lodan.

"You're welcome, Sir. If you care to leave your clothes here, I will have them cleaned for you."

"Thank you again."

The chamberlain bowed and withdrew. Lodan strolled to the great, arched window and looked out into the night. Rain was now lashing down, tapping incessantly against the hard transparency of the window. Another flash of lightning struck the ground just beyond the city and shot angry fingers of light onto the underside of the pillowed clouds. He thought again of Lorel and the privations that she must be enduring at this moment, while he was surrounded by luxury; the thought sent him into greater depression. How he wished she were with him now.

"Nasty night, is it not, Mister DeRhogai?"

Lodan swung round to face the intruder, a rotund fellow with absolutely no hair on his person. His eyes of startling blue observed Lodan steadily while his thick lips drew themselves into a reluctant smile.

"I am General Gerlic," he announced. "Excuse the intrusion; I have come to ask you to join me for dinner. I deplore eating alone."

Lodan stared at this strange, lugubrious creature. So this was Gerlic, one of the Five Generals of Rion; a most unlikely looking soldier. "I have not bathed yet."

"Of course, you have only just arrived. I will defer until your readiness is complete.

The general bowed slightly and withdrew, leaving Lodan intrigued. *An eccentric fellow,* he thought; but his principal concern was the fact that the general was here at all, in the capital of his deadly enemy, apparently treated as an honoured guest. He was anxious to interview the man to find out what exactly was going on because he now entertained the slither of a hope for Lorel and the defenders of Salom Gul. He stripped off and walked through the arched door to the bath.

"I listened to your speech," said General Gerlic as he pushed another morsel between his thick lips and began to chew while he talked. "It was most impressive for one so young; most impressive and persuasive."

"Not persuasive enough," replied Lodan.

The general smiled indulgently. "You never had a chance of success; you were sent on an impossible errand by naïve fools."

"So I see; and what of your errand? What is your progress? I assume you are here to negotiate much the same thing as I."

The general pursed his lips and raised a non-existent eyebrow. Not exactly, but it is true we both want the overthrow of Umbert Strellic."

"Then you are committed to the defence of Salom Gul."

Gerlic sucked another morsel into his mouth and considered. "Not exactly; Salom Gul will probably have to be sacrificed. Strellic is attacking as we speak."

This news deflated Lodan. "Is there nothing to be done?"

"You seem awfully concerned, young man; you are not a native so I wonder at your reason."

"I don't wish to see the destruction of my friends. They trusted me with this mission and I have let them down."

The general's white face assumed an expression of gravitas. "You have not let them down; as I said, you never had a chance of success. You stated in the Chamber of the Electors that you were brought here by a Moontrader."

"That's correct."

"Why?"

"I had some business with General Arkuna."

"Ah, the late general; a sad loss. What was the nature of that business?"

The probing was gentle and subtle, but Lodan was aware enough to be guarded. "It was a matter between my Great Grandfather and General Arkuna."

"Arms trading?"

Lodan nodded.

"And what happened?"

"The deal fell through on the arrest of the general; I was caught up in it and incarcerated."

"I always wondered how Arkuna balanced the books; I never thought he was an international arms dealer though. I always respected him, now I think he was a genius. The army has suffered greatly at his loss. But your story interests me too. How did his daughter engineer the break-out at the mine?"

"We found a way to neutralize the collars."

"We? You were with her?"

Lodan nodded.

"How, exactly did you do it?"

"Does it matter?"

"It does if we are to avoid such things in the future."

Lodan glared at the fellow. "The mine should be closed or mechanized; human beings should not be subjected to such horrors."

"Don't be naive, Mister DeRhogai, where else would we send all the reprobates, sub-humans and people we don't like?"

"You have designs on the leadership, how would you be different to Strellic?"

"Ah, I fear I am exposed. You are right; I will become the leader of Rion."

"What has it cost you?"

Gerlic grinned. "A small sum to cover the cost of a military intervention and the undertaking to re-instate the One True Faith in Rion."

Lodan's eyes widened in surprise. "Is that all? I don't understand."

"Of course you don't, my boy; you never have. You never asked yourself the question: how is it possible for a people to be at war for over a hundred years? Would not the physical and economic effort entirely destroy the planet and its people? Of course it would. One side would eventually prevail and dominate the other and periods of relative peace would be interspersed by uprisings and real destruction. On Tarnus we maintain equilibrium between our warring nations, occasionally exchanging a few salvoes just to remind the people we are at war. We fail to repair the physical damage, not because we can't but because leaving the ruins as they are leaves the people a constant reminder of conflict."

Lodan was so stunned at this revelation he hardly knew what to say. "You mean to tell me that this whole thing, this whole barbaric war is a sham, a hundred-year-old con?"

"That's a rather harsh and, if I may say so, simplistic assessment."

"Why? In the name of the Prophet, why?"

The general patted his mouth with a cloth then placed it slowly next to his plate. "The people of Tarnus are a dissolute, war-like lot, much given to flights of hatred. The belief that they are at war suits them and keeps them in order. It sates their natural propensity for hatred and causes them to make no excessive demands on their governments who are able to control them with the fear of invasion and brutal occupation. The rule of Umbert Strellic has briefly upset the elegant balance that the various governments of Tarnus have always maintained by mutual understanding. Strellic really does want to invade and conquer his neighbours; he is a power-hungry, bloodthirsty peasant who has no proper understanding of how government works. It has always been a constant battle to restrain his ambition and his wanton destruction of the One True Faith did not endear him to his fellow rulers.

"Your little insurrection has been a useful catalyst in the way of ridding Tarnus of Strellic, but the Electors are not about to allow the replacement of one problem with another. The accession of a woman to government is bad enough, but a woman who has suffered the deprivations of the Mine of Kusk and therefore might have liberal tendencies, well, that would be insufferable and dangerous. The Electors will never allow Lorel Arkuna to triumph; your cause is dead, I can assure you of that."

Lodan rose and walked to the gallery of windows. Outside the storm had passed, giving way to humid, nighttime heat. "It's monstrous," he declared as he looked out over the glistening roofs of the city. "It's truly monstrous. Lorel and the city are to be sacrificed for this?"

"For the long-term good of the people."

"The good of the people! Have you seen the condition of the population?"

"That is due to Strellic's mismanagement of our affairs; it is not really a product of the war. When I am Marshal, these matters will be put to right."

"What is to become of me?"

"You will be deported back to Kagan."

"I am not ready to go; I have unfinished business in Salom Gul."

"There will be nothing much left of it; nothing for you there."

"Even so, I must go back. Will you help me?"

"This is not your affair, Mister DeRhogai; your presence will not be welcome in Rion."

"I do not intend to stay a moment longer than necessary."

Gerlic narrowed his eyes on Lodan. "What business sends you so keenly back to Salom Gul? Is it the girl? Is it Lorel Arkuna?"

"Yes, if you must know."

The general smiled faintly. "The last time I saw her she was a gangly, headstrong teenager. Now she is a direct threat to my authority for no doubt, there will be some factions in the military intent on following her."

"You are wrong, General; I know Lorel, she has no real designs on power."

"She has become a figurehead for the rebellion; she has power even though she may not desire it."

"I happen to know that Lorel wishes to leave Tarnus. She will come with me; I guarantee it; you do not have anything to fear from her."

"She returns your affection?"

"Yes, she will follow me when I leave Tarnus. General, I appeal to you, save lives, do not start your administration with the blood of your countrymen on your hands. Don't let Salom Gul fall to Strellic's army. There are many fine men defending it, men who will pledge loyalty to you, their saviour," he added with considerable emphasis.

The word 'saviour' brought Gerlic up with a visible start; it had distinctly pseudo-religious connotations that, in a vain man, was bound to encourage visions of a messianic quality. In an instant he realised that, instead of being his nation's subjugator, he would become its liberator; its hero. He narrowed his eyes on Lodan and pointed his fat finger at him. "You, Mister DeRhogai, are too clever for your own good."

XXVIII

The bombardment of Salom Gul started as the sun slipped below the horizon. For many it was the last daylight they were to see, for the destruction was accurate and thorough. Strellic had surrounded the city and those that could hid in cellars and listened to the sound of war machines and the shattering of stone and the fabric of their lives above them. The sky turned red with flames as the city burned.

Lorel and Jodi watched the onslaught from the palace roof, occasionally taking cover as another salvo burst nearby and tossed shattered masonry and dust into the air. They both knew this was likely to be the end and they had made a pact to die together. A white-hot blast of light hit the building next to the palace and it began to burn. Acrid smoke billowed into the air and choked the atmosphere about them. It was time to take cover.

They descended to the basement where hundreds of soldiers had assembled and waited anxiously for their commander. They looked towards her, as if expecting her to produce a miracle; but she had none to offer.

Allrik approached them. "It doesn't look like Lodan was successful," he said. "They will be coming soon, we should deploy."

Lorel nodded and pulled herself up on to a stone plinth so she could address the soldiers. "You soldiers, you freedom fighters, I am proud of every one of you.

Together we have taught Strellic that he is not the master of Rion; we have taught him the cost of his debauched and corrupt rule. He comes now to try to re-take this city. Make him pay for every step with blood for he will show you no mercy. Fight honourably and do not be taken alive, for that will be the worst fate for all of you. I thank you for your support and I wish you good fortune."

The soldiers cheered as Lorel jumped down, grabbed her weapon and led them out into the blood-red night.

Strellic's army advanced into the city as the first hint of dawn touched the gathering clouds with crimson light. During the night the pounding hell of bombardment had devastated the fabric of the metropolis and stripped it to its ugly bones. Fires burned out of control and overspread the place with poisonous, acrid smoke that found its way into the eyes and lungs of the defenders, causing them to choke and vomit. Now the first volleys from the defenders resounded through the shattered canyons as the attackers came into range. From one ruined street to the next they were inexorably pushed back towards the centre. Atrocities of indescribable brutality were meted out to those defenders foolish enough to be taken alive and to the small rump of citizens who had stayed.

As the battle wore on Colonel Doric and Lieutenant Norgu were both killed and by the evening less than three hundred defenders remained alive, concentrated in and around the palace. Lorel, Jodi and Allrik had stayed together during the battle, each looking out for the other as they fell back from one position to the next. Allrik, one handed and grimacing with pain, had accounted for over thirty of Strellic's men on his own, but now he was exhausted and could go on no longer. Battle scarred and stained with their own blood as well as that of others, they ran into the palace and got ready the make their last stand.

Sarlat Strellic had watched the battle unfold with mounting anxiety. For him the business was a foregone certainty for even a military fool like his father could not fail to prevail over the poorly defended city. However, Sarlat had other matters on his mind. He could not rid himself of the conviction that Lorel Arkuna knew where the deep-space cruiser was and he meant to 'interview' her on this subject as soon as he could. In relative safety, he swept through the devastated streets of Salom Gul with his posse of Elite Guards and established a command post in a cellar just out of range of the defender's weapons. Here he issued orders that the attack was to stop immediately and the soldiers were to hold their positions. Gradually the weapons fell silent and Sarlat emerged from his cellar into the smoke-filled remains of the city and approached the palace. An officer was chosen and sent forward with a banner of peace.

The besieged fighters greeted the respite with relief and a good measure of scepticism. They allowed the envoy to enter the palace and conducted him into the presence of Lorel and a collection of her lieutenants who had assembled in what was left of the council chamber.

"I come from His Excellency Sarlat Strellic who sends you greeting and congratulations on a well-fought campaign," said the officer, reading from a tablet given to him by Sarlat. "I am charged by His Excellency to offer you terms of surrender under the following conditions:-

1. All hostilities are to cease immediately.
2. All Rebels are to disarm, vacate the palace and render themselves to government forces, where they will receive a guarantee of humane treatment.
3. The fugitive, Lorel Arkuna, is to render herself for fair trial by the appropriate authority.

Those are the conditions of surrender as dictated by His Excellency."

"By whose authority does Sarlat Strellic offer terms?" said Lorel. "Is his father dead?"

"No, Ma'am, the Beloved Leader is very much alive."

"Then I ask you again, by whose authority does he offer terms?"

The officer blinked nervously and regarded her with a look of confusion. "I don't know Ma'am."

"Tell him to shove it right up," shouted Allrik. "I don't care who issued the terms, Strellic Junior or Senior; neither can be trusted."

"Be quiet, Allrik," said Lorel angrily. She returned her attention to the envoy. "How long have we got to consider?"

"One hour," replied the man.

"Very well, we will discuss it and let you have our answer if you would be so kind as to return in one hour."

The envoy saluted and marched out.

"You're not serious," said Allrik when the man had left them.

"You shut your mouth," said an officer, "you're not of rank, you shouldn't even be here."

"I've as much right as you, you tin-pot general."

"Be quiet, both of you," said Lorel. "Squabbling will get us nowhere. We will consider the offer rationally."

A sharp discussion ensued with some clutching at the tenuous promise of survival and others pointing out the obvious pitfalls given the record of the Strellics. Jodi sat on a pile of rubble and listened with increasing impatience to the arguments going around in ever-decreasing circles until his patience broke and he stood up and interrupted them.

"You can discuss this all you want, but in the end, your fate is sealed. I am not of Rion, not even of Tarnus, so I speak only as a man who is about to die. It seems obvious to me that you have two choices before you; whether to die fighting, or to die at the hands of Strellic's torturers, for I assure you, that is where you will end up if you walk beyond the walls of this palace. If you think that the likes of Umbert Strellic has had a sudden epiphany of humanity then think again. The leaders among you will furnish him with examples that he will use to warn others against rebellion. Your deaths will not be easy at his hands. You waste your time with this discussion; you have less than an hour to live, take each moment and embrace it. Say goodbye to your friends and fellow soldiers and die like men. That is all I have to say."

He walked from the chamber and climbed up to the roof. He could see the field weapons and the soldiers crouching in the ruins beyond the palace compound, waiting for their final command to destroy the place and all its defenders. Within the compound he looked down upon the straggle of doomed soldiers, squatting pointlessly behind the shattered remains of the statue of Umbert Strellic. He heard a noise behind him and knew who it was.

"Quite a speechmaker, aren't you?"

He smiled and turned around. "Someone had to say it."

"Sarlat is after me; that's what this is all about."

Jodi looked away and nodded. "I'd rather kill you myself than let you fall into his hands."

"I might hold you to that. We don't have much time left," she said, smiling ruefully. "What did you say back there? 'Embrace the moment'."

"Something like that," he replied, taking her in his arms and kissing her. They urgently shed their clothes and she wrapped herself around him, shut her eyes and threw her head back as they joined for one final time. He was everything she had ever wanted and now this perfect union would last forever for they were about to die and time and change would never be able to sully it. She opened her eyes and looked up at the last of the daytime sky framed in the smoke of war and for the first time, saw the infinity of it. She knew that this would not be their last act of love, for that would be when he killed her out of mercy.

They clung together and kissed even as his passion ebbed inside her. Neither spoke for there were no words or thoughts that had not travelled between them. They were both ready to die now and as the final vestiges of ecstasy ebbed from their bodies he lowered her to the floor and watched her dress.

"We shouldn't die naked," she said, handing him his clothes.

He smiled as he took them and began to dress himself.

She cast her eyes to the south and looked out over the ruined city. "The hour is almost up now; what shall we do?"

He didn't answer so she turned. He had drawn his sidearm and had it trained on her. Tears had started to run down his cheeks, glistening on the desolate pain of his face.

"I love you," she whispered, as she closed her eyes and waited for the blast of searing, disruptive heat. He didn't reply; he couldn't speak and there was nothing more to say for she already knew how much he loved her. Seconds passed and she waited, but the blast never came. She opened her eyes, wondering if his nerve had failed, but Jodi wasn't even looking at her anymore; he was looking beyond her into the southern sky where half a dozen tiny specks began to grow larger and larger.

"Is that what it looks like?" he said, straining his eyes through the smoke.

"Fate preserve us," she gasped, "he did it; Lodan did it."

They saw the craft break formation and begin the attack. Fire rained down on the city once again, decimating the conquerors in their bunkers and newly-formed strong points. This was the sound of real war, making what had gone before almost inconsequential. Lorel and Jodi rushed from the roof and down into the basement of the palace. Soldiers were still streaming in from outside, cramming the place with hot, noisy excitement. Some hugged and kissed her as she passed and some even kissed Jodi, which he took in fairly good grace. Allrik pushed his way through to them and shouted above the din, but neither heard what he was saying; they laughed even as the ground and walls shook around them.

XXIX

Umbert Strellic heard the testimony of his spy with incredulous anger. He had half expected Gerlic to make his move but he had not reckoned on the barefaced duplicity of the man. He had gone crawling to the Electors of Trant and now the enemy was on its way. He considered a rant but time was against him; the army was in the city and would be easy prey to the sky-borne war machines of Trant against which, thanks to the rebels, they now had no defence. He had to get away; he had to get to the safety of the south and back to the bosom of the people who truly loved him.

Strellic had not yet entered the city for it was not yet completely safe; there were still pockets of resistance and the palace was still in enemy hands. His anticipated triumphal march through the ruins would have to be postponed for his army would be exposed to forces from above that they had no means to counter. He had no time or indeed, inclination to save his soldiers from their fate so he took a troop carrier and with six of his trusted, personal bodyguards, he slipped quietly away towards the Gul Valley.

They had been travelling about half an hour when he saw the craft approaching from Trant. He watched as the distant bombardment threw fresh clouds of dust and smoke into the air as his army and capital city were pummelled mercilessly. He spared a passing thought for his son, who would no doubt perish, but in truth, his overwhelming concern at that moment was for himself.

He arrived later that night in Hensk, the town of his birth, certain that once in the bosom of his own people he would be welcomed and could build his power once again. As his vehicle neared his palace in the centre of the city, it became clear that something was amiss. A rumour had broken out that the army had been destroyed and Strellic was dead. In wild celebration the people were rioting and the palace had been put to the torch. A mob were braving the flames and carrying from the burning palace items of its precious furnishing and decoration. In the park that fronted the palace a large number of bodies, half clad in palace livery, hung from hastily erected gibbets and tree branches, their sightless, bloodied faces lit by the flames.

"We need to get out of here, Sir," said one of the bodyguards. "It isn't safe."

Strellic posted his portly frame into the turret and looked out upon the riotous scene. "But my people love me; they love me," he whined in apparent incomprehension. He did not understand what his subjects were doing.

"Sir, we need to go," repeated the bodyguard urgently.

But, at that moment, Strellic was recognized and a crowd quickly surrounded his vehicle, shouting abuse and hurling stones. Strellic ducked inside, his face a study of mystification. "Why are they doing this when they love me?"

The guards, under no such delusion, fired on the crowd and tried to back out, but a quick-witted citizen had wedged a large piece of iron in the tracks of the troop carrier and it began to turn in a circle. Some fell screaming beneath its undercarriage and the people were angered more. They attacked the vehicle with stones and burning debris. More fell but still more came and the troop carrier began to burn. Soon the occupants were forced out. Strellic struggled out through the turret and tried to address the crowd from the top of the vehicle.

"My children…" he called, but that was as far as his speech was allowed to get. They pulled him from the vehicle and dragged him into the park before his burning palace. His clothes were torn from his body and a rope was produced. He screamed and blubbered in turns as the rope was tied around his right ankle and he was hoisted upside-down and suspended from a tree branch. Here, soiled and naked, he was flayed with batons of wood and stoned while he screamed, "What have I ever done to you?"

Finally, one citizen hurled a rock that hit him in the eye socket, smashing his skull and silencing him forever. His guards were hacked to pieces and their body parts hung up next to that of the Beloved Leader where they remained for six days and nights, until some distant relatives were permitted to take them away and burn them.

In this way ended the rule of Umbert Strellic, the Beloved Leader, Marshal of Rion. It was ended by the seed of rebellion, sown at the Mine of Kusk by Lorel, Lodan and Allrik, who had demonstrated that it was possible to alter the course of history by one small act of defiance; a defiance born of desperation and the exhaustion of the oppressed.

XXX

Unaware and uncaring of the fate of his father, Sarlat Strellic cowered in a cellar near the palace with a small cohort of the Elite Guard, while the machinery of war screeched over the city. Being close to the palace, his bunker was spared the destruction that rained down on the rest of the city and when the bombardment finally ceased, he emerged into the smoke and ashes of complete devastation. Of an army of twenty-five thousand, less than a thousand survived, buried among the rubble of the mutilated city.

Only the palace and a few nearby buildings had escaped destruction and as the defendants began to emerge and look beyond the walls they saw the burning wasteland that had once been the capital city of Rion.

Lorel, who had no strong affiliation with Salom Gul, stood in the square next to the ruined statue of Umbert Strellic and began to sob. "What have we done?" Her muffled words escaped from behind clenched hands.

Jodi put his arm around her. "What we had to," he replied. "What choice did we have?"

She shook her head. "There are always other choices."

"We would both be dead by now, had it not been this way."

"Perhaps that would have been better."

"I would have done it; I would have killed you. You know that, don't you?"

She attempted a smile and took up his hand and kissed it. "I'm certain of it."

"I don't care how many died or what was devastated, I was preserved from having to do that and I thank Fate for it."

"Fate and Lodan," she replied.

Allrik wandered up them and glanced from one to the other. "How did we survive?" he said.

"They didn't attack the palace; they must have known it hadn't fallen," replied Lorel.

Allrik nodded. "What happens now?"

Lorel shook her head. "I don't know, I really don't."

"Do you think Lodan is coming back?"

"I hope so."

"Do you? I came up to the palace roof before the bombardment. I was looking for you."

Lorel coloured a little. "I'm sorry you saw that."

Allrik waved a dismissive hand. "I have seen you both naked before, but not together like that. I love you both, but I also love Lodan. He is going to be hurt by this."

"I know," replied Lorel.

Four hours after the bombardment, General Gerlic's army rolled through what was left of Salom Gul. Units deployed throughout the city and began to pull the survivors from the rubble while the general took a division and headed for the palace. He stepped from the armoured vehicle on to the hallowed ground that had once been the centrepiece of Strellic's empire and looked about him grim-faced. Lorel, who had been sitting on the steps at the base of what remained of Strellic's statue, rose and greeted him. She remembered him from the last general's meeting on which she had accompanied her father and recalled how unimpressed she had been. Now he had become the most powerful man in Rion and she was still unimpressed.

"I am pleased to see that you survived, Miss Arkuna," began the general.

"Not much else has," she replied shortly.

"Stones can be rebuilt and lives replaced. You are a true heroine of the Revolution and I salute you."

As they spoke some troops disgorged from another vehicle and she saw Lodan amongst them.

"Ah, I believe you and Mister DeRhogai are acquainted; I am sure you have much to discuss."

He took his leave and walked towards the palace as Lodan approached.

"I knew you would survive," he said, taking her in his arms and hugging her.

"And I knew you would succeed," she replied as he kissed her forehead. She held herself close so that his lips could not find her mouth.

"It wasn't me," he replied, "Gerlic had already arranged things with the Electors."

She stepped from his grasp and frowned. "Are we to be invaded? What has he ceded?"

Lodan concealed his disappointment; he was aware she had not permitted him to kiss her even after such a separation and tribulation. "Rion will not be invaded," he replied coolly as Allrik grabbed his shoulder from behind. Lodan turned and allowed himself to be effusively greeted by his friend. "We have to talk," he said when Allrik finally released him and they began to walk together towards the palace. "Did Jodi survive?"

"He's in the palace," replied Allrik.

Lodan smiled ruefully and nodded, noting Lorel's mouth tighten. Was it possible that she had become attached to this boy; this child?

"No doubt he will be anxious to leave Rion," said Lodan, trying to gauge her reaction.

"I'm sure he will," she replied. "And you too. Lodan, you should know I believe I now know where my father hid the deep-space cruiser."

He frowned, stopped walking and turned to her. "Where is it?"

"In the Outlands, quite near where you crossed the border. There are a number of abandoned mines in the canyons that run through the massif; there is one in particular where my father took me there when I was eleven."

Lodan's frown deepened; he had not exactly expected this development. He had promised Gerlic to take Lorel away from Tarnus and had planned to take her to Barta Magnus where he imagined her odd resistance to his advances would gradually be overcome. Now a different prospect had opened up and his original purpose in coming to Tarnus could be resumed, and he did not welcome the news at all. "The Outlands," he uttered, and walked into the palace.

Jodi greeted him with reserved civility and congratulated him on his success. Lodan did not trouble to explain his part and they repaired to a private place on the roof.

The evening had now gathered in the heat of the day and the fires that burned throughout the city had begun to glow in the falling light. Below them soldiers strolled about in the plaza, eating and talking of their parts in the final victory; each expectant of a new future under a new and enlightened leader. Jodi looked out at the darkening scene; he had not discussed the future with Lorel, and up until now there had seemed little point since they both thought they were unlikely to survive. But they had survived and now he was mindful of his obligation to his sister, Matty, who was in danger from the murderous intentions of an Evangelist. He had been delayed on Tarnus and was now very late, but he still might be able to save her.

"What Lorel has just told me about the deep-space cruiser has taken me by surprise," began Lodan. "In my mind I had abandoned the charge placed on me by my kinsman, the Arkon of my family, but now, it seems, I may have an obligation to continue."

"Whether you continue or not," replied Jodi, "know that I will be going. My sister is in danger and I will not forsake her. Lodan, your father's ship lies in deep orbit; it is your rightful inheritance and will provide you with the means to go wherever you please."

"Thank you for pointing that out, Jodi," replied Lodan frostily, "but I believe the deep-space cruiser was provided for my use; it will not respond to anyone but me."

"That is undoubtedly true but my intention is to save my sister from certain death and for that I need the cruiser. If you don't wish to continue the mission you can re-assign it to me and I will take it, for after your capture, the Arkon entrusted the mission to your father and by implication, to me."

"What do you mean, 'to you'?"

"I mean, Lodan, that you and I are brothers declared by our late father in front of the Arkon himself."

"That is impossible, you are not blood; the Arkon would never have permitted it."

"The Arkon was given no choice."

Lodan glared and brooded. He had not taken to Jodi, he could see too much of himself in this headstrong young man. He reluctantly admitted to himself that, of the two of them, Jodi would have been more worthy of his father's respect and this revelation only made the wound sting more.

"This is semantics," said Lorel. "What does it matter who has a right to the cruiser?"

"I don't like this," put in Allrik. "You are both my brothers and I can't bear this bad feeling between you."

"I intended no malice," said Jodi. "I'm sorry if I've offended you, Lodan." He stepped towards his brother. "I would prefer that we did not become enemies."

Lodan was cornered and inwardly cursed. He knew he was being irrational and perhaps even vindictive. Jodi had done nothing to warrant such antipathy, except to be just too bloody perfect. He stood and took the young man's arm in a gesture of friendship.

"I'm sorry too," he said through gritted teeth.

"There," said Allrik, "now we are all brothers. Lorel, you haven't told us what you intend to do."

"Before you say anything," said Lodan, "you had better know that I have given an undertaking to General Gerlic to take you away from Tarnus."

Lorel shot him a look of surprised shock. "You had no right to do that."

"I know," replied Lodan, "and I'm sorry. But you must understand that had I not, the general would have allowed Strellic to overrun the palace and if you weren't killed he would have made sure you disappeared. You have the respect and affection of the people; you are a potential rival."

"I have no such aspirations," she returned warmly.

"Gerlic doesn't know that and he doesn't trust you not to use your popularity and fame against him."

Lorel thought for a moment then nodded sadly. "It's going to be Strellic all over again, isn't it?"

"I believe so," said Lodan, "except Gerlic will be worse; he has more ability."

"I miss my father," she uttered. "We will go, get away from this place; as far away as we can."

"If you can allow us a troop carrier and some supplies, we will leave early in the morning. No one will see her go."

General Gerlic looked up from the makeshift desk he had arranged in what was left of the council chamber. "She has agreed?"

"She has."

"Where will you go?"

464

"To the north; I have arranged a shuttle to my late father's ship. After that, probably Barta Magnus."

The general drew his thick lips into a faint smile. "I've always wanted to go there, but alas, I think I will be rather busy here. A carrier and supplies will be ready for you before first light. Make sure she does not return to Rion."

"She won't come back, I guarantee it."

"Will you be taking the other foreigner?"

"Yes and another fighter who wishes to leave. May I ask you something, General?"

"You may ask."

"Go and see the mine before you reinstate it."

Gerlic smiled but his startling, blue eyes displayed absolutely no mirth. "Goodbye, Mister DeRhogai," was all he said.

XXXI

They set out for the Outlands before first light the next day. General Gerlic had been as good as his word and provided them with a troop carrier and supplies for several days. A contingent of guards witnessed their departure; Gerlic had decided to make it known that Lorel was leaving of her own free will; fleeing the destruction for rosier opportunities elsewhere. It was the initial move in the subtle destruction of her character that caused those that once revered her to alter their high opinions.

But Gerlic's soldiers were not the only eyes on that scene of departure. A man dressed in the uniform of the victorious regiment, but not belonging to it, watched them and slithered away to tell others of what he had seen.

They struck north from the palace and trundled through the hot embers of the city and out into the desolate plain beyond. They had all travelled that way before, for this was the way to the Mine of Kusk, but no one alluded to that terrible journey. As they progressed, ghost-like figures emerged from the darkness; emaciated zombies heading back towards the city to reclaim the shattered remnants of their lives. Under Gerlic, Salom Gul would be rebuilt; the palace would be restored and dwellings would eventually rise from the dust; but now the centre of Salom Gul would host a new structure, one that had not been seen there for fifty years. A great temple would rise from the ashes of Strellic's reign and Rion would once again turn its face to the One True Faith.

As they pressed north the scant traces of human occupation gradually dwindled and they found themselves in the treeless, dry flatlands that stretched all the way to the bleak, frozen polar region. They veered from the road that would have taken them to Kusk and headed northeast towards the Northern Massif. Allrik was steering the same route that Lodan had taken three days before with Fornu and Terrik and they could follow the trace of the tracks of that previous journey.

There was much to talk about, but little was said. Lodan was moody and reticent and Jodi and Lorel seemed to be maintaining a studied distance that kept them unnaturally silent. Lodan quietly noticed this and his suspicions were further aroused.

At the failing of the light, they stopped and took a meal together inside the carrier. Lodan ate little and excused himself. He opened a flask of wine, walked out of the vehicle and propped himself up against a boulder some distance away.

He had drunk half of it by the time Allrik found him. Allrik settled next to him and looked up to the star-filled sky. "It seems strange that we will soon be up there, amongst all those stars."

"Strange to you perhaps," replied Lodan.

"Yes, I suppose you are a well-seasoned traveller."

Lodan glanced at him thinking he was being sarcastic, but he betrayed no sign of it and it was not in his character. "I have only made two star-trips," he replied, "hardly well-seasoned."

"Two more than me."

"I see you leave those two alone," he said, nodding towards the troop carrier.

"I don't know what you mean."

"You're a poor liar, my friend. They are making an art of restraint."

"They don't want to upset you."

"They are making it worse; treating me like a fool. Why has she chosen him, Allrik? Why not me?"

"I don't know, Lodan."

"All I ever wanted to do was protect her and love her, why is that impossible? Sure, even I can see he is handsome, but is that all that matters to a woman?"

"You are asking the wrong man, I was in the army and I have had little experience of women; to me they are a mysterious tribe."

"To us all."

Lodan took another gulp of wine and passed the flask to his friend.

"You know, Allrik, since the mine I have not had a single erection. Up until then my cock used to go hard at the slightest hint of sex. I only had to see an exposed breast or thigh and up it would go, begging for attention. On Kagan I had a different woman almost every night, sometime two or three, but none of them meant anything to me. Since meeting her I have lost my appetite for other women, but the odd thing is I get no reaction when I recall all the many times I saw her naked. It's unnatural."

"I think I know what you mean; it was odd how our nakedness in the mine robbed us of libido. I was never highly sexed but I too have suffered the same loss. Perhaps we have been affected physically in some way; perhaps we will recover in time."

Lodan reached for his friend and kissed him on the top of his head. "Perhaps we are better off without it."

Allrik grinned in the dark and took another swig of wine. He loved Lorel and Jodi but his affection for Lodan was deeper. It was a product of their intense struggle for survival in the mine; a unique bond that had grown slowly and invisibly between them during that terrible time. "You know, Lodan, you are my true friend, the best a man could wish for; but jealousy is an ugly thing and it hurts me to see it in you. If you truly love her you have no alternative; you have to respect her choice. Don't allow her to see you ugly. Perhaps, in time, she will tire of him and turn to you."

Lodan picked up a stone and flung it into the night. "No, my friend, they are soul-mates, even I can see that. She will never love me in that way. I'm tired and a little drunk, why don't you go back and make sure we don't burst in on them at an inappropriate moment? I don't think I could bear to see that."

Allrik recalled the little scene on the roof of the palace and smiled to himself in the dark.

In the early hours Jodi woke up inside the troop carrier. The others were snoring gently as he rose quietly and stole outside to relieve himself. The huge arc of the sky dipped towards the flat circle of the horizon as the world turned towards another day. There was no wind and the sound of his water splashing on to a rock was the only noise he could hear. It was a particularly long piss, one of those that seemed to go on and on, even when you think you have finished. It had turned cold outside and he was anxious to return to the warmth of the troop carrier when something arrested his attention. At first he wasn't sure, it was like a minute disturbance in the even light of the horizon, but as he concentrated all his senses on the spot, he became aware of what it was he was seeing. He quickly shook away the last drips and dived back into the troop carrier.

"Wake up," he shouted as his companions groggily opened their eyes. "We're being followed!"

Saralt Strellic emerged from the cellar where he and five of his Elite Guards had sheltered, into the burning wasteland of Salom Gul. Whilst buried, they had torn the insignia and regimental badges from their uniforms and blackened their arms and faces with the soot and ashes that leaked into the makeshift bunker in which they crouched. Unlike his father, whose image was universally known, Sarlat was recognizable to few outside the palace circle and with the addition of a low-peaked cap, the dusty, blackened mask of his face would have fooled even his own father into thinking he was a stranger.

The tiny cohort of Elite Guard who remained loyal was, in reality, only loyal to one thing. Sarlat had informed them of the treasure of General Arkuna but not of its exact nature and in following him the soldiers had visions of gold and jewels that Sarlat did nothing to discourage. His avowed certainty that the general's daughter knew of the location of the deep space cruiser spurred him to commit any necessary transgression in the pursuit of his goal.

Together, Sarlat and his band of fortune hunters insinuated themselves into the rump of Gerlic's army and waited. In the early hours of the day following the final attack on Salom Gul, one of them observed the departure of Lorel Arkuna. The acquisition of an armoured car had been a mere matter of a few slit throats in the night.

Allrik climbed into the steering position and gunned the motor into life. He turned on the lights and set the vehicle in motion.

"Turn off the lights," said Jodi, "they'll see us."

"I have to see where I'm going," replied Allrik, "if we hit a boulder we won't be going anywhere. Besides, they can already see us, they're following our tracks."

"Who the hell is it?" said Lodan

"It doesn't matter who it is," replied Lorel. "We can't allow them to catch us. As fast as you can, Allrik."

"This is the maximum speed; you'd better strap yourselves in."

The chase across the vast plain of Kusk began that early morning. By the time dawn broke they could see the rising swirl of dust coming from the vehicle behind them. It was obvious that it was a faster vehicle, for they could see it gradually gaining on them. Allrik swerved and swung the unwieldy troop carrier through the uneven terrain with his one good arm and the skill of a pilot well-used to handling such a vehicle. Those inside were bumped and thrown about in their seats as the bruising chase headed towards the Northern Massif.

At last, after over five hours of lurching torture, the Massif loomed on the distant horizon. Behind them the chasing vehicle could now be seen through a viewfinder. Lorel waited until a relatively smooth tract of ground lay ahead and climbed into the turret to take a look. She quickly returned and strapped herself back into her seat. Her face was grim.

"Well?" said Lodan.

"It's an armoured carrier," she announced.

"Shit!" exclaimed Allrik. "We'll be in range soon."

"We need more speed," said Jodi. "Chuck out anything we don't need; the water, the food and any on-board equipment that isn't fixed."

As the troop carrier veered through the terrain, parts of it were hurled out into the desert. Most of the water and all the provisions went first; bedding, excavation tools and anything not fixed followed. The speed increased a little with the shedding of the weight and Allrik began to take more chances with the stability of the tracks. He mowed over rocks that should have been avoided and pushed boulders out the way with an alarming crunch against the structure of the carrier.

They ignored the two most southerly canyons and headed for the third; the one that Lorel recalled from her father's last words. At last, the mouth of the canyon came into view and they veered towards it, Allrik extracting every last fraction of power from the pounding vehicle. A flash issued from the armoured vehicle behind them.

"Get down," screamed Lorel as the air above them cracked and the troop carrier lurched and almost turned over. Allrik fought the steering and brought it back on the straight, cursing freely at the slow response. Another salvo brought the disintegration of the forward screen and a cold wind blasted into the cab. Allrik jettisoned the back door by blowing its catches and swerved the carrier into the narrow mouth of the canyon. For a moment they were out of the direct line of fire.

"How far down?" he shouted over the howl of the wind through the vehicle.

"About four kilometres," shouted Lorel. "Just beyond that blind bend."

But four kilometres was too far; Allrik knew it; they probably all knew it; even so they nearly made it to the bend in the canyon when the final blast came. It hit the right track, melting and disintegrating it at the same time. Allrik lost control and the carrier began to swerve and tip. It rolled over twice and came to rest on its side. Those inside clung on as the carrier turned somersaults and came to rest on the sandy floor of the canyon.

"Out, out," screamed Lodan, unfastening his harness. The others followed but Allrik stayed still.

"I think my arm is broken again," he said through pain-gritted teeth. "Can you help me?"

Lodan unfastened his harness and tried to help him up, but Allrik screamed with pain as he tried to move.

"Get going," he said. "I'm not going anywhere."

"You're coming," bellowed Lodan, pulling him out and ignoring the man's screams of pain.

"Fuck it, Lodan, my knee is shattered. Now sod off while I give these bastards something to think about."

Lodan met his eyes and saw that Allrik knew his time was up. Breathing heavily to control himself, he shoved a sidearm into Allrik's hand and squeezed his shoulder. He ran out of the back of the troop carrier and after the others.

Allrik gritted his teeth and pulled himself around so he could see the approach of the armoured vehicle. Sweating and shaking with pain, he aimed at the forward track and discharged a full blast into it. The armoured truck shuddered as the track shattered, spraying super-heated metal shards into the air. It swerved and veered to a stop and its armoury quickly turned on its prey. Allrik fired again and hit the enemy broadside, but it was not sufficient to silence the more powerful weapon of the attacker. A bolt of light cracked the air around Allrik's head and a rush of heat passed through his body and that was the last thing he felt. His lifeless form slumped and the troop carrier began to burn.

Sarlat and his guards climbed out of the armoured truck and approached the burning troop carrier. They readied their weapons and waited for the occupants to emerge, but no one came out of the inferno.

One of the guards saw the footprints in the dust. He called out to Sarlat, "They went past that rock promontory."

Sarlat roundly cursed the dullard. Did he have to tell them everything? "Get after them," he screamed.

The soldiers ran to the promontory as Sarlat waddled and puffed behind. As they rounded it a pulse of energy felled one of them and the others dived for cover.

Beyond the promontory, Jodi and Lorel had taken a position behind a boulder to cover Lodan and Allrik's escape, but Lodan rounded the promontory alone and ran towards their position. A burst of energy shattered some of the boulder above them as he dived into cover.

"Where's Allrik?" said Jodi as Lodan picked himself up.

"He didn't make it."

Jodi's face darkened and took on the singular aspect of a killer. "Go; both of you." he said. "I'll keep their heads down."

Another pulse blasted the boulder, showering them with dust and shards of rock.

"I'm not going," shouted Lorel over the din.

Lodan saw that this was not a time for a discussion; Lorel was determined to stay with her lover and Jodi's face had taken on the same, murderous expression that it had worn as he had raced past him out of the Mine of Kusk. It was a face not to be argued with. He touched Lorel on the shoulder. "Good luck," he said and raced towards the chasm in the cliff face while Jodi and Lorel fired at the rocks that protected the position of their pursuers. They kept their enemy's heads down just long enough for Lodan to reach the chasm and then they stopped firing to preserve what was left of their sidearm's reserves. Immediately a brilliant light cracked the air above them and another part of the boulder shattered, cutting them with its splintering shards. Another blast shattered more of their cover, which was being quickly demolished. Their protection would not last much longer.

Lodan ran into the huge, cliff-face chasm and immediately entered a cavern of massive proportions. The half-light filtering from outside revealed all manner of wondrous features etched into the stone by countless years of toil. Lodan peered into the temple-like void and caught a glimpse of an incongruous sparkle close to the far end of the cavern. He had seen one of these fabled vehicles only in simulation and knew immediately that Lorel had been right. The deep-space cruiser was here. As quickly as he could he picked his way over the rocky slope that descended into the cavern and ran towards the ship. As he approached the elegant superstructure began to glow with life.

Its new master had arrived.

Jodi and Lorel crouched below the disintegrating boulder as the rain of energy bursts shook the air around them. The very atmosphere seemed to be burning as the heat intensified. Their weapons were depleted and they had not been able to reply for some time and now it was only a matter of moments before the end would come.

"Give me your weapon and make a run for it," Jodi shouted over the harsh sound of the bombardment.

"No, you go," Lorel replied.

They looked into each others' faces and knew that they would die together.

Suddenly the firing stopped and the sound of Sarlat's high-pitched voice reached their ears.

"Lorel Arkuna, surrender now and you will be spared."

The sound of that hated voice froze her blood. So it was Sarlat who had pursued them across the Outlands. "It's Strellic's son," she said to Jodi.

Jodi's face took on an even darker aspect. "You have an account to settle with him."

She nodded and he could see the pain of recollection in her eyes. "What do you want?" he shouted over his shoulder.

"Throw your weapons down and come out; it's your only chance. My men will not fire," called out Sarlat. "I wish to discuss the return of certain, missing assets that your father stole from the state."

Lorel laughed at the irony and the sheer presumption of the man. "Assets? What are you talking about? You son of a turd."

"Lorel Arkuna, do not anger me with your sour language; I know you have knowledge of a certain item illegally obtained by your traitorous father. I am prepared to make a deal with you; your life and the life of your companion in exchange for the asset. It is a fair exchange."

"Go fuck yourself, you fat cretin."

Behind his rock cover Sarlat struggled to control his temper, but he was a man not used to exercising self-control and the onrush of indignation overwhelmed his better judgement. "Kill them!" he screamed.

His captain turned towards him. "Excellency, she is trying to goad you into killing them so they can't be tortured into a confession. If we kill them we will never discover the treasure."

Sarlat could hardly believe his own ears; no soldier had ever questioned his orders before or had the temerity to point out the folly of them. His eyes bulged and he glared at the man. "I said kill that fucking bitch; NOW. You will be taken to the mine for disobeying my order when we return."

In those last few injudicious words Sarlat Strellic sealed his fate. The captain, perceiving that his future prospects looked somewhat bleak, took decisive action. He quickly stepped forward and fetched a blow to his commander's temple. Sarlat went down into the dust like a sack of vegetables, his face a mixture of alarm and fury. The other troops witnessed this amazing scene with trepidation; by his action the captain had condemned them all.

"You are a pathetic heap of shit," hissed the captain.

Sarlat began a tirade but two other troopers took up the matter and kicked him in the ribs whereupon he began a rather undignified sort of blubbering.

The captain looked down in disgust, ashamed that he had ever served this man. He turned and called out to the condemned pair behind the boulder. "Miss Arkuna, Sarlat Strellic no longer commands this unit. I wish to speak with you, soldier to soldier. Here is my offer of good faith."

He strode over to the recumbent figure of his erstwhile commander and pulled him roughly to his feet, then, with the sole of his boot, he propelled him out into the open land in front of their position. Sarlat staggered forward and fell into the dust once again. They could all hear him whimpering.

Jodi poked his head out from behind the boulder and saw the scene. "It's Strellic; it might be a trap."

Lorel shook her head. "He would never place himself in that much danger; his men have mutinied."

She looked out from behind the boulder and saw the man she hated wallowing in the dust. She checked her weapon; there was just enough energy left. She recalled what he had done to her and to her father and brought the sidearm up to take aim. But, at that moment, a low rumbling sound issued from the mouth of the cavern behind her and began to increase rapidly in intensity. They both looked around to see the sharp point of a beautiful, glowing craft emerge from the bowels of the rock. The ship cleared the cliff face and turned towards them. The air around it danced with light, filling the whole canyon with intense brilliance as it slowly edged forward and settled over their position. A ramp lowered from its belly and touched the ground just behind them. Jodi took Lorel's hand and led her towards the light.

Sarlat picked himself up and started screaming at the soldiers to shoot at the ship, but the troopers were struck into statues at the amazing sight of a deep-space cruiser floating above the canyon floor only metres from them. As it passed over them the air shook and the ground beneath their feet seemed to melt so that they were thrown down and had to cover their heads with their arms against the pounding pressure as the initial drive was fired. The ship began to rise and soon cleared the canyon walls as it climbed into the clear sky. Within a few seconds it was gone.

Sarlat Strellic had learnt nothing from his recent experience. He picked himself up and rounded on his former command and screamed at them in frustration and disappointment. "You fucking cowards; you could have stopped them instead of cringing behind these rocks. With that ship I could have ruled the whole of Tarnus; I could have been the emperor of the world. That was my ship, it was mine; it was mine!" He shook his fist at the sky and glared at the men who were staggering to their feet. "I will have you all sent to the mine," he shouted. "Give me your sidearms; you are all condemned as traitors."

The soldiers were bemused. Even with the entire arsenal of Rion at their disposal, instead of a cannon and a few sidearms, they still could not have brought the ship down and every man knew it. Now they were stranded in the middle of the most hostile wilderness on the planet with absolutely no hope of rescue and they were armed and he was not. The man clearly had no grasp of reality.

"You have led us to our deaths, you ignorant fool," said the captain, advancing.

Sarlat saw the malice in his face and on the faces of the other soldiers as they came towards him.

He backed away. "I am the son of the Beloved Leader; you will follow my commands."

The soldiers laughed. Sarlat retreated, squinting at them with a look of incomprehension. Why weren't they responding to his commands? He would make them pay dearly for their insubordination. He took a few more steps back until his boot hit a rock and he tripped and fell heavily on to his back. He looked up at the circle of grim faces looming over him. "You are all under arrest," he bellowed.

"And you are a fat, useless lump of turd," said the captain just before bringing his heavy boot down on to the unprotected face of his one-time leader.

They kicked him to death and left his mutilated body to be consumed by the shifting, wind-blown dust and sand of the canyon floor. And by this action the brief Civil War of Rion was ended and the last vestiges of the rule of the Strellics in the Division was finally extinguished.

PART FOUR

REVELATION

I

The death of Allrik tainted the relief of their escape from Tarnus and filled them with profound sadness. Lodan and Lorel had known him less than fifty days but so much had passed between them that it might have been an entire lifetime. Jodi had known him only a few days, but in their difficult journey from the mine to Salom Gul, he had bonded with the man to a greater degree than he would have thought possible with another of his own gender. Allrik's open and oft-declared love for them all had buried what reserve they might have felt, for it was noble love freely given from a noble soul and they would all miss him very much. Between them Allrik had been the peacemaker, the arbiter who might have brought about a truce, however uneasy, between Jodi and Lodan, but without his benign influence the festering rivalry between them would only deepen and become ever more toxic.

Jealousy and envy are powerful emotional forces for a man to hold at bay but, strong as they were in Lodan, they were not the principal cause of the process of Lodan's gradual estrangement from the other two. Ever since his escape from the mine he had increasingly turned towards the credo that had been instilled in him since the day of his birth. He turned towards the Prophet to whom he attributed his preservation. He reasoned that he had been spared to fulfill a purpose; a purpose that would be revealed to him in the course of time. Now, in the tranquillity of the ship, he began to devote himself to a form of contemplation practised by those who would aspire to membership of the Brotherhood of Mercy. This form of worship required solitude and abstinence; two qualities much suited to his present circumstances.

Both Jodi and |Lorel sensed a profound change in Lodan's demeanour and the journey through occupied space was characterized by a strained reticence, even between the lovers whose stilted conversations always seemed to return to the death of their friend. In their melancholy they might have turned to each other for succour, but they did not for neither was reliant on the other for emotional support. It was a sad time for all of them and so, when the time to go into stasis came, it was something of a relief.

As they disrobed and cleaned themselves, the expectations of what lay ahead differed in each of them. Lodan brooded on the heretical nature of the mission and wondered why the Prophet had spared him in order to undertake such a journey for it was base and wicked to question the infallibility of the word of Minnar. Lodan knew that Mankind was born in the Sea of Creation on Agon, so what was the point of this odyssey? Lorel had no religious indoctrination to colour her expectations and looked upon the journey as one of potential discovery. In truth, she would have followed Jodi wherever he wanted to go for she was already bound to him and his fate would be hers.

Only Jodi had real purpose. Since discovering his sister, Matty was still alive his entire direction had been to secure her safety and reunite himself with her. They were ninety-six days behind the Evangelist, Dax, and ninety-six days was a long time to survive the attentions of a man so driven by irrational, murderous intentions. He kept telling himself that she would find a way to survive, but even as he did, doubt gnawed at his belief.

The deep-space cruiser carried two spherical life-pods, one on each flank, each furnished with twelve stasis units. Lodan ordered that they should occupy separate life-pods: *In case of malfunction*, he said, but actually, given the state of their relationships at that time, it seemed natural that they would separate. He bad them a cursory farewell and took himself off to the starboard life-pod. He chose one of the twelve units, opened it and listened as it began to instruct him. He stepped into the unit, the door closed and the process began. He shut his eyes and went into the long, dreamless sleep of stasis.

II

Almost five years later Lodan opened his eyes and waited for the stimulant to take effect and for his disorientation to subside. He had read about coming out of prolonged stasis but had never before experienced it. It felt like the long absent soul returning to the body, as if a person could be reassembled from various physical and spiritual elements that had been scattered to distant places.

It seemed to him ages before the unit eventually opened and he stepped out. It warned him as he left that he would be uncoordinated and weak and recommended resting for twenty hours before ingesting food. He moved cautiously forward, rediscovering as he went the art of walking, as though having to instruct each leg in turn to move in the correct way. He made his way stiffly and awkwardly across the belly of the ship to the other life-pod. He opened it and saw that Jodi and Lorel had not been revived. He checked their vital signs, all seemed normal; the units were functioning correctly, so he returned to the central control to check where they were. They were under three days from their destination.

He repaired to his quarters, removed his clothes and looked at himself in the reflector. He was five years older and yet, but for a slight growth of stubble on his face, he looked no different; his body had aged no more than a week during the stasis. He cast his eyes downward and thought of Lorel's naked body. The mental stimulation stirred nothing below and he smiled grimly; the Prophet had spared him that distraction and stasis had done nothing to alter the situation.

He cleaned himself, dressed and laid down to rest, but the thought of Lorel nagged at him and he could not settle. He rose and went back to the port life-pod. He peered into Jodi's unit and saw the man lying there, eyes shut and still. It would be so easy; so easy, he told himself. All he had to do was open the unit and disrupt the process of revival; it would look like a malfunction and Jodi would experience no pain as his life signs gradually ebbed away. Lorel would then turn to him; it would be inevitable in this remoteness and even if she did not, at least he would have the satisfaction of knowing that no other man could touch her.

He stood in front of the unit for some time, weighing in his mind the consequences of what he was seriously contemplating. Under Kagan law his father had recognized Jodi as his son, so it would be fratricide, an act specifically condemned in the Book of Minnar. He recalled his father, his wisdom and the love he bore him; enough love to sacrifice his own life in the protection of his son's. He compared his father's actions to his own unworthy thoughts and was ashamed; Sevarius would never have contemplated killing a man that way; he would have challenged and fought his enemy openly. He looked at Jodi's lithe, muscular frame and recalled the ease with which he had killed his enemies. If they fought it would not be easy, not like fighting the soft-muscled Kagans he had so often vanquished. Given the provocation, this man would murder without thought or regret. The youthful, handsome face with its faint shadow of down belied the character of its owner; this boy was a killer through and through.

He turned to the adjacent unit where Lorel reposed. She was the only woman he had ever loved and she was the one he could not have. He studied her form carefully. The sight of her white, firm breasts hidden under the soft, flimsy clothing should have aroused in him an onrush of passion even if it could not manifest itself physically. But as he stared at her he realised that a change had been wrought deep within him that had brought about a more sober assessment. It caused him wonder if he had ever really loved her. He smiled to himself; the Prophet had released him from this shallow bondage but His purpose was not yet clear. He would wait and see what developed and then he would know, for the Prophet would eventually reveal to him the way forward; of that he was certain.

As he stared dispassionately at her, Lorel opened her eyes.

III

The warning sounded as they approached the destination star. It had become bright to them, singled out from the firmament of the billions of stars that surrounded it, and now its light caught the exterior of the cruiser making it shine in the darkness like a meteor in a black sky. They had entered the planetary system.

"There's an unknown, foreign object in orbit around the fourth planet," said Lodan as they assembled on the bridge. It was the first time they had all been together since coming out of stasis. Lorel had particularly noticed that Lodan had become even more distant and now avoided their company altogether. She suspected that something had radically altered his state of mind and that they had cause to be vary wary of him.

"A ship?" asked Jodi.

Lodan examined the signal. "Possibly, but it's entirely inert."

"The Evangelist is still here," said Lorel.

"If he is he must be dead," replied Lodan. "There are no signs of any energy at all. One other thing, if this reading is right, the object is enormous."

As the cruiser eased into high orbit above the fourth planet of the star designated KT153/2739, they could see below them the great scar in the surface that the explosion of a deep space cruiser had produced. New volcanoes had begun to form at the rim of the crater, spewing magma and hot ashes into the poisonous, frozen atmosphere of the planet.

"That's very recent," said Lodan. "There's only one thing that would produce an explosion of that signature and that magnitude; a cruiser, one that had been deliberately engineered to explode."

"That crater's over a thousand kilometres across," said Lorel. "Nothing anywhere near it would have survived." She placed her arm around Jodi's shoulder and squeezed tenderly. "I'm sorry Jodi, we're too late."

Jodi stared at the image, tight lipped. He had always known in the depths of his heart that he would never see his sister again. Now he was sure she had perished at the murderous hands of an Evangelist and an impossible sadness overcame him. "She has become part of the planet," he said quietly. "I hope she didn't suffer."

"She wouldn't have known anything," replied Lorel. "It would have been instant."

Jodi bowed his head and sat down. "I should have got away earlier," he muttered angrily. "It's my fault she's dead."

Lorel sat down next to him and hugged him too her. He put his head on her shoulder and sobbed while she comforted him.

Lodan observed the scene resentfully. This warrior; this hard-edged killer had melted away and been replaced by a little boy crying on his mother's shoulder. For the first time he understood something of the nature of their relationship; she had never wanted a man, an equal, a peer; what she had always desired was to be a mother to her lover and Jodi, with his combination of youth and virility, had supplied her need as no other could. He turned his back on them in disgust. It explained her behaviour in the mine and her coolness towards him and he gave himself leave to rejoice that he had escaped her clutches.

As the black-hearted, fiery-rimmed crater slipped towards the horizon, they got their first look at the tumbling hulk of the abandoned craft.

Lodan observed it in tight-lipped silence; it had to be a sign, but what did it mean?

Lorel released Jodi from her embrace and stood. "There are some marks at one end; can you magnify them?"

Lodan increased the viewer to its maximum capacity and the word written on the forward section of the hulk drifted across the three-dimensional image on the bridge. As he stared at it, the full significance of what he was looking at finally hit him. He recalled the blasphemous words of the Fourth Proposition and saw in this ship those words made real. The Prophet was revealing Himself, piece by piece. A message would soon be sent.

"It's not of our civilization," said Lorel.

"*Hyperion*," said Lodan so quietly that she barely heard.

"*Hyperion*? Is that what it says? How do you know?"

Lodan's expression was grim. "It is in the ancient form; I was required to learn it at the seminary on Kagan when I was studying for the Brotherhood. That word says '*Hyperion*'."

"What does it mean?" said Lorel.

Lodan turned to her with an intensely hostile expression on his face. "It means evil; pure evil. This is a black ship; it must be destroyed."

Jodi looked up with sudden resolution; his eyes were red from tears but fervent and shining. "No, it must not be destroyed; not until I know what happened to my sister."

"She's dead; forget her," uttered Lodan through clenched teeth.

"I'm going over there; I don't care what you think."

Lodan glared at him. "Then you will become part of the evil and it will destroy you too."

"So be it," replied Jodi.

Jodi eased the escape pod into the gaping hangar near the forward point of the ship and set it down, locking it to the metallic floor. It had been decided that he should explore the ship alone because the cruiser's system had detected explosive material aboard and he was not entirely sure that Lodan would not attempt to destroy the ship while he was on board. He needed Lorel to watch the man who was becoming increasingly intense and alarmingly strange. He secured the lifebelt about his waist and activated it and the protective envelope began to glow about him. He pulled a lantern from a locker, opened the life-pod door and floated out into the vast, empty hangar of *Hyperion*.

Through the open doors of the hanger he could see the faint light of the cruiser moving against the star-field as the hulk tumbled through its orbit. Jodi sent the lantern ahead and followed its stark light through the open portal and into the belly of the ship. As he entered the first corridor, he found the first evidence that someone had gone before him. Directional indicators pointed the way.

"Do you see this?" asked Jodi. "It looks like skin spray."

Lorel peered at the image that Jodi was generating while she monitored his progress on the schematic that the cruiser's system had produced from a probe. Lodan had refused to be present and had confined himself to his room saying that he would not suffer himself to be contaminated by such evil.

"Yes, I see," replied Lorel. "Turn right at the end, Jodi."

He passed into the labyrinth, along numerous interconnecting corridors until he finally entered the crew's quarters. The ancients who had once occupied the ship had left little of themselves behind, but as he floated through the various chambers he came across the one vital piece of evidence of recent occupation. He was arrested by four words scratched on the front of a locker in modern script. The words said, 'look at the stars'. He opened the locker and pulled out the two items inside; the ship's log detailing journey of Jun Siu and Solon Bru and the life history of Matty that Jun had recorded. The other item was an unusual, lozenge-shaped object. As he peered at the ancient object, it began to glow and the strange images of ancient times floated in the frozen, airless confines of *Hyperion*.

"I am glad Matty found love," said Jodi, as their viewing of Jun Siu's account concluded.

Lorel took his hand in hers and kissed it. Jun Siu's account of Matty's life on Ennepp with her brother had moved her to tears and she began to know and understand aspects of Jodi's early life that, either from shame or lack of recall, he had not shared with her before.

"Jun Siu was not like me," he continued with a frown. "I wonder why Matty loved him."

"He was a Suran; I have never seen one before, but I have heard of their strange attitudes and traditions. Jun Siu can hardly be typical of that race; and as for Doctor Bru, he looked perfectly normal to me. According to this account his body should be out there, quite close by. Perhaps we should retrieve it."

Jodi shook his head. "Leave it be; let their wishes be honoured."

A profound silence fell between them and he would not look at her. She studied his bowed head, not really knowing what to say. She could tell that the discovery of the violent nature of his sister's death had affected him greatly, redoubling his self-admonishment and guilt at not being there to save her.

"Do you want to talk about it, Jodi?" she whispered.

He shook his head slowly. "No." His reply was barely audible.

She wanted to share his grief but he had shut her out, excluded her from that corner of his life and she felt denuded by it. She sensed that she was intruding on his grief; intruding on a bond of love that pre-dated hers and would persist through all the turns in Jodi's life. She saw that he would never be entirely hers. She rose quietly and left him to his melancholy.

The personal record of First Officer Johansen, which had resided on *Hyperion* for over one-hundred-and-twenty thousand years, came as profound surprise to them. The manner of its reactivation when Jodi held it in his hand and its eclectic contents were a revelation to them both and for the first time, they truly grasped what it was they were doing in the outer reaches of the galaxy. In this matter neither were burdened with philosophical prejudices; Lorel had been raised in a fiercely secular tradition and Jodi had no tradition other than the childish superstitions of the Native race and his understanding of the writings of the Prophet which he had gleaned while learning to read on the farm in the south of Ennepp. They entered the new landscape with open minds. But Lodan was different. He was the product on intense indoctrination into a faith that could brook no dissent and as the physical evidence began to chip away at the bastion of his beliefs, so he built ever-stronger defences in his mind. He closed his eyes and ears to the truth that was being uncovered before him for he knew that these were falsehoods and the sure path to damnation. The intensity of his faith could brook no challenge and now he began to see the purpose the Prophet had always intended for him; he now saw why he had been spared. *Hyperion* was not the primary source of evil; it was merely a signpost to a greater blasphemy; a blasphemy that must be expunged from the universe.

He began to plan.

"What does he mean, 'look at the stars'?" uttered Jodi time and time again, as he searched through the extensive spectacle of Johansen's life.

"Perhaps he meant there was something in the stars around here, something unusual we should be looking for," replied Lorel.

Jodi turned and glanced at her, he had thought himself alone. "There is nothing unusual about this region, other than its relative lack of stars," he replied. "No, there's something on this… this record. That is the logic of scratching those words on the face of the locker I found this in. And, one thing's for sure, Surans are creatures of logic; I just wish Jun Siu had been more specific and not assumed we are all as clever as they are."

"What do you think he was guiding us to?"

Jodi gave her a look of puzzlement. Had she not understood? "The source of humanity of course."

She raised a sceptical eyebrow. "Do you really think that such a thing exists?"

"It has to."

"But all the way out here? I mean in the outer galaxy. Why here?"

He shrugged. "Why anywhere? It's just a matter of chance; the conditions for the successful development of higher life forms seem to be extremely rare. In our own region we have surveyed tens of thousands of planetary systems, many of which display past or present signs of organic life and yet only a handful have developed life-forms beyond what might be described as extremely primitive and none of those have evolved beyond basic, free-swimming creatures. There is no particular merit attached to any region of the galaxy; all that's needed is a stable star and a world with the right conditions."

"You really believe that, don't you?"

"I don't know; I really don't know what to think." He turned back to the flow of images and sounds generated by the lozenge-like object. "Where's Lodan?" he asked.

"Still in his cabin," she replied.

"I'm getting very worried about him."

"He's sulking."

"Is he? Are you sure that's all it is?"

"What do you mean?"

"You heard what he said about *Hyperion*; he called it evil. He's changed; changed out of all recognition. I see the way he looks at us and, I assure you, it is not jealousy that motivates him. I don't like the way this is going. I've got a bad feeling about it."

"He'll come round; give him time."

"I don't know that time will make any difference; there's something extreme about his behaviour. I think he's losing his mind. He controls this ship; it's going to be difficult."

Lorel took his hand and kissed it. "He's had a lot to cope with; the death of his father and Allrik and…" she bowed her head, "his disappointment; he's taken it hard."

"These are heavy blows, but I think it's more than that. I think it has something to do with his faith."

"Lodan is not religious."

"Isn't he? I've been to Kagan and Sevarius told me about the seminaries and the indoctrination of the young. Lodan is not as strong minded as his father or the Arkon; I don't think he has escaped his upbringing; I think, at a fundamental level, he still believes in the Prophet."

Lorel frowned. "If that's true we have a serious problem."

Later on Jodi awoke and the images of Johansen's record swam about in his brain. He observed Lorel breathing peacefully next to him, her breasts exposed in the soft, shadowy light of the cabin. Increasingly alarmed at Lodan's irrational behaviour, they had resolved to stay together when asleep for mutual protection, but an idea was beginning to form in his head and he knew he would get no sleep until he had resolved it. The sight of her stirred him physically but he did not want to wake her so he rose quietly, pulled on his britches and went back to the bridge to study the record in further detail. It had suddenly occurred to him where he might look for Jun Siu's clue, but as he wandered distractedly into the room he found it occupied by Lodan, who was looking intently at one image in the section designated 26, 'Historical'. He contemplated returning to his quarters but the sight of the image impelled him forward. He had seen the image before and now Lodan had found it too.

Lodan did not acknowledge him or even seem to notice his presence. He just kept staring at the image of a dead tree in silhouette against a night sky of stars fixed with fine detail.

"Look at the stars," said Jodi.

Lodan suddenly looked up at him. His eyes were glazed and his person was unkempt. He smelled of a peculiar cocktail of body odour and incense. Some words spilled from his mouth but Jodi could not understand them. They sounded like the ancient priestly language he had heard used in incantations.

"You've found it," said Jodi.

Lodan's eyes suddenly focused on him. "I should have killed you in stasis; there was nothing to stop me."

Jodi took a step back; he sensed the awful hostility in the man. "True enough, it would have been easy and you could have made it look like a malfunction. But that would be a coward's way and you are not a coward, Lodan. You're my brother, I will not fight you and if your intent is to murder me, I will not prevent it."

"You could not prevent it. You are a blasphemer. Go back to your whore."

Jodi took a step towards him. "My brother, you are not well."

Lodan stood suddenly and threw the lozenge to the floor; the image faded and disappeared. His eyes blazed with hatred. "You are not my brother; do not say that again. You are base and soiled in the mind; you intend to destroy the word of the Prophet. You are an instrument of evil."

Jodi tensed at the expected attack but Lodan passed him and left the bridge without another word.

When he was gone Jodi sat down in numbed silence. He was now sure that Lodan had become unstable and represented a serious threat to his two crewmates. He controlled the ship and his irrational behaviour might bring disaster. He picked up the lozenge and the image of the dead tree against the night sky sprang into the room. He gazed at it in contemplation for some time and then he started work. Three hours later the navigation system had found the solution; the only place in the galaxy where the night sky would have matched the sky in the image one hundred and twenty thousand years ago. Star reference KT65/7674.

When he returned to Lorel he found her awake.

"Where have you been?" she whispered drowsily.

He undressed and snuggled beside her. "I've found out where we have to go. Lodan found the image that Jun meant us to see."

"Lodan!" she returned surprised.

"He was on the bridge."

"How is he?"

"Not good; we *do* have a serious problem."

Jodi made two more visits to *Hyperion* during which he searched the craft for treasure. He found a number of items from the crew's quarters and brought them back to the ship. These were mostly implements of a personal nature left behind by the long departed crew; a hairbrush; various items of clothing; a stuffed toy in the form of a strange-looking creature. He also brought back several of the geological samples he found in the laboratory; mostly igneous rocks that had once interested the ancient crew of *Hyperion*.

During this period they saw nothing of Lodan who had, once again, withdrawn to the sanctity of his quarters where he spent his time in a form of contemplation designed to distil his faith into a concentrate of pure, unadulterated devotion. He asked the Prophet again and again for guidance but received no divine answer. He knew that the infidel, Jodi Saronaga, had discovered the location of that which must be destroyed, but he was by no means certain of his worthiness to be the instrument of his Lord. He had suffered in the mine but had not embraced the suffering; he had not welcomed it as a true soldier of the Faith would have done and this truth convinced him that he must now go beyond the confines of his own spirit; he must step beyond the threshold of his narrow existence and become that which the Prophet had always intended. He must perform the rite that his father had forbidden.

As he stared at his own image he saw nothing in the vacant eyes looking back at him. They were the eyes of a stranger, an impostor. The body that Lodan DeRhogai had once inhabited was a foreign thing to him. It was a foul and evil thing polluted by an instrument of pleasure that could no longer be tolerated even though it was now dormant.

He removed his soiled clothing and cleaned his body thoroughly. When he was satisfied he arranged before him the instruments of the Rite; a razor-sharp knife and a thread. He took up the knife and shaved himself all over so that no adornment should taint the purity of the deed. When this process was complete he began an incantation while he took the knife and drew two deep cuts into the flesh of his abdomen from the base of his penile shaft to his waist just above the pelvic bone. He watched the blood flow from the flesh and drip down his legs on to the deck where it formed a pool around his bare feet. He waited until the blood congealed and the flow stopped before performing the next part of the Rite. As the last drops of blood splashed to the floor, he took up the thread and tied it around the base of his penile shaft. He welcomed the pain as the thread bit into his flesh. He knotted the thread securely in the manner used by Evangelist novices and taking up the knife with his right hand and stretching the sacrificial flesh with his left, he placed the knife beneath the shaft and sliced decisively upwards.

Jodi and Lorel had not seen Lodan for four days when they fell into a discussion about what to do. They were both anxious to leave this star system with its ancient hulk of a ship and painful memory of Jodi's dead sister and to journey to the new system that Jodi had identified with its prospect of great discovery.

"He has not left his cabin for over four days," said Lorel, "I think we should check on him."

Jodi nodded. "He hasn't eaten, the rations are untouched."

"I'll go in," she replied. "He's more likely to tolerate my presence."

"I'm coming with you; I'll stay outside in case you need me."

They made their way to Lodan's cabin and tried to open it, but it was locked. Lorel banged on the door and called out, but could get no response.

"He's not dead," she said. "The ship's system confirms that."

"I'm going to get a sidearm," said Jodi.

She touched his arm. "No, it might provoke him; I'm sure he won't try to harm me. We're going to have to force the door."

Jodi fetched a hammer and smashed his way into the control mechanism by the side of the door. When he had exposed its workings he pushed the hammer into the lock release until he heard a distinctive click. He held the hammer in place to keep the lock open.

"That's it, open it," he said.

Lorel placed her hands on the door and pushed it to one side. In the subdued light she could see Lodan sitting straight-backed, cross-legged on the bed, his vacant eyes staring at nothing more than the blank wall in front of him. She saw the large pool of blood on the floor and blood-soaked cover below Lodan's naked body. She approached slowly and cautiously until she stood directly in front of him. She looked down and flung her hand to her mouth to suppress a scream when she saw what he had done.

"What is it?" said Jodi rushing into the room behind her. "Oh fuck!" he whispered when he saw the gruesome sight.

Lorel covered her face in shock as Jodi passed her and approached Lodan. He slapped the man gently on the cheek to get his attention. Suddenly Lodan's vacant eyes focused on Jodi and his face darkened with hatred.

"Blasphemers!" he screamed and, too late, Jodi saw the knife in his hand. He felt the blade enter his side and he reeled away clutching at the wound as blood oozed between his fingers. Lorel grabbed Jodi and pulled him out of the cabin as Lodan turned his head to watch them. She briefly caught sight of his eyes; vacant eyes that registered no recognition of her. They were the dead eyes of an Evangelist.

She helped Jodi back to the bridge and he slumped into a chair, his wound bleeding profusely.

"The arsenal," he said through gritted teeth. "Get a sidearm, quickly."

She ran to the arsenal and opened it. Not a single weapon of any description could be found there. She searched around frantically but Lodan had removed all of them. Jodi looked up and saw Lodan enter the bridge. He was a gruesome sight, his naked torso and legs were caked in dried blood; his wild eyes seemed to burst from their sockets as he saw his quarry. He lurched forward, his knife raised and ready to stab. Jodi stood and met him, grabbing his arm and parrying the forceful blow. Lodan twisted him and grabbed him around the neck while Jodi hooked his leg out from under him, sending both of them crashing to the floor. Jodi felt the raw strength of the man as Lodan's arm tightened around his neck, he knew he could not let go of the arm that held the knife for that would be the end. Lodan rolled him over and pinned him down with his full weight. Jodi was losing strength fast and desperately tried to get free but Lodan was too strong for him. Eventually he let go of the arm and felt the searing pain as the knife entered his body just below his armpit and then again at his thigh. He was being stabbed to death and there was nothing he could do to stop it. He stopped fighting and waited for the next blow.

But the next thing he felt was the full weight of Lodan's body slumping onto his; He heard and felt the man's hot breath in his ear; there was a groan that seemed to issue from the depths of his soul.

Lorel stood over the bodies of her lover and his attacker panting heavily. She held in her hand one of the geological samples of rock that Jodi had brought back from *Hyperion*. It was now stained with blood from Lodan's head. She threw away the rock and pulled Lodan off. She turned Jodi over and grabbed his head. He looked up into her eyes and blinked.

"Is he dead?" he asked weakly.

She checked Lodan's pulse. "No, he's alive. You're badly hurt; I'll get the medical kit."

She hurried and was soon by his side cleaning his wounds and dressing them. As she worked with the efficiency of her army training he watched her impassively. Before she had finished Lodan groaned and began to stir. She grabbed a tranquilliser phial and discharged the full amount into his neck. He groaned again and was still.

She helped Jodi into a seat and finished dressing his wounds.

"He would have killed us both," said Jodi, staring at the blood-soaked form lying on the floor.

"Yes, I believe he would have. I wonder who that was? Because it certainly wasn't Lodan."

"What are we going to do? We have to get control of the ship."

"I'll think of something, in the meantime I need to get him cleaned up and secured."

"Are you going to try to reattach it?"

She shook her head. "I don't have the knowledge; curiously we didn't cover that particular operation in medical training." She smiled weakly. "The best I can do for him is to suture it and make sure the wound isn't infected."

"Make sure you keep him tranquillised."

"Don't worry; he'll be out for hours."

She turned down the gravity control until Lodan's body was light enough to handle easily, then taking him under each arm, she pulled him from the bridge and into the nearest vacant cabin. Here she cleaned him in the unit and placed him on the bed before returning the gravity to normal. Jodi had lost quite a lot of blood and she found him asleep in the seat, so she returned to Lodan with the medical kit without disturbing him. Within the kit she found the information she

484

required and, following the instructions step by step, she performed the operation as best she could. When she had finished she stood back to admire her work. The stump was swollen and ugly but the swelling would subside and the urinary tract was clear. She pumped some painkillers into him, covered him with a sheet and left him to sleep.

Jodi was awake by the time she returned to the bridge.

"How is he?"

"He'll live."

"I wonder what possessed him," said Jodi reflectively. "I mean it's such an extreme act."

"I don't know much about Evangelistic practices, but it's clear he's lost his mind."

"Have you found the missing part?"

"I haven't looked."

Jodi's mouth widened into a rare grin. "He might want it as a souvenir."

She forced a smile.

"I once knew a man who had to have his genitals removed; he kept them in a jar of preservative on a pedestal, like a trophy."

"That is weird but I don't think Lodan is so self-obsessed. This act was some sort of atonement; a punishment for something in his past."

"It's possible. Allrik told me that the mine had made him impotent, perhaps the same thing has happened to Lodan."

She nodded reflectively, recalling for a moment the horrors of that dark place. "I did notice that in all the guys after several days. I just put it down to the onset of weakness. It makes we wonder what other damage was done to our bodies."

The insistent, searing pain awoke Lodan from the depths of the drug-induced coma. He opened his eyes slowly and blinked at the light above him. His head felt heavy on the pillow and he found that he lacked the strength to raise it. As his eyes adjusted to the light he discovered that he was not alone; the female infidel was sitting in a chair near the end of the bed with a weapon in her hand. He tried to move his arm but found that he had been bound so that none of his limbs could be moved. He watched her without speaking and waited for her to make the first move. She seemed in no hurry, content to allow the silence to speak for itself; eventually she spoke.

"How are you feeling, Lodan?"

"Why have I been tied this way?"

"You tried to murder Jodi."

Lodan searched his memory and the image of the attack on the male infidel returned. "I don't remember."

"You attacked him with a knife."

"Is he dead?"

"No, he's alive."

Lodan cursed him silently. "I don't remember. Tell him I'm sorry."

"Are you telling me you don't remember anything you did?"

"Nothing."

"You do realise you have impaired yourself, don't you?"

"I am in pain."

"You have impaired yourself by cutting off your penis. Why did you do that, Lodan?"

Lodan stared blankly at the Infidel; this stupid female had no idea what he had done, how at long last he had committed himself to the Prophet. "Can I see?"

She approached and peeled back the cover. He looked down and saw the angry scars from the cuts across his lower abdomen and the newly sutured, truncated member. He concealed his elation.

"I have done my best," she said, "but I am not a surgeon."

"Thank you."

She replaced the cover. "What made you do it?"

"I don't remember."

She returned to her seat and eyed him contemplatively. "Will you direct the ship to a new location?"

"Where?"

"KT65/7674."

"I'm guessing that is the system from which the star image was taken."

"You remember that?"

Lodan held her gaze; she had almost tricked him. "It is a memorable image." Well?"

"Will you release me if I command the ship to go there?"

"You will go into stasis."

"For how long?"

"Until we are sure you have recovered your senses."

"I am, as you see, fully recovered, but I completely understand your caution. I will direct the ship and go into stasis as you wish."

"Thank you. Do you require any more pain-killers?"

"No," replied Lodan quickly; he did not wish to dilute the exquisite suffering that his devotion required, but instantly realised he had betrayed himself. "You are a skilful surgeon and the pain is tolerable," he added quickly.

She arched a sceptical eyebrow and rose, leaving him alone.

He watched her go and sank back into reflection. The Prophet had chosen to spare the infidels and shackle him. Clearly he had acted rashly and mistook His purpose. He did not understand the reason, but clearly he was to enter the very heart of the blasphemy. He must enter the very Jaws of Damnation.

IV

The star designated KT65/7674 was growing ever brighter when Lodan woke up. As the reviving serum coursed through his bloodstream he opened his eyes and saw through the transparency of the stasis unit the figure of Jodi holding a sidearm. *So, they have found the weapons,* he reflected; *no armaments will save them from their fate.*

Moments later he stepped stiffly from the unit as Jodi raised the weapon and pointed it at his midriff.

"Do not worry, brother, I will not harm you," said Lodan, "I have fully recovered my senses."

Jodi made no reply. He stepped back and gestured with the sidearm towards the bridge.

Lodan smiled at his caution; it was justified. "I am sorry I attacked you, my brother; I hope that you can forgive me."

"I will judge you by what you do now, but I do not trust you, Lodan."

"I understand."

They entered the bridge and Lorel turned from the image of the bright star. "How are you feeling, Lodan?"

His tone was stiff and formal. "Thank you, I am well."

"Do you require any pain relief?"

"No, I am not in pain."

She returned to the navigator and changed the image. A distant world appeared three quarters lit by the star; blue and white with oceans and clouds. "This is the third planet; it appears to be the only one capable of naturally supporting life."

Lodan stared at the image; it was like a jewel, a wonderful, tempting jewel. He smiled inwardly at the genius of the Prophet; that He should bring these Infidels to their end with such a temptation: a world finer than any they had ever seen. "And that is your true destination. So be it."

As the image of the world grew larger and they began to see it in closer detail, its beauty only increased. They began to see green-swathed continents with golden-brown deserts and snow-capped mountain ranges; there were seas and lakes and vast river systems and ice at the poles.

"It's beautiful," said Lorel.

"Yes," replied Jodi, "I have seen nothing to match it; not in any image of the galaxy. What is the atmosphere?"

She read off the atmospheric analysis; it indicated perfect conditions for life.

Lodan studied the world intensely and said nothing. He saw the evil beauty of it and now he knew why he had been spared and why he had been brought to this place

"Could it be occupied?" asked Lorel. "The conditions are perfect for humans."

"If it is they cannot be advanced," replied Jodi. "There are no lights of any kind in the dark quadrant. Even so, we should be cautious."

"I agree; we should survey as completely as possible before we attempt to land. Lodan, will you direct the ship to bring us into orbit?"

Lodan smiled and glanced from one infidel to the other. He also looked at the sidearm in Jodi's hand and decided that the time was not yet upon them. He commanded the ship to approach and orbit.

The atmosphere on the bridge was strained and brittle as they watched in silence as the destination grew larger and the detail of its surface increased. The world's single, barren moon appeared beyond the planet's rim, its first segment caught in the intense sunlight. It was a world without atmosphere, a barren and lifeless globe, cratered and pockmarked by countless impacts. But as it hove into view they saw something astounding. In the centre of one of its craters was a pattern laid out in the dust; a pattern preserved for millennia. It was the distinct imprint of a city.

"There are people here," cried Jodi moving to the image for a better look.

Lodan smiled at his foolishness. The Prophet had provided the distraction he needed. He grabbed Lorel with such raw speed and power that she had no chance to defend herself. He wrapped his right arm around her neck and held her head with his left.

"Drop your weapon," he commanded, "or I will break her neck."

"Shoot him." The words choked from Lorel's mouth brought greater pressure from Lodan's powerful arms. Jodi hesitated; he could see he had no prospect of aiming at the parts of Lodan not protected by Lorel's body before the man could carry out his threat.

"Drop the weapon; you have one second."

Jodi loosened his grip on the sidearm and let it fall to the floor.

"Kick the weapon over here, Infidel."

Jodi toe-poked the sidearm towards Lodan. "Let her go."

Lodan released Lorel and propelled her towards her lover. He picked up the sidearm and pointed it at them. "When the Prophet spared me from the death sentence of the mine I knew a higher purpose was His design. Sit down, for you will soon be judged."

Lorel and Jodi sat next to one another; he took her hand and held it fast.

Lodan noted the gesture and smiled thinly. "You cling like children entering a dark tunnel. I should thank you, Jodi, for removing the temptations of the flesh from my head; I now see that it has swamped my mind all these years and cost me a time of grace and purity. I have put such low temptation behind me. I now see the true path; I now see the way to the summit of enlightenment. I am His instrument and I will cast His enemies into the depths of Damnation. This blasphemy must be destroyed; utterly eradicated from the universe and I have been chosen for this glorious task."

"Lodan, consider what you are doing," pleaded Lorel, "think about what we are about to discover on that world."

"It's no use, Lorel, he's gone quite mad," said Jodi.

Lodan steadied the weapon on them and sat down. "I feel sorry for you both; you are without faith, without direction, without the grace of the Prophet. You exist for copulation and shallow pleasures for when it comes to the evils of pleasure there is nothing to equal the debauched influence of females. Did you really believe that I would collude in the destruction of the One True Faith? That I would sink so low and debase myself with this foul conspiracy?"

"What are you going to do, Lodan?" asked Lorel; she could now see fine detail on the world they approached, they were getting close.

Lodan glanced at the image and grinned. "By the grace of the Prophet I overrode all the systems of self-preservation while you were distracted with that hulk."

"That is not possible," said Lorel. "Not even a Suran could do that."

"They are infidels and not guided by His hand."

"You're mad; you have lost your wits, Lodan. Think of what you are doing."

"His work," replied Lodan quietly. He glanced at the fast approaching world. "Not long now."

The ship careered towards the planet with the speed of an asteroid and they now saw his intention. Unlike an asteroid the craft would not break up as it entered the planet's atmosphere, it would become a fireball that would impact on the surface, the ship's propulsion core would be compromised and there would be destruction. It would be as if a new sun had been created on the face of the world, the atmosphere would burn and everything on the surface of the planet would be destroyed.

"Don't do this, Lodan," said Jodi as calmly as he could. "Think about what you would be destroying."

"I know exactly what I am going to destroy," replied Lodan just as a shudder passed through the frame of the ship. They had entered the upper atmosphere at a shallow angle. The image of the world's horizon shimmered and faded from view as the exterior began to heat up. An alarm klaxon sounded and a voice began to announce warnings as they plunged towards the surface. The buffeting became more violent as the ship entered the upper stratosphere and the atmospheric resistance turned it into a brilliantly gleaming fireball.

Lodan began to laugh. He had finally triumphed and soon they would all be consumed by the conflagration. Then suddenly he stopped abruptly and his expression took on an aspect of disbelief and horror.

A fourth person had appeared on the bridge.

Jodi saw his chance. With immaculate speed he reached into his boot and with one single action withdrew the knife he kept there and sent it on its way. It hit Lodan in the stomach, burying itself up to the hilt.

Lodan looked down at the hilt and the blood issuing from the wound. This was surely not part of his Lord's plan; how could it happen? He looked up; his enemy was already on his feet; Lodan raised the sidearm and fired.

The bolt hit Jodi on the side of his torso, sending him twisting into the air. His flesh burned and bubbled as the pulse of energy shot through his body. Lodan watched in fascination as his victim writhed on the floor. He heard the woman scream. Why was she screaming? She could not save him; she could not even save herself. He looked up at the fourth figure on the bridge with its stern, deeply lined face and now he saw that he was in the presence of the Prophet Himself. He lifted his arm and his awestruck face lit up at the sight but the spectral figure remained impassive.

"Why do you not speak, Lord? Have I not pleased you? Am I unworthy? Speak, I beg you."

A violent shudder coursed through the ship. The spectre shimmered, disappeared and then returned and now Lodan realised who and what he was looking at. His face darkened and he stared at it in disbelief. He had been tricked. His eyes turned back towards the Infidels but of them there was no sign.

Jodi stopped writhing about halfway down the passage that led from the bridge to the starboard life-pod. His body went limp as she pulled him, using every ounce of strength in her body. At any moment she expected the bridge door to open and madman inside to lurch through it, sidearm blazing. She held him tightly under his arms and hauled until she came to the life-pod lobby. She pulled him inside as the klaxon pumped its urgent warning into the air. Once inside she closed and locked the door before she hit the emergency escape sequence. The life-pod door behind opened and she pulled Jodi's inert body inside. The door closed like a guillotine. The interior was alive with warnings preventing launch. She overrode them and the pod burst from its host into the high atmosphere of the world.

The engines roared as the pod tried to gain equilibrium but the speed of descent was too great and the craft was over-powered by its own velocity. It became a fireball streaking across the sky, twisting and turning out of control. She threw herself on to Jodi's body and hung on as the white heat screamed outside.

The burning life-pod hit the ocean near a promontory of land. It struck at such an oblique angle that it was thrown high into the air like a skimming stone while plumes of steam and vapour were thrown into the black, smoking trail. The pod hit the water once again and was once more bounced into the air, but now the ocean had given way to land and it cleared a promontory and crashed into thick forest behind a beach, setting the landscape ablaze and leaving a long trail of destruction before finally coming to rest.

Above the crashed life-pod another larger vapour trail scarred the clear, blue sky above the storm clouds and, disappeared beyond the eastern horizon. On board the deep-space cruiser, Lodan remained in his seat clutching his blood-soaked stomach. The spectre watched him impassively as he awaited the impact that would end his suffering and propel him to Paradise for his deed. Even if the Infidels had survived the landing they would not live long on what would be left of the planet. He thought of his Lord the Prophet and gave thanks.

At last the spectre spoke. "I always knew that you could not be trusted, Lodan."

The time of impact had passed; he looked up into the stern, disapproving face of his Arkon.

"Did you really imagine I would rely on your fragile abilities? I always knew you were weak-minded and liable to the temptations of foolish belief and empty ceremony. You have seen the world of human origin but you have denied the evidence of your own eyes. You have chosen superstition over reality and truth and you will never walk on its sacred soil. You will be brought back to Kagan and your failure and disloyalty will be punished with total severity by my successor."

With these words the grim image of the Arkon of the DeRhogai faded and left Lodan sitting in stunned and bitter silence. The man had indelibly imposed his spirit into the heart of the deep space cruiser. Lodan's untutored tinkering would never have produced that which he desired; even if he had caused the ship to crash, its core would never have been compromised. The planet would survive whatever he did. His face twisted with the agony of failure; the Prophet had abandoned him and now it was the Arkon's bidding that was being done. He had failed and now he would have to answer for it; he would descend to the iniquities of the After-world there to writhe forever in torment. He looked at bright image of that which he should have destroyed but the world was already no more than a distant point of light in the cosmos.

PART FIVE

THE GARDEN

I

The first sensation that hit Jodi was intense pain. It felt to him as though his whole body had been immersed in scalding oil while someone had been pummelling him with their fists. The air surrounding him was hot and difficult to breathe. A few feeble lights blinked pointless warnings. He opened his eyes and recognised the interior of the escape pod. Lorel was lying close by; he could see a gash on her forehead from which blood was slowly dripping. A sudden tremor of fear ran through him as he was seized by the thought she might be dead.

He raised himself and crawled over to her, ignoring the pain that darted through him as he moved. She was still breathing. Despite his pain he felt an instant flood of elation; she was everything to him now and the thought of living without her was impossible to imagine. He cradled her head and licked the blood from her wound; it was a deep cut and would require attention. He gently lowered her head and slowly pulled himself over to the other side of the pod where he found the medical kit stowed in the correct place. He opened it, brought out the analgesic and delivered a dose into his arm. Instant euphoric relief coursed through him and sent him into temporary rapture. He rolled his eyes and started to laugh although he had no idea why; there was nothing particularly funny about his present situation; they had crashed on to an unknown world in a region of space so remote that there was absolutely no prospect of rescue and the only saving grace was that they were both still alive.

He peeled off his shirt and looked down at his damaged skin. A large area stretching from his waste to his navel on the left side was burnt where the blast from Lodan's sidearm had glanced him. It was an ugly sight. He took up a phial of new skin and sprayed the area generously. It tingled as it repaired the damage and began to form a new dermal layer. There would be some scarring, another imprint on the violent history of his body. He checked himself for other wounds; there was some bruising and a few superficial cuts and scratches sustained during the buffeting in the centrifuge of the sphere as it hurtled to ground, but nothing to cause him particular concern.

He moved over to Lorel, cleaning the gash in her forehead before sealing it with another phial of new skin. Then he checked her for broken bones and other injuries. He could find nothing beyond a few minor cuts and bruises so he left her to recover in her own time.

He put away the medical kit and tried to look through the small view-port in the door of the sphere. The heat of the landing had rendered it opaque, but he could see strong light through it. He checked the exterior sensors but all had failed; he had no way of knowing what awaited him outside. He knew they were on dry land, also that the atmospheric composition was favourable to human life, which was more than could be said for the stifling interior of the pod. He had to get out; he had to get away from this impossible, airless heat. The manual escape mechanism was still too hot to touch so he wrapped his shirt around his hand and began to turn the handle.

The door eased inward and began to slide to one side. An intense light entered the vessel and made him squint; a rush of air blew into his face. He breathed it into his lungs; it was hot and smoky, like the stinging air one breathes when too close to a campfire. As the door drew to one side more smoke curled into the pod and he began to cough. He put his arm over his nose and mouth and retrieved two respirators from a locker. He put one on himself and the other on Lorel and then wound the door back fully.

Smoke enveloped him and he could see nothing of the world. Heat rose through the soles of his boots and caused him to speculate that they had come to rest in the crater of a volcano. He had read and seen images of the volcanoes on Agon and knew something of the conditions one might expect to find in such features. But the air was not sulphurous and the heat not sufficiently intense for a volcanic crater; it was organic and the ground beneath his feet was soft, like the softness of the forest floor of his youth. The residual heat from the exterior of the pod was beginning to burn his skin so he cautiously moved away from the pod.

As he gained distance the smoke began to clear and he saw the first hint of the cloudless, vibrant, blue sky above him, polished by the early morning sun. The intensity of the colour stunned him; he had never seen its like, not even in the clear, cold evenings of the Southlands of Ennepp. He moved on and the smoke dissipated enough for him to gain his first view of the world.

The violence of the landing had carved a scar of devastation through the landscape and there was a large impact crater where the pod had hit the ground for the final time before rolling to its present position. Fire had raged until quenched by the torrent of a storm passing in the night and now the pristine forest had been replaced by an avenue of smoking and broken, black stumps. He was surrounded by a wasteland, but beyond the charred remains of the forest, through the tracery of smoke, he could see a deep green swathe of conifers shrouding a gentle slope in the land that ended, beyond the trees, with the unmistakable glint of a turquoise sea.

Jodi took off his aspirator and breathed in the smoky air. At that moment he knew they had arrived in Paradise.

Suddenly an extraordinary sound, like a cracked scream of desperation filled the air above him. He instinctively crouched in alarm and steeled himself for battle, but when he looked up to find the source of the scream he was astounded to see a creature flying through the air without the assistance of any sort of machinery. He watched it wheel away towards the sea where others of its kind joined it, squawking and crying as they effortlessly soared. It was the most extraordinary thing he had ever seen but it was just the beginning of the wonders to be discovered on this new world. He took a few steps and looked around him and looked back towards the smoke enveloped life-pod. Beyond it the land rose, with an increasing gradient, towards forested hills and craggy peaks. The beauty of the untarnished landscape almost made him weep. It seemed they had landed in the very garden of the universe.

And now he was impatient for Lorel to see it too. He replaced his respirator and returned to the pod. It was filled with smoke and he had to feel his way to her. She was still unconscious and hadn't moved so he picked her up, hoisted her over his shoulder and carried her out of the vehicle. He brought her down the gentle gradient towards the sea until he came to the edge of the forest where the charred trees were still standing. Here he gently laid her on the ground and removed his and then her respirators. He tapped her face gently and spoke her name several times until she opened her eyes and groggily focused on him.

"Where's Lodan?" she whispered.

"I don't know," he replied. "He didn't crash the cruiser."

She slowly took in this information and frowned. "He may be back; he will find us."

Jodi nodded; he had not thought of Lodan. "He may come back, but we have been here some time and he has not come for us. My knife got him in the gut; perhaps he's dead."

"What about your injury?"

"It's fine, I've taken some analgesic and sealed it." He pulled up his shirt to let her see.

"I'll dress it properly for you."

"It's fine; it doesn't hurt. You have a split head."

"I can't feel it. Where are we?"

"It's beautiful, Lorel. Look at the sky; have you even seen anything like it? She admitted she had not.

"And there's a sea nearby, and trees and everything. It's like... it's like the sort of place you read about in The Book; it's like where all the good people go in After-World."

"Perhaps we are dead."

He shook his head and smiled at her foolishness. "No, we are not dead; we are home."

A piercing cry above caused her to jump; she stiffened and her eyes opened wide in alarm. "What was that?"

Jodi pointed to the creature high above. "Men that fly without machines."

She gazed up at the extraordinary sight. "When I was young my father read me stories of such things; things of myth and legend."

"These aren't myths Lorel; they're real; as real as us. Let's go to the sea."

He helped her to her feet, but she held back. "Wait, there could be monsters here."

He laughed. "Monsters are myths, they don't exist."

"Yes and neither do men who fly without machines. We have no weapons to defend ourselves. They could be dangerous."

He released her hand. Alright, you stay here and I'll go and check."

No," she cried, "if we are to be killed by monsters we might as well be together."

He smiled and took her hand and together they entered the swathe of coniferous forest that led down to the sea. Inside the forest, away from the crash site, the air became fragrant and the soft earth beneath them gently crackled as they disturbed the thick bed of rotting needles. All around them they heard the sound of small flying creatures; the buzz of wings and chatter of strange voices calling to one another. Each discovery was like a new miracle until their senses were overwhelmed by the variety and fecundity of the place.

Jodi picked up a fallen branch and broke it to form a rudimentary club. "Just in case," he said.

They walked on and the intense, azure sea began to stretch out before them. They broke through the trees and stepped onto a narrow beach of pale, gold sand curving gracefully to form a bay encased by two rocky promontories. The sound of wavelets upon the sand now filled their ears and they saw the flying men floating on the water and walking on the shore nearby and they saw that they were not like men at all. Jodi tried to approach one but it waddled away and took flight, soaring into the sky with a piercing call to join others circling above. He picked up a pebble and threw it at another. The pebble missed its target and the creature flapped its wings and rose into the sky, out of his reach.

"Why did you do that?" said Lorel in an admonishing tone.

"I wanted to kill it to see what it's made of," replied Jodi.

"Leave them alone, they don't belong to us."

Jodi smiled and kissed her. "You're wrong, this whole world belongs to us, for there's no one else here. There's nobody to tell us what to do; what to think; where and how to live. There's no one to make us get off their land or detain and starve us in purgatory; or to send us to our deaths in a filthy mine stinking of shit and human misery. We have left all that behind, a million light years behind; we are the gods of this world, the rulers of an entire planet."

He took off his boots and stepped into the water; it was pleasantly temperate. She watched him anxiously as he stooped, gathered some droplets in the palm of his hand and put it to his tongue.

"It's salty, just like the sea on Ennepp," he declared.

"Spit it out, you don't know what's in that water."

He laughed at her foolish caution; didn't she understand that in Paradise nothing could harm you? He kicked off his pants and in moments was wading into the water.

"Jodi, come back," she screamed desperately, but he just laughed and waved and splashed like a child and soon disappeared under the water. She saw his head bobbing between the waves and then he suddenly vanished from view. She called and called with mounting concern but the sun shone on the bright surface and dazzled her with intense light. Anxious to gain a better vantage point, she ran to the end of the beach and began to climb through the grassy scrubland of the promontory. Some of the bushes were thorny and she arrived panting and scratched on the high headland and looked down into the clear, turquoise waters of the bay. And there, to her horror, she saw monsters; large, black shapes moving lazily through the water just below the surface. All the blood seemed to drain from her body as she squinted against the glare of the sun on the surface of the water, searching for some small hint that Jodi was out there. But no matter how long she searched she could not see him. She sunk to the warm sward, entirely drained, for grief had numbed her brain; she knew instinctively that the monsters had got him and she was now entirely alone. How cruel that they had come all this way together; survived everything that Fate could hurl at them, only to die in this remote paradise.

She buried her face in her hands and cried bitter tears. She cried until she could cry no more and cursed the mocking beauty of the place that had so quickly ensnared them and fooled them with its deadly hand. This was no place for people; it never had been and it was certainly no paradise. She could not live here; she could not be the lone survivor; there was no point to any of it.

Hardly knowing what she was doing, she approached the edge of the cliff and looked down at the tumble of boulders below. She could not continue without him and it would be so easy to do it now; to hurl herself on to the rocks and end her life in this strange and cruel place. She readied herself and looked for one last time at this new world; at the sleek, black monsters in the bay and the creatures flying above in the cloudless, blue sky; the sunlight dancing on the languid sea. She looked back across the stretch of sand where the dark, green-grey forest ended; a forest so full of life. Her eyes were drawn along its verdant edge, along the long sweep of the bay towards the boulders below the far promontory.

From behind a boulder a figure emerged and began to walk along the shoreline. Her heart pounded at the sight and a sudden euphoria almost paralyzed her and then she wept.

She met him on the beach near his discarded pants. She was so angry with him that she hit him hard on his arm before he could even speak.

He staggered back in surprise. "What was that for?"

"I thought you'd been killed and eaten. Didn't you see those monsters? I can't believe you could be so rash."

"I saw them, they won't eat me; I am the king of them."

"You don't know what they're thinking or what they'll do. It was stupid, just stupid." She began to cry, conflicted by anger and relief.

He saw that he had really troubled her and was contrite. He put his arms around her and kissed her. "I'm sorry," he said.

She caught the fragrance of the salty sea on his flesh as she buried her head in his chest. "Promise you won't do that again," she said through her tears.

"Don't cry, I won't die; I won't leave you here alone."

He lifted her face to his and kissed her again with hard passion. Their need for each other became urgent and soon they were making love on the sand under the stare of the sun. It was a hard edged, brilliant passion born of a freedom neither had ever known in the other. They were alone in the world, free of censor and inhibition and now it seemed to her that her lover was no longer immature for he had grown to fill her whole being and she could never see him again as a boy.

After their lovemaking they walked to the sea and bathed in the warm sunlight before walking back through the forest to the life-pod. The sun was beginning to wane when they arrived for they had stopped frequently to inspect many of the new things they saw. The fire beneath the pod was beginning to lose its energy and the dense smoke had been carried away on the breeze. That evening they sat outside the blackened hull and watched the world turn and the sun illuminate the forest as it fell beyond the horizon. They spoke of many things; of what they had seen and what they would do in the future. They were stranded on this remote world and no help was ever likely to come. The thought did not depress them because they had all they wanted in each other and in everything that surrounded them. They had rations enough to last twenty years and Jodi had found fresh water in a stream letting into the sea at the far end of the bay.

"I wonder what happened to Lodan," said Lorel as they watched the stars gradually emerge in the darkening sky.

"Maybe he bled out and died and the ship's system took over and prevented the crash. We'll probably never know."

"I am sorry for him; he looked out for me in the mine. He was a friend."

Jodi did not pursue the subject; he had his own opinion of Lodan, a man who had allowed blind faith to destroy his basic humanity. "I wonder what happened to the people who lived here. Did they die or did they leave?"

"Perhaps they are still here, as ghosts."

Jodi smiled. "Ghosts and monsters, Lorel, you have a vivid imagination."

"Well, we've seen the monsters, why not the ghosts?"

"They aren't monsters; they are just beings who are not like us."

Just as she finished speaking a new sound was heard. Several creatures started howling, their plaintive, chilling calls echoing through the darkly forested hills. They looked at one another and Jodi took her hand.

"I wish I had my knife, there are things in the forest. We will sleep inside the pod this night and when the sun comes back I will attend to the making of a weapon."

That night the creatures who had not been killed by the impact and fire of the crash-landing, or fled from the devastation, began to return. A single brown bear padded cautiously across the wasteland and sniffed the air and ground around the pod. As if some deep ancestral memory triggered its senses, it fled the scene and did not come back. A small pack of wolves soon followed, prowling the darkness for new quarry or an injured animal. They crossed the charred, ruined land and disappeared into the forest. Nothing else came into the clearing that first night; the clearing smelled of death.

The night was short, shorter than the nights on Ennepp or Tarnus and by the time the sun illuminated the hills behind the beach, the air was already warm and fragrant with the fresh smell of pine. The pod and the surrounding land had cooled and the fire that had taken hold in the soil beneath the pod was out. Jodi was the first to wake and emerged from the pod barefoot. He felt the warm soil underfoot and let it creep between his toes, enjoying the sensation. He walked around the back of the pod and urinated while he looked towards the hills caught in the rising sun. The morning chatter and song of the birds had returned to the forest and he listened with pleasure to their conversations and wondered just what they were saying in their strange languages.

He finished urinating and looked up towards the crest of the nearest hill. Near the summit he discerned a rocky platform that did not look entirely consistent with the natural form of the landscape. It was about two kilometres away and would afford a commanding view of their surroundings. He resolved to go there as soon as possible.

He went back into the pod and discovered Lorel just waking. The interior was still warm and she was curled up on the floor without clothing. He observed her quietly, enjoying the curve of her taught body, strong, muscular thighs and firm breasts. What a handsome woman she was, feminine without being delicate and strong both in physique and mentality. He had loved Matty, but he saw now that it was an immature love and quite unlike his love for this woman. This woman was his partner, his equal, rather than his responsibility and his respect for her drew from him a height of passion such as he had never before experienced in his short life. He nestled at her back and kissed her neck while pressing himself between her buttocks. She awoke, surprised by his approach.

"In Rion this is not allowed," she murmured.

"We are a long way from Rion," he replied.

As the morning heat gathered, they shed their clothes and returned to the beach to bathe in the sea together. As they walked back to the pod, hand in hand, Jodi suddenly stopped, knelt and inspected the ground minutely.

"Look at this," he said, pointing out the paw-prints of the lone bear that had wandered into the clearing during the night. "Something came here last night." He placed his own foot next to the paw-print. "Something quite large I would say."

Lorel looked down at the track and shivered involuntarily. She sensed a menace in their paradise but did not voice her concern lest he should disapprove of her caution.

He went on all fours and described a similar track in the sandy soil next to the original. Rising, he looked at her and smiled provocatively. "A monster, no doubt; one that walks with its hands and feet."

"You might not be smiling if you came face to face with it."

He nodded. "Perhaps you are right. We had better search the pod; there should be tools aboard and maybe a knife or two."

A thorough search of the life-pod produced a collection of rudimentary tools stowed in a locker under the floor. The tools were such as might be necessary for a small group of survivors to sustain themselves in an alien situation. There was a digging implement that could also serve as an axe; various cutting instruments including three knives of different lengths; there was a fire-starter and even a set of vessels for cooking.

Jodi held up the knives and beamed. "We can gather food and conserve our survival rations."

"We don't know what can be eaten on this world."

"We will observe what the creatures eat and try that."

"We are not the same; what they can eat might be different."

"True, but we will have to find out if we are to survive here and if men lived here once they must have survived on the fruits of this planet."

She conceded the logic of his argument but declared that it must be done with caution; that is to say, eating minute amounts and recording the effects of each food source.

Until the sun was high they worked in the pod, searching it for every last item that could be used for survival. When this was done Jodi took up the spade-like implement and dug a latrine a good distance away and down-wind of the pod while Lorel set about gathering some wood. Their domestic arrangements completed, they sat together on the ground and shared the last of their water.

"The aquifer is damaged, I can't make it work. We will have to collect water from now on and sterilize it for drinking. There's a freshwater stream at the other end of the beach; I noticed it yesterday as I was coming back to you."

"It's quite a way off; a shame we did not land nearer."

Jodi agreed but added that he might have an idea. "If I can dam the stream, I can cause the water to follow a different path into that impact crater. Then we will have fresh water much nearer."

"A canal; It will be a lot of work," she observed.

"But worth it. Do you see that rocky outcrop with the flat surface up there?" he added pointing towards the nearest hilltop.

"Yes."

"I have a mind to climb up there and take a view of our surroundings."

Lorel looked at the progress of the sun and took a bead on the distance. "We'll go at sunrise tomorrow; the journey may be difficult and we might not get back before the night if we go now."

Jodi, who was all set to go immediately, saw her wisdom and did not press the point. Tomorrow would be soon enough for they had the rest of their lives to explore their new world.

Later, they lit a fire and listened to the strange sounds of the forest as the sun conceded to the stars. A thin crescent of light rose as they conversed well into the night. It was the first time they had seen the moon as the ancients would have seen it, long before science explained its mysteries.

The next morning they armed themselves with knives, packed rations and a water carrier and set off towards the interior. Away from the beach the forest was thicker and they had to hack their way through stretches of dense undergrowth. The trees surrounding them were filled with the calls and chatter of many flying creatures; the scent of the trees and bushes with their garlands of flowers sweetened the warm air as they began to climb the rising gradient. They collected water and followed the shallow valley of the stream into the interior and heard, as they advanced, the rustle of creatures in the undergrowth, scurrying away in fright at this unfamiliar sound and scent. On one occasion they saw the brown, furry body of quite a large animal fleeing as they advanced. Jodi instantly gave chase but the animal easily evaded him.

"Did you see it?" he said as he returned from the chase.

"Yes, it had four legs but no arms."

"Just like the prints near the pod."

"But this was much smaller."

"It could be a juvenile; there couldn't be more than one creature like that."

Lorel, taking exception to his assumption, pointed out that they had seen many different types of flying creatures. Jodi considered her argument and conceded that there could be more types than one, but not many.

Higher up the slope they discovered something that radically altered their view of this new world and taught them something of its ecosystem. Their route had taken them a little distance from the stream for they had come upon and begun to follow what looked like a natural path through the forest. As they advanced, they came to a small clearing where a group of large, black flying creatures had gathered in one spot, arguing noisily over something on the ground. Flapping and cawing they jostled over the prize until Lorel and Jodi approached at which point they fluttered away into the surrounding trees, complaining bitterly at the interruption. They came up to the spot and looked. On the ground they saw the remains of a creature with had four thin legs and what appeared to be an insubstantial, handless arm just above its backside. Its body and head were covered in brown, variegated fur; it had large, pointed ears on the top of its head; at least they assumed it was the head for it was a shape they had never seen in their lives. The creature's belly was ripped open and the bloody remains of its contents stained the ground beneath it.

Jodi knelt down and felt it. The fur was soft to the touch and the body still warm indicating that it had met its end recently. He began to inspect it, checking the feet and pulling the legs apart to see what lay beneath. As he observed the physique of the animal it struck him how similar it was to his own physique. The animal was male and the arrangement of its genitals and their relationship with its anus was much the same as his. It had four limbs a head and a body, as did he; it had two eyes, a nose and a mouth with teeth and a tongue and two ears on each side of its head. He looked up at Lorel. "This is a person," he announced.

She laughed. "Don't be silly, Jodi; it looks nothing like us."

"You're wrong; it has the same physique as me, it just looks a bit different. These are the people that live here and maybe this is what will happen to us if we stay.

"That's ridiculous."

"Is it? Then what happened to the people like us that lived here? Where have they gone?"

"I don't know and neither do you."

"Those black flying creatures were eating his flesh."

Lorel knelt beside him and stroked the face of the dead animal. "They can't have been; flesh is not digestible, it is not a source of food."

Jodi looked into her eyes and in a moment they were both transported back to the mine. "We both know that's not true."

She nodded. "We have much to learn and no doubt much of it will be disagreeable. Let us leave this poor creature in peace and continue."

They rose and walked on and saw the flying creatures return to their feast. They watched the loud, squabbling birds from the edge of the clearing; it was clear that they were eating the animal's flesh. After some time another hairy animal slunk cautiously across the clearing and the birds scattered. It bore little resemblance to the dead animal; it was smaller in stature but looked more powerful. Its head turned cautiously from side to side as it moved. It had come to regain its prize.

"I think there are many different creatures on this world and they eat one another to survive," observed Lorel. "They are not people like us."

Jodi stared intently at the grizzly spectacle of carnage as the newcomer began its meal. He was thinking; *if they can eat flesh, so can we.*

Beyond the clearing another sound filtered through the trees and scrub. It was the insistent, low murmur of running water. They followed its source and soon came upon a pleasant, rocky glade where a pool received the waters of the streamlet that tumbled over a rock-wall and fell three metres into it. Strange, brightly coloured winged creatures flitted about filling the air with their muted buzzing. One landed on Jodi's arm and began to preen itself. He grabbed it, crushing its delicate wings beneath his grasp.

"You killed it," said Lorel, observing with disapproval the twisted, broken form lying in his open palm.

"I didn't mean to, it is a delicate animal," he replied, inspecting the strangely shaped, elongated body. "It is weightless, that is how it flies."

"Well that one won't be flying anymore. You should be more careful; you don't have the right to kill anything you like."

Jodi did not agree, but stayed silent. They had never argued about anything before and he did not enjoy the prospect of her disapproval. He reached down and tasted the water. It was sweet tasting but he did not dare swallow it; he had drunk tainted water many times before and regretted the results and neither of them knew what dangers lurked in this apparently harmless source.

They sat quietly on a rock and watched the busy activity of the pool while their feet cooled in the soothing water. Their stillness and silence soon brought a reward when a larger version of the dead creature in the clearing, suddenly appeared out of the bush, sniffed the air and began to drink at the pool. It raised its head and looked straight at them for a moment before ambling back into the cover of the undergrowth.

"It saw us but didn't run away," said Jodi.

"It has no reason to fear us... yet," she added as an afterthought.

"It drank the water," he added in a hopeful tone.

"Yes it did; it would be better if we didn't have to sterilize it; our supply of the chemical is limited."

They filled the water carrier, dried their feet on leaves and left the grotto by a path that led them around the rock wall and began to climb more steeply. Gradually they noticed a change in the vegetation that had passed from pine to more broad-leafed trees. Some trees appeared to be in fruit; strange, dark-brown, bulbous pods dangling pendulously from branches like roasted scrotums. Some had fallen to the ground and burst open and were being devoured by swarms of small, flying creatures. Jodi climbed the tree and secured a fruit, breaking it open and touching the contents with his tongue. It was sweet and delicious, not unlike some of the sweet gourds of his native forest on Ennepp. He spat it out, picked a few more and threw them down to Lorel.

"They taste nice; I think we will be able to eat them." He said as he descended. "We'll take them back and try them a small piece at a time."

He took off his shirt and turned it into a sack by knotting the sleeves and passing the knotted end through a stick, he placed the fruits into it and they moved on. The path grew steeper until it met the base of a rock-wall where it appeared to transform into an unnatural staircase weathered by a million storms. Here and there the path was difficult, but they made the ascent and at last, found themselves on the rocky platform that could be seen from their home near the beach. No trees clung to the bare, gnarled rocks of the platform but scrub and tufted grasses sprung from cracks and from the shelter afforded by the tumble of weathered boulders that occupied the surface.

From this elevated, treeless vantage point, they could see the lie of the land surrounding their home and the sparkling sea beyond which was dotted with islands as far as the horizon. The land beneath them undulated with forested hills that were truncated by further capes and bays to either side of their own. Inland, the topography gave way to higher, rock-encrusted peaks, each crowning the other as the ranges tumbled into a mysterious, impenetrable interior.

"We are the kings of all this," shouted Jodi, stepping close to the precipice and holding his arms up to the sun. For the first time in his short life he was absolutely free; nobody could bid him or chain him or starve him or thrash him until he welcomed death; he had everything that he had ever wanted and the joy in his heart burst forth with his echoing words.

Lorel gently drew him from the edge and they embraced. "It is beautiful," she said.

"It is lovely beyond words," he replied. "And all ours."

They turned their faces towards the odd tumble of boulders that occupied the platform. There was something about them that did not fit with their surroundings. Lorel noticed it first, discerning that the prevailing geology was sand coloured, whereas the boulders were off-white. As they walked around the place they began to understand for even though the boulders were weathered there was still enough of a vestige to interpret what they had once been.

"These rocks were once a building," she declared.

"You could be right," he replied as they walked among the incongruous formations. He spied something at the base of one of the larger rocks, pulled it from its resting place and showed it to Lorel. It was severely weathered but its shape was unmistakably that of a human arm.

"They made images of themselves using stone, just like our own civilization," she said as she inspected the find. "I wonder who lived here. Do you think they were like us?"

"It looks like it," he replied. "I was wrong, those hairy creatures are not people at all; they are something different. Let's see if we can find any more pieces."

They searched the ruins and retrieved several more pieces of sculpture. They brought them all to one spot and tried to assemble them on the ground but none of the pieces seemed to fit together very well. There was a nose and an eye-socket from one face; the mouth and chin of another; three sections of torso and three unrelated leg sections. Some were barely discernable as human parts, while others, occupying more sheltered places, still clung to the hand of their creator.

"These are pieces of many statues," declared Lorel.

Jodi inspected their work and looked about him. "I have seen this type of thing before. When Sevarius took me to Kagan I saw such things as these might once have been; Images of the Prophet carved in stone and housed in great temples."

"You think these are images of the Prophet?"

Jodi smiled and shook his head. "These were made a hundred thousand years before the birth of Minnar. These people knew other prophets and perhaps this was their temple. It seems to me that men need such things in their lives and always have needed them."

She sat down on a boulder and gazed out at the land beneath them. "We were not permitted such beliefs in Rion."

"No, you had to worship Strellic."

She nodded sadly. "Or die."

He caught her reflective tone and knew she was thinking of her father. He sat beside her and put his arm around her shoulder, drawing her close to him. "There are many who should be here to see this, but they're all gone now and only we two are left alive."

Tears moistened her eyes at his words as she thought of those they had left a long way behind. "I wonder if anyone else will ever find this world."

Jodi reflected. "Lodan is the key; he has the lozenge that guided us here and the knowledge of this place. I pray he is dead and we are never discovered."

She was surprised by his words and turned, catching him gazing distractedly into the distance. "There is enough room here for many people."

He nodded without taking his eyes from the vista. "True enough, but people always fuck it up, even though they don't mean to."

They explored the plateau until the afternoon sun began to weaken and then they made their way back by the route they had come. At the waterfall they stopped and bathed beneath its cool flow and gathered various fruits to test on themselves. The carcass in the clearing was now entirely gone with no more than a hint of blood on the ground remaining. By the time they returned to their camp the afternoon sun was beginning to lose its strength and a cooling breeze was drifting in from the sea. Jodi ate half of one of the dark pods and declared it to be very tasty; he was all for consuming the other half but Lorel stopped him, reminding him of the consequences should it be toxic. In the event, they discovered it to be both pleasant and nutritious, as were many of the forest fruits and, over time, they gradually built their knowledge of the edible flora, discarding what was bitter and unpleasant and avoiding what upset their digestive systems.

During these early days Lorel made frequent use of the medical kit, applying its contents to the painful and annoying bites of insects and to their digestive systems to relieve the symptoms of dysentery and other unusual ailments that manifested themselves in that strange and new environment. Over time their immune systems began to adapt and the effects of the alien ailments became more tolerable, but by then the medical supplies had been dangerously depleted and, eventually, they had to ration themselves.

In the days following their arrival they made a number of expeditions into the surrounding area, visiting the adjacent bays and taking other routes into the hills. On these trips they discovered many new and amazing properties of the natural world but no other trace of the human beings who had once lived on these shores.

On the seventh day of their new lives, they started digging the canal that would direct the waters of the stream into the impact crater left after the crash-landing of the life-pod. The work was hard and cost them much sweat under the burning sun, but in five days the trench was complete and all they had to do was dam the stream to force it to follow another course. With rocks and soil they gradually blocked the flow of the stream until, at last, nature conceded and water began to fill the trench and gradually crept towards the crater. They sat together on the edge of the crater and watched with pleasure and pride as the first rivulet of water trickled into the depression. It would take some time to fill, but now they had fresh water nearby and a place to bathe.

Jodi's next project was to erect a hut next to the pod where they could shelter from the heat of the sun and from the occasional storms that swept in from the sea. Using the spade-axe, he chose and cut suitable branches from the surrounding forest and built a framework tied together with twisted vines. The framework was buried for stability and thatched with woven vegetation. A low, rock wall surrounded the entire structure that was furnished with a table and two seats made from a dissected tree trunk. These domestic comforts were finally completed on the twenty-fifth day after their arrival and that was the same day that Lorel became sick.

At first she assumed that she had eaten something untoward, but Jodi pointed out that she had not eaten anything different from him and that it was not anything that they had not safely eaten before. It was not regarded as serious for she soon recovered only to be sick again later that day.

She puzzled over her condition. "It can't be anything to do with our diet; I don't have the runs and my intestines don't hurt."

"It must be something: I'll get the medical kit and look up your symptoms."

And then she suddenly realized what was happening to her. She held his arm and pulled him down to her side. "Don't bother, I know what it is. We are going to be parents."

It hit him like a bolt; for some reason it had never occurred to him that their frequent coupling would result in this. He gawped at her with a mystified look on his face. "I didn't expect that," he declared when he recovered his tongue.

She regarded him quizzically. "Why?"

"I don't know; I just didn't think about it."

"You do know that sex often leads to pregnancy?"

"Of course I know," he replied shortly.

"Then what, Jodi? Did you think you were different?"

"No, I just didn't think about it, that's all."

She laughed, somewhat derisively.

"I don't know what you're laughing at. We have to stop doing it now."

"Where did you get that idea?"

"I might damage the baby."

She grinned and took his hand. "The baby will be fine; you can't damage it that way."

"Are you sure?"

"Yes."

He considered for a moment. "In that case, I kind of like the idea." And then gaining enthusiasm, he added, "We will have lots of children, and then they too will have children, and this world will be populated again and we two will have been the beginning of it."

In the days that followed the revelation of Lorel's condition, the charred wasteland surrounding their camp began to return to life. Dormant plants, discovering new sunlight, eased their delicate arms above the dark soil and the land gradually turned green. They noticed, also, that the sun no longer climbed so high and the days seemed to shorten. The air, though still warm, began to lose the oppressive quality of the mid-day heat and became more temperate. This was novel, since neither hailed from worlds subject to marked seasons and they wondered how cold it would get before the return of the high sun.

As Lorel's condition progressed and her belly began to swell, Jodi increasingly went out foraging on his own. He would leave the camp in the morning wearing his ragged clothes with a knife tied about his waist and would disappear into the forest armed with a spear made from a sharpened bough. He had quickly adapted to his new environment, casting aside all trappings of civilization and reverting to the savage that he had always been in his soul. He began to wander further and further from the camp, always noting his direction of travel, using his innate sense of geography to find his way back.

On one such occasion he came across the tracks of a large animal similar to those he had seen in the clearing on their first day. He was intrigued to see what manner of creature had made these prints on the ground and, without thinking of the danger, he followed the trail.

The tracks led him into the interior of the forest, further than he had ever ventured. He moved stealthily, sniffing the air frequently and listening for any sign of the animal. He followed it through the sunless forest, into a steep-sided valley where a recently storm-fed stream splashed over rocks and tumbled into a small pool. Here he drank and as he cupped the sweet water to his lips he saw, at the bottom of the pool, the unmistakable glint of gold. He reached down, pulled it from the silt and brought it into the air. It was a tiny figurine cast in the shape of a naked woman, much worn and damaged, but unmistakably human in form; a token of the distant past, washed out of the soil and carried to this place by the water.

As he squatted by the pool, inspecting his new treasure, he was interrupted by the sound of a violent argument nearby. He dropped the figurine and instantly turned his attention to the quarrel. He set off into the bush towards the sound, drawing his knife and readying his spear. A few metres on he saw the creature; a large, evil-looking thing with dark; brown hair and a long snout; it was eating one of the fleet-footed, thin-legged animals that he had seen in the forest but had never been able to catch. The she-bear stopped eating at his approach and eyed him uncertainly. It had never seen anything quite like this before and didn't know what to do; the strange, hairless creature just kept getting nearer. She snarled a warning, but this didn't stop the creature. She had driven off the dogs that had killed the deer but this animal was not so easily discouraged. A sharpened stick suddenly came through the air and hit her in the ribs. It didn't penetrate her flesh but it was enough to demonstrate that she was outmatched. With a roar of complaint, she fled into the bush.

Noting its lack of success, Jodi picked up his spear and began to inspect his prize. It was a large animal with a pair of strange, many-pointed growths springing from the top of its head. The kill was recent and little disturbed other than a lacerated jugular and ripped stomach through which its entrails spilled on to the ground. Ever since he had witnessed the other animals eating flesh he had wondered if such a thing could sustain them. He took his knife and began to cut. He removed the best part of one of the animal's legs and one of its antlers and took them back to the stream to wash away the blood; then he picked up the gold figurine and started back.

It was dusk by the time he reached camp and received a reproving look from Lorel.

"You are late," she said.

He kissed her and threw the meat from his shoulder and it landed on the ground with a thump. "Sorry, I went further than I have ever gone before and look what I found."

"An animal leg. Why have you brought that back?"

"I'm going to eat its flesh, just like the animals do."

"There is plenty of food in the forest; we don't have to eat flesh."

"The fruit is falling from the trees and rotting on the ground. It doesn't last and we may need other sources of food."

He handed her the antler he had hacked from the deer's head.

"What is it?"

"I don't know; it was attached to an animal's head, like a crown."

"Did you kill it?"

"No, an animal killed it and was eating its flesh. It was the same animal that made those tracks; a large, hairy monster with big teeth."

"I've told you to stay away from creatures like that," she replied angrily.

"Don't worry, I threw my spear at it and it ran off. All the animals know I am the king of them."

"Yes, this time it did, but maybe next time it will attack you."

In a moment his expression darkened. "Then I'll kill it," he growled, drawing his knife and stabbing the air.

She regarded his taught, muscular form, rehearsing the fight and, at that instant, realized that he had grown at one with this world and the forest that surrounded them. He had become an animal like the creatures that stalked the dense woodlands; an instinctive being apparently lacking in self-awareness.

He caught her quizzical expression and stopped his dance of death. "What?" he said.

"Nothing," she replied. "Go and wash, you have the creature's blood on you."

He pulled the tiny, gold figurine from his belt and handed it to her.

She gave it close interest. "It's pretty; where did you get it?"

"I found it in a stream up in the hills. It's gold, isn't it?"

She shrugged. "It looks like it."

"I will get more."

"What for? What use is it to us?"

He nodded resignedly at her wisdom and walked off to bathe in the crater.

Later, as they sat by the fire in the gathering dusk, he cut a piece of flesh from the leg and tasted it. It was chewy and he did not care for the bloody taste. He spat it out into the fire.

"I told you," she remarked in suppressed triumph. "You'll probably get the shits now; or something worse and it serves you right."

Jodi stared at the morsel of flesh as it sizzled in the fire. "Do you want to survive on rations? There's a cold spell coming; I can feel it. The days are getting shorter and the sun weaker. The trees do not replenish their fruit. It will be a fallow time and we will not get food from the forest."

"The animals live and so will we; we do not have to eat their flesh."

Jodi did not agree but judged it prudent to drop the subject. He picked up the antler and studied it. "I think I will be able to carve this into a fine point. It will give keenness to my spear."

His fascination with death and killing sometimes jarred her sensibilities and tainted her love for him, but she said nothing. They had never had a difference of opinion and she did not want to start now. She realized that his fierce nature was part of him and could not be tamed and should not be. She recalled the first time she saw him, running, like the wind, out of the mine and into the barracks where he sated his lust for revenge with blood. He had not changed and never would and, in a way, she saw that it was for the best. Their present situation called for a man of his character and any attempt at moderation would reduce his capacity to provide for her and the child growing inside her. She watched him begin to whittle the antler into a point and was suddenly contrite at her disapproval. She picked up a knife and cut another chunk of flesh from the animal's leg and placed it into a pot and added water. Setting it on the fire to boil, she said, "If we are to eat flesh it should be made safe by boiling it first."

He nodded and carried on whittling. She had conceded to his argument and he did not wish to discomfort her with any overt recognition of that fact.

With boiling the flesh became soft and edible. Jodi tried it first and discovering no ill effects, Lorel ate some two days later. Now they had both eaten flesh the animals of the forest would, once again, suffer on the point of a man's spear.

As the days passed it became clear that Jodi's prediction of a colder season was correct. The sun's path across the sky passed increasingly closer to the horizon and the time of daylight became shorter. The rainfall increased and cooler breezes sang mournfully through the pines. As her condition matured, Lorel ceased entirely to accompany Jodi on his expeditions and confined herself to the life-pod, the cabin and its surroundings that she had begun to coax into the form of a garden.

Jodi passed to her his knowledge of cultivation and saplings of fruit trees and other edible plants were brought from the forest and planted in the soft, dark earth surrounding the camp. Some survived and some failed, but gradually the patchwork of a garden started to appear. Now their diet consisted of the flesh of various animals that Jodi had trapped and killed or found, freshly slaughtered, in the forest. They stored the animals in the stasis units where they were perfectly preserved until required for the pot. They discovered that the inedible pelts of the animals could be dried and used as clothing against the cold and Lorel made them rudimentary suits of fur that they wore over their increasingly ragged clothes.

It was not long before Jodi discovered another source of nutrient during one of his frequent trips to the sea. He had often tried to catch one the myriad creatures that darted through the water with such ease, but they had always easily eluded him. He tried spearing them and throwing rocks at them, but always missed his target, until one day, squatting on a rock above an inlet, he discovered the principle of refraction and managed to spear a substantial animal as it swam lazily in the shallows below. Its flesh was quite unlike the flesh of the land creatures but it tasted good and soon became a favourite source of food.

As the cold season progressed Jodi augmented the shelter next to the life-pod, strengthening its structure, sealing the roof against the rain and building up the dry-stone walls until it more resembled a rudimentary shack. He built a hearth with a smoke outlet on which they could cook their food and keep warm during the darker days. Lorel, coming from the ambient heat of Rion's climate, seemed to suffer in the lower temperatures, but Jodi only thrived more. His childhood in the southern flatlands of Ennepp had taught his body to resist the cold and he would often swim in the sea and run naked and wet through the forest in the rain, eventually returning to the camp when he would stand by the fire while she dried him. And when she expressed her concern he would brush them aside telling her how much colder he was as a boy-slave on the Doah Farm. In fact they had been fortunate in the location of their crash-landing, for the temperatures rarely fell to freezing and the cold season was short.

As Lorel's belly swelled with the child, so the season turned and the world began to warm once again. The garden surrounding the camp sprung to life with a variety of plants, many of which had not been introduced by them. The forest sung with life and the heady perfume of blossom filled the air. With the coming of longer daylight, Jodi began to range into the distant hills once again, exploring and searching out new quarry, bringing back his kills for his heavily pregnant mate. But one morning was different for it was to change everything in their lives.

After embracing his mate, Jodi set out in the early sunshine in the direction of the pool where he had encountered the she-bear towards the end of the warm season. He had been there several times since but never again come across her beyond the evidence of tracks in the soil or the rustle of undergrowth. He reached the pool where he had found the golden figurine and stopped and drank, then he pressed on, winding his way further up the steep-sided valley.

He first heard the disturbance in the bushes to his right and swung around, drawing his knife instinctively. He knew it was she, but instead of timidly retreating into the bush the creature growled angrily and charged. She was upon him with a speed he had not expected, knocking him to the ground while burying her teeth into his shoulder and ripping her claws across his stomach. As he went down beneath her huge bulk he lunged upwards with the knife and buried it deep into her chest. She roared in agony as he plunged the knife into her again while using his other arm to fend her gnashing teeth from his face. Her teeth closed about his arm and ripped at his flesh as he desperately stabbed again with the long knife. Then suddenly she stopped and her full weight slumped down on him, pinning him to the ground. Her breath, hot and fetid, stung his nose as he struggled out from beneath her bulk. He had punctured her lung and blood poured from her mouth in frothy globules as the life gradually left her body. Jodi, gasping for air, sat upon the ground next to her and looked down at his own injuries. His abdomen had been opened and he could see the sickening sight of his own intestines as blood poured from the wound; his shoulder and arm were lacerated and were also bleeding profusely. He was beginning to feel light headed from the loss of blood but knew he must not pass out for he would surely be eaten by other creatures waiting for an easy meal. He gingerly eased off his ragged, torn shirt and wound it around his waist, tying it as securely as he could across the gaping gash in his flesh. The last moments of life rattled from the bear and she was still so he used her body as support while he pulled himself to his feet. Bent double and gritting his teeth, he surveyed the dense forest around him and wondered how he was going to make it back. He had ventured further into the interior of the forest than ever before and it was going to a long walk. He pulled the knife from the lifeless body of the bear and staggered back down the ravine.

Nearby a single cub waited for its mother to return to the den and, smelling blood, the wolves came down from the higher slopes.

As the sun sank below the horizon and dusk crept over the forest, Lorel tasted the fish stew she had prepared for their meal. She had learned over time how to improve the taste with leaves gathered from the nearby forest and shoreline and thought, with a nod of appreciation, that this concoction was one of her best. As she prepared for his homecoming, she looked out frequently towards the direction he would emerge from the forest, but as the light grew dim, she still did not see his familiar figure against the dark trees. He had never returned so late before and she knew instinctively that something was very wrong.

The child moved in her belly as she removed the pot from the fire and set it down upon a stone. She wrapped a cloak of deer fur about her shoulders and placed the knife she used for cooking into her belt and set off towards the forbidding wall of trees. Despite her history of incautious behaviour during the war on Tarnus, Lorel had always been prone to pessimistic expectations, choosing to emphasise in her mind the inherent dangers of any situation rather than the benefits of bold actions. As such she had always half expected something ill to happen to them and with the late coming of her mate, was now certain that something untoward had occurred. Jodi had never before returned to camp after sunset and she now imagined all manner of misfortunes.

She entered the forest and began to call for him. At the sound of her voice, echoing among the trees the night calls of the animals ceased as they listened to the unfamiliar call of another animal. As the darkness descended, she followed the well-trodden paths through the trees, stopping regularly to call and listen for his reply. No sound reached her ears save the chatter of night insects. She wandered further and deeper, disregarding the dangers of the night, intent only on finding him. He was out there somewhere, in trouble, injured and waiting for her to come, she was certain and she would not give up until she had found him.

She heard sinister noises as she advanced, strange grunting and rustling undergrowth, but her purpose would not be diverted. A frail moon, occasionally glimpsed through the glowering canopy of trees, cast an insufficient light for navigation and after three hours of wandering, she was exhausted and completely lost. She sat down on the ground and ran her hands over her belly. The baby inside her shifted again and then her waters broke.

The child arrived quickly, slipping from its womb as she screamed and pushed while squatting over her fur cloak. It opened its mouth and cried as she cut the cord the joined it to her and took it into her arms. She could not see it well enough to determine its gender so she felt for its genitals. It was a girl. She pressed it into the warmth of her body and wrapped the fur cloak over them. Exhausted and unmindful of the dangers of the night forest, she closed her eyes and slept.

Jodi lay on the edge of the pool and stared despondently at the ragged, blood-soaked shirt that covered the ugly gash that had opened his abdomen. He was weak and light-headed from the loss of blood and the pain of movement had not allowed him to get far from the site of his fight with the bear. With his feet dangling in the water, he eased off his pants and surveyed his lower torso, reflecting with a wry smile that at least the monster had spared that part of him. Using his good, right arm, he rinsed his pants in the water, took up his knife and began to cut them. First he fashioned a bandage for his arm that he tied using his teeth and one hand; then he made a pad for his shoulder that he held in place until the seeping blood fixed it. Finally he cut a larger pad from the remaining leg, untied the blood-soaked shirt from his middle and eased it gently from the wound. The nauseating sight of his own exposed guts greeted him as the wound seeped more blood. He placed the pad over the gash and retied the shirt over it to keep it in place. He knew that every movement would cause more blood to flow from it and that he had no choice; he had to take his chances in the forest and stay where he was. He eased himself away from the pool and into a small nook formed between two boulders and propping himself against the rock to keep the wound closed, he settled down to wait for the night hoping that the flesh-eaters would be content with the carcass of the monster he had killed.

He spent the night in fitful sleep, waking at every rustle and disturbance. He saw the dark shadows of creatures drinking at the pool in the sad light of the waning moon; he heard the eerie howling of dogs nearby as they descended upon the carcass of the bear and found its defenceless cub. The long night seemed endless, punctuated by fitful sleep and long periods of painful drowsiness but, as the first light of dawn brushed the tops of the hills, Jodi had stayed undiscovered; he had survived.

He rose carefully, holding his wound as he moved and cupped some water from the pool to his lips. Then he started the long journey back to the camp. His movement soon opened the wound in his belly and it began to seep, dripping on to the ground as he trudged through the brush and leaving a trail to tempt the gorged animals in the ravine above. There was plenty of meat for all from the bear and its cub, but a wounded animal was always a temptation even in a time of plenty.

Further down the valley, Lorel and the newly born child had also survived the night. In the first, pre-dawn light, she opened her eyes and saw her baby for the first time. She was perfect with a screwed-up face below a shock of jet-black downy hair. She slept peacefully under the warm deer fur, her swarthy skin still stained with the trauma of birth. Gazing on the sleeping infant almost robbed Lorel of her immediate anxiety, but she was soon brought back to reality as the bleak desperation of her situation returned. She rose stiffly from the forest floor and took off her shirt, tying it together in such a manner as to fashion a rudimentary papoose with the two sleeves forming a sling around her neck. Now that she could see the form of the hill about her she had an idea of exactly where she was. She took her bearings and set off towards the valley.

Six wolves had left the pack and followed the scent of blood down the valley towards the sea. Since the arrival of the new animals and the explosion and fire that had accompanied them, the wolves had stayed well away from that part of the coast. Even after a season of cold weather and new growth, it still smelled of danger and death. But now one of the hairless animals had encroached on their range and it was injured; they meant to eat its meat. They caught the hairless creature near the mouth of the valley; it was standing by a tree watching them. It was cunning but it was doomed.

Jodi stood with his back hard against a massive tree-trunk, clutching his stomach wound and watching the advancing animals. They were smaller than he, but he could see they were armed with sharp fangs and too numerous for him to fight off. Even healthy the contest would have been difficult, but he was weak and injured and knew that this was where it ended for him. Now he saw the nature of the world in which they lived. He was not the king, he was just another vulnerable creature who could be killed and eaten and the cavalier attitude that he had adopted since they had arrived was stupid and arrogant. He thought of Lorel and their unborn child; the child he would never see and bitter regret seized him. He had failed her and failed his child too; it was a heavy thought to carry in his last moments of existence. He drew his knife; he would not die cheaply.

The first animal led the attack. Snarling it rushed from the brush and leapt for his throat. He thrust his knife upward, piercing the wolf's throat as the weight of its charge knocked him to the ground. The others were not discouraged by the swift fate of their leader and quickly closed on him. He felt teeth rip into his buttocks and legs as he curled up to protect himself. A jaw closed on his arm as he swung the knife again and heard the yelp of pain as another animal met its death. But Jodi had run out of time and energy and had nothing left to fend them off. The predators circled him slyly observing the wounded creature, getting ready for the kill.

Without warning the sound of rustling in the scrub nearby turned into a blood-curdling scream and rocks flew through the air like missiles, striking two of the wolves in quick succession. The ferocious mate of the hairless creature was descending on them like an angry bear. The contest was over; they had plenty to eat elsewhere. They turned tail and fled into the bush, back to the safety of the high ravine.

She pushed aside the bodies of the two wolves and knelt beside him. Taking his bloodied head in her arms, she kissed him again and again. He looked weakly up at her and saw the head of the child, peeping from the papoose.

"The baby came," he whispered.

"Last night, in the forest, as I searched for you."

"I'm sorry; I should have been with you."

"Yes, you should have been. It's a girl."

A faint smile touched his lips. "I am glad."

She began to examine his wounds. Blood was oozing from the gash across his stomach and his flesh hung in ugly chunks where the wolves had rent his skin. He was almost entirely covered in blood, his own and that of the animals he had killed. "Can you walk?" she asked.

He nodded and she helped him to his feet. They set off together on the long walk back to their camp, stopping frequently to rest while Jodi gathered enough strength to go a little further. The setting sun was touching the tips of the nearby trees when they finally stumbled from the forest into the refuge of their home.

He slumped down on a rug of fur while she placed the child into the rude cradle that Jodi had hewn from a log. She began to cry but Lorel had no time for her now. She fetched the medical kit from the interior of the life-pod and went to work, cleaning and suturing the gash in his stomach and the various bite and claw wounds on his body. She knew every scar on his body; the healed knife cuts from his youth in the land of the Pal; the lash marks from his days of slavery and the punishment he had suffered before his brief incarceration in the Mine of Kusk; the ugly burn on his side at the hands of Lodan; she knew them all intimately, they were part of him, a living testimony to the harshness of his life. Now there would be a few more scars on him to get acquainted with and she would have to learn to love those too.

"I told you not to go up there," she admonished as she worked. "What were you doing up there? You were going after that monster, weren't you? I told you time and again to leave that animal alone."

He grimaced in pain as she sutured another deep cut but said nothing. She was quite right, he had been reckless and he knew it.

"Did that hurt? It serves you right," she continued as she worked. "Look at the state of you. You nearly died out there. I'm so angry with you. What would I do here without you; left alone in this wilderness on the edge of the galaxy?"

"You won't be alone; there are three of us now."

"Yes, and no one to look out for us. You will be laid-up for days; at least until that wound across your stomach knits."

"It'll be alright in a couple of days; you'll see."

"It will not and you won't be going anywhere until I tell you."

She continued to scold him while she worked. He watched her in silence, noting how large her breasts had become recently. All the while the baby cried in its cot.

"What shall we call her?" he asked at length.

"Baby," replied Lorel. "She can choose her own name when she's old enough."

"Is that what you do on Tarnus?"

"No, it's what we'll do here," she replied decisively.

"What will we call the next one? We can't call them all 'Baby'; it'll get confusing."

She stopped work and looked into his eyes. "We won't have any more if you pull another stunt like this; she'll grow up without siblings."

Her reply forced him to recognize that he was now a father and had the responsibilities of a father. He reached out and touched her arm. "I'm sorry," he said. "I promise I will be more careful in the future."

She took his hand and kissed it; she could never maintain any angry feelings in his presence.

She covered him with another fur and fed the baby at her breast. By the time she and the child settled next to his warm body beneath the fur, he was fast asleep.

He woke in the night while the stars still shone in the clear sky. He was shivering and sweating at the same time and felt so weak that he could not raise himself from the bed to go and urinate. Beside him Baby and Lorel slept peacefully; he could see the tops of their heads under the ragged edge of the fur cover. Not wishing to disturb them he shut his eyes and tried to return to sleep but the insistent pressure of his bladder would not allow it. Reluctantly he stirred her from her slumber.

"Lorel, I need some help," he whispered.

She opened her eyes at the sound of his voice and sat up. "What's the matter?"

"I need to piss and I can't get up."

She eased herself from under the cover and knelt beside him. Even in the faint starlight she could see he looked terrible. She placed her hand on his forehead. "You have a fever," she whispered.

"I just need a piss," he replied almost inaudibly.

She got up and retrieved one of the cooking pots from the hearth. "Can you move?" she asked.

"No, I don't think I can."

This frightened her. He was so weak and looked so ill. She pulled back the cover, rolled him carefully on to his side and placed the vessel so that his urine would pass into it. He could not even raise his arm to hold himself so she did the job for him.

"I'm sorry," he whispered as the last drops splashed into the pot.

"It's alright, my love," she replied tenderly.

He had never heard her call him that before; they never used such expressions of tenderness with each other, nor had they ever declared their love; it had simply been understood from the beginning. Now, however, it seemed oddly appropriate and he was glad to hear it.

She put the pot to one side, turned him on to his back and stroked his curly, black hair. "Go to sleep, you will feel better in the morning."

But the morning saw no improvement for a fever had taken hold of his body. He did not wake up with the sunrise as usual, but seemed to have slipped into a sort of disturbed coma. She placed Baby in her cot and pulled back the cover. His wounds were sound and but looked angry and there were strange, red blotches appearing on his skin. She went to the medical kit and pulled out the last phial of universal antibiotic. She had hoped not to have to use it lest the child needed it, but something had got into Jodi's body and was poisoning him. She delivered the contents of the phial into his thigh and covered him. Afterwards she attended to the child and prepared some food. She had not eaten for over a day and felt a little light-headed.

Jodi woke up two hours later. The fever had subsided and he had gained enough strength to sit up. She gave him some water and wiped his face and body with a cool, damp piece of fur.

"You would have made a fine doctor," he observed as she worked. "You have made an excellent job of these injuries."

"My father always insisted that his men were instructed in basic surgery."

"A wise command for men in battle."

She smiled. "No one ever fought in Rion; it was all a charade; Lodan discovered that when he went to Trant. The only war seen in recent memory was the one started by us."

"Are you not proud of your hand in Strellic's overthrowing?"

She stopped dabbing at his leg and sat back on her haunches. "What difference has it made? No doubt General Gerlic will prove just as corrupt and self-serving as Strellic; the only thing that will change is the face on the statues."

"You may be right, but at least, your father acted admirably."

"I don't know; he gave me no hint of what he was doing. Sometimes I feel I didn't know him at all."

"He was protecting you as any father would."

"I know, but it doesn't make it easier to accept."

She resumed her work, drawing the dampened fur up and down his legs. He watched her intently, noting the fall of her blonde hair, now almost to her shoulder and the fuller swell of her breasts.

"Your breasts have got bigger," he observed with studied casualness.

She looked up sharply. "Don't even think about it; you're too weak and I'm certainly not ready."

"I wasn't," he lied, recalling with chagrin the extended length of time since they had last made love. He knew that abstinence was normal during this period, but it still frustrated him.

She finished washing him just as the baby woke up and started to cry. She picked her up and put her to the breast. As he watched the tiny human suckling, he was reminded of a distant memory of his own mother suckling his younger sister in their rude hovel in Faloon Pal. How far he had travelled since then; halfway across a galaxy to come to this paradise and to a new home with those he loved.

"Let me hold her," he said.

Lorel gave him the child and he wrapped her in his arms, rocking her gently and inspecting her little fingers and toes while Lorel prepared some food.

"She looks like you," she remarked as she stirred a pot of deer meat.

"She better had," he replied with a broad smile.

She too smiled, watching them together as the sunlight slanted through the opening of the cabin they had built next to the life-pod. Now he was back and they were safe and the garden blossomed outside.

In the afternoon, his strength had returned sufficiently to allow him to rise and sit outside the cabin. It was a warm day and they sat together, listening to the chatter and calls of the creatures that shared their garden and the distant murmur of the sea.

Jodi, in silent thought, stared out towards the azure glint of water for a long time. He was given to periods of reflection and this time of enforced idleness prompted particularly deep thought. At length, collecting himself he remarked; "This world is full of dangers. In our worlds the danger comes from the things that human beings do to each other; here, it is the creatures that pose the threat." He took up her hand and kissed it. "If I die you must carry on; for your own sake and the sake of our child. Promise me you will do that."

She pulled her hand away. "Don't talk about it; you're not going to die."

"I will one day; we both will."

"When we are old and our children have had children."

"I hope you are right; I hope that you will see me grey and toothless."

He grinned at her but in his dark eyes she saw a disturbing shadow of what he knew his fate was to be. It was the shadow of death.

She turned her face away from his; she could not bear to see it.

She awoke during the night, disturbed by the unusual quality of Jodi's breathing. He was normally a quiet sleeper, rarely given to the snoring and snorting of the barracks, but that night his breathing was short and irregular, as if he was struggling for each lungful. She placed her hand gently on his forehead so as not to disturb him and felt the heat and moistness of it. The fever had returned.

Quietly she rose and took up a fur cloth, dampened it with cool water and dabbed his face. He briefly opened his eyes and she saw the ghostly reflection of starlight in them before he closed them again. In that moment despair seized her for she knew that she had seen death. She stayed with him until the grey dawn brought rain upon the garden and dressed the leaf and blossom with pearls of water. She cradled his head and rocked gently to and fro while she wiped the beads of sweat from his fevered skin. From time to time he would open his unseeing eyes and utter some words of deluded meaning that trailed off with the exhaustion of the effort as the poison in his blood gradually closed his body down. She remained with him all that day and all the next, rising from him only to feed the child when she cried. In that afternoon his breathing became so shallow that she could hardly hear it. The springtime sun, hard in the crisp air, lit the cabin through the small window that he had fashioned and fell across his face. He opened his eyes and a whisper, barely audible left his lips. "Is that you, Matty?"

Jodi Saronaga died in the afternoon of the two-hundred-and-seventy-fifth day of their life on Earth. Lorel did not cry, she was emotionally exhausted and had nothing left inside. She held him as his body cooled and the baby cried in the crude, wooden cot. As the setting sun set the treetops glowing, she lay him down and took up the spade and went into the garden. Choosing a place near in the orchard, close to a fig tree, she began to dig, working with mindless regularity until she had sufficient depth and space to properly accommodate his body.

She completed her task as the last vestiges of ghostly, grey twilight stole away to the west. A new moon had risen and stars dotted the sparse sky. She returned to the cabin; the baby was asleep in its cot and the place was silent. Jodi's body lay uncovered on the fur rug; the grey light had turned it to marble.

She knelt down and kissed the cold flesh, running her hands over its familiar undulations and scars. Now her tears fell upon the sculpture that he had become and grief overwhelmed her; all she had of him were memories; she would never know his touch again; or hear his voice; or feel his love inside her.

In the maturing night, she carried him to the graveside; heavy though he was she would not drag him. She stood in the hole and brought his body gently to its floor and climbed out. In the near darkness his features were hard to see as she stared into the grave to look upon him for the last time. Then, with bitter resolution, she took up the spade and began to cover him with the black, fertile soil of the garden.

When she returned to the cabin, she found the child crying in her cot. She picked her up, put her to the breast and lay down beneath the fur cover that still smelled of him. He had told her to survive and she would honour his wish, even through the pain of his loss. She would honour his wish but she would never again live in the full light of the world.

PART SIX

THE HEART OF HYPERION

I

Keymer Dorkanlu, the captain of the salvage vessel 'Arc', stroked her chin and surveyed the two other individuals on the bridge. "Well, what do you think, gentlemen?"

"I don't like the look of it," replied Turkon, a gangly fellow with a large, hooked nose and long, streaky-black hair. He looked older than his thirty years and, like Dorkanlu herself, was a misfit, a fugitive from the cosmetic perfection of his native Barta Magnus. "We've never salvaged a deep-space cruiser; no one has."

Dorkanlu unclasped her hands from the back of her bald, shiny head and passed an enquiring gaze to her second in command; a flattering title since the three on the bridge represented the entirety of the crew. Pirate, her Number Two, a lumbering, ancient, grizzled cove of indeterminate age who had once, reputedly, served time as a Moontrader, stared at the minute white dot in the middle of the image. "I dunno, Cap," he said. "A deep-space cruiser; it's not right; it's just not right. What have they told you?"

"Not much," she replied, swinging her feet from her chaotic desk. "You know what Surans are like; secretive bastards the lot of them. They claim it was sold to the DeRhogai of Kagan and now falls to government of Suran after the default."

They all knew what she was talking about; after the death of the Arkon, the house of DeRhogai failed catastrophically, pulling down a number of planetary economies with it. The international financial system had still not fully recovered.

"They told me it was traded through an arms dealer on Tarnus," she continued, "then it disappeared. It hasn't been traced for over ten years. Apparently the cruiser was purchased on unsecured credit so it reverts back to the Surans. You know the law; to secure it we have to physically board it; machines will not do."

"What about the crew?" put in Turkon.

Dorkanlu shook her head. "The Surans claim they don't know anything about who or what is on board. We can't scan it, the hull is too dense and it hasn't responded to a hail. The only thing we know is that one of the life-pods is missing."

Pirate absently put his hand down his pants and scratched his testicles. "I say we go," he declared.

"That's alright for you," responded Turkon. "You're old; it doesn't matter if you die. I'm still young and if that bloody ship is rigged the blast will be seen halfway across the galaxy."

"Deep space cruisers can't explode like that and anyway, I don't think the size of any explosion is particularly germane," replied Dorkanlu flatly. "Small or large, the result will be fatal. The Surans are paying us well to secure this ship; very well, in fact, *and* they pay promptly. Since this financial melt-down we've been living on scraps; we don't have any other work in prospect."

Pirate pulled his hand from his pants and grabbed his colleague's arm. "Come on Turk; you're the explosives expert; don't be a limp prick. We need your vote."

Turkon pulled his arm away quickly. "Don't touch me with your cock-soiled hands, Pirate." He slumped on a rubbish-strewn sofa and looked moodily from one to the other. "What the fuck," he declared resignedly. "But if I see anything I don't like, we're out of there. Agreed?"

The other two nodded.

The sleek vessel, decelerating as it approached the star region of Kagan, appeared on the starboard side of the shuttle as Captain Dorkanlu expertly turned the vessel to rendezvous with it. They were close enough to see with the naked eye the black scars where the port life-pod had blown itself away from the ship.

"Looks like they left it in a hurry," observed Pirate.

"Look at the hull," said Turkon. "What are those marks?"

"Atmospheric scorching," replied the Captain. "It's been flown through a dense atmosphere at high velocity."

"The plot deepens," muttered Pirate under his breath.

"We'll go in via the empty life-pod dock," said Dorkanlu. "Any objections?"

The two men had none; Turkon gloomily observed that it was just as likely to be rigged as any other access point.

Dorkanlu carefully eased the shuttle close to the empty cavity in the ship's hull where the life-pod had once been housed. She stabilized the shuttle and locked the two vessels together so that the access points coincided.

"This is it, gentlemen," she said as she rose from the controls. "Full kit for this one I think."

They repaired to the aft of the shuttle and donned lifebelts, blast suits and helmets; checking each other's equipment thoroughly. When they were satisfied Dorkanlu opened the outer door and they saw the access port of the life-pod about three metres in front of them. Behind the transparency that was set into the port, they saw nothing but black.

"It's running dark," said Pirate. "Probably no life support."

Dorkanlu sent a lantern out and they followed, floating across the void between the vessels. She placed a universal key on the bulkhead next to the port and, with a sideways glance towards the others, activated it.

The port slowly opened. She could hear the heavy breathing of her colleagues through their communicators as the door slid to one side to reveal the black interior of the vessel. She sent in a lantern and they followed it into the ship.

They found themselves in the life-pod corridor, a freezing vacuum that, at first bore no evidence of the violence that had taken place on board; but as the life-pod door returned to its place they all saw the bloody hand-prints that smeared its interior surface.

Turkon pulled his weapon from its keep.

"What are you doing, Turk?" said Dorkanlu.

"You can't be too careful," he replied. "It could be a trap."

"The ship's dark," said Pirate gruffly. "Put it away before you hurt someone."

Turkon scowled and replaced his weapon and they began to search the ship, carefully opening each cabin door and peering inside. All were empty until they came to the furthest from the bridge. When they opened the door the first thing they saw was a large pool of blood that had dried on the cabin floor. More blood stained the bed and a cover that floated above it like a frozen ghost. The glint of a knife blade caught the lantern light and Pirate pushed himself into the cabin and grasped it as it floated near the ceiling. He showed it to the others; the blade was dark with blood.

As they looked about the cabin, Turkon spied a strange object floating near the floor in one corner. He reached for it, closed his hand around it and brought it close to his face for a better look. Then he saw what it was.

"Oh crap!" He exclaimed, suddenly breaking the heavy silence and instantly releasing the object.

"What?" cried the other two in chorus.

"Oh shit! Oh fuck! I told you we shouldn't be doing this," he wailed

Pirate grabbed the tumbling object and peered at it, then silently presented it to his Captain.

She held up the frozen piece of anatomy between her gloved thumb and forefinger and frowned. "Odd what the cold can do to a man, isn't it?"

"You think this is a time for jokes?" spluttered Turkon. "Don't you see what this is?"

"It's a severed cock," said Pirate helpfully.

"You fools, we've been tricked. This is an Evangelist vessel. Oh fuck! Oh fuck, fuck, fuck."

Dorkanlu observed her crewman's meltdown with calm disdain; she had seen its like many time before. She waited until the panic subsided somewhat before speaking. "You may be right, Turk, this is a Kagan ship, after all." She propelled the member back towards her crewman. "But I fancy that a deep-space cruiser is not the usual place to perform the Sacrificial Rite. This is more likely to be the result of torture."

Turk dodged the advancing piece of anatomy and scowled at her. "Is that supposed to make me feel better?"

They searched the remaining cabins where, in one other, they found evidence of past occupation. Finally, they entered the bridge and there they discovered the owner of the missing part. Lodan's body was floating near the ceiling, the knife still buried in his flesh. His eyes were shut and his face serene; it was the face of a man who had accepted death. They pulled him to the centre of the bridge and Dorkanlu nodded to Pirate.

"Will you check please?"

Pirate eased the frozen pants apart and peered inside. He looked up at his Captain and frowned. "His cock is missing, but it wasn't torture; it was surgery."

"I told you," put in Turkon.

"Shut up, Turk," snapped Dorkanlu. "What's that he's holding?"

She prized something from the frozen fingers of Lodan's right hand and held it up in her own. As it warmed in her grasp, the lozenge-shaped object began to glow.

II

Keymer Dorkanlu was the product of an elite military academy on Barta Magnus. Abandoned as a young child by her elderly parents unable to cope with her wild temperament and exasperated by her stolid refusal to take an interest in her appearance, she drifted through a series of government institutions until she finally entered the military academy where she was to blossom. Having served for thirty years in the army, she used the generous pension she received to put down a deposit on the Arc, an ancient salvage vessel. Ten years later she stepped on to the deck of a deep-space cruiser and her life was to change forever.

Following the return of the cruiser to Suran jurisdiction, she was surprised to be approached by the head of the High Council. This august being questioned her personally on many aspects of her life, particularly her religious affiliations and beliefs. Being satisfied with her answers the commission was offered with a fee so generous that it would enable her to pay off her debts and retire anywhere she cared in some style. She did not require any thought. She left her vessel in Pirate's hands and chose five ex-marines for the task. And now, over five years later, as they approached the given co-ordinates, she saw for the first time, the world to which they had been sent.

Besides her five marines, the ship's compliment consisted of forty-two Suran nationals; all scientists with a variety of specialities. She did not care for them much with their monosyllabic answers and distant superior attitudes, but, as they mostly kept to their own individual spaces, she did not see much of them. Her job was to oversee the safety of the Surans; not to like them. Now, at the final approach, two Surans had appeared on the bridge to monitor the process.

"What is the time to orbit, Captain Dorkanlu?" asked one.

"Two hours and thirty four minutes," she replied.

"And the initial scan?"

Dorkanlu checked her readings. "They should be coming through in three point two minutes."

The Suran nodded solemnly, betraying no emotion or outward sign of excitement. The bridge fell silent as they all peered at the distant point of light beneath the star. At last the first readings started to emerge. The Surans began to read and discuss the results of atmospheric probes and planetary morphology in unintelligible technical detail until one of them gasped in amazement and the other responded with uncharacteristic animation.

"What is it?" said Dorkanlu, slipping from the captain's chair and joining them.

They were so distracted that they didn't even notice how uncomfortably close she had got to them.

"It's the biomass reading," said one. "This figure, do you see it?"

"Yes."

"It's the fauna quotient."

"I'm sorry?"

"The occurrence of free moving animals," explained the other. "This figure should be minute, less than a hundredth of one percent."

Dorkanlu re-checked the figure. "So there are quite a few free-moving animals on this planet?"

"You don't understand," said the Suran. "There are trillions upon trillions!"

III

"Stay here, trooper."

"But Captain, there are two of them," replied the man by her side.

"Just stay here; put a lifebelt on, just in case. We can't afford any contamination. Come only if I get into trouble."

Keymer Dorkanlu secured the lifebelt about her middle and checked her weapon. She entered the shuttle's airlock and waited while the air was drawn back into the vessel and the pressure equalized. The outer door opened and she stepped from the vessel onto the pristine sand. Above her a seagull screeched and dived down towards the water. She drew her weapon in alarm, but her alarm soon turned to wonder at such a sight. With her senses heightened, she began to make her way towards the crashed life-pod. The sounds of the creatures in the forest trees assaulted her senses; behind her the shuttle rested on the beach beneath the relentless sun while the sea beyond sighed gently in the soft breeze.

She moved carefully, her weapon drawn, just as she had been taught in the military academy, alert to any disturbance in the undergrowth. Soon, she emerged from the trees and entered a clearing, where the trees of the forest conceded to cultivation and unfamiliar vegetation. In the centre of the clearing stood the life-pod and a crude, hut-like structure from which issued a curl of pale smoke that drifted into the warm, languid air. She approached warily, knowing that they must have seen and heard the craft land on the beach, but other than the smoke, there was no sign of human presence.

Suddenly, to her left, the odd sound of a strangled derisory laugh cracked the air. She approached its source and was met by an extraordinary sight; a hairy creature with four legs and an oddly shaped head was tethered to a post. It was chewing something but momentarily stopped to watch her before resuming its meal. She stared at it, barely able to believe her eyes; such creatures were the stuff of myth and legend.

Her path eventually led her to the open door of the crashed life-pod. She stepped inside and approached the first of the stasis units. Through its transparency she could see the furry body of a large beast, quite similar to that tethered outside. The other units contained more bodies of beasts in varying degrees of dismemberment. It was both bizarre and grizzly. Muttering to herself in disgust, she emerged from the life-pod and passed through the crude door of the adjacent hut. A low fire burned in the hearth with a pot placed above it to warm containing something she could not readily identify. In the corner a bed consisting of what appeared to be the furry skins of the creatures showed signs of recent occupation. The place smelled disgusting, quite alien to anything she had ever experienced.

Suddenly she became aware of the presence of another person. She swung round and fleetingly saw the form of a naked girl silhouetted in the doorway against the brightness of the sunlit garden. She was on the cusp of puberty, with a mass of tangled black hair and a wild look in her dark eyes. She silently vanished as quickly as she had appeared and Dorkanlu, rashly forsaking her training, pulled her weapon and ran to the door in pursuit. As she emerged from the hut, a hand from nowhere knocked the weapon from her grasp and spun her to the floor. The knife at her throat was wielded by a naked woman of about thirty years of age, with long, startlingly blonde hair and skin ulcerated and scarred by too many wild encounters with nature. She had a deranged, murderous look in her pale eyes and her cracked lips were drawn into an expression of wild aggression.

"Who has sent you?" she demanded through clenched teeth.

Dorkanlu was so taken aback she failed to answer quickly enough for her attacker. The knife was pushed against her throat, drawing a trickle of blood.

"*Who has sent you?*" repeated the mad creature with greater urgency.

"Surans," replied Dorkanlu, regaining her wits..

The wild-looking, black haired child reappeared and looked down at her in triumph, as if she had just become their quarry and was soon to be disembowelled.

"Surans?" repeated Lorel. "Not Evangelists?"

"I'm a woman," replied Dorkanlu.

Lorel eyed her; she was indeed a woman, though not at all feminine. "Surans you say? This is a trick."

"It's not a trick. Let me up," said Dorkanlu, "others will soon be here and you will be in danger."

"Others? Do you mean the dead soldier in your vessel?"

Dorkanlu gazed into the wild eyes and knew she was in serious trouble.

"Kill her, Mum," screamed the child.

"I will when she has answered me. What others?"

"Scientists and soldiers. If you kill me they will come and wipe out everything you have here. They will take you back and you will be separated from each other and imprisoned."

"Liar; you are alone, I see it in the fear that is in your eyes."

"Do you think we came half way across the galaxy in a shuttle? You killed the Kagan, didn't you? And cut off his cock."

At this Lorel blinked and a distant memory sparked in her addled mind. "Lodan? He's dead then?"

"Quite dead."

"That is as it should be. He tried to destroy this place."

"Mum, stop these words; kill her now," shouted the agitated child.

"Be quiet, River," commanded Lorel and the child moodily slumped to the ground and began stabbing it with her knife while eyeing her potential victim with deadly intent.

Lorel speared the woman beneath her with a ferocious glare while she pondered the matter. Dorkanlu forced herself to remain calm; her attacker was strong; her scarred body lean and muscular; it would be a difficult fight if she could not convince the woman to see sense.

"We did not expect to find anyone here," said Dorkanlu. "I have been sent by the Surans to claim this world, not to destroy it."

Lorel continued to stare into the eyes of her victim while she commanded the child to pick up the weapon.

"What weapon?" asked River.

"The thing she dropped," prompted Lorel.

The child retrieved the sidearm from the ground where it had fallen.

"Give it to me."

Lorel rose quickly, grabbed the weapon from the child and pointed it at Dorkanlu. "Get up and put your hands behind your head."

Dorkanlu obeyed while Lorel stood over her and levelled the sidearm at her head.

"Why is your lifebelt active?"

"We have been instructed to avoid any contamination of the environment."

"It's a bit late for that. Are you in communication with anyone else?"

Dorkanlu considered lying but knew the lie would soon be found out. "No," she replied.

Lorel visibly relaxed. "Now, tell me who you are and what you are doing here."

"My name is Keymer Dorkanlu; I have been commissioned by the High Council of Suran to bring here a group of scientists to survey and lay claim to this planet."

"How did you find this place?"

"On the Kagan ship we found an object in the dead man's hand..."

"The recorder?"

"Yes. The co-ordinates were extrapolated from an image contained in the object."

"The image of the tree and the night sky?"

"I think so."

"So it has fallen into the hands of the Surans; I suppose there is some justice in that."

"That may be true, but they will not be pleased to find this world occupied. In Suran law you have first claim to this planet. You have the right to say what is to be done here."

"Mum, I don't like these words. Why can't we kill her now?" pleaded the child.

Lorel's eyes flickered towards her offspring then back to Dorkanlu. "She is speaking her way out of death, my child."

The young girl's face dropped in disappointment and she got up and sloped off into the garden, kicking angrily out at clump of herbs and sending their heady scent into the air.

The two women eyed each other.

"May I drop my hands?" said Dorkanlu

Lorel nodded. "I still have the weapon, remember."

"Who are you?" said Dorkanlu after a pause.

"My name is Lorel Arkuna of Rion on Tarnus."

Dorkanlu stared at her in disbelief; Stellic's campaign against the Rebellion of Rion was taught as an example of how not to conduct a military operation. "You are the daughter of General Arkuna?"

"Yes."

"You are supposed to be dead; it was announced by the government of Rion some time ago to quell the rising faith in you. You became a cult figure; I think there's even an unofficial shrine to your memory."

"I am pleased to hear it," replied Lorel and the hint of an ironic smile creased her cheek.

"So your father was the agent between the Arkon and the Surans?" said Dorkanlu, beginning to put it all together at last.

"Yes."

"And who was the man you called Lodan?"

"A descendant of the Arkon of the DeRhogai. He was charged with a mission to discover this world."

Dorkanlu smiled and nodded as another piece of the puzzle dropped into place. "And the dismemberment?"

"Lodan was devout; he could not accept the reality of what we had discovered. It disturbed the balance of his mind. He performed the rite on himself."

"And is that when you had to kill him?"

Lorel stared out into the garden as she recalled a distant, painful memory. "I didn't kill him; Jodi did that to protect us."

"Jodi?"

Lorel let the weapon drop. "Come, I will take you to him."

They stood together next to the cairn of stones that marked the final resting place of Jodi Saronaga. The fig tree by the grave dappled the ground with filtered sunlight.

"It must have been hard for you," said Dorkanlu as she looked upon the grave.

Lorel nodded slowly as tears moistened her cheeks. "I wish I had died too," she said quietly.

IV

The expedition led by Keymer Dorkanlu remained on Earth for almost two years. During this time fragments of the shattered civilisation that once existed gradually emerged from long burial. In the years between the death of one civilization and the coming of another, two ice ages had advanced even to the shores of Africa, crushing and sweeping all before them and scouring the land of much of what had once existed. Nature reclaimed the world and, disdaining the feeble works of Man, crushed them beneath its careless heel. In the places untouched by the ice sheets, other agents accounted for the shallow imprint of humanity. Wind, rain and countless generations of forest quickly reclaimed the environment and dismembered the vast cities that had once polluted the land and the skies above the land. The world fell silent and the small clatter of mankind disappeared from its surface and from the surfaces of nearby worlds reached by over-proud technology.

The Earth fell silent. An extinction occurred; one of a series that had characterized the history of the planet. But this extinction was unique for it did not come about by result of natural processes; no asteroid impact or volcanic outpouring or ice age caused it, for this extinction was induced by a phenomenon far more powerful than any that had gone before. It was engineered by the power of knowledge.

Lorel Arkuna took her daughter's hand as they stood together in silence looking down at the cairn below the fig tree beneath which rested the remains of the only man she had ever loved or would ever love. The dark soil had claimed his flesh but the memory of him was still keen in her thoughts. The expedition was about to leave Earth for Suran and she would accompany it for her daughter's sake. Despite her socialization with Dorkanlu and her crew, River was still wild and needed an education and contact with other, more refined human beings. As she gazed at the stones, Lorel wondered if she would ever return to this wilderness where her lover rested. The Surans had offered to disinter his remains and transport them back to civilisation, but she had refused to allow it, she could not face the prospect of seeing what his body had become beneath the dark earth and this, after all, was the place he had loved best in his short life. He belonged here; he belonged to this world and no other.

It was summer and the sun warmed the fertile ground of the garden as Lorel and River walked down the well-worn path from Jodi's grave to the shack. Hand-in-hand they stood inside for some moments, both silent and reflective. They had not lived in the shack for two years and already natural forces had begun to dismember it. There were holes in the roof and weeds sprouted from the compacted earthen floor. She recalled the daily conflict with nature and the grim struggle to stay alive; she remembered the beautiful evenings when she and River would sit outside and eat while they talked of many things. It was all history now; the stuff of a different life. She wrapped a tender arm around her daughter's shoulder and led her out of the shack towards the beach and the waiting shuttle.

And so the first expedition left Earth. It carried with it artefacts of human origin and many samples of the animals and plants it had found. Just as the Arkon had predicted, these were to become great treasures that instilled greater power and wealth to Suran. But the greatest treasure of all was yet to be discovered.

They found *Hyperion* still in high orbit above the fourth world of star KT153/2739. The great, black hulk turned impassively against the stars as Keymer Dorkanlu and five Surans crossed the void towards it. They docked in the open bay and began to search the ship. They found what they were looking for in a chamber below the floor of the bridge. It was a single, crystalline structure no bigger than a man's head. It was the long dormant heart of *Hyperion*. They took it back to the ship and placed it in suspension for the long journey back to civilisation.

They found the frozen body of Solon Bru near *Hyperion*. It was intended to repatriate the remains and inter them in a mausoleum that was to be built in honour of Doyen Lim, Bru and Jun Siu, the Suran youth whose remains were never discovered. In the event the erection of a mausoleum was considered too vulgar for the conservative populace and nothing more than a small memorial was eventually raised outside the main entrance of the Museum of Humanity.

On her return, Lorel was afforded the unique honour of addressing the assembled members of the Suran High Council. No foreigner had ever before received such an invitation. She began, somewhat nervously, by outlining the circumstances that led to the discovery of the Earth and continued by describing the tastes various types of flora and fauna that could be eaten whilst bringing before the increasingly incredulous Surans preserved examples of such creatures. But Lorel saved until last her final surprise, saying to the assembly, "For those of you who have not seen enough to wonder at; behold this!" With those words she opened a large crate and two birds with plumage of scarlet, blue and green, sprang out of the crate and flew up into the ceiling of the hall above the astonished assembly. I shall never forget the mischievous grin of triumph as my mother calmly observed the pandemonium.

The long-stilled heart of *Hyperion* was brought back to Suran and given new pulse. The discovery of the Earth was momentous but it had little effect on the ordinary lives of the billions who lived within the human diaspora.

It was in the heart of *Hyperion* that they found the real treasure; the treasure of which the Arkon DeRhogai had dreamed but was too late to see. In that single object the sum of ancient knowledge and experience was discovered. In the writings of ancient philosophers and theological teachers they found the monotheistic tradition that caused the establishment of an entirely new religion that encompassed a new doctrine based on tolerance and love. The tight strictures of the old faith were largely abandoned and worlds long denied cultural liberty now found themselves exposed to a wide variety of secular experiences. Instead of the monotonous chants of the faithful the temples began to echo with the music of long-dead geniuses; the halls and public squares resounded with the works of literary giants issuing, in translation, from the libraries of Suran. Now they see Henry the Fifth and Twelfth Night on Barta Magnus and even on Kagan, the last bastion of the old faith, the Arkons, finally capitulated and embraced the new order.

It is natural for an intelligent species to ponder upon the source of its own existence and, in the absence of reason, to generate mythical explanations to account for it. The early settlers of the five planets were not able to rely on the elegant theories of Charles Darwin and Alfred Wallace, nor had they any fossil record to guide them. They chose, instead, to rely on the pronouncements of a man who lived in an age of relative ignorance and by the power of indoctrination, maintained their allegiance to that credo for over two thousand years. Faced with overwhelming evidence, the powerful and wealthy institution that flourished as a result of the Prophet's teaching eventually accepted the truth of human origin but skilfully adjusted its position, declaring that the words of the Prophet were metaphorical. The theologians declared the Prophet to be the last in a long line of messengers of a higher being and adopted the monotheistic culture of the Ancients, wondering why they had not thought of it for themselves, for no amount of scientific analysis could gainsay the existence of a godlike Creator of All Things. Such a notion is a matter of faith and any discussion as to the existence of such a being is ultimately sterile, for it is impossible to prove or refute by the application of any process of reason. So they turned their prayers and imprecations towards their new, more powerful god without pausing to wonder if an entity capable of creating the entire universe would require worship of any description at all!

From the heart of *Hyperion* a lost civilisation has been reincarnated and the spirit of human joy, long smothered by superstition and oppression, has been replanted and now people everywhere can sing and dance once again.

V

At the age of sixty-six, my mother and I joined one of the numerous research expeditions and returned to the Earth. She was now a wealthy woman and fated throughout civilised society, but her time in the Mine of Kusk and the privations of her struggled life on the Old World had removed from her the expectation of old age. She was slowly dying and the sentimental attraction of the world on which she had shared her life with Jodi had become impossible to deny. She knew she had to go home.

I recall her eyes filling with tears as we walked together from the shuttle, up the familiar beach and into the garden that she had distilled from the fertile soil over thirty years before. It had been left untended and nature had reclaimed it with wild, lush uncultivated growth. The life-pod had long since been removed and taken as an exhibit in a museum, but the stone foundation of the little hut my father had built still traced the ground below the vines and myrtle. She looked down at it and smiled wistfully as the memory of their time together turned in her mind. I took her arm and we walked on until we found the fig tree, now mature and laden with arms of ripe fruit, below which stood the cairn of stones that marked the last resting place of my father. I pulled the tumble of undergrowth from the stones while my mother watched me in thoughtful silence.

"We will make the garden again," she said quietly.

In the years following her return to civilisation, my mother travelled extensively as she delivered more lectures to larger and larger audiences. Indeed, it is true to say that she became the most famous person of the era. During this time she continuously worked on her account of what was to become known as the Revelation, visiting places of significance and speaking to people who had a direct or indirect connection with the events. One particular person proved a fruitful source of information, providing her with copious details of Jodi's early life. She discovered Laon Cour Son living in some comfort, under an assumed name, on Barta Magnus. Their first meeting was guarded until she explained who she was, whereupon he effused great surprise, pride and sadness at what had become of his ward. It was clear to her that Laon's paternal love for Jodi had not diminished and they became firm friends until the end of her life.

VI

And now I look up from my writing desk and see my mother's garden as it is today, radiant in the late afternoon sunshine. Flowers bloom where the tangled shrubbery once choked the light and the forest has been cleared all the way to the sea where a single-dwelling house stands next to the beach. There are two cairns beneath the branches of the fig tree now, side-by-side in the dappled sunshine where my parents lie together in death; their spirits at one.

I turn from the garden and look down the steps of our home towards the shining sea where my husband plays on the beach with our two young children. He is a scientist, one of ten thousand or so who have come here to maintain the integrity of this world and to uncover the wonders yet to be discovered beneath its soil. He sees me watching him and waves as our children shout for more games. I wave back and smile; for what greater, more joyful corner of the universe could ever be had than this garden?

This Paradise.

This Earth.